DEAD HARVEST

a collection of dark tales

Edited by MARK PARKER

SCARLET GALLEON PUBLICATIONS, LLC

DEAD HARVEST

Published by Scarlet Galleon Publications, LLC
FIRST EDITION
Edited by Mark Parker, Cover design by David Mickolas
Scarecrow image created by pumpkinrot.com. Used by permission.

ISBN-13 978-0-692-32338-0
Printed in the U.S.A.

Acknowledgements

Sincere thanks go out to:

Richard Chizmar and Brian James Freeman of *Cemetery Dance* magazine for their kind and gracious support of this project from the start.

David Mickolas for his incredible cover design and additional graphics, including the Scarlet Galleon Publications LLC logo. (And to pumpkinrot.com for kindly permitting us to use their chilling scarecrow for our cover).

Brian Moreland for the Herculean task of formatting the print and digital manuscripts of *Dead Harvest.*

Michal Evans of *Grinning Skull Press* for his patience and generosity in answering my many, many questions.

Erin Sweet-Al Mehairi for her generous guidance.

The contributors of *Dead Harvest* without whose talent this book would not exist.

In loving memory of my parents,
Claudette M Parker
William J Parker
Mom and Dad, I wish you both could be here to see this.
And for my sister, Trina, who has been my champion from the beginning.
I could not have done this without you. I love you!

Table of Contents

Autumn Lamb

E.G. Smith

Winter

Millard braced the .223 rifle on the gate and winced, regretting how hard he shoved the butt against his arthritic shoulder. He switched on the spotlight beside the gun's barrel. The lean, shorn sheep were huddled in the far corner where a willow extended its red-barked limbs over the woven-wire fence. They were skittish and grew more so in the glare, their spooked eyes smearing gold streaks as they jostled against each other, bleating and snorting.

"Show yourself before one of us freezes to death." Millard's whisper fogged his bifocals.

He cast the harsh beam back and forth across the pasture. Waiting became agony as cold stung his bones and stiffened his joints. Despite the ache in his back and the tremble in his hands, he refused to concede, even to himself, that the farm work and the winters were more than one worn out old man could bear. It was his farm to work and to protect, and no one else's. If a man couldn't take care of his property and his stock, what reason did he have to be alive?

A flash of red drew the old man's cheek to the icy stock. Squinting through the scope's eyepiece, he tracked the fox as it slunk along the back fence line, undulating over the frosted turf. He struggled to keep the crosshairs on the animal as it moved away from the flock, passing behind the hay feeder. It crested a hillock and turned its burning eyes into the light, lifting one paw and exposing its flank. Millard aimed between the elbow and shoulder, exhaled and fired. The pelt fell in a heap as the blast echoed off the house and the outbuildings.

With the gun smoking on his shoulder, the farmer latched the gate behind him and crossed the field, weaving between gopher holes and frozen piles of manure. The spooked ewes milled and surged away as he passed, leaping over each other. Skunk stench preceded the corpse by five paces.

The fox sprawled at the weedy crease of turf and wire, its body wrung like a towel and its snout fixed in a snarl. Millard leaned his rifle on the fence and hoisted the limp animal by its tail, playing his gun's light over the long, ruddy fur. Something dripped onto his boot. After another drip, and another, he traced the leak to the fox's ribcage, where two identical holes oozed yellow goo that smelled of menthol. There was no blood.

Millard wondered at the twin wounds, both of which were kill shots bound to have hit the heart or lungs or both. He'd only fired once that evening, he was sure of it. If this was a fox he'd shot on a previous night, how could it have survived to hunt again?

With the fox dangling from one hand and the gun cradled in the other, he walked toward the sheep, his boots sinking into snow that lingered in the shadow of the fence. He picked up a trail of pink drips near the rusting feeder and tracked them past a series of purple clots to the remains of a month-old lamb. Entrails bulged steaming from a gash in its belly. A glazed eye gaped upward, branded with a glowing sliver of moon.

The farmer's long sigh hazed the world, then dissipated. There'd been foxes and coyotes on the property every night that week. Two lambs taken, and now this one ripped. What would he tell Ida?

Millard slung the rifle on his shoulder and trudged back to the gate with the fox swinging from one hand and the lamb swinging from the other. He emerged from the pasture and hobbled to the barn, favoring his clicking knee. The galvanized metal trashcan clanged as he tossed in the flaccid corpses and slammed on the lid. That would do for now. He needed sleep.

He turned toward the house, where the master bedroom window now glowed yellow. The drive was a patchwork of frozen puddles that crunched underfoot. Muttered curses puffed a trail of swelling, rising clouds that wove upward through the silhouettes of bare maple branches.

Ida met her husband at the front door, her stringy hands drawing together the lapels of her flannel robe, her long pewter hair gleaming in the moonlight.

"I heard a shot." Her teeth chattered.

"I got a fox, but not before it got a lamb."

Before she could ask the dozen questions he saw welling in her throat, he grunted, "I'm beat to death." He slipped past her into the foyer, discarding gun, boots, hat and coat as he made for the stairwell.

The following morning, Millard let the alarm beep for twenty minutes before he rolled off the bed, hissing and favoring his bad hip. Breakfast was eggs from their hens, toast and bland decaf. The doctor said decaf-only and that's all Ida got at the market anymore. As he sipped and scowled, it occurred to him that aging was a series of cruel dockings, as if the most vital parts of your life were being pruned away: a bad knee, so no hunting; a sensitive gut, so no hot sauce; gout, so no beer; cataracts, so no driving at night; and high blood pressure, so no real coffee. How long before he was nothing but a stump propped up in the TV room, like the bare ficus in the corner that Ida said was bound to leaf out any time?

"What are we going to do about the foxes?" Ida asked from across the table, rattling the spoon in her cup. "That's three this week."

"Four." Millard sopped up gooey yolk with his toast. He wasn't letting on about the second wound in the fox. He didn't know what to make of that so it wasn't worth telling.

She stirred harder. "Please say it isn't the one we promised to hold for the Henderson boy's 4H project."

"No, it was a different one. But we can't afford to lose any lambs, not with all the singles we had this year. To lose stock to cold or to scours is one thing. But to lose them to predators…it makes it all seem to be for nothing."

"I know you're against it," Ida said, "but Clara swears their goats haven't been pestered since they got a dog."

"No dog's going to do my job." Millard sipped his bitter coffee and stared out the window at the yellow sun welling over the horizon.

Ida left for work at the school library before Millard finished eating. He pulled on the same coat, hat and boots and headed outside. A frigid breeze rattled the maple limbs and stung the farmer's eyes. In the barn, he loaded a sack of grain and three bales of hay onto the tractor's upturned blade and steered out the door and toward the pasture. As he drove, he considered whether to worm the sheep that day or the next. His right hand still ached from working the banding pliers over forty-three tails and twenty-odd scrotums.

The tractor lurched, then rolled to a stop, idling hard before stalling out. Millard cursed the silent machine, which was slipping out of gear more often each day.

A clatter, loud as close-by thunder, almost knocked him off the seat. He climbed down and traced it to the trash can, then edged up to the shuddering metal, expecting to see a cat scavenging the carcasses. The lid, which he'd placed on the can only hours before, was now upside down on the ground and he nudged it aside with his boot. He peered over the rim. Inside, a lamb turned circles on a pile of sawdust and stumbled over an empty feed bag. The dead fox was gone.

Millard gathered the lamb into his arms and hugged it tight until it gave up struggling. He carried it into the barn and stretched the fail body across a hay bale. It was a wether, its dry, shrunken scrotum dangling below the ring of green rubber he'd stretched on a couple weeks before. Its ivory fleece was matted with streaks of dark brown and its belly was wide open, with no sign of healing. Each time the lamb fussed, a mass of shriveled, leathery viscera protruded from the gash, along with dribbles of the same thick yellow ooze he'd seen on the fox. It was the same lamb he'd found dead the night before. How it was alive was beyond him.

Expecting the animal to keel over any moment, the farmer drew its black, crusted skin together with a row of surgical staples and put it back in the pasture. The lamb wobbled on rickety legs to the center of the enclosure, spun crooked circles trying to chew at its belly, then sprinted toward the flock at the feeder, scattering them. The other ewes and lambs formed a wide circle around it, shifting to maintain their distance as it approached the feeder. Its own mother shied away despite her swollen udder.

The lamb looked back at Millard and gave a shrill bleat that sounded like a pig's squeal.

Spring

The maple budded, flowered, leafed and spun its samaras toward ground that turned from ice to mud to dust. Still the lamb tottered around the pasture, driving the terrified flock like a collie. The rent in its underside refused to heal. After a week, most of the staples fell out and two or three dangled loose, dripping the yellow ooze. Millard never saw the lamb eat but somehow it kept going. Shunned by its mother, whose udder had withered, it wandered the field only sniffing at grass and grain. Ida begged her husband to call Jim, but the farmer didn't know how he'd tell a common-sense country vet that one of his stock was walking around dead.

As longer days greened the fields and choked every untrodden inch of ground with weeds, Millard's battle with the vermin continued unabated. Spring chores kept him busy past supper, and mayhem in his pastures kept him up half of most nights. In years past, the farm went weeks without an attack. Now, a quiet night meant only one fox or coyote or weasel or raccoon. Often, a menagerie of predators descended on the fields, sending the henhouse into hysteria and spooking the sheep. By Easter, Millard didn't bother kicking off his boots and going back to bed, but sat in the parlor with the gun across his lap, staring at the moonlit front windows and awaiting the next cackle or cry.

Some mornings the animal he'd shot the night before remained where he'd left it, more often it was gone. One coyote carcass had five bullet holes, three .223-sized and two smaller, meaning it had taken a couple of hits at another farm. Millard tossed it in the metal can and weighted the lid with a cinder block. By dawn, the can lay on its side with its lid three yards away and no sign of the corpse. After that, the farmer built a bonfire in the can and burned all the remains he found, stirring them with a hoe to make sure the flames reduced each body to charred bone. He wondered how many holes the varmints could endure. How much animal needed to remain for it to keep going?

And how long could his own body hold out? The work left him drained like a tire stuck with a rusty nail. His joints grew stiffer each day and some nights he seemed to cough more than he breathed. He stopped taking his blood pressure with the home monitor Ida bought at the drugstore and logged values that sounded good, but not too good. There was no sense in raising her pressure too. He figured it was a bad year all around and that the troubles, with the wildlife and with his health, would smooth over soon enough. A farmer learns to take a bad year in stride, even when he's on his knees.

Apart from a story about a plague of gophers the next county over and a piece about a nearby hatchery losing half their pullets in a night, the

Argus Gazette offered little corroboration and no insight. Millard and Ida's neighbor on one side grew alfalfa and had no stock, and their neighbor on the other side, rarely seen outside his broken-down trailer, wasn't much for chat. Millard made weekly trips to the feed store seeking information as much as supplies.

One Saturday morning in May, he walked an aisle in the hardware section, passing rows of steel shelves that held nothing but a chipped coat of beige paint. Millard set his plastic hand basket, half filled with boxes of .223 cartridges, down on the linoleum floor. He squatted and checked the back of the lower shelves, but they were bare save for a few streaks of grey powder and a pile of bright blue granules.

"Millard, what can I do you for?" The clerk smoothed the tractor and barn embroidery on his polo shirt, then fiddled with the knobs on his walkie talkie, squelching its crackle.

Millard struggled to his feet, leaning hard on a bowing shelf. "Howdy Larry. I'm looking for something for foxes, and maybe coyotes. Do you have any traps that size?"

"Leg traps or the cage type?" Larry clipped the handset back on his belt.

"Whatever you've got."

After a half-hearted search of the cardboard cases above the shelves, the clerk shrugged. "I'm afraid we're out of anything that size. Best I could do is a gopher trap. Every kind of trap's been flying out of here the last few weeks."

Millard eyed the blue granules. "How about strychnine bait?"

"Same deal, I'm afraid." Larry clanged his knuckles along the empty shelves. "Not that we carry anything labeled for canines, but the farmers have been buying up the gopher bait, the rat bait, slug bait, any kind of poison they can get their hands on. And to be honest, it doesn't sound like poison's working for them anyhow. Coyotes giving you trouble?"

"Yep." Millard took off his cap and wiped sweat from his bald spot. "But foxes mostly. More in the last couple months than in all my years on the farm put together."

"Out by Mayr Junction it's coyotes. Lots of dead stock." Larry pointed toward menswear, then waved his hand at tack and fly control. "Out toward the highway, I hear it's feral cats going after poultry. It's a bad year for everything except selling traps and bait. Of course I can't sell what I don't have."

The clerk blurred, stretching and splitting in two like a funhouse mirror reflection.

"Can't seem to shoot them—" Millard reached for his basket's plastic handle and missed, "—fast enough." His face was dripping, his heart racing.

"You ok, Millard?" Larry's four, then eight, arms reached toward Millard. The farmer's rubber legs buckled and he slumped against a cardboard box filled with blister-packed mouse traps. He hit the floor with his face against the display's plastic sign, eye to X'd-out eye with a dead mouse caught in the crosshairs of a rifle scope. The traps were two for ninety-nine cents. Limit four per customer. While supplies last. No rainchecks.

After four hours at the ER, the doctor said it was his blood pressure, and increased the dosage on several of the half-dozen medications he took. Ida arrayed the multicolored pills in a grid of wells in a plastic box on the kitchen counter, seven days across with rows for morning, noon, evening and bedtime. Millard had no time for the prescribed bed rest and no stomach for the heart-healthy diet. Ida protested, but shopped for eggs and steaks and beers anyway, her motherly instinct fearing starvation more than heart failure. Her husband said it was real food or nothing, spiting the body that had betrayed him.

By himself, propped against the shower wall waiting minutes for his stream of urine to arrive while the water pipes made a deafening screech, he was afraid that this might be his last year watching over the farm. He only hoped that he'd drop dead bucking a hundred-pound bale of hay and not wither away in a wheelchair in the parlor or in a nursing home bed. He'd wring his own neck before it came to that.

The first government people came when Ida was checking her tomatoes for hornworms, picking the squishy caterpillars off in her leather gloves and dropping them into a bucket of soapy water. Millard heard the voices, dropped his hay fork and circled the house, brushing his wife aside to ask for credentials. The man in a dress shirt said they were from the Department of Agriculture and the woman in the coveralls said they were asking farmers if they'd seen more predators than usual that year. The farmer answered their questions, but they said little in return when he asked what they thought was causing it, and what could be done.

More bunches of letters came and went: IFG, DHW, IDA, CDC and some Millard had never heard of. All of them jotted on clipboards and some of them asked to tour the property. The farmer said no, that he was too busy, and watched them drive away, their white pickups and black sedans kicking up clouds of dust. Ida asked why he turned them away. Millard said he didn't need help, an explanation he'd given so often over the years that it had become the gavel that adjourned their conversations. But it was more than stubborn self-reliance. It was the lamb.

One late-spring afternoon, Millard leaned against the rail fence, dry under the canopy of the maple as light rain fell over the grazing sheep. The injured lamb stood in an empty corner of the pasture, its tiny cotton ears twitching away drops. Should he still call it injured? The tear in its stomach never healed, but it never sickened.

Millard saw something in the strange lamb that he dared not express to anyone, even Ida: a solution to his infirmity, and the hope that he might work the farm forever. The lamb did more than refuse to die. It refused to grow, to age. In the months since it had been attacked, the lamb hadn't gained an inch or a pound. While its flockmates gorged on grass and grain, fast approaching market weight, it remained frozen in eternal youth, divorced from the cycle of consumption and elimination, development and senescence, life and death. Millard believed the lamb might stay that way forever. Could he do the same?

Summer

By June, repeated applications of herbicides began to turn the tide against the weeds, blanching and shriveling them into straw. Ida's tomato plants spilled onto brick pathways, their stems buckling under heaps of overripe fruit. As the swamp cooler rattled at full speed, losing its battle for the house with the scorching sun, the shade beneath the maple remained the only cool spot on the acreage.

One morning, Millard sat on a camp chair in the green glow beneath the tree, his elbows on his knees and his head in his hands. The sun was already high overhead, lost above the leaves, and the yard beyond the tree's shadow was too bright, too exhausting to squint at. He pressed his palms against his temples, as if trying to shove the sweat back into his pores. His mind wandered from one chore to another: fence repair, roof patching, changing a stuck sprinkler head. The drive needed grading before it turned into a swamp. It would take days just to take the tractor's rusted engine apart, much less find the problem. And what was to be done about the pipes? How many yards of plaster and lath would have to be torn off to find the source of their wailing? Between the heat and his fatigue, Millard felt up to none of it.

The idea struck him just as a hen raced from the barn, cackling that she'd laid. He didn't stop to pick the notion apart or hammer out the details. He set to work right away, before Ida came home from work and before he could talk himself out of it.

Millard crept through the gate and across the pasture, angling to corner the lamb between the fence and the shed. His quarry inched away as he approached, then pronked and fled. The other sheep ran screaming in all directions as the farmer pursued the lamb three times around the pasture, finally driving it toward the willow. He dove and caught a hind leg, tumbling over the grass and manure as he gathered up the other flailing limbs. He limped to the barn and shut the door behind him.

Millard wedged the squirming sheep under his left armpit and rifled through the piles of vet supplies on his workbench. As he pored over syringes and empty vaccine vials, light from a chink in the roof struck metal. A #10 blade, still sealed. With his teeth and his free hand he opened the packet, dropping the scalpel onto the bench top. He shifted the lamb around until he held the triangular blade in his left hand, braced against the table's edge.

"This'll only hurt a lot," he told the gnomish sheep.

With a grunt, he drew his right forearm across the scalpel's tip, opening a two-inch slice in his skin. As the wound trickled blood over feeding tubes and half-rolls of army gauze, he reached underneath the lamb, probing its belly. Knuckle-deep in its gut, his right index finger stirred its intestines with no reaction from the animal save for a stiffening of its gangly legs. His finger emerged covered in yellow goop that ran down and mixed with the blood striping his arm.

The wooly ear twitched as he spoke into it. "Here goes nothing."

Millard took a deep breath of air suffused with hay dust, then rubbed the glop into the throbbing cut on his arm.

He returned the lamb to the pasture, then stapled and bandaged his arm. It was slow work left-handed and he kicked himself for not doing it the other way around. Instinct told him to inject himself with some of the penicillin he kept in the kitchen fridge, but he thought better of it. Antibiotics might be the antidote to the pungent fountain of youth he'd just smeared under his skin. He'd take a chance on a secondary infection.

By noon, he felt like he was burning with fever even though the thermometer said his temperature was three degrees low and dropping. His skin tingled and his heart skipped half its beats. By the time Ida came home, he sat in his easy chair, pretending to watch the news but secretly scrutinizing his body, awaiting the next symptom.

"Did you cut yourself again?" She said before kissing his cheek.

"That tractor's engine has it in for me," he lied.

"Does it need stitches?" She straightened a seam on the bandage. "And do we know if your tetanus booster is in date?"

"Everything's under control," he told her. He hoped it was.

Millard only picked at dinner. The food tasted bland, like clay, even though it was Ida's fair-winning lamb casserole.

She fretted as she cleared the table. "You usually have seconds or thirds, but tonight not even firsts."

"Not hungry." He stood and weathered a rush of dizziness, leaning against his chair. "Not feeling myself today is all."

Millard never felt himself again.

Soon blood no longer flowed in his veins, replaced by the yellow sludge that made him kin to ripped sheep and riddled varmints. It leaked from shaving cuts and jaundiced his eyes. The wound on his arm never healed, and it took a roll of gauze per day to sop up the fluid from the incision and the staple holes. His digestion petered out, with no desire or need to supply one end or eliminate from the other. His urine thickened and dwindled until it ceased altogether.

What he lost in normal human functionality he gained ten-fold in vigor. His knee grew silent, his hip no longer ached and his heart rate slowed. He leapt out of bed in the morning, skipped his after-lunch naps and marched around the acreage so fast that the horseflies could never catch up to bite him. He stopped taking his medications, pocketing each fistful of pills and capsules and tossing them into the burn barrel to blacken and shrivel along with the corpses.

One evening he mashed his toe on the leg of the coffee table, and it dawned on him that he hadn't felt so much as a twinge in weeks. The next day he tested it, squeezing a fold of skin on his belly with fencing pliers as tight as he could, then twisting the jaws all the way around. There was no pain, only a pair of rectangular dents that lingered like a brand.

Ida suspected, of course. How could she not? Millard left his meals untouched, always saying he wasn't hungry and would eat later. He cancelled regular doctor appointments, claiming he didn't have the time or the need. Citing the ever burgeoning onslaught of predators, he took to sleeping on the downstairs couch to be nearer the door. But he never tired, and by August he spent the entirety of each night rocking on the shadowy porch and pacing the moonlit acres. He could only guess at his wife's fears.

He vowed to tell her the truth, but first he wanted to be sure about what he was dealing with. Was he invulnerable? Immortal? He needed a test, certain beyond a doubt, so he'd know what to tell her. A gunshot was no good, for if he survived it would leave a mess he'd have to live with forever. The same was true of jumping off the barn roof, throwing himself under a cattle truck on the road, and so on with every method of savaging of his flesh. This stumped him for weeks, as he considered the lethality of every implement, machine and construction on the farm.

One afternoon in September, as he carried Ida's canned tomatoes down to the cellar, the solution caught the tip of his boot and sent him stumbling across the cement floor, juggling the mason jars. He lined a dusty shelf with the tomatoes and turned to the plastic bottle that he'd kicked over. It was a gallon container of Annihilator Max herbicide concentrate, more than half full. He held the label up to a grimy bare bulb.

If inhaled... Call a poison control center or doctor for treatment advice.
If on skin or clothing... Call a poison control center or doctor for treatment advice.
If in eyes... Call a poison control center or doctor for treatment advice.
If swallowed... Call a poison control center or doctor for treatment advice.
If person is not breathing... Call 911, then give artificial respiration.

This was the good stuff, the only thing he'd found which would even wilt the mallows that were invading the lawn. The warning label even had its own hotline number.

Millard climbed the bare lumber steps and locked the cellar door, then descended. He pressed and unscrewed the cap with ease as his knuckles had un-swollen and the tremble had left his hands a month before. He peered into the bottle's mouth, swirled the reddish-brown liquid and sniffed the sulfurous fumes deep into his lungs. He pressed the bottle to his lips and drank mouthful after mouthful of thick fluid that tasted of nothing, like swallowing mineral oil. The yellow ooze that had replaced his saliva had done his taste buds in.

Millard set the bottle down and leaned against the washing machine for a long while. Orange sunlight from a window across the cellar glinted through jars of preserves. When he was satisfied that he'd suffered nothing worse than a distended belly, he climbed the stairs. He sat down at the kitchen table, grabbed a napkin from a sheep-shaped holder and wiped poison from his lips. He called to his wife, and as her footfalls approached from the parlor, he decided to start at the beginning. That was always best.

Autumn

The leaves of the maple turned yellow, starting on the branch that overhung the barn and progressing across the tree until no green remained. Most fell to heap the ground, while a few clung to their branches until torn loose by squalls that rained down dead limbs and abandoned nests.

As an Indian summer lost its grip and autumn grabbed hold, Ida seemed to resign herself to her husband's transformation. She said so little about it that Millard worried he'd frightened her away, and that he'd soon find her dresser drawers empty and a note saying she was going to live with her sister. But she stayed and adapted to his peculiar new vitality. He sat with her while she ate breakfast, counting the animals he'd killed the night before on the fingers of one, and some nights two, hands. At dinner, he read the paper while she ate her meal-for-one. Every evening they kissed goodnight at the front door, husband carrying his rifle toward the fields while his wife padded upstairs to bed. Millard wondered if she understood the full scope of his change, if she knew that he'd long outlive her. But they never spoke of it, and their lives forged new channels and flowed onward without scrutiny.

With Millard on perpetual vigil, no more lambs were bitten that year and the burn barrel smoldered day and night. A plume of greasy smoke reeking of singed hair lay over the farm and seeped into the house. Ida never complained, but kept the windows shut and latched.

As darkness came earlier each day, making night of afternoon, Millard's euphoria dimmed. Time seemed to slow, no longer running like stream, but oozing forward like the sludge in his veins. The farmer lost his zeal for the chores, telling Ida it was best to leave some of them for the spring. The tractor, the pipes and the drive could all wait. The truth was he had the energy to do the work, but was fast losing the desire.

By November, he spent most days sitting on the porch and staring out over the field with the rifle in his lap. The flock labored under the weight of their thick coats, waddling to avoid the autumn lamb, the eternal lamb, as it crisscrossed the cold-blanched turf. Ida stayed out of the cold, knitting in the parlor or puttering in the kitchen. Millard could no longer feel chill on his skin, and most days he didn't bother with his coat, hat or boots, but just rocked in his long johns. His bare toes made prints on the frosted planks. With each arc, his solitude nudged toward emptiness, and from emptiness to despair.

Like the varmints and the lamb, Millard was disconnected from the living world. Without joy or pain, hunger or satisfaction, life or death, they all went through the motions of life without purpose. The predators killed without eating, the lamb pastured without grazing. The farmer burned the former and nurtured the latter with no satisfaction, no joy. He'd made a devil's deal with the yellow ooze, winning a new youth but losing his desire to make use of it. He was like the brown, curled leaves, scuttling across the porch, a husk of what he'd been.

Autumn gales brought storms that drenched the soil and threatened to rust the rifle in his hands. One afternoon as Millard sat and rocked on the porch in his nightshirt, watching the puddles in the drive merge into ponds and lakes, he resolved to do more than watch over the property like a scarecrow. The drive needed grading and the ditches on either side, as it wound up toward the road, needed re-trenching. Ida shouldn't have to hopscotch her way to and from the car. He would put himself to good use.

Half-naked but oblivious to the cold and wet, he splashed to the barn and started the tractor. The engine putt-putted and the hydraulics whined as he raised the blade. Millard steered up the drive toward the road. Squinting into the rain, he aligned the blade's edge with the ditch and lowered it with a squeal until it clunked on the ground. He drove forward, bucking in the seat as the steel rasped through dirt and caught on stones. After ten yards he looked back and considered the shiny smear of mud, judging that the blade's angle wasn't steep enough. He left the engine in neutral, raised the blade a hair, then jumped down and wrestled with the giant pin on the mount. It wouldn't budge. Cursing, he crawled underneath the chassis and wriggled onto his back, unbothered by the gravel that raked his spine. He raised his foot and kicked up at the blade's mount, pounding it with his heel.

He spat drips of mud from his mouth and shouted, "Come on. I can't lay here all day."

The pin shimmied loose and one side of the blade dropped down with a clang. Millard hooted and began to drag himself out from under the machine, but something was wrong. He was crawling one way, but instead of moving the other way above, the underside of the tractor was gaining on him. He squirmed faster, but made no progress as chugging metal hulk rolled over him.

He'd never gotten around to fixing the slipping gears, and the machine had put itself in reverse.

The farmer raised his head off the soupy ground and saw that the tire had already crushed his leg and its deep treads were chewing up toward his waist like giant black teeth. The absence of pain made the ordeal far worse, confirming that his flesh had long been as good as dead.

With a scream, the farmer curled sideways, clawing toward the ditch as the wheel planted his pelvis into the earth like a thumb poking a bean seed. The canted blade followed, its tip tracing a deep furrow along the tire track before cutting Millard in half.

When Ida came home from work she must have passed his legs on the drive and seen the tractor tipped sideways and smoking in a field before finding his upper half grasping at the porch steps. Millard couldn't think of anything to say that would stop her from crying. He asked her to lift him onto the rocker, but she collapsed beside him. He asked again and again until she gathered herself and dragged him up each riser, across the planks and bear hugged him into the chair. Her jacket and skirt were covered in the yellow ooze that drained from his hewn body, slimed the porch, ran down the spindle legs and pooled like spilt syrup under the rockers.

Millard rested his head back against the top rail. "I've got to watch the sheep, Ida. Bring my rifle. I think I left it by the stove to dry."

She stared at what remained of him, dazed, then staggered through the front door.

"And there's a box of cartridges on the sideboard," he called after her. "Bring those too."

The rain shushed him as it fell harder, blurring everything beyond the porch rail. He knew what little remained of him and what little remained for him to do on the farm. He could shoot what he could see from the porch, which wasn't much, but what else was he good for? Not bucking hay or driving the flock or fencing. Sure as hell not shearing the sheep before they lambed. He was eternally useless, like the lamb that never grew fat.

Ida returned, handing him the box of ammunition and leaning the rifle against the rocker.

"Thank you, dear," he said, patting her trembling hand. "Now go on in and clean yourself up. Shower. Change into dry clothes. I'll be fine here. Don't you worry."

She hesitated on the threshold, then went back into the house.

Millard gave the box a shake, trying to judge by its rattle and heft how many shots it would take. Balancing his sheared torso on the swaying chair, he hoisted the gun and turned it backwards, pressing the muzzle to his breastbone with one hand and fingering the trigger with the other. A squeal from the pipes upstairs told him Ida was showering.

After twenty-odd rounds, the bolt knob sizzled his fingers each time he worked it. What was left of Millard slumped on the chair seat, as he found that very little of him needed to remain to keep going.

He shoved another yellow-slimed round into the chamber.

Villianwood

Benjamin Kane Ethridge

Katrina forced the mask over his face, ignoring the child's protests.

"This one hurts, Mommy," Adam said. A muffled whine went through the rubber. The eyes behind the ninja turtle's sockets welled.

"Sorry, honey." Katrina tugged at the mask several times before it came free. She turned away from her child. If she saw his face, it would only make her more desperate. Considering the other two masks—a pirate and yellow spaceman helmet—she lifted them for Adam's inspection. Back still turned to him, she said, "Which one then?"

"Do I have to wear a mask?"

Katrina plopped down on the couch. "We talked about this. You're out of school, there's no babysitter, and I might have to go to Los Angeles any day now. This is my big chance, remember?

"You don't want them to see my face."

She rubbed her eyes. "No, honey, that's not it."

"I can wait in the car."

"Not in this heat." She shook her head. "Not in the city. No."

"They won't let you in their movie if they see me, will they?"

"Don't talk like that. Adam, I just don't want them staring at you, okay? You've had your feelings hurt too much lately. It's tiring. Okay? Just... really...tiring."

Her six-year-old son shifted in the threshold of the kitchen, backlit by the harsh canned light overhead. Neurofibromatosis had left Adam's face looking like a bunch of flesh-colored grapes. It started progressing around three years of age and now looked more gruesome than ever. After countless days of trying to get used to it, she'd gotten into a bad habit of looking away from him.

At least she was still here. She hadn't packed up and left his father alone with a three-month-old baby to take care of. Although Derrick demanded otherwise, Katrina sent him photos of Adam every few months. Most of the time they'd go ignored, but sometimes Derrick would call her, irate, and threaten to cut ties to them completely if she didn't stop sending the photos.

But he'd never do that.

Coward that he was, Derrick did love his son. He *had* to look at the photos. And Katrina had the right to inflict at least some of her pain on the son of a bitch.

Whatever. All that was just amusement. She loved Adam and was in this for good. There was no need pretending it wasn't difficult though. Every day. *Every single day.* Dealing with it. Watching her boy sleep and being robbed of that warm feeling a mother should have when her angel is in dreamland. Instead she sees Adam's ravaged face and fights the notion it would be better if he never woke up.

She did love him. She did. She wasn't lying to herself. She wasn't.

"I guess I like the pirate one." Adam crept up to the counter, went on his tiptoes, and slid the mask toward him so he could look at it again.

Katrina got up from the couch with a soul-spent sigh. "Thanks, baby. Keep your fingers crossed I get the call." She dipped down to kiss his forehead, paused, and moved her lips to his dusty brown hair. Her eyes pooled for a moment as she wondered if he had picked up on that detour.

"Do you want some mac and cheese?"

The boy nodded as he intensely considered the empty-eyed pirate head.

"Okay, then I got to get back on the phone and find you a sitter."

"Why?"

"Vacation is up next Monday."

"I want to see your restaurant."

"You will. I'll take you sometime. It's a nice place."

A dark crescent cut through the bubbly flesh around the boy's lips. His smile appeared toothless and frightening.

She hurried away to the pantry.

"Where'd Darlene move to again?" Adam asked.

"The same place as I said before. Texas."

Darlene was a sweetheart. She'd always come over to ride bikes with Adam and watch TV. After her father got stationed at a different Air Force base, they'd moved and Adam had been pining for her return ever since. Nobody had ever been as nice to him as that little girl.

"Do you think she'll come visit?"

Katrina got out a large pot and the colander. "Maybe we can take a trip someday when we have more money."

A knock at the door almost made her drop the pot in the sink. Adam bounced with excitement. "Maybe Darlene's here now!"

"Please go to your room." Katrina rounded the counter.

"But I want to see!"

"Go. To. Your. Room." She pointed.

Adam let out a furious grunt and sprinted down the hall, pirate mask in hand.

Katrina leaned up to the peephole.

Larry Barten from next door. *What the hell does he want?*

Larry was a tall man, who might have been attractive had he not been one hundred pounds overweight, his striking face half-submerged in dough. He had an eight-year-old son named Tyler who was the antithesis of Darlene. Tyler refused to play with Adam and frequently called him *oatmeal face,* which embarrassed the hell out of his parents, Larry especially. So embarrassed, in fact, that anytime the wind changed direction in their town, Larry felt obligated to brief her. It was annoying, but she understood he was saving face for his brat.

Katrina checked her hair in the mirror under the coatrack before unlocking and opening the door.

"Hi, Kat. Hey, sorry to bother you." Larry took a sucking deep breath after every sentence, which made every conversation painfully long.

"No, it's okay. What's up?"

"Are you having any root infestation in your house?"

"Root?"

"Like tree roots coming up from the floor?"

Katrina shook her head and fought the urge to make an expression showcasing how thoroughly irritated she was with this visit. "No. There aren't any trees on our property, Larry. I don't think you have any either."

"We don't, but trees're popping up through the whole town. It's completely weird. This AG professor I was talking to at Rite Aid, he told me it's all the same tree, like, do you know about aspen forests?"

Katrina gave a tight-lipped smile. "Not really."

"The entire forest is one tree—one living thing—the roots are all connected to one parent tree. It's called a colony."

"Here in Southern California? Aren't aspens like a Colorado tree?"

"This isn't an aspen, and it grows different stalks very far apart. These trees are popping up like half a mile away from each other and growing really, really fast. I also heard they draw a lot of wildlife out of hiding. Possums, raccoons, and—"

"Okay, thanks." She smiled a little dismissively.

"Serious. Turn on the news tonight at six o'clock. I had a five-minute interview with one of the local networks. I don't know if they'll use it."

"That's exciting."

"Yeah, nobody knows what this tree is—I just thought since so many people were having major property damage, you might want to double-check your insurances, just in case the colony grows out this way."

"Thanks, I'll keep that in mind."

"Um…" Larry looked over her shoulder apprehensively. "Where's the little guy?"

"Playing in his room."

"Still feel horrible. I think Ty was just grumpy that one afternoon. We should get them together again and give it another shot."

"Sure. Kids are kids."

"Yes they are!" Larry nodded. "Okay then. The wife is coming back with groceries soon, so I better be there to help her or I'll be in for it."

"Oh yes, better go. Thanks again."

"No problem."

Katrina shut the door.

"Mommy?" Adam called down the hallway.

"Yeah, hon?"

"I know what Larry's talking about. It's pretty cool."

She didn't have time for this, but still felt bad about the mask thing, so she walked down the short hallway into his room. She jolted to a stop in the doorway.

A young tree had sprouted through the center of the floor, four feet into the air. At its base, thrusts of splintered wooden planks peeled away from the brown carpet. Adam sat near it, engaging two wizard action figures to climb its length.

Katrina could hardly find the words. "What . . . what is that? When did *that* get here?"

Adam looked at the tree and shrugged.

She thought back to the last time she'd been in his bedroom. Adam had slept in her bed the last three nights. She'd done laundry last weekend. It had to be at least four or five days since she'd stepped foot in here. Still, with a rich black trunk almost a foot thick, that it had grown to such a size was disturbing. Five branches stretched from the top, like fingers spread to steal light from the atmosphere. Leaves, so astonishingly green they nearly hurt the eyes to behold, tipped the branches in random places.

"Come out of here, baby," said Katrina.

"Why?"

"Because I said so."

"I like the tree. Don't get rid of it. Please?"

"Adam Jeffery Bailey, get your butt up and come out of there."

Her son's eyes cast down amid the colossal deformity of his face. Making his fingers go dead, he dropped his toys and got up.

This was a nightmare. The headache, once located square between Katrina's eyes, had migrated across her entire skull and traveled down her neck. The pain made her nauseous and she'd massaged her forehead raw. Third daycare in a row, and this one seemed to be shrinking away too.

"I give him the medication for the seizures in the morning and . . . uh-huh . . . Adam hasn't had one in almost two years . . . yes . . . he isn't special needs though . . . the last time he'd been checked with the MRI, yes . . . Look, his tumors are mostly on his face, neck, and shoulders. Goodness, no they don't need to be drained. Inside he's a healthy boy. And a good boy. He'll help with chores and . . . can you just let me finish? Wait, you don't know how difficult it's been . . . please? It *isn't* contagious . . . I told you already, there aren't any special day classes available that work with my job . . . You can look it up online. You have? I'm pretty sure it came from my husband's side of the family . . . Ex-husband, I mean . . . Yeah, I know it might be hard for younger kids . . . Well you shouldn't judge just by images from WebMD. If you . . . but . . . listen please . . . Oh, the hell with !"

Katrina pushed "End" and threw the phone onto the couch. Crossing the kitchen, she took a deep breath. She opened the fridge, got the water pitcher, and grabbed the bottle of ibuprofen from the cupboard.

The phone rang before she could take the pills.

She rushed over to the couch and quickly picked it up. The number didn't look familiar, nor did the area code. Was it Roger calling to tell her about the part? Or the studio itself?

She answered.

A voice with a slight Mexican accent replied, "Pedro's Tree and Stump removal, calling back a Katrina Bailey."

Her shoulders sunk. "Yes, that's me. I called about this tree that has come up through—"

"Ah, yes. The villainwood trees?"

"Villain—what?"

"That's just a nickname around town, Mrs. Bailey. We've been getting calls all morning. For now, I can only put you on our call-back list."

"Is there anybody else in town? It has grown pretty fast already—"

"Rogers Landscaping and Green Castle Cultivation, but I think they're up to their necks too."

"Really? This crazy tree will probably tear through my roof . . . I have a credit card. I can pay right now, today."

"Just got ten calls in since we've been on the line. Look, I can put you in our system. We can probably be out there in a few days."

"A *few* days?"

The man's chuckle trailed into a sigh. "I was actually being generous with that time frame. The roots are like concrete and go down so far, we have no idea where they came from, where the parent tree is."

"*Wonderful.* I guess we'll be getting a big hole in our roof then."

"You won't be the first, sorry to say. The city is setting up something for families at the community center. You should check there."

Katrina was numb, couldn't think of anything to say. This was unreal.

"So put you in the system?"

"Yeah," she answered.

"Okay, I'll use the information from your message you left."

" 'Preciate it, she said."

"Good luck."

She ended the call and strode into the hallway. *Where was that boy?*

"Adam? You're not messing with that tree, are you?"

"Bathroom," a small voice returned.

Katrina sat on the couch and remembered the pain relievers on the counter. She felt too exhausted to get back up.

A series of thumps, a scampering, registered above.

She sat up in the returning silence. "Adam?"

"Whaaaat?" the boy complained.

"Nothing." She leaned back again. Splendid, now there were probably rodents in their crawlspace, brought into the house from this damned villaintree or whatever they called it. This was not the kind of shit she needed right now. Sleeping here with it growing out of control? Rats or possums or bugs getting into the house?

Having only a landline nowadays made her feel so damned impoverished. If she wasn't waiting on that call from Roger, she'd probably have taken the city up on their community center. Derrick's child support check scarcely covered the mortgage, and with amassing medical bills and how little she made at the restaurant, it wouldn't surprise her if their days were numbered in this house. Things had been so much easier when she was a dumb young girl goofing around in her theater group. The whole universe felt open and available. Now it was a solitary confinement cell.

The house let loose a resounding series of snaps; the walls buckled, flexed, and resumed their position. She paused in mid-flight from the couch. *Not a quake.* It had to be that tree, screwing her entire house up from the foundation all the way to the rafters.

This was it. She couldn't stay in this house much longer. If Roger didn't call by seven o'clock tonight, she would call him and try to get the studio rep interested again.

But a couple hours later there was no need.

The casting department called.

* * *

"I don't want to boast or anything," Katrina went on with a fake laugh, "but the restaurant I work at has been featured on the Food . . . So if the video I sent is interesting, I'm ready to come down to audition. I mean, it's better to narrow this down . . . right . . . you're going to get people off the street, but with all my theater background we spoke about . . . yeah, exactly . . . you're at least getting someone who has seen the ins and outs. Probably doesn't mean much, but I also got third place in my high school drama competition. Both freshman and sophomore years . . . Why, thank you."

Dressed in yellow pajamas, Adam hovered over her, a red muppet firmly held to his chest. She didn't want to look beyond the layers of his face and meet his needy eyes. She knew it would break her stride; this conversation was going better than she could have ever hoped for. Out of fear of the very nice casting rep hearing her, she just wanted to yell Adam out of the room.

The rep told her they were still building a list of names. It was a process. And she understood. Completely. In the end, he'd call back tomorrow with a date and time for live auditions.

"Can't wait," she told him. "And, thank you."

As soon as she hung up, she stared at her son in quiet rebellion. For a few moments, he was a different person to her. Couldn't he see how close she was? Didn't he care?

His tumors looked like a pale colony of aquatic eggs in the diffuse light of the living room. He was always gawking at her, always hoping to get answers; she didn't have any. He was six, yes, but he should have known by now that she was powerless to help him.

"Okay. *What?* What, Adam? What? What is it? Why can't I just have one conversation without you on top of me?"

"I hear whispering in the ceiling," he said.

Most men couldn't wrap their arms around the villainwood's trunk by now. The bark was a curious looking configuration; it didn't look like any plant Katrina had seen before. Bands of coarse onyx tightly wound around brighter red inner skin, a freshly flayed column of muscle that bulged painfully between dark tourniquets. Tangles of roots swelled around the ground, several of the larger plunging all the way through the walls, one spearing

Adam's twin mattress in the rightmost corner. Near the floor, smaller, weaker roots met the running boards like freeze-frames of a spaghetti collision. Overhead were three visible branches extending across the room that hadn't yet penetrated the drywall. More of the blinding green leaves pushed out from thick stalks, fibers hanging down from their bases like the scraggly hair of an old witch. While all the light seemed to emanate from the leaves, the rest of the room clamored with hands of shadow.

A simple ladder made of diminutive cut roots had been hammered with brass nails into the side of the trunk. The ladder ran up its length, past shredded wood layered in latex paint, into the empty outrage in the ceiling.

Adam whimpered, but Katrina couldn't stop staring, blinking, staring, blinking, tilting her head. Her thoughts spilled out of her: "Who put that ladder there?"

"The elves, Mommy."

She looked down at her disfigured son. He gripped her hand tightly and pressed into the sides of her legs. His face hadn't changed. He might have been happy, mad, frustrated, or suicidal, but all she saw were the useless tumors that made him as devastatingly unique as this tree was.

"Adam, you're saying there were people in here? You saw them?"

"They were whispering. I saw an elf last night, outside the bathroom. I thought it was a dream, but the whispers today sound like the one I saw."

"Are you making this up?" she asked. "It isn't funny, hon."

When he didn't answer, she reached down and shook his shoulder. "Tell me."

"No, Mommy."

"But you were dreaming?"

"I don't think so."

"You saw one?"

"Yes. But I hear more than one."

"How many more?"

The little boy shrugged one shoulder and leaned his head against her hip once more. Katrina backed away from him and went out of the room. Adam followed.

That's what those thuds had been. There were transients living in their ceiling space. The bums must have found a way in somehow. Maybe the tree had popped through the roof and they climbed inside. She almost didn't want to go outside to see, but she had to get to the bottom of this.

Calmly she headed for the front door.

"Are we going outside?" Adam cried out cheerfully.

"No, no, you stay in here."

"Oh," he said.

Katrina slid the dead bolt out and stopped, hand on the handle. She said no so often, she'd forgotten when to say yes. She nodded with a short smile. "Okay, come on outside Adam."

"Yay!" The boy skipped toward her.

An earthy odor billowed in as the door opened. She sneezed violently two times, her eyes going wider with what she saw. A matrix of branches had grown over the threshold, creating a deep barrier. Adam, once more, pressed into Katrina and gripped her leg. Saying nothing, she looked to the two windows in the front room. The white shades were drawn, but from the crisscrossing shadows beyond, there was little doubt of what grew over them.

"I don't know, Kat," Larry muttered. It was difficult to see him through the cross sections of oily branches. Just a shifting ghost face. "My tree trimmer's wearing out. The branches almost look, I don't know, *thicker* than before?"

"Please don't tell me that."

"Did you call your ex-husband? Maybe he's got something better—"

"On a Hawaiian cruise," she snapped.

"Okay, okay," Larry said, trying to sound reassuring. "I'm going to give the police department a call."

She sighed and leaned on Adam's aluminum baseball bat like a cane. "Don't bother. I already tried."

"How's that?"

"I said, DON'T BOTHER, WE'RE FUCKED!" She picked up the bat and struck the door. A divot of wood came free with the blow.

"Come on, Kat."

"Really?" She threw the bat nosily into a corner. "I've got homeless people living in my roof."

"I've been up and down the ladder. Just a bunch of branches twisted up in the rafters. These invaders would have to be the size of spider monkeys to live inside such a small space. Probably just squirrels. Just don't freak out."

"Ha! Say that on this side of the branches!"

"It's going to be okay."

"STOP saying that stuff, Larry. Just go away if you can't help!"

Adam started whining. The sound of his voice made her more upset. Katrina groaned. "We're the only ones in this whole damn neighborhood who get this shit!"

"Kat, the trees are all over town—"

"Why is this happening to me? Everything happens to me."

Larry's shape dissolved through the branches. "I'll get back to you soon."

Tears slalomed down the orbs and craters of Adam's face. His mouth hung open, a steady stream of drool slipping out. Over his shoulder she spotted the photo of them together at his first birthday. He had only a few of the tumors then. She had thought they were some type of warts—shamefully feared some kind of clandestine venereal disease had been transferred from Derrick through the womb—back then she wanted him to take the blame somehow. Yet, the smile on her face in the photo, Adam's goofy grin, the coned blue birthday hat leaning off his downy hair, the light around them at the kitchen table, it was a different cosmos with different people. Had it ever been possible to be that happy, to feel anything but dread for the years to come?

By now, she almost absorbed the grating noise Adam had been making.

The house settled in a series of trembling clicks that followed with rolling thumps.

Footfalls?

Adam ramped up his fit and Katrina went to him. How could she protect him from the world when she hadn't succeeded with anything yet? It wasn't fair. With that in mind, however, if Adam couldn't count on his mother, who could he count on? She'd chastened his father for being unable to deal, well goddamn it, she was going to deal!

She got down on her knees and hugged Adam close to her. It had been a while since she initiated this and it felt good. He deserved this. He was just a little boy.

Just a scared little boy.

You have to be the one to make this right.

Her cheek brushed a bank of tumors along his jaw-line and a shiver ran down her spine.

"Can we call Dad on the ship?" he asked.

"Adam, we can't hope for him to come back. It's just us."

"Will you ever marry someone else?" His voice sounded hopeful. There were no new revelations about his father, and though Adam was still curious, he had done his own part to move on.

"I might. You never know."

How could I meet anybody now?

"Do you think someone will marry me when I grow up?" Adam asked quietly.

Katrina almost couldn't answer. She looked away, heart folded to bits in her chest. "Of course someone will. Of course."

"And she'll be pretty, like you?"

"Prettier," Katrina replied, voice cracking.

He pulled away and she met his eyes with a quick, feeble glance.

"I love you Mommy."

She didn't want to think this way, but he looked so chilling right then. His face, while probably expressive and thoughtful, looked deep with menace.

"Love you too, honey. Let's go to bed."

"But the elves—"

"Just squirrels. We'll lock the door anyhow."

They walked to the bedroom. The hall smelled of ancient smoke, of aged cherries, of fresh wounds. But this was a wonder, for the air was crisp and clear, the hanging branches in the hall bore no fruit, and so far, no blood had been spilled.

Katrina spent the next day pouring any chemicals she could find on the tree. Bleach, detergent, dish soap, rubbing alcohol, even shampoo. With a butcher knife she managed to sever a few of the leaves, but the hard stems made the blade go dull after an hour of cutting.

She sat on the edge of the couch, hands burning from the bleach and the soreness of the blade work. When the phone rang she'd hopped up quickly, all thoughts of the tree leaving her mind, and ran *so giddy* to pick up the call.

A campaign for financing had failed and a sole producer pulled out on the same day. The entire project dissolved.

Sorry. Not even a bit part in an indie movie.

She twisted the phone around in her hands, wanting to kill it.

A giggle went through the hall. A smallish voice. A snort.

Katrina waited a moment for more sounds. When nothing else came, she got up silently and peered into the hall. The door to Adam's room was open.

She went to the closet and pulled out the baseball bat. Careful to avoid the whiny floorboards under the carpet, she made her way across the hall. She sidled up to the wall and glanced into the room.

Adam stood in the dark bedroom between two large roots that dipped like wooden waves. Something shadowy and spherical hovered before him. Katrina thought it might be a part of the tree at first, but then it moved, twisted around, and she could tell it was a being of some kind. The little monstrosity was about a foot shorter than Adam. Sharp horns, or maybe ears, stood at either side of its head. Loose, burlap clothing hung from its body in tatters. Adam giggled and jumped up and down. He held hands with it and danced in a circle.

After the frolicking stopped, it *whispered* to her son. Like bent rusted nails, fangs interlocked inside the wide mouth with every word. She didn't like how those words sounded. Slow popping bubbles through tar, the release of primordial air, which was then followed by a snicker of devilish insinuation. A slender, yet rough hand fell on Adam's shoulder and patted him.

The figure, which Katrina could now see was indeed an elf, drifted away from Adam, raising a hand in farewell, and then climbed the tree ladder, swiftly going up and out of sight.

Katrina didn't know it then, but the next two evenings would end in the exact same way, with her boy communing with the fiend from the tree, and her, crouched in the hallway with the bat, watching, waiting, and feeling nothing inside.

* * *

"We need to be serious, hon. You aren't giving them our food, are you? We might be trapped in this house for who knows how long."

"You've been watching us?" he asked.

"Had to. I've never seen anything like them before."

"Aren't you mad?"

"I am," said Katrina, narrowing her eyes at her son. "But what difference does that make? We're here and they're here."

"You're right. Do you want to meet them?"

"Of course not. They're monsters."

"Then . . . why do you let me play with them?"

"Don't ask silly questions."

But Katrina asked herself the same thing.

What am I waiting to see happen?

Adam languidly stirred his macaroni and cheese. It was the last box and a very thin concoction since they'd run out of milk and butter yesterday. He'd only taken a single bite and Katrina was taking it personally. Every tumor in his face pissed her off. They were sickening. Just like his giggles when he was playing games with those elves from the villainwood tree. If she wasn't such a loving mother, she might have said they deserved each other. That clammy gray skin and those endless needle teeth like something out of a whale's mouth; how they clutched on to Adam's action figures with such barbaric intensity and made grunting sounds for imaginary play; the sardonic shimmer in their too-green eyes that seemed to suggest murderous betrayal was waiting right around the corner.

Her boy didn't see them as monsters, but he wasn't stupid. Only recently had he really opened up and let the elves into his personal space. Growing more comfortable around them had simultaneously made him less comfortable around Katrina. Over the course of a couple days he had pulled away from her noticeably, but still, she never, never ever, would have expected to hear these next words as he laid down his fork.

"I want to go with them, up the ladder," said Adam, his voiced edged and more mature than she remembered it. "And I don't ever have to come back down, if I don't want to."

Katrina's fork clattered on her plate of wax beans. "Are you joking?"

"Are you, Mommy?"

"What do you mean by that, young man?"

"That's what you want. For me to go away. So you don't have to be a Mommy."

"That's nonsense, Adam. That's really, really stupid, of you to say."

"I don't think so."

"Well I do!"

"They like me. They like me more than Darlene did. More than you and Dad. I want to go, Mommy. They aren't monsters at all."

Katrina stood and put both her fists knuckle-down on the table. "How dare you. You haven't even known these things for a week and you're ready to give up on me? Well that's bullshit! I never gave up on you, kid. I never did. How could you betray me like this?"

Adam sat there pensively. Maybe he didn't understand the word *betray.* Maybe he did. Either way his eyes clouded with tears.

"I'm locking that door and we aren't going into that room until someone comes and gets rid of that goddamn tree. You're saying goodbye to them tonight." Katrina picked up her terracotta plate, went over to the sink, and dropped it in.

"Just let me go."

She froze, fighting the trembling in her lower lip.

"Eventually, someone will get us out of here. There are smart people who will find a way. When those people come to rescue us, they'll see that I did my job, as a mother."

Though she didn't look at him, she could tell by his thickened voice he was crying. "Why then? Why'd you let me play with them? Did you want them to hurt me, Mommy? Are you mad that they didn't?"

"Oh Adam!" She caught her mouth and shook her head frantically to rid her mind from all the darkness. "Stop saying such horrible things. How could you?"

A few minutes of silence passed before Adam added, "Please, they're my best friends. They love me."

Katrina dragged her wrist over the tear trails on her cheeks. The emotion that had brought them had fled. "Tough shit. This ends tonight. Now eat your mac 'n' cheese."

* * *

Adam poked her ribs again. Katrina kept her eyes closed and forced out a heavy breath. He put his hand on her cheek. "Mommy, you awake?"

She turned away from him, digging her hand under the pillow. The bed flexed as Adam slid off the side. Katrina kept her eyes at slits, seeing nothing but the digital clock on the nightstand across from her. Adam stood bedside for five long minutes before stepping away.

"Love you, Mommy," he whispered.

Tears broke through the slits.

She heard the door slightly squeak as he went into the hall.

More tears.

Of anger. Not at Adam, but at herself. Where had her mind gone? She'd almost given him away. At the time it had been opportunistic instinct, but now she realized how evil the notion was, of not bearing any responsibility for what might have happened. Allowing her son into a dangerous situation. When rescuers came, how would it look for her to have lost him? She wouldn't let Adam do that to her.

She turned, ever so slowly, to see if he watched her from the hall, but he was gone. Blood pulsed hot in her face. Shame. Rage. She could have used this in her audition, had she had one. Had she just had a chance to even try. Had she not been blindsided. Always blindsided. Had she known when she met the father of her child . . . had she had an inkling.

She hated the word *had.*

Katrina took the bat from under the bed. Walking into the hallway, she noticed a few more roots had broken through the wall. She tripped over one and regained herself by grasping the door frame.

Inside the room, she saw the elf descend the ladder, its sinuous shape bouncy with excitement. Adam stood on top of a root with a plastic grocery bag loaded with his belongings. The elf leaned in and hissed something into Adam's ear. On the snaking roots it looked a nightmarish abstraction.

Katrina bent low, keeping the bat behind her back. She approached from a lower vantage afforded by the messy intertwine. The elf gently took Adam's hand in its own, the cindery flesh sparkling like high-mineral dirt. Slowly, Katrina grasped a low-hanging branch from the villainwood tree and pulled herself to a higher vantage.

Adam didn't notice her rise behind them. Not at first. But the elf saw immediately. Its head inclined a bit, and its eyes, the same color of the tree's blinding green leaves, focused on her, seeming uncertain and very certain at the same time. Her son just began to turn as the bat crashed into the elf's head.

"Oh!" Adam said, shocked.

Something fluid and dark ran over one of the green eyes and the elf looked around, drunk on pain. Katrina lifted the bat again and delivered another blow that forced the creature down, its body draped over a root.

"Mom!" Adam squealed. "Mommy!"

"Hush, you're safe now!" Katrina hooked her arm around Adam and pressed her hand over his mouth, for once the fleshy barnacles on his lips not bothering her in the least. She had a clear shot for the elf's head, and she took it.

The darkness exploited no gore, but wetness gloved Katrina's hand. In that same absence of light, the wrecked skull before her was a tuft of gloom. Blood pitter-pattered on the roots below.

Adam struggled in her grip. He'd slip out soon. She had to finish this, and she couldn't do that with him carrying on.

With great effort she stumbled over to the hall with her son in tow. He sobbed through her hand but Katrina was numb to the sounds. He didn't know what these things would do to him. He was just a boy. She couldn't be held responsible. She couldn't fail again. Not again, goddamn it. She didn't want to ever say the word *had* once more in her life—and feel it infect her from the guts out.

No!

She opened the closet and pushed Adam inside, the door doing little to muffle his wails. She wedged her foot against the bottom and grabbed the nearby wrought-iron magazine rack. As she heaved it across the carpet, copies of Entertainment Weekly fluttered off the sides. She tucked one of the rack's iron bands under the handle to barricade the door.

"I'll let you out later, honey," she told the boy. "I made a mistake, okay? I shouldn't have let it go this far. We can't have those things in our house. You know that, Adam."

Her son let out a panicked cry and slammed into the door. The magazine rack shuddered but held against the impact.

"No Mommy. No Mom. *Mommy!*"

Adrenalin flooded her body as she stormed back down the hall and back into the bedroom. The shape of the dead elf still lay across the roots where she'd left it. Katrina stepped over it, her resolve growing as she made her way to the trunk and grabbed the first rung of the ladder.

The hole into the crawlspace was almost too small to get her shoulders past. Gnarls of roots gathered around her, all flickering with soft candlelight. Using the bat, Katrina pulled up through them and spotted a small passage along the rafters. She ducked and shimmied through a narrowing between the mass of branches and the wall until she reached a corner that gave her just enough clearance to kneel. Her eyes darted around the attic, searching. The candlelight expanded and clarified an alcove where two elves sat at a child-sized table set for four, their eyes hungry and sly, as though waiting impatiently for their meal to begin. Something told her one was the father and one was the mother, by their respective sizes compared to the other.

The father gently rapped his stumpy fingers on the table, while the mother moved a greasy black lock of hair off her face.

Katrina awkwardly moved the bat around her body and shifted her position. The elves' sharp ears perked at the sound of her stepping forward. Heads turned, they raised their startling green eyes up to the giant before them and smiles faded from their gaping, fanged mouths.

The father tried to say something, but the sound ended, just a sharp whistle of choked-off steam. Katrina hit him so hard his body came out of the chair and flew into the branches behind. The mother wailed and scrambled over to a chopping block with a roasted pigeon upon it. She drew a knife out of the side of the dead bird and turned—

Right into the end of Katrina's next swing.

This strike only clipped the elf's jaw, sending her staggering into a circle. Katrina moved forward. The father, prone on the floor, attempted to raise his head and then vomited over the branches before passing out. The mother elf tried to grab the carving knife, but Katrina caught up with her and connected better this time, driving soupy purple brains around the bat in a flourish. The mother dropped dead there, but she kept beating her until the head puddled on the floor.

She went back to the father elf, and though he already appeared dead, she beat his head in just as she had done the mother.

Katrina stood there, hunkered over the table, which had oddly not been disturbed in all the violence. Every fork, spoon, knife and plate ready and unused, and every dark corner of the crawlspace now silent.

It had only taken minutes, but she knew more peace right now than she'd enjoyed in a long time. Bizarre, but it seemed she'd needed to kill these monsters her entire life.

With morbid satisfaction and adrenaline still surging, she climbed carefully back down the ladder.

She went into her bathroom and thoroughly washed her hands and face, but didn't bother changing into a nightgown.

Adam was asleep in the closet, his bulging, tumorous face still wet with tears.

Katrina was too exhausted to haul him into the bedroom. He stirred a little, but otherwise he was out like a light and would sleep until tomorrow. Even in the most stressful times, when a kid sleeps, they sleep well. She wished she knew how that felt again.

Exhaustion finally covered the nerve-shocked energy that had been powering her. Katrina stretched out over the living room floor and pulled Adam on top of her, holding him just like she had in the hospital after he was born. It was warm and surprisingly comforting to have him draped over her like that, so she left him there, and slept with him close that night.

Slept like a child.

It was sometime just before dawn that Katrina realized roots had grown around her and Adam. Some underneath them, a few thin, taut ones between them, and a dense swathe over them. The villainwood had pinned mother and son in such a horrible way that even squirming became impossible.

For a solid hour she was in shock. Once she regained focus, she tried not to cry or panic.

As sunlight leaked through the holes in the ceiling, Katrina saw that Adam was awake. Roots had grown under his chest, lifting him at an angle so that he was looking down at her from above. "Somebody's going to find the parent tree," she told him. "They'll figure it out. We'll be okay, hon. Okay?"

Everything inside her told her otherwise. The roots had tightened even after a short while and breathing became harder.

She lifted her head and kissed Adam on the bubbly flesh of his right cheek.

"I love you so much, honey."

He said nothing to her.

Besides roots, the only thing in Katrina's line of sight was her son's face. That was her world right now. That face. The face she'd made. The face she was responsible for. Her legacy to cherish and preserve. She had little other choice but to seek the truth there. It didn't take long. In his eyes, all that was once alive on her behalf had entirely departed, never to return.

Not even if they had a lifetime to spare.

Learned Children

Ronald Malfi

Soon after, he began to question his sanity.

Holes, Paul Marcus thought. *Craters. A few more months of this and it'll look like a blitzkrieg.*

It was about the missing girl, of course. The scarecrow was a dream—he couldn't think of it otherwise without compromising his sanity—and he wondered how much of the actual digging had been done in some sort of fugue state, for he could only recall what he had done on the mornings that followed, waking in bed with mud dried to his feet. Once, he'd awoken in the field, his skin gritty with hours' old perspiration, his arms and shoulders sore from digging.

Digging holes, he thought. *Craters.* Trembling.

He was what the townspeople called "a distant"—a person from elsewhere who'd come to roost among them. A drafty old farmhouse with more bedrooms than he would ever need and a position of schoolteacher that needed filling were the things that brought him here. A *distant,* he supposed, was better than *intruder,* was better than *trespasser.* Nonetheless, he felt his own intrusion in his bones. His students did not make him feel any more welcome, either. Blank, moonfaced dullards, he often felt like he was preaching to a classroom of earthworms. Even creepier was when their slack disinterest turned to brazen effrontery.

"Can anyone tell me what Blake is trying to say in this passage?"

Ignoring the question, one of the piggish little gnomes toward the back of the classroom said, "They talk about you in church."

The comment caught Paul Marcus with his guard down. "I'm sorry?" He still did not know all their names, mainly because they refused to sit in their assigned seats. "Someone has been talking about me?"

"In church," repeated the boy.

"I don't understand," Paul said.

"Your car has a broken headlight," said one of the girls.

"Your shoes are funny," chided another.

And so on…

It was his students who first brought the missing girl to his attention. They kept her empty desk at the back of the classroom like a shrine; sometimes, after recess, some of the girls would bring flowers in with them from the schoolyard to decorate it. Hardened fingers of bubble gum hung like stalactites from the underside of the desk and someone had carved JANNA IS DED on the desktop.

Of course, since she was never found, no one knew for sure that she was dead.

"Who's Janna?" he asked upon first noticing the inscription. "What happened to her?"

"Someone got her."

"What does that mean?"

"She was here one day," said a boy as he dug around in one nostril, "and the next day, she was gone."

"When?"

"Month ago."

"Who took her?"

The boy shrugged. "Why is your hair gray on the sides but black up top?"

The students snickered.

There was no Janna on his roster. Were the little cretins messing with him? He didn't put it past them. There had been frogs in his desk and, disturbingly, a baby bird with its neck broken in his coffee mug one morning.

But they were not messing with him.

"It's true," said George Julliard one afternoon in the teacher's lounge. He was working around a mouthful of peanut butter and jelly. "Abduction is the sheriff's best guess."

"She isn't on my roster."

But he found out why later on: his roster had been carefully rewritten to exclude Janna's name. His roster was not the original. The original was found crumpled in a ball in Janna's desk, her name clearly legible. When Paul brought this to the principal's attention—a middle-aged woman with thinning silver hair—she only laughed and said kids will be kids.

"Did any of you change my roster?" he asked his students the following day.

"What's your favorite color?" asked one of the girls.

"Do you like cats?" asked a boy.

Holes, he thought. *And the scarecrow.*

It was a dream, surely. The scarecrow was just a slapdash thing strung to a post in the east field, its clothes tatters of flannel, its face a featureless burlap sack. Something so innocuous even the crows nested on its shoulders and pecked at it. Yet at night, in Paul's dreams—for surely they were only dreams—it would appear framed in Paul's bedroom window, its respiration—*respiration!*—impossibly fogging up the glass.

In a state of near-somnambulism, Paul would climb out of bed and, barefoot, follow the lumbering dark shape around the side of the house. That first night there was a shovel leaning against the porch. Paul took it as a weapon. The scarecrow—nothing more than a smudge of darkness—moved onward through the stalks of corn.

It wasn't until Paul reached a sparse clearing in the corn did he realize the scarecrow had disappeared. Something about the softness of the ground troubled him. The shovel, it seemed, was all too conveniently in his hands.

He dug, thinking of the missing girl, thinking, *Janna is ded.*

In the end, he found only an empty hole in the earth. And in the morning, despite the filth on his feet, he wondered if it had all been a dream.

But it was no dream. And it continued for the first month. When he tried to stay awake, the scarecrow did not appear. It was only on those nights where, bested by exhaustion, he would slump over in a chair only to awaken at the sound of the creaking porch as someone circumnavigated the farmhouse. A shape would lumber past the windows.

Scarecrow, he thought, shuddering.

He was supposed to find the girl—that much was clear to him. Each night, the scarecrow led him to a different part of the field. Often, Paul could discern patches of barren earth between the stalks, and he would commence digging. Other times, he found himself uprooting stalks to cultivate his craters. By the end of the month, and with the harvest moon now full in the sky, the field was pockmarked by his obsession.

"She lived in your house, you know," said one of his students...and how simple was he that he hadn't already come to this realization? It gave his obsession a heart and a soul.

"You're getting warmer," said another student, and this caused the hairs on the back of Paul's neck to rise. As if they were watching him at night while he dug like a grave robber in the cornfield.

He wanted to ask them, *Is the scarecrow real?* He wanted to say, *Is that what got Janna?* But he didn't. He would be driven out of a job for being a madman.

Again, night came. The scarecrow appeared shifting through the corn at the edge of the field. This night, Paul waited for it, sitting on the porch with the shovel across his lap. Again, he followed it into the field. When he lost sight of the creature, he began digging.

Janna is ded.

There was nothing beneath the ground.

Above, ravens cawed.

On a Tuesday, someone put a rotten apple on his desk. Someone else had stuck used flypaper in X formations across the windowpanes in the classroom. Again, the principal laughed and said kids will be kids.

"No one handed in their homework," he said to the class. This wasn't totally accurate—someone had handed in a ream of paper on which they'd pasted cutout photos from glamour magazines. Paul found this alarmingly sociopathic.

At the end of the day, as they filed out of the classroom, one of the girls smiled at him. Her front teeth were blackened and there was a bruise on her left cheekbone. "Tick tock goes the clock," she said to him.

"What?"

She smiled horridly then fled from the classroom.

He no longer waited for the scarecrow to make its appearance; he spent his evenings digging trenches in the cornfield. By the second month in the farmhouse, there was very little corn left.

Exhausted, sore, he dragged the shovel behind him back toward the house, stopping only when he saw the scarecrow hanging from its post in the east field. Its form was slumped under the weight of countless black crows. Despite his tiredness, he went to it. The crows were bold and did not fly off immediately. Paul scared them off eventually by swinging the shovel.

"Get," he said. "Go on."

It hung like wet laundry, its pant legs sprouting straw, its flannel shirt tattered. The featureless burlap sack of its face seemed to sag under the weight of its existence.

It does not exist. Not like that.

He reached up and pressed a hand to its straw-filled flannel shirt.

Not straw-filled.

Paul went cold. He dropped the shovel in the dirt.

Reaching up, he peeled the burlap face away to reveal a second face: a head turned funny on its neck, reminding Paul Marcus of the dead baby bird left in his coffee mug.

The next Monday, after a weekend spent at the sheriff's office filling out paperwork, he stood before his classroom. The earthworms were suspiciously quiet this morning. Nothing had been left on or in his desk. The flypaper had been removed from the cracked windowpanes.

"I want..." And his voice cracked. "I want you all to turn to chapter five in your texts," he continued, trying hard to sound in control. He was sweating through his tweed coat and his throat felt constricted. "I *want—*"

"Dogs can sense fear," said the boy toward the back, picking his nose.

"My mother had an abortion when she was a teenager," said one of the girls.

Paul Marcus offered them a wan smile and wondered, not for the first time, whatever happened to the schoolteacher he had replaced.

Into the Trees

Tim Lebbon

Dying, Toby Sugg was drawn back to the only good place in his life, and the only good thing he had done. He had always known where his final resting place would be. That tree was a knot in his memories.

He parked close to the canal, remaining in the car and readying himself to walk along the towpath. He wanted to enter the wood unseen. Opening the window, he closed his eyes and breathed in scents that took him back through the years, inspiring a rush of memories that brought a startled sob. Toby hadn't cried since his father's death when he was fourteen years old. He'd made people cry--he was very good at that--but he'd believe that something about the old man passing had hardened him up.

Maybe all it took was something special.

Cut grass, dank canal water, and the perfume of blooming bluebells stripped away the years and scars and showed Toby hints of what he might have been. His face cracked in a rare smile. It felt strange against his lips and cheeks, like a stranger forcing itself out. He wondered if perhaps he would open his eyes and see more of the past. But when he looked, the old shed close to the canal bridge was gone, and the 'No Horses' sign he'd once peppered with air rifle pellets as a kid had been replaced. The new sign was spray-painted with a crude set of balls and a spurting cock.

Toby sighed, and wondered what childhood had become. He chuckled, feeling old. Then he closed his eyes against a new wave of pain. Age was no longer his concern.

Hand pressed to the wound in his gut, he opened the door and stood from the car. He'd promised himself he wouldn't cry out, but the agony was great, and stiffness had set in on his long drive from London. He groaned aloud, bit his lip and leaned against the car, glancing down. No spooling guts, no gush of fluid and blood and shit. If the knife had pierced his intestines, he'd likely be dead already.

I'm going to bleed to death, Toby thought. It was a vague idea that no longer troubled him. He had been dying since he had left Lucy Hughes with a splinter gone bad in her finger.

Time for the bleeding to end.

"This is my favourite place," Toby's father says. "I found this tree when I was nine, thirty years before you were born. I'd be out walking with my dog. Kids were allowed out then, not like now. I'd go out in the morning and be told to be back for tea, and I'd make my own fun. Building dens in the woods, cycling along deserted roads--not so many cars back then. Summer holidays would stretch forever, and every day would be filled with sun stuff. I'd get burnt and go home aching and shivering, and my mother would smear calamine lotion all over my shoulders and arms and neck. *That's* the true smell of summer. Calamine lotion." He looks at Toby, standing patiently nearby. "Your mother would never let you get sunburnt."

His comment held a note of accusation, and that confused Toby. He didn't *want* to be sunburnt.

"And it was one of those days I found this tree. I'd come into the field..." He points across the rolling landscape of wide open fields, overgrown hedges. The tree stands alone in several acres of bright yellow rape, like something forgotten. "Used to be a barn over that way, by the gate onto the road. I stopped there for a piss and fell asleep in the shade. Then when I woke up I saw the tree, and it was like..." His father leans back and looks up into the stark branches. "It was my tree."

Toby looks as well, and sees nothing remarkable. There are a few branches bearing leaves, but even more that don't. Surrounding the tree's wide trunk, lying on the ground are the remnants of fallen boughs. Perhaps it is diseased or has been struck by lightning, but Toby suspects this tree won't last many more summers.

"Found these," his father says. He waves Toby closer with an impatient grunt. Toby does as instructed. "See? What do you think they are?"

Toby has seen things like this before, but they're usually sprayed on motorway bridges or the backs of garden walls. He's never seen them carved in wood, and he wonders at the effort it must have taken to put them there.

"This one," his father says. "*A.M. long boy, 1954.*" He raises an eyebrow at Toby.

Toby shrugs.

"This one. *Peter for Mary, '33.*" His father circles the tree, reading other carved initials and strange words, nodding now and then, grunting on occasion. "A few newer ones," he says. "Not many. Nowadays, kids don't have the patience."

Toby follows him around the tree, then sits on a gnarled, exposed root next to his father. They share a chocolate bar.

"It was the whole time thing that bewitched me. Who are these people? Why is A.M. a long boy? Where are they now, and what have they done since they carved those initials?" His dad shakes his head, looking out across the undulating field as if waiting for someone.

"Don't know, Dad," Toby says.

"This tree doesn't give a shit about time," his father says, as if he hasn't heard his son. "It stands here and accepts the names, and those that carve them go on through life, living its joy and grief, and die. And the tree doesn't care, or change for them. It's just here. And it keeps the ghosts of those people here, just as they were when they carved those things. In that moment, forever. Doesn't matter what they become."

Toby shivers. He frowns and looks away, not wanting his dad to see that he is unsettled. He feels the bulk of the tree behind them, and its limbs' shadows reach out in a timeless embrace.

"Doesn't matter," his father says again, quieter.

They stand to walk home, and even at that young age Toby has an inkling that his father is not quite the man he pretends. His knuckles are twisted and scarred like old oak, he has mean eyes, and harsh men pay calls when Toby is supposed to be sleeping.

After his father dies, Toby visits that field one more time. It is early spring. The field is freshly ploughed and planted, and a small metal-framed barn has been built close to the gate. On the old tree, he finds a set of initials that his father did not read aloud on that early summer day. And he perceives the shape of a troubled face, so reminiscent of his father's, in the bark of its old knotted trunk.

It isn't fear that kept him from ever visiting again, but troubles of his own.

It took him a couple of minutes to open the gate onto the canal's towpath. The spring on the catch was heavy and stiff, and trying to pull it back tensed his stomach muscles. That aggravated the wound, made more blood flow, and hazed the world. *Soon the haze will fall and stay down,* Toby thought. But he would not give up now.

He left the gate open and turned left, passing beneath the stone road bridge and walking slowly, steadily, along the canal. He had come this way many times with Lucy, and not once since. In the years since leaving here he had thought of this place rarely, and only in moments of extreme violence, his mind seeking some unconscious retreat from chaos. He'd always pulled back, not wishing to mar his memories with coughed blood and ground glass thumbed into eyeballs. But he'd known that he was seeking the good.

An explosion of duck and ducklings across the water startled him. He looked around, suddenly feeling terrible exposed and guilty. He remembered sitting in the woods with Lucy, just in sight of the canal, glancing around with a similar sense of delicious guilt as she removed her top in front of him for the first time.

Dog walkers and cyclists and runners, he thought, listing everyone he was likely to meet in the few hundred yards between here and the gate entrance to the wood. However much he tried to exude normality, no one could ignore the swathes of dried blood across his jacket and trousers. The last thing he wanted was to die in a hospital.

He could throw himself into the canal, but he was not yet close enough to Lucy.

The wood began to his left, an explosion of bluebells at its edge smearing the landscape with beauty. He paused to look, amazed, aghast at how gorgeous it was and how he had not appreciated such beauty since leaving this place. Other things had taken his mind. Women and drugs and booze, violence and torture, executions. He had considered beauty in the pain of others, as he poured shredded metal and acid into their throats and pushed shattered glass into their frantic eyes.

It was always about the splinters.

Walking, holding the wound that was killing him, Toby could not remember her voice. The smell of her breath, the look in her eye when he said something amusing, the feel of her lips against his throat, the warmth of her hand against him through his jeans, he remembered all that. But not her voice. He imagined it still reverberating through these woods, back and forth between trees from twenty years ago. Too faint now to be heard, but insinuating itself into his mind nonetheless, those words of love Lucy had whispered to him, and endless devotion. Near the end, he had returned to listen.

He reached the old gate into the wood, and it was almost the same as before. Twenty more years of use had smoothed the timber to a sheen, and one of the cross-struts had recently been replaced. Beyond, the path wending between trees seemed more worn than before, as if the wood had been discovered. The secret roots of trees showed through. *I'm almost there,* he thought, and felt suddenly apprehensive. What if the tree had fallen? What if someone had cut it down?

What if his own actions had killed the tree? He had a talent for death and pain.

He rested his bloodied hand on the wooden handle and pushed the gate open.

Sixteen, confused, pleasantly perspiring in the summer sun, the centre of the universe, troubled, careless, Toby hurries up the road to meet Lucy in the small wood they have made their own. Paths criss-cross the woodland, but they are mostly overgrown, and rarely trodden. They can hear the road from inside, and from most places can see the regimented line of trees marking the route of the canal. But when they are in there alone, theirs is the whole world.

He is in love with Lucy. He's told her, and she has whispered those words back. She is beautiful and innocent, sweet and succulent, and each time they have met here, things have gone a little further. Her coy smile drives him to distraction. Her warm, hesitant hand is his dream.

Toby carries a rucksack containing a blanket, a bottle of cider, some food, and a knife. He always carries the knife. His dead father's legacy insists upon it, but today Toby tries to shrug his father away. Such darkness has no place here.

He runs through the band of bluebells that edges the wood and enters its shadowy embrace, heading for their tree where he knows she will be. It is an ancient oak, part of its trunk hollow and roomy enough for two to lie down together. *One day we'll go inside,* she said a few days ago, and her voice had been loaded with delicious promise.

Toby races through the wood, and minutes after entering he sees her waiting for him beneath the oak. She is wearing a light summer dress and sandals, and sunlight cutting through the canopy speckles her hair and face with gold. He pauses a dozen steps from her, returning her smile, breathless from his dash from the village. But the true thief of his breath is Lucy's beauty.

She is the thing that gives him hope, when everywhere else darkness gathers. She has spied the shadows on occasion, biding their time deep within him, scarring his perception if he ever lets it stray beyond their time together, their wood. *It's just family stuff,* he has told her. *Don't worry about it. You make it all go away.*

But it waits beyond the wood, always.

"Close your eyes," she says.

Toby does so, breathing deeply. He hears a whisper, and the woodland holds its breath. When he looks again, Lucy is pulling her short dress up over her head and shoulders, and she is naked underneath. He has seen her breasts before, held them, kissed them. He has delved between her legs, stroking the soft down and the wetness. But she has never revealed herself to him so openly and fully, and he cannot hold back the gasp.

"It's a lovely day," Lucy says. She stands slightly awkwardly, but her coy smile betrays the subtle power she has over him.

"I..." Toby says. He drops his rucksack and starts forward, but she holds up one hand.

"You too."

He looks around them, expecting eyes everywhere. A hundred feet away through the trees, the canal marks the southern edge of the wood. He can see no movement there, but that doesn't mean no one is watching.

Lucy tilts her hip and raises one expectant eyebrow.

Toby strips quickly, not at all shy beneath Lucy's frank, innocent appraisal. Naked, both of them, cool breeze drying perspiration from Toby's skin, she takes his hand and slips sideways into the cool embrace of the old oak tree.

It is quick and clumsy and beautiful, and afterwards they hold each other, Toby kneeling and Lucy sitting astride his lap. They kiss. It is perfect, and he cannot believe either of them will ever leave these woods again.

"I love you," she whispers into his ear. "I'll always love you." His heart falls, and he is struck with a terrible, sudden sadness. It's as if she knows it cannot last.

"I have to get something," Toby says. He eases her from him, awestruck by her softness and curves and gorgeousness. Outside the tree, he slips his hand into the rucksack and grips the knife.

The bluebell carpet made him weep. It was a long time since Toby had cried, but he felt no shame. Not here. Back in the city, surrounded by hard people and where appearance and reputation were the currency, he'd have cut out his own tongue rather than be seen shedding a tear. Being a cold-hearted bastard meant survival. And whenever he was doing something foul, and he thought of this place and Lucy and the last good times, he would see away any sadness with another slash of his knife across some poor fucker's throat, or another handful of powdered glass pressed into a wound by his gloved hand. The screams would drive those memories down, because they were too precious for such brutality. And his employers would smile, and comment on the black heart that must beat in Toby Sugg's chest.

After the deed was done, he would never dwell on what he had remembered.

He walked slowly, holding his wound, afraid that memory would leak from it. Somewhere a woodpecker hammered, and other birds flitted through the trees' canopy, singing to the sun. The cry of a distant buzzard broke in. Toby could not recall the last time he had heard a buzzard, let alone consciously acknowledged the call.

There was a new bridge over the stream, where before there had only been a rotting log dropped into its flow. It was made from two railway sleepers side by side, and a metal mesh was nailed to them to prevent walkers slipping on slimy wood. The path to and from the bridge was well worn. It made

Toby sad that others had found this place, yet the wood was still treasured. There were no beer cans, no vandalism.

"Not far to the tree," he whispered, remembering the last time he and Lucy had been here. He breathed in the scent of bluebells, but could not find the purity. Perhaps passage through his nose corrupted the smell. She had been naked and innocent before him, offering him her greatest gift, and he had taken it greedily and then...

"It wasn't my fault," he said, louder. He paused and looked around at the trees waving gently. As a child he had spent long periods just staring at trees, enraptured by the way they moved so fluidly, gracefully, in the subtlest of breezes. Even now, they did not judge.

When he reached the tree, its familiarity took his breath away. He sank slowly to his knees. The oak was unchanged, timeless, rooting him to the past, and its immutability made him mourn everything he had done since last leaving this place. All the cowardly decisions he had made, the schemes he had agreed to, the times he had obeyed instead of standing firm, in that moment he would have thrown away everything to be back here again as a teenager, the future bright and wide and seemingly endless. Now it was all ending, and he could never go back. That was why he had returned here to die. It was not an apology, or a plea for forgiveness from a god he did not believe in, or the girl he still loved. He simply wanted to be somewhere good one more time.

"I'm sorry, Lucy," he said to the woodland. He stood again and moved towards the tree, circling so that he could see the entrance to its large hollow trunk. "I just hope you never know me older than I was then."

All the things he had done. All the people he had hurt, and those he had killed. His father's friends had demanded payback for all he had stolen from them, and even at that young age, outside the wood Toby had been more like his father than he could have suspected.

Lucy had told him that she would always love him. He hoped that was not the case, because he was not worth loving.

The base of the oak was surrounded by untrampled bluebells, and he tried not to step on too many as he approached the old trunk. He pulled his cigarette lighter and leaned against the tree, looking back the way he had come. There were not even footprints to mark his way. That was good, because he might have never existed.

He heard a car in the distance, and a barking dog from the direction of the road. High overhead, a plane made its lazy way across the blazing sky. Toby ducked into darkness inside the trunk, flicked the lighter's wheel, and found what he had come to see.

"My dad told me these will hold the ghosts of us here, forever, just as we are now." The light inside the tree is faint, filtering in from several cracks higher up in the trunk. But it is enough to see by, and enough for him to make sure the initial are finely cut, and deep enough to last. He has chosen the smoothest spread of wood he can find. "He had his own tree. But this one is ours."

Lucy hugs him from behind and watches him carve, and he can sense her delight. He can also feel her breasts, warm against his back.

"You first," he says, carving a large L and H. Wood peelings fall away, exposing the lighter flesh beneath. He always keeps his knife sharp. He feels Lucy's breath against his neck as she rests her chin on his shoulder.

"Loves," she says as his knife pauses beneath her initials. So he carves 'loves', and then his own initials below that. She hums her satisfaction, then runs her hand across the newly carved message.

"Ouch!"

"What?" Toby turns, and Lucy has her hand pressed to her mouth. She is beautiful. He looks her up and down, where light breaks in through the opening to dapple her slender body.

"Splinter," she says, taking her hand from her mouth and showing him. "Come here." She puts her hand somewhere else, and Toby lobs the knife outside. It sticks in the ground, as young and innocent as Toby. But both of them will know blood.

The carving was worn and aged, a dark scar against dark wood, but he leaned against the tree's insides and remembered every stroke of the knife, and every caress that had followed. It amazed Toby that they had found room to make love in here, twice, but he supposed time might have lifted the hollow tree's floor, and it always made things smaller.

His vision blurred. The pain he'd been living with for almost a day surged in again, recognising the end of his journey and settling with its hooks and barbs, and sending its splinters through his core and into his brain. It was always about the splinters.

He slid down against the rough trunk, and shards of rotten wood showered down onto his shoulders and head. Something scurried into his collar and tickled down the tangle of hair on his back. He'd always been hairy, just like his father. One of his employers had named him Yeti, and the name had stuck. He'd never liked it. Once, he'd broken a man's arm for using the name in front of a room full of strippers.

Toby was thirsty, and coming to rest gave his thirst room to expand. It burned his mouth and seared his face, making sandpaper of his tongue. *I'm home,* he thought, but he still did not want to close his eyes. One hand pressed to his stomach as if to hold his life inside, he splayed the other against the ground. Fingers working, old leaves and dead things cool against his skin, he felt the history of the tree's insides rising about him.

Old names, old ghosts, the things this tree had seen.

"Stupid fucking prick," McGrath says, leaning in towards his face. Toby tries to move but cannot, his arms held behind him. He'd let McGrath's son get caught in a drug bust, the last in a string of disasters to hit the bastard's network, like sickly dominoes declining to fall the other way. "Why the fuck didn't you do something? It's what I pay you for, what I paid your stupid fuck of an old man for before the cunt ran away. But he couldn't hide, eh?" McGrath leans in closer, so that his lips are pressed against Toby's left eye. "Couldn't hide."

Toby eases back then butts forward. McGrath grunts. The chair tumbles, his arms are free.

Knives. There are no guns here, because McGrath hides in plain view, a nice pad in Kensington. Guns are noisy.

A flurry of violence. Toby takes his knife from a man's broken hand and kills him. Then McGrath, coming at him with a butcher's cleaver, his trademark grin echoed as Toby trips him and cuts his throat. He watches his former employer bleed out, stepping just out of reach several times as McGrath crawls for him.

He looks at the knife in his hand and sees it scoring wood inside a tree, but blinks away the memory. It is an enclosed shell of goodness in the blank his life has become.

Toby feels rage rising, something that doesn't usually happen. Usually, he's cold.

"You stole me away from everything," he growls. McGrath pauses in his determined, red crawl, and then Toby falls on him, finishing him in moments but stabbing for a long time after.

As he stands, the knife in the gut from McGrath's fourteen-year-old daughter. She sneers at him as she tugs it out to stab again, and Toby carves his signature one more time.

The world changes. In the midst of his blazing agony, the good place calls to him, the last good times singing through the years. If only he had stayed with Lucy. Her splinter had been his fault, and he should have made her better.

He came to lying across the hollow, face close to the opening. His view of woodland was framed with the dark blue of bluebells, and the pale blue mosaic of late afternoon sky between leaves. His thirst was consuming him. The pain had grown, seemingly expanding larger than him and becoming a part of the tree as well, its aching limbs and tired old roots.

Lucy rode by on a bicycle.

Toby smiled at the vision. It wafted a scent of blooms and perfume at him, and he remembered the scent of her breath against his. Her hair was longer than he had known it, tied in a ponytail. She wore jeans and a loose blouse, and carried a rucksack. Her face was older, perhaps a little wiser, just as beautiful as ever. He imagined her passing here every day, existing only in this wood where their ghosts had been carved into the tree. Perhaps somewhere, sometimes, she saw him as well. He wanted to sing her name, and then he heard the clank of gears changing, and the scrape of a loose chain jumping.

"Bugger!" Lucy said. She disappeared into the trees.

Toby could not breathe. She had stolen his breath, leaving him winded. His knife wound caught fire again, and he groaned, reaching out one hand.

"Lucy?" he asked. Perhaps she still lived in the village, came through here to work every day, passing their tree as surely as a ghost. She haunted his memories deep down, and haunted their memory here. "Lucy?" For the first time in twenty years, the memory of good almost outweighed the bad.

Toby felt himself leaking into the ground and seeping amongst the old tree's roots. He was spreading, and the tree's hollow became smaller. He closed his eyes and drifted willingly into unconsciousness.

Walking through the village the next day, he is in a daze. His mother has sent him to the shop to buy the newspapers. She takes five papers every day, and spends much of her time glued to the internet. *Watching out,* she tells him. *Keeping my eyes open in case they come to collect.* She never elaborates, and Toby does not ask. He knows that his father was involved in dark things, but since his death, Toby and his mother pass through each other's lives like shadows.

Now, Toby cannot shed his smile, and neither does he wish to. He feels as if he's carrying a glow about him, brighter than the summer sun and hotter that Lucy's hottest part. Their secret time in the tree has refreshed the world for him, and today he sees it as somewhere new.

As he walks past the park a car approaches behind him, he turns around, and his heart leaps. It's Lucy's parents, and peering from the open back window, Lucy. Her father's face is set grim, but he is forced to slow to let a car pass from the other direction.

"Hi," Toby says, waving. Lucy smiles. His own smile is hot, face red. Beneath her parents' awful glare, he feels so obvious.

Her father lowers his window. "You leave her the fuck alone."

"Dad!" Lucy says.

"Shut up." He points at Toby, his hand shaking just slightly. "Stay away from my girl. I know you. I knew your scumbag old man."

Toby can't help looking at Lucy. Though upset, she is still smiling at him, and there's an almost unbearable look in her eye, a sharing of secrets and a promise of more to be made.

"Splinter gone bad," she says, holding up one hand and showing him the plaster on her palm. Her father mutters some curse and then screeches away, bouncing across the back of a sleeping policeman.

Lucy turns to wave, and those are the last words they ever share.

* * *

Toby stirred. Darkness. Night sounds. The smell of damp, and the scent of a fox. He used to know what a fox smelled like before he was taken to the city. He lost everything there, and more. All his childhood knowledge, and the things that had made him Toby.

He tried to open his eyes, then realised they were open. He couldn't move. The pain in his stomach was a void in the night, a black hole swallowing perception and understanding and hope. He still managed to orbit, but was falling quickly. Beyond the black hole lay nothing.

The tree grasped him to itself, pulling him inward with gentle sharpness. He could hear it growing in the night. It was an old thing, but this new sustenance was feeding it well. The hollow pressed around him as if he had always been part of the tree, his flesh its flesh, his sap its blood.

An animal urinated on him. It was warm, and then cold.

He loved her, and they took him away.

When he returns home with the papers, they are already there.

His mother is grim-faced and statue-like. She tells him that he always had it in him, seed of his bastard father. Toby pretends not to understand. One man tells him his name is McGrath, and he punches Toby in the face. Again, again, and when he's on the floor they start kicking him in the guts, the back, hard but not hard enough to make him pass out.

He pulls the knife his father told him to always carry, and McGrath laughs and takes it from him, stabs him through the hand and pins him to the floor.

Toby screams, and a cloth is stuffed into his mouth.

His mother leaves the room.

They bundle him into their car and leave the village, and they beat him all the way to London. He drives thoughts of Lucy down. He does not want her to see, to know, and they tell him that he is his father's payment to them for the money he stole years before. They tell him there was nowhere for his old man to hide, and there's nowhere for him to hide, either. They say that they'll kill his mother if he runs, and though he believed he did not care for his mother, he finds suddenly that he does.

McGrath whispers into his ear, "Lucy Hughes." That is all he says, and only once.

Toby becomes a terrible man. His father's son. McGrath's voice naming his love keeps the memory of her deep, deep down, apart from those times when he is doing awful things and he grasps that memory, the last good time, and the last time he was good. The memory becomes ripped and torn.

It is always about the splinters.

Can a bad man be good? He sometimes wonders. And for years he knows that it is only death that might bring the answer.

He was awake the next morning when Lucy cycled past again. She was wearing leggings and a hoodie, and the rucksack was slung over her shoulder. She wore sunglasses, but he knew the colour of her eyes.

He had woken inside the tree and found himself unable to move. Perhaps blood had dried him against the wood. Some of his muscles seemed to have petrified. He was a statue. He'd thought that death would come on in the night, but seeing Lucy again drove away his dreams, and surprised him with a sudden rush of panic.

Toby did not want to die.

The tree held him close, and he felt irrevocably joined to its ancient growth. *Surely it has all my blood,* he thought as Lucy disappeared from view.

The temptation to let himself fade into the tree and out of the ruin of his life was immense. But he had the knife. And after having been taken away from her all those years ago, he still had something to say.

The carving took some time. His letters were uneven and rough, but it was the message that counted, not the manner of its giving. With every splinter that fell, he felt Lucy standing behind him, her beauty touching his shaking, sickening flesh.

Later that day, the squeal of brakes roused him. Clouds hid the sun. Toby could not move, but he could see. It was the most beautiful sight he could imagine, and he knew then that he could die happy.

Lucy stood astride her bike, staring back at the tree. She must have passed it and then applied her brakes, pausing to stare at the place that, he hoped, still meant something to her. A husband, children, a life... perhaps she had them all. But he also hoped that she still had him somewhere in her heart.

She smiled. She could not see him, and that made the smile more precious, because it was all for her. Then she turned her back on the tree and cycled away through the wood, heading for the road home.

"Lucy," Toby whispered, but his voice was too weak to leave the tree. He wondered whether he could really have driven all the way here from London.

One day, Lucy would return closer to the tree. Outside, maybe she would see a knotted, gnarled spread of bark that vaguely resembled the face of the boy she had loved.

And if she ventured inside she would see what he had carved.

We are always as we were here.

Putting the Ground to Sleep

Bryan Clark

Jim Cafferty cussed and dropped the wrench back into the battered old toolbox at his side.

"What is it, papa?" This from Jim's daughter Frannie, who was on the other side of the Farmall F-30 with a can of oil.

"This damn machine your uncle sold me, that's what. Regular my ass. Expand your operation, he said. Great investment, he said. Well, now I've got a hundred and fifty more acres that need tilling and this contraption can't leave the shed, and we've wasted damn near the whole day working on it. Light's too far gone now, but tomorrow we'll have to start early and get the horses hitched up. Season's getting away from us and we still need to put the ground to sleep."

"I've always liked those words," said Frannie. "They're so...evocative."

"They're going to evoke one hell of a hard spring if we don't get it done. I've had enough of this thing for one day. Hell, the rest of my days. I've made it this far with my horses. Harry can have his damn tractor back. Should have never trusted a machine to do a horse's job. Let's go see if mama's got supper ready."

As Jim and Frannie put their tools away, their black spaniel mix Sam lifted his head from the pile of old coats he usually lay on while they were doing shop work and looked toward the open door of the shed.

"Hear something, Sam?" Frannie knelt down next to him and ran her fingers over the dog's soft hair. Ignoring her attention, Sam jumped up and trotted toward the door. He froze just inside, looking out over the field and growling softly in his throat.

"Frannie, shut the light off," Jim said as he walked to the door, following the dog's gaze. All he could see as the lone bare light bulb went out was the moon hanging in the darkening sky, and the occasional husk blowing through the standing stalks in the field. Nothing he could see that would raise the dog's ire. Frannie followed him as he stepped outside, nudging the dog back behind the door and pulling it shut. As he reached to latch it, something seemed to move out of the corner of his eye and he turned to the field once more. Did the ground at the edge of the yard swell for a moment? Jesus, not already. It was too early. There was still so much to do.

"What did you see?" Frannie asked.

"I could have sworn...*No.* It was nothing. Eyes are getting old and tired. We better make sure Sam stays locked up at night though. Don't want him running off and coming back rabid."

When they entered the house, the smells of cooking greeted them. Rebecca Cafferty was placing a dish of green beans on the table. She looked up at them. "Good, you're in early. Saves me having to yell out the front door like I was calling hogs."

"Early tonight and late for the next two weeks, most likely. That blasted tractor broke down again. That brother of yours is a crook."

"Harry is a good, God-fearing man and he meant well. He was thinking of your best interests."

"He was thinking of the interest he'd make financing the payments is what you mean." Jim winked at Frannie across the table.

"I saw that. You two go wash up now. What would God think of you folding your hands for grace with axle grease all over them?"

"You suppose if we clean up real good for Him, maybe He'd come down here and lend a hand? A miracle is about what it's going to take to keep ahead of the freeze."

"Jim Cafferty, you will not blaspheme at my table, or you will not eat at my table!" Rebecca had gone from her usual tight-lipped tolerance to red-faced and trembling slightly. "It's bad enough you have our daughter out there doing man's work when she should be in here with me, studying her Bible."

"You know I got no one else to help me out there. There's more work than one man can do by himself now I have those extra acres, and I can't afford to pay help."

"You wouldn't have to take on those extra acres if you'd just—" Jim whirled to face her, and the look in his eyes pulled her up short.

"I like the work, mama. It feels good to do a day's honest labor."

"I did not ask for your mouth, young lady. You will not talk back to me."

"I wasn't talking back. I'm fifteen, mama. I'm not a little girl. I can do the work. I want to do the work."

Rebecca drew back as though she were about to slap Frannie. "Jesus H. Christ, Rebecca," Jim snapped. "Calm down. You never used to act like this. It's not just Harry, it's his damn wife too, with all her Bible studies and going on like she knows more than the preacher. She's got you spooked something awful."

"That's enough! I told you about blaspheming at my table! Supper is ruined!"

"It ain't ruined, dammit! The food's still hot."

"Don't matter if it's hot, it's not blessed! Your filthy mouth has driven God from our home tonight!"

"You think God gets scared off by a man cussing at the dinner table?"

"Mama…papa…stop it! Can't we please just eat supper?"

"I believe I've lost my appetite," Rebecca turned and went into the next room.

"I'm sorry, papa. I didn't mean to make her angry."

"It's not your fault, darling," Jim said. "Your mama's got a lot of funny ideas from your aunt Catherine lately. Ever since she went to that tent revival last summer, Catherine's been spitting fire and brimstone down everyone's throats. That woman's got a cat in her brain and she's doing her damnedest to give it to your mama. Let's just have some supper and get to bed. We have a long day tomorrow."

The sudden fight between her parents shrank Frannie's appetite too, and after eating a small plate and clearing up the kitchen, she went to bed. She could hear her parents' voices downstairs.

"If you would just get us out of here, Jim Cafferty, you wouldn't have to worry about the ground."

"Just where are we supposed to go, Rebecca? World ain't exactly brimming with opportunities for a man who never finished the fourth grade."

"Then you know what has to be done."

"I need to put the ground to sleep is all."

"And what if you can't?"

"I've done it every year of my life and this year won't be any different."

"The days are getting short."

"You think I don't know that?"

"Then if the time comes—"

"That nonsense Catherine's been putting in your head about the wrath of the Lord and sacrifice is just that—nonsense. You think after all these generations someone hasn't tried it before? There's a reason it's done the way it is. The pattern of the work is the only thing that puts the ground to sleep. Blood ain't got a thing to do with it. That's only what it takes after. You try to feed it, you'll just wake it up more."

Frannie stopped listening then. She'd never heard her father talk like that before, and it was scaring her. She didn't know what it meant, but it was worse than all of mama's God-fearing talk lately.

That night Frannie dreamed of the earth. She was standing in the middle of the field, looking toward the house. She could see her father standing in the yard, splitting firewood. The loud *CHOK* sound of the ax smashing through the logs echoed between the buildings and bounced out across the field to her ears. Then she heard another sound, quiet at first but building until it was much louder than the splitting wood. It sounded like bellows in a smithy, deepening and growing in volume until it became a giant's breathing. The ground beneath her feet rose and fell in rhythm with the sound. To her left, an eye as big as the tall steel wheels of the tractor opened in the ground, trickles of earth running into it. More eyes opened, all across the field, then the dirt rose up in front of her and swatted her into the ground.

A glowing grapefruit sky greeted Jim and Frannie the next morning. The dream was already fading from memory, although it had left her feeling shaken. She looked over the field in front of the house. The fence line looked wrong somehow. Had the ground moved overnight? Was it encroaching on the yard, moving closer to the house somehow? It must be the leftover feeling from the dream making her see things. A cold gust of wind bit through her flannel, and the chill chased the unease from her.

Frannie never tired of the view out across the gently rolling patchwork of Iowa farmland. It stretched for miles in three directions to the horizon, interrupted only by the low, sparsely wooded hill that marked the northern border of the property. Some of her friends thought it was dull, but to her it was beautiful. It had been the life of her family for generations and she wouldn't have traded it for all the forests and mountains in the world. She lingered on the sunrise a moment longer and hurried to catch up with her father, who was already opening the barn doors.

The horses seemed unwilling to leave the barn, as though something was making them nervous. Frannie thought of Sam's unusual behavior in the shed the night before. This morning he was less skittish, although he seemed to be paying an unusual amount of attention to the field. Clyde and Ben allowed themselves to be harnessed but when Jim tried to direct them toward the cultivator, they shied and dug their hooves in. Eventually he got them grudgingly into place to be hooked up to the implement, and then the fight started all over when he got them near the edge of the field.

"What in the hell is wrong with these horses today? They're hardly better than the tractor," Jim grumbled.

"They're acting like Sam was last night, papa. Something out in the field is upsetting them."

"It's upsetting me too. Feel that chill in the air? This ground will be hard as stone by the end of the week. We don't get it turned over now, we'll have to blast it loose in the spring."

"Yes, papa."

"While I get these stubborn horses to work, I want you to see if you can get that tractor moving. We get that engine running, there's a chance yet we'll beat winter to the finish line."

As Frannie turned to walk to the shed, she thought she heard her father mutter under his breath, "And live to see another one."

"Papa?"

"Yes, Frannie?"

"What were you and mama talking about last night after I went to bed?"

"Nothing for you to worry about for a while yet. Get to work, now."

At least an hour had passed when Frannie heard her father's voice, faint and far away, swearing. She also heard the horses whinnying. They sounded afraid. She ran to the door of the shed, following the sounds to her father and the horses in the middle of the field. At first she couldn't figure out what was wrong with the sight. Her father was still standing on the plow platform, and the horses were both still hitched and moving along. Then she realized what was wrong. They were moving backward, as if the plow was dragging the horses across the earth instead. Their hooves dug in, jerking and straining against the harness, but they couldn't resist whatever it was that was pulling them farther out into the field.

Sam ran around her legs barking as she bolted to the edge of the yard where the grass stopped and the stalk-stubbled earth began.

"Papa!?"

"Frannie, get away from the edge!" Jim called to his daughter as Clyde was swallowed up to his chest in the churning soil. He screamed in terror, flecks of spittle flying from his mouth as his eyes rolled wildly. Ben tried to break free but the harness held him fast. Jim ran to the horse's side, frantically trying to loosen the buckles. Ben's back legs started to sink just as Jim got the harness off and leaped onto his back. Grabbing a double fistful of mane, he urged the horse back toward the yard.

"Papa, what's happening?" Frannie cried.

"It's too late now, just run for the house! Get inside!"

Frannie turned and bolted for the house, the fear in her father's voice, like nothing she'd ever heard before, was all the motivation she needed. As she ran, she called out for Sam, who came barking at her heels and followed her through the door.

The ground rolled under Ben's hooves, and the horse fell forward, tossing Jim over his head to land face first in the dirt ahead of him. Jim heard his collarbone break with a wet crack, and managed to roll aside just in time to avoid being flattened by the tumbling horse. Crushing the pain between gritted teeth, he forced himself to his feet and began running toward the yard, hearing the horse screaming with fear behind him. He cleared the last fifty yards and was nearly at the grass when the ground pitched beneath his feet again and sent him sailing. He managed to keep his balance and land running, although the pain swarming through his collarbone like a colony of fire ants nearly made him black out.

Jim ran up the porch steps and slammed the door behind him, leaning against the smooth wood, panting with exertion and desperately trying to keep the pain from his broken bone under control. He clenched his jaw and marched across the floor to the kitchen, tying an old coat from a peg by the back door into a makeshift sling. Then he opened a cupboard, took out a bottle of the Miller brothers' moonshine he kept for special occasions, pulled the cork out with his teeth, and took a long pull.

When the fire in his throat had helped some to quench the fire in his collarbone, he took a deep breath and focused on his surroundings. The first thing that swam into focus was Frannie's face. Tears filled her eyes and her mouth was quivering. Then he realized that her fear was not only from what she had seen outside, but from the hand sickle her mother had held to her throat. Sam hid under the kitchen table, whining.

"Rebecca, what the hell are you doing?"

"Sacrifice. The Lord is angry, and will be satisfied with nothing less."

"She's our daughter, Rebecca!"

"What more meaningful sacrifice could we give our Lord, James?"

"What did I tell you about blood? Enough with the Abraham and Isaac shit, that's not what it wants!"

"The Lord—"

"The Lord ain't got nothing to do with this!"

A piercing scream from outside drew Rebecca's attention. For a moment, Jim stopped to look out the picture window too. Ben had milled about in the yard, dazed by the confusion and waiting for Jim to come back to put things in order. He had begun to graze on the lawn and gotten too close to the edge of the field. The living earth had caught one of his legs and was trying to drag him down, but it only had the one leg and Ben was a tremendously strong beast. He yanked the trapped hoof free and bolted from the yard, heading for the road beyond the hill and safety.

Jim took the moment of distraction to grab Frannie away from Rebecca, pulling the blade away from her throat and shoving his body between them, then twisting the sickle from Rebecca's hand and pushing her down onto the sofa.

"Frannie, get me some bed sheets from the linen closet!" he barked to his daughter, before turning on Rebecca, who was bucking against his weight and making his broken bone sing a lullaby to his brain. He fought his way back up through the encroaching blackness at the edges of his vision and bellowed, "Goddammit! *Enough!*"

She was temporarily subdued by the fury in his voice. Time enough for Frannie to return with the sheets and help her father tie her mother's hands behind her back, and her ankles together.

"Papa, what's wrong with mama?"

"Nothing's wrong with me, dear," Rebecca said softly. "The Lord is angry. He has thrown the land into upheaval and demands a sacrifice to tame it."

"He demands no such thing!" snapped Jim.

"You are the most precious thing we have," continued Rebecca, ignoring her husband. "The greater the sacrifice, the more it will please the Lord. Your blood—" She was cut off as Jim knocked her unconscious.

"I...I'm sorry," he said. "I didn't know what else to do. You're scared enough as it is."

"I don't understand," Frannie said.

"I know," Jim sighed. "I was hoping I wouldn't have to put this on you for a few more years." The house shook as the ground beneath it shifted. Plates and glasses fell from the cupboards in the kitchen and smashed on the floor. Frannie yelped and put her arms around Jim. He winced and continued.

"This land has been in our family for generations. Our kin have been the custodians of it since white men settled here. The ground here, it lives, but not in the way all ground lives. There's something mean in it, something dark. They figured out how to tame it way back, how to reap a living from it so long as they put the ground to sleep at the end of the season by working it in a certain pattern. We don't know why it works anymore, or how they found it out in the first place. That was forgotten long ago.

"Thing is, if it's not done on time the ground starts to wake up. All spring, all summer, it's satisfied to have things growing on it. But when the harvest is done and the crop is all gone, it gets restless and hungry. If the pattern isn't made, the ground wakes up and it eats. Your mama's wrong, though. It don't want no sacrifice. It don't care a bit what it takes into it, and it wouldn't stop at just one body. Just eats whatever is there, whatever can't get away. Winter eventually puts it down again, but every time it's allowed to wake up all the way, it spreads. The restless ground gets a little bigger." The house shook again.

"I just thought I had a few more years yet before I needed to teach you the pattern."

"So what do we do, papa?"

"You have to get out of here. Take your mama and Sam in the truck and drive as far as you can, hope you get to safe ground and find somewhere to stay. Did you get the tractor working?"

"I think so, papa, why?"

"Because I have to try to stop this. If I start the work maybe that will calm it enough to let me put it back to sleep."

"Papa, no, you can't! It ate Clyde and it'll eat you too!"

"I have to try. No telling how far it'll spread before the freeze. You know the sunken spot that's always giving us so much trouble with the tile lines? That spot is from the foundation of the old homestead. You were probably too young to remember the year we had to stay at your Aunt Sally's while we built this house. That's how far it spread the last time."

This time the house didn't just shake, the whole building shifted. They could hear the walls of the basement cracking.

"We have to move now! Get your mama to the truck and go!" With that, Jim ran out the door.

"Papa, no!" Frannie yelled, watching her father bolt out the door and across the yard to the shed. Sobbing, she put her mother's arms over her shoulders and hoisted her off the couch. The house lurched again and Rebecca's eyes opened. "What's happening?" she groaned.

"We have to get to the truck, mama. If I untie your feet will you come with me?"

"We must placate the Lord's anger, child."

"Mama, shut up with that shit and come with me or stay here!"

"How dare you speak to me like that!" Rebecca had been working at the hastily tied sheet binding her wrists and got them loose. She came at her daughter screaming, fingers crooked like claws. Frannie pelted for the back door, grabbing the truck keys off the hook on the wall. Rebecca paused to grab the sickle off the floor and followed.

Frannie reached the truck, the ground beginning to roll beneath her feet, as the sound of the tractor coughing to life echoed out the corrugated tin doors of the shed. Sam leaped over her lap onto the seat beside her, barking a warning. She looked up as she turned the key in the ignition, seeing her mother running toward her with the sickle raised over her head. Frannie braced her foot against the door and kicked it out into her mother's face as she reached the truck. The sickle flew out of her hand and she collapsed to the churning ground, stunned. As Rebecca began to regain her senses, the soil around her was working up into a boil. She tried to get to her feet, but the earth had her. Her legs and left arm began to sink, and she reached her one free hand pleadingly up to her daughter.

Frannie looked at her sinking mother with tears in her eyes. She made for the outstretched hand, then stopped.

"Mama, I can't. I'm afraid..." But the restless earth took the decision out of her hands as her mother disappeared. Sobbing, she settled back behind the wheel of the truck and started up the engine. Then she looked out the window.

Her father was racing across the field on the tractor at top speed toward the abandoned plow. He and Frannie both saw it at the same time. A rolling wave of soil four feet high, surging across the field toward him like a breaker in a storm at sea. There was nothing he could do to avoid it. The wave of earth surged under the wheels of the tractor, sending it lurching down the backside of the wave and tossing Jim from the seat onto the ground.

"Papa!" Frannie yelled, leaping from the truck and running into the field to her father. Jim was struggling to his feet, the pain from the impact on his broken collarbone blurring his vision and making his legs unsteady. Then he heard his daughter coming toward him.

"Frannie, dammit, go back! There's nothing you can do out here, get going!"

"Papa, I can't leave you here!"

"You have to, who else is going to put this ground to sleep when I'm gone?"

"But I don't know how, you never showed me!"

Sam stood on the edge of the field barking, dodging away from the black soil as it moved in like the tide. With a final bark he turned and ran off toward the hill. They both felt the pull as the earth began to swallow their feet. Jim looked down at his own legs, gone up to the ankle. Then he looked to his daughter, struggling to free herself from the inexorable grip of the soil.

"I'm so sorry, Frannie," he sobbed. "This is gonna hurt, girl, but you gotta run!" Jim launched himself forward and hit Frannie with his good shoulder. The ground shifted toward him to hold him tighter, and that and the impact were just enough to allow him to knock Frannie free. She toppled backwards and landed on her rear with a stunned grunt. "Run to the tractor! Run!"

Frannie scrambled to her feet without question and ran for the tractor, only yards away but seeming like miles.

"Papa, what do I do?" she cried, swinging herself into the seat.

"In the tool box is a map showing our plot of land. I drew the pattern over top of it. I'm sorry there was no time for me to teach it to you but you're a smart girl and I know you can do it! Just hang on tight and don't let it buck you out of that seat!"

Frannie backed the tractor up to the abandoned plow and stood on the frame while she dropped the hitch pin in place, seeing the soil churn just inches below her feet. The ground rolled under the tractor again and nearly tipped her off, but she held on until the wave passed and jumped into the seat, wrapping her ankles around the frame to hold herself in place as the machine was bucked and tossed by the earth. She slammed the throttle forward and the tractor roared across the field toward her father, who was now almost to his waist in the ground.

"Frannie, what are you doing? The pattern!"

"I was scared and I let it take mama. I'm not going to let it take you too! When I drive past grab onto the plow and hang on!"

Frannie guided the tractor past the writhing figure of her father, bringing the plow right alongside him but afraid to slow down too much in case the earth started dragging her like it did with the horses. Jim grabbed the plow frame with both hands as it rolled by and held on so tight he thought his joints were going to crack. The earth fought to keep him, squeezing tighter and pulling him from below. The pain from his broken shoulder was incredible, and he choked back vomit as tears rolled down his face. His strength was almost gone when he felt his legs begin to slide out of the earth, and then he was free. His feet slipped out of his shoes and his trousers tore and came off, and the hungry earth swallowed cloth and leather as flesh and bone gained freedom.

"Papa!"

"That was some fine work, Frannie," Jim gasped from his position sprawled across the top of the plow and hanging on with every last ounce of his remaining strength. "Now get to the map!"

Reaching into the tool box, Frannie grabbed the map and spread it across the steering wheel. It was covered with strange, jagged lines and swooping whorls drawn in red ink.

"Right now we're about where that big arc in the middle starts," Jim yelled. "Start with that. The ground should start to calm behind us as we go if you do it right."

Frannie turned the wheel and began to trace the esoteric symbols laid out on the map, and it was just as her father said. Every time she made a pass, the earth behind them stopped heaving and churning, and laid still. Several times big waves like the one that knocked Jim off the tractor tried to swamp them, but each time they were prepared and rode them out. Finally, almost an hour later, the last bit of head land was made quiet. Frannie pulled the tractor into the yard and turned off the engine. Exhausted, shaking, the blood drained from both their faces, Frannie and Jim staggered away from the machine and collapsed next to the porch.

Frannie looked at the ripped up patch of ground near the pickup and started to cry. Jim put his good arm around her as tears rolled down his face also, making streaks in the dirt smeared on his cheeks.

"You did everything you could, Frannie. This place has a way of getting to you after a while. Your mama just lost it. It's a terrible thing, but it's not your fault."

"I was so close. I could have taken her hand."

"I don't think she'd have let you. She was too far gone. But look at what you did today, Frannie. You saved me, and you saved our farm. Next year I'll start teaching you all about this land and how to work it."

"I don't know if I can, papa."

"I know you can. You'll have to. I won't be around forever, and someone has to be the custodian of this place. Not too many people I would trust to take care of it, and I would hate to think what would happen if there was no one here to work it. Who knows, it might spread to the whole rest of the country, even the world."

Frannie sighed and leaned her head against her father's side, closing her eyes. She was too tired to argue. They had survived, and right now, that was enough.

A familiar bark opened her eyes again, and she turned to see Sam trotting down the hill toward them, his tail wagging, with Ben close on his heels. She held out her hand to the dog, as the horse reluctantly trotted past, and he lay down beside her with his head in her lap. She stroked his hair as the four of them stared out over the sleeping ground.

The Raincatchers

Greg F. Gifune

I used to think the rain would wash me clean, make it all better somehow, maybe even set me free. The tears of God—that's what they told me when I was a kid, and I believed it. Years later, slowly dying and wasting away in my own misery, I finally figured out what He was crying about. The words of warning those nuns had whispered to me every night when they tucked me and the rest of the kids nobody wanted in for the night were branded into my memory like all the other mantras we'd learned.

He cries for the damned.

That day there was nothing left but the goddamn rain, trickling from pewter skies, spattering pavement, soaking the greenest grass I'd ever seen stretched across a small, empty park—weighing down branches, dripping from shiny leaves and blurring the world like smoke and mirrors from some cheesy magic show. For a while I'd even blocked out the sound of it tapping the canvas awning, but it always feels the same. Can't ever shake the way it feels, the rain.

Six days out of Bangor, stuck in some quiet little town between Boston and Cape Cod, me and Cowboy just sat there, watching the rain, waiting for what we'll never know. Never did, really. After more than three years on the road the days all blended together without meaning or purpose, except for those days when we did our thing, when it just happened and we found ourselves raging against everything and anything. Those days you remember. Still, it don't matter. We were way beyond redemption, had been since the whole thing started, since the first time we took it from fantasy to reality, and we were in so deep there wasn't no turning back, no matter how much we might've wanted to.

"How long we gonna sit here, Jimmy?"

His voice broke my concentration, ruined the moment like it always did, and dragged me kicking and screaming back to reality. Me and Cowboy huddled under a big blue canvas tarp stretched over some recreation building at the outskirts of a public park. Leaning against a cinderblock wall, just feet from what would be public bathrooms once the construction was finished, trying to figure out what the hell to do next.

"Why, you got an appointment or something?"

Cowboy picked at his fingernails, or what was left of them. Bastard was always chomping on the damn things like some nervous schoolgirl. He stared down at his hands for a minute, then, with a sigh, turned and looked out across the park. In three years he'd aged twenty from the looks, eyes all bloodshot and saddled with big black puffy bags, his stubble-covered skin creased and battered by life and weather and all the other shit that haunts people like us. He leaned against the edge of the cinderblocks and folded his arms, and that's when the rain got him, trickling onto his old leather hat, dripping from the brim onto his nose and chin, dangling and clinging to him like a lover in the dark. A lost puppy, drenched and shivering in the rain.

There were times I hated the motherfucker.

"I miss Nikki already," he said softly.

"Don't want to talk about that right now."

"Ain't never gonna find another Nikki, man."

"What the fuck did I just say?" I settled back against the wall, hard and cold as a corpse against my back—even through my denim jacket—stretched my legs out and crossed them at the ankles, knees cracking like twigs.

"So what are you thinking about then?"

I shot him a look. "Don't never ask me that, I told you before."

"It's the rain, ain't it?" Cowboy turned, gazing down at me with those sad dark eyes, forever the scolded child. "Three years road doggin' with you and I still don't know what this shit is you got with rain."

"It's nothing you'd understand."

"I ain't stupid."

I let that one go, but the battle in my mind was already raging. Visions flickering through the rain like strobe lights, coming and going, living and dying with every blink of my eyes. Times I didn't like to think about. Times before they took me away from my mother and stuck me in that home with those nuns. Times when I'd sit on the porch of that old shack and watch the rain while my mother did her business with whoever was passing through town. She did what she did; I never hated her for it. Somebody's got to be the town whore, just so happened it was her. Damn fine woman, my mother, just had her problems like the rest of us is all.

I pulled a crumpled pack of cigarettes from my shirt pocket. Only two left. I rolled one into the corner of my mouth and struck a match, watching the flame battle to survive against the light breeze. We all have our addictions, I guess, all got our weaknesses. *Crosses to bear,* the nuns called it. Least my mother never told me I was born evil. Even sitting in that dingy back bedroom, shit strewn from one corner to the next, her frail body straddling an old chair, draped in a stained and faded slip, hands shaking and trying to find a vein in all that bruised and swollen skin stretched tight over bone, she always told me I was an angel.

One of God's little angels, she used to say. *And can't nothing ever hurt you long as you remember that.*

Least she believed it. I guess back then that was enough.

"Think they found her yet?" Cowboy asked.

And then just as soon as I'd chased the visions off, they were back. Nikki, with those big blue eyes painted black, sexy little birthmark between her nose and upper lip, smiling that *fuck-me-baby* smile. Goddamn waste, just like everything else, don't know why I'd ever thought she'd be any different. "It played out," I told him. "Let it go, Cowboy."

He turned his back on the rain, and if I hadn't known him even better than he knew himself, I would've thought he was challenging me. "That was fucked up, Jimmy. Nikki was one of us, she—"

"Nothing lasts forever," I said. "How many times I got to tell you that?"

"I just don't see—"

I know he was still talking, still pissing and moaning, but his voice faded away, absorbed by the rhythm of the falling rain. And I was back in that shitty little motel in Bangor, sucking down the first beer I'd had in weeks, sprawled out on a bed that wasn't nothing special but beat the hell out of sleeping on the ground, TV showing some old black and white movie. Nikki was sitting naked in front of the mirror, doing up her eyes like she always did when we ran into enough cash to afford her makeup. Big black long-legged spiders surrounding those baby blues, catching my attention in the mirror and giggling like a toddler come Christmas morning.

"She wasn't like the rest of them," I heard Cowboy say. "Nikki was special, man, she was one of us. She was..."

Just another bitch we'd snagged on the road. Young and pretty and stupid and dreaming about being a big star in Hollywood. A hot little tramp hitchhiking and running from some backwater town down south, running from a step daddy who loved her a little too much and a town where girls like her ended up pouring coffee at the local diner for the rest of their lives...or ended up like my mother.

The only reason she lasted as long as she did was because she had the same disease festering inside her that me and Cowboy got, and those eyes and that ass and that smile and those tits came in handy on the road. But she wasn't never one of us.

I knew Cowboy was in love with her and that's why it had to end. Can't love nothing in this life if you want to survive—or even if you don't. But he'd never see it that way. All the rest he could go along with, but Nikki he'd never get over, never forgive either one of us for. So I tuned him out and listened to the rain.

Nothing quite like that sound. Rain.

Made me think about being a kid again, sitting on the front porch of that old shack. My mother had a regular named Earl something, big fat slob, a traveling coffee salesman who drove through town in his piece of shit black Cadillac every few weeks. He'd waddle across the yard, toss me a can of coffee, muss my hair with his sausage fingers then go inside and roll around with my mother for an hour or so.

I kept every coffee can the fucker ever gave me. Once they were empty I'd stack them out behind the house. My mother couldn't afford much in the way of toys, so I played with them fucking cans. Didn't matter anyway, there weren't any kids in town I could call friends, so I was pretty much on my own. The rain—the rain was my friend. My best friend.

It rained the last day I saw Earl. When he pulled up he noticed all the coffee cans scattered across the weed infested dirt lot we called a front yard, rain pinging against metal. I had a plan to catch me some rain.

"What the hell are you doing, boy?" he asked, hurrying as best a man at his weight could, to the shelter of the porch. "They turn off your indoor plumbing or something?"

"Just playing, sir," I told the fat fuck. "Catching some rain."

His pig eyes laughed at me, same way my mother's laughed at him once he was gone and she was counting his money. "Can't catch something like rain, boy. Like trying to catch the wind, don't you know that?"

Worst part is he was right. Even after the rain, when I took all them cans back behind the house, careful not to spill them, the shit inside wasn't rain, not anymore. Once you caught it, it became something else. Something common, something missing the magic that made me want to capture it in the first place.

Even days later, when the water had turned dull and murky and had all sorts of small flying bugs floating dead along the top, I kept the shit. My mother asked me why once, how come that rainwater was so goddamned important to me. Never did give her an answer, but not because I didn't have one.

"What the hell we going to Cape Cod for anyway?"

I looked at Cowboy, his face all scrunched up into a grimace. "There's still another couple months before the tourist season hits. Nice and quiet out there now," I said. "Plus, it rains a lot there this time of year."

"You and your fucking rain." He let the cinderblocks support him, his eyes darting back and forth, scanning the park. "I don't like these small towns, man. Guys like us stick out like titties on a ten-year-old. Always feel safer in the city, Jimmy. Cops in a big city don't give a shit about guys like us, but in these places they love fucking with—"

"Quit bitching," I snapped. "Where you want to go?"

Something kind of like a smile twitched across his lips. "I was thinking heading back toward Boston. Hang around there for a while, see what we can see. Remember how Nikki wanted to go to Boston for a while?"

Nikki.

Doggin' it with us for more than two months. Crazier than we were. She could pull down enough cash working a truck stop for a few hours to keep us in hot food and motel sheets for days at a clip. Between what the truckers paid her for head and what she could steal when they weren't looking, she was a moneymaking machine. But it wasn't until the first night we did our thing, her picking a guy up at a bar and luring him outside to his car where me and Cowboy were waiting, that I knew she was special. All of us piling into that car and driving him way out onto the state highway. Pulling into a rest area and dragging the cocksucker out into the tall grass between pavement and forest. The three of us—for the first time, the *three* of us—circling him, raining down on him until he didn't cry or scream or beg no more.

And Nikki, even better at it than me and Cowboy, even more turned on, drowning in the rush of power and the high you can only get from watching the life slip from somebody, and knowing you're the one who stole it.

I knew then we couldn't just use Nikki up and toss her aside like all the pussy before her. I knew she'd stick for a while…but I also knew there'd come a day when I'd have to cut her loose.

"Tell you what," I sighed. "You want to go to Boston for a while? Then that's where we'll go."

Cowboy turned, crouched down next to me, grinning with them brown teeth. "You mean it, man?"

"Yeah," I told him. "Besides, what the fuck did peace and quiet ever do for us, right?"

Somewhere along the line his laughter turned to screams.

Nikki's screams.

Getting up from that table, eyes and lips painted black, dancing and laughing, taunting me at the foot of the bed. Cowboy watching her—a love struck kid as always—his chest heaving; eyes wide, soaking in that body and all the evil that went with it.

Nikki giggling and crawling across the bed like some panther in heat, talking shit about the next mark we found and how sweet it could be, her hands all over me, her head dropping into my lap and her mouth on me. Cowboy looking away, jealous and wishing it was him instead. The phone by the bed suddenly in my hand—and all that fucking blood.

Cowboy cradling her in his arms, crying and asking me why I had to do it this time, why her, why now? Me, standing in that tiny bathroom, looking at myself in the mirror, covered in her blood. Feeling the high, the release, and the anger slipping away into the closest thing to calm I ever get.

Just beyond the far end of the park, movement caught my eye. Some yuppie asshole in a designer sweat suit jogging through the rain, moving slowly up across the grass before turning onto a path that cut through a cluster of trees. I looked at Cowboy. He'd seen him too.

I stuck my hand out, and he helped me to my feet with that look he always has right before we do our thing.

"Let's get it done," I said, that high already tingling, tempting me.

"Then Boston."

I nodded. "Then Boston."

"We stay here afterward, we'll get caught."

But just like everybody else, what Cowboy never understood was, couldn't nobody ever catch me. Like the rain, once you had me I was something else. The magic gone. And just like the shit floating in them coffee cans, wouldn't nothing ever get me clean.

Without another word, we left the safety of the tarp and headed for the path.

Bathed in the tears of God.

Crosshairs

Amy Grech

Standing with one eye shut in front of the shooting gallery at the county fair, Billy Hogan felt the crotch of his jeans tighten and raised his air rifle slowly. He didn't budge. All the while his father's words echoed in the confines of his mind: *"You've got to get 'em when they don't expect it, son! Ask yourself what Jesus would do and your aim will be true!"* His father stood directly behind the boy with his brawny arms folded. Billy felt his hard stare driving him to succeed. He stared at the yellow ducks passing by, watching them with deadpan eyes but seeing nothing, and knocked them down without missing a beat.

On one of their frequent trips into the dense woods behind their house, Billy's father, a big bearish man with a grizzly beard, usually bagged a deer, or sometimes a bunch of squirrels, with four bullets, one for each of his victims. He *never* wasted a shot, no matter what.

Mr. Hogan taught his son how to focus on his target, at all costs. He stressed the importance of waiting until the prey appeared in the center of the telescopic site before taking the shot. "Like a martyr on the Cross" was the phrase he used to make the concept easier for young Billy to grasp. In Sunday school, he learned that a martyr was someone who endured great suffering for a cause they believed in—just like Jesus had.

Billy watched in awe as his father raised his Remington Pump Action Shotgun swiftly and silently. He froze, shut one eye, squinted with the other, took a deep breath, switched off the safety, and waited until his prey, a deer this time, entered the crosshairs in the telescopic sight before he exhaled, squeezed the trigger and the young buck fell down, dead.

Sometimes he would let Billy hold the rifle on his own when the magazine was empty, the muzzle still smoking from a recent kill. The boy loved the feel of it, sleek and heavy, and hot in his hand. It was a man's gun, not a child's toy, cheap and light, like the BB gun he'd had his eye on at the fair.

His father stood behind him, guiding his movements while Billy struggled to hold the gun level. Billy felt his breath hot, whiskey sour in his ear. "Don't worry, boy, you'll grow into it before you know it."

Billy nodded. "I can hardly wait."

"Be patient, son. I know it's hard, but you can't rush perfection. You've got to take it as it comes." He shook his head. "Always remember, practice makes perfect."

The boy grinned. "I know, Dad."

His father placed his callused index finger on top of Billy's tender one and together they caressed the trigger before squeezing off a shot.

The old man behind the counter at the fair, dressed in a red and white pin-striped shirt and black pants, was aghast as he watched the tall, lanky kid standing in front of him knock everything down there was to hit—including the mechanical mother goose that flapped her wings—right between the eyes. A crowd gathered around to witness the freakish occurrence, this being the first time someone had ever hit everything the first time up.

Before he knew it, the man was shouting, "We have a winner!" He unlocked the glass case that housed the Grand Prize—a BB gun complete with telescopic sight. Billy'd had his eye on it since last year's fair, but at that time he had not been skilled enough to win it.

But a lot had happened since he turned ten this past summer. His penis had started getting hard for no apparent reason, when he least expected it, and he was frequently roused from exciting dreams about guns or girls by a warm dampness in his underwear.

The man behind the counter bent down to whisper in his ear, "Be cautious when handling this gun, boy. It can be extremely dangerous if not used properly. Someone could get hurt if you're not careful."

Billy nodded with a sly grin plastered across his face. "Look what I won, Dad!" He grasped the gun tightly in his wiry arms and pointed it at a slight angle before bringing it over to his father.

"You've earned it, Billy. That was some fancy shooting back there. I'm impressed. You've got talent, son, that's half the battle. Now you've got to whet your appetite for the hunt." His father patted him on the head.

"I aim to please." He tucked the BB gun under his arm.

On their walk back through the woods, Billy's father nodded his approval. "I see you've finally learned how to shoot your load."

"Yeah...right, Dad." Billy blushed and kept his eyes on the ground, embarrassed by his father's choice of words.

"I'm talking about the prize you just won!" He pointed to the BB gun. "I think it's time we had a talk about the birds and the bees." His father winked.

Billy rolled his eyes. "No one calls it that anymore, dad. Stop trying to disguise sex. I already know the basics. I'm a real fast learner."

Mr. Hogan snickered. "I'll *bet* you are!"

The boy climbed the cracked cement stairs that lead to the back door, dug his house keys out of the front pocket of his jeans, careful not to aggravate his raging hard-on, and unlocked the door. His father closed it gently behind them without saying a word, walked over to the fridge, pulled out a root beer and handed it to Billy. Then he grabbed some ice from the freezer, dropped it into a rocks glass and topped it off with a generous serving of single-malt whiskey, a clear sign their little talk would be involved, and probably boring.

Billy decided to get comfortable. Setting his new BB gun across his lap, he felt self-conscious about his erection, although he doubted his father noticed it from the other side of the table.

Billy opened his root beer and took a long sip.

His father took a swig of whiskey, set his glass down on the table, and pushed it aside, more intent on the task at hand.

"Let us pray for forgiveness and strength." He made the sign of the Cross, closed his eyes, and bowed his head.

The boy mimicked his father's movements.

Together, they recited their favorite prayer: "Our Father, Who art in Heaven, hallowed be Thy name. Thy kingdom come, Thy will be done, on earth as it is in Heaven. Give us this day our Daily Bread, and forgive us our trespasses, as we forgive those who trespass against us. And lead us not into temptation, but deliver us from evil. Amen."

Billy's father opened his eyes and cleared his throat. "Good sex with a woman is even better than that adrenaline rush you're probably still feeling after your impressive performance at the fair."

Billy smirked, guilty as charged. "The thrill of the kill really gets me going."

The man grunted and continued his lecture. "When you handle a gun or a woman, if you've enjoyed yourself, you'll shoot your load without thinking about it. Of course the gun requires your undivided attention. You've got to zero in on your target at the exact moment it's in your sights, or else you'll miss your chance at the kill."

His father paused to down the rest of his whiskey and wipe his mouth with the back of his hand. "When you're with a woman, you've got total control. You've got your bullet in her chamber, pumping her full of lead—so to speak. Do you follow me, son?"

Billy finished his soda. "Uh…I think so. Handling a gun is more of a challenge because you have limited control over what you're after. But when you're with a woman (and you've got more experience than I do) the challenge isn't always there, but the excitement is."

Billy's father reached slowly across the table and patted one of his son's bony shoulders. "Well, son, I couldn't have said it better myself."

Armed with his father's words of wisdom and his brand new BB gun, Billy ran out back to the woods where he could pursue livelier game before it got too dark.

"Ask yourself what Jesus would do…and your aim will be true."

He paused when he heard something rustling to his left. A tiny chipmunk wiggled its nose and looked around, sensing danger, but not knowing who the enemy was.

Instinctively, setting his sights on the disturbance, Billy aimed in that direction and pulled the trigger. The furry creature, concealed by dead leaves until the shot blew its cover, yelped and tried to flee, but Billy launched a BB directly into its tiny hindquarters, paralyzing it instantly. He clutched the gun in one hand and grabbed his prize, still squealing, by the scruff of its neck, in the other. He rushed home, dropped the dying thing down on the back stoop, and ran inside to get his father, who was busy in the kitchen making venison stew for supper.

"Dad, come see what I got!" Billy grinned, finding it nearly impossible to contain his excitement.

His father stepped outside, looked down at Billy's catch, gritted his teeth and said, "Wounded game is nothing more than a wasted shot! Bring me back something that's dead tomorrow—or I'll take that BB gun away and give it to a boy who knows how to use it properly!" He kicked the writhing chipmunk off the stoop into a pile of dead leaves, ignoring the dribble of dark blood left in its wake, and went back inside, slamming the door shut behind him.

The next afternoon, not wanting to disappoint his father again, Billy snatched his BB gun from its usual spot against the wall next to his bed and crept out to the woods in search of an easy target. He felt his penis get hard in anticipation of the hunt. Perched high in a tree directly in front of him, Billy spied the perfect target: a squirrel nibbling on an acorn.

He took a deep breath and set his sights on the tiny creature, waiting anxiously for the exact moment when his target became a *martyr on the Cross.* His trigger finger twitched as he struggled to hold it still until the time was right.

Billy fired.

Still clutching the acorn, the squirrel hit the ground with a soft thud. Billy scooped up his catch and rushed back to the house, eager to make his father proud.

"Dad, look what I got!" He held the dead rodent up for his father to see.

"Nice shot, son—right in the eye. Kills 'em every time! Remember that and you'll never go wrong!" Billy's father grabbed the carcass and admired the BB shining dully in the socket where the squirrel's left eye had been. "This little fella's a keeper!"

Billy licked his lips. "Can you stuff and mount him for me, so I can keep him on the dresser next to my bed? A trophy is sure to inspire me."

"You betcha!" His father winked.

* * *

The sun resembled a blood-red orb sinking slowly in the western sky when Billy went out to the garage to swipe his father's Remington Pump Action Shotgun for a little experimental adventure in search of the *ultimate* fair game. The gun was much heavier than the BB gun he was now used to—because it was a *man's* gun—not a toy. Billy hardly noticed the extra weight; tremendous excitement filled him with a sense of deeper purpose.

While he set out on his mission, Billy tried to think of a place with targets that moved faster and were tougher to hit than the ones at the shooting gallery. He camped out in the tall grass a few miles away from the woods and waited for a commuter train to pass by. He decided that would do quite nicely. Billy set up his father's camcorder on the tripod he'd brought and adjusted the focus, so he could record himself in action for posterity.

A few minutes later Billy heard a familiar whistle not too far off in the distance. He walked a few feet in front of the camera and stood off to the right, ready to open fire as soon as the train appeared in his sight. When it sped by in one big silver blur, Billy locked on to a random window, thumbed off the safety, and fired in rapid succession. It was much harder to hit something moving so fast, but Billy managed to rise to the occasion.

That done, Billy shut off the camera, grabbed his gear, and headed for home. He reloaded his father's rifle carefully, so he wouldn't suspect a thing, and put it back in the rifle rack out in the garage before heading into the house.

As usual, his father was in the living room watching the news and drinking single-malt whiskey. He turned around when he heard the back door slam and glared quickly at his son, not noticing the camcorder case in Billy's hand. "Where you been, boy? You had me worried."

Billy shrugged. "I had a train to catch."

Mr. Hogan nodded vaguely and turned back to the television with a sense of wonder. "Get a load of this, son. An unidentified sniper just shot six passengers on a rush hour commuter train. Turns out he only fired six bullets—one for each victim. He must've been quite a shot."

Billy glanced at the raw footage and grinned. His father had a keen eye.

"Let me show you where I've been." He took out the videotape he had just made and popped it into the VCR, so his father could see how much progress he'd made in the week since winning the BB gun at the fair. Billy pressed PLAY and sat down on the couch next to his father to admire his handiwork up close.

Billy's father was speechless as he watched his son stand off to the right, hidden by the tall grass, poised, ready to open fire as soon as the train was in view. When it sped by, he saw his son lock on to a window and start firing in rapid succession. His father winced when he heard gunfire and saw glass shatter. The passengers' shrieks were drowned out by the noise of the rumbling train, but the camera angle managed to catch one bloody face locked in a scream, providing a silent soundtrack to the carnage.

Slowly, still in shock, his father turned off the television, finished his whiskey, and shook his head. "How could you do something like this with my good rifle?"

"It was easy," Billy said with pride. "I waited for the right moment when my target became a martyr on the Cross—just like you taught me. Then I shot my load without thinking about it. I sure caught those folks off guard, didn't I, dad? I was so excited…I didn't know I hit the train until I played back the tape, just now." He started to laugh. "I really wanted to impress you. It looks like I've exceeded your expectations."

"This is no joke, son. Shooting animals is sport. But shooting people is *different.* It's murder, plain and simple. You've committed a very serious crime." His father's scrunched-up face tried to drive the message home, but from Billy's blank stare, Mr. Hogan could see the boy didn't understand what he had done at all. "You know, son, you could go to jail if anyone finds out you did this. What drove you to go out and shoot up a train?"

Billy stopped laughing. "You did."

"I never told you to shoot anyone! You always twist my words around into something else! You don't listen. You're too busy hearing what you want to." Billy's father shook his head in bewilderment.

"You told me to ask myself what Jesus would do and my aim would be true. That's exactly what I did. It worked wonders every time." Billy grinned. "I wanted to make you proud, Dad."

"Well, you went about it all wrong. If you'd only asked me I would've taken you out to the woods and let you shoot some deer, instead of watching me do it. This time you've gone too far!" He shook his head. "You've got to think about the consequences of your actions, boy. I thought you knew that by now, but I guess I was dead wrong!"

Billy buried his hands deep in the pockets of his jeans. "I…uh... don't know what came over me. I guess I got caught up in the moment."

"Come on, show me exactly where you found that rifle!" He grabbed his son by the arm and dragged him out of the house, to the garage where he kept his guns.

With his trigger finger, Billy pointed to the rifle rack hidden in a dark corner of the garage. "It was empty when you showed me how to shoot." He bit his lip.

"You still don't want to be pointing an empty gun at people, boy!" Without giving it much thought, Billy's father grabbed the gun his son had taken without permission, switched off the safety, and leveled it directly with the boy's face, pausing a moment for emphasis.

Billy felt the crotch of his jeans tighten. He stared at his father with vacant brown eyes, knelt down on the cold, dirty floor of the garage, spread his arms wide, and waited.

His father's hand shook uncontrollably. And accidentally, the loaded gun discharged.

A single bullet lodged in the boy's left eye.

Billy hit the ground with a soft thud, a pool of blood spreading out from his head like a glistening halo.

A similar wetness spread across the crotch of Billy's jeans, as the final jolts of his body caused a wan smile to stretch over his proud face.

Finally, Billy had become the martyr on the Cross.

Just as his father had taught him.

Bringing in the Sheaves

Richard Thomas

Ever since I was a little boy, the cornfields filled my nightmares with the sounds of rustling stalks, and the stench of something decomposing. I guess you could call it a recurring dream, the way the empty fields would fill my head with gentle hot winds and stinging scratches up and down my arms. I blame it on my younger brother Billy—it was his idea after all—his fault. But I don't hold onto that grudge. I see the girl, Margie, every once in awhile, hanging out in front of the 7-11, or maybe down by the bowling alley. Small town living doesn't offer up many options, but back then she was one of them. Today, less so.

Doesn't really matter, the name of our town, they're all the same, dotted across the Midwest, filling up the middle of Illinois, long arteries of dust and despair stretching out in every direction. Bluford. Cairo. Dakota. We all worked the fields, tending to chickens, hogs, cows and the like. It was a lot of early morning chores and dark nights where we tried to kill ourselves one way or another.

My younger brother Billy, only three years my junior, he'd tag along whenever he could. Sometimes I needed somebody to shoot hoops with on the back of the barn, or to blame the broken window on; that's how it went. He was always falling down, his simple skull filled with ideas, massive forehead constantly scratched and riddled with scabs. I didn't treat him like a simpleton, but he was definitely slow. I'd hear a thud or a slam, something creaking or snapping in two, and I'd go running for the barn, running for the tractor that kept moving into the cornfield with nobody on top of it, as it disappeared into the unforgiving folds. A tine of a pitchfork jammed through his meaty thigh, trying to fly out of the loft into a pile of hay below. An angry raccoon disappearing down the dirt road, unwilling to be his pet,

Billy's face and arms bleeding, his wide grin stretched taut over bones that knew no failure. One dead animal or another, cradled in his arms—a hen with a snapped neck, or field mice staged around a tiny table sipping at tea, a stiff cat swung around by its tail—he didn't mean anything by it, just curious, I guess, as we all were.

The girl lived down the road a bit. She was always dirty, constantly lifting her torn skirt over her head, showing off her dingy underwear to whoever would look. But she was sweet on me, sweet on Billy. Margie was a year ahead of me. She probably just wanted somewhere quiet to go where her daddy couldn't touch her, where her mother couldn't lay her dead eyes on Margie's thin arms and pale skin. So we let her come over, after school, or in the summertime. We'd pal around with her down by the creek, looking for tadpoles, or frogs to put in jars—left out on a shelf where they'd dry up and leave our room stinking of something gone foul—rotten and thick.

When she asked us to tie her up, we thought she was joking. We were older now, sixth grade for me, about twelve, and Billy still only nine. I had seen a filmstrip in class once, bad illustrations of flaccid penises, the scientific data going over my head, our stunned faces flush and embarrassed by the idea of a naked woman's body, the idea of what we were supposed to do. It was dirty. And yet, it was spectacular.

We'd seen her underwear before, it wasn't a big deal, and we weren't interested in putting our tongues in her mouth. Gross. But we had nothing else to do, so we tied Margie to a post at the back of the barn, and turned to each other, mute, as she smiled in the dimly lit space. We ignored her for a bit, leaving her to squirm, to test the knots, moaning and grunting. She was our kidnapped ransom, so we went about the barn fortifying our defense, leaning broken broom handles against the wall, our weapons, gathering shovels and baseball bats, and a lone, rusty pitchfork, still stained with a bit of Billy's blood.

Billy finally approached her and licked her face, from her chin to her eyebrow, and she giggled and turned her head away. He spit into the dirt.

"Salty," he said, smacking his lips.

He picked up a stick and started poking her, in the belly at first, and then he raised and lowered her faded skirt.

"Billy?" I asked.

He glanced at me, then back to Margie, a dirty grin easing across his face.

"What? She started this."

Margie turned to look at me, her eyes tiny fragments of coal.

"Leave him alone, Rodney," she said, "We're just playing."

"Yeah, Rodney," my brother wheezed, bending over, and raising her skirt. "Let's see what she's got."

I crossed my arms. I wanted to see too. I glanced to the house, it was quiet, nobody in sight. Billy held her skirt up with the stick, as Margie smiled, and took his other hand and placed it between her legs.

"Nothin," Billy said. "She ain't got nothin."

A car skidded into the yard and Billy let her skirt fall back down, and quickly untied her from the post. His face was splotchy and red, as was hers, but I was cold and pale, on the verge of throwing up.

"I better get home," Margie said. "Almost dinner."

She leaned over and kissed me on the cheek, and skipped out of the barn, into the sunlight. I wiped my face, the sticky residue of strawberry bubblegum, Billy's eyes on me, glassy and empty.

It was all Billy could talk about—Margie. All summer long. I didn't see her again, not for a while, but he went looking for her whenever he could. He looked for her at the grocery store with mother, or whenever we went for a ride with dad, fishing or off on some errand. He leaned out of the beat up Chevy Nova like a dog, his tongue flapping in the arid wind.

My father always plowed a section of the back forty, a path out into the corn, with a patch of it cleared out, like his private sitting room. There wasn't much in the space, just a rusty metal chair and a crate filled with empty beer bottles, a hole dug into the earth filled with cigarette butts and spent matches. I don't blame my father for wanting this space, somewhere away from our mother, who had an endless list of things for him to do—broken latches and busted screens to fix, buckets of paint that needed to be emptied. As far as I know, he'd just sit out there in the dark, staring up at the stars, drinking and smoking, wishing to be someplace else. *Anywhere* else.

On the rare evenings when the two of them would go upstairs, turning the television set up loud, hand in hand as they climbed the stairs, all giggles and fists of flesh, Billy and I would head for the fields, to sit in his chair, and stare up at the dark sky, dotted with pinholes of light. It was as close as we'd get to the man, as close as he'd let us get. We'd find half smoked butts and smoke them, coughing and spitting onto the ground. We'd drink the warm remnants from the bottom of the bottles and cans, sweet and sour and forbidden.

When Billy started disappearing, this was the place I went. I often found him covered in blood. He wouldn't say anything, just hold his palms up to me and grin. I'd take him back to the house and get him cleaned up, hosing him down until he started to cry, and then I'd slap him until he shut up.

Margie started showing up again, and she and Billy would disappear into the barn. They had secrets now; things would go quiet when I walked into the barn. We'd still take walks together, to the creek and into the woods, even out into the cornfields, lost and scratched by the sharp stalks and ears, hollering for each other, hiding, as we choked on the dust and the heat. Inevitably we'd end up in my father's room, lying by the chair, the walls of corn around us a fortress against the rest of the world. I only saw them kiss once, but it made my stomach curl. He was too young, I thought, and even though he was my brother, he was clueless about Margie's advances. I barely understood them myself.

I cornered Margie one afternoon and warned her off my brother. She put one hand on her hip and asked me if I wanted that attention, if her time spent with my brother was something I'd prefer she reserve for me. I told her she was crazy, but she wasn't wrong. And on an afternoon when Billy wasn't around, she and I ended up in the hayloft, our wet mouths on each other, my stomach in knots, telling myself this was what I needed to do in order to protect my brother—my hands on her dirty, sweaty body, our tongues a slick disaster.

Daddy had been on the road now for weeks. Business trip, local fair, something to do with the price of our harvest and subsidies, I didn't understand it all. I knew that the house was quiet—that we were bored to death—and I knew the bottle of whiskey hid above the fridge was slowly emptying as our mother sat quiet at the kitchen table.

We siphoned off part of it, and replaced it with water, disappearing into the fields when she went to sleep. We choked it down as we lay in the darkness, waiting for something to happen. When I drifted off, his hands found my neck, his knees on my shoulders—the air in my lungs disappearing into the night. He'd found out about us, Margie and me, there was nothing else to explain it. He was stronger then I remembered, his eyes bulging in his head as he clenching hands squeezed on my neck, showing no sign of letting up. I finally brought my knees up, banging him in the center of his back, throwing him off of me, as air rushed back into my lungs.

"Dammit, Billy," I choked. "She's not worth it. You're too young, anyway."

"Fuck you," he murmured, looking up from the ground, the darkness swallowing our sweat and our tension.

"She's my girl," Billy muttered. "Don't touch her again."

"You'd choose flesh over blood?" I asked. "She's just some stupid whore from down the road."

"Shut your mouth, Rodney."

"I'm sure I'm not the only boy she's kissing. I told you, she's no good."

Billy lay there.

"That's for me to decide," he said.

Daddy never did come back from that business trip. And that wasn't a good thing. Billy wasn't talking to me. Instead, he drifted about the property like a ghost, chucking rocks at anything that moved. For three days we didn't talk, until I walked past the barn and the stench of rotten meat engulfed me.

I'd let him have the barn, somewhere to go where he didn't have to look at my face. In the middle of the sweltering barn lay a large metal bowl of cat food, dusted with white powder, and surrounding it was a ring of dead cats, their grey tongues protruding from their tiny, still mouths. Flies buzzed my face.

Billy.

I yelled for him, but he didn't answer. I headed for the cornfields as sweat pushed out of every pore.

I found him standing over Margie, her arms tied behind her, sitting in the metal chair, buck naked and crying. Billy was holding a pocketknife in his hand, looming over her, poking her skin with the sharp blade. Her whimpers were lost on the wind, but her eyes bore into me.

"Billy," I said. "Enough!"

He turned to me, his jaw clenched.

"We're just playing," he said. Margie shook her head back and forth, afraid to speak, and Billy backhanded her across the face.

"Stop it, Billy," I said. "It's over, let her go."

"She came here," he said. "She took off her own clothes, she sat in the chair. This is what she wants," he whined.

"No, Billy, it isn't. You've gone too far."

"No, this is going too far," he said, leaning over the girl. I started running to him, but I wasn't fast enough. He put the blade under her left nipple, her breasts hardly anything at all. Her eyes went wide as his thumb held the tiny pink protuberance, and he sliced it clean off and flung it to the ground. She gasped, unable to scream, as blood ran down her pale skin. He looked up at me, smiling, and I was on him, and we were rolling to the ground, my fists beating about his head, the tiny blade stabbing my back, my arms, until I knocked it out of his hand. I beat him until he stopped moving, and then I stood up.

Margie was crying, snot running down her lip, blood pooling in her lap.

"It's all right," I said. "It's over."

I picked up the blade and walked to her, cutting the rope that bound her trembling flesh. I knelt down and held her as she sobbed into my shoulder. Straightening up, I held her face in my hands.

"Margie, don't come back here. You hear?"

She nodded her head and quickly got dressed.

With daddy gone it didn't take much for mother to drift away too. She'd picked up a job at the local diner, and we saw her less and less. Strange men came for the harvest, and we watched them descend on the farm like locust. Billy and I didn't talk any more.

When the summer ended and a cool wind started to fill the space that used to be our family farm, I went to the barn in search of Billy, ready to bury the hatchet, to move on from these transgressions, to erase from our minds what had happened out there in the fields.

A shadow swung back and forth across the opening of the barn. The stiff bodies of the sacrificial cats were long gone, but the rotten stench still remained. I swallowed, a lump in my throat, and stared up at the rafters, at his still body, the rope around his neck, his purple face, and a stain of urine in the dirt below his dead body. I took a breath, exhaled, and lowered my head. It didn't have to be this way.

Or maybe it did.

A Knowing Noah

Mark Patrick Lynch

One morning in early fall, when the leaves were still lighting up the trees and the cold hadn't yet pressed in and set a marker for the coming winter, I learned that if you ask Liddy Tibbs what she thinks of Lionel Travis she'll tell you straight out.

"Oh, that Lionel, he's a no-good. Has been since the day the midwife slapped him on the ass."

"Don't hold back any, Liddy," I said.

"I taught him for three years, same as I did his daddy before him, and believe me, if there was any kind of misdemeanour in class, I knew where to hunt out its cause. Nine times out of ten, it'd be Lionel, face as innocent as a peach's skin. That boy..." She released her frustrated memory on a stream of breath and hooked a finger every bit as bent and gnarled as she was, toward the centre of my chest. "In fact, you ask me now and I'll tell you something else too. The thing about Lionel, he's just like his father—a Knowing Noah—always was, always will be. And *that's* why you should go talk to him."

When I didn't say anything to that, she glanced at me and shook her head.

"What's that raised eyebrow about, Wilson? I seen that eyebrow skedaddle up your forehead since you were knee-high to a grasshopper, and it always means the same thing. You're confused."

"I can't hide anything from you, can I, Oh Wise Confucius."

"No reason to get smart. Just because you're smiling when you say it and you've a Sheriff's badge on your chest, don't mean it ain't a wiseass remark all the same. And you ain't answered the question. Don't think I haven't noticed. Just because it takes me longer to climb a staircase these days, don't mean the treads don't run all the way up to the attic."

"Sorry, Liddy. My bad."

She slammed down the point of her walking cane and came to a stop. "And I don't want to hear you talking off like you're a teenager. That kind of language, and with grey starting to show in your hair, it's not a good match. A man in your position should be setting an example."

I resisted the urge to sink my hands into my pockets and hang my head, knowing if I did Liddy would be on my case for that too. I walked slowly beside her as she started to shuffle along the sidewalk again. The first rain of leaves had settled in the gutters, burnishing the edges of the streets. The shadows were already lengthening with the age of the year, and the sun weighed heavier in the air, as if it was tarnished bronze rather than airy gold. In the distance the wind ruffled the tops of the pine trees that surrounded our town and ran for miles up and down the mountainside.

"Go ahead," Liddy told me. "Tell me what's got your head so knotted."

"It's what you just said. I've heard a lot of things in my time—been *called* a good few of them as well—but I never heard that phrase before. *A Knowing Noah.* What's it mean?"

She hunted out my eyes in the shade cast by the brim of my hat. Liddy's own eyes were a clear, unblemished brown—the eyes of someone at least half a century younger than her actual age. I've seen teenagers with stares more faded than Liddy Tibbs's. Now I saw a fascinating and disorienting depth in the woman's pupils, as if she were pulling the world inside herself and taking its measure. I couldn't believe I was talking to someone who was over a hundred years old and every bit the witch folks around town claimed her to be.

"It means, Wilson, that if there's trouble coming, Lionel Travis's got wind of it from somewhere, and right now he's building whatever metaphorical ark he needs to, to save his tootsies from getting wet."

Breakfast had been scrambled eggs and a couple of nicely browned slices of toast that morning. It was waiting for me on the tabletop after my wife, Maggie, had headed out for her stint assisting Doctor Appleman at the health centre. As breakfasts went it wasn't much, but it was enough to set me up for a good day after a weekend of righting the wrongs of a small, woody mountain town—a place where, until recently, nothing much happened.

I'd hardly got through the department door before Lou-Lou Ginty, the telephone operator and desk jockey, called out to me.

"Got us another one, Sheriff."

That brought me up short for a second. There'd been nothing for a couple of weeks now. I'd almost let myself believe things were quietening down, rationalising away a lot of things that probably couldn't be rationalised. I'd come to tell myself all the crazy stuff that'd happened would wind up as an odd set of stories, ultimately doomed to remain unsolved and enter into the town's folklore as the "Summer of the Manifestations," assuming it ever had cause to be remembered at all.

I got a churning in my stomach, making me thankful Maggie had left me only a light breakfast. And, yes, I'll openly admit to it, a sense of dread and excitement rushed through me.

"Who is it this time, Lou-Lou?"

"Carrie Fletcher. At the Portsman's." She handed the printed details across the desktop to save me coming through the gate to look over her shoulder at the monitor.

I noted the time the call had been logged. "Yeah, I know Carrie. Says here she called quite early." As soon as she knew someone familiar would be in the station, I figured. "She go into more detail than this?"

"All she said was that it'd happened to her last night. She was calm on the phone. But underneath…she sounded *fur-reeked.*"

Didn't they all? I tapped the sharp edge of the paper on my chin, thinking as Lou-Lou watched me.

"Sheriff?"

"I'll go over there now."

She called after me. "Oh, and Mr. Parsons has lost Biggywig again! It happened yesterday." Before the door swung all the way shut, I heard her add, "He swore he had his leash on this time, but Biggy just ripped it out of his hand in the park and lit off."

The kettle was coming to a boil on Carrie's stove. We'd been at high school together and had dated for a while, pretty basic stuff, nothing beyond a couple bases. When I went away to college, I hardly saw her again—though I'd hear tales about what she'd been up to; who she was running with; how she'd married and lost a baby girl in childbirth; and that she'd gotten divorced a couple years after that. That kind of bond in high school never really leaves you, however many roads you go down in life. It can stretch thinner with the years, but it never really snaps, even if all that's left is an ever tautening, fraying thread you barely feel snag you as you pass by each other on the street.

Right now, her hair awry and her face free of makeup, dressed in the first thing she'd found to put on that morning, Carrie's mind wasn't on our past at all. "Thank you so much for coming," she said to me again. She'd been thanking me ever since I'd rapped on her door and she'd grabbed me by the hand and led me past the seating, which was still stacked on the tables, and into her private kitchen. It looked like the Portsman's wouldn't be opening for fresh apple pie and the finest cup of joe this side of Boulder today.

A marmalade cat brushed between my legs as I sat waiting for Carrie to tell me what had happened. Carrie wrapped a towel around the handle of the kettle and lifted it off the stove. She poured boiling water onto coffee granules in two striped mugs, added milk, stirred, and carried them both over to where I was seated, handing me one of the mugs.

"I haven't slept a wink," she told me.

"It happened in the night—woke you?"

"It wasn't a dream. There's evidence I can show you. But it was so...you know...*weird.* I just, well, I was there. I surely can't deny all that happened. But it was wrong, such things cannot happen. I didn't know the first thing to do."

"You hadn't heard about anyone else, the things going on around town?"

"Running a joint like this, you hear all the gossip, but that's all it ever is. *Stories.* I mean, it's all just so outrageous. Who'd believe such a thing unless they saw it with their own eyes?"

Without makeup to hide them, her freckles showed. I remembered how she hated her freckles when we were kids, and how she did her best to cover them up. I'd always liked them, but try telling a teenage girl they make her cute when Bo Derek's considered the perfection of womanhood and has not a blemish to her face. See how much you're believed then.

I took a sip of the coffee. It was good, even out of granules from a jar, worth her place's reputation. I said, "Hard to accept until someone unloads a bucketful of strange on your living room carpet, then gets a stick and stirs it all up?"

She released a single sharp yelp of a laugh. "Yeah! And then stomps it into the rug too. There's nothing you can do but accept it at that point, which is why I called the station. Did I do right, Wil?"

"You did right. Now tell me exactly how it happened."

She did, and when I asked her to, she escorted me upstairs and showed me the marks, the flaring on the bedroom walls, the discolouration on the ceiling that could've been soot but we both knew was not. Then she pointed to the side of an old dresser. "It was my grandmother's. All I could think when I saw it, was thank god my mother's no longer alive. She'd scream at the state it's in now," she said, letting me see where the piece of furniture was scorched and warped, and beads of sap or glue—or perhaps it was lacquer from the veneer—had bubbled and left trails, like blood seeping from a wound.

I was willing to bet that even the best French polisher in the state couldn't repair the damage. "How long did it last?" I asked her.

"At the time? For-*ever.*"

"But if you were to put it into minutes."

"You know...I'm not sure I could. Strange, isn't it, but I really couldn't say it lasted ten seconds or ten minutes. Or ten *hours* for that matter. I was alone and scared. It was in the middle of the night, and you know how fear seems to be ten times worse in the darkness of night—only this *was* real," she said, before stumbling over a hitch in her throat. "However absurd it might sound...it happened. It really happened!"

"I know it did," I said.

She looked at me with a sudden, penetrating incisiveness, sizing me up in a way that she hadn't felt the need to before. "It's happened to you?"

"No, but you hear a crazy story told by separate witnesses enough times, and you get to figuring something's gotta be going on, even if you don't know what exactly it is. And more and more of these things, they're leaving evidence behind. No one's dreaming any of this, Carrie."

As the sun moved around the edge of the building, the light fell through the cream netting over the windows. But even as the room brightened, it did nothing to make the location of the *manifestation* (as folk had begun to call these things) any less aggressive and obtrusive than it was.

Carrie put a hand out to me, tugged tentatively on my jacket. When I unglued my gaze from the stains on the floor, I saw tears streaking her face. Her lips were downturned and her teeth were all but chattering as she made an anxious grimace. I could feel how much she was trembling, just from her fingers.

"Wil, I've someone coming around later, someone close. But please, could you hold me a while. I'm scared."

I drove around in the cruiser, not particularly looking for anyone or anything. I just wanted time to think. For two months, the *manifestations* had been occurring, witnessed by the townspeople. Probably it had been going on longer than that. In fact there were rumours of six months at least of all this oddness. Officially, however, according to our first reported sighting, it'd been two months.

Most of the *manifestations* occurred in people's houses, during the night, but not exclusively so. In Chattergee Park, over by the stand where the band played on nice August evenings, one of the biggest *manifestations* had taken place in the middle of a Wednesday afternoon. There had been ten witnesses, six of whom I would've taken seriously if they'd told me Bigfoot had come and kidnapped them in a UFO and taken them to a city on Mars.

That no two witnesses agreed on what form the *manifestations* had actually taken was somewhat of a convincer in its own way. It made me dismiss the notion that any of it might be a practical joke, by those who'd called in the reports. One man had claimed he'd seen Jesus standing before him, while another had witnessed a pair of rotating loops of light that intersected and pulled and tugged at a small fiery ball, hurtling in and out of the loops, and another had claimed to have seen some sort of giant bird from prehistory running around with its tail-feathers on fire, while yet another witness had seen a smooth pyramid glittering and dancing on its points until it was too bright to look at.

The youngest witness, Thandi Conners, had seen a windmill with a laughing scarecrow riding around on the sails. She hadn't been the slightest bit frightened in making her report. And now, for the first time since the reports had started to filter through to the station, there was genuine physical evidence left behind. There were scorch marks on the side of the bandstand, and where the grass had been touched by its appearance, all the blades had curled around in a tight circle. It was perhaps the most unnatural thing I've ever seen in my life. Prosaic maybe, yet subtly menacing. If before I'd at least tentatively been able to put it all down to the skewed musings of the population smoking too much bad grass—such things have happened before, though certainly not on such a scale—this physical evidence changed all of that. It was also some kind of tipping point for the phenomena as well, because now when someone witnessed—or was chosen for—a *manifestation,* there'd be some sign of its presence left behind.

But how come no two people ever saw the same thing?

For Booty Myers a burning tree with eyes and a snapping mouth had grown out of the walnut desktop over which she conducts business in Myers' New and Used Books—before fragmenting and splintering to nothing, leaving behind as evidence a grazing to the desktop that looked like it might've been caused by the presence of tree roots.

"Moonshine" Johnny Parris had been fishing out of his skiff on the *Triburn* river when "a bare nekked lady" had materialised, trapped inside a pillar of ice, and had pressed her fulsome bosom up against the ice while screaming screams Johnny could hear, but distantly, from inside her prison.

When I asked him if the skiff had tilted over and he'd taken on any water—something to suggest actual weight and a real physical presence—he shook his head and scratched his whiskers and told me he couldn't "rightly recall," on account of all he'd been thinking was that there was a bare nekked lady right there in front of him.

Ray Brick had seen a sea-lion, or a walrus—he wasn't a hundred percent sure which, the "one with tusks" was the best he could ascertain—on the hood of his Ford Sedan when he crossed the town line driving back from work.

Jill Dawes had found her postal round interrupted by a mailbox *manifesting* into a tableaux of her deceased relatives, sort of melded into one amorphous mass, like a bunch of plastic dolls put too close to a flame.

Carrie Fletcher's bedroom had been lighted in the night by a whirlwind of colour and nebulous forms that had looked like flapping sheets one minute, then like the hooked talons of a giant eagle the next.

There was no consistency to any of the reports, nothing to give us a clue about the how's, whys, or wherefores. All we knew was that something strange was going on. But *what?* I was prepared to go further and state that for every reported *manifestation* there was probably at least another two or three we never learned about.

As I drove down tree-happy Maple Street musing on things, the shadow of the forests surrounding town was a shifting haze in the distance. Through it, I spotted a familiar figure shuffling along the sidewalk and pulled the cruiser over and shifted it into PARK. I climbed out to talk to Liddy Tibbs, thinking if anyone had an inkling of what might be happening here, or at least help guide my thinking on it, it would surely be Liddy.

"Hey, Liddy."

She stopped and turned around, an action that took her no small amount of time, but which, upon seeing me, still brought a smile to her face.

"Sheriff. Nice to see you. All important in your big shiny car."

"It's not that shiny, Liddy."

"Uh huh. I see that. You don't have no one to wash it for you?"

"I do it myself."

"But you been too busy of late…"

"I heard you'd not been too well, Liddy. Been meaning to come out and see you."

"Ach! Doctors, they tell you things, but you don't have to believe them."

I nodded. "So you've taken yourself out for a walk. Against doctor's orders."

"I'm dog-hunting. Biggywig's gone missing again. I heard about it, you know how it is."

The town's party line. Rumour had it that Liddy Tibbs was a wise woman and had a third eye. She might well be a wise old lady, but I knew from borrowing her telephone one time that she had no such thing as a third eye. I'd found that when I picked up the receiver of the old bakelite instrument Liddy refused to replace, you could hear plenty of other voices down the line before even dialling a number. Liddy smiled when she saw the comprehension light in my eyes as I put it all together and she said, "Now, don't you breathe a word to anyone about what you just heard, Sheriff, or my reputation's done for."

I was flattered she trusted me, and I never said a word to anyone, and never will, at least not while Liddy's still alive. And, now that I think on it, I doubt very much I'd say anything after she's passed either.

"You seen him yet, the dog?" I asked her.

"Does it look like I've found him?"

"Got me there, Liddy."

"And you a *po-leece* officer too. Which is why you've really pulled up to talk to me, ain't it, Sheriff? You wanting my advice, I can tell by that look you're wearing. I remember it from when you were in my classroom." She snorted, collected her bosom and muscled it ahead of her, saying, "You'll have to walk with me if you want my advice. Got a stray hound to find. Citizens have to do for themselves, you know, on account the police force in these parts have trouble finding the seat of their own pants with the help of a mirror and an extra pair of hands."

"Okay, you're right," I said after we'd walked past a few of the generously spaced maples. "I'm sure you've heard all the talk, so tell me what you think of these things folks are calling *manifestations.*"

"I wondered when that'd come up," she said, and in a few more steps got down to things.

Eventually Liddy told me to go see the Knowing Noah, Lionel Travis, and see what he was up to. "The boy ain't been blessed with smarts, but he's got cunning like the rest of his family. Wouldn't still be alive after all this time if he hadn't got them. He'll maybe not know what to do *in-tell-lect-chu-ally,* but that animal part of his instinct, it'll've kicked in and he'll have something set up to protect himself, whether he knows it consciously or not."

I nodded, said, "What do you think of him, Liddy?"

She told me. Which is where we came in and I won't repeat myself by bothering you with it again.

Driving over, I watched as the thick clouds overhead lowered themselves across the mountaintops, stealing away the peaks and what would soon turn into the snowline, settling just above the pines, brooding in company with the shadow-darkened trees.

"Sheriff."

"Howdy, Lionel. Good to see you."

The jut of his chin and his searching gaze told me he wasn't so pleased to see me. He was wearing bib overalls and a plaid shirt with the sleeves rolled up. The fine hairs on his forearms were fuzzed with sawdust and the veins on the back of his hands stood out, weathered with the years. He was tall and blonde and blue-eyed and brought a trail of the dust out onto the porch with him. If Hansel and Gretal had been in a position to use that to find their way home instead of breadcrumbs, they would've never have gotten lost.

"Caught you at a bad time?" I asked, nodding at the ballpien hammer he held loosely in his left hand. It was known that Lionel wasn't one for honest labouring, hadn't been when he was a young man, and wasn't now that he was at an age where most people who'd worked in a paying job all their lives would be looking to slow down, being sure to shore up their finances for retiring. Most other days, my question would've been seen as humorous, maybe a mocking challenge to him. Today he appeared not to notice it.

"You haven't caught me at anything," he said, staring at me like I was a wall that'd suddenly sprung up along an alleyway he was used to walking down.

"Glad to hear it….So what're you doing?"

"That your kind of business these days, Sheriff?" he said, forcing a cordial smile. "What a man does on his own dime?"

I took off my hat, pinged the band. "Well now, Lionel, I'm sure you know there's been some odd business going off in town lately. Most everyone knows someone who's been affected, or else they've heard about it. Tell you honestly, I've a pile of odd reports I don't have the first clue about what to do with. Don't have the right kind of tray for them, you know? IN…OUT…I've got those, BUT no tray for: YOU GOT ME!"

"So you came here? Do I look like the FBI or the National Guard? Your worries ain't nothing to do with me, Sheriff."

"Maybe not," I said on the back of a sigh. "But humour me nonetheless, and tell me what're you making, Lionel?"

"Who says I'm making anything?"

I pointed out the evidence—the hammer, his work clothes, the fine and thick freshly-sawn dust everywhere, and finished by saying, "It's what they train us to notice in police school."

His face seemed to be chewing on itself as he came to a decision whether to lie or to be damn obstinate, or to come out and tell me the truth from the start. Something that looked like cunning crossed his face—or maybe he'd just seen an opportunity and was now looking to take it.

"I suppose it don't hurt for you to have a look around, Sheriff, if it'll settle your mind any. Maybe it'll interest you, or you'll know the right person to talk to about it. Maybe we can do some business."

Around back of Lionel Travis's house was the fattest, if not the tallest, totem pole I've ever seen. It was swollen and warped and, all in all, one mean piece of carved wood. It stood maybe eight feet tall, being nearly as wide as that too. Apparently, Lionel had been at work on it with a chainsaw, then had gone to it with a hammer—the one he carried now, I deduced, Sherlock Holmes-like—and various wood chisels. A couple of axes were scattered around the area as well.

"I didn't know you were Native American, Lionel."

He shook his head. "How'd you get to be sheriff with such a smart ass mouth on you?"

"I wonder that myself sometimes. S'ppose it helped that no one else was running for the position too, I admit."

"I got Cherokee blood in me. It's thin, but it's there."

"No shit. And you being so tall and blonde and all."

"No shit."

"My blood, it's thinned by the drink, but there's still some Irish in there somewhere. Doesn't mean I like planting potatoes and donate to the IRA though. Why a *totem pole,* Lionel? You're not exactly known for your hobbies."

He shrugged. "Sometimes a man finds a calling."

I whistled admiringly at his construction. "You sure started ambitiously. You ever carved anything before?"

"Funny you should ask, Sheriff. Started a few months ago; been making some things up ever since."

He showed me into a dilapidated barn. Through splinters of light coming down from the poorly maintained roof, it was easy enough to make out four other carvings, carefully honed and buffed to a polished finish. Three were painted, one seemed to be awaiting that particular attention. Even before I examined them I knew they were cut to the same design Lionel was aiming at with the giant outside.

"Know what a totem can be used for, Sheriff?"

Straightening up, I looked at him. His own face might've been carved from wood right then. "Tell me," I said.

"My forefathers—" (I managed not to look too cynical when he said this) "—believed they could ward off spirits."

"*Evil* spirits?"

"Didn't specify which, far as I know. Evil all depends on your perspective, don't you s'ppose, Sheriff? Just telling you the job totems did—still do—the right totems. Of the right make and design." He examined his fingernails, before huffing them on his overalls, then he squinted at me. "Anyhow, you seen what I'm doing, Sheriff. Thought that was what you wanted to know. Seems to me you got some investigating to get back to, from what you were saying earlier. All those *manifestations,* or whatever. Ain't it what people've been calling them? You got that to go back to, find a way of preventing any more of them before they start causing some harm to folks and not just a few scorch marks here and there."

"Lionel..." I wondered how he could've known about the scorch marks, but couldn't think of what else to say. It was undoubtedly the town's party line, up and running as well as ever.

He saw that, couldn't keep the smile from his face. It was the smile of the man selling you gasoline for every cent he could, because he knew you'd only ever be passing by his gas station once and your car was running on empty.

He said, "Totems are for sale. You want a word with the Selectmen, see about buying them off of me? I'm working quickly, so I'd say—oh, five, six more days—they'll be finished, painted up and ready for collection. I can think of some places around town where they'd sit pretty nicely. Sort of like they're looking after things heading this way from *out there,*" he said, motioning to the various layers and heights of the pines climbing the slopes of the hidden mountains behind them. "No telling what you want to keep in the woods—and out of town," he said. "Be sure to be in touch, Sheriff. Good day to you."

We put Lionel's main totem up in the middle of the park and some smaller copies of his masterwork at equal distances around the town—at equidistant *cardinal points*—the theory being they covered enough ground to offer up protection. Why it worked, we didn't know, assuming that those totems did work and it wasn't just luck the *manifestations* stopped once we'd planted the damned things. But it was good enough for us.

Spirits or whatever you fancied calling them, *something* had been challenging us, making that first incursion from their realm into ours. And though I don't know what lives in the forests—either in physical form or in some indefinable existence of the soul or spirit—what I do know is that those woodlands stretch in all directions for miles, and however well a man might think he knows them, he doesn't know *everything* that happens within their shadows, every day of the year, in every season, and in the hush of night and the first hesitant light of dawn. It's just not possible for any man to truly know of those things that are bigger and stranger than we can rightly imagine—the creatures that might live out there who just might view us as curiously and cautiously as we view them—if only we knew where to seek them out and observe them.

The totems have been up six months now and there've been no reports of any other *manifestations*. Spring's well under way. Mr Parsons's dog Biggywig—who you'll recall ran off in the park the day I went over to Carrie Fletcher's and then Lionel Travis's—was found outside the deli in town. He was snacking on scraps the good patrons of that establishment fed him as they left with their purchases. He's since run off twice more, and has been found twice more again.

Carrie Fletcher announced her engagement to Tim Deaking, the handiest carpenter in town, and even though I'm in a fine marriage I count my blessings for every day, a little frayed old string tugged on my heart when I heard the news.

Liddy Tibbs is defying all doctors' predictions, though she's walking slower each time I see her. Myers New & Used Books had an author signing with a New York Times bestseller, a nice little guy from Dublin who charmed everyone off their feet, and Booty Myers sold out of every one of his books on the day, and had to take signatures on pieces of paper she promised to glue into another batch of books for customers as soon as they came in.

Lou-Lou Fernick on despatch keeps me busy with the usual low level crimes and neighbour disputes that rack up in a forgettable little town like ours—population still 10,347. Everything is pointing up for a good summer too. Except now, it's been raining constantly for three weeks without relief. The storm drains are dangerously close to overflowing, and one or two people are keeping an anxious eye on the *Triburn,* fearing it's going to breach its banks before too long. What we'll do then, I don't know. A lot of folks stand to lose their homes if it happens. All of us are praying for a let up in the weather and most folks are expecting it too, waiting for the clouds to break apart and the sun to glide a nice clearing beam of light through the heavens. But I'm not one of them. Tell you the truth, I'm somewhat worried, on account of a number of rumours I've heard recently—and which I'm going to go and check out to see if I can validate or not.

Way some people are talking, it seems Lionel Travis is at work again in his back yard. This time the reports coming back say it looks like he's making himself something huge, the likes of which none of us have ever seen.

Word is Lionel's building himself one helluva great big boat.

Bad Salvage

Wayland Smith

Some say a good deed is its own reward. And, at times, a bad one can be its own punishment. Not just for the doer, but for those around them as well. That was the lesson Cullen Davies not only learned too late, but his entire town suffered through too.

Cullen was what some called a *banker.* In this usage, the term had nothing to do with a bank, although it did with finance—in a way. Others called him a *land pirate.* Cullen thought of himself as a salvage man. The fact that he caused the salvage in the first place was something he chose not to trouble himself with.

Cullen's family was from Wales, and he'd learned his trade—if you could call it such—from his grandfather. Cullen would take a lantern, and hang it from the neck of a horse, and walk the beast up and down a sandbar. Helmsmen would see the bobbing light, and mistake it for a safely docked ship. The ship would come to grief on the sandbar, and, lo and behold, there would be salvage for the taking. Years later, this custom would give a name to the town of Nag's Head, for the horse's head that bore the lantern.

One particular evening, having had little luck fishing, Cullen decided to see if he could catch something different. He collected his horse, his lantern, Young Robbie, and Grim Linus. Linus was a towering figure of a man, barrel chested, heavily muscled, with a wild patch of dark hair atop his large head. He also had the most unceasingly dark outlook on life and its prospects. Robbie was a lad of eight or so, with bright blond hair, ragged clothes, and always willing to earn the odd coin.

Cullen fastened the lantern to his horse's neck, but kept it shuttered. No sense advertising their presence until there was a reason to risk it, after all. It didn't pay to invite competition or nosy sheriffs, revenue men, or what have you, certainly not before there was any sort of prize in sight. An hour passed, another, and Cullen wondered if this was to be another fruitless night, when Linus called out in his deep, rumbling voice, "A light!" and pointed. There was just enough starlight to make out Linus' arm, and Cullen looked in that direction.

He was about to curse Linus for a fool seeing visions, when he caught the faint lantern bobbing off the coast. Cullen breathed in deeply, the moist salt air filling his nose. "Let's try our luck," he said, opening the lantern's shutters. They waited, watching, the sand crunching beneath the men's boots and the horses' hooves. Minutes passed, and then, finally, the ship turned. Linus chuckled, and Cullen nodded. Maybe their luck would change yet. He turned to the boy.

"Robbie, look sharp! Run and tell the fools down at the Sea's Edge that we may have us one." Robbie nodded once and started running, his legs churning, kicking up a spray of sand behind him as he quickly disappeared into the night.

The ship slowly approached, looming larger as it neared. In the privacy of his thoughts, Cullen began to allow himself some doubt. The ship was larger than he'd thought at first. Still, nothing ventured, nothing gained—as he'd heard said—and he had no intention of showing weakness before Linus at any rate. Finally, after what seemed several nights worth of waiting, the vessel ran aground and shuddered with a creak of wood. The impact was violent; the sails had been nicely filled before the grounding.

As the ship crashed to a stop, Cullen heard the shouts behind him. Robbie had delivered the message, and the other bankers were arriving. At the front of the group, as ever, was Michael, who many suspected had once been a pirate in earnest before coming to the small town of Holly Ridge, in the Colony of North Carolina. Michael had a rope with a hook on it, and a large knife thrust through his belt.

"Well spotted, Cullen!" he shouted as he swung the rope around once, twice, and let it fly. His arm was practiced, and the hook landed solidly, biting into the rail by the bowsprit. He scurried up the line like a rat after cheese.

The sailors aboard ship had been stunned by their sudden stop, and then had begun seeing to their damaged vessel. Michael was on them before they knew it, and he was an artist with the knife. More of the robbers climbed the line behind him, not as gracefully, but spurred on by greed. The battle, such as it was, was short. The rough townsmen had done this before, and some of the sailors were still stunned from the impact.

After the unfortunate men on the deck were defeated, the bankers moved below decks. They broke into smaller groups, searching the captain's cabin, the galley, and the holds. Michael found nothing of interest in the powder magazine. Gunpowder was bulky, and, while useful, it wasn't as valuable as some other, more easily portable items he was hoping to find. He moved on to the main hold to see how the others were faring. He expected a lot of searching and some possible squabbling over whatever spoils they had found. What he found was so very much worse.

A man with darker skin than Michael was used to seeing, but not black like a slave, was standing over a large metal box of some kind. Fat John—to distinguish from Blond John or Tall John, the name being popular—was lying flat on top of the box, and the stranger had just finished cutting his throat. Blood flowed from the wound down onto the box. Michael bellowed in rage and charged forward, knife in hand. The stranger flicked his hand and Michael felt a searing pain as a knife spun through the air and embedded itself into his shoulder.

The others heard Michael's yell and came to the hold. James fell with another thrown knife in his throat, but the force of numbers from the rest overwhelmed the man, for all his clear skill with his blades. He fixed Michael with a glare as his breath bubbled out in blood, and said "My master will come for you all…" as he died.

"Ship coming!" Young Robbie called from the deck where he'd been left as a watchman. Rather than risk being caught by the Navy or simply better armed and like-minded thieves, the men hurriedly grabbed whatever they could lay hold of and fled over the ship's side. Michael kicked the man as he left, pain radiating through his arm.

As they fled, no one was there to see Fat John's blood seep down carved channels in the large metal box beneath him. The blood was sent down cleverly wrought runnels that drew it deep inside the box. There, it dripped into a still mouth, which suddenly began to show signs of life—a thin tongue licking the liquid.

* * *

The Royal Navy ship *Swift* pulled in as close as possible to the wrecked merchant vessel. The captain sent a small boat to check for survivors and see how badly the ship was damaged. Ensign Hamish Alexander was a man with keen eyes for a chance at supplementing his meager pay from His Majesty's Navy. As the small search party fanned out, he quickly made his way to the main hold. If the pirates who had run the ship aground had left anything, it would be down there, and his for the taking if he was quick enough.

His lantern illuminated a hold that had clearly been ransacked, and he cursed. But then, he saw something on the far side of the space. Quickly moving to it, he tried to make sense of what he was seeing. Before him was a large iron box, the top split open in to two halves, each now standing upright. "What would you need an entire box of metal to protect?" he wondered aloud, hope and greed tinging his voice. Moving closer, the lantern light slowly fell into the box's interior. It was a mostly hollow space, with an elaborate series of trays that ran down from the hinged lid to the bottom, which was divided into two sections. The far section was empty, but, straightening up and peering over the lid, Hamish saw the most beautiful woman he'd ever laid eyes on lying on the side closest to him.

He moved around to the end of the box, leaning down to see her better. She had golden hair, and a breathtakingly wonderful face. She was dressed in fine clothes, slightly old-fashioned, like something his grandmother would have worn, if she could have afforded it. He squinted, bringing the light back up to her face. Her eyes were wide open and staring at nothing, not reacting to the light in the least. They were a deep blue, like a summer sky, but slightly glazed. He moved the light and the eyes remained still. Was the woman dead? He leaned closer yet, and realized he couldn't see or hear her breathe. But if she *was* dead, she must have passed recently. Her body looked flawless, if her skin was slightly pale. What could this mean, he wondered? Some rich noble had died in the Colonies and was being sent home for burial?

Hamish never heard his death approaching, staring, bewitched, at the beautiful woman in front of him. At the last moment, the hairs on the back of his neck stood up and he started to turn, but it was far too late. A powerful hand seized him by the neck, the other grabbing his arm in a vise-like grip, crushing his wrist. His cry of pain died before it started as he was slammed to the floor, his wits dazed from the force of the blow. Somehow, his attacker had caught the lantern, and lowered it gently to the deck. The last thing Hamish saw were fine black leather boots and then a face rushing down toward him—pale skin, mouth open, eyes burning red, and impossibly long teeth getting closer and closer.

The vampire drove his fangs into the sailor's neck, drank for a moment, then forced himself to stop and held the man over the box. "Drink deep, my love," he said as he used his talon-like fingernails to open the man's throat wider. Blood poured down into the woman's open mouth, and she suddenly coughed, then opened her mouth wider to drink more freely, her body shuddering.

She reached up, feebly at first, and grabbed at the sailor, bringing him down to her mouth, sucking on his neck, her eyes slowly focusing. Finally sated, she tossed the man casually to the deck and stretched languidly, like a cat, pulling her clothing tight against her in several places the other vampire couldn't help but admire. "Are we in the Colonies?" she asked, licking a stray drop of blood from her lips.

The vampire frowned. "Not quite. We somehow seem to have run aground. Some damned fools tried to take the ship, and Jorsca died feeding me enough to wake me." He gestured to where the dead gypsy was slumped on the deck. "We are quite close, however."

She sat up, took his hand, then stumbled trying to exit their traveling coffin. "Why am I so weak after feeding that much?"

"We've been traveling over the sea. The running water is still affecting you. I'm older and have fed more."

She pouted. "Not sharing your meals with me?" she asked with a flirtatious tone in her voice.

"Listen, there are others moving throughout the ship. Enough to sate us both and fight the water-weakness."

Hours passed and Captain Wade paced the deck impatiently. "Damn them, what can be taking so long to search a simple ship?"

His first officer, Mellor, tried to think of some explanation he hadn't offered the last several times the captain had asked the question. "We could send another boat, sir," he ventured after a moment or two of tense silence.

The Captain whirled. "Do that! Take a boat, find out's what become of Ensign Alexander and his men, and tell him if he doesn't have a damned good explanation, I'll have the lash on him!"

"Me, sir?" Mellor took a half pace back at the captain's vehemence.

"Yes, *you.* Get in a boat, go to the ship, find the ensign, and report back to me. Are these orders understood?" The captain's voice raged, and everyone anywhere nearby hastily found something to attend to elsewhere.

Mellor swallowed and nodded, moving away slowly. He'd hoped for a more even-tempered captain after Captain Douglass had finally given up the sea, but Wade flew into rages at the slightest provocation, making the crew uneasy. Rounding up three sailors, Mellor climbed into the pinnace and was lowered to the water, the sailors sliding easily down the ropes to join him.

Shortly, the boat traveled across the water to the grounded ship. "*Sea Spectre,*" Mellor read as the lantern light fell on the transom, and he shivered. When the men rowed the boat into position, he grasped the line hanging down from the deck and climbed, wishing for a proper ladder the whole way up.

Once on deck, he was greeted by the surprising sight of Jones, one of his men who usually had to have any sort of respect beaten into his thick Welsh skull, standing by the hatch to the main hold, at attention, musket held tightly in his hands. Fed up with the night, and wishing to be back in his cabin with what remained of his bottle of port, Mellor snapped, "Well, report! What did you find? Why are you standing there like that?"

Jones' thick Welsh accent sounded curiously flat, none of the usual edge of insolence in it. "The Master told me to guard him while we wait."

"What *master?* While you wait for *what?* Talk sense, man!"

"The master. You're an officer. He'd like to speak with you, sir. Down below," Jones gestured to the hatch, his flat eyes never leaving Mellor.

"Oh...very well. I'll talk to the ship's master and get this affair over with." Mellor went below as he heard the rest of his party making the deck after securing their ship.

Below, Mellor stopped in disbelief. A man in a fine green shirt and leggings of a sort he didn't recognize lounged at a table, idly leafing through what appeared to be the ship's log. At his side, a striking woman was flipping a long blade into the air and catching it with no apparent effort, her blond hair flowing unbound over her shoulders. Around them, Williams, Harper, and Jackson stood rigidly.

"What is the meaning of this?" Mellor asked. "Why are you men just standing around?" He might as well have not spoken at all for all the reaction he got from his men. "Who are you?" he demanded, stepping closer to the seated man. Williams and Harper moved to stop him, but, before his rage could spill over into the words burning in his throat, the man waved his hand negligently and the sailors stepped back.

"I am Johann Berkholt," the seated man said. "My wife and I slept when our vessel struck ground here, and your men have kindly assisted us." The man's voice was calm, reassuring, and Mellor felt his anger draining away as he met the man's gaze. Such deep brown eyes the man had…somehow so compelling.

"Would you be so good as to tell me your name, sir?"

Mellor was abashed by his lack of manners. "Your pardon, sir. I am Walter Mellor, First Mate of His Majesty's Ship *Swift*." He raised his hat respectfully.

"I see, Mr. Mellor, thank you. Perhaps you would clarify a point for us?" Surely it was reasonable to answer the man's questions, then offer him aid? He was clearly a gentleman of some kind, for all that he was a foreigner.

"How may I be of service?" Mellor asked, not noticing that his voice was assuming the flat tones he had noted in Jones' on deck.

"I am not precisely clear on where we are, and your men, while helpful enough, are not well versed in fine navigation."

"Yes, sir. It's not a skill everyone can master. We are off the coast of North Carolina, near a small township called Holly Ridge."

Johann nodded. "We have reached the Colonies, then?"

"Yes, sir. Well, just shy of them. Your ship here is on a sandbar, not the shore itself."

Johann nodded. "Indeed. My thanks for your instruction. Greta, is there more we need of the officer?" The blond woman shook her head, catching the blade again, not deigning to look at the Navy man. "Very well. I know you're still weak from the trip, would you care to feed?"

Mellor wasn't clear witted enough to appreciate what happened next, which was a blessing. One moment, Greta sprawled in her chair, the next she was standing before him, pulling him in as if for a kiss. At the last moment, before their lips could meet, Greta bent his head to the side and Mellor felt a sting of pain in his neck, then a warmth of great pleasure spread through him. And then the world slowly went black.

A tiny corner of Jackson's brain remained his own, and he screamed silently as the woman drank Mellor's blood like a drunk offered a free round, gulping it down quickly. Johann turned to Jackson. "How long is this Davison going to be?"

Jackson was forced to answer, his slight resistance no good to him here. "I can't say, Master. He needs to scout the way and come back, it could be some time."

"And how long until dawn?"

"I would say some three hours, Master."

Eternity seemed to tick by for Jackson, captive in his own mind, until finally Davison returned. "Sir, the way is clear, and the tide not yet run low. You could leave now if you hurry yourselves."

Johann rose. "And the water is not on the path? We prefer to keep our feet dry, you understand." He laughed, but at what Jackson wasn't certain.

"Yes, you can cross from the shoal to the shore on but damp sand if you make good time now," Davison assured Johann.

"Very well. If more of your crew come calling, delay them for us, won't you?" The question was asked softly enough, but there was no possibility of resisting it. Johann held his hand out to Greta, who had dropped the luckless Mellor's body to the deck. "Shall we, my dear?"

There was a blur of motion that made Jackson even more certain that this was a ship of the damned, crewed by devils, and they were gone. Jackson tried to regain control of his body, but felt helpless, moving with the others as they climbed back to the main deck, staring across at their own ship, guns at the ready.

Cullen winced as Sarah bound his arm. The cut was long, but not too deep. One of the sailors had proved to be much better with a knife than it looked at first glance, and Cullen had almost paid dearly for his poor estimation. He'd fled when Young Robbie had shouted his warning, and come away with little more than the coins he'd gotten from the dead sailor.

Michael was excited, his own wound already bandaged. “You should have seen it. A great box of iron. It must have a treasure in it!”

Cullen was tired, and in pain. Sarah smiled as she finished tying the dressing on, and then gathered her supplies and left to give the men privacy. “We can check after the damned Navy leaves. Why are they still out there?” Young Robbie was once again acting as lookout, and so far, he'd not come back to give the all clear.

“Who knows why the Navy does anything?” Michael shot back. “We need to get back there before someone else gets to it!”

Cullen was trying to find the right words to calm his excited friend when a whimper came from the door. Both men spun to see Sarah being held off the dirt floor by a blond woman with a hand clamped around her throat. Beside her, an impressive figure breathed in deeply, nostrils flaring, eyes closed. He opened them, staring at Michael. “We have a debt between us.” His voice was accented, powerful, and cold. Cullen found his skin crawling at the mere sound of it. Michael looked scared, something Cullen had never seen before. The two strangers stood framed in the doorway, looking into Cullen's small hut.

“What would that be?” Michael rasped, his attempt at bravado undermined by the quaver in his voice.

“You killed my servant. I require recompense.” Sarah's legs kicked feebly as the other woman held her casually, showing no strain, watching the confrontation with a cruel smile on her face.

“I didn't kill anyone,” Michael protested.

“I have your scent. You left blood at the scene of your transgression.” The voice was even but brooked no argument, steel beneath the soft tone.

“What do you want?” Cullen asked, stepping forward, trying to prevent things from getting worse. He glanced worriedly at Sarah, who was turning red in the face, her struggles slowing.

“Vengeance. A blood debt must be paid.”

“I understand that. But surely Sarah never killed your man.” He tried to keep his voice subservient, giving himself time to figure out what to do next.

“Greta,” Johann said, and the woman released Sarah, who fell to her knees, coughing, wheezing, hands going to her bruised throat. “And what do you propose, landsman?"

Cullen licked his lips, trying to fight back the unfamiliar fear that threatened to choke him as thoroughly as Sarah nearly had been. "You're just arrived, you'll need a place to stay. If he killed your servant, you'll need a new one, won't you?"

Johann considered the words. "You seek to bargain with me?" he smiled, something feral and terrible in it.

"We can come to some arrangement, can't we?" Cullen almost pleaded. Sarah slumped on the floor, and Michael looked back and forth between Cullen and Johann with fear and hope warring on his face.

"If we are to negotiate, will you show me the courtesy of asking me in?"

Cullen swallowed, looking around, wondering what he could possibly offer the man. "Please, come in, let's talk like men of business."

At his words, some of the tension left Johann and Greta, and they stepped inside. Johann cocked his head to one side, as if thinking carefully. "Here is what I propose," he began. Suddenly he was standing in front of Cullen, arm swinging in a fluid blur of speed, sending Michael flying into the wall. "I take my price in blood, you become my new servant, this place becomes our home while we learn what we need to of this New World, and you live to serve me." The voice was cold, implacable.

Cullen looked at Sarah, then at Michael, and swallowed. Whatever his visitors were, they were simply too powerful for him. "I agree."

"Tell me, does your town have a priest?" Johann asked.

"No, sir, we're too small a place to have our own church or clergy."

Johann laughed a deep sound that sent spasms of ice down Cullen's spine. "Excellent."

Holly Ridge had always been a small, unremarkable town. If the people of the town after that night grew quieter, more withdrawn, no one in the surrounding countryside really made note of it. If they were all somewhat paler, well, it was a harsh winter, food was short. And if they hurriedly broke off conversations when a rare outsider passed through, such as the Naval officials investigating the disappearance of the good ship *Swift,* well, every town has its secrets, doesn't it?

The Man with X-Ray Eyes

Richard Chizmar

My father died when I was just a boy.

There was an accident at the mill where he worked. One man lost a leg. Another lost the vision in his right eye and most of his scalp. My father got the worst of it, though—he was crushed to death.

We buried him two days later on a sunny June morning. After the service, most of our friends and relatives came back to the house. A somber parade. They stood in the kitchen and sat around the living-room and the den, whispering, crying, nibbling on little sandwiches and drinking from paper cups.

I stayed outside mostly, sitting in the shade of the front porch.

Most folks didn't know what to say to an eleven-year-old who had just lost his father, so they pretty much left me alone.

After a time, my grandfather came out and sat down next to me on the step. He put his arm around me and we sat there in silence, listening to the grass grow and the birds sing. After a while, I asked him if he felt like crying. He slowly nodded his head and told me what it felt like to bury his only son—how his heart ached with sorrow and swelled with pride all at the same time. He told me that my father dying the way he did was a cruel reminder that life has a way of playing tricks on all of us, that sometimes things aren't the way they seem. And then he told me how much he loved me, how proud he was of me, how much I reminded him of my father.

That was just like Grandpa. He always knew the right thing to say, the right thing to do. And he was right—life does have a way of playing tricks on all of us.

That was a long time ago; seems like forever. I'm much older now, just turned forty-two last month. My grandfather is gone, of course, and so is my mother. I stayed with her in the old house until she passed away from ovarian cancer in the autumn of '76, and then I sold out to a young couple from somewhere east of Boston. I left town at the age of twenty one and spent the next five years at the university.

After graduation, I moved back to Coldwater. Just across town, on the other side of the tracks, right next to where the old Lexington Bed and Breakfast used to be. A nice, little house with a decent yard and a white painted fence.

I've been there ever since.

I don't date very often. There's just not many opportunities in a small town like Coldwater. At least not for a guy like me. Last time I had a date—six months ago, at least—was with a woman I met at the library one evening. Anne something-or-other. A tall redhead from over in Windhurst. We went to a movie and then out for pizza. She spent most of the night staring at her wristwatch and playing with her hair. We never had a second date.

I'm not lonely, though. I guess I've gotten used to this kind of life. Besides, I always have my kids. I see them at school five days a week and around town most every day. They call my name and wave and sometimes stop to talk. So, it's a rare day that I feel alone or without company.

I teach history over at Coldwater High School. Six classes a day, three with the seniors and three with the sophomores. Been there almost fifteen years now.

My teaching philosophy is simple: work hard and have fun. I try to make all my classes interesting for the kids, plenty of films and graphics and student participation. I think they learn more that way—and that's what's important.

Every year the kids tell me I'm one of their favorites. And every year it means the world to me. My co-workers don't talk to me much, but that's okay. Sometimes I think they're just jealous.

I've never seen a UFO.

I've met a few people who claim they have.

Roy Weldeman, a gym teacher from the high school, swears he saw one fly directly overhead one night when he was crappie fishing out on the lake. He told me (and this is a direct quote): "Hell, I almost shit my pants right there in the boat. That's how scared I was."

A lady down the street from where I live—an old friend of my mother—told me she was actually abducted by a UFO when she was a teenager. Said it flew down and landed in the field behind her house early one morning and when she walked out there to investigate, she was zapped unconscious and abducted. Said she woke up in bed, naked, all covered in grass and dirt, her feet cut and bleeding. When she checked the alarm clock on her nightstand, four-and-a-half hours had passed.

Weird stuff, huh?

Sure, like most folks, I've seen them on television and in pictures, but I've never seen a UFO up close and personal.

I wish I would.

I'm not sure how the aliens got here, or when they first arrived.

I saw my first alien the summer I turned sixteen.

Her name was Jenny Glover, and she was new in Coldwater. The weekend after the Fourth of July, her family moved right across the street, into the old Sumner place. She was fifteen, and just like me, an only child.

God, she was beautiful. Long, shiny hair the color of summer wheat. Eyes like an angel. And she liked me. She actually liked me. She always used to say that I made her laugh.

Those first couple weeks, we spent all our free time together. Showing her around town. Going to the movies. Playing card games in my basement. I can still remember how my heart felt every time she came close to me or brushed against my skin—like it was going to jump right out of my chest. Jesus, she drove me crazy.

But then, one day, everything changed.

We were walking on the dirt path that runs alongside Hanson Creek, taking a short-cut back from the grocery store. About halfway home, we took a break and sat down on an old, fallen log. For a long time, we just sat there, shuffling our feet in the dirt, not looking at each other, talking about nothing. Then she took my hand in her hand, and I knew we were going to kiss. If I didn't faint first.

I looked up into those ice blue eyes, *really* looked for the first time—

—and I saw something that wasn't human.

Somehow I *saw.*

And then in a flash of sudden understanding, a flash of absolute knowing, I *knew* what she was, what she intended to do.

And I knew right then and there that I had no other choice.

So I killed her.

The second one was many years later.

I was in college at the time. It was summer break, and I was at Fenway Park, watching the Red Sox and the Mariners. An extra inning game in the middle of a gorgeous August afternoon.

Between the tenth and eleventh innings, I moved down a couple dozen rows to a better seat along the third base line. I excused myself and sat down next to a plump, bald man with a smear of mustard on his chin. The man looked up and smiled at me.

I nodded, but didn't return the smile.

He was one of them.

After the game, I followed him home to the suburbs and killed him in his garage.

I've only been wrong once.

And once is enough, believe me.

Happened about a year ago. I was vacationing by myself in Florida. I'd never been to Disney and had always wanted to go.

There was a little girl at the park with her family. Cute as a button, and about that small. Maybe six or seven. She was waiting in line ahead of me with her older sister and brother. She kept looking at me and smiling… looking right into my eyes.

And I knew.

Later on, back at the cabin, I discovered my mistake. And it almost killed me. Honestly it did. I couldn't believe it.

Somehow, I had been wrong.

She wasn't one of them after all.

I had killed a human being.

The doctors and the detectives like me. Despite what they suspect, despite where they fear all this is leading, they can't help it. I can tell. I can see it in their eyes.

They asked me to write down everything in my own words.

They recorded all of our conversations, but they want something down on paper. Something official, I guess.

First, they want a little history about me. About my life—past, present, future. That's easy enough.

And, then, about the aliens. They want to know every last detail, starting with the first one I killed out by Hanson Creek when I was sixteen years old, and ending with the old lady from just last week.

They want to know how many others I've been able to find over the years. Where? When? How?

They want to know where I've traveled to during my summers off from teaching. Visits with relatives? Vacations? They want to know all of it.

And they want to know about the eyes. The *eyes* are very important, they tell me. How do I know the things I know? How do I see the things I see?

They're all very nice to deal with. Very pleasant. And they're patient, too. They never rush me with anything.

Of course, I'll give them all the answers they need. They're on my side now. Or at least, they will be very soon.

Earlier this morning, when I finished telling my story, I gave them directions to my grandfather's cabin in the woods. They left a few hours ago by helicopter, so they should be there by now.

Any time now, I expect a phone to ring somewhere down the hall. Then they'll come for me again. With more questions, I'm sure.

After that, I expect a lot of phones will be ringing. All over the country, probably.

Or maybe not...some things are better kept secret.

I took precautions, of course.

Aliens walking our streets is not a very believable story—*Jesus, don't you think I know that?*—so I took some safety measures, just in case.

I cut off their heads.

Each and every one of them. Cut off their heads and saved them. Took them up to my grandfather's cabin. Took Polaroids. Then stripped the flesh away with chemicals. Then I took more photos. Carefully labeled each one of them. Date of death, gender, age and identity (whenever possible).

Inside my grandfather's cabin, I have all the proof anyone will ever need.

Skulls. Hideous looking things.

Skulls of various shapes and sizes—none remotely human, none constructed of anything resembling human bone.

Skulls that will forever change our history.

Over forty of them in all.

They're back from the cabin.

About twenty minutes ago.

They haven't been in to speak with me yet, but I can see them talking outside in the hallway. The two detectives and the doctor with the long hair.

They're scared. Real scared.

I can see it in their eyes.

Red Fuel

Jonathan Templar

They had driven too far.

It was supposed to be a quick run out past the fields—a swift escape with an equally swift return—but the early evening was a rare beauty. Like a lover who can't bear to say goodbye, the sun was reluctant to pass over the horizon. It burnt the sky a blistering orange, which made the fields glow as if they were aflame. Driving into the sunset felt a little like driving into heaven—and a little like driving into hell. Either way, the three of them kept on going, although the horizon drew no closer.

It was Eric's car. He had inherited it from his father, who had passed it down to him in the nature of a lesson. It was an Oldsmobile Sedan, far older in years than its current owner, and it had known many, many better days. Eric's father, who was a wise man in lots of ways, perhaps far wiser than his own son would ever grow to be, explained that taking possession of an old and weary automobile would force Eric to better appreciate the mechanics of her function, to learn her curious quirks and how to appreciate the complexity of her assembly; how to fix her when she broke, as she often did, and how to care for her and discover her secrets. *Treat her like a lady,* his father would've said. *Learn how to make her purr.* That way, when he could afford to trade up to a younger, more demanding model, Eric would have a better appreciation of how to keep her happy, as well.

Eric thought his father was a tight-ass son-of-a-bitch. The Oldsmobile was held together by rust and hope, and the only thing Eric would learn from being her owner, were the dozen new curses he spewed each time she broke down, which happened just about every other day. But Eric was young, and at least he had a car of his own. On a day like today, when driving felt like the only cure for the horrors of a summer lost to a dead-end job that would fail to pay his way through even a semester of college, let alone a year, that was enough.

The job was character building, his father liked to tell him. What character he thought his son was going to build preparing sandwiches for eight hours a day, surrounded by a bunch of dead-beats who couldn't even speak English, he was less than forthcoming about.

Josh had it far better. He had an internship at his father's law firm—the law firm that would no doubt offer him gainful employment once law school had spat him back out, regardless of the quality of his degree. Josh got to wear a suit and sit behind a desk and didn't stink of jalapenos at the end of his working day.

But Selina had it better still. Her parents expected nothing more of her than that she not hang around the *palace* they called a home all summer long, that she got out from under their feet as often as she could, which she did.

Josh and Eric didn't quite move in the same circles anymore. They barely shared the same orbit. But they had been friends once. Good enough friends that the echo of their friendship still remained, even after they'd drifted apart.

Selena was one of the new spheres Eric's old buddy orbited now, but she remained one that offered Eric nothing but a poisoned atmosphere, no matter how appealing her surface might appear. Josh had moved on to better things; better people who didn't spend the summer slicing baloney while wearing a paper hat. Josh had become a mostly silent number stored on Eric's cell phone—a memory of simpler times. They saw each other every now and then, but each occasion might have turned out to be the last and neither of them would have noticed.

But Josh and Selena—for all their billing as the best and brightest, despite all the promise of the future that seemed to owe them everything—neither of them owned a car.

For that, they still needed Eric.

They had just meant to go for a spin, but the day had invited them to go further—to go out of town, into the farming country, and perhaps even further than that. They'd left behind the working farms, the vast fields where the corn still rose well above head height, where the crop was still harvested not by the old families who had built up the community the three of them had come from, but the corporations who now owned most of this land, and had encouraged the community to expand and diversify. Nobody around here was what you could call a farmer anymore. They were proud to have grown beyond the old ways.

But the cultivated fields passed them by, and soon they were driving through what had become very much a wilderness. The fields were no longer tended this far outside of town. Some of them had grown wild, some simply lost to hard, barren ground.

The road was long and straight and undemanding. Not a single vehicle had passed by for half an hour or more. The three of them no longer sipped furtively from their previously concealed beers. They could afford to relax; to let the scenery pass them by in a blur and just enjoy the sense of freedom that came with an open road to nowhere in particular.

And then the engine started to cough.

"Shit!" Eric hissed, tapping the fuel dial. The dashboard was a series of lies, each gauge telling a story that had little relationship to reality. The tank was showing as a quarter full, and Eric had chosen to trust it today. But then he knew they certainly hadn't been cruising at a steady twenty-five as the speedometer had been insisting, and the milometer had been boasting no more than thirty-thousand miles for twenty-five years now. One tap and the arrow in the fuel gauge fell to its rightful place—deep into the red.

The Oldsmobile started to rumble with hunger.

"We're out of gas," Eric said to the two in the back.

"How the *fuck* are we out of gas," Josh asked. "I thought you had a full tank."

"We did have a full tank," Josh bemoaned. "But then we started driving."

There was a round of recriminations, but it got them nowhere.

"Turn around, dude. We need to find to a gas station."

"You seen one recently? We gotta keep going, and hope we find one before the fumes dry up."

But the old bitch was listening to Eric, and decided fumes weren't going to be enough. With a painful rattle, the Oldsmobile gave up and stopped in the middle of the road.

"What the *fuck* are we gonna do, Eric?" a shrill voiced Selena asked. "We're fucking miles from anywhere!"

Eric opened his mouth to snap back at her, but before he found the words his unconscious mind poked at him. *You saw something!* It said. *Can you remember what you saw?* Eric shut his mouth again and pondered. There *had* been something hadn't there? Something that, at the point they passed it by, had been useless to him—had been filed away by a brain busy with other pursuits—but now he needed it. Eric backtracked, retraced his mental steps, and there it was—about a quarter of an hour ago. Something they'd passed by in the long line of abandoned fields they'd sped by. A skeleton of the old days of agriculture left to decay. *But for how long?*

"I saw a *thing,* a tractor maybe, in a field a few miles back. We could see if it's got some fuel left in the tank, siphon it off," Eric suggested.

"What, you think we're gonna walk? I've got heels on, Eric!"

"I'm not going on my own!" Eric said.

Selena looked toward Josh, to see which way he'd go. He shrugged, a haze in his eyes that suggested he'd already downed one beer too many. "Doesn't seem fair for Eric to go on his own, 'Lena. We should all go together."

Selena glared, pulling off her heels, which weren't that high, really. As she bent over, Eric got a view straight down her top—a glimpse at what kind of flesh the prospect of a law degree and a promising future at an up and coming firm your father happened to be a senior partner in could bag you. He tried to turn away, he really did. He hated himself a little for looking, but he looked all the same.

"I get blisters, you two can fucking *carry* me back!" Selena said, standing upright.

Eric rummaged in the trunk and pulled out a rubber hose and the tin full of engine oil his father had provided along with the car. "Got to make sure you keep her oiled up, Eric," his father had said. But Eric had never bothered. The tin was sticky with residue, and he took it to the side of the road and emptied it onto the dusty ground, ground that swallowed the thick liquid hungrily. Eric hoped it would hold enough gas to get them home. He tried not to think how unlikely it was that the tank of the abandoned machine would still have *any* gas left for them to pilfer.

He asked the other two to help push the car off the road. Josh helped.

Selena crossed her arms and watched. And then they headed back along the long road to find the briefly glimpsed hope of salvation.

They walked for longer than they could judge; the surrounding landscape refused to change, so distance was meaningless once the car was no longer within sight. The dusk settled, but night seemed reluctant to follow. Their shadows grew longer on the road, but the light didn't fade. By the time they spotted the frame of the machine peering above corn that rose high above their heads, Eric had started to think he imagined it.

"There she is!" he said, craning his neck. He had a few inches on Josh, more on Selena, and they rose on tip toes to look over the wall of corn. The top of the machine stood out, the last of the sun making shadows of its frame.

"This is it?" Josh asked. "This is what we've walked miles for? Shit, Eric, that thing's a pile of fucking rust! There's no way there's anything left in its tank."

"I didn't hear anyone else offering up ideas," Eric said. "Let's check it out…there might be something left."

Selena was behind them. She looked miserable and ready to drop. "We got the gas yet?" she asked.

Josh threw a thumb at the rusting behemoth in the fields. "Got about as much chance of getting milk from the thing as we do gas. For fuck's sake, Eric!"

Eric pushed his way through the wall of untended corn. It was brittle and sharp. He had to shield his face as he made his way through. Within a few feet, he was lost. The now fading light and the high stalks robbed him of any sense of direction. He just pressed ahead, almost glad to have some distance from the others, determined to find a way out of this predicament, thinking that perhaps if he willed it strongly enough, he'd find gas in abundance out here in this elephant's graveyard.

He stumbled into a clearing he hadn't expected to find—a circle, or close enough to one, the ground flattened, the corn stamped into the dry soil to make a jagged carpet. It couldn't have been a natural occurrence, this crop circle. The machine was at the centre of it, the corn had been flattened outward from its bulk, as if the stalks had fallen backward in its wake. Now that Eric could see the machine in all its glory, he knew what it was. A combine harvester—the roof of its cabin, once painted green but now peeling and sad with lost glory—was what he'd seen poking above the corn, as they'd driven by. Up close it was wider than it was tall. The front of it, equipped with a rotary head, the sharp twisting blades that had been used to harvest these fields in days gone by, was now tainted by rust and dulled by the elements. The corn that circled them blocked any wind from entering the clearing. It was still and silent and heavy as Eric stood there looking at the combine blankly. He felt as if he had trespassed into an empty church built to some unfathomable and long forgotten deity.

Josh broke the silence, stumbling into the clearing. "Fuck me! Look at that monster!" he said.

"Impressive, huh?"

"Yeah, if you're some fucking redneck with a hardon for farm machinery. Thing's like a fucking rusted out dinosaur. Hey, maybe we should just drive *it* home instead. I'd love to see my old man's face if he woke up and found this parked in the driveway."

Selena was behind him, less impressed by the giant before them, her feet itching and aching from having to step across the sharp stalks littering the ground. "Is there any gas in the thing, or not?' she asked, wanting this all to be over with.

"Let's see," Eric said, stepping carefully toward the harvester. There was something foreboding about it; something that made senses he didn't usually acknowledge, cry out warnings he didn't understand. But as he got closer, the evidence of his own eyes gave him reason to recoil.

Around the far side of the harvester, where its shadow would fall during the height of day, there were dead things. They littered the scorched soil as if they had been tipped here by a dump truck—two or three deep in places, a festering mound of spoiled flesh and bone, the tattered remnants of fur removed from the skins and thrown aside. Most of them were small things, cats perhaps, small dogs at a push, it was difficult to tell. One skinned beast stripped of its flesh looked much the same as another. Jawbones screamed up from the dirt, but they were indecipherable, jaws that could have screamed the agony of their death in the language of any number of beasts. But their death had surely been agonizing. In fact, the air still stank with their suffering.

"That's some sick shit..." Josh said, peering tentatively over Eric's shoulder.

"What do you think it is?" Eric asked.

"Fuck knows. Some hobo's larder by the look of it. They like their meat to come with whiskers out this way."

"What is it?" Selena called, still at the edge of the clearing.

Josh and Eric shared a look. "Dead cat," Josh called, raising eyebrows to his old buddy. *No need to freak her out,* his expression said. Eric agreed, reluctantly looking back at the rotting body farm.

"Let's look in the tank, get out of here as fast as we can."

"On that my friend, we're in total agreement."

The tank was to one side of the cabin. Like the roof of the machine, it was dented and the paintwork was peeling away in rusty strips. Eric banged it with a knuckle. It clanged a response that encouraged him. "Doesn't sound empty..." he said, knowing he only had a limited understanding of what the fuck he was doing.

He unscrewed the cap. He didn't even need to look inside the tank to know it was full. There was gas right up to the very lip.

"I'll never doubt you again, bro," Josh said, patting Eric on the back.

"Here, hold this for me." Eric passed the oil can over to him. He pulled out the hose he had tucked into his jacket pocket and dipped it into the tank. Then, carefully as he could, he sucked enough liquid into it to start it pumping. "A can of this should easily get us back to civilization."

Josh nodded eagerly. The gas filled the can, slowly but surely. The boys were silent, willing the task to be over. This clearing smelt of things they didn't understand, and they wanted to be away from it before comprehension began to dawn. Selena seemed oblivious; she was busy picking corn from flattened cobs and smearing them to pulp between perfectly manicured fingers. "This is, like, the fattest corn I have ever seen," she said, but the boys weren't listening to her.

Long minutes passed, and then the can was full. Too full. It began to overflow; the fuel ran over the top and started to coat Josh's hands. At the sight of it pouring over him, Josh let out a cry that was very nearly a scream and dropped the can, recoiling in disgust.

"What the fuck is *this?*" he wailed.

Eric dropped to his knees, picked the can up before too much of the stolen contents were spilled. "Jeez, Josh, calm down."

"It's blood!" Josh held his hands up, palms inward, and waved them at Eric. The liquid running down his hands was a thick syrupy consistency, and even in the ever fading light, the scarlet colour was unmistakable. Josh looked as if he'd pushed his hands wrist deep into a bucket of gore. Its *blood!*" he wailed again.

Eric snorted laughter. Josh took a step back, having expected a different response.

"What the fuck are you laughing at?"

"It's not blood, you retard. It's red fuel."

"Red fuel?"

"Sure. They put dye in it, so you can't steal it. Farmers and shit, they pay less for gas but you can only use it off road. My dad told me about it one time."

Josh looked at his hands again, feelings of repulsion replaced by equally unwelcome pangs of humiliation. "Red fuel. What do you know?"

"You can get a fine for using this stuff. Once it gets into your tank, it leaves a permanent trace. It's a big risk using this, Josh."

"You know what? You get us out of here and back home before nightfall, I'll buy you a new fucking car myself."

"That's assuming this stuff doesn't just poison her for good."

Josh put his hand on Eric's arm. "No way, dude. Luck is on our side tonight."

Then Selena screamed.

The boys darted back to the other side of the harvester. She was where they had left her, but she was no longer idly picking at the crops. She pointed off to the side of the clearing, where the reel at the front of the harvester was aimed. Someone else had joined them, had pushed through the thicker stalks that lay deeper in the field.

"What the fuck is that?" Selena called to the boys, and they could see where her confusion might lay. What had come through the corn was a man, technically, although a lot of him was missing. He had a barrel chest upon which stood a grizzled head, a yellowy white beard that seemed to have grown over too much of his face, as if it were a spread of mould rather than hair, but was thinning in a number of patches, through which flaking, scabrous skin could be seen. He wore a cap on his head, the visor hiding his eyes, which might have been a mercy. It certainly could have done with obscuring his mouth, which was toothless beyond a few rotting stumps, and dribbled thick and foamy spittle across the beard as he moved toward them.

None of this mattered though, because their attention was stolen by the rest of him. Or rather, what was missing from the rest of him.

He had no legs.

He burst into the clearing on stumps formed from random sections of wood, clumsily tied together with rope and wire. One *leg* consisted of a table leg attached to the butt of a rifle, which stood in for a club foot that he hobbled forward on. The other looked as if it was several wooden banister rails and perhaps a broom stick, wrapped in green wire with the head of a long tin leaf rake stuck to the end, which flapped erratically with each lumbering step. In addition, one arm was missing, and dangling from the shoulder, tied by a harness that was either too big or too weathered to do what was asked of it, the lifeless replica from a mannequin hung uselessly, the hand missing from the wrist, the flesh coloured paint faded and cracked. He looked as if he had been broken and had then been forced to repair himself with whatever he happened to find tucked away in his garage.

"What have you done?" the half-man asked in a voice like an autumn leaf. "What have you done to her, you little bastards?" The word sounded more like *buzzards* coming from that toothless mouth, words ran into each other inside his slobbering drawl, but the meaning was clear all the same

"Shit!" Josh grabbed the can of red gas from Eric's hands and without a moment's hesitation sprinted back into the high crops and away from the clearing. Eric didn't react; he was still trying to process the walking yard sale spitting brown flecked drool down its chin. But Selena's eyes widened as her boyfriend fled. "Josh?" she called after him. Then she looked over at Eric. "Eric?" she asked, his name a question to which he didn't have an answer.

"Who...who are you? What do you want?' Eric asked the old man.

The old man turned his head and squinted, as if Eric was just a dot on his horizon. "What did you do to her? I'd only just filled her up."

There was a coughing, rumbling sound from behind Eric, and he felt a tremor in his toes, the ground beneath them starting to shake at the promise of what was to come. The rumbling grew, changed pitch, and then it became a roar.

"Get out of her way, into the corn 'fore she sees you!" the old man screamed at him, and Eric didn't want to turn around, didn't want to see what was slowly coming to life over his shoulder. He did as the old man said, ran across the flattened corn and whether he had intended to or not, he grabbed the petrified Selena as he passed, pulling her by her porcelain arm, an arm he could have wrapped his hand around and seen the fingers join together she was so slender. He threw her down, onto the narrow corridor between two rows of twisting corn, and she did not offer so much as a peep of protest. Eric dropped to his knees, looked through the barrier the high stalks created, but he could see nothing. The sound had become deafening though, as if it were an engine enclosed in a steel box, echoing back and intensifying with every grating revolution. The air was thick with the stench of burning fuel, like a suicide's garage. Eric wanted to cough that taste out of his mouth, but he knew he daren't make a sound.

The old man staggered up behind them, moving like a broken toy. "She was full," he said again mournfully. "It's only vermin blood in her tank, but she was sated all the same."

"What the fuck are you talking about, what's full?"

The old man looked at him, and Eric could tell from his eyes, the way they couldn't stay still even for an instant, that this man had left his sanity a long way behind and a long time ago. "It was a trying time, we was all losing our land, our homes. I prayed every day, prayed to God to send us help, to show us the way out of our misery. But he never answered me. So I started to pray to... other folk as well. And one of them answered me. She made these old fields shoot up like I never seen before, more than I could ever hope to gather. But she asked a terrible price, one I had no choice but to pay."

The shadow of the harvester fell over them as it made its way through the abundant corn, looking to harvest more than the soil of this land could ever provide for it. They couldn't see it from their vantage point, but they could each feel its terrible hunger.

"I tried to keep her fed…tried to keep her from wandering. Gave her as much of me as I could afford to give, and then I hunted the fields for vermin when there wasn't enough left of me. She was sated. I thought she might have had enough that she'd sleep awhile. Why'd you have to come and wake her?"

Eric could barely hear him over the thundering engine that powered the harvester, the savage sound of its whirling rotor blade as it tore itself a path through the fields. But he heard enough, and somehow he understood more.

"Where's it going?" Selena whispered.

"It's going to feed."

Josh ran through the corn, though he had no idea which way he was heading. When he found himself on the freeway, the sudden joy of hard concrete beneath his feet was almost enough to make him fall to his knees and weep. But he didn't. He kept on running, the can of precious gas held tight to his chest.

It was one of the precepts his father had drilled into Josh. No matter what the situation, no matter what the provocation, no matter whose honour might be at stake, you always, always, run from a fight. "Only an idiot stands and fights," he had told Josh. "You want redress? You want to get your revenge over some meathead who can only think with his fists? You do it later, and you do it legally and you do it comprehensively. You screw the fucker, son. You don't end up facing an assault charge that steals your future out from underneath you. The first sign of trouble, you run like the wind."

Now, Josh and his old man didn't see eye to eye on many things, but on this one issue they were in complete accord. There was nothing and nobody he wouldn't leave behind in a heartbeat. It was Eric's car, his fucking carelessness that had stranded them out here. Let him deal with it. And he could deal with Selena too. Shit, he hadn't taken his eyes off her tits since they'd set out. Maybe this was his chance to earn some access to them. He hoped Eric had better luck than he'd had so far. No, as far as Josh was concerned this was all someone else's problem to solve. He had the gas, he'd be more than happy to fill the tank of Eric's car with it, he wouldn't hesitate to start her up and get the fuck back home without a glance over his shoulder at who he'd left behind. If he was pulled over, if the contents of that tank were examined and their tell-tale colour exposed, he didn't know anything about it. It wasn't his car, after all.

But he didn't have the keys. That hadn't occurred to him until now. Could he hotwire the Oldsmobile? He didn't think so. He'd seen it done enough times on TV, but then he could say that about a lot of things. Perhaps Eric had left the keys in the ignition. It was possible. It wasn't as if the bitch was going to go anywhere with an empty tank, and who in their right mind would steal her anyway? It was worth holding out some hope. Otherwise, he'd just have to keep on walking until he got some reception on the cell phone, make that shameful call to the old man to request a lift back to town. That, or maybe someone would pass by and he could flag them down. Just a stroke of luck was all he needed. He was used to being lucky. It came with the territory.

So Josh wasn't that surprised that after walking little more than a brisk half mile along the road, he heard the distant sound of an engine approaching. It was coming the wrong way, though. Ideally he wanted to head back into town, rather than further away. But right now, with throbbing feet and a dry mouth aching for another beer, he couldn't really have cared either way.

He looked back down the road. It ran straight into the distance, the evening light fading but still enough to see there was nothing there, no lights signalling an approaching vehicle. Sound must carry a long way out here, he figured. He kept on walking, not prepared to stop just yet, not until he could see his saviour clearly. But the sound of its engine grew louder, and still Josh couldn't see anything but miles of asphalt up ahead. Surely sound didn't carry that far? Maybe there was another road, parallel to this one, on the other side of the fields. He craned his neck, but the corn grew too high for him to see over. He could hear it more clearly now though, and realized that it wasn't an automobile he'd been waiting for, that the gas guzzling chorus was industrial in origin, that there was something working the fields that they must have missed on their journey out here. This was as just as welcome. Any sign of civilization was better than nothing.

Josh stopped, pondered if he should make his way back off road; see if there was some hick farmer back there with a landline he could use. He didn't have to ponder for long. The harvester came out of the field as if hell itself had spat it out. It reared up over Josh, and his vision was filled by the spinning blades on the front of the rotor, blades that looked rusty but quickly told him what he was looking at wasn't rust—just like what sat in the tank slowly nourishing the beast was not fuel.

It hadn't needed to hunt, not for a time, its needs had been taken care of and it had been allowed to sleep. But it hadn't forgotten the art. Josh's last seconds were spent wondering just how this day had gone so horribly wrong.

Then, with a whirring sound of churning blades, his luck ran out for good.

The Hawthorn

Marie Robinson

Some of the townsfolk gathered at the low, ivy-strewn cemetery wall while Michael, the gravedigger, readied a proper hole for the nameless man. Old Mrs. O'Conor was quaking in the chill dusk air, her gnarled hands simultaneously clutching her shawl tighter around her throat and stuffing a handkerchief beneath her nose. In a voice that crackled like the autumn leaves beneath her boots, she declared this was the first suicide in Windhollow.

"Could have been the first visitor, too," Herne, the stableman, added. "Besides, it doesn't count, he wasn't a local man."

Poor Ryan Flynn, the shepherd's boy, found the stranger swinging from a hawthorn tree as he was returning to the house with the sheep's milk. His father reproached him at first for dropping the bucket, but softened considering the circumstances.

Several of the older men cut the corpse down and carried it over to the churchyard, where Father Tarmon—a withered old man whose once commanding voice now rose scarcely above a whisper—took pity on the stranger's soul and blessed him and promised him a grave.

Orrin saw the hanged man for a moment as a fierce gust tore the shroud back from his face. His eyes were open, skyward; his face was streaked from the tears that had run down his dirty cheeks. Around his neck he wore a gruesome ring of bruises, like an amulet of sorrow.

"He's only a boy!" Old Mrs. O'Conor wailed before she began to weep into her kerchief. Orrin sadly observed that the dead man's features were frozen in youth.

Michael whirled about to find that which had disturbed her. With a fleeting look of sadness, he tugged the shroud back over the stranger's stricken face and continued with his work.

"Why d'ya s'ppose he did it?" Poor Ryan Flynn slurred, as though his lips had suddenly grown too big for his face. His cheeks were dotted with roses and his long eyelashes drooped on heavy lids. Everyone at the tavern felt sorry for the boy's gruesome finding that morning and each man there had bought him a pint. After his fifth drink most of the beer had ended up down his shirt instead of his throat.

"I'll bet it was on account of a broken heart," Sweet Scarlet, the barmaid, sighed as she rubbed a pint-glass with a rag. "Sufferin' from the loss of his love."

"More like driven mad by one!" Poor Ryan's old man grumbled; his weatherworn face was lined like papyrus under his cap. He had developed bitterness in regard to women after his wife, Fiona, left him when his son was hardly old enough to speak. Only the wild and brave dared to leave Windhollow, and Fiona Flynn had been just that—or so the stories said. Orrin, too, was quite young when she had gone, but he remembered her; she was beautiful, with dark, lush hair, and shining black eyes a man could fall into like a well. Though the memory played back with the ethereality of a dream, Orrin recalled the day he saw her swimming in the lonely pool out on the moor. He had been crouching in the heather, trying to hide but she must have sensed him watching her, for she turned, her eyes finding his between the flowered stalks. She smiled, her strange eyes twinkling, and tossed back her head and laughed, the sound as soft and charming as bells. It was the only time he had ever seen a naked woman.

After the night she ran away, tearing out of the house like a mad crow in bare feet, everyone had his or her theories as to why she'd fled. Some said it was because her husband had a heavy hand, others insisted she was running off to meet a secret lover. The women in the town were always whispering about Fiona, even before she vanished. They talked rumors of her having a bastard son in another town, and some accounted her aberrant and unruly behavior on having Sidhe blood in her veins. The men had much to say about her, as well, but listening to their talk embarrassed Orrin and stirred up images from that day by the pond.

Before anyone could offer any additional theories on the subject of the hanging man, Poor Ryan spilt forth all five-and-a-half pints just as he had spilt the sheep's milk that morning at the hawthorn. His father grabbed him roughly by the shoulder and yanked him out of the tavern, letting a breath of crisp autumn air slip in as he opened the door.

Everyone cleared out of the way as Sweet Scarlet approached Poor Ryan's mess on swishing skirts with a bucket, rag, and a grimace. Orrin left a few extra notes for her on the bar and slid off the stool as she bent down on her knees to soak up the sick. He blushed as the remaining men fixed their eyes on her round bottom hoisted up in the air.

When he left the tavern, Orrin found the air to be brisk and pleasantly cool, and he thought the sounds of the wind-tousled night to be charming in their familiar way. The wooden rattle of the clacking tree limbs, the whisper of rushed grass, and the faint squeaking of some loose barn door were just a few of the inviting noises that caught Orrin's ear, and he decided to go for a walk before shutting himself inside his quiet, lonely room.

The two pints he'd consumed at the tavern had filled his body with satisfying warmth, and an easy smile now rested on his freckled face. He thought of Poor Ryan vomiting in the tavern and fancied that his own current state was much more pleasurable. However, the boy was only sixteen; he still had plenty of years in this remote country village to learn how to drink. Or, so went the discussion that Orrin carried on in his head.

He was shaken from his stream of consciousness when he noticed a jagged silhouette cresting the approaching hill. Orrin believed he had been wandering with no particular destination and was startled to find himself at the hawthorn tree by the Flynn's farm—the same hawthorn where only a few hours ago a strange man had swung on a rope. In the sweeping wind he could hear an eerie squeaking he had previously assigned to a loose door, but now imagined it being the sound of a swinging noose. He brushed away the goosebumps that sprouted on his skin and reassured himself there was no significance in his distracted body carrying him to that haunted place. Orrin was going to turn toward home when a shimmer caught his eye, and his flesh resumed to creeping when he spotted a figure in the moonlight.

Standing in front of the dark, twisted tree, was a woman. Her long hair lashed about her head, the silver strands in it flashing with a likeness to the starlight. Her frame was swallowed in a long, loose gown. Open at the neck, it flapped in the wind and teased Orrin with glimpses of pale flesh. At her side was a white dog—a shepherd-like creature with pricked ears and a lolling tongue. The pair stood statuesque, gazing out into the night. Orrin followed their line of vision and found a boy at the other end of it. It was Poor Ryan. He was barefooted and in his bedclothes, with a look of entrancement on his face as he gaped back at the ghostly woman.

Orrin turned his eyes back upon the woman and found she'd raised her arms in the air, causing her sleeves to drip down from her wrists like candle wax, and held them out in front of her, as if inviting the boy into an embrace. While the rest of her face maintained features that were soft and smooth—emanating an almost maternal reassurance—it was the woman's eyes that terrified Orrin on sight. They were two holes of stark, swallowing black.

He tore his eyes away from her petrifying stare, and looked back to find Poor Ryan shuffling back up the hill. Orrin's heart started pounding against his ribs and his thoughts began to whirl like leaves picked up in a gale. He knew he ought to throw himself in front of Poor Ryan and press his hands against the boy's chest to stop his march. He wanted to run forward and help the boy, grab him by the shoulders and shake him from his stupor, but he could not will his feet to move as much as an inch. When Orrin looked back once more upon the woman cloaked in moon glow, he was overcome with a sense of dread as he anticipated her eyes turning from Poor Ryan, to fall upon him instead. The idea flooded him with panic, and before her cursed gaze could shift in his direction, he turned and fled from the spot, and did not stop until he collapsed on the other side of a locked door.

Orrin spent the rest of the night lying stiff and paralyzed upon his bed. Sobered by fear, his eyes flitted between the closed door and the solitary window of his room. From where he lay, he could see only the black, star-spattered sky outside, but he waited with apprehension for a figure to appear on the other side of the glass. It seemed to him that every crunching leaf and every gust of moaning wind was most assuredly the woman's approach.

Though she never showed, Orrin was haunted by the thought of her standing by the hawthorn. He recalled each harrowing detail of what he'd seen: the flowing dress like a shroud; the white dog (either her servant or sentinel); and her *eyes*—two gaping holes in her porcelain face. Then he thought of Poor Ryan—glassy-eyed and slack-jawed—and winced at the image of the boy staggering unblinkingly toward the strange woman. The emotions etched into Poor Ryan's face remained fixed in Orrin's mind, but what they conveyed was beyond his current comprehension. Poor Ryan had been consumed by some driving force, but trying to decipher the source of its coercion left Orrin mystified and wide-eyed on his bed until he finally relaxed at the winking eye of daybreak.

He woke to the soft, familiar sound of his mother's voice. She was speaking to another woman out in the garden. Their speech was muffled, so Orrin crept from his bed over to the window and slid it open as soundlessly as possible to listen.

"Missing? How awful!" Orrin's mother exclaimed with a gasp. "Poor Ryan is only a few years younger than Orrin. Do you suppose the boy ran away?"

"No," the other woman said. Orrin recognized the nasally tones to be those of Widow Browne. "I fear something strange is happening in this town. I truly fear for our children."

Orrin reached up and eased the window shut. Balled up on the cold floorboards of his room, he began to tremble, his mind once again brought to unrest. Poor Ryan was gone and Orrin alone had witnessed his abductor, and somehow he sensed he daren't tell another soul about it.

That day the townsfolk searched tirelessly for Poor Ryan. While everyone else paired up, Orrin slunk off alone to the moor. As he traipsed away from Windhollow, he felt the hawthorn looming at his back, and a sensation of being watched. He tottered over the knotted landscape until he reached the lonely pool, which lay flat and dark among the heather like an oculus.

The place was silent and still, as if time had abruptly stopped. Orrin cupped a hand over his mouth, believing his breath had become devastatingly loud. His movement was very much the same as it'd been upon seeing Fiona Flynn in her bare flesh, in an effort to not be seen which had not worked. Holding his breath, Orrin walked to the water's edge and peered down into the mirror-like surface. He was observing his darkened visage, eyes wide and palms pressed over his lips, when the water began to softly quake. Beneath the trembling surface Orrin thought he saw something stirring, and soon a cloudy white shape began to form.

A sharp cry escaped from his hand-covered mouth, as a pale, ghostly face rose to kiss the surface of the pool. Orrin turned and fled before he could watch the woman open her vacuous, black eyes.

When the sun finally fell on their fruitless search, the men of Windhollow filed into the tavern with weary hearts and empty stomachs. The women served food while Sweet Scarlet served drinks, and the room was nearly silent, except for heavy sighs between gulps.

The somber stillness was broken when the tavern door flung open to reveal the stableman, Herne, panting in the doorway. His hulking frame nearly filled the opening, forcing his bloodhound, Arthur, to scramble inside through the space between Herne's legs. The stableman shuffled in and collapsed onto an empty barstool, gasping and sweaty, his wild eyes troubled by something unseen—and *unnatural.*

Folks remained quiet but exchanged worried glances while they waited for Herne to speak.

"I was in the woods," he began, once he caught his breath. His voice was hoarse and Sweet Scarlet offered him a glass of beer, which he raised to his lips and emptied in a single swallow.

"I thought I would have one last look around for Poor Ryan before the sun set. Mind you, it had already begun its descent, and the world becomes a shade darker when those trees close in around you. It was so still and quiet, I was overcome with the sensation of being watched by unseen eyes. Then, Arthur took off and bolted deeper into the woods. I ran after him, forgetting my unease for a moment, thinking he could've caught scent of the boy.

"I followed Arthur as best I could. I couldn't see him anymore, but I could hear him rushing through the leaves. It was getting dark fast, and as I chased after Arthur, I could only really make out the dark outlines of the trees—until I saw a glare of light up ahead. At first I thought it was the moon, but it was much too low for that.

"As I got closer, I heard growling. I saw Arthur turned toward the light, snarlin' at it with his tail between his legs. Then I realized it wasn't light he was looking at, but rather a woman with skin that glowed white. She had long, silver hair, but she wasn't old—she was young and very beautiful. She even seemed sort of *familiar* in an uncanny way."

Herne closed his eyes, as if recalling her image in his mind. A tear slid down his ruddy cheek. "She wore a long, white gown and, her eyes…oh, god, those eyes!"

Orrin shivered, listening to the man.

Herne's face became pained as he described them.

"I've never seen such eyes. They were all black, blacker than coal, without a stitch of color, and oddly *deep*, like the night sky. They terrified me, but I couldn't look away—I didn't want to. I noticed she was smiling at me, a clever smile, and despite my fear I found myself smiling back. At her feet were two dogs, their lips curled back in snarls."

"*Two* dogs!?" Orrin blurted out—everyone shooting berating glares at him.

"Aye," Herne answered, "with pelts as white as bone."

Orrin shrunk back into his chair, withering under the glares of the townsfolk. He swallowed a meek apology and another gulp of beer, but distress and confusion trumped his embarrassment. He recalled the ghostly woman and the single hound at her side, and he was certain there had only been the two of them atop the hill—and Poor Ryan scrambling up to meet them.

"I asked her if she needed help," Herne continued, "but she didn't answer me. She just kept staring, with those black eyes of hers. I felt like I was on the other end of a fishing line, with the hook cutting right through my heart, and before I could stop myself, I started walking toward her.

"Her dogs began to growl with even greater ferocity, milky saliva dripping from their jaws, like they were just waiting for the chance to leap at my throat. The woman shushed 'em, and stroked each of their heads with long, white fingers, before turning and walking away into the trees, the dogs and the eerie light following after her. I wanted to follow, too. I even tried, but she disappeared and I was left alone in darkness."

When Herne was finished with his story he laid his head down and wept.

Orrin's father, Patrick, and Michael, the gravedigger, dragged Herne to his cottage by the stables after he'd become too drunk to walk. The rest of the men stumbled home and many of the women—including Orrin's mother—

stayed behind to help Sweet Scarlet clean up the tavern.

Orrin was apprehensive to walk home alone to an empty house, but it seemed he didn't have a choice, his father had already left to help get Herne home, and when Orrin asked his mother if he could stay and help the women tidy up, she insisted the ladies could manage on their own. A few short years ago, Orrin would have been welcomed to stay behind, to listen to the women chatter and giggle while they cleaned the tavern, but now that he was no longer a child, the women thought of him—even *looked* at him—differently.

When his mother firmly sent him away, he glanced at Sweet Scarlet before leaving; perhaps hoping she would invite him to stay. But he was surprised to catch an unexpected twinkle in her eye, and a clever little smirk on her rosy cheeks. Orrin felt a short, sharp tug in his stomach, and quickly turned to leave, before the barmaid could catch sight of his face flushing red.

He strode along the path toward home, his head humming with the pints he'd consumed. It was nearing early morning and Orrin could sense the heavy presence of the waxing moon stalking him from above. He could almost feel it growing larger with every step he took, as if he carried it on his very shoulders.

Spread out on one side of the path was a towering wall of darkness—the forest, wild and tangled, yawned with a maw full of tall, twisted teeth. Peering into it was like squinting into an abyss; for its darkness was complete, save a few skulking shapes which Orrin could only hope were trees. He fixed his eyes on the steady marching of his feet and trained his ears on the *pit-pat* of his shoes hitting the earth. The sound was steady and soothing, like a metronome, and was doing well to calm him, until he heard the sudden, subtle snapping of twigs under the weight of phantom feet somewhere off to the side of him.

He stopped and looked to the dark line of trees. Pressed against the shadowy veil of the forest, was the ghostly woman with her two white hounds poised on either side of her. She was staring out at Orrin from the edge of the woods; her silver hair swirled around her head in the breeze and her gown hung loose about her shoulders. Orrin's heart pounded like a hammer in his chest. At once, she was both daunting and bewitching. Though frightened, Orrin could not keep from meeting her magnetic gaze. Her obsidian eyes absorbed him. His terror rose to a paralyzed panic as he was quickly drawn into their abysmal darkness. Powerless against her silent seduction, his blood began to churn hot and fierce inside him, and suddenly he was sweating profusely and could hear his own heartbeat thrumming inside his head as his muscles began to pulse frantically.

"*Orrin,*" a soft voice called—so quiet that he wasn't sure if it had actually sounded out loud, or had merely conjured in his head. He was consumed in the hungry gaze of the ghostly woman and could focus on nothing else. Even his physical distress, which had been so horribly intense a moment ago, was now fading. Windhollow had all but melted away; there was nothing more of the drab, sleepy town. The realm Orrin was being drawn into was dark and sensual. He felt a sensation of formlessness overtaking him, as if he was floating in water. He was relaxed to the point he thought he might finally fall peacefully asleep, but just before he sank into total unconsciousness, he was startled to feel someone—or something—tearing at his clothes. Unseen fingers grasped tightly around his arms and shook him, and a voice rang out in his ears. It sounded to be that of his father's.

"Orrin! Wake up, boy! Wake up!"

"Da—" Orrin mumbled.

"Son, you need to go home. Run straight home." Patrick instructed his son in stern, paternal tones, but the fear on his face could not be obscured as the moonlight washed over it.

A velvet voice crooned Orrin's name from the woods. He peered around his father and saw the woman in white beckoning with a long, white finger.

"Come on, boy!" Patrick barked, and began to run toward the cottage, tugging his son along behind him. A shrill, menacing cackle ripped from the phantom woman's throat and filled their ears as they both fled into the looming light.

Finally reaching the cottage's dappled porch, Patrick flung his body against the door and it flew open with little resistance. Once inside, Orrin ran into his father's open arms, and together they fell against the door in a quivering knot of limbs.

On the other side, the two hounds were throwing themselves against the wood, tearing at it with their claws, while their jaws dripped and snapped. The woman continued to jeer and shriek as she went from window to window, raking her long fingers against the opaque glass. They shivered in one another's embrace until the door finally lay still behind them and the hideous laughter abated.

The pre-dawn air fell into a pained hush, and after much anxious waiting for the phantoms to return, their bodies finally gave away to exhaustion. They fell asleep on the cold floorboards, Patrick slumped against the door with his son curled up beside him. Orrin slept deeply and dreamed of cold, murky water, and dogs with watchful eyes.

They were awakened by heartbreaking wails and pounding on the door. They clasped each other in a stab of terror, but relaxed when they noticed the sunlight pouring in through the windows.

Patrick opened the door to find the Widow Browne crumpled on the front step, weeping into hands that were bloodied from beating on the cottage's doors.

"My baby," she blubbered. "She took my baby!"

All work was put aside to look for the child, but the search lacked the previous day's composure. The townsfolk searched frantically, tearing through the brush with trembling hands, eyes opened wide. Anticipation of finding the baby gnawed at them, as did the terrible prospect of a grisly discovery. At sunset, at the close of another hapless search, they filed into the tavern yet again, with weary bodies and broken hearts. It wasn't until after supper that Widow Browne offered up her awful tale, for that was when the appropriate time seemed to be. After every fork was set down and the only sound in the place was the crackling of the fire, Widow Browne sniffled once more into her handkerchief and lowered her bloodshot eyes.

"I woke to the sound of my baby crying," she said, pausing to choke back a sob before she went on, "which isn't unusual, of course. It was pitch black and quite cold in the room. I lit a candle and took it with me. As I approached the door of the nursery, the temperature grew colder, and the light changed—a sort of soft, silvery light, like moonlight.

"I always see the window before I see the crib, which is tucked away in the corner, and with horror, I beheld the window wide open, letting in a terrible wind. When I rushed forth, a frigid gust snuffed out my flame, but there was no trouble seeing for the room was filled with that strange, ethereal light.

"It was only when I stepped through the doorway that I saw the woman leaning over the crib. The glow was coming *from* her! She was smiling down at my baby, and I screamed as she reached down to touch him. When she looked up, at me, I saw that terrible face. Her lips were pulled back into a sneer, like that of a hungry animal. Worse yet, were her eyes! They were stark black and empty, like hollow sockets. I heard a low growling and at first thought it was coming from between her bared teeth, until I glanced down to discover the two snarling dogs at her feet. The woman reached down and picked up my son in fingers thin and terribly long. I dropped the candle and moved to snatch my baby away, but the dogs leapt at me with their gnashing teeth. I was too frightened to make another move, so I watched, paralyzed, as the evil woman pressed my baby boy against her breast and carried him to the window where she crawled out, her hellhounds leaping out after her, leaving me alone in the shadows."

Several pints of beer brought a bit of much needed cheer into the tavern, and even inspired a rosy-cheeked smile from Widow Browne, which was quite unthinkable given the circumstances of her missing child. The heavy silence had been replaced with an almost pleasant hum of conversation. Orrin took the hop-induced moment of merriment, as an opportunity to slip through the front door unnoticed.

The cool night air greeted him with a sigh as the silken hands of the wind caressed his face with an unsettling intimacy. His sobriety became painfully apparent as he looked out over Windhollow to the swell of land from which the hawthorn stood upright, its spindly branches reaching upward, in an almost desperate attempt to embrace the star-strewn sky.

Carried on the wind was a mournful song of baying hounds. Orrin's heart ached at the sound, and with great effort he began to march toward its source.

The moon hung fat and full, spilling down its silver light to drench the moor. As Orrin crunched his way across the scrubby grass, the howling grew louder. And when he descended the hill that was adorned with the cursed tree, he could see the moonlight reaching like a sharpened blade across the soundless surface of the pond.

Three white hounds lined the edge of the water, each lifting their snouts in turn to sing out a long, sorrowful note. They stopped, their ears pricking to his approaching footsteps, and turned their heads to fix gleaming eyes on him as he drew near. Looking into their all-too human eyes, Orrin froze in place, finding a brief, paralyzing moment when the dogs were not meeting his panicked gaze. They seemed, instead, to be focused on something—or someone—behind him.

Orrin whirled around, his heart thumping audibly in the soft, silent night, to face whatever loomed there. The only figure at his back was the gnarled silhouette of the hawthorn itself.

The eerie silence was shattered by a sudden burst of laughter that echoed across the moor. It was the same laugh he had heard on that day when he was a child—the charmingly wicked little snicker that had escaped from the lips of Fiona Flynn. Following it was a large splash of water, as if someone had jumped into the pond.

Orrin whipped around once again to find himself even more alone than before, for the brooding hounds had vanished. The water was as still as ice. Surely he couldn't've imagined the noise, could he? He inched up to the water's edge, searching for a ripple on the pond's placid face. The image of the moon glared on the surface of the water, making it impossible to see even an inch below its surface.

So determined to find *some* evidence of the splash, Orrin bent down on hands and knees, his nose hovering just above the pond's glow. His eyes burned from the sharp moonlight reflected up at him, and a dark, organic smell that abruptly rose to meet his nostrils.

His lowered head cast a long shadow on the silver-stained water. He willed his eyes to pierce the sealed surface, but only had a fraction of a moment to see anything at all, before something quickly rushed up through the mirror image of his face, and grabbed him roughly by the hair. It was a hand, white and slender, with long, cruel fingers.

He cried out, only for his voice to be reduced to pathetic gurgling as he was pulled underwater. He thrashed about in the bone-chilling water until he wrestled free from the wicked grasp that held him. He opened his eyes and released another muffled scream that issued from his mouth in a stream of bubbles. Floating inches from his own face, was another, the pale skin tinted a sallow green in the murky water. The eyes, black as coal, stared unflinchingly into his own, and he waited in transfixed terror for whatever was to come next.

It was then that the horrible scene shifted. Much to his surprise, the ashen eyes grew unfocused and the face began to drift lazily downward. He watched the body of the woman in the tattered white gown sink gently down to the bottom of the pond, her hair swirling around her face.

With a gasp of air, Orrin burst through the surface of the water, grappling for the shore as he gulped painful breaths of air into his heaving lungs. He sucked in one last heaving breath and dove back beneath the water's obsidian surface.

The moonlight pierced the cloudy water in silver spears. Orrin followed one like a length of rope to the bottom of the pond. He expected to find the pallid corpse, but all that was left was a pitiful pile of bones scattered among the rubbery weeds.

Gently, he scooped the haphazard skeleton into his arms and rode the moonbeams up to the surface of the water. The bones clattered when Orrin laid them in the tall grass. They were brown and slick with algae, and only the largest and thickest had stood the test of time.

The three hounds had returned. They stood silently in a row, boring into him with their solemn stares. Orrin, too exhausted to feel any kind of fear, leaned back in the brittle grass and fought once more to catch his breath.

Before he had a chance to do so, one of the dogs broke free from their frozen state and leapt forward. Orrin threw his hands up over his face, anticipating teeth tearing into his water-slick flesh, but the attack never came. Instead, the dog snatched up a bone from the pile and ran off, clutching it between its chewing jaws. The other two jumped forward and did the same, their ivory forms shooting off over the darkened moor with the vaporous grace of a fading apparition.

Forgetting the searing pain in his chest, Orrin grabbed the rest of the bones, cradling the grinning skull in the crook of his arm, and took off after the spectral hounds.

The trek through the moonlit moor was a blur of shadows; the bones clacked in his grasp as he ran. His eyes were fixed on his destination, which quickly revealed itself to be the hawthorn atop the hill. Orrin stopped abruptly, and the rattling bones fell silent. Before he saw the sprawling silhouette crowning the hill, Orrin believed he had almost forgotten his fear, but it all came flooding back like the cold pond water that had just engulfed him.

Beneath the tree, the three dogs poised expectantly, their eyes gleaming in the darkness. He marched up the hill to the tree with slow, deliberate steps, recalling Poor Ryan as he did so. He thought back to that night when he watched the boy traipse toward the ghostly woman with the black eyes. Orrin looked down at the skull in his arms, which gazed back up at him with empty, shadowed sockets. They did not have the same hypnotic affect as when the face was framed with long, silvery hair, or wrapped in snow-white flesh—the now slimy skull, featureless and frail, was in reality quite pathetic.

Sorrow replaced the fear in Orrin's heart as he thought of the wild woman who the skull had belonged to…of her body decaying alone and unknown at the bottom of the pond…and the menacing phantom that was born out of her presumably tragic death.

The dogs had set to digging a hole at the foot of the hawthorn. When they finished flinging the rich, black dirt through their claws, they let the bones fall from their slobbering mouths with a sickening thud.

Orrin inched up to the edge of the shallow grave and kneeled forward. He arranged the disarrayed skeleton as neatly as he could, placing the black-eyed skull at the top of the pile, then grabbed a fistful of cold soil. He was never old enough to know the real Fiona Flynn, to him, and perhaps everyone else in the town, she'd been merely a myth. She was a local legend. Her living self had been rumored to be wild, sensual, charming and untamable, while her ghost had appeared seductive, hungry, and wicked.

The only person who knew the *human* Fiona, was her cruel husband, who most likely drove her to her watery death.

Orrin let the handful of earth sift slowly through his fingers, wishing silently for the lost spirit to find her bones and come to an easy rest and a deep, eternal sleep, once and for all. When his hand was empty, he shoveled the rest of the upturned earth into the hole with his arms and patted it down flat. He then stood and gazed from the top of the hill out over the village. Orrin realized that Fiona Flynn was perhaps his favorite part of Windhollow. She was the only thing that made him *feel*—be it terror, lust, or awe. She provoked in him a longing for adventure, and as Orrin peered out over the sleeping village, he knew he could never return to his humble rural life as it'd once been.

Turning his back on the thatched roofs and smoking chimneys spread out all around him, Orrin set off down the hill, where the dogs had raised their snouts and, were once again, set to howling. He began to crunch over the moor in his wet boots, but stopped when he noticed the mournful song of the hounds had abruptly ceased.

Orrin looked back over his shoulder and found the hill above him empty, save for the gnarled hawthorn tree, reaching up with twisted branches toward the gleam of the now full moon.

Reaping a Quiet Lunacy

Martin Reaves

"By believing passionately in something that still does not exist, we create it. The nonexistent is whatever we have not sufficiently desired."
- Franz Kafka

"Hell is empty and all the devils are here."
- William Shakespeare

"I don't know if I'll make it back."

Jesse Cokely pauses the digital voice recorder, gripping the ferry railing with his left hand as a fist of autumn wind punches the boat. He lifts the recorder to his lips. "Assuming I make it there at all. I swear it's like something doesn't want me at Seaview." Another pause. Then, slowly: "*She* wants me there. I know she does. That wasn't her in the loft, it was just a shell she used to inhabit. It wasn't her, and that wasn't her blood. Someone like Chloe doesn't end like that."

He clicks off the recorder and drops it in a pocket.

The Staten Island Ferry rises and falls gently in the wind-chopped water. Millions of people make this trip every year. And they all eventually come back. But few of them make the trip with the sole purpose of spending the night in Seaview Hospital. Occasional ghost hunters, sure. They come to the crumbling haunted wreck in the hopes their shaky-cam, night-vision videos will go viral on YouTube. Maybe some actually experience phenomena or maybe they scare themselves into thinking they have.

Jesse is not going in search of a ghost. He's brought one along for the ride.

* * *

Earlier that morning, bleary-eyed after his shift tending bar at a Greenwich Village strip club called The Rumpus Room, Jesse stood street-level looking up toward Chloe and Dray's loft. Dray was the headline stripper at The Rumpus Room and failed to show for work the night before. The club's manager, Florent Degoode, had been in a high state of worry at her absence. And Jesse knew why.

Dray's partner, Chloe, had apparently gone off the rails. Early the previous morning Florent had confided in Jesse after Chloe had some kind of massive breakdown, claiming a character from a story she was writing actually spoke to her. She'd been so terrorized by whatever she thought had happened she passed out. Dray understandably freaked and called Florent, her closest friend other than Chloe. Florent came over and while trying to make sense of what Chloe saw in the story she'd been writing they discovered a second manuscript. According to Dray, Chloe claimed she had been writing both stories in a fugue state, she herself completely unaware what she was writing, the only bit of information she could give being that she thought she had created something, or unleashed something. Florent asked Jesse's opinion on those writings, both of which seemed to support the idea that the brilliant Chloe Sender had lost her marbles.

When not tending bar Jesse's field of study was Chronic Mysticism, which essentially investigated why and how fearful legends endure, ultimately asking the question: *Can a prolonged and fearful way of thinking actually create the thing we fear?* Jesse believed there was no stronger emotion than fear, and chronic thought backed by emotion had the potential for enormous creative power.

So Florent had come to him, thumb-nailing how Chloe had been sleep-writing these two manuscripts—one a kind of psychotic memoir, the other a tale of a demonic conjuring—both pointing to a host of suppressed childhood memories involving the most horrific sexual abuse Jesse had ever heard of. Jesse had kept his cool, spouting rhyme and reason in the face of apparent madness. What he couldn't tell Florent—what he hadn't really admitted even to himself—was that he had been in love with Chloe for several months. Months back, Florent had sent her to him to see if he knew who might have a translation of an ancient piece of twisted Akkadian literature called The

Codex of Forbidden Knowledge. Jesse not only knew, he had a translation, one he had translated himself from a French translation of the original Akkadian text. The book read like an instruction manual in depravity, with passages actually detailing how to conjure a demon through the act of gang rape, with another section that seemed to suggest a method of having sex that was so intense it could bring forth visions of the underworld—and it only degenerated further from there.

He had no idea what someone like Chloe would want with such a book, but he was happy to share it with her if only to be in the company of someone he considered one of the finest of the new breed of intellectual writers. They had met clandestinely several times, Chloe no doubt fully aware that he was in love with her, lesbian or not.

At their final meeting Chloe had placed a flash drive in his hand. "Copies of some of my writings," she told him. "Experimental stuff. Prose poems, stream of consciousness, stuff like that. Stuff I can't really do anything with. I honestly don't know what all is on there. If you stumble on anything really embarrassing, keep it to yourself."

He went home that night and read through every piece on the flash drive, becoming more unsettled and disoriented with each increasingly twisted sentence. He'd known back then something was wrong. But he couldn't ask her about it. They'd had their last meeting; Chloe made that clear.

And that meeting was the last time he saw her before finding her dead, in a pool of congealed blood, her body caved in on itself like something had crushed her from the inside.

Jesse descends the ramp from the ferry to Staten Island. He locates the nearest car rental counter and picks up the cheapest car available that has GPS. He considered driving from Manhattan, but he wanted to make the journey as Chloe had, across the water.

Assuming her stories are true, he thinks.

He punches in the coordinates for Seaview Hospital on Brielle Avenue. A few minutes later he is moving southeast on Bay Street along the Hudson River. In less than half a mile he turns right onto Victory Blvd, headed southwest for another six miles into the island's wooded center. The wind is now at his back, seeming almost to urge him on. One hand on the wheel, he pulls the recorder from his pocket and begins to recite one of Chloe's writings from memory, a haunting piece likening the Staten Island Ferry trip to a boat ride to Hell:

> *"Charon's Charge: A Midnight Ride to the House of Broken Corridors by Chloe Sender*
>
> *Charon stands at the helm, in fine foul garb*
> *A gnarled fist to the wheel*
> *I cannot see his face*
> *I cannot feel*
> *Another ride*
> *Midnight Crossing*
> *Gentle swells urge us on*
> *Over Styx, foghorn moans*
> *Bright Lights into Dark Wood*
> *At Seaview terminus doomed to roam*
> *Along tainted shores and Broken Corridors."*

"So tell me about Chronic Mysticism."

"Ah, I see Florent has been telling my secrets." Jesse had looked at Chloe, trying to determine if she really wanted to know or was just making conversation. Her eyes, too intense to look on for more than a few seconds, urged him on.

He'd been embarrassed at first, then warmed to the subject. "You won't find C. M. on any curriculum. I coined the term to try to explain—to myself, I guess—how certain ideas or beliefs come to be. More than that, how they *linger*, you know? For instance, we're all familiar with the standard idea that departed spirits leave an imprint, right? Whether through trauma at time of death, or unresolved issues, whatever. They supposedly leave a sort of psychic watermark that hangs around and it's what we think of as ghosts. That type of thing doesn't really interest me. What C. M. questions is how the belief itself came to be and then remains as part of our psychic structure. It investigates the hypothesis—my hypothesis—that long-held beliefs can actually create the thing or entity in question. What I'm interested in is the many thousands of years of deep-seated fears and whether dwelling on them can actually make their objects...real. There is no stronger or more creatively deadly emotion than fear."

Jesse had remembered those damning words as he stood looking up at the loft where Chloe lived. He wanted to go in to check on Dray, to see why she hadn't shown for work, and maybe to see Chloe, to see if she would acknowledge him with a look, maybe the tiniest of smiles that said, *I remember the time we shared.*

As he stood debating whether to go up, the street door opened and Florent Degoode emerged. But this was not the man Jesse knew. Florent was a gentle gay man with an astonishing sense of decorum. Jesse had known him for years and the man walking toward him was somehow *wrong*. There was a stiffness to his walk, like someone just regaining the use of their legs. Jesse was about to call to him then stopped. Florent walked by within a few feet without acknowledging Jesse until he was even with him. His head turned slightly in Jesse's direction, his eyes meeting and locking on Jesse's as he passed, his head swiveling to maintain that contact even as he continued by. Jesse turned to watch him go, telling himself that Florent's head couldn't possibly turn that far around, he was imagining it, just as he was imagining the tendril of pink-tinted drool running over Florent's bottom lip.

A brittle dusk is settling in as Jesse steps from the car. Before him stretches a path littered with fallen leaves and bordered by ancient black walnut trees. At the end of the path stands the hulking shell of Seaview Hospital. Jesse consults his mental guidebook and pulls the recorder from his pocket, speaking into the microphone in a whisper:

"First a poor house, then a tuberculosis hospital, now a decrepit and abandoned New York City landmark. Seaview Hospital and New York Farm Colony has a history of haunting. The farm colony/poor house (originally designed as a means of rehabilitation for the mentally ill) was established in the 1830s and the hospital opened in 1913. The complex has sat in decay since 1975, but due to a landmark designation in 1985 nothing can be torn down. Workers of the hospital claim to have seen old patients wandering through the hall; now it's a rotting asylum left to the elements."

Jesse begins walking along the path, whispering to himself. "So tell me,

Chloe. If this place closed down in nineteen-seventy-five, well before you were born, how is it that you were here some fifteen years later, experiencing your own version of hell?"

He lifts the recorder again to his lips:

"The Taste of Mad Dreams by Chloe Sender

He waits outside my door
I've told this tale before
Of windows and faces and rusted braces
Red-headed whores dancing; legs spreading; blades lancing
This is how it happens
This is why it happens
First the pain, then the rain
Of tenderness
First the blade, then the trade
Of flesh for blood. Blood for desire
Each caress apposite payment for a moment's distress
All leading back to the long, long flight
Past broken faces and lunatic light
Across enraged waters, down fractured corridors
Where he waits…behind Seaview's doors
Savoring the taste
Of the mad dreams
Of children."

When he was sure Florent would not turn back, Jesse entered the apartment building. In the elevator he began to shake.

Florent's eyes.

The way he had looked at him, almost taunting him.

"That's wasn't Florent," he said as the elevator ascended. "I know it *was* him, but…it wasn't him." He dug his knuckles into his eyelids until black spots began to bloom behind them. "God, I'm losing it."

He smelled it a few seconds before the lift stopped outside Chloe and Dray's loft. He almost pressed the button to descend back to the ground floor, to leave the building and not look back. Then his hand pushed the grating back with a protracted screech. Chloe's door was directly in front of him, slightly ajar. He walked forward slowly, his feet trying to rebel and move him in any direction other than straight ahead. He nudged the door with his foot and it swung open soundlessly. The reek of blood and evacuated bowels was so intense he could almost hear it. There was a dense buzzing in his ears that he realized was actually in the room with him. Without intention or decision he continued into the loft's large central area. The buzz came from a black swarm of flies feasting on a large red-brown patch of liquid under a low leather chair. The flies were so thick they obscured the delicate feet resting in that congealed puddle. His eyes remained on those feet for as long as he could manage before climbing the slender ankles, up to her knees, and Chloe's perfect fingers resting in her lap.

He made himself look away. And that's when he saw Dray. At her easel, facing away from him, slumped forward.

Dray was more than a stripper. She was an artist. How could I have forgotten that?

But the canvas did not show the work of a talented hand. On the easel, in shaky splashes of red and green, was a small child with large dark holes for eyes. At the bottom of the picture, in a spidery script as a child might do, were the words:

Peek-a-boo, I see yooouuuu!

Jesse clicks on a penlight as he walks down the decimated corridor. He is looking for the central chamber described in one of Chloe's narratives. This particular piece of writing on the flash drive is date stamped the day before she gave him the drive. Like the rest, it seems an exercise in surrealism. But a thread runs through all the fragments of story and poem on the drive. Taken by themselves he can almost believe they are no more than literary experiments.

But he knows too much. Florent told him too much. The stories are evidence of a mind becoming unhinged.

And maybe they are more than that. Maybe they are a sort of stylized diary.

The timbre of Jesse's footsteps alters slightly, becoming less sharp, lingering a bit longer on the air. He snaps his fingers and the sound echoes. The skin on his arms prickles as he realizes he is now in a large chamber. He has no memory of walking through a doorway, or of turning off the long hallway, but somehow he is standing in the center of a cavernous room.

"Okay," he whispers to the air, "this is the money moment."

The thin beam from his penlight illuminates very little, until suddenly it does, as though the simple presence of the beam has begun to create physical objects. And of course they are all right where he imagined they'd be.

Where she said they'd be.

She wants me to see everything as she saw it.

He shakes his head. Stop it.

Still shining the light, picking up more and more detail, he pulls the recorder from his pocket, speaking as quietly as possible:

"A Prisoner of Seaview by Chloe Sender

Now I lay me down to sleep
on a diseased mattress.
In the far corner of this cavernous space,
this dark echo chamber whispering in drips and creaks, sighs
and groans.
Walls sway under a weight of years and decay.
A deep, mournful moaning calls from far off.
A ferry's horn.
Outside this space, outside this central world,
numerous hallways and corridors, all stretching away from
my filthy bed,
like a spider's legs expand out from its belly.
Here, in the belly,
floating in festering venom.
A scatter of dancing shadows thrown by the propane lantern
he holds out before him.
Him.
Footsteps echo. Voices from the corridors echo off high ceilings.
A door opens somewhere,

rubber shoes squeak across polished tile as the door closes.
And a latch is turned.
He's here.
This is all from before. I'm not here now.
But in this here and now, in the central chamber...
There. See the sink along the nearest wall?
The small bowl that might have once been a toilet?
The rusted frame supporting the decaying mattress
on which some version of me now sits?
It's all here, just as it has always been.
And there, right there, dangling from the rail just to my left:
the frayed and blood-crusted remnant of a strap, dull light glinting
off its tarnished buckle.
The low horn moans again.
This is my bed. This is my room. Where I belong.
Where I have always belonged.
I lay me down, but only for a moment.
He approaches. Though still far across the room in elongated shadow,
he is somehow beside me.
I smell him.
His smile, it has texture and sound.
He has come to me once again,
reaching deep within,
to savor my dreams.

Jesse clicks off the recorder. His hands fall to his sides, the need for light forgotten.

"How could any of this happen to you?" he whispers. "And how did you survive it all? A father who did what he did, driving you not only to attempt suicide at such a tender age, but to go on attempting it so you could return again and again to doctor in a psych hospital who showed you some form of kindness..."

His voice breaks. Without knowing he is doing it, he lifts the recorder again. "But that doctor was not kind at all, it just seemed that way to a child who didn't know any better. No, he was just another fucking psycho. A pedophile preying on his patients. Or…maybe it was just Chloe. Maybe she was his sole conquest."

Something rattles just ahead of him. He lifts the penlight.

And there it is, just as it was described.

Now I lay me down to sleep
on a diseased mattress.

A strap with a rusted buckle hangs from the frame, swaying for no reason at all, the buckle tapping against the rusted metal frame.

He sways in time with the buckle, a sudden onrush of dizziness causing him to stumble back. That bed was not there a moment ago. He would've seen it.

But it is there now. In some version of reality, that bed is here. *She described it and now I see it, simple as that.*

"She's still creating," he whispers, the narrow beam from his penlight dipping and glinting off a pair of eyes under the bed.

He drops the light and hears it shatter at his feet.

In the loft, Chloe and Dray dead, flies buzzing.

Jesse wasn't sure how long he stood, frozen into a terrified immobility. But it was more than terror. It was sickness and heartbreak and terror all rolled into a new emotion with no name. The urge to vomit was overpowered by fear fueled by the proximity to violent death, which was in turn overpowered by a colossal sense of loss as he understood how much he had truly loved Chloe.

He should call the police. That's what he should do.

His eyes moved around the room, looking for a phone. What he saw instead was two sheaves of papers, stacked neatly beside each other.

Manuscripts. These must be the stories she was apparently writing in her sleep.

His feet took him toward them. The larger of the two stacks had no title page. He read the first sentence:

The child snaps awake at a dead run, lurching into consciousness out of a vast shadowy emptiness. From a pitch-black void into glaring illumination, she is thrust into a cacophonous now, *running away from or toward something unknown.*

The top page of the much smaller second manuscript seemed to glow. He knew it was not glowing—it couldn't be—it was simply the words themselves, so much like the short snippets of prose he'd found on the flash drive.

This is her true voice, he thought, *the voice of a child so broken she would attempt suicide just to be taken back to a doctor who would then do the unspeakable—maybe much worse than what was actually happening at home.*

He lifted the sheet in trembling hands, his eyes scanning and picking out individual sentences that seemed to jump into his vision:

"In the House of Broken Corridors by Chloe Sender (Part One)

He waits just outside my door.
In the long hallway that never ends.
Sometimes I get lost, but I always find my room.
Or my room finds me. It wants me to be here.
He's always here.
Sometimes I am here first.
Sometimes he is waiting.
Outside. In the hall.
He paces in front of my door, dragging his fingernails against the painted metal.
Scraping and then tapping.
The shadow moves from left to right, right to left.
I hear him breathing.
I hold my breath, watching the doorknob, watching the shadow, waiting for either to move.
Not breathing. Like Dolly doesn't breathe.
My head pounds from not breathing. Fog from under the bed wraps around me.
It feels good. Like awake sleeping.

The corridor is empty.
He's not there.
I'm not here.
I'm somewhere else, awake-dreaming, not thinking these thoughts,
not remembering.
Pretending I'm not here and never was here.
But I think I want to be here.
I just have to be brave enough to do the thing that makes me go back.
It hurts, this thing.
But it's the only way.
Watching the shadow that isn't there, I pull Dolly closer, pressing
her cool porcelain face
against my cheek.
I whisper, "What do I do?"
She doesn't answer.
She almost never answers.

Jesse holds his breath, listening.

Those weren't eyes, my light just reflected off something, maybe some broken glass.

Everything in him wants to turn and run. But it's getting darker and he knows he will only succeed in hurting himself if he bolts.

He releases his breath and hears the sound of his exhale come from somewhere in front of him.

That's just an echo. Breathe, man, come on. You knew shit might happen here…not because there are ghosts, but…

But what? Sure, I actually started to believe Chloe had created something, at least in her own mind, but why did I think I might encounter something?

Because of the footprints.

Jesse picked up both manuscripts, knowing at that moment that he was not going to call the police. Not yet. He knew he could be arrested for disturbing a crime scene, but something in him knew this wasn't a crime scene, not in the truest sense of the word.

He would call later, anonymously. Chloe and Dray couldn't be left here like this, but he didn't have to be the one to discover them. He didn't know anything the police could use, but he'd be held for questioning indefinitely.

He actually didn't know anything at all, not yet. But the manuscripts in his hands would get him closer to knowing.

He backed away toward the door, unable to avoid seeing Chloe one last time as he turned toward the door.

He froze. *No, I didn't see that.*

He turned back slowly, eyes clenched shut.

Just go, there's nothing else to see. You imagined that.

His eyes opened, staring at the floor in front of him. Just a wood floor, a bit scuffed, nothing out of the ordinary. His gaze inched ahead, toward where a cloud of flies swarmed over a darkening pool of blood that had once been inside a woman he loved.

And there, a few feet before the blood came into view, tiny footprints, like those of a very small child, a child who stepped in a puddle and walked out, leaving a fading trail, a trail headed straight toward him.

He ran.

He doesn't know if the footprints were there when he entered the loft and doesn't really care.

Something had been there. And something left.

He sees Florent again in his mind, walking toward him, then passing, his head swiveling as he continues on.

Jesse stoops to find his flashlight. His fingers locate the tube, but it is empty, the batteries having scattered when it hit the ground.

A footstep sounds behind him and he freezes.

"Chloe?"

No answer. Did he really expect one?

Still in a crouch, he closes his eyes, shutting them in darkness. After what might have been several minutes or maybe only a handful of seconds he opens them again. After the total darkness behind his lids he can see a bit of the room surrounding him. All normal items. The sink, a toilet, the bed.

But none of those things were here before, you said it yourself.

"Fuck it," he whispers, stands and approaches the bed.

He sits, waiting for something to grab him from underneath, knowing as he thinks this that he is acting like a child.

The bed creaks next to him. He feels the mattress depress with the weight of another.

My imagination. What else ya got?

He hears a door creak, then rubber-soled shoes squelching across the floor to his left. The rattle of squeaking wheels to his right, maybe an I.V. stand, maybe something else.

"I'm here," he says softly, immediately hearing the phrase echoed from every corner of the room.

He waits.

There are no more sounds. He tries to stand and falls back to the bed.

In the darkening gloom he sees that the strap has been buckled around his wrist.

"Oh Jesus."

A voice—Chloe's voice—whispers in his mind:

This is how it happens

This is why it happens

First the pain, then the rain

Of tenderness

Another voice, this one his own, issuing without his will from his lips: "You wanted to know, Jesse. Now you can know. She gave you hints all along, through her writing, through her simple brief presence in your life. She was a living breathing expression of pain, of irreparable damage. She created the very thing that took her life, of course she did."

With trembling fingers he manages to pull the recorder from his pocket, his voice almost non-existent as he speaks:

"It's here. In the room with me. Is this how it ends? Maybe. The darkness is absolute now, a suffocating blackness I can taste. Are my eyes opened or closed? I can't tell. I can hear it now, its breath so like the early autumn leaves scudding across the broken stones outside this tainted place. A liquid inhale followed by a crisp, brittle exhale. It's all of them compressed into a single manifestation. Her dad, the doctor, maybe even that fucking doll. Every ounce of foul and potent dread Chloe experienced condensed into one horrific and deadly force."

He paused and felt something like a doll's porcelain fingers slip into his shackled hand. His bladder let go and he began to weep.

He drew a shaky breath and continued. "Yes, you can write your dissertation now, Mr. Cokely. You were right all along. This kind of emotion-fueled creation is possible. But, why the hell did you think the death of the creator would mean the death of the created?"

A voice from behind him, lips tickling at his ear:

"Just lie back now. This won't hurt a bit."

Ablation

M.L. Roos

Amara sat at the bar, sipped a martini, and casually scanned the room for possibilities. She was bored. She needed a challenge. Tonight did feel different. Must be the double hit of the All Hallows Eve Blue Moon, she thought. But this couldn't possibly be the place where she'd find her next project. She was usually directed to out of the way, hole-in-the-wall dives on the outskirts of town, where she had to dress like a five-dollar crack whore. Tonight she was actually able to wear a decent dress, Jimmy Choo shoes, and had her hair and makeup done. It was nice feeling like a lady for once and not an undercover cop looking for meth.

Amara giggled to herself. The place wasn't the Ritz, but there was an actual piano player in a tux, playing a poor rendition of a Billy Joel song, but he still managed to have a few barflies hanging around him as if he was the next Henry Connick Jr.

At the other end of the counter—speaking too loudly and reeking of desperation—stood the cowboy, complete with hat, gold tooth, and pressed Levi's. *All hat and no cattle,* thought Amara, smiling. Another urban cowboy living in the city, impressing the ladies with the 'aw shucks ma'am, t'weren't nothing' dialogue, and probably getting away with it too. He was trying to hit on this gorgeous dark haired girl who giggled at his jokes but kept darting her eyes around the room, looking for anyone else but him. The cowboy was losing and trying to hang on. The girl was trying to get away. Another night, in another bar, in another city.

By the piano sat a very handsome man in an Armani suit. Latin, or Italian, dark hair, beautiful, smoldering dark eyes, square jaw. He glanced at Amara and gave her a quick smile. Amara turned away—the secret female signal for *get lost.* Armani man read the gesture accurately and went back to his drink, albeit in somewhat of a state of surprise, not used to getting turned down. That was the purpose of the $300.00 haircut and the $5000.00 suit. It practically guaranteed an easy pick up of anything he desired.

Amara sighed and took another sip, then noticed the gentleman across the room. He was alone. Amara took a quick inventory and decided he was the one. Nearing middle age, potbelly, wrinkled shirt, fat stubby hands—and an air of loneliness.

Amara walked past Armani man, who could only look further surprised, confused and ticked off, as she strolled past his table, walking toward the bereft-looking fellow. He saw her approach, gave her a sheepish smile, which quickly turned into a bewildered look of terror tinged with hope.

"Hi. Are you alone this evening?" Amara asked.

The man took a quick inhalation, and said, "Yes,"

"Then maybe we can spend some time together."

The man's face turned myriad shades of color. He quickly looked down at the table in front of him, picked up the half-empty glass he'd been nursing, and spun it mindlessly in his fat, pudgy hands. If he didn't stop soon, the amber liquid would be all over the table, and himself.

Amara reached out her hand and placed it ever so gently on top of his. He stopped the glass mid-spin and looked up at her. Her velvet eyes trapped his and he was immediately ensnared in their gaze. "No need to be so nervous. I won't bite." Amara said, smiling and stroking his fingers, barely touching his skin. It was a calming gesture which seemed to help. "Now, there, isn't that better? What should I call you?"

"Brent…My name is Brent….From Alberta," the man stammered.

"Well Brent from Alberta, my name is Amara. What brings you to Winnipeg? *Business?*"

"No. I'm just driving through, on my way to North Dakota. I have a truck I'm delivering to a company." Brent stared at the table again, trying not to look directly into her eyes. It wasn't every day—hell, it never happened!—that a beautiful woman spoke to him. He knew what he looked like—and what he represented to women. He was short, overweight, and had no social awareness of anything. At least, that's what his mother had told him all the time.

"I see. So maybe you would like some company for the evening? Being transient, it must get awfully lonely when you're out on the road." Amara leaned forward and ran her long, red fingernails lightly across Brent's arm. Light sweat appeared on his brow and upper lip. He could not help but notice Amara's breasts, pale white against the scarlet of her low cut dress. Brent quickly looked away and wiped his forehead with his hand.

"What do you say?" Amara asked.

Brent looked around nervously in disbelief that this beautiful creature was asking to spend the night with him. "Come on slugger. Take a chance and see what happens." Amara laughed and stood up, holding out her hand. Brent tentatively reached out for her. He still thought this was a joke. Any minute he expected to see a camera crew appear out of nowhere, with a celebrity host telling him he was on TV, and that his friends were going to come out laughing. Except Brent was a loner. There were no friends who cared enough to play a practical joke on him. There was no family members that would put one over on him, either. *There was no one.* Ever since Brent's mother died two years ago, he was alone in the world.

"Are you a hoo…hooker? I ain't got much money" Brent said. "I mean no disrespect. It's just that…" Brent's voice trailed off in a whisper.

Amara's laughter was a soft tinkle from across the table, a beautiful comforting siren's song of promise. She sat back down, grabbed his hand and said, "No, honey, I don't do this for the money. I don't need to. You just look like you could use a friend, and I thought I could help you. Maybe give you another perspective that you normally don't get to see. Think of me as a Halloween gift."

"A gift?" Brent laughed nervously. "Nobody ever gives me gifts." He rubbed his hand through his hair, then wiped it on his pants.

"Well then, today's your lucky day, now isn't it?" Amara flashed him another smile.

Brent looked at her. A momentary coldness flashed across his eyes, and disappeared just as quickly, and he said, "What's in it for you? If it ain't about the money—what is it, then? Nothing comes for free…everyone has an angle…even someone as beautiful as you. *Especially* someone as beautiful as you."

"Listen Sugar, if you don't want to get together, that's fine. I just saw you sitting here, alone, and thought you could use some company. Besides, it's Halloween. I thought we could spend some time Trick or Treating—I'm in the mood for *Treats.*" Amara started to stand up. "But if you prefer to be alone, that's okay too. It's not my nature to force anyone to do anything against their will." She pushed her chair back from the table and turned to leave.

Brent watched the curve of her dress as it slithered down her back and clung to her ass.

"Wait!" he half shouted.

Armani man and the cowboy looked in his direction, then at each other, a comical look passing between them.

Brent stood up. He grabbed Amara's hand and grasped it tightly, in case she changed her mind. They walked out the door together.

Brent lay on the bed. He was afraid to move, afraid to breathe in case Amara disappeared, or he realized he was dreaming. But he did not remember any dream that he ever had that included red neon lights blinking in the window against the dirty yellow curtains. The ceiling appeared blotchy in spots. In the corners, black fungus-like matter was slowly spreading outward. Any day now, the fungus would meet and the ceiling would cease to be white. A taped up faux leather chair sat in the corner next to a cigarette scarred end table full of ring stains from countless glasses and bottles put down wet—dreams lost and destroyed at the bottom of a bottle in this soulless room.

"Now Brent, I want you to tell me a story. Do you think you can do that?" Amara sat on top of him, straddling his chest. Brent was cold. He was naked and bound lightly at his wrists and ankles to the bed frame, secured by silk-corded ropes. Amara's satin panties felt hot against his expansive stomach and the heat of her thighs pressed against his ribs. The purple satin, half-cup bra was too small for her large breasts—it seemed like any minute now they would fall free from the thin piece of cloth they were encased in. Amara leaned over and stroked Brent's damp forehead. Her breasts were nuzzled against his mouth and nose. He could smell her scent, warm and heavy. It reminded him of exotic flowers, spice and warm honey on a humid night.

"What story am I supposed to tell you?" Brent asked weakly. His heart was pounding so hard, he thought it would explode in his chest. He was now sweating profusely, even though he felt cold. His face was flushed, his pupils dilated to the point where it looked like his eye colour was black rather than the washed out blue they usually were. His breathing was shallow and quick. He didn't know if it was from fear or excitement. Probably both. Either way, this was a good way to bring on a heart attack—especially at his age.

"Well Brent, tell me what turns you on. What do you fantasize about most? What gets you hot?" Amara breathed against his cheek. She sat upright and ran her hands down his chest and protruding belly.

"*What?*" Brent asked, stunned by the request. He must've misheard; no one had ever asked him that before. *Ever.* Even when he was a teenager, experimenting with girls in the back seat of his dad's Buick. Or the one time he managed to get lucky and got invited into Mrs. Stewart's house, located right across the street from him. She was a newlywed in her early twenties. He was sixteen at the time, and out working in the yard, cutting the lawn. She called him over and offered him an ice cold drink of lemonade and as they were chatting on the porch, she casually mentioned that her husband was gone for the weekend and would he be a dear and look at the window in her bedroom? She placed her hand on his arm and said, "It gets so stuffy in there at night, and I just don't have the strength in my arms to push that darn old window up—but I'll bet you do." She followed him up the stairs, closely. He was annoyed at first because she was in his personal space, but when he felt her hand on his shoulder, he understood. It became all too clear when he turned into her bedroom and the window was wide open. He turned around and she was naked. Heart pounding in his chest, his breath dried in his mouth, she grabbed his hand and placed it on one of her breasts. He felt like he was going to die and go to Heaven all at the same time. It never happened again. But that was one memory he cherished.

"Come on, Brent. What do you think about those nights you sit home alone watching TV on a Friday night? Or when you've been driving all night to make your next delivery? What runs through your mind? You can tell me…I can keep a secret." Amara knelt down and ran her tongue up Brent's chest. He inhaled sharply and struggled helplessly against the ropes that held him to the bed.

Brent laughed nervously, "Um…you know, the regular stuff." His face and chest flushed, turning bright red, competing with the glow of the neon sign.

"I bet you have girly magazines, don't you?" Amara asked in a sing-song voice. "Or girly books—maybe a few videos? What about your friends? Do you trade magazines and movies with them?" Amara sucked in her breath and sat up. "Why, I bet you do, Brent from Alberta. Why I bet there are a group of you guys who get together on a regular basis and trade tips and ideas, movies and magazines and everything. Pretend I am one of your guy friends. What kinds of things would you tell me?"

"Um I don't usually talk about..."

"Oh sure you do. I bet you guys get together on a regular basis and talk about all kinds of things, maybe even get together on fishing trips and such. Come on, you can tell me. It's not like I know where you live, or who you really are. Heck, I don't even know your last name. Is it because I'm a woman? Is that why you can't tell me your secrets...your fantasies? The things that drive you mad with desire?

"Amara, I am getting a little freaked out here. Do you think you could untie me now?"

"But I thought we were getting to know each other. Don't tell me you've changed your mind because I was asking a few questions? What if I turned off the lights? I know that always helps me get comfortable confessing my darkest secrets to someone. And do you know what your reward will be, Brent from Alberta? I will fulfill *every...single...one...of...your...fantasies.*" With every word, she trailed her finger closer and closer to his groin area. "Now doesn't that sound like fun?" Amara squealed and jumped off the bed, ran to the light switch and flicked it off. She then reached under the bed and pulled out a roll of duct tape, tore off a strip and sealed Brent's eyes and perched back on his chest.

"*What the hell!*" he screamed, and tried to kick out, a useless gesture.

"Shhhh, sugar plum. Shhhh..." Amara placed an index finger across Brent's lips and held it there. "There, there, little lamb. It's okay. I am doing this for your own good. This way you can tell me everything you need to tell me, and you can do it in the dark. Pretend you are talking to yourself in the middle of the night—or pretend I am a priest—confess your sins, your sexual desires, and I will fulfill them. I will be your dream come true. Think of me as your genie in a bottle, except you only get one wish, not three. Still, that's not so bad, is it?"

Brent's heart hammered in his chest, but he was quiet. A weird sense of calmness and peace descended over him. His breathing became shallow, less erratic. "I...can't." His mind was racing a million miles an hour—fear, anxiety, excitement, hope, terror—all battled to take top honor. *What the hell had just happened?* All he wanted was a drink and a good night's sleep. Now he was in the *Twilight Zone* version of *The Love Boat*. Nothing made sense.

"You can't...or you won't? Once you tell me your sexual fantasies, we can get on with it. Come on, Brent. *Please...*" Amara begged. "This is every guy's dream, being tied up and naked in bed with a gorgeously hot woman, willing to do—or be—anything you want. This is your lottery win, Brent. This is your once in a lifetime, Big Fish story. The one to tell the grandkids about. Well, maybe not the grandkids." Amara giggled. "Can you honestly tell me there aren't a thousand other men who would willingly trade places with you in a heartbeat? I'm giving you a golden ticket, and you want to throw it away." Amara pouted. Brent could hear disappointment in her voice, and visualize her luscious, lower lip jutting out.

Amara got off Brent's chest. He felt the springs of the bed move and heard her footsteps pad lightly across the floor.

"Where are you going?" he asked in a mild panic.

"Nowhere, love. Just here, sitting in a chair, watching you. Thinking about you and how to get through to you. What do you think Mike would do in this situation"?

"Mike? Mike who?" Brent asked.

"Come on Brent. Mike Faraday. Your best friend and confidant in Alberta. Your best buddy. Partner in crime. The custodian at all those elementary schools. *That* Mike."

"How do you know about Mike?" Brent hissed. "I thought you didn't know anything about me." He struggled against the cords holding his wrists and ankles, but with each yank, the cords bit deeper into his flesh. "Dammit!" he screamed. "These things are killing me. Loosen them!" The skin had started to abrade around his wrists and ankles, turning the flesh an ugly reddish purple.

Amara laughed a low, throaty laugh. Her voice dropped a register and she growled, "I know more than you think, lover. I need to hear you say it, though. I need to hear your *confesssssion* on this very special evening." The words slithered from her and became something inhuman.

The temperature in the room dropped twenty degrees. The sound of rattlesnakes filled the air along with the rhythmic beating of drums. "*Confesssssion isssss good for the sssssoul, Brent.* You do have a sssoul. And you have a choicccccce. You can keep it. Or you can give it to me. One night…one chance."

"What the *fuck* are you talking about, you fucking bitch? Let me go!! Brent screamed. He pulled at the cords some more, and cried out in pain. He started to sob, hitching his breath and slobbering all over his face and shoulder.

"Darling," the Amara voice was back and all other sound ceased. "PLEASE! Why make this so difficult? Oh you poor thing. You poor baby. Little lamb." She kissed his wrists and slowly the skin knit back together. Then she licked his ankles and they healed as well. "There, now Sugar Plum. Doesn't that feel a little better? You really need to stop making such a fuss. You are going to make yourself sick and then mommy will have to take care of you." This time, the voice belonged to Brent's mother. Immediately Brent was nine years old, lying naked, tethered to his bed, while his mother tended to his needs. He had a fever of 103 and felt like he was on fire. His mother kept sponging him down with cool water, dousing his legs, stomach, forehead, chest and arms with water, all the while telling him to stop making a fuss. The fever lasted two full days, and his mother stayed with him every minute, singing lullabies to him and dousing him with tepid water, as he thrashed about in fevered delusion, until his fever broke. He was soaked, and so was his mattress, to the point where it had to be thrown out. But his mother saved his life.

"Please let me go. I don't want this. I never wanted *this.*" Brent started sobbing.

"What *did* you want, Brent? A quick jab between the sheets? What good would that have been? Wouldn't have changed a thing. And that's what this is about, Brent. *Change.* I need to see you change. I need a commitment…an oath…a pinkie swear…*anything* that will assure change. Because if I don't see it, what's yours will soon be mine."

"What change? What oath? Oh my fucking GOD, what is going on!?" Brent screamed.

"Well yes, you are partially correct. God does have something to do with this. Contrary to popular belief, He can only be in so many places at once, so He sends a group of us down—or up, in this case—to collect what He thinks is justice. You know, it's funny but God and Satan really do like each other and they do agree on a vast majority of things, and in some cases, even agree on the collection method. I know *I* was surprised." Amara laughed softly.

"There are some things, Brent, that are more evil, than evil itself. Did you know that? There are some things that defy forgiveness, that immediately keep a human from being, well, human. For these non-humans, God has made a pact with Satan. They were talking in a bar one night, enumerating the sins of the world, and the one sin they agreed on, the most heinous sin of all, was the one they decided to tackle together—to attempt to eradicate it one person at a time. Satan wanted to wipe it out all at once, but God wanted people to have a chance at redemption, so they chose a group of us." The sound of ruffling feathers unfurling filled the small room and a light breeze filled the air. "Are you familiar with the Six Things That God Hates? Well, that's the censored version; there are actually Seven Things That God Hates, but humans, translating the scrolls for the Bible found the information, either to be so abhorrent or of no consequence that it was omitted. You should have seen God that day. Not a happy camper, I tell you.

If he could curse, he would have, believe me. He was so angry and distraught, we heard him all the way downstairs, and Satan went up to see what was going on. God ranted for a while and Satan suggested they go out for a drink, talk things over, see if maybe another solution could be agreed upon. You know, I think God was grateful for having a sounding board, and for having someone to agree this was important, when it was obvious humanity that did not. From that meeting, *we* were created, both in Heaven and—that *other* place." Amara giggled.

"We are sent here to *help* the unfortunates confess their sins and secrets. And, if they do, in return they get to become human once again. God will take them back, but they must confess, and they must *change.* And we only get one night a year to make this change. I know this is a difficult choice." The sound of wings lightly flapping filled the space. "But really, what choice do you really have, Brent? Stay as you are, slowly devouring piece by piece, until there is nothing left of you upon your death? Are you willing to sacrifice your eternal soul for a few inches of flesh? Remember, this is for eternity. There are no going back-sies."

Brent lay motionless, afraid to breathe. Amara walked over and tore the tape from his eyes. Brent yelped in pain, blinked rapidly, his eyes tearing up. Amara bent over and wiped them with a tissue.

"So…are you ready?" whispered Amara. Her black and white wings were fully spread out and spanned the room from corner to corner. Brent's eyes were wide open, mouth agape, exhaling in staggered breaths. He was frozen in fear, humiliation, and weakness.

Amara's outspread wings *shimmered.* It was like they were vibrating at a higher frequency than could be seen by the human eye. The beauty and grace, the aura of brilliance and peace that surrounded her, was overwhelming to Brent. He wanted to fall on his knees and confess all his evils to the world and sleep in her blessed arms forever.

"I am your once chance Brent. Your one salvation. And time is running out. I have others on my list," Amara said.

Brent gasped. "This cannot be happening. This is not real." He closed his eyes tightly and repeated over and over again, "This is not real…this is not real."

"Brent, this *is* real. And I will not allow you to lose your mind, because that would be too easy. You have to choose. Remember, little lamb, *not* making a choice, is making a choice. Think of all the good you could do with this one act of kindness. All the redemption you could apply to all the souls you have damaged. Doesn't that mean anything to you?"

Brent sobbed openly and whimpered. "I deny you and everything you stand for! Get away from me you devil's spawn. *Get behind me, Satan!*" Brent was wailing, tears streaming down his face. "You are a stumbling block to me. You do not have in mind the concerns of God but only human concerns." He knew he was denying his salvation, but the cowardice in him overtook the common sense. Or was it greed? Did he really think what he did didn't hurt anyone?

"Oh, Brent…you poor, weak, disturbed, hairless little monkey. I really tried with you." Amara looked up at the ceiling. "I did try, you see that, right? I gave you all the prerequisite chances, asked all the right questions. Brent, I don't get a free toaster oven for saving your retched soul. Believe me, it's not worth it. If I had it my way, I'd just as soon throw you in the pit myself and leave you there for all eternity. But I'm the middleman here, I don't have any decision making powers—*yet.* I'm afraid you're appealing to the wrong person. Think of me as a Messenger of Piece," Amara winked. "*Piece* with an *iec* if you catch my drift."

Brent thrashed on the bed; the ropes that bound him were cutting deeply into his wrists and ankles, leaving ragged wounds behind, thick with blood. The smell of copper and feces filled the air, as Brent's bowels let go. He howled at the injustice of it all. All he ever wanted was to be left alone—and to be loved. This was all wrong. This was against his will. Mike was the one who came up with the idea in the first place. All those lonely girls at the bar just looking for a little attention. He could spot them a mile away. Brent didn't really want to go, but Mike made it seem so easy. And Amara was right…they did look at the girly magazines…and found websites and video tapes. Everyone always looked so happy. That's all Brent wanted…happiness for a few, short, sweet, blessed moments. That wasn't wrong, for fuck's sake! Everyone generally got what they wanted in the end. *Everyone.* And why should he be any different? No one got hurt. But this…this was horribly wrong. He wasn't about to admit to anything that was perfectly normal and decent. He paid his bills on time, and his taxes. He looked after his mother until the day she died, and was even kind to the elderly neighbors on his street. He was a *good* person. He showed up to work on time, worked hard every day, and he minded his boss.

"You know what's going on don't you, Brent? Look at me. *Look at me, Brent!*" Amara slapped him across the face, leaving a glowing red swatch across his right cheek. Brent opened his eyes and looked straight into her eyes. Her breasts began to shrink until there was no breast tissue at all. The purple satin bra changed to a t-shirt. Amara started to grow smaller in stature, breath by breath, until she was the size of a twelve year old.

"This is what you like, isn't Brent? Someone smaller and weaker than you. Someone who won't talk back, ask you questions—or make you accountable for your behaviour or actions? Isn't this what you really want?"

Brent was openly sobbing now. "Please leave me alone. Please. I'll go away. You'll never have to see me again. Just please let me go." He was surprised to notice he was getting an erection.

"Let you go? Do you really want me to let you go? It doesn't look like you do." Amara slapped his penis and Brent let out a yelp. "Or would you rather *live,* Brent? That's your choice. More choice than you ever gave any child you molested. Think about it. I let you go, you will die. You stay tied up...and you may live. I can't guarantee it. But it depends on how fast the paramedics can get here to stop the bleeding."

Brent screamed again. "*PLEASE...*I just want to go home!"

Amara took off her panties and slowly positioned herself on top of Brent. "Now if you move this will hurt a great deal more than if you just lay back and relax," Amara laughed. "Isn't that what you usually said to the girls, Brent? Ironic, isn't it?"

He was thrashing back and forth, bucking, trying to throw Amara off of him.

"Ok, I guess you don't want to play nice." Amara sank all the way down on his erection. The barbs on the Rapex condom Amara was wearing clamped down hard at the base of his wildly throbbing penis. Amara quickly jumped off him.

"I had to modify the condom, because it just didn't work to my satisfaction. Be thankful I've perfected the technique. The first guy I tried this on was really left messed up. He still has his penis, but it's a useless, shredded knot of flesh. I think he keeps it in a jar on his desk. Unlike yours, Brent, your penis severed quite nicely, and if they find you in time, you may still get a chance to pee standing up, but it won't be of any other use to you."

Amara walked through the hallway of the empty Gorden Bell Elementary School, wearing a tight jean mini skirt and white halter top. She popped some bubble gum and carried a backpack and strolled around the corner when she ran into the janitor. He was a big man, wearing clean, blue overalls, with the word Mike stenciled over the right hand side of his chest. Amara smiled, and adjusted her skirt and ran her red fingernail across his sewn on name.

"Hi, Mike. I'm Amara. Your friend Brent asked me to look you up if I was ever in Alberta. And here I am."

A Sacrifice for the Soil

Jason Andrew

The lively band of blond, wild-haired children shrieked like delighted banshees as they stomped and trampled through the aisles of the crowded curiosity shop. They halted their rampage to gape over a grimacing shrunken rubber head carefully keeping their distance while daring each other to stick a finger in the thing's mouth. Abram Wakefield coughed politely to stifle the powerful urge to laugh at their harried mother's attempt to wrangle them toward the exit by bribing each of them with a small, ostentatiously branded plastic bag filled with white powder with the dubious name *Authentic Hoodoo Farting Powder.*

He had never imagined yearning for a child of his own. Abram spent most of his life rejecting anything connected to his family. Did he really want to bring a child into this newly forged life? *Strange that watching the children brought him such unexpected bittersweet joy,* he thought.

Abram waited patiently between the framed Technicolor poster featuring the Mummy as played by Boris Karloff and the display wall of refrigerator magnets containing ironic warnings of the prophesied zombie apocalypse. The shop proprietor turned his attention to the mother to haggle over the wares.

Infantilizing monsters for the entertainment of children seemed unwise. At fifteen, he had witnessed the mummification ritual to hardened souls for the journey to Leng used by his mother's branch of the Wakefields as a child and remembered blanching for nights afterwards refusing to close his eyes to sleep.

Zombies were wretched creatures that straddled the line between the living and the dead. The unscrupulous leveraged them for cheap labor or herculean tasks requiring unnatural fortitude. His father had sent him to

Haiti that summer to learn the family business from his Uncle Anton.

The restless dead worked tirelessly throughout the night in the sugar cane fields. It had been his job to feed the zombies their allotment of monkey flesh mixed with the brains of those who displeased the family. *A not-so-subtle reminder from father that the Wakefield wealth required sacrifices.*

The shop proprietor knelt down to the children and whispered a thoughtful, but playful instruction on the safe application of the powder. He spoke to each of them in turn and later bid them a warm farewell as they exited. "Excuse, Mr. Borri? I was hoping I could have a word with you about a private matter."

Borri was a thin, frail man that somehow radiated a calm power of authority that even the children instantly sensed. He wiped the messy mop of chestnut brown hair from his eyes and gestured for Abram to come closer. "Welcome to the Curiosity Shop, Mr. Wakefield." He pointed to a display of colorful illusionist tricks, playfully snatched a large set of metal rings, and presented it to him. "Might I interest you in the Rings of Mystery? Only the most skilled magician can separate them." He skillfully pulled the rings apart and then joined them together once more. "Quite perfect for entraining children of any age."

Abram knew very little about Remington Borri. He was rumored to be the world's great alchemist and one of the oldest residents of Seattle. Few creatures, man or beast, would dare to raise a hand against him. If half of the legends were true, surely Borri could resolve his dilemma without getting gored by the horns of the beast that was the Esoteric Order of Heavenly Delight.

He cautiously stepped closer, holding his hands up to show a deference, not certain if he'd offended Borri. "No, thank you. I'm not here for an illusion, Mr. Borri." He swallowed and wet his lips preparing to say what he had come for. "I need your discretion and your help."

Borri raised a single questioning eyebrow. "I had wondered why a Wakefield would deign to enter my humble shop of curiosities reserved for children and tourists." He sighed and turned his attention toward restocking the shelf. "I don't usually discuss business here in the open. I have an entrance in the Underground for such concerns."

"I'm afraid if I visited the Underground, the family would notice." Abram avoided contact with the family and the Esoteric Order of Heavenly Delight. How did Borri know him by sight? How much did Borri already know about his problem? "A member of my family cursed my wife causing her to turn barren and it's killing us."

Borri shook his head disapprovingly. "I have a non-aggression geis contract with the Wakefields to specifically avoid getting involved with their internal disputes as long as it doesn't involve outsiders. I'm an honorary member of the Esoteric Order of Heavenly Delight."

"You wouldn't be technically breaking your agreement, Mr. Borri," Abram argued. "I left the Order when I reached my majority and refused to accept mystical investments from any of the family patrons. I'm just a contract lawyer."

"You are technically correct that it wouldn't be a violation of the geis," Borri admitted with great reluctance. "However, it would place my interests in the middle of Wakefield politics and that certainly could make my life difficult." He opened the cash register and began to tally receipts. "Thank you for stopping by, Mr. Wakefield."

"Why do you run this store?" Every discussion was a potential sale. The trick to turning a no into a yes was to make the conversation personal. There was something about this frightening immortal deigning to work a cash register that just didn't feel right. "I'm not talking about the real curiosity shop in the Underground, but this place with electric buzzers, fake magic tricks, and tacky rubber heads?"

"Tax purposes, of course. I might have a small measure of power and influence in this world, but I certainly don't want the drudgery of an extended conflict with that dreadful Internal Revenue Service." He smiled as though admitting an uncomfortable secret. "I think it is important to plant the idea of wonder in the minds of children. My last child died in the Great Seattle Fire. I have great, great grandchildren with gray hair that barely know my name."

Abram walked around the curved counter to try to get Borri to look him in the eyes. "Haven't you ever truly loved someone? Imagine that moment when you look into their eyes and know you will do anything to make them happy or shield them from the darkness in the world."

"I've lost nine wives to the predator that is time." Borri wiped his glasses on the sleeve of his shirt. "I'm familiar with the concept."

"Heather, my wife, is a beautiful soul. She doesn't know anything about magic or the dirty politics of my family." Abram blinked, surprised this was working. Merely speaking about the curse choked his words. "I don't even know why they did this."

"It has been noted that your elder brother Kirby is unable to perform with his new wife," Borri revealed. This wasn't exactly shocking or new news to Abram as Kirby had never been interested in women. "It is unlikely he will be able to produce the required heir for the Wakefield seat for the Order—especially given his most recent interactions with the Omega Watch."

Despite the bad blood, Abram still felt worry for his brother. It surprised him that they would keep such a thing from him. How long had it been since they'd spoken? Three years or more? "What happened? Is he alright? Why didn't the family tell me?"

"You have been excommunicated from the Order as you've said. Naturally such things aren't discussed with outsiders," Borri explained. "Kirby attempted to break though the Great Barrier to reach Leng."

Abram shook his head. "Wouldn't that destroy any protection this world has from the Old Ones?"

"Politics tend to confuse the mind of those caught in the moment."

"I have three brothers that can take up the slack," Abram protested. "Why attack my wife?"

"You might have left the Order, Mr. Wakefield, but your blood heirs could one day claim a place of leadership." Borri slipped his glasses back on his face and examined Abram once more. "If you truly wanted to shield your wife from the darkness, you should consider adopting to avoid the issue entirely."

"Mr. Borri, I planned to never have children, certainly not blood heirs as you say. What if the madness of my mother echoed in their eyes? What if my father's bloodlust awakened in them? I always thought it would be safer to avoid such things."

"What caused you to change your mind?"

"My wife." Abram glanced about the shop as though worried an enemy might overhear him. "Heather grew up alone. Her parents died in a car crash. She had no family. Before we married, she was alone in the world. Children were a dream of hers. To know there was someone in the world who shared the same blood. It's killing her to not be able to conceive children with no medical explanation for it."

Borri closed his eyes for a moment and rubbed his temples, as though suddenly overcome by a migraine. "I suppose it couldn't hurt for a consultation. He closed the register, locked the front door, and then gestured toward a set of stairs near the back. "Follow me to my office."

Abram scratched his head imagining an entrance to the Underground would be a hidden passage or at least protected. "That leads to the Underground?"

"There is a Befuddle glamour cast over the area," Borri explained. Only magical creatures and sensitives can see it."

They descended stairs through a concrete hall away from the garish commercial displays into a crowded homespun shop that appeared more like a magician's workshop than a tourist trap. Every spare inch of room was crammed with artifacts of interest and various knickknacks from all over the world, such as enchanted eye-glasses that promised to spot vampires, chattering skulls that whispered secrets of the dead, and watchful stone gargoyles that turned their heads skeptically as Abram passed.

Borri removed his glasses slowly and cleaned them with a white handkerchief. He opened his mouth to say something, then shook his head. Instead, he gestured to a large glass door near the back of the shop. "Please follow me."

Abram followed him into an elaborately decorated office. Borri sat at his oversized oak desk and began searching through a drawer. "Please sit while I gather my files. I may have a number of different options for you and then we can discuss payment. I trust you've tried the Wishing Chair in the Chinese Room?"

"I proposed to Heather while she sat on the Wishing Chair more than a year ago." The Chinese Room was a small room decorated with onyx and marble panels, adorned with hand-carved occidental art at the top of the Smith Tower. The main attraction of the tourist location was the famous Wishing Chair. A dragon and a phoenix were carved together out of a majestic dark wood that brought forth luck and fertility. Legend had it that this special chair could help you conceive if you wished hard enough. "I didn't suspect anything until I realized a year had passed without her telling me she was pregnant."

"Did you speak to Amaterasu?" Borri asked.

Amaterasum the White Lady was a tupla manifested from the legend of the Wishing Chair. Tulpas were sentient creatures often cast and shaped by the imagination of the masses. The Wakefields dealt with a number of tulpas to use their magic for their purposes. "She felt a curse upon Heather and so we went to the Doctor and discovered nothing wrong with her. She's never been sick a day in her life."

"It is a pity that the Prefontane Fountain is still dry." The Blue Lady was one of the two patron tulpas of Seattle and the Prefontane Fountain her place of power. She was known to have a special interest in children. "The Blue Lady remains a prisoner of Cenotaph. Perhaps you could use your family's connections to secure her release to heal your wife?"

"This is why I came to you." The thought of involving either the Esoteric Order of Heavenly Delight or the dark wizard Cenotaph turned his stomach. What further harm would they inflict on Heather? "I came to you in order to avoid that entanglement. Neither my wife nor a child should be bound to my personal obligations to the Order. What sort of life would that be for them?"

Borri found the file he was looking for and placed it between them on his desk. "Unfortunately, I am strictly prohibited from using the method I have personally used to cure this affliction."

How could he tell Heather there was no hope? Abram reached across the desk grabbing onto Borri's shoulders. "Why can't you help us?" He realized the offense and released Borri ruefully. "Sorry…I can't stand the thought of Heather suffering because of me."

Borri scoffed and waved away the offense. "You didn't listen to what I said, Mr. Wakefield. I said I couldn't *personally* cure your wife—not that I couldn't help you."

"How can you help without curing her?

Borri cleaned his glasses once more, half-smiling. "Mr. Wakefield, I've lived over eight hundred years as a man and immortal. There is little that happens in this world and others that I've not yet seen. You've wisely placed your trust in me. Above all else, I'm a professional."

"You want something for this help I presume?" Abram asked.

Borri nodded. "Payment is required, as it should be. The city government has denied certain permits for the Bread of Life Mission downtown near Pioneer Square. They need a lawyer to address this issue."

"This is something for the Order, is it?" Abram asked suspiciously. "If I am going to live free, I can't be bound to them."

"Actually, I suspect this deed would be against the Order's overall interests in Seattle," Borri admitted with a rueful smile. "Mr. Bang has personally requested I ensure the mission remains open."

Mr. Bang was the other patron tulpa of Seattle. Some whispered he was the modern incarnation of Death. Why would he want a mission to remain open? "I can make an attempt, of course. But I can't promise to succeed."

"If you accept the job, you should note that Mr. Bang isn't known for his mercy."

He was willing to take the hit for Heather. If things didn't work out, Heather could always find another husband and perhaps the Order would remove the curse. "Fine."

Borri slid over the folder. "You should find everything you need in there."

Abram glanced over the map and the detailed notes. The magical principals were sound, but he found the idea of it somewhat disturbing. Heather was worth it. "You knew I would come to you, didn't you?"

Borri shrugged. "I am a professional."

Abram Wakefield circled the brick water tower around the concrete wading pool, near the almost empty reservoir, before he finally checked Borri's map for an entrance to the legendary tunnels. He paused at the bronze statue of a misshapen donut and stared across the bluff at the glittering lights of Seattle and the black expanse of the Puget Sound. The famous saucer of the Space Needle illuminated the night.

Once he orientated himself, Abram followed the concrete path toward the glass conservatory where scientists and students tended to unusual specimens of plant life from around the world in five distinct environments. Each step forward crunched the brittle yellow and orange leaves underfoot signaling the arrival of autumn. It was cool enough that his face felt refreshed, but warm enough that he sweated under his leather jacket.

He checked his watch. There were a lot of cars in the parking lot considering that Volunteer Park had closed thirty minutes earlier. What if someone saw him? What if he saw someone he knew? His hands shook. Why should this frighten him so?

He'd heard rumors of a local gay cruise spot hidden in the wild places between the trees, but he hadn't imagined they would be so close to the rest of the park. Heather's favorite picnic bench was positioned just at the edge of the tree line, where she could see the blue waters of the Puget Sound on a clear day.

The so-called tunnels weren't actually underground, but open spaces between overgrown patches of trees and shrubbery protected from the weather by a large brush canopy. He stepped between a cluster of trees that grew close together and formed the outline of a bowl. *I must be getting close,* Abram thought, *that looks like a womb!*

His heart raced as he stepped between the trees and pushed forward through the brush. The snap of a twig seemed to echo loudly like a cannon. An older man with grey hair and a slight paunch passed Abram with a knowing smile as he straightened his tie. Abram blinked and then pressed forward into the tunnel surprised by the sense of motion around him.

He turned toward the trees and brush near the abandoned tennis court, then climbed up a trail that seemed to lead to a strange dip in the land. Abram pulled on the ivy growing along the trees to keep his footing until he managed to duck completely into the green.

The earthy smell of the wet soil mixed with salty sweat and heat from naked flesh nearly overwhelmed him. Thin streams of light from distant street lamps and buildings shone through the leaf canopy. Pockets of illumination crisscrossed like spotlights from hand-held phones and flashlights. Abram felt the power of this place.

Masculine forms shrouded by shadows touched themselves and each other in the sacred grove with wild abandon. Abram measured their pleasure by their moans, grunts, and screams of delight and ecstasy. As he stepped closer, the mist dissipated and shadows revealed themselves as flesh. They groped and kissed in the darkness, soaking in that blessed touch from another stranger in need.

Mystical tantric energy flowed through the soil and the greenery, causing a tingling sensation in his flesh. Could he possibly collect what he needed without actively participating? Would the components he gathered from the aftermath keep the same potency? Borri's notes indicated that the power was in the ritual and sharing the experience. Decade after decade, men seeking secret pleasures gathered on this exact spot to sacrifice their seed and lust to nature and the universe. Borri had explained that such a place had stored power that could be leveraged if used properly. This was a place Abram could tap into in order to beg for help to power the ritual to cure Heather. He had the training and the will, but not the fortitude to resist the curse. Abram needed to power the curse through an invocation to a higher power that might take pity upon his plight.

This grove was sacred to the Green Man. Some cities had patron tulpa—small gods that protected them and adapted to the needs and fears of the dreamers. The Green Man had been worshipped ages before there were roads or wheels. He was part of the eldest instinct of man to love and live. The ritual depended upon calling on this tulpa. He had many names and faces. *Jack in the Green. The Horned One. The Stag.* Abram needed to gain his favor.

Abram never really thought much about touching another man sexually. His brother Kirby indulged in such pleasures, although it was never discussed except as his private vice.

Abram stepped into the sacred grove. There were a dozen men in various stages of undress with their pants open stroking themselves. Would they find him attractive? He worried about getting hard, but surprising that wasn't difficult. They accepted him into the circle as a brother in lust and worship. At first, he imagined Heather naked and ready for him and then every other woman he had ever kissed. Abram found himself lost in the moment of the warm flesh surrounding him, until he realized everything in one final scream.

Dawn's light poked through the brush canopy by the time Abram stood at the sacred grove alone. He knelt down to the wet soil and collected a sizable sample in a plastic bag. Borri's notes indicated the soil was infused with the essence of those who'd pleased the Green Man. A rustle of leaves alerted Abram to the presence of another. He turned toward the trees, but saw nothing. "Is someone there? I don't want to hurt anyone, but I don't want to be hurt either," Abram said.

A smiling face emerged from the brush with green eyes, a wide smile, and a beard made of leaves. He nodded approvingly and then laughed. Abram felt the power of his voice. This was the legendary Green Man in the flesh. "It is good to love your wife. You will have a child and the sacrifice required."

Abram Wakefield paced the sterile room. He couldn't look at the doctor or the ultrasound machine that flashed an image of his child. Heather sniffed. Her big beautiful blue eyes welled with tears. Her blond hair seemed to droop with helplessness. He remembered the day he first saw Heather. She'd reminded him of a painting of a Gibson Girl with her rosy cheeks.

"The bleeding may have been caused by a placental abruption," the doctor said. "It is exceptionally dangerous for both the mother and the fetus." He continued to explain in calm rational terms the circumstances. The chances of the fetus surviving were low. "There are a number of options we can take from this point to increase the chances for the fetus and protect the mother."

Abram listened to the doctor speak in cold facts and statistics about the chances of Heather's survival. Why would the Green Man bless the pregnancy and then allow it to die stillborn or possibly kill his wife?

He recalled that early morning months ago and remembered what the Green Man had warned. *The soil required a sacrifice.* Abram listened intently to the doctor, then escorted Heather back to their condo. He brought her dinner and later that night rubbed her feet until she slept uneasily.

Once he was certain she would sleep the night, Abram dressed and then opened the trunk in his closet. It contained the one artifact he'd kept from his days in the Esoteric Order of Heavenly Delight. The Dagger of Azathoth. It was a wicked blade forged with dark magic from a black meteorite containing metal from a world of terror and torment.

A Wakefield learned from an early age how to make a proper sacrifice for his family.

Wind whistled shrilly through the leaf canopy. Rain drizzled through the limited protection soaking the grass creating a field of muck. Abram Wakefield waited impatiently at the sacred grove soaked and shivering.

He knelt down once more to the wet soil and cried for the Green Man. "Please hear me! I understand now, I promise! I'll do it…whatever is required to save my wife and child. I know how to sacrifice someone." He held the Dagger of Azartoth in his hand. "The next man that comes here will be for you. Please, let my child live."

Motion rustled the brush and leaves. Abram stood grimly. The inclement weather seemed to have prevented most of the regulars from coming to the grove, but now finally someone was approaching. He hid the dagger under his coat and waited.

Remington Borri stepped from the bushes as though this was merely another section of his curiosity shop. He wore a white shirt and an old fashioned vest. He smirked and wiped his glasses with a handkerchief. "Heather is worried about you, Abram."

"Did you come here for revenge against my family?" Abram asked.

"Indeed, but perhaps not how you expect."

"You knew the baby would get sick!" Abram accused.

"All babies get sick." Borri frowned, annoyed at the rain and the wind. "That is the way of the world."

Abram drew forth the dagger. He didn't know if he could kill Borri, but if doing so could save his family, he would make the attempt. "They could *both* die..."

"That's the risk of life," Borri conceded.

"You cheated me!" Abram accused. "I did what you wanted. I saved that mission! They'll never have trouble with the IRS again."

"You did your job well, Mr. Wakefield." Borri stepped closer, holding his hands up in front of him, indicating complete surrender. "That's the reason I'm interfering."

"I'll do whatever's required to save my child."

"Indeed—as any father would. I'm not certain that blade would actually kill me, but I know it would be agonizing. Please don't stab me. That would be rude since I'm here to help." Borri waited until Abram lowered the dagger and then continued. "I'm here to explain the choice available to you, Mr. Wakefield. You did your job, I can do no less."

Abram shook his head. "You won't stop me. Jack said he needed a sacrifice. Blood for blood. I know how this works. I learned it at my father's knee."

"That is indeed a mighty and proper sacrifice for a Wakefield—and it would work. But I'm hoping you are more than that." Borri coughed and then cleaned his glasses again. "You would never be able to look your son in the eyes. Certainly you can kill me, if that's what you choose. I won't even try to stop you."

"What else can I do?" Abram asked. "Let them die?"

"You don't understand the Green Man. He cares not for blood alone. He cares for *life.* If you want his patronage, then you must sacrifice what matters. Your life. Your wealth. Give up the easy life. Live better."

"And that will save them?"

"You'll have to buy their life each day."

"*How?*"

Borri smiled. "You did the impossible for the Mission. Do the same for the land. Protect this place and others like it. Use the tools you have."

"How does being a contract lawyer help my child and my wife?" Abram asked.

"Become Jack's contract lawyer. Fight for the environment. Keep the sacred groves such as this safe. A life for a life."

"Will that work?"

Jack's face appeared in the trees around them once more. "A sacrifice is required."

Borri stepped closer to Abram and gestured to the Green Man in the canopy of trees.

"Trust me, I'm a professional," he said. "Now, allow me to introduce you to your new employer."

House of Nettle and Thorn

Todd Keisling

"Are you sure this is such a great idea?" Jim Auster peered up at the old Victorian at the end of the street. "This doesn't even look like a sorority house."

Nick parked the car along the curb and checked the GPS. "This is it, bro. 220 Stine Way. Just like Krystal said."

They were a few miles from campus, tucked away in folds of suburbia that Jim didn't recognize. While the house itself didn't give him the creeps, the empty neighborhood certainly did. Streetlights were on, illuminating the cul-de-sac that, at the moment, was devoid of human presence, other than their own. The other houses sat lifeless and mute, their lights extinguished at such an early hour, yards teeming with overgrowth. Jim checked his watch and saw the time was barely eight o'clock. Frowning, he turned back to the sorority house.

"What time did she say the party starts?" Jim asked.

"Sunset," Nick said, trying to downplay his excitement—but Jim knew better. He'd only lived with Nick for a couple of months, and he already knew how to read the guy. Not that there was much there to read. In the little time they'd been together, Jim was privy to all sorts of stories about Nick's sexual prowess, recalling his high school conquests and legion of online girlfriends. *The internet is an untapped resource,* Nick had once told him. *There are chicks everywhere looking to get laid! Social media just makes it that much easier, bro!*

Some men, Jim decided, were meant to do great things—cure diseases, walk on celestial bodies—but Nick Edgleman's contribution to the great human identity would equal to nothing more than a crusted stain on a pair of boxer shorts and overuse of Axe body spray.

"I owe you for this," Jim said, coiling his fingers around the car door handle. He sighed. "I was supposed to study with Megan tonight."

They climbed out of the car and stood on the sidewalk. Nick put his hand on Jim's shoulder and gave it a tight squeeze. "Forget about Megan. It's her loss. Just relax, bro. Be my wingman tonight, and I'll introduce you to some of the ladies in my history class. They put Megan to shame."

"Thanks," Jim said, recalling his roommate's complaints about the "lack of quality vagina" in History 101. "You're a real *bro.*"

Walking the length of the moss-covered wall that separated the sorority grounds from the sidewalk, Nick was too caught up in the moment to catch Jim's sarcasm. Jim followed his roommate to the large wrought iron gate in front of the house. He paused when he saw the symbol emblazoned between the black iron bars.

"What sorority is this again?"

Nick scratched his head, staring up at the darkened house. "I don't remember. Sigma-something."

Jim traced his fingers over the symbol. "These letters don't look Greek… they look like *flowers.*" They *were* flowers. Three of them. Blossoms each supported by an odd jumble of vines. Entangled in the center of that sinewy mass was the figure of a man on all fours. It was all Jim could do to not laugh at the image.

A cool October breeze rustled the trees around the house, limbs scraping against the old Victorian's gray siding, startling him away from the effigy on the wall. The tree limbs produced a scratching noise akin to nails raking down a chalkboard. A slow chill crawled up Jim's spine as he peered up at the home of Sigma-something sorority.

Nick's phone chirped. He reached into his pocket and thumbed across the screen.

"It's her," he said, grinning.

"What'd she say?"

"'*Where r u? Party is dope!*'"

Jim looked up at the second floor windows, listening for signs of life. All he could hear were the continued scraping of tree limbs and the crackle of brittle leaves being dragged across the empty suburban street by the breeze. Sitting in his dorm, pining over the one that got away, was beginning to look more and more appealing.

"Some party," Jim mumbled. He looked back at Nick. "Listen, I'm starting to get a bad feeling about this. No one else knows we're here, and this girl from the internet...she could be anybody."

Nick rolled his eyes. "Put your tampon back in and relax! I've done this before. Besides, would you turn down tits like that?" He held out his phone, revealing a photograph of a pasty-pale woman from the neck down, her naked breasts like cantaloupes on the screen.

Jim felt a twinge of envious need stir in his groin. "No," he said, his eyes lingering for a little too long on the photo. "No...I don't think I would."

Smug, Nick lowered the phone and began to type out a reply. "That's what I thought. Looks like there's hope for you yet, bro."

Jim forced a smile, but deep inside he was raging against a well-known fact of life: *Hot girls always fell for the douchebags.* The sting of Megan's rejection was still fresh, and her choice to date one of Nick's fraternity brothers had been a shotgun blast to his pride, even though she said she still wanted to be friends. *Of course she did...* He was well acquainted with the dreaded friend-zone. He'd spent a week wondering what he could've done differently, gorging himself on a diet of fried comfort food, while wallowing shamelessly in self-pity. *What must it be like to be on the other side of the fence?* He wondered. *To actually be* wanted *by the opposite sex, instead of merely tolerated.*

Nick's suggestion that he stop sulking and get out of the dorm for a while had seemed like a good idea at the time. After seeing the bare breasts of Nick's once and future conquest, Jim wondered why a girl like that would be cruising the university's social network looking for guys. But, then again, who was he to question it? Maybe she saw something in Nick's profile photo she liked—with his face painted blue and white to match the university's colors, while wearing three polo shirts with the collars flipped up, flashing a cocky sideways grin at the camera. Or maybe it was his listing of "Hot Bitches" as an interest on his profile that had led this Krystal person to send him a private message in the first place. Hell, perhaps she even saw a hint of intellect in those narrowed eyes and arched eyebrows.

Or maybe she was just a desperate nympho, Jim mused.

In any event, Nick was one lucky son of a bitch.

"All right, I texted her back and asked if we have the right address—"

The porch light switched on, blanketing the yard in a warm, golden glow as the front door creaked open.

A figure appeared at the threshold. "Nick?"

He climbed the porch steps in two strides. Jim followed cautiously, running his hands along the porch banister as he ascended. An old, dry vine had wrapped its way along the length of the railing, its surface leathery, almost prickly to the touch.

"Are you Krystal?"

Jim rolled his eyes. Of course she was, her profile said as much. He paused behind his roommate, taking in the sights while they introduced themselves. She was taller than he expected, but evenly proportioned. Her emerald green dress clung to her body in all the right places. Her hair was pulled up in a cascade of curls, accented with a trio of purple flowers tucked behind her ear. Jim was immediately drawn to her cleavage—not because of the ample real estate, but because of the glimmer of light reflecting off the amulet wedged in the canyon between her boobs.

"I'm so happy you could make it!"

Krystal stepped forward and wrapped her arms around Nick. She kissed his cheek, whispered something in his ear, and emitted a soft, coquettish giggle. Then her eyes met Jim's, and her playful demeanor vanished.

"Who's this?"

Grinning, Nick turned back and put his hand on Jim's shoulder. "This is my buddy, Jim. His girlfriend just broke up with him and he's feeling a little lonely." That was a lie, of course. He and Megan hadn't actually gone that far in their relationship. In fact, *relationship* was a loose term in this sense. Jim's cheeks flushed. "Thought maybe we'd introduce him to some of your friends."

He shot Jim a wink, but his roommate didn't catch it. Jim was too focused on the caricature of the girl standing before him—not quite entranced by her beauty, but by the *façade* of her beauty. He squinted, trying to determine if her face was real or just a mask. No doubt Krystal was gorgeous, borderline perfect in the eyes of a horny nineteen-year-old, but something about the way she was staring at him, and the way she recoiled when she saw him, made him uneasy. There was a flicker in her eyes, a glint of hatred he hadn't accounted for, and certainly didn't understand. Within a moment of meeting this girl from the internet, Jim wanted nothing more than to turn on his heels and run away like a scared child.

"So whaddya say, babe? Can my bro join the party?"

Krystal flashed a liar's smile from ear to ear, giving Jim the once-over. The flicker in her eyes was there for just a moment longer before it vanished. "Of course," she said. "I'm sure we can find someone to keep him company while we party."

"Listen, I don't want to impose," Jim said. He could take a hint; it was clear he wasn't welcome here. And he didn't want to be here anyway. Not now. He looked at Nick and shrugged. "Give me your keys. Text me when you're done, and I'll come pick you up."

"No way, bro." He looked back at Krystal, who was tangling her fingers in the amulet's silver chain. "She said it's no problem. Right, babe?"

Krystal flashed that smile of hers again, looking down Jim. The heat on his face intensified as a cold snake of apprehension coiled itself around the length of his spine. The phantom serpent tightened, hardening his guts to stone. He wanted to protest again but the words just weren't there.

"No..." Krystal said, "It's not a problem." She gave Jim another once-over before taking Nick by the hand. "Come on in. Let's party."

The foyer gave way to a large sitting room on the left, replete with candelabras on the end tables, a staircase to their right, and a hallway straight ahead. Jim had never set foot in the sorority houses on campus, but he'd been in his share of fraternities and they were all one safety inspection away from being condemned. He expected sororities to be tidy, but not *this* tidy. This house was immaculate, and far more elegant than he'd expected. Even for a sorority that operated off campus.

A gold chandelier hung above the foyer. Glass sconces adorned with red roses lined the soft green walls, leading a path of light down a hallway beside the staircase like a proverbial golden trail of crumbs. A purple velvet curtain separated the foyer from the hallway, muffling the vibrant tones of classical music that was coming from somewhere in the house, the notes flitting through the air like butterflies. The room was thick with a ripe, sweet smell Jim couldn't quite place.

"Wow," Nick said, craning his neck up to the chandelier, "Nice digs."

"Thank you," Krystal said, "it's been in our mother's family since the last reconciliation, a reward for a bountiful harvest."

Last reconciliation? Bountiful harvest? Jim wondered what the hell she was talking about. He let Krystal and Nick walk a few steps ahead of him as he edged closer to the door. Krystal excused herself for a moment, promising to return after she told her sisters about the arrival of her *boyfriend.* Once she'd disappeared behind the velvet curtain, Nick turned to him with his hand held up in the air, grinning like an idiot. Jim stared at him, frowning.

"Oh come on, bro, don't leave me hanging."

"I don't think I should be here," Jim whispered. "Did you see the way she looked at me? And what's this shit about reconciliations and harvests?"

Nick reached out and pushed Jim back against the door. "I came here to have a good time and that's what I'm gonna do. Go ahead and be a little whiny bitch for all I care, but don't fuck this up for me! Maybe getting laid would do you some good, bro. That way you'd stop being so uptight and get over that bitch who dumped you."

Jim clenched his teeth. He pushed Nick back and held out his hand. "Leave Megan out of this," he growled. "And I'll stay out of your business… but only if you give me your keys."

"You're not drinking?"

"No. And if you know what's good for you, you won't either."

"What, you think I'm gonna get roofied?"

Footsteps echoed down the hall. Nick dropped his keys into Jim's hand and playfully slapped his cheek. "You can't rape the willing, bro."

Krystal emerged from the hallway and held out a plastic cup. "Follow me. I'll introduce you to my sisters."

Nick took the cup and followed, looking over his shoulder to mouth the word "sisters" to Jim. The hallway stretched the entire length of the house, and the deeper they went, the more Jim felt like an outsider. Was it the way Krystal glared at him? Was it the house? A strangely familiar scent filled the air, and he was about to say something when he saw the grin on Nick's face. *Just stop it,* he told himself. *Try to have a good time.*

"There's the kitchen," Krystal said, pointing to their right.

Jim stuck his head into the room, and observed a pair of women standing around the island in front of the sink. A dark green liquid rippled in a punch bowl. The women, both brunettes, thin and pale and dressed in snug emerald gowns, offered Nick the same rehearsed smile as Krystal, before zoning in on Jim's presence. The first brunette ladled some of the green punch into a plastic cup and offered it to Jim, without as much as a smile. "Drink? It's rich. Loosens the soil. Good for the roots."

"Maybe later," Jim said, shrinking back into the hall with Nick and Krystal.

"And here is the study," Krystal continued.

Jim turned to the room opposite the kitchen and stuck his head in the doorway. Other guys, some of them barely college age from the awkward look of them, were paired off with Krystal's sorority sisters, drinks in hand, laughing and chatting. Two sofas lining the opposite walls were occupied with couples, their limbs entwined, heads pressed together, kissing.

"This looks like my kind of place!" Nick said, peering in.

Nick turned to Krystal and grinned as he lowered his hand to the small of her back. She ran her fingers through Nick's hair and leaned forward to whisper something in his ear. When she was finished, she flicked her tongue lightly against his earlobe.

"Is this my date?" A new, kinder voice lilted from across the room as they entered the study. A thin girl with raven black hair seemingly floated across the room, her green dress whispering against the wooden floor. She wore a smirk on her face and a purple flower tucked in her hair, and within moments of taking her in, Jim forgot all about Megan and studying. The girl was beautiful.

"Jim," Krystal said, "this is Gemini."

Gemini, he thought. *Hippie parents. Must be a flower child.*

He stuck out his hand to shake hers, but she twisted her way into his arms before he could react. She caressed the back of his head, cradling him for a kiss. Her lips were wet and warm, and her tongue slipped into his mouth for just an instant—so quick, in fact, that he later wondered if it'd actually happened. The girl's skin was petal soft and smelled of honeysuckle and summertime, but her tongue left a taste in his mouth that was almost metallic, gritty. He was struck with a brief sense of euphoria, and his head felt ten pounds heavier.

Gemini pulled away from him and smiled. "Nice to meet ya,

handsome."

"Uh, hi." He realized his hand was wrapped around her waist, her hip pressed up against his stomach, and the sudden heat between his legs could only mean one thing. He dry-swallowed, waiting for the embarrassment to set in, but if Gemini felt his erection, she made no sign. This mysterious girl had managed to fill his mind with her own form of light, and for a while, his thoughts of Megan were reduced to fading shadows, vanquished to forgotten corners of his memory.

"Sweet." Nick raised his hand again. "You gonna leave me hanging again, bro?"

Stunned, his mind lost among a series of dark waves lapping against the inside of his skull, Jim didn't leave his roommate hanging this time.

"Maybe you'll have something in common," Krystal remarked, before tugging on Nick's arm. "Come with me. I want to show you something."

"I'll see you later, bro," Nick said.

Jim watched them leave the room and disappear into the dim hallway. He turned back to Gemini. "So," he said, "did you grow up around here?"

The girl ran her fingers through the back of his hair, sending chills all the way down to his groin. "You could say that," she said. "Most of us grew up here. But some of us are transplants. And some of us are hybrids."

The orchestral music swelled from the stereo speakers at the far end of the room, and the couples on the sofa gradually became more intimate as the tunes rose to a crescendo. One of the girls pulled away from her date—his eyes were narrow slits, one corner of his lips turned up in a half-cocked grin, his cheeks flushed—and kept eye contact as she lowered herself to the floor and slid her hands down the front of his pants.

Jim watched in awe. *Holy shit. Is this really happening?*

"Let's give them some privacy," Gemini whispered. "Want to see the rest of the house?"

He didn't have a chance to respond before she took him by the hand and pulled him from the study. She led him through the house, wandering from room to room, seemingly at ease, and at other times incredibly giddy as she gave him the tour.

Jim didn't care. His head was reeling from all he'd seen so far. These girls were unlike the others he'd dated, and that fact simultaneously terrified and excited him. Red flags of alarm still flew up in the back of his mind, but the more he listened to Gemini's voice, the less he focused on them. He thought she was beautiful and the most real girl he'd seen all evening, light years beyond the likes of Megan Whitfield. Gemini's syllables seeped into his bloodstream and brain like a fine gin, and by the time they reached the sitting room, he was drunk on her words, captivated by every breath.

"—And this is our wonderful mother, Iris."

He followed her gaze to the portrait over the fireplace. The painting depicted a large, blossoming flower, its purple petals interwoven with a series of prickly needles protruding from within, while a number of vines faded into the earth.

Jim stepped closer, inspecting the painting's finer details. Several dark hands were buried in the earth with the vines, their fingers crooked as claws, trying to pull themselves free of the soil. Small, grayish tendrils were threaded between the fingers, pulling them back down into the earth.

He remembered the insignia on the gate and turned back to his date. Gemini smiled, proud of the portrait, and although Jim found her warmth disarming, he also found her ease with the macabre scene unsettling.

"So...Nick mentioned you're part of a sorority, but he couldn't remember the name. What Greek organization is this?"

"We are the House of Nettle and Thorn. True daughters of Demeter."

Jim paused for a moment, waiting for her expression to crack and reveal the big joke, but her smile never faltered, her eyes never narrowing to betray a con. "Right," he said, forcing a smile. "That sounds like a great organization."

"It truly is," Gemini went on. "Our seeds are scattered across the world, but here our roots run deepest. They have since the last reconciliation, and will continue to until the next."

Jim kept smiling while idly checking his watch, wondering where the hell Nick had run off to. *You know where he went,* Jim scolded himself. *He's probably upstairs somewhere, suffocating himself between Krystal's enormous tits.*

Gemini laced her fingers with Jim's. "Would you like to see our garden? It's in the back yard." She looked up at him with dark violet eyes and a smile that made his stomach flutter. If she was crazy, crazy never looked so beautiful...or smelled like the sweetest of flowers.

Flowers. Yes, that's what he couldn't place earlier in the hallway. The floral smell of the house reminded him of a greenhouse—or funeral home.

That familiar cold serpent from earlier coiled tighter around his gut, but his senses were dulled and his mind clouded by the experience he was having. This mysterious girl both excited and unnerved him. Finally, after chasing Megan for more than half a semester, he'd found a girl who was willing to show him the attention he craved and deserved—a girl who wanted *him* for a change. Forgetting about Megan and the uncertainty tightening in his chest, Jim gave himself over to this beautiful girl, permitting himself to be led by the hand down the hallway, through the kitchen, and out the back door.

The cold air took his breath away. He hadn't realized how warm it had been inside the house. Gemini let go of his hand and floated down the back steps that led onto the patio. At the edge of it was a large flowerbed that stretched on for the entire length of the backyard. Jim knew little of horticulture, but he could spot a rose anywhere—and she was dancing among the flora, her body moving in time with the muffled tunes coming from inside.

He took a seat on the steps, watching her odd dance, wondering if this night could get any stranger. But he didn't have to wonder for long. He was staring up at the stars when she stopped moving and stood directly in front of him. When he looked at her, he was startled to find an odd flickering in her eyes. No matter how hard he tried, he simply couldn't look away.

"Do you like me, Jim?" Her lips parted into an innocent smile as their eyes met. She walked over to the edge of the flower bed, lifted her dress, and stepped out of her slippers. She curled her toes in the dark earth.

Confused, eager, frightened, intrigued—these were but a taste of emotions filling his mind, setting his heart on a race to escape its chamber while his blood migrated south. He'd had so many false starts with Megan, so many promising nights that ended in disappointment and masturbation, that when the opportunity finally presented itself, he found he didn't quite know how to react.

"Yes," he whispered, his mouth suddenly dry, the tip of his tongue aching to taste her skin.

"I like you," she said, kneeling before him, her eyes never leaving his while her hands worked independently, first unclasping his belt, then unzipping his jeans. She held his gaze a moment longer, her mouth turned upward in a playful smirk, her lips full and glistening. "I *want* you."

Gemini took hold of him and he almost came right there. He bit his lip to hold back the wave, groaning as his swelling length throbbed in the warmth her hand. The last thing he saw before losing himself in a blizzard of mental static was the clarity of her gaze and the shimmer of violet in her eyes.

She closed her mouth around him, lapping her tongue against the underside of his shaft before taking him deeper into her throat. Jim felt the pleasure of her full lips for only a moment before the pain shot through him like a bullet—white hot and searing—every nerve standing at full attention, screeching in agony. Needles. Thousands of tiny, hot needles jabbed into his sensitive flesh. Gemini moaned softly as he struggled to push her away, mistaking his discomfort for pleasure. The more he resisted her, the deeper she sucked him into her throat. *She's going to swallow me alive,* he thought frantically, and for as irrational a thought as it was, Jim truly feared she might actually engulf him, starting with his most prized appendage.

Tears filled his eyes as he writhed in agony, squirming to free himself from the vice of her mouth. In a moment of desperation, he did the only thing he could think to do. He gripped a handful of her hair and yanked as hard as he could.

She moaned once more, tightening her grip, sending a new wave of blinding pain up to his gut. The pressure spread through his groin and down his thighs. Splotches of color danced before his eyes, and a single calm thought occurred to him as the darkness came to claim him. *She's going to suck me dry.*

The absurdity of it is what saved him. He blinked away the tears, closed his fingers around the flower in her hair, and tugged. Gemini cried out in pain, shooting backward in surprise, releasing his bloody member to the night air.

Jim rolled onto his side, his hands drawn instinctively to his crotch, curled up as if that might hold back the burning, throbbing—and blood.

"Why would you do that?" she cried, grasping the flower in her hair. He looked at her through a blur of tears. The purple blossom hung limp to one side. He'd cracked the stem in two.

"Why would you do *this?*" he growled, lifting one leg to examine his wound. He was now flaccid. Dark beads of scarlet oozed from a thousand pin-pricks, and the flesh of his cock was pruning.

Gemini climbed to her feet, and when he looked up at her, his blood went cold. Pale green veins had surfaced beneath her forehead and cheeks, accented by two thin streams of green tears oozing from her tear ducts. She held her head, nursing the flower as if it were still attached.

Oh God.

The painting over the fireplace flashed before him, sending his heart into the pit of his stomach, where it continued its frantic hammering. The green drinks—*good for the roots*—the floral smell, even the gritty metallic taste of Gemini's tongue that he now realized must've been dirt. The pieces were all there, jabbing into his brain, completing a grotesque portrait of horror that made his heart plummet.

Jim met her stare. "What the fuck *are* you?"

Gemini's face screwed up as she began to sob. She looked away, tears falling onto the rich earth. Small vines snaked out of the soil and blossomed around the droplets, drinking in her sorrow. She turned back to the stalks of foliage in the garden with her face buried in her hands, her cries echoing into the night to the rise and fall of the muffled orchestra still bellowing from inside the house.

Jim wanted to feel bad for her, but the sharp, prickling pain at his groin told him he shouldn't.

"Y-You didn't have to hurt me," she stammered. "We could be part of something greater, forever. You could join our harvest, be part of our next reconciliation." She turned back to him as a clump of green vines rose from the earth and curled around her legs and up around her waist, blossoming into a full bloom of deep purple flowers.

Jim scrambled to pull up his pants and fasten his belt.

"Where are you going?" she asked.

Jim wanted to respond, but his words failed him. His mind raced with more urgent matters. He hoped his wounds were superficial, but even that wouldn't rule out a hospital visit, never mind how the hell he was going to explain this to a doctor. As soon as he found Nick, they were getting the hell out of there. His stomach lurched. Where the hell *was* Nick?

"Please don't leave me..." Gemini cried, but Jim didn't listen. He scrambled back across the patio and up the stairs, leaving his date rooted in the garden.

"We haven't seen him," the brunette with violet eyes said, offering him a plastic cup full of green liquid. "Have a drink."

Jim waved the girl away with a grimace. "He was just here half an hour ago. With your friend, Krystal."

"Oh..." Violet Eyes gave him a vacant look before downing her own cup of the green punch. "Maybe he left."

He reached into his pocket for Nick's keys. They jangled against his fingers. "No," Jim said, "he didn't leave. He's still here."

Violet Eyes shrugged. "I don't know what to tell you."

No, he thought, *I suppose you don't.*

"I like you," Violet Eyes said. Her cheeks darkened, looking up at him with a mischievous smile. Jim glimpsed faint green lines sprouting out from her eyes. He offered her a weak smile in return as he edged his way out of the room, wincing with every step, the prickling, burning pain of his wounded groin still shooting through him. *First Nick,* he thought, *then the hospital.*

Jim avoided the study, wandering instead down the hall toward the staircase.

"Nick?" His voice echoed in the empty foyer. A grandfather clock ticked idly from the sitting room. Jim stood at the bottom step and called up into the dark. "Nick? Hello?"

Silence. He waited, listening, and when Nick didn't respond, he turned for the door.

A low abrasive hum gave him a start, the hairs on his neck to standing at attention.

"What the hell?"

The hum fell silent for a moment, then started up again. Jim stepped away from the staircase and toward the hallway. A cabinet sat in the corner recess where the hall met the foyer, its surface adorned with a number of trinkets including a collection of shiny silver baubles. As he drew near to the source of the hum, he realized it wasn't a hum at all, but a rough vibration. Something was vibrating in short bursts.

He pulled open the cabinet drawer.

There were at least a dozen phones in the drawer of varying sizes and ages, the oldest of which was a huge Motorola the size of a brick. There were others, including several iPhones, some scuffed, some engraved, and some with rubber cases. One case in particular caught his eye. It was a blue and white case with N.E. imprinted on the back.

That cold, uneasy feeling rose up again in his gut, forcing the pain of his groin out of his mind for a few precious seconds as he held Nick's cell phone in his hand reassuringly.

"You wouldn't leave without this," Jim whispered. He turned on the phone and read the display. Two missed calls, one of which was from less than a minute ago.

Jim chewed his lip and tried to ignore the pounding in his chest as he thumbed through the menus. In some ways he felt ashamed to be invading his friend's privacy, but the situation necessitated drastic action. He opened the social media app and navigated to his roommate's direct messages, scrolling through a number of conversations until he found what he was looking for. *Krystal Demeter.*

He scrolled past a number of nude images she'd sent Nick, as well as several perverse messages, until he reached the end of their chat history, and the beginning of their conversation. Krystal had been the one to initiate contact with Nick, casting her line across that great expanse of the internet in hopes that someone would bite.

Hey I saw u at school and I think ur cute. Want 2 B Friends?

Jim sighed, frowning at his roommate's stupidity. The conversation went downhill from there, none of it providing insight into his friend's current whereabouts. In the end, all Jim had was his roommate's cell phone and car keys, but not *him*. Defeated, Jim slipped the phone into his pocket and turned to leave—but something else in the drawer caught his attention.

Most of the phones were dead, their batteries lifeless and corroded, but there was one that flickered to life. There were twelve missed calls and thirty-two unopened text messages.

Jim wasn't sure what led him to open the phone's social app. Curiosity, maybe, or the evening's bizarre turn of events, lending credence to all the personal alarms firing inside his mind—or perhaps it was almost having his penis ripped off by a mutant plant-girl. Either way, when Jim flipped through the phone's private messages, his blood stopped cold in his veins.

Hey I saw u at school and I think ur cute. Want 2 B Friends?

No, he thought. *Please no.*

He thumbed down through the messages, pausing on the same dimly lit photo of Krystal's naked breasts. Shaking, he pulled Nick's phone from his pocket and compared the messages. His heart sank. They were identical except for the time stamps. The other phone's messages were dated almost a year ago.

A loud shriek startled him. He dropped both phones. They clattered to the floor. He stood there like a rodent caught in the open, waiting for one of the sisters to find him rifling through their things. Except these phones didn't belong to them. They belonged to the dozens of other young men who'd fallen prey to whatever the hell they were.

An uncomfortable sting rose up in Jim's groin, and he pressed his hand there to hold back the pain. Something squished in his pants, and he knew if he didn't find Nick soon, he could forget about ever getting laid again.

Another scream filled the hallway. Jim's heart surged, thumping in his chest to the beat of what he thought was the Blue Danube waltz. Against his better judgment, he pushed aside the heavy curtain and walked quietly down the hallway. Adrenaline coursed through his veins.

"Take their seed, sisters. Take it all."

Violet Eyes stood at the study's threshold and clapped her hands softly as more screams overpowered the classical waltz. A lump manifested in Jim's throat, filling his airway like a ball of cotton. Violet Eyes smiled at him before turning her attention back to her sisters. Jim thought he was ready for what lay beyond the threshold. He was wrong.

The men in the room were entangled in a series of vines protruding from the arms of the sisters, thick ropy tendrils squirming and digging their way into their victims' exposed flesh. One of the guys—Jim was horrified to see he was the one with the half-cocked grin from earlier—turned toward him and moaned in agony, his arms twisted at impossible angles while his date took him relentlessly in her mouth. His eyes rolled up into his head as his cheeks sank inward, his body cavity imploding at the draining will of his attacker, collapsing into himself like a deflated sex doll.

Violet Eyes turned to Jim, smiling proudly. "They learn so fast," she said. "This harvest will be the best yet!"

Jim tried to speak but words failed him. His mouth was dry, and any attempt to find his voice was met with a dull ache shooting through his groin. The other girls were sucking their guests dry as well. For a moment, all that raced through Jim's mind was that it could've been him.

Violet Eyes traced her fingers along his arm. She smiled and licked her lips. "My name's Holly, by the way. I like you…"

"He's mine, Holly." Gemini shuffled into the hallway, the hem of her dress caked in soil, and her cheeks streaked with an atlas of green tears. The broken stalk of the flower in her hair hung limp to one side. She avoided Jim's gaze, focusing her stare on Holly. "Krystal paired us."

"But I haven't paired—"

Gemini struck her with the back of her hand. The slap echoed down the hall, but did nothing to interrupt the deathly orgy in the adjacent room.

"He's *mine,*" Gemini growled. "Now leave us alone."

Holly stepped back, speechless, nursing her reddening cheek. She retreated through the kitchen, and just before she exited to the garden, Jim saw a hint of dark green ooze dribbling down her chin.

He looked back at Gemini, unsure of what to say. He wasn't sure if he wanted to kiss her or run away. "Where's Nick?"

Gemini sighed. She took his hand and rubbed her thumb across his fingers. "He's with Krystal. He was paired with her…just as you are paired with me. Our special ones are taken to the basement to meet Mother Iris. Come."

"To the basement? I don't understand. Why—"

Her lips pressed against his forcefully and for an instant he forgot all about the pain coursing down his thighs, and the fear racing through his mind. For the moment, there were only the two of them, a quiet center of the universe, separate from the pain and confusion he'd felt since first following Gemini out into the garden. Her tongue darted into his mouth, accompanied by the metallic taste of soil. He wanted to pull away, but didn't. A sick warmth overcame him, filling his head with hot desire, displacing all thoughts of Nick and Megan. *This is what it's like to be wanted,* he thought. Opening his eyes, he lost himself in the subtle glow of Gemini's violet gaze. Their lips parted, and Jim felt himself lean forward for more. He *wanted* more. He *needed* to taste her one last time, but she wouldn't let him.

Gemini looked away and squeezed his hand. "I'm sorry we couldn't spend more time together, Jim. Come with me."

He tried to kiss her again, but she held him back.

"I *insist,*" she said.

Jim tried to lean in once more, but paused when he saw they had an audience. The other girls from the study watched from the doorway, their cheeks swollen with light green veins, their violet eyes glowing in the dim light.

"Harvest him, sister."

Gemini closed her eyes, green tears spilling down her cheeks. "I know, sisters. I know." She tugged at his hand. "Come, Jim. It's time for you to meet Mother."

Gemini led the way down the basement stairs. The walls were aged and cracked, and a thick musty smell of soil permeated the air. Jim hesitated in the doorway as he stared down into the dim abyss, his heart rapping so hard against his chest that he had trouble catching his breath. Part of him wanted to find a way out of all this. There was a voice somewhere in the back of his mind screaming like a frightened child, begging to find Nick and leave.

Forget Nick, a voice whispered, soft and soothing, yet spoken with authority. *Come to me, child. Let me look at your beautiful face.*

Jim pivoted, turning back toward the kitchen where the other sorority sisters watched. They looked less human now—more green veins had surfaced on their porcelain skin, their violet eyes bulged, and small gray tendrils snaked down their necks and arms. They stared at him with rabid urgency. One of them was even licking her lips.

"Go on," she said.

"Meet our mother," said another.

"Jim, come with me," Gemini said from below.

He turned back and looked down the stairwell. Gemini was on the landing, peering up with her hand held out. The tears had aged her face, filling in every line, giving her cheeks a pale green complexion. He remembered

Krystal's face when she'd first met Nick at the front door. He'd thought she wore a *façade* of beauty. He'd wondered if there was a seam somewhere he could find, half-tempted to reach out and pluck the flesh right off her face, but he resisted the desire out of fear for what he might find staring back at him.

Behind him, eager fingers traced the back of his neck and shoulders. He felt hot breath on his skin as the other girls' flirtatious whispers urged him on. "Go, sweetie. Go."

Jim took a breath, whispered a prayer, and descended the steps. He took Gemini's hand, and together they went down to the last landing. Another large velvet curtain hung from the basement ceiling, cordoning off the rest of the room from the stairs.

"Mother Iris," Gemini announced, "we've come to pay you a visit. I have my paired special one for you. The last of tonight's harvest." She pulled back the curtain, revealing a large space illuminated with bright UV lights—and an enormous bulbous *thing* planted in its center.

The world Jim thought he knew had already been shaken that night, its foundations cracked by almost having his penis ripped off by a mutant plant woman. But what he saw waiting for him at the bottom of the stairs, just beyond the curtain of the basement, all but finished the job, sending his concept of reality teetering into an endless, blackened void of further doubt and confusion.

Nick was dead. He could tell from the way his roommate's deflated, bloody limbs were sticking out of the creature's maw. Arms and legs were compressed side by side in an unnatural pose—the fingers on one hand still twitching. Until that moment, Jim hadn't even considered the possibility his roommate might've suffered a similar fate as those unfortunate young men just one floor above. He didn't know what he expected to do when he finally did find Nick. Persuade him to leave? Had he been so naïve to think that might actually work, given his friend's insatiable appetite for sex?

Standing at the threshold, staring at what he presumed was Mother Iris, Jim heard her voice in his mind, urging him to let go. *Just let it happen,* the being cooed. *We want you to be one with us, child.*

Something gave way in his mind. The sensation was subtle, the faintest crack in his mind, through which the last of his sanity would undoubtedly seep. He suddenly felt very small and very young, like a child having wandered across the borders of a dense, dark forest. Even if he somehow managed to break through the throng of ravenous women above, some part of him knew he could never go back to his life as it'd been—not really.

The dark green bulb that had devoured Nick's last remains was bisected down the middle. It split open for just a moment, revealing seemingly endless rows of sharp thorns, their amber color tainted with a hint of scarlet. Surrounding the bulb were large vibrant petals that fluttered erratically, filling the room with an anxious rustling noise that made his ears itch. To either side of the flowering mass was a human leg bent at the knee, the flesh wore a pattern of dark green veins, muscles tightening and convulsing in time with the rustling petals.

Jim's mind finally caught up to his senses, and he realized he wasn't looking at two disembodied legs. The legs and the flower-bulb thing were connected to the same mass. The crack in his mind splintered outward as his stomach began to churn. *She's giving birth to that thing,* his mind screamed. And although his mouth hung agape, no words came to him.

He was partially correct. Mother Iris lay on her back, legs spread and exposed to the room, but she wasn't giving birth to the creature protruding from her womb. The flower was a part of her, used to satiate her divine hunger for centuries, feasting on the blood and bones of hapless men who were drawn into her trap, their sweat, lust, and semen a delicacy to her taste buds.

Jim's terror was surpassed only by his sudden, inexplicable desire to become one with her.

Krystal appeared from behind the writhing creature. She was nude, her body pockmarked with leafy wounds oozing that same viscous green fluid. Her breasts peeled back, blooming into patches of swirling vines and small, violet flowers. A thick green tendril coiled out from behind Mother Iris and wrapped around Krystal's legs, inching its way up her body with the power of a python. A small, green nodule at the tip of the vine latched onto the purple flower in Krystal's hair, enveloping the petals as it fusing to her head.

A second green tentacle lurched out of the flickering shadows and beckoned toward Gemini. She let go of Jim's hand, walked obediently across the room, and bowed her head. The elephant-like trunk wrapped around her thin body, wrinkling her dress. There was an audible *shurp* as the tendril latched onto her flower's broken stem like a leech.

Both girls went limp as the appendages lifted them off their feet, twirling them in the air like discarded dolls. Their eyes drained of color, transforming into the milky white of cataracts, and their mouths flapped open and shut as Mother Iris tested their muscles. They were a part of her now, and when Mother Iris spoke, she did so through their vocal cords.

"Come to me, child. Let us have a look at you."

Jim wanted to run, but a voice from within suggested the impossible, the insane: *Why not stay?* His feet were unwilling to move, and for each moment he stared into the many eyes of this monstrosity, the desire to remain grew ever intense, building with each successive heartbeat of the creature. He forgot about the prickling pain in his groin. That was just a flaw of the flesh. Besides, what good was it to him now, if instead he could become part of something divine?

The bulb furled open and excreted one of Nick's loafers. The damp shoe was covered in gelatinous ooze. It plopped onto the basement floor in front of Mother Iris with a sickening *thud.* Jim stared at down at it, a part of him horrified—while another part envied Nick's place within the goddess.

"Take me," he muttered. A chill ran through his body as he lowered his gaze, feeling wholly unworthy before the writhing goddess. Everything he held dear and had hoped for up to that moment—school, family, losing his virginity, the girl he thought he wanted—now seemed so trivial. He was but a grain of sand at the edge of a vast ocean of possibility, and Mother Iris was a voyager of those strange, wondrous waters.

"Take me with you," he said, his hands trembling.

Mother Iris considered his proposal, her tendrils swaying in the air, carrying Gemini and Krystal like marionettes. "Do you seek our glory?" the gaping maw said.

Jim fell to his knees. He wiped tears from his eyes and bowed his head. "I want to be with you, Mother. Please take me with you."

The crack in his mind splintered further, separating his heart from all matter of logic. The reasonable part of him—that screaming young man tucked away in the shadows of his mind—grew distant, shrinking away as he became blinded by the glory of Demeter's daughter.

The bulb split wide open and flared its prickly thorns at him. A long, slender vine protruded from the center of the leafy maw and inched its way across the floor toward him. He closed his eyes and relinquished himself to Mother Iris. The tendril curled around his wrist and began to pull him across the spew-slickened floor. Inch by inch, Jim Auster was dragged to his fate, a destination to which he would have gone willingly.

Within a moment he would be a part of something greater than himself. Beyond all this, he would never again feel rejection or sorrow. There was only the warm bliss of Mother Iris' acceptance, which was all he'd ever wanted. Lost forever amid the nettles and thorns, he welcomed the unspoken invitation to be devoured sweetly within the belly of a living goddess.

Retribution

Dana Wright

Lissa was drowning. The water pulled her under, dark and swirling. She gasped, her arms flailing out into the black abyss. The prom dress she wore twisted and bunched around her ankles, holding her down amid the plants. Her legs beat wildly against the weeds dragging at her feet, drawing her deeper still. Mouth open in a silent scream, she fought for air as more fetid water forced its way into her mouth, choking her. Water turned to mud. Mountains of silt poured past her lips. Razors slashed at her arms, creating a bloom of rust in the water. The scarecrow held her, pulling at her to come up, his dark fathomless eyes the only assurance she had in the black ever after.

She clawed at her throat, fingers useless. Her eyes closed and the landscape shifted. The drowning pool became a sea of cornfields. The wind whispered through the dry husks, beckoning her to listen. Her witchfire hung, useless. It wouldn't come…until after. Birthed in her virgin's blood, the fire awakened as it bled out into the earth. The scattered conversation of the cornhusks chittered, showing her the way back to herself. She struggled to reclaim it here in this landscape of mind-numbing pain and terror. Memories tugged at her—remembered horrors washing over her body in waves. *Her father. The pressure of his weight pressing down on her. The violation of her body and soul. His laughter. The scarecrow's arms around her, saving her…*

"No! No!" She tried to scream, but her throat wouldn't make a sound.

"Lissa."

It was a familiar voice, a focal point for her panicked mind, a light in the hollowed out spaces of the terror. There were far too many memories piling together. Too much blood and pain and hate.

She struggled to breathe, fighting against the pressure in her chest and the fullness in her throat. If only the darkness would close in—allow her to let go. She tried, but something kept tugging on her to return. If she cut deep and hard enough, she thought, *maybe.* Anger burned in her belly. *I want to die.* Her finger tips were numb, itching to react. But instead, they hung there twitching. Something was in her hand. A razor? Cold, dark and sweet, with its shiny handle and long sharp blade.

"Lissa, look at me."

She fought to open her eyes. The darkness bore up, too strong. Images of blood and death battered her with memories long since buried. *Running through the cornfield. Her throat raw from screaming. Her dress ripped and soiled. Where was she? Oh God! What had he done? The old house speaking to her with walls of silence and secrets. The outpouring of love from the fields themselves. The scarecrow's tender hands as he rescued her. But how? Her mother invisible as a ghost, walking the house's empty halls. A wail rose up from Lissa's very soul. No…not her! No!*

"Lissa! Wake up!"

There. Her lover's face appeared just beyond her vision.

The slideshow of the cornfield and the drowning pool became one. Ingrid. *Her long blond hair fanned out, pink prom dress floating in the shallow water, the once sparkling green eyes faded into vacant dead orbs.*

The specter reached out her hand and trailed icy fingers down Lissa's cheek. She glanced at the razor in Lissa's hand and shook her head. *"Remember your promise, love."* She leaned forward and pressed her cold lips against Lissa's. Her mouth held the ghost of cherry lip gloss. Sweet and bitter, Lissa's heart contracted with the need to touch her, and be touched, to revel in the warmth of Ingrid's outstretched hand. The floral scent of her favorite perfume wafted around the girl's ghostly form. She could give up the razor if she had her love back again.

Ingrid… Why did you leave me?

"Ingrid!" Lissa cried out, her voice little more than a sob.

"Remember..." Ingrid closed her eyes and the apparition faded, leaving Lissa to sob into the empty darkness, the silver blade still clutched in her hand, witchfire burning deep in her blood.

Lissa woke. The sheets lay tangled in a heap around her ankles. Cold sweat covered her body, making her skin sticky and uncomfortable. The nightgown she wore bunched around her hips. She tugged the cotton gown down to cover herself, not that it mattered here, but old habits died hard. Her breath was reminiscent of an ashtray, foul and disgusting. Lissa's pulse pounded. She inhaled a deep lungful of air to try to calm her breathing. Her off and on girlfriend Heather laid alongside her. Tonight they happened to be on.

The razor. *Shit.* She glanced down at her hand. Not there. *Where was it?* She reached into the nightstand drawer and lifted it out; the silver handle glinted in the moonlight. Lissa knew it was like playing Russian roulette keeping it next to her bed, but she needed to be sure where it was at all times. It was the key to everything she'd ever been—or ever would be.

She slipped it back into the drawer and rubbed at her arms. *Not tonight.* The dried scabs of her last cutting festival were just beginning to look semi normal. There was no need to ruin the look—not yet—while the dreams were still manageable. *If you called dreaming about your murdered girlfriend manageable.*

"You okay, Lis?" Heather's voice groggy with sleep.

"Yeah…I mean, I think so." Lissa angled herself up by her elbows and looked at the luminous number of the bedside alarm clock. 1 AM. She'd been in bed an hour. *God.* What had she been dreaming? It'd felt so real. She reached for the bottled water on the nightstand with a shaking hand, and the dream came flooding back.

"Ingrid…" She hadn't said that name aloud in a very long time.

Lissa squeezed her eyes shut against the barrage of nocturnal memories. She pressed her fingers to her lips. Still cold. She could taste cherry lip gloss.

Heather slid a hand on her back. "Bad dreams again? You want to tell me?"

"Yes, the dream." Lissa swung her feet over the side of the bed and smoothed the nightgown down against her legs. "And no." *Hell no!* "No, thanks. It's okay, but I really don't feel like talking about it." She wasn't about to travel down that road. It'd taken her years to put the trauma of those events behind her, and one dream wasn't going to take her back again. Fuck the cornfields! Fuck the evil bastard who continued to lurk in the darkest chambers of her memories! Freedom from him had been her ultimate goal. Instead, she'd been forced to live with what he did to her each and every day of her godforsaken life.

Fingers tingling, she pushed the witchfire down again. Heather didn't need to realize just what kind of freak she shared her bed with. Bad enough with the nightmares, she didn't feel like adding fuel to the fire.

"Hon, are you sure you're alright?" asked Heather.

Not really…

Ingrid's hollow eyes swam in front of her vision again.

"Hon, it was a nightmare. You know it can't hurt you, right? Heather patted her back. "Come back to bed. It's only been an hour, you need more rest."

"I know…" Lissa said. Even after all these years, memories of Ingrid still had the power to frighten her, or at least move her to a place of deep sadness, considering all Ingrid had been forced to endure because of her—then lose her very life to it all. Lissa had been all too willing to leave it behind when she'd survived the cornfields and had emerged back into the world, at least in some fashion. The only thing she'd taken from that time had been the razor that now sat in the drawer next to her bed. The whole sorted nightmare had been her version of a twisted Cinderella horror story. *Fight the right shoe and make it fit.* Only her shoe had never been found, so the fit couldn't be established. All she had were tattered memories of an horrific event, wielded at the hands of her very own father. The bastard who'd taken her fairytale away for good.

The cell phone on the nightstand began to chirp. Lissa picked it up and swished her finger across the touch screen. Her fingers were shaking. No one called at this hour unless someone was dead.

"Hello?"

"Lissa?" The voice crackled on the line familiar but she still had trouble placing it.

"Who is this?" Still shaken by her dream, she put niceties aside. Heather shifted back onto her side with a groan.

"Honey, it's Aunt June."

"Aunt June?" Her legs grew weak and Lissa sank back onto the mattress. She tapped the touch light on the bedside table and sat blinking in the soft glow. "Hi. It's been…"

"Oh honey. You don't have to say anything. Your mother." She paused, her voice faltering. "She's gone."

Tears prickled behind Lissa's eyelids, the shock jarring her to her core. "How?" Lissa asked, her voice weak.

There was a deep sigh on the other end of the line, followed by a moment of marked hesitation. "She found out you were still alive and wanted more than anything to right old wrongs. To find you. But something went wrong. He—" Her voice grew to a choked sob. "After what he did to you..."

Cold horror slid down Lissa's insides. Ingrid. The dream. "Aunt June... *please*...I don't want relive it." Lissa shrank into herself, the fear for her mother warring with her own anger. She'd allowed her father to bully her, knowing what he would do. Lissa loved her mother, but the betrayal still carved a deep groove into her heart. She realized she might never be able to find forgiveness for either of her parents, which was a realization that hurt her more than anything.

"What did he do to her?" Lissa asked, closing her eyes and steeling herself against what her aunt might tell her. She was more than aware of her father's proclivities, so she held her breath and waited for her aunt to answer.

Finally Aunt June spoke. "They found your mother's body this morning, honey. She called me last night in a panic. Your father had been acting strange, your mom had said. He'd accused her of cheating on him—as if she ever would. She was getting ready to leave him. To find you and start a new life."

Too much...too little...to late, Lissa thought. "What. Did. He. Do?"

"Old Daisy Forbes came by with some strawberry preserves. She made sure your father was still working out in the fields. Daisy said it felt off when no one answered the door. She found your momma with a plastic bag over her head in your old room. Daisy called the police right away. Your dad is claiming it was suicide."

"What?" Tears slid silent down her cheeks. *Her mother. Gone.* She couldn't discern even the first emotion tumbling through her brain. Remorse? Hate? Love? Relief? A tangle of heart and mind that would never fully make sense.

"You have to come home, sweetheart. Your mama didn't kill herself." Her aunt's sweet voice quickly turned bitter, filled with secrets and memories they shared. "I understand I'm asking a lot, honey, but your mama...she needs you to put her to rest."

Almost without noticing, Lissa stood up. "I'm coming," she said, without hesitation, her fingertips tingling with the unreleased power coursing through her body.

Lissa flipped on the bedroom light and dragged her suitcase out of the closet.

Heather turned over, concern written across her smooth features. Her long, red hair splayed out across the pillow, eyes narrowed in concern.

"Do you want me to come with you?"

Lissa froze in the middle of stuffing clothes into the suitcase. "No, I don't want you anywhere near him. I appreciate it, but this is something I need to handle." Her mind traveled back to the ramshackle farmhouse and the endless cornfields. The house with walls that told her when to lock the door, when to run, and whispered of darker things to her, whenever they threatened. Things buried deep in the cornfield, same as her lover.

"How long will you be there?" Heather asked.

"I'm not sure." *Lissa knew the words were a total lie.* She looked into the girl's eyes, possibly for the last time. She pushed the thought from her mind. There was no time to linger on what could have been between them. She'd been running ever since that night so many years ago. Heather's eyes lingered on her as she moved around the room, collecting what she would need—the bare essentials—just enough to get by for a couple of days, then she would have to see where fate took her.

Lissa filled the rest of the suitcase and snapped it shut. Numb, she went into the bathroom and turned on the shower. Maybe the warm spray would erase the sensation that crept along the back of her neck. *Home.* What a crazy thought. The ties that bound and gagged and never, ever let you go, was more like it. The scars on her arms tingled and she fought the urge to pick up the short razor on the shower tray. She promised Heather she wouldn't do that anymore. *"Remember you promise!"* Ingrid's soft lips whispered in her memory. Bitter tears fell from Lissa's eyes like so many invisible secrets, like rain disappearing into the ground of the cornfields she was about to see again.

* * *

Some things you never forget. The road to her father's house being one of them. Every bump along that dirt road had always set her teeth just a little more on edge. Dried husks of corn whispered their secrets as she maneuvered down the uneven path. The scarecrow placed on the edge of the property watched with soulless eyes as her small Kia got closer and closer to her destination. *Her own personal Savior in a sea of maize and death.*

The two story old Victorian farmhouse had once been her home. Lissa could never remember it being a particularly happy place—even before the abuse had begun. Any joy she'd felt while living there had come from the classes she'd taken while in high school, always filled with the relentless dream of one day getting away and moving to the big city.

And don't forget the kiss of the blade against your skin. Blood dripping onto the floorboards, feeding the house that said it loved you. That it cared about what happened to you, in only the way protective walls can. Escape!—the walls urged. Leave this place and be free...

Then her last year of high school came along, with Ingrid and her fuck-the-world attitude. They'd become inseparable. Lissa's father hated Ingrid on sight. "That girl's a lesbian whore, and I won't have any daughter of mine seen with such trash!"

Trash being the operative word, Lissa thought bitterly, as her car dodged yet another crater in the unpaved Memories flooded back like a plague of locusts. The pink shoe sat in the seat next to her. It was time to deal with her past, once and for all. She had gone to countless therapists, and for what? To forgive? To move on with her life? What a fucking joke! She'd tried the forgetting part, and even the forgiving part, which was all but impossible to do, with her scars constant reminders of what her past had made of her.

"Fuck this!" She spat, continuing toward the farmhouse.

Now her mother was dead.

Her mother had never understood—not really. As battered as her daughter was, she was forever making excuses for her husband, about his temper, how exhausted he was from working the fields nonstop. On numerous occasions, Lissa begged her mother to stay home on her bridge club nights. But she acted as though she hadn't heard her daughter's please. It never failed. The glowing red taillights of the family car disappearing down the long road along the rustling cornfield, was the green light that freed the monster sharing the house with them. From the front room, the television blared, while even louder music blared from two large stereo speakers. The yelling would start whenever her father watched wrestling. But first came the drinking. Hard alcohol or beer—it didn't matter. He would drink and drink, constructing a cycle that never seemed to end. The drinking fueled the yelling which fueled even more drinking.

Lissa did her best to ignore her father's rants. Alone in her room, she would try to concentrate on her homework, refusing to even think about stepping foot out of her room. The thunderous noise continued from downstairs—and so did drinking.

When her mother finally did come home, she would go immediately into her room, and close the door behind her. Lissa had school in the morning following most of her father's rages, but first she had to get through the endless night ahead. She never knew when he would come into her room—only that he would. The doorknob would twist and the walls of her room would cry out.

Wake up, girl! And wake up, she did—if only to pretend to be asleep. She'd learned over the years to be still as he touched her body, his alcohol-infused breath clouding her face. The even cadence of feigned sleep was an art she'd perfected. If she stirred, other things would happen, less savory things she didn't want to think about. Her only escape had been the icy kiss of the razor on her skin. Then *Ingrid.* Her one true love. Her only hope for a future beyond this hell.

Lissa remembered the day like it was yesterday. Ingrid propped up on her bed, eyes lowered over her algebra textbook, pretending to study. Her own pulse thrumming in her veins as she observed everything about this enigma of a girl. Sunlight falling across Ingrid's silky blond hair, and the way she would curl long strands of it around her fingers whenever she thought too hard on a problem. The subtle habit Ingrid had of catching her bottom lip in her teeth, Lissa's breath catching in her throat each time Ingrid's full lips would curve up in a smile. She wanted more than anything to feel them against her own.

Lissa was forever pulling her long sleeves down, so Ingrid couldn't see the scars from the razor. She didn't want Ingrid to worry about something neither of them could do anything about.

Her father had almost caught them sharing their first kiss outside the back door of the farmhouse that fated day. He was supposed to be in the fields for another hour or more. It was supposed to be safe. She thought they had time alone. But it was never safe. Not with that bastard who called himself her father. Not *ever.*

Only with Ingrid, did she forget the fear that was her life. Ingrid had turned to Lissa and let her fingers slide along the soft curve of her face. Lips pressed against hers so quickly that Lissa couldn't be sure if she was dreaming or if it'd really happened. Ingrid stepped back with a slow smile widening. They'd been seeing each other for weeks, the tension between them growing.

"You are so beautiful," Ingrid whispered. "If you can make it, my parents are hosting a book party. Mom's been published again."

Lissa grinned. "What does she write?" Her stomach was doing butterflies and something was wrong with her knees; they kept shaking. Her eyes drifted to the swell of Ingrid's tee shirt and she swallowed heavily, glancing away.

"Don't ask." Ingrid giggled. "Just come."

Her father came out from behind the barn without a sound. His eyes watched the girls as they talked. He glared at Lissa and shot a loathing glance in Ingrid's direction.

Ingrid left then, Lissa watching as she made her way into the cornfield. Anger and fear churned together crafting a determination in Lissa's gut to get out—break free from this prison of a life. Lissa stared off into the distance to the scarecrow that watched over the fields. Sending a prayer that her love would be protected, she went back into the house, mindful of the threat that would soon lurk within.

Ingrid welcomed Lissa into her home the night of her mother's book party. Any night she could escape the confines of her house, and the dread that lived there, Lissa would make her way to the family's farm through the cornfield. Bright and airy, it was practically another world from the strict confines of her own home life. From the groping horrors that plagued her nights, and haunted her waking moments.

Because of Ingrid, she slowly stopped using the razor for release. With her, Lissa felt freer than she ever had before. With Ingrid, she could forget.

"You should date my daughter," Elisabeth, Ingrid's mother, told her one day. "Then you could call me Mom." Lissa remembered standing stock still as Ingrid froze, shooting her mother a glare. She understood how much that would cost Lissa if her father ever found out. Impulsively she reached out and planted a kiss on Ingrid's lips. Emboldened by the sheer happiness she felt from the accepting comment Ingrid's mother had made. Lissa agreed, thinking how nice that would be.

"Sealed with a kiss," Lissa laughed. "Now you have to take me to prom," she said, looping her arm through Ingrid's.

"I love you," Ingrid whispered. They walked out into the setting sun, and began to talk about their plans after graduation. In just a few short months they would be free and could leave for the big city—get jobs, move in together, maybe even check out the local nightclubs, and finally get out from under the shadow of Lissa's father.

"He's not going to let you go," Ingrid sighed, stepping into the sugary pink prom dress at the bridal shop later that week. Her parents had graciously footed the bill for Lissa's dress, too, after her own parents had refused.

"I won't say a word," Lissa said. "What he doesn't know won't hurt him." But what he *did* know could hurt her, she relented. Just thinking about his disgusting hands on her body made her want to retch.

Ingrid's brow furrowed in concern. She let the dress slide to the floor and stepped out of it. "He knows about us, Lissa. The way he watches me when I walk you home, I know he does. I swear, you have to be careful with a man like that. He's an animal. You can never turn your back on him. He always looks like he's ready to pounce…and I don't like it."

Lissa snorted, grabbing the peach confection from the hanger, "I don't care about him."

"You'd better!" Ingrid scowled. "He hates me, I know he does. Which means he hates that you love me…which could prove dangerous for you if you're not careful. "

Lissa did her best to shrug off the worry Ingrid was conveying. "So I'll meet you at the cornfield and your parents will take us, no big deal. He'll think I'm there trying to find a guy to dance with and we can hang out. Nothing's going to happen."

* * *

The night of the prom Ingrid's mother got stranded with a flat tire. Lissa's mother was pulling laundry from the line, then she was going to go play bridge with her friends. The house was quiet. Lissa finished putting the final touches on her makeup and tucked a loose curl in her up-do. She angled her body toward the mirror above the desk in her room, admiring the way the gauzy peach fabric hugged her curves. The silver strappy sandals made her look taller, too. She smiled and grabbed the tiny evening bag she'd borrowed from Ingrid's mother for their special night.

"You think you're going somewhere, girl?" Her father's voice rasped from the hallway. He pushed open the door and confronted her full on, his jaw clenched in anger. His clothes were streaked, covered in dust and grime from the fields—and something else—something *darker.* Was that *blood?*

"Yes, sir," Lissa said, continuing to check her reflection in the mirror. "I'm going to the dance at school." *Keep calm,* she told herself. *Just get past him and out the door and everything will be fine.*

Just sensing his looming presence in the doorway made her skin crawl. She tried not to think of all the nights he'd snuck into her room to watch her—not always at a distance—and *touch* her, which was even worse.

"No you're not!" he said, springing into the room, shoving her viciously. Lissa was flung back against the desk, her back hitting the corner. "I know what you've been doing," he spat. "You and that blond haired slut!"

Lissa gasped for air, trying not to vomit all over her dress as she clutched the edge of the desk to stabilize herself. "Don't touch me!" she screamed, wheezing as she tried to get to her feet. On her way up, she grabbed a large dictionary from the desktop and swung it as hard as she could. Much to her surprise, she the book connected with his face. His head snapped back and his eyes turned dark. Coming at her again, he backhanded her. The impact of his large, clenched hand rattled the teeth in her head. Suddenly she was falling again.

"Whore!" His eyes narrowed in rage, as he rushed at her again. This time his fist connected with her stomach.

Lissa screamed, her dress tearing as it caught on a drawer latch. She struggled to right herself, scrambling to find purchase on the hardwood floor before he reached her. Everything was a blur. One second she was falling, the next she was fighting him off. Lissa kicked out with both feet, knocking him back a few paces and out the door into the hallway. She stumbled on the fabric of the dress as she staggered into a standing position. She darted out the door past him before he could get back on his feet. The coppery taste of blood flooded her mouth. She spit it out and kept on going. Her lip stung where he hit her and her guts swam in her midsection like they were on fire.

Fucking bastard! She thought.

Run! The shadowed walls of the house cried out.

Waves of electric light flickered at her sides, and her fingertips itched.

Danger!!!

Lissa fled. She had to get to the cornfield and reach Ingrid before he did. They would leave together tonight. Her stocking feet slid on the polished wooden floors as she tried to make her way out of the house. She scrambled out the front door and took off into a run. Gravel bit into her feet causing angry tears to flood her eyes. *How dare he, that sonofabitch?* Her mother's car was gone, which wasn't a surprise. Little help was to be had from that direction anyway. She stumbled once, falling to her knees, scraping them raw, tearing her nylons. A bloom of bright red fanned out as the fabric tore.

Staggering to her feet, she took off in a run again. The breath in her sides hitched, but she was focused on the ground in front of her. She just needed to get a bit further, then she and Ingrid could leave this place and begin their life together.

Wait…something caught her attention…a blur of something pink. *A shoe?*

She stopped.

What?

Horror laced down her spine.

"INGRID!" Lissa screamed.

The path along the cornfield was littered with pink. A barrette. A second shoe. A broken corsage.

Oh God! What had he done?

Lissa dove into the rows of corn. "Ingrid!" Her voice was a sob. Tears ran down her face making it difficult to see. She was drowning in terror. Then behind her, came the sound of boots on gravel. He must've gotten out of the house.

"Where are you girl?!" his voice echoed through the rows of tall corn.

Lissa wiped at her eyes and ran until she reached the break in the middle of the field, where the small drainage pond they used to help irrigate the crops was located. There floating in the water, surrounded by her billowing pink dress, was Ingrid.

Lissa darted toward the edge of the pond and stopped. *"Ingrid!"* Silent tears wracked her body. Lissa heard him coming. She was numb. He'd done it. He'd killed the only person she'd ever loved.

"You bitch!" Hands scooped her up, swung her around, and threw her back down onto the muddy grass again. This time, on her back. In a flurry of motion, his full weight was on top of her. The sound of ripping fabric and the weight of another person pressing down on her was all she could hear and feel. Her legs were suddenly parted violently in a burning invasion of body and mind. Within seconds of rough thrusting, she was broken, used. Hands clutched her throat, cutting off her air. Then there was no more sound. She'd let it all fade away. Besides, what did it matter now? Her terror-glazed eyes stared into the cornfield, the chill of dusk settling over her.

"Got what you deserved, you little bitch!" He kicked her in the side over and over again, then she heard his footsteps retreating back toward the house.

Lissa lay there unmoving, letting her own blood seep into the ground, maybe even nourish it. She welcomed death. Her love was gone. There was nothing left to live for. Her eyes drifted shut as welcomed blackness slowly crept in.

The tingling in her fingers brought her back. That and the movement of being carried. Fearful he had her again, she twisted, but only the scratch of hay and the moldy smell of old fabric met her nose.

What?

Lissa opened her eyes to meet the dead stare of the scarecrow that'd watched over their fields ever since she was a little girl. His gate was steady as he pressed on through the fields, corn whipping at her body with every step he took. At the end of their short journey, the scarecrow stopped and set her down gently. A pink shoe was dropped in front of her, and Lissa stifled a sob. It hadn't been a dream. *Ingrid.* Her Ingrid.

She closed her eyes to blink away the tears. When she opened them again, the edge of the corn was empty. Her fingers tingled and arched with a blue fire.

"*What is that?*" She whispered, her eyes transfixed on the power flickering beneath the skin of her trembling fingertips. *Did I call him—the scarecrow?* Her eyes scanned the edge of the corn, but nothing moved. She got up and took off, walking in the direction of her aunt's house. Looking down, she saw that she was still gripping the pink shoe the scarecrow had dropped in front of her. She couldn't believe Ingrid was gone.

"I'll come back for you Ingrid. You have my promise."

Lissa had survived that fated night. She'd spent a lifetime pushing past the horror, determined never again to set foot back in the cornfields—unless it was under her own terms. The dream of Ingrid had been a sign, telling her the time was right. Ingrid's pink shoe had kept vigil the entire trip, as still was, as the Kia pulled up in front of the farmhouse of her horrifying childhood.

Cinderella has returned.

Lissa's feet hit the dirt and the ground beneath them trembled. She was back at the house of her upbringing—and the house remembered her. Whether for her blood, or the creature the land had made of her, was yet to be determined.

The house loomed in front of her, dark and brooding. She knew he was there. Inside. It was time to see if the proverbial shoe fit. Slamming the car door behind her, Lissa turned toward the front door, ready to finally face him, after all these years.

Sure enough, the front door swung open and her father emerged. Weather worn and slightly grayer, he approached where she was standing.

"Who's there?" He bellowed out, his voice slurred from drinking.

"It's your *daughter*, Lissa!" she spat.

"No..." he muttered, staggering backward, falling onto the tattered welcome mat in his haste to back away from her. "You're—"

"*—Dead*" Lissa finished, letting the blue witchfire flicker at the ends of her fingertips. "No," she continued. "But certainly no thanks to you." She sauntered toward the house, reveling in the enjoyment of watching the blood drain from his face, as he got a good look at her. "You're not seeing a ghost, *dad*. Yes, it's me. The daughter you raped and left for dead."

A spark flew from her fingertips, hitting the dirt beside him.

"You devil bitch! I should have drowned you myself."

"Like you did to Ingrid?" Her voice dropped dangerously low. "You murdering *bastard!*" she hissed.

The crunch of dead leaves and the whisper of rustling fabric approached from behind her. A shadow appeared over her shoulder and Lissa smiled. *She should have known he would come.*

"I'm glad to see you again my old friend," she said, turning around, holding out her hand as the lumbering scarecrow did the same. "Thank you….you saved my life!"

His soulless dark eyes scanned the man on the porch, his dry, cracked lips sinking into a flat line that could have been disgust.

"So now my mother rests beneath the corn," Lissa said to her father. "How fitting that you should join her."

"No…" her father's eyes grew wide as the scarecrow dropped Lissa's hand and began his slow journey toward the porch.

"Blood of the land cries out for vengeance…" Lissa continued.

"I never killed nobody that didn't deserve it," her father slurred

"Now, dad, it's not nice to tell lies." Her fingers twitched again and the witchfire found him.

He gasped and fell to his knees as the lightening-like energy coursed through him with a flash.

The scarecrow climbed the first stair…

Her father screamed.

Then a second…

"NO!"

The creature's large gloved hands pulled her father from the porch, dragging him unceremoniously down the wooden stairs, to the unkempt yard below.

"Put me down!" the man howled, his face contorting in rage.

"I don't think my friend is listening…*Dad.*" Without hesitation, the scarecrow dragged the flailing man into the dark swaying stalks of corn.

Lissa followed, shoe in hand. The tall rows of corn whispered their secrets to her in the breeze, and they dipped to caress her arms as she followed the scarecrow and her father into their folds. She was whole again. Saved by the land that loved her.

A scream echoed in the field.

Lissa found herself standing at the foot of a newly hewn scarecrow stand. Hanging from the wooden posts above her was her father. Strung up with rope, he fumed with rage.

"GET ME DOWN FROM HERE, GIRL!"

The scarecrow stood on the wooden structure, his dark eyes intent on his task. Slow and steady, he worked until his replacement was tied down. He reached around and forcibly opened her father's mouth, muffling the curses that were pouring forth from his lips. The scarecrow had his tongue. A flash of metal and the deed was done. Blood flowed from the hole in his face, mute grunts and primal cries deafened by the quick work of the blade.

"I don't think so," Lissa said, approaching the dais and climbing up carefully. "You forgot something..." Her hand closed over his bloody mouth, witchfire spreading through his body in a dark blue river of light. His eyes were wide with terror, as she took back what he had taken from her. *Her innocence. The love of her life.*

Lissa pulled back her hand after the witchfire had stopped flowing. She reared back and drove the pink heel of the shoe she'd been carrying straight into the socket of her father's left eye. At that same moment, the scarecrow flashed its blade and eviscerated him, his foulness spilling forth for the whole world to see.

"If the shoe fits…" Lissa said, stepping down. And the scarecrow joined her.

"Come on, my protector. Let's go find Ingrid."

Together they moved through the tall walls of corn, her companion at her side. She knew somewhere in the green-gold maze was her love. At long last, she would find her.

Just as she'd promised.

Extreme Times, Extreme Measures

Andrew Bell

I never thought the day would come when I'd have to prove my own sanity. As day quickly turned to night, I almost thought the opportunity would pass me by completely. I hadn't slept for over twenty-four hours, but with the aid of copious amounts of caffeine and pain killers, I thought I might just survive. I wandered the bustling streets of Kent, trying not to lose my temper at passersby. I was forever amazed at how they pretended to be following something important, shrouded in cheap perfume or old school aftershave, needing to be somewhere forty-eight hours ago. Hell, they wouldn't recognize something important if it crawled beneath their skin and poked their eyes out.

*Easy...*I thought to myself, breathing in the scent of my own deodorant and aftershave. I wasn't wearing any; the co-mingled scent was coming from the bag I was carrying. I focused my senses on the movement of my feet, watching one foot follow the other, dodging the squeaky leather shoes and squelching trainers, as they busily—aimlessly—passed me by. *Easy...*I thought again, nudging their swaying bodies from out of my way, ignoring their language, however colourful, feet disappearing in gutters now choked with trash and dark brown leaves. Everyone had somewhere they wanted to be, yet nobody really needed to be there. I *needed* London. I needed the sky and air and noise. I needed time and space in which to think, and these people were draining it all away with each and every passing breath.

If one more person bumped into the plastic carrier bag I was swinging, I was going to bite their fucking nose clean off—straight to the goddamned bone. I saw the neon lights winking in the gloom up ahead, and felt a little relieved I'd made it this far. To peel off from the bustling crowd of the side street, especially on such a cold and miserable evening, was what I needed right now.

I entered the store and heard the jangling of the bell above the door, harsh fluorescent light shining down, dazzling me. *"Just take it easy,"* I whispered to myself, looking down at the bag—noticing something that turned my stomach and sent goosebumps across my body like a rash. Maybe I wasn't as perfect as I'd previously thought. I wondered just how careless I could be.

"Just get the stuff you came for and keep walking," I mumbled, as I made my way down the aisle toward two large coolers. *"Screw it."*

Andy and Carl had requested eight cans of beer, but judging by the weight in my pocket, six cans would have to suffice. I took the ice-cold beverages from the cooler, ignoring the small bloodstains on my fingers, and made my way up to the counter. I couldn't believe that less than an hour ago, I was standing in the hallway of the noisy house I shared with three other students, buttoning my overcoat, listening to the blessed silence of their absence. It was Friday night and they'd left for home already. We'd reached the end of our second year of college without killing each other. We gave each other a wide berth, which made such things possible. I didn't give a damn about their interests or the time they invested—or, rather, *wasted*—studying physics and classical education. They could fill their heads with as much of that nonsense as they wished, but art was where the heart was. That's what kept me there, and nothing else.

We had mounting bills to contend with, and that's pretty much all we had in common. September was almost over and I'd be leaving the bright lights of London for the rain soaked streets of Newcastle soon enough. I could already detect the scent of burnished steel from impending storms that always battered the coast. It was something to escape to, certainly, but first I had twenty-four hours to put an end to the misery that'd turned my life completely and utterly upside down.

Andy, Carl, and I were promising artists, all of us. Even Lenny—when he could be bothered to turn in for his lectures—was a good film maker, although he kept to the special effects make-up side of the art. Of course we knew we were no big deal. Heck, we spent our days sleeping mostly, occasionally working on unfinished projects here and there, and our evenings working. I worked in a factory, Carl as a doorman at a local nightspot. How we managed to get this close to our degrees, I'll never know.

We were supposed to be study partners, but tonight—as rare as rocking horse shit—we were sitting around the fire, at least what passed for one. The three-bar heater glowed brightly in the centre of the poorly lit room like a beacon on a misty night, trying its damnedest to stretch its warmth more than two or three inches outward. The scent of burning dust permeated the air as its workings groaned like some pre-war generator, teasing us with the promise of it saying intact for another hour or so, or the terror of it exploding into a hundred, cheap plastic shards, killing us all. The damned thing kept us guessing, alright, and like Neanderthals, intrigued by this new thing called *fire,* we were powerless to take our eyes from it. Any distance we drew away from its comforting heat was like wading naked through an icy lake. Besides, power was rationed in this little abode, so it was a case of either put up or shut up. We chose the former.

The smell of whatever Andy was burning in the kitchen—or *cooking,* I should say—drifted on the cold draft that always managed to squeeze through the balcony doorframe at the far side of the flat, no matter how tightly it was closed. As a rule, we would make sure Andy was aware of our discomfort, from the smells emitting from the kitchen, but on this occasion I decided it was wise to keep *my* opinions to myself. After all, the less attention I drew to the smell *I* was carrying with me, the better.

Candles flickered on a small table built for two—romantic to some but practical to Andy. The hours he could steal working behind a bar not two blocks away, did a better job of stealing from him. The pitiful article of furniture, which seemed to prop up the wall beside the single glazed door leading to the balcony, leaned precariously to one side. A stack of dog-eared Art and Design textbooks and secondhand Hollywood Make-up paperbacks spilled over the edges of the table, about to topple onto the floor at any given moment. Apart from an old leather sofa, and an even older stereo, there was little else to speak of in the place. Spartan was not the word I would use to describe the room. The words *shelter* or perhaps *kennel* were closer to being right.

When I actually noticed a faint breath billow from Carl's mouth, I reached into my jacket pocket and produced a pack of cigarettes, shook one from the box and lit it, if only to generate a little more heat from the lighter near my face.

It was about to get colder.

"What's wrong, smelly? You only have change for *two* tins of deodorant this morning?"

I looked up, blue smoke dancing before my eyes. It was Andy, standing in the doorway of the tiny kitchenette, his skinny body silhouetted by the bright yellow light of the room behind him. He shook his head, grimacing. He could've been just an extension of the darkness surrounding me and Carl—something to be afraid of—that was, until he opened his mouth. He was born and raised in Newcastle, only a few streets away from me, but was as far from a Geordie as a Geordie could get. He hated the city, the people. At least that's what he insisted. But it was a little like a smoker being unaware of the smell of cigarettes after a time. And just like an ex-smoker, as irritating as they could be to the smoking people, he wasn't afraid to voice his opinion, as though he'd seen the error of his ways and everyone else was foolish to continue their habit.

Here in London he always sounded like the actor Jimmy Nail, and we would constantly remind him of it, too. That's why we called him Jimmy. Besides which, he had a massive bald patch he fought daily to conceal. That's where they hit the nail on the head. At least that's one of the many puns we tried to nudge into our conversations.

"Yeah, Blobba," Carl said, frowning. "You don't have to go to such lengths for us, you know? You're turning out like that mad monk over there!" He nodded toward Andy who graciously raised two fingers, unsmiling.

"Been a long shift's all. Get's a bit close in the factory," I said, drawing deeply on my cigarette, hoping they wouldn't notice the blood stains on my fingers. It wasn't a complete lie either. Temperatures soared in that damned place and everyone got sweaty. "You should take a blast of the women! Christ! Y'want one?"

Andy shook his head as I held out my hand, rattling the almost empty box of cigarettes. "Go on then," Carl sighed heavily, grabbing the pack before I could protest.

He was a big bloke, a gentle giant, one might say. Standing almost seven feet tall, everyone and everywhere seemed smaller when he was around. Since clipping his hair down to the wood, he resembled a large bullet, although nobody actually told him that to his face. They wouldn't dare. The cigarette he'd just taken from the pack looked like a toothpick in his hand. It would only last about three drags before burning all the way down to the filter. I hated smoking round him because the cigarettes never lasted very long. We were all students, so money was plenty hard to keep hold of.

As for me, I stand about five feet seven. Some of the others at the student house, thought I could actually be taller laid on my back, the cheeky bastards! Okay, for a penniless student I was a tad overweight. That's why they called me Blobba. I hated the name, but it did have a certain *charm* to it—at least that's what I told myself. It could've been a lot worse. I admit the old folks knew how to feed me when I ripped up sticks every month and rode the train home. If it's on my plate…it's coming with me. And who would I be to refuse? After all, I didn't know where the next meal would be coming from. Just because I worked shifts at a godforsaken circuit factory to keep me in college, didn't make me king of the world—not by a longshot. My family thought I was doing okay for myself, being fat and all, but nothing could have been further from the truth. This was also something I kept to myself.

Secrets, you see? Some weren't as bad as others. We all had them. But tonight there was one in particular I needed to share.

"It's getting late, Blobba," yawned Jimmy, hearing the elevator beyond the rooms paper-thin wall shudder to a halt before continuing on its merry way. He sighed, rubbing at the corners of his eyes. "Got a lecture after dinner tomorrow, so—"

"That's after one, you lazy bastard," Carl piped up, shaking his head. "We get together when there's something the matter, right Blobba?" he said, flicking the spent cigarette in the saucer beside his knee. He gave Jimmy a wink. That's when I should've known—

I should've known!

"Like I told you both earlier," I said, suddenly feeling colder than ever before at the very thought of what I was about to tell them, "This won't take long."

"Pass me another beer from the bag then, fatty," Jimmy said, sighing heavily.

I crawled over to the carrier bag I brought along, being careful not to disturb its contents, and picked out another tin, wiped its cold surface on my jumper, then quickly inspected it for residue before passing it to Jimmy.

"Go on then, Blobba. Haven't got all night."

"Remember when I told you I thought I was being followed home after my shift?"

"Ah, not that *bullshit* again," said Carl, shaking his head again. "I thought this was something *serious!* You been acting all weird the past week or so..."

"Fine," I said, taking another cigarette from the pack and lighting it.

"Look, mate," said Jimmy, sitting down heavily on the battered leather sofa in front of the heater. "You're here now, so just have out with it."

"I don't think you guys will be making fun of me when I tell you what I did last night."

There, I said it...

"Nothing you could do would ever surprise me," Jimmy said.

"You're not making any sense, mate," Carl said, pointing a finger at his temple. "These cheap cigarettes have gone to your bloody brain!"

"Just listen to me for one minute," I said, trying to keep my voice down. I glanced over my shoulder for a second, holding my breath, distracted by a tiny scratching sound at the door leading out to the balcony. I turned toward the heater again, exhaling loudly, before going on. I had to relax, even though I could feel my entire body shaking. "You're my mates, okay? This has been on my mind for some time now. Hell, I can't remember the last time I felt this afraid. It's over...I know it's over...but..."

I heard a shuffling noise, except this time it was coming from just outside the front door. I froze, unable to breathe for a few moments as my heart suddenly skipped a beat. Then the noise stopped.

"For godssake, Blobba, it's just those two daft kids from the flat next door," Jimmy said, yawning. "One of these days I'm going to smash their tiny empty skulls in with a baseball bat. I swear I am..."

"You probably wouldn't do a friggin' gram of damage," Carl grumbled.

Jimmy rolled his eyes.

Carl got the message and shut the hell up.

"So...last night," I said slowly, choosing my words carefully. "I finally did something about it."

"Right...And? You did something about what?" asked Jimmy, shrugging his shoulders.

"I'm not the crazy fat guy that everyone thinks I am," I said.

"Yeah," Carl chuckled, firing a glance at Jimmy. "Nobody thinks you're crackers, mate. Fat on the other hand—"

"Like I told you," I said, calmly. "It lasted for about a week."

"And now it's over, and we can all go to bed—separately," Jimmy teased.

Carl grinned.

"Yes," I said softly, feeling the rock roll off of my shoulder. "Yes, it's all over now."

"You don't seem convinced," Jimmy countered.

"I am, Jimmy," I said, taking a deep breath, "I am."

For a fat guy I could move pretty quickly when pushed, and the evenings being as dark and cold as they'd been of late, I'd pulled out all the stops. Hell, I'd even opted to wear my training shoes instead of the standard-issue toe-capped work boots they thrust at me after my first shift. I'd slip them on at the factory, but then kick the buggers aside when it was blessed tools down *time.*

My locker was broken, but I didn't care. If it would spur me along quicker, then the training shoes it would have to be. Besides, staying back those extra couple of minutes, hanging round the locker room, so to speak, ensured me I'd be on my own along the road, which suited me just fine. I preferred to brave the inclement weather. After all, a kid of nineteen, studying to be an artist, his whole life ahead of him, wasn't exactly a popular amalgamation in such a place, whose population could barely see beyond their own noses, let alone what could be lying there on the horizon if only they'd take a peek.

The number of petty squabbles that'd escalated into full blown fights outside the workhouse was ridiculous. Everyone was a potential punching bag, therefore every worker needed to tread carefully. The industrial estate was nothing more than a bleak cul-de-sac, comprising of four standard sized units, sharing a single lamp post at its centre—I would use the term heart, *but it had none to speak of.*

When the klaxon told us it was the end of the shift and we all spilled like ink onto the path, it wasn't wise to drag your feet, so we moved out without ceremony. Like the warm fingers of Jimmy's heater, the overhead lamps' beam only stretched so far before severing ties and leaving you to the mercy of the surrounding darkness. I wrapped my coat tightly around myself and headed off along the estate, just the way I'd done for over a year. Even during the summer months, when the night's light made the area a little safer to roam, I still kept my head down. But this particular night was different. I knew something was happening. But this time I was sure I was right—it wasn't just in my head.

Upon passing through the estate's tall iron perimeter fence, a small lamppost to my left flickered as though a firefly had been caught within its globe, and had been burned against its bulb. I glanced to my right before crossing the road, where other small establishments were still operating after ten o'clock evening—the graveyard shift now in full swing. At least their neon signs would light my path a bit, *I thought.*

That's when I noticed something moving at the corner of my eye.

Just get moving, *I told myself.* For crying out loud, whatever is going on is going on. Probably has been for a week, so tonight's no different! Of course it's happening again, you're letting it!

I felt my body shudder as if I'd stepped on a live wire. The hairs on the nape of my neck stood erect, and I could feel the hairs springing up across my scalp. Goosebumps rose along the length of my body, from head to toe, and I could see bright flashes swirling before my eyes. This reminded me of the way I'd felt my first day at the factory—being shown around—eyes following me like I was a pedophile being lead to his jail cell. Poisonous, bitter souls, watching my every move, seeking out some chink in my armor.

As I set out walking, I could smell something strange in the air around me, like a rancid piece of meat left to roast in the noonday sun. But there was also the tang of citrus riding its shoulders too.

*Despite the sound of the industrial wheels grinding and moaning in the factories to my right, I was aware of the occasional bang and clatter, as though—*Don't! Just don't think about it! Keep moving your feet. That's it. Left, right. Left, right. Left, right.

It felt like someone, or something, was following me.

*That…*thing *is following me! I heard heavy footfalls behind me.*

They're NOT footfalls, for crying out loud! It's all in your bloody head, man!

I quickened my pace, feeling the slush of the wet leaves and soil seeping through the soles of my training shoes, chilling me to the bone. My heart raced in an effort to catch up with the waning moon on my left, which always seemed just one step ahead of me. I suddenly felt as though this was one race I'd already lost. I could see the old warehouse which marked the corner of the adjacent industrial estate, knowing that if I reached it I would be safe and sound. It was strange how I'd walked this road over three hundred times and had taken the trek for granted each time. Now it felt like it was a matter of life and death. And, hell, who knew, perhaps it was.

Nobody's going to die tonight, or any other night!

You're letting your mind run away with you.

There, you've nearly made it!

Standing opposite the warehouse, my lungs burning as they fought to control the rush of air I craved, my pounding heart knitting a tattoo against my ribs, I saw the thing directly in front of me. It stood, a silhouette against the moon, hot breath billowing about its head like the exhaust from the industrial chimneys behind it. Eyes like diamond chips sparkled in what I can only describe as its head. Teeth, long and glistening, dripped with saliva, splitting its lower jaw in two. And that's when it disappeared into the shadows of the warehouse.

The nights passed, the shifts rolling into one, and my holidays were almost here. All I needed to do was make it to the factory shut down, then I knew I'd be alright. But I'd hear that sound—that thundering of feet—hear them quicken, keeping up with me as I, too, hurried along. The warehouse just up ahead, getting closer. That distinct smell of meat and citrus making my stomach churn. I would turn and see that same creature staring back at me. Those eyes*—like diamonds.*

I'd told Jimmy and Carl, but only when I knew the first sighting had been more than just a coincidence. That's when I realized a problem shared is definitely a problem spread around the whole damn college! Yes, I took the jibes—the games—the stickers and notes left on my locker and attached all over my over coat. But I knew *it was real, it was happening and most of all, it was happening to* me. *I was on my own and it was up to me to prove I wasn't losing my mind.*

So last night I didn't run. I walked along as nice as you pleased. After all, if the thing was going to hurt me, I'd be dead already.

THUD!

CRUNCH!

Make all the noise you want…

The moon kept pace, always one step ahead.

This circus had gone on long enough!

As I stood at the corner, about to cross the road, I swiftly stepped into the darkness surrounding the warehouse instead, not knowing where the hell I was going or what I was going to do when I finally got there.

Stepping through the door, the place felt as cold as a meat locker. In fact the temperature seemed colder here than it did outside. It was free from the elements at least, I thought, slowly stepping through the small hallway, catching my reflection in a shard of broken glass which might've once served as the screen of a reception area or office.

I almost jumped through the fucking thing, when I glanced up and noticed objects as large as cattle suspended from the darkness above me. The chains holding them, as if for dear life, were motionless. Slivers of moonlight pouring through the cracks in the ceiling high above glistened off their metal links, forming a shimmering pool of silver on the floor in front of me. I could almost hear voices whispering in the shadows of the long hallway, despite the crying wind seeping through the cracks in the floorboards and ancient walls. Whatever the place had been used for in the past was still present in the chilled air. I wrinkled my nose at its lingering stench. It couldn't be feces, surely? The stench seemed to be coming from directly behind me. I spun round, eyes wide, not daring to utter a word, let alone breathe. There was a flash of movement to my left, but I couldn't quite discern it.

I don't like this, Blobba!

Then my heart skipped at the sudden snap of cloth to my right, like the sound of wings or a sail caught in a stiff ocean breeze.

What the hell are you trying to prove, lard ass? Get the hell out of there!

"Not yet," *I whispered to the dank air. And that's when I took the long, serrated kitchen knife from the small rucksack I was carrying. Not fully sure what I intended to do with it. Or even if I'd use it.*

I tried to concentrate on the sounds swirling around me; somehow detect the source of whatever it was that moved through the darkness. The seeping wind caught what it could, and carried some of the sounds away, leaving me to the screams of my own reeling mind, and the slants of silver light glistening viciously off the blade in my unsteady hand. Then I saw the figure standing in the silver pool before me.

I wanted to turn and run, but I couldn't move. The messages from my brain had lost contact with my body, and now I stood like something carved from stone, a statue with a beating heart. The damned thing was staring directly at me, hot breath billowing about its face like steam. As it slowly stepped out from the disc of ice-cold moonlight it was standing in—becoming one with the darkness—all I caught were the sparkling eyes as it came for me.

I wasn't about to move. Not now. I held my ground, and the knife—in both shaking hands—waiting for the creature's gleaming teeth to tear me apart.

Move your arse! *was all my mind could manage.*

I closed my eyes, took a deep breath, and made my way forward through all that black, determined not to stop until one of us was dead.

That's when Jimmy and Carl burst out laughing.

"What? Care to share the frigging joke!"

"Are you going to tell him, or shall I?" sniggered Carl, almost choking on a mouthful of beer. He dropped the can beside him and shook his head.

"Yeah, *you* might as well, mate," replied Jimmy, sitting back on the sofa, closing his eyes. "It's *old* news now, joke's over. To be honest, I can't be bothered with the whole thing anymore."

I felt the rock suddenly roll back up onto my shoulder once more, my blood turning to iced water.

"What *whole thing*? You're not making any sense!"

"Will you keep your voice down?" Jimmy whispered, sitting forward now, his face close to the heater. "I've got to live here, you know!"

"The whole thing was a joke, Blob," Carl said, flatly.

"A—*joke?*"

"Yes. Remember those? Funny things you laugh at."

"No…this isn't happening, Jimmy. This isn't happening." I heard my own words as they repeated themselves over and over in my head. I started pacing back and forth, shapes and colors appearing before my eyes as I did. I ran my fingers through my hair, again and again. "*This isn't happening. This* can't *be happening!*"

"Is he for real?" Carl scoffed, looking to Jimmy for answers.

Jimmy got up and stepped in front of the heater, blocking its heat for a second. I knew he was approaching me, trying to catch up as I paced, but I had to keep moving. Like a shark, if I stopped, I'd suffocate and die. My heart was about to explode in my chest. And I felt like I was going to die.

You're not going to die! You're panicking!

"What's happening, mate?" Jimmy grabbed my shoulders with the power of a vice grip. "Are you going to be okay?" Pain lanced through my muscles, but it seemed to draw me slowly back down to earth. "Fucking *LOOK AT ME!*" Jimmy shouted. "What's the matter with you?"

"A—*joke?*" I repeated, blankly.

"Yeah…Lenny should be proud of himself, getting you to wet your pants like you are now. In fact, I think I'll get the bugger on the phone, and clear everything up," Carl said, laughing, grabbing his mobile phone from his pocket.

"Don't bother, Carl," Jimmy said, his eyes never leaving mine. My shoulders felt numb as his grip tightened. "I already tried calling him last night…and again this morning. No answer. Bastard's not answering his phone…"

"Lenny was…Lenny was in on the bloody joke, too?" I asked. "Why did you guys do it?" I asked, my voice barely a whisper. "Why did you make me prove to you—"

"Prove what? Prove you can't take a bloody joke?" Jimmy asked. "Well, we've certainly proven that, haven't we?" Jimmy added.

"Prove to you that I'm not a fucking psycho!" Carl shouted.

"Carl, shut the hell up!" Jimmy spat over his shoulder, not caring about the noise they were making. The fucking neighbors could complain to his landlord all they wanted.

"Carl, get me a lager, would you?" I said, my voice cracking—maintaining eye contact with Jimmy the whole time.

Carl sneered.

"Just do it…please!"

I heard the other man give an exaggerated sigh before crossing the room to the carrier bag I brought along tonight, which contained the beer.

He reached inside the bag and froze.

* * *

I knew they wouldn't phone the police. After all, their lives—*all* of our lives—would've been over if they did.

Dead.

As dead as Lenny.

Yes, it was a shame about Lenny. Good old Lenny Spencer, as crazy as the day was long. Never around when you needed him, always hanging about when you didn't. He could dish out the jokes as much as take them. The poor fool was due to stay with his family in Ireland for the autumn holidays, but he'd decided to fuck with my head instead. Shame. He was a talented special effects make-up artist. He could've easily worked in Hollywood, or for one of the UK movie houses.

"Never dare a fool" he'd say. "A ten pound note and I'll do anything."

"Yes, you were good, Lenny. Too bloody good, if you ask me." I muttered the words, closing the door softly behind me.

I made my way to the stairs and slowly descended, giving the squeaky fourth step a wide berth. I didn't know why I was being so cautious—the neighbors in the building wouldn't've been able to hear me over the screams coming from Jimmy's flat anyway.

Now Lenny didn't have a head to fuck with. It was in the carrier bag.

I was one less fool they'd fuck with. That was for sure!

Hodmedod

Stuart Keane

"Urgh…shit…where am I?"

The acidic, fuzzy taste of a hangover lingered in his throat as his tongue peeled away from the roof of his mouth and rested lazily between his teeth. He sucked air between his lips in order to circulate some saliva, his mouth emitting a soft slurping noise. Stagnant, warm air entered his mouth and caused him to cough. Four soft coughs were enough to bring him out of his stupor.

Nicolas opened his eyes.

The world was a blank white canvas.

Must've rolled under the duvet after that sick night, bro!

Nicolas reached for the blanket. Nothing happened. His arm wouldn't move. Grinning, he realised he must've rested on his arms throughout the night. They were both stretched out beside him. *Give it a moment. The blood will start flowing again soon enough.*

Nicolas struggled to remember the previous evening. How did he get back to his bed? Despite the fog that shrouded his brain, short bursts of memory returned. He recalled partying with Paul and James in London, their home city, the latter celebrating his bachelor party. The wedding was imminent—only three weeks away—so they'd indulged liberally with strippers, drugs, and enough booze to shame a fraternity. Shreds of information returned to Nicholas, but one obvious memory raged in his throat.

Man, I need some water.

Why are my arms still numb?

Nicolas tried shaking his arms.

Nothing…

What the hell?

Surely, the blood should be flowing by now.

But, it wasn't. His arms were inert at his side. Not numb or dead.

Tied down. Restricted.

Tied down? There's no way...

The familiar feeling returned to his arms and they started to feel heavy once more. Gravity took its course and all of a sudden, his equilibrium returned.

Hang on...I'm not laying down, I'm upright. What the hell?

Needles prickled and poked at the muscles beneath, causing him to yelp with the sudden discomfort. Normally he'd shake the pins and needles away, but today he couldn't. The prickling, interspersed with slight shivers, created its own little torturous ritual. Gritting his teeth in anger and confusion, Nicolas rode it out until his hands felt normal again. He sighed. His hands were flexing and closing, bringing blood back to the tips of his fingers. Once everything felt normal, he tried to lift his arms. They wouldn't move.

What the fuck?

That's when he felt the binds around his wrists. Soreness exploded down both limbs. His wrists felt raw and swollen. Numbing irritation tickled his body from both arms, and that's when he realised his wrists were bleeding and bruised. The tender skin felt mushy beneath the mysterious manacles.

James and Paul have a lot to answer for!

Nicolas felt the unnerving cloud of fear and panic enveloping his mind's eye. His breath became ragged and short—raspy. He tried pulling his arms forward, but tight restriction greeted him. Whoever had bound him had done an excellent job. Despite the panic, growing irritation, and confusion, Nicolas felt a grin spreading across his lips.

"Ha ha, nice one, fellas. Great joke. You fucked up though. You're supposed to prank the groom, not the best man."

Silence.

The only sound, faint as it was, emitted from the wind. He could feel it on his legs. It caused his jeans to ruffle occasionally. That's when Nicolas realised he was outside. A sudden chill breathed up his legs, raising the coarse hairs on his calves and thighs. He felt his scrotum shrivel and the hair on his head retracted a little. A resounding shiver rattled his body.

A wooden pole bumped his spine. Nicolas couldn't bend his back. When he tried leaning forward, nothing happened. The unfamiliar, cold object stretched the length of his spine and remained there, snug and tight.

Shit, they've crucified me? They've literally crucified me!

The fuckwits!

The wood felt cold and damp. *Must be the morning dew? If I'm outside, that is.*

Carefully, he elevated his left leg into the air. His ankles weren't bound. He slowly lowered the foot back to its normal position. He repeated this with his right leg. His feet were balancing on a knob of wood. Removing both would send him falling to the ground. With the tightened shackles around his arms, doing so would be a dangerous idea.

You don't know how high you are. So be cool.

Famous last words...

He breathed out, the white visage rippled with his warm, sour breath. He inhaled and coughed once more. For some reason, he imagined beer breath was worse than bourbon breath and thanked himself that he'd opted for liquor. Whenever he breathed, the white visage flapped slightly.

And what the fuck is this white thing over my head?

Nicolas shook his head left and right. The obstruction moved slightly but stopped fast under his chin. Much like his wrists, he felt a small tightness cup his jawline. The white thing, probably a pillowcase, was strapped on. The faint smell of fresh cotton confirmed his suspicions.

"Seriously, guys, this isn't *fucking funny* anymore."

Nicolas felt like freaking out but didn't dare. One wrong movement and he'd topple to the unseen ground. Who knew what lay down there?

Right, summarize. You're a lawyer. C'mon, you do this for a living—this is your livelihood, for heaven's sake. Why would James and Paul crucify you? Use the minimal evidence. You don't believe in God but Paul does. That's one possible reason. Churches scare you. True, another possible motive.

Maybe they're a bunch of cunts who took a sick joke one step too far.

A gust of wind rocked the wooden device, and Nicolas felt his body swaying left for several long seconds before settling again. Nausea swept through his bloodstream as his body believed he was going to topple from the unknown height. Strong, cold breeze snaked up his legs, lifting his jeans somewhat and rifling his boxers. The white pillowcase shifted significantly, the bind beneath his jawline slipped and slid to his lower lip. Still lodged, Nicolas felt it digging into his teeth.

Oww, fuck!

A trickle of blood oozed over his teeth and tickled his tongue. His gum was bleeding. The copper taste combined with his hangover made him retch. His cranium bounced back against the wooden pole with a *clonk.* He cursed under his breath and exhaled, riding the pain. He swallowed the small dosage of blood.

The gust diminished. Nicolas listened for any noise, any indication of where he was. He heard an ever-present rustling, an eerie, calm noise on the wind. *What was that?* He recognized the sound but couldn't pinpoint it.

Fucking hangover.

"Paul? James? Anyone? If you bastards are listening, this isn't fucking funny anymore, get me the *fuck* down!"

Suddenly, drinking a bottle of Jack didn't seem like a wise idea anymore. The sweet taste of Jack emerged from his stomach, floating on his breath, mutating with the curse of a hangover and when the essence escaped his lips, it was pungent, sickly.

The hangover kicked in.

Nicolas vomited into the pillowcase. The puke shot from his mouth like hot water from a hose. His head moved forward, inches from the vomit impact spot. The weight of the liquid pushed the material back down to his jawline

Within seconds, the vomit rolled down the white cotton, nestled against his chin, and dribbled down his neck, seeping beyond the bag and trickling down his chest, beneath his shirt. He could feel warm goo and lumps of food—probably the last-minute kebab from Abdul's—congealing into his two-day stubble.

The pillowcase, weighed heavy with acrid, bodily fluids, floated closer to his face. The bile slicked the tip of his nose. The smell was awful and made him vomit again; the proximity of the white visage caused the second dousing of bile to spatter his face. It oozed from his eyebrows to his nose, and some went in his hair. He closed his eyes and felt warm fluid streaming over his eyelids. The putrid smell of meat, chips and alcohol engulfed his facial prison.

Nicolas coughed and hacked, choking on the fumes.

"Who's there?"

Nicolas opened his eyes. The fumes immediately brought tears to his eyes. He coughed violently. Before he could respond, the strange voice prompted him again.

"I can hear you…answer me, who's there?"

Was he imagining that? Did someone just speak?

Nicolas cleared his throat. "My name's Nicolas. Who's that?"

"Nicolas? Oh, thank the Lord! Nic, mate, it's Paul."

"Paul? Paul, you piece of shit, get me down!"

Silence for a second. Nicolas spat into the pool of vomit, aware it was slowly leaking out of the pillowcase onto his chest. The warm bile was growing cold and lumpy. He tried to place his mind elsewhere. "I…I…I can't," Paul responded.

"This isn't the time to fuck about, Paul! I'm covered in sick and my wrists are fucking bleeding. You better be ready to get a kick in…"

"I can't because I'm tied up, too."

The revelation slammed Nicolas in the heart like a sledgehammer. His breath shot out of him, inflating the pillowcase a little. He moved his head back, not wanting the puke-covered whiteness to slick his nose again.

"What do you mean you're tied up?"

"I can't move. My arms are strapped down or something. I can't see. There's a bag or something over my head."

"Paul, calm down. I'm in the same position as you. Is the bag white?"

"Why in God's name does that matter?" Nicolas heard Paul apologize to God as he said that, taking the Lord's name in vain.

"Paul, listen to me. It's not important but snap out of it, God isn't going to get you down from there. *Listen* to me. Mine's white. What's yours?"

"Mine's pink. It could be a pillowcase or something…it's moving on the wind."

Nicolas knew some small talk would keep Paul distracted. Being a man of the Bible, Paul didn't like confrontation, he was the wimp of the group and Nicolas always acted like an older brother to him. Paul was a nice guy, loyal, innocent and friendly. And he knew how to have a great time, but sometimes he lived for his religion and in certain circumstances, it wasn't appropriate.

Like now.

Crucified in God knows where.

The irony wasn't lost on Nicholas and he grinned. "I think it's a pillowcase or something. It's warm, like when you wake up with your head between piles of pillows."

"True. Wait, what did you say?"

Nicolas frowned. He felt drying vomit crack in the crease lines. "I said we have pillowcases on our head."

"No, before that. Did you say God won't get me *down?*"

The emphasis was there and Nicolas knew where Paul was going. "Yes, Paul. Don't panic but I think we…we've been crucified!"

Two seconds of silence. Then, "*Arghhhh fuck,* fuck, fuck. Get me down, get me *down!*"

Paul never swore and the cursing made Nicolas jump. His left leg lifted from the knob and nearly sent him falling. He quickly regained his footing. "Paul, calm down, it's okay, we're only tied down. There's no nails or anything, okay?"

He knew that last sentence was a stupid one. He would've know, if his hands or wrists were shafted with spikes of metal. It seemed to work, though. The screaming stopped and Paul calmed down. His breath was hardly audible.

"Paul, you have to stay calm, okay? I don't know how we got here but James is probably behind it. Probably did this because he thought we'd tie him up somewhere. The groom getting one up on the best men. Crafty sonofabitch."

Paul was still breathing heavily. He didn't speak.

"C'mon, Paul. Chat with me. It'll keep us occupied until James comes and releases us. He's getting a fucking cleaning bill, though."

"Why would he do this to us?"

"I don't know. I hate churches…no offense, so for me, it's an easy prank. For you, I suppose there's some joy in crucifying a man who's in love with Jesus."

Paul didn't say a word. Nicolas knew he was nodding. He did that a lot.

"So we just wait until he comes back?" Paul's voice was jittery.

"I suppose so. But we're in this together, okay? Talk to me." Nicholas tried to reassure Paul, knowing the slightest issue could push him over the edge.

"Are your wrists hurting?" Paul's voice was calm.

Nicolas closed his eyes. "Yes, they're a bit sore, yes."

"Mine too. He could have loosened the binds somewhat. What a cock."

Nicolas smiled. Cock was a mundane word. He preferred cunt, fuckface, or shithead. "Yes, he's a right cock."

"I didn't even want to come out. I had Mass this morning and I'm missing it for *this.*"

Nicolas felt his eyes widening in surprise. "You can miss Mass? Isn't that against your religion or something?"

"Nah, we can miss the odd one. We can always make it up another day."

"But we're co-best men so it's worth it, right?"

"Not now, no." Nicolas agreed with that. Paul was right on the money. "My arms better heal before the wedding."

Nicolas nodded. "I suppose a week is enough."

Silence filled the unknown distance between them. Paul coughed. Nicolas started to breathe through his mouth. The vomit had dried now, caking the white surface. His neck felt lumpy and stiff. "Hey, Paul?"

"Yep?"

"Is your pillowcase tied on?"

"I think so. I can feel the restriction on my neck."

"I puked in mine…if that helps."

Paul laughed, an insane and crazy laugh borne of frustration and disbelief. Nicolas had to admit his situation was pretty funny. After a moment, Paul calmed down. "You're joking, right?"

"Nope, vomited right here in the bag. Abdul's kebab paid me a visit."

Paul gagged. "Seriously? I told you those things were bad for you."

"Yeah well, after this I won't be eating another one."

"Think of it as a dietary decision. You'll be better off for it. The Lord will see you onto the right path."

Nicolas rolled his eyes. He said nothing.

A gust of wind rocked him again and this time, his body hung in the air to the right. The pillowcase loosened and slipped again, the binding slapping the bottom of his nose. It scraped some of the dried puke from his chin, grinding into his stubble, making Nicolas wince. His mouth tasted the fresh, open air and Nicolas gulped in huge mouthfuls of it. It felt cool on his sweaty, vomit-soaked skin, and the gust stopped, returning him to his upright position. Goosebumps prickled his cold skin, making him shiver.

"Did you feel that?" Paul asked.

"Yeah, the wind keeps swaying me around. The crucifix isn't very secure."

Nicolas expected another panic attack from Paul. He was surprised when he came back with, "Mine's secure. It didn't rock much; I felt the wind going up my legs. It's chilly, like morning air. You don't think it's too late, do you?"

"I don't think so. You're right…it feels too cold to be afternoon. Who knows, though, we hit the bar pretty hard last night."

"I'm never drinking again. Becks has a horrid aftertaste."

"Well, you did drink seventeen of them."

"They were small bottles, though."

"Yes, but you didn't indulge in one of Abdul's disgusting kebabs. You know that's the cure for any hangover right there. Well, in moderation." Nicolas slapped the roof of his mouth with his dry tongue. He opened his mouth again, letting the chilled air soothe his throat.

"I heard the guy jerks off in the mayo. Why would you risk eating that shi—stuff?" Paul uttered in revulsion.

"It's an urban myth. He'd have the health inspectors down his neck quicker than a whore's drawers hitting the deck."

"I don't think Abdul would give a toss. Or maybe he would, considering the rumour. I suppose you're right though. I prefer a steak myself. None of that processed rubbish."

Nicolas said nothing. Despite the hangover, he felt pangs of hunger in his stomach. "Man, I could murder a kebab now." He stifled a smile.

"You're kidding, right? You're an animal, Nic." Paul laughed.

"I suppose so. Wouldn't say no to a cheeseburger either…"

The wind rocked Nicolas's crucifix again. He moved backward this time, tilting back, similar to being in a dentist's chair. The pillowcase flapped against his half-exposed face. Nicolas wished the cotton sack would slide off and leave him be. It loosened slightly but held. The crucifix returned to its standing position.

No such luck.

Nicholas felt tightness in his legs; his muscles were starting to seize up.

"There goes the wind again," Paul chirped.

"I'll vomit again if it doesn't let up," Nicolas responded. He poked his tongue out, lapping at the fresh air. The pillowcase sat strapped diagonally across his face, pushing against his left nostril. Small pangs of pain shot through his face as the grip tightened.

"Stop talking about vomit. I'm feeling queasy." Paul hocked in his throat. Nicolas grunted in revulsion. "Now *that's* disgusting."

"Where do you think we are, Nic?" James's back garden? His workplace?"

"I don't think Megan would allow this to go on, especially with a baby on the way. James has matured a lot recently, and she lets him off on certain things, but crucifying his best friends in the garden for a prank…yeah, that's pushing the boundary."

Nicolas rolled his tongue over his teeth, feeling the morning fuzz. He heaved again and continued. "Not to mention he wouldn't want us disturbing Mrs. Farnsworth. Stupid old bat would drop dead and sing a Hail Mary at the sight of us. Mind you, it's his stag do so Megan might not be home. Who knows?"

"True. I don't think it's the workplace. He works on an industrial estate and I haven't heard a single car since we've been holding our impromptu mothers' meeting. Just that fucking creepy wind." Paul started whispering again, repenting his vehement sin.

"I recognize the wind. There's a familiarity to the sound. I just don't know where I know it *from.*" Nicolas lifted his legs again. Left, then right. Keeping the blood circulating. His wrists were numb now, the pain almost bearable. His legs were growing tighter, relieved slightly by his movement. He winced.

Paul spoke. "I like Megan, though. You weren't wrong; she's helped James grow up a lot. The guy deserves someone like her after the shit he went through."

"Yeah, Aimee was an absolute bitch. She took him for granted…"

Paul interrupted. "Not to mention she fucked his boss…stupid whore."

Nicolas nodded, aware no one could see the motion. "Megan's a good match for him. I can't wait to meet their kid. They're going to be so happy together."

"I heard he's calling the kid Jesus. How cool would that be?"

Nicolas snorted. "In your little world, very. I wouldn't fancy its chances in school, though. Mind you, growing a beard in adulthood may provide some interesting career choices."

Paul laughed. Silence returned for a moment.

The wind blew in the background. The rustling grew and subsided, several times over. Nicolas was aware of the lack of technological sounds—no cars, no cellphones, no machine noise, no hum of power lines. He noticed his brow creasing in thought.

The wind picked up again. Familiar with the routine, Nicolas waved his head from side to side violently, trying to shift the pillowcase. The wind rocked the crucifix and the cotton slipped, gave and flew off his head. A whipping noise sent it to the unseen background and Nicolas was free.

Yes!

The cold morning air was refreshing on his face. His eyes squinted, cautious of the sudden glare. He closed them for a moment to let the cool air soothe his sweaty, puke-encrusted skin. After a moment, Nicolas opened his eyes a fraction and took in the surroundings.

"Thank fuck. Paul, my pillowcase just came off. I'm free."

"Yes. Well, it's a small result. Mine isn't going anywhere. What can you see?"

"I'm just letting my eyes adjust to the light." Nicolas looked down at the ground, avoiding eye contact with the sky.

His eyes cleared and his vision returned. The colours faded in like a bad film cut until his vision sharpened and his focus took over. "Thank God, I can see."

"Oi," Paul exclaimed in anger.

"Sorry, mate. I apologise. Let's see where we are."

Nicolas couldn't see his feet.

He frowned, feeling the stiffness of the vomit on his brow.

A dark-brown, wooden pole stretched to the grassy ground below him, his feet hidden behind a flailing white sheet peppered with blue flowers.

He shifted his left foot to confirm his suspicion. A stout wooden stub was secured to the pole itself but he could only confirm by touch alone. As he moved his leg, the sheet billowed out from his touch. It covered him from neck to toe.

That's not a sheet…it's a huge white shirt.

He saw a pair of oversized brown trousers below him, starting from the bottom of the shirt to the ground. Attached to the pole, they touched the ground, crumpling because they were too long, swelling occasionally with the wind. He estimated his feet were three or four feet off the ground, a sizeable fall. A jolt of concern seized his brain.

This looked a bit strange.

The ground was grassy and dry, the tips of the grass yellow with age. The grass was tatty and damaged from overuse. Like someone, something, or both passed through here regularly, wearing a groove into the dirt.

Nicolas looked up.

He was in a cornfield.

"What the fuck?"

"What?" Paul answered.

But Nicolas didn't answer.

His tired, alcohol-abused eyes fell on a dilapidated house in the background. A farmhouse. The paint on it was white and flaky, milky with age and neglect. The wooden roof was in a serious state of disrepair, tiles were missing and a small hole was visible above the front door. Planks and nails barricaded the glassless windows. The grass and foliage around the exterior was long, unmaintained, overgrown, and messy. A shopping trolley, upturned and rusted, sat tangled in the grass. A dirt path, nearly invisible behind weeds and a cracked brick wall, wound its way to the main road that ran parallel to the building itself.

The road snaked past their location, between two cornfields. They sat in one, the other stretched into the foreseeable distance. On the horizon, the sun was rising behind three small hills, casting an ambient red glow on everything in its path.

In another situation, the view would have been beautiful and magnificent.

"Holy shit," Nicolas uttered, caught up in the moment.

"What do you see? Where are you?"

Nicolas snapped out of his stupor. He craned his neck to the sound of Paul's voice. His eyes settled on his friend.

"What in God's name…?"

"I told you not to…"

"Shut up, Paul. Just shut up a minute."

Paul remained silent. Nicolas closed his eyes and squeezed them shut. He reopened them, not believing his eyes.

The scene was familiar. Paul was dressed in identical clothing to Nicolas. Long white shirt dashed with blue flowers, long brown trousers that upended when they hit the dirt. However, from this angle, the full, horrifying picture became clear.

A huge crucifix, Paul's arms outstretched and bound to it, stood off to Nicolas's right, just within his peripheral vision. To the eye, he looked crucified. However, the long sleeves of the white shirt smothered his arms, drowning them in their inflated size.

Straw protruded from the holes in the arms. Nicolas' eyes glided central to the arms and saw the pillowcase. A cartoonish, almost creepy face was scribbled on it, its crude felt-tip mouth permanently crafted in a smirk of malice. The eyes were merely dots centered in egg-shaped circles. A brown fedora rested on Paul's head. Nicolas guessed that due to the inflated size of the monstrosity before him, it lay on the peak of the crucifix.

Nicolas realised his original guess had been wrong.

They hadn't been crucified.

They were dressed as scarecrows.

"This is fucked up. Right, Paul…you mustn't panic, okay? You promise you won't?"

Paul said nothing. His movement was almost imperceptible beneath the gigantic clothes that covered him. Nicolas wondered if he was looking in his direction, following the sound of his voice. "You're fucking joking, right? You say something like *that* and expect me to remain calm?"

"Well, some new information has come to light…but at least we aren't crucified." Nicolas considered his next words carefully. "We're dressed up as…as scarecrows."

Paul laughed hard. "You fucking what?"

"Easy, Paul. Don't you want to—?"

"—No, I don't fucking want to repent my sins. Jesus *fucking* Christ, Nicolas. First we're crucified for whatever reason is going through James's twisted little mind. That's fine, I get the reason behind it, ha ha—fucking hilarious. I'm religious, you ain't, and it terrifies you. Well done, score one for the groom."

"So why is this worse?" Nicolas looked along his arms and realised straw was poking out of his makeshift arms too. He couldn't feel the straw on his hands.

"You really are a dickhead aren't you? The crucifix had a reason. It worked in the context of a prank. This doesn't. What in the name of Satan's scrotum does this have to do with *anything*? It doesn't. And I don't fucking like it."

Nicolas realised his friend was right. He looked up and opened his mouth to say something…his eyes focused and looked to the right of Paul.

He screamed.

A loud, guttural, horrific scream.

"What? Did you fall?" Paul asked innocently. "Don't tell me you broke your arm or something?"

"My God…*James!*"

"Oh he turned up, did he? It's about bloody time. Okay, James, this is a great prank and all. Now, do you think…?"

"James! What the fuck!"

Paul stopped mid-sentence. "Nicolas…what, you're scaring me."

James's impaled corpse sat on a crucifix inches from where Paul stood, inert. If not for the pillowcase, Paul would have smelt or seen the dead, bloated corpse that sat before him. His face was a mutilated mess. Someone had ripped his jaw off, leaving his top teeth and bloody, drooping muscle in its place. A piece of sinew wobbled on the intermittent wind. Unlike Nicolas and Paul, James wore his own clothes, his wrists savagely impaled to the crucifix with brutal looking pairs of pliers. Someone had forced the metal claws through his flesh, severing the skin and muscle, and dried blood had congealed around them.

His shirtfront, previously a white polo neck, shone red with slick blood and bodily fluids, probably from the vicious jaw removal. The shirt was now a dark shade of red and brown. Someone had removed his trousers and severed his penis. It sat on the ground inches from the foot of his crucifix. Sagging and limp, it was obvious the body was dead and had been for some time. The dead eyes stared off into the distance, at nothing in particular.

Nicolas vomited. The vomit splattered his shirtfront, the brown trousers below and rasped onto the grass below him. The sound echoed across the cornfields, startling a few crows nestling in a nearby hedge. It also piqued Paul's attention. "Nicolas, talk to me, what's going on?"

"It's...James."

"Is he going to get us down? James, you prick, this isn't funny..."

"He's dead." Nicolas uttered, dejected and shocked.

Silence. The familiar wind came back to Nicolas and it registered. The sound was corn blowing in the wind. Strangely familiar before, the new situation made the sound all the more eerie. Nicolas struggled to look up. When he managed to, he expected to see evil eyes peering out from the corn.

None did.

This isn't a Stephen King movie.

Why the fuck are we here?

"He...he can't be dead. We literally only saw him...minutes, no, hours... ago."

Nicolas nodded, exhausted. He couldn't muster any words.

Paul and Nicolas heard footsteps approaching from behind them. Small dainty footsteps, breaking dried grass and scuffing dry dirt. A new, muffled voice broke the silence.

"Seven hours ago, Paul. It was seven hours ago when you last saw James."

Nicolas strained to turn his head but couldn't. The sun was higher now, stark and bright in the morning sky. Nicolas squinted against the glare. The cornfields glowed a wonderful yellow and green. The wind rustled the entire field in unison. The sound reverberated in Nicolas's ears.

Paul spoke first. "Who are you, what did you do to our friend?"

The footsteps came closer and suddenly the person walked into view. Nicolas saw movement in his peripheral vision as the stranger made their presence known.

"Hello, Nicolas. My, you look a little...peaky."

Nicolas recognised the voice. A jolt of fear shot through his scrotum, through his stomach and prickled the hairs on his arms. A cold hand of betrayal and horror snaked up his spine. His eyes focused on the new arrival, recognition apparent on his face. "No fucking way."

"That's no way to speak to the bride of your best friend, is it?"

Megan, James's fiancée, stood inches from his restrained body. She wore a white wedding dress. The dress, strapless and snug, made Megan look like a princess. She wore a diamond tiara on her head, her hair bunched up in a tight, neat bun. Her bronze shoulders stood proud above her dress. She flicked a strand of black hair from her face and smiled, her perfect, arrogant smile infuriating Nicolas, who sneered, contempt present.

Her left hand rested on her hip, her legs positioned in such a way she looked like she was idling, waiting patiently for someone to walk up to her. Her eyes were on Nicolas, occasionally Paul, with a short flit to the right, as she sized up her captives.

In her right hand was a black stun gun.

"We need to stop meeting like this, Nicolas. My fiancé might think we're fucking behind his back." She looked over at James, his dead form unmoving. "Well, actually I don't think he'll be thinking anything anymore."

"What are you talking about?" Nicolas spat, dry vomit tingling his lips.

"Megan, thank fuck. James is dead, I think. Get the police! Nicolas..."

"Shut the fuck up, Paul. I'll get to you in a minute. Stop bashing your fucking bible too, God isn't going to help you today." Megan looked at Paul for a long, hard second before turning her attention back to Nicolas. "Now... where was I?"

"How did you get us *up* here?"

"I have my ways...and a tractor. Hell, I have a whole set of farm tools. My family owned this place once upon a time. I know my way around the machinery. Hoisting you up was child's play." She flexed her arm, mockingly. "Now, answer my question."

"What question?" Nicholas licked his parched lips.

"Where was I? Or do you like disobeying an armed woman?"

"You were chatting shit..."

"Ah yes, me and you, fucking. It would have been so nice, so amazing. I would have given you the best night of your life…and you turned me down. Shame on you." Megan slid a hand down her body, a body that curved and radiated in the tight white dress. "To think, you could have had this…been inside this…oh well, it's your loss."

Without warning, Megan stepped forward and pushed the stun gun into Nicolas's crotch. The aim was good, despite the buoyancy of the clothing around him. The weapon attached to his pubic region, an inch above his penis. The shock shot through him, scorching his veins, burning his skin while dribble and spit erupted from his mouth. A vibrating noise sounded, filling the cornfields with the sound of pain and electricity.

"Nicolas…what's going on?" Paul sounded confused.

Megan pulled the weapon away. Nicholas coughed and Megan folded her arms. "How did you enjoy that?"

Nicolas coughed and sputtered. "Wha…why…are you…?"

Megan sneered. A hand shot up and patted her hair back into place. "C'mon. Like a good little whore, spit it out."

Nicolas looked up, his face red and sweating. His eyes were watering and his hair was fluffier. He fixed his gaze on Megan. "Why are you doing this?"

Megan smiled. "Why? *Why* do you think? My fiancé was a fucking piece of whore-banging scum, that's why. He fucked whores on the side and it's all *your* fault. You and that religious cunt over there." Megan pointed the stun gun at both men in turn. "My husband-to-be was pure before you cunts got your claws into him. Pure and clean, undamaged."

"You're wrong," Paul said, flatly.

Megan swiveled, her evil gaze resting on Paul. "Oh … and why is that?"

"We didn't do anything. James is James…we don't persuade him or control him. He's a man who acts how he wants when he wants. We didn't do a thing to him. If anything, he changed for the better because of you," Paul finished.

"Paul…she killed James. This is all down to her. The scarecrow bullshit, the pillowcases, the fucking *Children of the Corn* setting." Nicolas drooped his head again, still in pain.

Silence filled the air. Megan smiled and placed the stun gun on the ground. She stepped back into Nicolas's view. "This one…this one…he's a bit special at times, isn't he?"

Nicolas glanced up, his teeth bared. "Leave him the fuck alone."

Megan skipped a little. Nicolas couldn't help notice her breasts jiggling as she moved. Megan, he had always thought, was a beautiful woman. Angelic in appearance, an image he found hard to envision right now, she'd come onto him one night when James was out of town. Insecure in the knowledge, or lack thereof, that her fiancé was playing away—he wasn't, he was on a business trip and was one hundred percent faithful to the love of his life—she'd gotten drunk and flirted with him. In another situation, on another day, and if she'd been single, Nicolas would have reciprocated. But he didn't. James was his best friend and he wasn't about to ruin that for a quick lay, no matter how beautiful, and especially considering it was James's fiancée.

"What did I ever do to you?" Nicolas uttered.

"Nothing—which is my point. You should have done something to me. You should have fucked me hard, made me beg, and made me scream. My fiancé was doing it to some filthy rotten *whore* so why didn't you do it to me?"

"James never cheated on you," Nicolas said, sincere in his conviction.

"Don't fucking lie to me. I know what he did."

"You're wrong." Nicolas considered the danger of arguing with this clearly unstable woman. His friend's honour seemed relevant in the wake of his death. "He loved you."

"He did, he loved you, Megan," Paul said. "You were his life."

Megan looked at the ground, a stoic look on her face. *Contemplating?*

Nicolas twisted his head to see Paul. He was still hidden under the scarecrow outfit. He turned his attention to Megan. A tear rolled down her cheek, smearing it with mascara. Nicolas felt a lump in his throat. "You realise he loved you, right? He'd never hurt you. The old James, sure, he might have, but he was a changed man when you came along. Completely changed. For the better, not the worse. You *do* know that, right?"

Megan didn't look up. She sniffed, wiping the tear from her face. One glance at Nicolas and she smiled, a sorry, forgiving smile. "Thank you, Nicolas. I needed that."

Megan walked past Nicolas and disappeared. Nicolas breathed a sigh of relief and slumped on the cross. "What's going on, Nic? Damn this fucking pillowcase."

"I don't know...I think she had a moment of clarity or something." He heard the wood creaking beneath Paul's weight.

"Wrong, muthafuckers."

A sloshing sound filled the empty, soundless void in the cornfield. Fear coiled through Nicolas's veins again and a quiet, splashing sound filled his ears.

Suddenly the strong smell of gas filled his nostrils, pungent, sickly.

Oh God, no!

"Nic...Nic, what's that noise?" Paul sniffed the air. "Is that *gas* I smell?"

Nicolas couldn't see Megan but it didn't take a genius to figure out what she was doing. "Megan, Megan...don't do that. Come over here...we can..." The sound of liquid hitting dry grass and clothing was stark in the silence of the cornfield.

"Nic, what's going on? Why can I smell gas?" Paul's voice had risen one octave.

Megan snorted. "Talk? I doubt it. I don't speak to liars. You think you can lie to me and I will walk away? No fucking chance."

"You were crying...doesn't James mean anything to you?"

"Nic...Megan...stop ignoring me. What's going on?" Paul was fidgeting now, waving his head around, panicking.

Megan ignored both men. The sloshing stopped and a loud, metallic clang rang off the horizon as she threw the gas can against an unseen surface. Three crows flew up from a tree ahead, scratching the sky with their wings. Nicolas tried again. "Megan? What about James?"

Megan stepped into view. A small trail of mascara smeared each cheek. The tears had been genuine. She wiped the wetness from her face. "What about him?"

"You loved him. He loved you, ever *so* much. Why did you kill him?"

"I didn't kill him. I set him free." Megan said, matter-of-factly. "He kissed other women so I ripped his jaw off. He fucked other women so I removed his cock. He even loved a bit of strap-on action, not with me mind you, but his whores. So I drilled a hole in his anus and stuck a dead chicken up there. He got everything he deserved."

"You did *what?*" Paul exclaimed.

Megan lifted the stun gun into the air. "You know I caught chlamydia from my prick fiancée? *Chlamydia.* It's ruined me, infected me with a whore disease and as a result, I can never have a kid. It's destroyed me. Therefore, not only can I not have kids with James—I mean, I'm kinky but I wouldn't fuck a corpse—but he's also ruined me for all men, more deserving, faithful men. Forever."

Nicolas coughed. "I don't get it…you're having a kid with James, right now…"

"Not anymore." The statement was flat, drenched in regret and scorn. Megan looked down and sniffed, wiping her eyes with the back of her hand. Her head raised and her eyes bore into Nicolas. "I lost our baby because of your best friend. My little bundle of joy…gone. Miscarried, dead, an afterthought for the father. While he was off fucking his fancy, I was incubating a baby for him. When he came home, he gave me this…this fucking disease and it killed our baby. *Killed it!*"

Nicolas felt a wave of surprise and warm guilt fill his heart. He'd thought James had changed, he really had. If Megan was telling the truth, then his friend had been lying to him all this time, jeopardized his future for the sake of quick temptation. "I'm sorry, Megan. I didn't know…seriously I…we didn't know. Tell her, Paul."

"He's right, Megan, we didn't have a clue."

Megan breathed out, deep and loud. "That's okay. He killed our baby and I killed him. Tit for tat. We're nearly even."

Nicolas felt a twinge of terror in his gut. He didn't say anything.

Megan sniffed and looked up. "And you're next." An evil smile crossed her lips.

She threw the stun gun into the air and it arced in a large circle, flying beyond Nicolas, and landed at the feet of Paul. Nicolas watched it go, terror in his eyes. "No, *no!*"

The stun gun sparked and ignited the gas-soaked base of the crucifix. Yellow flames licked and tugged at the wood, the clothes, scorching the brown, crumpled trousers. They crept higher, burning the material, becoming more vehement and orange before the first fire lapped at Paul's feet.

"Nic…help me, Nic, it's getting warm in here." Realisation dawned on Paul. "Argh…fuck. *Fuck! I'm on fire! Help me!*"

The flames engulfed the scarecrow, taking Paul with it. They wrapped around the arms, torso and head, melting the pillowcase onto Paul's face and burning through his skin. The crackling of wood and flesh erupted, making Nicolas retch and gag. Paul screamed in raw, unfathomable pain, as the flames engulfed his body, burning him alive. After a minute, he was dead. The flames licked and scorched at the torso, crackling and popping. Black smoke plumed into the air.

"Paul, *Pauuuuuuuuuul. No! No…no.*"

Megan watched in glee, a smile on her face.

Nicolas turned his head to her. The stench of burnt flesh and bone was strong and acrid in the air. He could hear and smell Paul burning beside him. "You bitch."

Megan looked at Nicolas and licked her lips. "My, oh my, that was a lot of fun. Really gives me the urge to fuck…but I have other plans for you. You had your chance to have this." Megan held her hands out in front of her and pointed the fingers back. "You blew it."

"What did Paul ever do to you?"

"Well, aside from corrupt my fiancé? I just didn't like him much. You know he told me to hold the wedding in a church or we'd go to hell. I mean, who says that to a bride-to-be?"

"You know what he's like."

"I don't give a shit. The guy needs to learn to keep his mouth fucking shut. I don't think he'll have a problem doing *that* anymore." Megan laughed and skipped a half-circle before looking back at him.

"You're sick. Fucking sick."

"Maybe I am, but no man has the right to cheat on me. No man has the right to violate my body with any sexual disease. This is your fault. You only have yourself to blame." Megan stepped past Nicolas. "And it's time for me to finish this"

"Hold on…"

Megan stepped past Nicolas and out of sight. He felt fear spiking his soul. The smell of Paul still lingered in the air and he felt nausea overtake him once again. He was about to vomit when a new noise changed everything.

The revving of a chainsaw broke his concentration.

"Megan…*Megan!*"

She didn't answer. Nicolas hardly had time to react when the chainsaw sliced into his side like a hot knife through butter. Blood caught the chain and spun into the air, spattering Megan and her white dress. His ribs shattered behind the pressure, sending bone fragments into his organs, shredding them. The pain took a second to ignite and by that point, his intestine slipped out of the gouge in his abdomen. It unraveled like a hose and slapped the dry ground several seconds later.

The life ebbed away from Nicolas as he witnessed the blade tear through his left ribs, spraying blood and viscera all over the ground before him. Blood dribbled from his mouth as his body became limp and sagged on the makeshift cross. His legs gave way, he fell, losing balance, and toppled. He stopped fast, his arms snapping at the wrists, still bound as the weight dragged him down. The cracks were sickening. After a moment, his dead body hung limp in the listless breeze.

Megan wiped the blood from her face. She spat on the ground in front of Nicolas. Stepping forward, she gripped the broken corpse by the chin and moved her face in close. "Hodmedod, or the scarecrow, is supposed to scare birds, warn them away. You did no such thing for my James. You only brought them to him, the birds or women or whatever you fuckers call them nowadays. You see why I had to kill you, end you all, yes? Your primary function and you couldn't even do that. You have failed me." She licked his puke covered, deceased mouth—her tongue relishing the taste; savouring it—then released Nicolas's dead, bloody chin.

"Yummy."

Megan smiled. She placed the blood-soaked chainsaw on the grass beside her and laughed. The laugh almost drowned out the sound of the cornfields rustling, at peace and tranquility with one another.

Almost....

Nails

Jeff Strand

"Ew. Clip those things."

"What are you talking about? I just cut them—" Ricky glanced at his hand. His fingernails were about a quarter-inch long. *Had* he cut them yesterday afternoon?

Yes, he'd done it while he was watching the otter video on YouTube. He distinctly remembered that. Unless...he'd gotten out the clippers, sat down with the intention of clipping his fingernails, and then been so distracted by the amusing otter antics that he forgot.

Weird. He was pretty sure he'd clipped them, but nails didn't grow this much overnight, and he liked to believe that his life wasn't so boring that he could say with one hundred percent certainty when he clipped his fingernails.

"All right," he said, pulling aside the blanket and sliding his legs over the edge of the bed.

"I didn't mean to do it right now," said Maggie.

"I need to get ready for work anyway."

It was still strange having Maggie in his bed on a workday. She'd been sleeping over on weekends for the past four or five months, but it was only within the past couple of weeks that she'd been here on mornings that required setting an alarm. He wasn't sure if he liked it or not.

They both had office jobs, but hers started half an hour later, so she got to stay in bed while he got ready, and then she'd get up right before he left the apartment. Which was fine—it wasn't as if he thought she was going to steal his TV or something—but it still felt kind of invasive. Plus, it was one great big step closer to "So when are you going to put a ring on that finger?" He didn't want to put a ring on that finger. He liked Maggie a lot, and would never consider being unfaithful to her, but he had every intention of trading up at some point in the future.

Ricky clipped his nails, shaved, showered, and got dressed in his slacks, long-sleeved shirt, and tie. None of those were required by the dress code. Employees were allowed to wear jeans (unripped) and short-sleeved shirts (without logos), and ties weren't required except when bigwigs from New York City were visiting the office, but Ricky always wore business attire. If you were a professional you should dress like one.

He gave Maggie a kiss and left the apartment.

As long as it arrives first thing in the morning, Tuesday is not a problem, Ricky typed in the e-mail. *If it is not here by eight, though, we will have to—*

Ricky's fingernails were making an annoying clicking sound on the keyboard as he typed. He held up his hand and inspected them.

They weren't as long as they had been when he woke up this morning, but they were close. That was insane. Nails didn't grow that fast. He was freaking *positive* that he'd clipped them after Maggie's comment. He'd even spent a couple of minutes trying to find a nail that hadn't landed in the trash, just so Maggie wouldn't see it on his bathroom floor.

He would never, ever become the kind of person who would cut his fingernails in the office, so he didn't keep a clipper in his desk. What was the deal? Had he changed his diet in some way that affected his fingernail growth rate? Ricky had never heard of this sort of thing happening, although to be fair, it was not a subject he'd ever really researched.

He typed *rapid growing fingernails* into his Internet browser and skimmed a few of the search results. It could be that he was somehow healthier now. That would be nice, although he wasn't sure why he'd be suddenly healthier now. He was pretty much eating and exercising the same, and his stress level was actually a bit higher now that Maggie was getting closer.

Or it could be hyperthyroidism. That wasn't so cool.

"What'cha doin'?" asked Gary, startling Ricky so badly that he nearly knocked over the cup of coffee that was three feet away from his keyboard. Gary was a short, tubby guy who waddled rather than walked, yet he possessed a ninja-like ability to suddenly materialize in those very rare occasions when Ricky used his work computer for something non-work-related.

"Nothing," said Ricky, which was the same answer he'd given to the same question asked by Maggie recently when she'd walked in on him looking at pornography.

"You don't want to mess with hyperthyroidism," said Gary. "Better get yourself checked out."

"I will."

After his usual lunch of a salad and bottled water, Ricky returned to his cubicle and began to type, stopping after a few keystrokes.

He couldn't quite see a difference, but his nails were definitely longer. How the hell did somebody's nails get noticeably longer in two hours? That's not how fingernails worked! It was freakish and unnatural!

Ricky considered biting his nails to get them back down to a length where he could type without inconvenience, but decided against it. Chewing your nails was nasty.

By the time he shut down his computer, his nails were half an inch long. That was utterly bizarre. No way could this be explained by a vitamin surplus.

He clipped his nails as soon as he got home. 5:13 PM. He'd keep track of how quickly they grew.

Maggie arrived at 5:48 PM. No phone call or even a text message; she just assumed that it would be fine to stop at his place after work instead of her own. At some point they were going to have to discuss this. Not tonight, though, because she was wearing the green blouse that showed off the maximum allowable amount of cleavage without being unprofessional.

She cooked him dinner (nice), had sex with him on the couch (very nice), and then they watched one of those stupid competition cooking shows to which she was addicted (not so nice, but worth it for the dinner and sex).

"Look at this," he said, holding up his index finger during a commercial.

"Ew," Maggie said. "I thought you were going to clip those."

"I did."

"No, you didn't."

"I did! Seriously!"

"Nobody's fingernails grow that fast," Maggie informed him.

"Mine did. It's weird as hell."

"Maybe you just imagined clipping them."

"I think I can remember when I cut my own nails."

"Really? Is it an activity that weighs heavily on your mind?"

"Do you want me to prove it to you?" Ricky asked. "Do you want me to go get the clippings?"

"I don't. I really, truly don't."

Ricky got up off the couch. "I'll be right back."

"Seriously. I believe you. I don't want to see them."

Ricky hurried into the bathroom. He knew that digging his own fingernail clippings out of the wastebasket in the bathroom was the kind of thing that would negatively impact his chances of having another round of sex tonight, but he needed to prove that he wasn't some kind of hygiene-ignoring slob.

He sifted through the contents for a couple of minutes, hoping his hands wouldn't come into contact with anything too horrific, and managed to find four of the ten clippings, which was enough to prove his story. He walked back into the living room, holding them in his cupped palm.

"See?"

"C'mon, Ricky, that's gross."

"But do you see them?"

"We're not supposed to be at this point in our relationship yet."

"But you believe me, right?"

"Yes. Yes, I believe you. Jeez. Be careful—you're gonna drop them on the couch."

"It's my couch. If I want to cover it with fingernails and water them every morning, that's my right."

Maggie sniffed a few times.

"What are you sniffing for?"

"Pot."

"I'm not on pot. All I'm trying to do is prove that my fingernails are growing at an accelerated rate, and as my girlfriend, you should believe me *without* me having to hold a handful of clippings up in front of you."

"How do I even know those were from yesterday?"

"Fine!" said Ricky. He wanted to angrily fling the fingernails to the floor to demonstrate the power of his conviction, but, no, then he'd have to awkwardly drag out the vacuum cleaner. "You're going to watch me clip them, then you'll see how they look in the morning."

"I don't want to watch you clip them."

"Too bad."

Maggie sighed. "You haven't had an interest in any kind of fetishes since we've been together, and *this* is the one you pick?"

"I need you to believe me."

"I think you're attaching way more importance to your fingernails than they deserve."

"I'm going to get the clippers. Don't move."

"No. I am not going to watch you clip your nails. I'll gag. If this is so important to you, show me what they look like when you're done, and we'll compare them in the morning."

Ricky nodded. Yes, that was a much better idea than making her sit there and watch him. He wished he'd thought of that before he'd proposed the grosser plan.

He went into the bathroom and clipped his nails. His toenails didn't seem to be affected by the growth spurt, but he cut those, too. Then he returned to the living room.

"See them?" he asked, holding up the handful.

"Seriously, Ricky, that's the kind of thing you need to not do. For real."

"But you see them, right?"

"Yes! I see that you have, indeed, clipped your fingernails. Do you want a pat on the head and a cookie?"

"No. I mean, I do want a cookie, but not for this."

"Throw them away, please."

"All right. I'll throw them away, but I won't take out the garbage yet."

Ricky threw away the clippings and then washed his hands with the good soap. Had he acted deranged? He hoped not. If Maggie had said something like, "Wow, you're right, that is pretty odd; maybe you should see a doctor," everything would've been fine. But he couldn't have her doubting his honor. He wouldn't make up something like this. He wasn't some loser, desperately seeking attention. He had something strange going on with his body, and if she expected him to put a ring on that finger—he knew that was never going to happen but she didn't—she needed to not call him a liar.

Okay, to be fair, she hadn't called him a liar. He was overreacting.

Anyway, tomorrow morning she'd *have* to believe him.

To Ricky's great surprise, there was a second round of sex after they went to bed. Nothing too exciting; just a few minutes of medium tempo missionary, without her encouraging him to go faster or deeper, but still, it was much better than the nothing that he expected.

He woke up before the alarm. 3:13 AM. Crap. He had to go to the bathroom. If he got up he'd have trouble falling back asleep, yet he probably couldn't fall back asleep while he had to pee. Catch-22.

He tried to hold his right hand up in front of his face, but couldn't move it.

What the hell?

It was too dark to see clearly, but his fingernails seemed to be...buried in the mattress? He tugged. Couldn't get them free. How deep in there *were* they?

He tugged on his left hand and couldn't move that one, either. It had gone through a pillow, which was just a fluffy feather pillow, so there was no reason it should be holding him in place so firmly, except that—

Was that blood on the pillow?

Was that *lots* of blood on the pillow?

Ricky tugged a few more times. Maggie's head wobbled with each tug but she didn't open her eyes or make any sound.

"Maggie...?"

He tugged some more. Her head continued to wobble.

"Maggie!"

Ricky tried to reach over to turn on the bedside lamp, but since he couldn't move either of his hands this attempt was unsuccessful. Until his eyes adjusted to the dark, he wasn't going to be able to confirm that his fingernails had gone through Maggie's head.

He felt that he was remaining remarkably calm under the circumstances, although at least ninety percent of that calmness came from his belief that this was a dream. Just a strange dream. Think about your fingernails before you go to sleep and you'll dream about them growing through her head during the night—that's the way it works.

It had to be a dream. Otherwise he'd be screaming and sobbing and stuff.

He pulled on his right hand as hard as he could. Slowly, very slowly, his fingernails started to withdraw from the mattress. Three inches. Four. Five. Six freakin' inches? Seven? Eight? Had they gone all the way through the mattress?

Ricky twisted his hand, trying to snap them off. The only one that came off was his pinky nail, which tore off at the source.

The pain was significant.

Though he didn't shriek, exactly, he definitely did not respond in a quiet, dignified manner. Maggie didn't move. She'd always been a light sleeper, so the fact that she didn't react to his cries of pain did not bode well for her head being in pristine condition.

"Maggie, please, wake up," he said. "Don't be dead. Please don't be dead."

He tugged again. Her head wobbled again in a very corpse-like manner.

How had she slept through this? What kind of person would let fingernails grow through their head without waking up? How fast were these things growing?

His pinky fingernail had already grown to the length of a normal fingernail, so the answer was, pretty goddamn fast.

"Help!" he shouted. "Somebody help me! Call the police! I'm trapped!" He didn't think that providing complete information—*"I'm trapped by my insanely fast-growing fingernails!"*—was a wise idea and settled for being vague. "I'm trapped!"

He forced himself to take a deep breath. He'd be fine. Maggie wouldn't, probably, but he'd be okay. Somebody would find him, they'd cut his nails, and the hospital would give him some kind of medicine to stop their growth. Maybe they saw this kind of thing all the time. No doubt there were countless medical marvels about which Ricky had never known.

He'd be fine. He'd be totally fine.

Now his eyes had adjusted to the darkness well enough to clearly see that the nail of his middle finger had gone through the side of Maggie's pillow, then up through the top, and into her ear. He sat up and saw that it had emerged from the other side; not quite from her ear, but just below it.

She was dead. The girl he hadn't wanted to marry but whose company he'd enjoyed a great deal was dead.

If only she'd believed him. If only she'd said, "Holy shit! Nails aren't supposed to do that! Let's get you to the emergency room right away!"

He called for help again.

Had his habit of playing really loud horror movies and being rude when his neighbors knocked on the door and asked him to please turn down the volume come back to haunt him?

He looked at his pinky finger. He could actually see the nail growing. It didn't hurt, but it was certainly a disturbing sight.

He pulled again as hard as he could on the hand imbedded in the mattress. Now the nails weren't budging at all, and he wondered if they'd curled on the ends.

Oh, why didn't he keep a pair of fingernail clippers next to the bed? Or a pair of scissors? Or shears? Or a knife? Or, hell, even a gun. If he had a six-shooter, he could blow off the remaining four fingernails and still have two bullets to spare.

Ricky could wait for help, or he could twist.

He decided to twist.

He squeezed his eyes closed, and turned his hand. The pain was unbelievable, but he forced himself to push through it. They were just fingernails. They'd break.

Swiveling his wrist as far as it would go didn't do the trick. The nails twisted but didn't snap.

He bent his fingers, whimpering in agony. He'd managed to go his entire life without suffering any ghastly accidents or undergoing any horrific medical procedures, so he didn't necessarily have an accurate point of reference, but this *had* to be an above-average amount of pain for somebody to go through.

The nail on his index finger snapped.

The nail on his middle finger did not snap. Like the pinky, it tore off entirely, taking a patch of flesh with it. Two thin trails of blood ran down his finger. Ricky hadn't cried over Maggie's death a few moments ago, but he cried now.

Two more. Only two more moments of excruciating pain and his hand would be free. He couldn't quit now. Now that he knew what to expect, the next two wouldn't be nearly as bad.

The nail on his ring finger tore mostly off, taking some skin and leaving behind a small piece of nail. See? It was hellish pain, but not as hellish as the middle finger had been.

Only his thumb remained. He gave it a violent tug.

Snap.

The snap was his bone, not his thumbnail.

Ricky let out a bellow that echoed throughout the room. Or maybe he was just hearing an echo because his sanity was slipping away. Either way, it was a very loud bellow.

Four fingers free. One broken thumb still stuck. The process of tugging was probably going to hurt a lot more now.

It did. In fact, it hurt so badly that he blacked out.

When he woke up, his nails had *not* grown back through the mattress, which would have been frustrating but also admittedly kind of amusing. Two of them had, however, grown right through one cheek and out the other, protruding out about six inches. The lower of the two fingernails had also gone through his tongue.

Ricky hadn't choked to death on his own blood, so that was something, anyway.

He sat up and leaned forward, draining some of the blood he hadn't choked on. The nail on his broken thumb was still stuck in the mattress, so he'd have to move his head instead of his hand. Very, very, very slowly, neurosurgeon slowly, he leaned to the side, sliding his fingernails out of his cheek and tongue. He tried to will his fingers to stop trembling, but they didn't really cooperate.

Finally, the nails slid free. Ricky resumed his efforts to call for help, but his cries came out as a bloody gargle. Nobody would hear him.

Okay, so, he was going to have to give the thumb another try—force himself to stay conscious this time—otherwise, he was dead.

He took a deep breath, braced himself for the pain, and tugged.

Ricky had prepared himself for the pain of a thousand red-hot pokers jamming into a thousand tight orifices, and so when the pain wasn't *quite* at that level, it was a relief. He let out a blood-spraying incoherent wail as he acknowledged that even a broken thumb wasn't supposed to bend like that, but the nail did tear off.

One hand was free.

He could, presumably, just pull Maggie's corpse off the bed and let it drag behind him as he went for a phone, but that seemed disrespectful. So he tugged on the other hand. All that did was pull Maggie's dead body closer to him. He rolled her onto her side, bent his knees, placed both feet against her back, and pulled.

Her neck bent backwards until it snapped, which was probably more disrespectful than if he'd dragged her into the living room.

He kept pulling and pulling, groaning with the effort, until finally, all at once, his middle fingernail popped free.

Free!

He spat out some blood and then got out of bed. He staggered into the living room, leaking all over his carpet. It took him a few moments to find where he'd left his phone, but he finally located it on the kitchen counter and quickly punched in 911.

Thank God. Thank God. He'd be fine. They'd send over an ambulance, get his wounds stitched up, give him some medicine to stop this freakish growth, and everything would be perfectly okay. The worst of it was over. Thank God.

Ricky held the phone up to his ear.

That turned out to be a very bad idea.

The Flower Dies

Kyle Yadlosky

The Unmarked Grave

The wind strikes hard in Brierfield, making the rain fall sideways in thin spears that slash my skin, chill my bones, and soak my suit through to my chest. The dirt road ahead, and grass fields to either side, are encased in a sea of endless black. A shaft of moonlight stands pale over one large tree that juts crooked and gnarled from the ground. I rush beneath its thick branches, pushing my hat down to my ears to keep the howling wind from tossing it into the dark.

Rainwater splashes and pools on the ground around me, drowning the grass and spilling beneath my boots. I hold myself against the trunk of the tree, standing on its rolling roots that rise like boulders from the earth. I catch my breath, rub my chilled palms together, and look out across the deep, sapphire night. The rain had pelted down from an angry sky as I made the drive out, and it hasn't let up a bit.

I light a match on the side of the tree and shield the flame from the plummeting drops. The flame licks the tip of my damp cigarette but gives it no life—the crumpled cylinder droops from the thick moisture of the rain. I drop it; it flips, falls, and then disappears into the grass. My fingers slip inside my coat, thumb over the damp leather of my journal. I don't even want to open it, but out of habit my fingers pull at the cover, opening it just an inch, and all the black ink runs down the soaked paper, bleeding into the guiding lines of each page. *There goes the country heritage piece,* I think. A story on the biggest Pumpkin Festival in New England washed out with the renewed downpour.

Lightning flashes, blasting the sky to a piercing white. In these seconds of nature-made daylight, my eyes catch the sheen of water on wood—more gnarled bark, crudely pounded with thick black nails, into a crooked, makeshift cross. At the base of it, a mound of droplet-flattened dirt churns to mud, flooding over a cluster of grey, withered roses. A pocketknife inscription in the ravaged wood reads: THE FLOWER DIES.

Another flash of electric daylight in the downpour shows spear-tipped black bars fencing off the cracked grey stone and sloping red roof of a small church. The rain still pelts me with a fearful coldness between the tree's branches. I press my hands over my head and dash for safety and the hope of warmth.

An old man wearing a light brown suit, thick grey hair standing short on his head, waits inside the church, watching the rain through the panes of a window. As I slam the door behind me, he glances over his shoulder and offers a wide grin.

"Some rain, fellah," he says.

I nod. "Some rain."

His eyes turn back toward the window. A lightning flash reflects over his pupils. "Don't know when it's supposed to stop."

"No..."

My footfalls echo as I weave between pews, under the patter of steady rain on the roof. A small fire flickers behind its grate at the far end of the room, behind the pulpit. "Roads got wiped out. My car's still out there, stuck."

"Sheriff's office got a big truck. Sure they'd be happy to tow you when it's all finished." He waves a hand toward the fire. "Warm up. Don't want you going to the Lord over a little rain, fellah."

I walk in the direction of the heat, crouch down, and rub my hands together. "You a preacher?" I ask.

He nods, watching between the window and me. "The only one Brierfield needs. In for the Pumpkin Festival?"

Thunder roars as lightning stabs the stars.

I throw my coat off and set it to dry on the floor next to me. "Was," I start, as I unlace my boots then set them in front of the grate. "You all had a good turnout."

He grunts. Our voices fall to the music of the storm.

I drape my socks over the grate; lift my bare toes to the heat. "You handle funerals around here?'

"All who died before I lived."

"You know the one with the weird cross and the dead roses?"

His lips fall, face hardens. His eyes catch more lightning. "Must've been before my time." His voice runs a low rumble.

"With that inscription? THE FLOWER DIES…" I pursue. "The grave looks new enough that grass hasn't had time to grow. The soil all turned to mud."

"Right," the preacher grunts. "But why talk about the dead?"

"Just caught my interest." I shift in front of the fire, rub my palms together again. My hair has dried to a mass of strange brown barbs that stick up from every angle. My shadow plays a crouched monster across the entrance door.

The preacher sighs. "I didn't meet the girl. All I know was her funeral was almost unattended."

"Who *did* attend?"

"Me. Doctor. Sheriff and his deputy. No one who knew her."

"But that inscription..."

The preacher shrugs. Rain pelts the window.

I pull my dried socks from the grate and slip them back on. I replace my boots and jacket. The rain slows to a drizzle, and I take my leave of the preacher and his church. I have a hike back to town, down to the sheriff's office—then back out to my car.

I pass by the large, gnarled tree again, and stop to look over the unmarked grave. The dirt covering it still stands as a basin of soup with the small cluster of roses blooming from within. In the gloom, I think I spy one rose showing petals of a lively red.

The Deputy

Richard Reyes watches his pencil roll from side to side across the front desk at the sheriff's office. Only his cruiser stands in the lot. The yellow light over his head is all that illuminates the interior of the otherwise dark building.

Reyes raises his eyes to me, moves a pale hand toward a chair in a dark corner. "Relax," he grumbles. "Another storm's coming. Not sure if it'll be worth the trip up. But we'll move your car off the road—at least make sure it don't get flooded."

"I'd appreciate that," I say with a smile. He ignores it. I look around the dark room, toward closed doors that undoubtedly lead to other dark rooms. "Here alone tonight?"

"Yep, yep." He pushes his pencil. "Everyone takes off for the festival. It's fine, though, always quiet the night after."

"You watch the office alone every year?"

He nods again. "Yep, yep."

The pencil bowls from one hand to the other.

"You work here a long time?" I ask.

"Ten...eleven years."

"You never take off for the festival?"

"I'm not much a fan of—" he shrugs. "Plants, I guess. Planting."

"Sure."

He opens a drawer at the bottom of the desk, pulls a jingling cluster of keys free. A grunt breaks from his throat while he stands from the swivel chair. His back cracks in a little rattle of firecrackers. "Not really supposed to lock up," he grumbles to his boots. "But I'm not gonna wake anyone up tonight." He flashes a crooked grin. "If anyone dies tonight, and I'm not around to stop it, you're to blame."

I laugh.

With those words holding in the still air of the office, we take up our coats and walk around the back of the station to a fully built plow-ready pickup. The light rain patters in deputy's hair, weighing down the spots where he must have grabbed and pulled at his bangs earlier in the night.

The windshield wipers slosh away the raindrops that splash down as we drive toward the old church. My mind recalls images of that gnarled tree... the grave...and those roses.

Dead roses.

"So, you were at the funeral for that unmarked grave?" I ask, gnawing at a fingernail as we drive.

If he wonders why a stranger is asking so many questions, he doesn't let on. He glances at me. His lips drop to show the crooked teeth in his lower jaw. "I go to plenty of funerals."

"You'd remember it," I go on. "Strange cross. Dead roses."

He shivers. His fingers play against the steering wheel. "Let's not talk about that."

"What was it?" I ask.

"Just a girl."

"What was her name?"

The rain patters the windshield. The engine rumbles. The truck lurches as it hits the mud, catches, and slides. Luckily the tires continue to roll forward.

"How'd she die?" I try.

Reyes' lips barely twitch. "No one loved her."

The rain quickens its battering pace against the hood of the truck. Lightning flashes just as we pass the gnarled tree and the grave. And I see the cluster of roses sprouting from the mud. Now three stand red. Before I can check my eyes, the flash fades, and the grave disappears in the darkness.

The Dead Body

I stand at the checkout of the Brierfield grocer. Just a bottle of water and a candy bar. The man behind the counter stands with his back to me. His flannel draped shoulders, his grey hair are what are facing me; his eyes stand fixed on the wall behind him.

I ring the bell on the counter. "Ahem, excuse me," I start. "Excuse me."

The man doesn't turn around.

I ring the bell again. "Sir!"

The man stands facing the slats of brown wood on the wall. I glance over my shoulder at the others waiting in line. The backs of their heads face me as well. I don't know if this is some ritual for them or what.

I ring the bell again.

The man still doesn't turn.

I leave my candy and water on the counter and step back out into the street.

A smile and wave: Now Entering Brierfield Village.

The sign reads those words rolling into the small cluster of houses spread out with long patches of fields in between. Now, only straight faces cross my path—no eyes meet mine. Pedestrian shoulders and knees knock mine, spreading bruises over my shins, jostling me across the sidewalk. One shoulder wheels me around, and the man who hit me walks on without even looking back.

This is the day after their festival. The deputy dropped me off. I can finally get my car, and get the hell out of here. I want to see if I can learn more about that strange grave, but no one will speak to me. They won't even *look* at me. It's as if I'm not even there. Every walking body that ignores as it passes by, marches in the same direction I am. I follow the crowd, hoping to see what is causing this town to neglect me. The swaying mass of bodies, maybe fifty total, march toward a ramshackle house painted white, its grizzled yard choked with yellow crabgrass. They stop short of a ribbon wall of police tape. An officer standing, arguing with a bystander, catches my eye and turns his back to me.

I step up to the mailbox. 406, Richard Reyes.

The crowd silently watches. The screen door opens, one beige-uniformed officer holding the door ajar. Two more walk out across the threshold, over the warped planks of the porch, and down the stairs. They carry something long and brown behind them. Bits of it fleck off, fall like the skin of an onion to the damp dirt. The officers set the body on the ground, and an old man, perhaps a doctor, steps over it. He picks up one crumbling appendage, lets it fall.

I sidestep through the crowd, all eyes fixed toward the lawn. I nudge closer to the police tape. Everybody moves with my approach, as if weary of feeling my touch. I look over the strange, contorted remains. The corpse has the long arms and legs of man with withered, wrinkled skin, running with cracks and flakes. More layers of brown, darker and darker, lay beneath. I can see the outlines of muscles in the stomach, arms, legs—veins in the neck. At the top of the body, I see a twisted mouth, gnarled nose, and closed eyes of a human face.

Deputy Reyes lies like a rotten, sun-dried husk before me. The doctor nods to the deputies and walks away from the corpse. He looks toward the crowd, but closes his eyes when he crosses in front of me. His eyes open again, and then survey the street.

Two officers stay with the body. One lights a match. He flicks it off his fingers and the tip touches the dried skin of Deputy Reyes. It immediately catches, sparks, pops, runs with white fire. It eats his torso, his body, throwing up thick, grey smoke. It consumes his face, throws what's left of the man up into the swirling air in the form of large black clumps of ash. His spine pops with orange sparks. Soon, only a clump of black remains where the deputy once was.

That and the acrid smell of burning crops.

The Mother

The row of trees that hedge me in on either side as I drive out of town, are no less eerie in the daylight. Fog swirls around their white bark, that's twisted in wrinkles like petrified skin. I can see straight out to where the lone grave with its crooked cross stands apart from the grass, beneath the gnarled tree I took protection under just nights ago. A figure stands near it, a woman bundled in black. I see thick hands with loose skin clutching a shawl pulled around her shoulders. The woman turns her pale face toward me, and I catch her drawn eyes. They trail back to the grave as I pull over to the side of the road.

I turn my eyes in the direction of the grave, and see that it's open. I cut the engine, step out of the car, and stand there for a moment.

The woman looks at me, which both shocks my heart and makes my stomach jump.

She actually looks at me.

I walk in silence toward the opened grave. Upturned dirt runs in scrambled chunks across the grass, and red rose petals blanket the edges of the opening.

We both stare down into the black soil, not a word shared between us. Inside is a small white coffin, its lid shattered and heaved aside.

The woman pushes rose petals with the toe of her shoe. "She shouldn't've come back up." Her voice trembles in the cold air.

"They take her?" I ask.

The woman shakes her head. "You bringing her up to Poor Richard...She touched him once. You made him want her back. And she needs so much after spending so long in the ground."

The woman turns her back to me and walks from the grave.

I follow her across the mist-laden grass. She wanders between sections of gravestones, stops at one, and crouches near it. I walk to her side, feeling like an intruder as she wipes at the grave marker with a silk cloth. The gravestone reads Harold Greeves.

She glances up at me. "My husband."

"How'd he die?" I venture.

Her eyes wander back to the open grave with the small white box. "She killed him."

A cold chill snakes between my shoulder blades. "…I don't understand."

She shakes her head, scraping dirt from the base of the tombstone. "Best not to talk of it. Talking killed Richard."

"How?"

The woman matches my eyes. "I shouldn't even look at you."

I stand, holding a cold silence over her. She glances back toward the open grave again.

"I don't want to keep silence. She is—was—my daughter. In a way."

I crouch at the grave next to her. She clutches my hand as her throat gasps for air. Her voice drifts to me in a thin whisper. "I loved her. He loved her."

"Richard said she died because no one loved her."

The woman looks off, drifting back into her memories.

"She grew straight from the fields themselves. My Harold went out to harvest the pumpkins; a full day of work for us. Well, halfway through our toiling, under the high sun, he dragged through to find a cluster of bright red roses growing in the pumpkin patch. Lost in those flowers, my Harold found the thin white hand of a little girl amid the flowers. He dug her up himself, washed her off, holding her close to his chest, whispering in her ear that she was safe. By the time he brought her home, the sun had set. The girl was naked and pale in his arms, her red hair falling over her shoulders. She couldn't have been any older than fifteen. We made a room for her. We thought she was a gift from God. We both loved her. Harold loved her to the point that people whispered—but people always whisper—degenerates, drunks, spreading rumors to make their own misgivings seem less awful. But Harold, he got slower, weaker. And our girl—Fiona, we named her—grew more beautiful by the day.

"The way she spoke, you wouldn't believe she was nobody's child.

Perfect words, a smooth voice. She drew everyone's attention with her looks and kindness. She was the flower of Brierfield. But, like I said, Harold grew weaker. He couldn't plant on his own anymore, but Fiona's charms were enough to bring a number of eager hands around the farm to help. In two years, my husband aged to sixty. And, in three, he was dead. It was the strangest occurrence. We found him, a bundle of brown flesh in the pumpkin patch, poor Fiona kneeling over him balling her eyes out. I told folks there was something awful in her, but no one believed me. I told them that girl from the ground had a monster lurking under her skin. They paid me no mind. I kept my love hidden from her. I slapped her every once in a while just to keep myself safe. And she would cry, and it would hurt my soul. But it kept me alive.

"She married soon after Harold died. Omar Wright. He was a dumb man—huge dent in his broad forehead—and Fiona was the only woman to pay him mind. He aged thirty years in the first year of their marriage. They had two children. Those babes didn't survive two months. They came out the same brown husks as Harold. We found them baking in her back yard and her screaming over them. That brought her and Omar closer. The dent-headed man was dead in another three months.

"Fiona, so beautiful and smart, was distraught for days. Then, she'd forget—she never had children, never had a husband, never had a father. She'd start getting close to someone else, looking for that love. All the while, she'd become more and more beautiful and youthful, sucking the life from those she'd grew close to. She began making eyes with Richard when the village finally turned to me. You have to understand that I loved her, but I knew we had to turn our backs on her. And we did. We showed her no mind. We didn't speak to her. We didn't show her love. It broke my heart, watching her age from it. Her hair withered from red to crabgrass yellow. Her eyes sunk into her skull. Her skin stretched tight to where you could see her bones through it. Her teeth fell out. She screamed and raved, grabbed people, begging them to look at her—to love her. But we stayed strong, and our flower died.

"The police, the priest, and the doctor came to her funeral. I didn't go…I was too afraid of crying. I didn't want to give her any reason to come back. She was buried in a flimsy coffin, dropped in a deep hole. The priest threw up a rickety cross. I was the one who carved that inscription, and after doing so, those dead roses grew. It was all a terrible mistake."

Still kneeling in front of the tombstone, the woman wiped at her face with the same square of silk she'd dusted the stone with, dragged deep breaths of mist-laden air into her fragile lungs.

"We shouldn't talk about her," she went on. "You talked about her…and it brought her back."

"Where is she now?" I ask, voice faint.

The woman looks up at me, holding the filthy rag to her face. "She'll find you." She squeezed my hand. "Don't find her….don't talk to her. Let her die. Let her die again."

The Flower

Amid the throngs of dirt-smeared Brierfield inhabitants, I catch sight of a small pale face in the crowd—and a pair of large green eyes catch sight of me in return. A shy smile plays across rose red lips, as the lithe body slips through the doorway of a weathered bar on Main Street.

I shove my way past each person on the street, as I near the building and slip inside. No one inside the bar bothers to turn when the door opens to admit either one of us; the girl is several steps ahead of me. They don't throw as much as a sideways glance in our direction. Even the bartender stays facing his well-stocked whiskey rack behind the bar, his broad back to the room.

The girl, her red hair cascading down her shoulders and wrapping around clenching fingers, sits at a small table in the back—a dark, dusty spot, only made bright by her presence. Those eyes, they bewitch. Looking directly at me, they bore through to my very soul. My legs slowly draw me closer to her, as if powerless not to, her eyes never losing sight of mine. They grow wide as I close in.

I sit across from her. She moves her pale hands toward mine; her fingertips touch me. As if caught in a stiff wind, her wild, long red hair whips up and falls in tangles across my the back of my knuckles in thick curls, the tip of each strand pierces, then penetrates my skin—sucking at the blood beneath—draining my hands of life, until their stiff and cold. Each strand of hair digs in deep, feeding. I can't break free from her gaze—or her obvious power over me.

"You're the one," I mutter.

Her lips peel a ripe smile. "I am."

"You died."

Her eyes cast a tender look down at my hands. She runs her fingers over the back of my knuckles once her hair has pulled out. "You're nice," she says. "You look at me. Everyone here is so rude. No one ever looks at me."

Her voice is soft, like a song to my ears. It's more musical tones than actual words.

"You kill people." My lips barely move.

Her eyes match mine. A tear, capturing the colors of the light, hangs in her eye.

"I'm so lonely..." she whispers.

My mouth opens. A shallow breath drifts out. "I'm here."

Sitting with her, without a soul paying attention to either one of us, I feel alone. We could lock ourselves away somewhere and I'd feel the same. Her eyes seem to caress me. Her hands, cupping mine, radiate warmth, like from between her thighs. Her smile excites me.

"Have you been married?" I ask with a hollow voice, knowing the answer I've already been told.

"No, never," her lilting voice sings.

"Kids?"

"None."

"Family?"

"None."

Her eyes fill with tears.

Sweat streaks my forehead, runs over my nose, salts my lips, and dampens the front of my shirt. My legs begin to shake beneath the table. An animal need blossoms in my loins. I want to throw myself across the tabletop, lunge at her and tear her clothes off—meld my flesh with hers on this filthy hardwood floor.

"Can I deflower you?" I hear myself ask, weakly.

"Of course you can," she says. "I don't know you, but I know I love you."

I lurch across the table, my jacket falling to the floor. I kick my boots off, whip my belt from its loops, tearing at the front of my pants before they fall to a pile on the floor.

Her clothes seem to dissolve into her skin.

I touch her…and don't want to let go. I can't let go.

"Fiona," I murmur.

"Yes," she sings.

Is she above me? Am I inside her? Is she inside me? I can't see or think any of this—only feel it. When my body presses to hers, I don't move. I don't pull to separate myself from the wet glory of her warmth once I'm in it.

Her wild red hair tangles and prickles like bloody barbs from the stem of a rose, poking out, biting into my exposed flesh, draining me. My skin draws tight around my bones. My eyes feel dry to the air, their sockets growing snug around them. My breathing grows labored.

"I love you," she whispers her angel's song. "I love you…I'll always love you."

Our lips touch. They sting. Heat bubbles across my lips, and I can taste my own blood flowing forth.

"I love you, too…" I tell her.

In a flash, feet stomp around us, pounding the floor. Dust pelts my skin from above. Chairs screech across dried wooden planks, and glasses hammer teetering tables. Not a soul moves to stop us. Even in her nakedness, I can only see her eyes. The irises expand, blooming into colors I can't rightly describe, while her pupils swim with the blackest black, threatening to pour out and engulf me.

A lace of fear coils in my stomach, drawing heat from my trembling body. Icy chills snake down my spine. Closing my eyes, I hold my breath.

"No," she whispers. "Look at me..."

I keep holding my breath.

"Look at me!"

I cover my ears.

"LOOK AT ME!!" she shouts.

I get to my knees, and stand up. I can hear a loud hum racing through my head that all but silences her voice. The heat rushes from my body. A sob carries through the room. And, in an instant, I know she's gone. She's left the bar. I know this because my body suddenly feels empty.

Regretful, I open my eyes.

The room is filled with the same patrons as before, but now they're all turned toward me, each nodding their heads in unison, raising their glasses in cheer. "Good for you!" they shout. "Good for you."

I run from the bar. Red hair flashes in the night before. I follow. It floats up the hill, out of the village. It sweeps down the dirt trail, through the gnarled trees, back toward the grave. I stop short, catching the outline of her figure in the mist.

She dips a foot toward the grave. My chest heaves with ragged breaths, and my arms rise to reach for her. My legs ache to follow, but they feel sluggish.

Fiona.

A whimper breaks from my throat.

My legs shove off, arms clawing the air in front of me. My eyes jerk open as I sprint to rescue her, but to no avail. My legs are too slow. My boots crumple the grass, and clop to a halt. I stand there, a chill numbing my fingertips, while my gaze falls to the grave. Below the cross inscribed with the words THE FLOWER DIES, the dirt once again sits packed, and over it, a bed of velvety roses has been laid out—one in their midst a deathly ash-grey.

I kneel over the grave, eyes streaming, blurring my vision. My fingers wrap the stem of the single dead rose. I lift it to my nose and breathe in its bitter bouquet, crushing it in my fist.

After a moment, the old woman from earlier comes to gather me. She presses an arm to my lower back, and helps me to my feet.

"I love her…" I whisper. "I love her."

"I know," Fiona's mother responds. "We all do."

Reunion

Bear Weiter

Stepping around the corner, Edward took everything in: his wife stood just outside their doorway, the flickering gas lamp above twisting her look of confusion into aghast. A few steps down, at street level, a man spoke to her, his back to Edward.

"Mary, are you all right?" he called, running across the street.

"Edward?" she asked, her expression draining from her face as she sagged toward the ground.

Edward had not quite made it to the curb, but the other man leapt up the stairs and caught her before she hit the stoop. He held her up with one arm, keeping polite space between his body and hers.

"I believe she fainted," the man said, turning to face Edward.

Edward didn't blame her. He too felt a moment of dizziness, and had to grasp the railing to steady himself. Standing before him was his mirror image—his twin, Edgar—who had disappeared twenty years earlier.

They had been inseparable as kids, but during adolescence Edgar became distant, and selfish. By the time they went to college, neither could stand the other's presence, and each took a distinctly different path—Edward headed off to medical school, and Edgar entered the seminary. Neither finished their terms.

One month after the fire that had devoured the family home and their parents within it, Edgar suddenly vanished—along with every last bit of fortune their father had amassed. Penniless, Edward's remaining years in school also evaporated into nothingness, erasing his future as a doctor, as if it were a fevered dream.

That was the last Edward had seen of his brother—until this moment. He had no doubt that Edgar was behind the theft of inheritance, and while he could not bring himself to accuse his twin of the fire, the suspicion had never fully left him.

"You don't look so good yourself," Edgar said, a slight bemused smile teasing the corners of his mouth.

"Were you expecting a warm welcome, brother?"

"I expected nothing, actually, but it's been too long to catch up out here. Please, let me help your wife in and we can discuss matters more comfortably." There was no hint of a question, or request to be invited in.

Edward waved him on, taking Mary's other side as they walked through the entryway and into the front room.

Mary had begun to come to her senses by the time they set her on the divan. Her eyes drifted between the two men, unable to resolve what was before her.

Edward opened his mouth to speak, but Edgar spoke first.

"Please accept my humblest apologies, Mrs. Janus. It was not my intention to surprise either you or my brother. After all of this time I should have announced my intention to visit with a letter."

Mary shifted her gaze back and forth a few times, before settling on Edward. "Your brother?" She glanced once more to Edgar. "But you look identical."

They were in nearly every way—though standing next to each other, their dress and mannerisms distinguished them. Edward slouched next to Edgar's upright and assertive posture, and where Edward's eyes contained weariness, Edgar's sparked with interest. As always, Edward was dressed in a handsome wool suit, but it paled by comparison to the expensive hand-tailored work of his brother's

"This is my twin, Edgar," Edward said, a hint of a sigh trailing out with the words. "Edward, this is my wife, Mary."

Edgar took Mary's hand in his. "It is a delight to meet you, my dear."

Mary cleared her throat, and sat up a bit straighter. "It is nice to meet you, Edgar. Forgive my earlier surprise. When I answered the door and found you standing before me, the mirror image of my husband but in unfamiliar clothes, and then saw Edward coming from across the street, it was all too much. To be honest," her cheeks colored as she continued to speak, "I did not know Edward had a twin. My understanding was that his only brother died many years ago."

Edward looked at his brother. "I never said you were dead, only that you could have been. I had no way of knowing."

"Perhaps it was a fancy of his," Edgar said, smirking, and gave Edward a friendly pat on the arm. "It was not under the best of circumstances that I left. I do not blame him for giving you that impression, nor for refusing to acknowledge me. I'm certain I would have done the same had the situation been reversed. But this does bring me to the reason of my visit. I have come to make amends, for both my absenteeism and my past misdeeds. We two have been apart for far too long, my dear brother, and I'm ready to do everything in my power to reunite us."

Mary stood, smiling, and touched them both on their shoulders. "Well then let me welcome you back. I was just preparing supper, would you care to join us? It's not much, but it would be a pleasure to have your company."

Edward was unsure about this most recent exchange, but with both Mary and his brother looking at him, he nodded, and attempted a smile of his own. "Yes, stay for supper."

"I would be delighted, to say the least."

They dined on day-old stew, though the bread was fresh, and Mary had pulled out their best china and silverware. Polite conversation was the order of the night, and Edgar remained both charming and engaging. It made up for Edward's quietness.

"I guess no one ever called either of you 'Ed' as a child?" Mary asked, laughing at her little joke.

"It does seem to be rather cruel to have such similar names, I'll grant you that." Edgar said. "As a child, I hated it. I was fiercely independent. While I loved my brother, I wanted to be known as an individual, and did what I could to stand out on my own. It is a shame I carry to this day, to spurn someone so much a part of myself." He shook his head. "I must refine my brother's statement from earlier and say you were right, Mary. We are more than twin brothers. We are identical, in all the ways biology says. For a very brief moment in time, we were one."

Mary's brow creased in confusion, but Edgar continued on to answer the unasked question. "Science, my dear lady! It is amazing what they continue to discover. Scientists now say that Edward and I came from the same fertilized egg that very early on as our cells divided in growth, we separated, and continued to grow independently of each other. But, for all practical purposes, we were one at first."

A rosy blush had bloomed on Mary's face. "Oh my."

"Pardon my salaciousness. I suppose it is not a subject of discourse fit for the dinner table. I do get carried away when it comes to matters of science."

"Well it is fascinating, to say the least. So many advances, I just don't know what will be left to discover in this new century."

"It does seem like that at times, does it not? But I must say I believe there is far more for us to learn. There are areas of knowledge I just don't see science ever being able to explore thoroughly."

"You mean religion? God?"

"I *was* once a man of God, many years ago. But, no, I mean beyond what the various good books have to say. I have traveled to many places in this world, strange locales that are far different than what we know of here. Which reminds me—I have brought something for the both of you. Will you please excuse me for a moment?"

"Of course."

Edgar stood, nodded his head in a bow, and went to the front room.

Edward breathed out. He realized he had been sitting frozen in a rather upright and uncomfortable position during much of the conversation. His brother had been a perfect gentleman, polite and gracious, a nearly flawless veneer that nonetheless covered something hidden below. After all of these years, Edgar had more than a simple reunion as reason for his visit.

While he was away, Mary leaned toward Edward. "It's wonderful to have him here, don't you think?"

"Wonderful is not quite the word I would use," Edward said. "But he has changed, and so I'm trying to give him the benefit of the doubt." He hoped the words sounded sincere anyway.

"Was it that awful, when he left?"

"In all honesty, it was actually a relief when he disappeared. He was a terrible brother, and he left me in a bad spot, but his vanishing act was a relief of sorts."

Footsteps on the wood floor announced Edgar's return, and Mary sat back in her chair. She smoothed the napkin in her lap.

Edgar resumed his seat. He had two small boxes in his hands, and he slid one in front of each of them. The box before Mary was wide and flat, painted a glossy black, and hinged on one side. Before Edward sat a smaller square box wrapped in black velvet.

Mary beamed, looking up at Edward. He gave her a small nod and she undid the latch on the front and tilted the lid open. Lying on a cushion of red fabric, an ornately carved silver pendant glittered in the lamp light. A blue gem had been set in the center, and it hung on a thickly-braided silver chain. "Oh my," she said, holding the pendant in one hand. She glanced at Edward once more, and again he nodded. With care to center it just so, she hung it on her neck. It settled just below the hollow of her throat, and made everything else she wore look that much more drab in comparison.

She, however, glowed.

"Open yours," she said, all eagerness.

Even the box felt expensive, much more so than the gifts that would normally enter the house. He lifted the lid, revealing a ring of similar style to her necklace. Its design was a snake, coiled three times, with a head on either end. In the mouth of one was a blue gem, with all the cut and clarity as the one on Mary's pendant.

"Go on, try it on," Mary said. Her excitement had not dissipated in the slightest.

He slipped the ring on, choosing the middle finger of his right hand. It settled there as if it were custom-made to fit by a master jeweler. Though it appeared to be crafted out of metal, it felt soft, and warm to the touch.

"It's charming," he said, more for Mary's benefit than anything else.

"It's the mirror of my own," Edgar said, showing his left hand. There, entwined on the middle finger, the same serpent resided, but with a red gem instead of blue.

Edward nodded, about as much enthusiasm as he could muster at this revelation. He dropped both hands in his lap before tugging on the ring. He was ready to hide it away in the box it came in, but it didn't budge. He pulled harder, giving it a twist. The ring seemed to only tighten its grip. He lifted both hands into the air, not caring about how big of a show he made out of it.

"Is there a problem, Edward?" Mary asked, followed by a quick tittering laugh that gave away her embarrassment.

He ignored her. With as much grip as he could muster from his left hand, he held the ring firm and pulled. And pulled.

Again, the ring only tightened its own grip.

Words grunted out from Edward in short bursts. "What is this damned thing?"

"My dear brother, please. I'm sure you're making your finger swell with all of this. Perhaps we can search Mary's cupboards after dinner for some kind of cooking oil to ease it off."

With a huff, Edward dropped his hands onto the table. His finger had indeed swelled, puffing up and around the twisted form of the ring.

"The rings come from the Orient, and they may share properties with a Chinese finger trap. But I assure you, it will come off." Edgar slipped his own ring off with ease, held it up in the air, and slid it back on.

The conversation turned to travel, and all of the places Edgar had visited. Edward stopped listening. While Edgar talked, Mary occasionally glanced down at her necklace, and each time she'd light up with joy. Edward had been able to supply them with a small house of their own, and put food on the table, but his gifts to her had always been mindful of the budget—flowers, books, or trinkets made from pewter. Precious gems were out of the question; and something of that size…? He could not compete with Edgar, both in gift giving or travel. And he hated him more than ever for being reminded of his treachery.

His hand returned once more to the ring. With each tug, each twist, the thing tightened further. It was not painful or even discomforting physically, but he wanted nothing to do with it—or his brother. He counted down to the time when Mary would turn to clearing away the dishes and he could talk to dear Edgar privately.

It took much longer than he cared for, but finally Edward caught Mary's attention and nodded toward the empty plates. She took the hint perfectly.

"Please excuse me while I clear the table."

"Thank you for such a lovely meal," Edgar said.

"It wasn't much, I'm sorry, but the company made it all the better. And thank you for the wonderful gifts!"

"A small token. A small step toward a new beginning."

Edward bristled at this, but smiled at his wife as she left with the plates. Once she was through the door and into the kitchen, he turned to Edgar.

"Enough," Edward said, his voice low. "You've only come because you want something. Get to it, and then get out."

Edgar flinched, and raised his hands in mock defense. "Dear brother, I am sorry if I've offended—"

"You come here unannounced, after years of absence, after stealing everything I had, after our parents' deaths, and you try to buy me off with gifts?" Edward pulled on his ring once more, ready to throw it across the table if only it would budge. "Goddamn this ring!"

"Forget the ring for a moment. I have something more important to discuss. I'm honest about mending our split. But it's time sensitive."

"What are you talking about?"

"This." Edgar rummaged an inside coat pocket, and pulled out a small brick of notes. He placed the stack on the table, just before Edward and tapped it with his index finger. "There's more where this came from. A lot more. I want you in on this with me."

Edward looked at the stack. Without thumbing through it, he guessed the amount totaled more than a few years of his salary, perhaps several. He didn't touch it, but wanted to. His recent burning anger cooled at the sight of the money.

"And the catch?"

"Come with me tonight. Let me show you. I promise you this will be beneficial for both of us, the opportunity of a lifetime."

"You can't tell me here?"

"It's too substantial. It's something I need to show you. Plus, I don't want to mix Mary into it until you've made the jump. If it doesn't work out, you keep the money. But trust me; this will change both of our lives."

Edward ran his hand across the bills. He knew the amount alone would bring big changes for him and Mary—if, what Edgar promised was true, everything would be different. While his issues with his brother ran deeper than money, the financial blow Edgar had dealt him years ago had been the final knife in his back.

He rose and opened a drawer in the dining set, ready to stash the bills back behind the silverware. He didn't want Mary to know about any of this yet, and with all of their finest utensils out, she might just find it there. He slipped it into his own coat pocket instead. "Show me."

"I shall show you a new life," Edgar said, patting his brother on the back.

Mary was in the kitchen cleaning up. Edward called out to her. "Darling, I'm running out with Edgar for a little while. I'll be back before long." He refused to say "we" until Edgar proved himself a new man. Mary said something in return, but it was muffled through the walls.

They grabbed their coats and headed outside.

"My automobile is just around the corner," Edgar said, pointing out the direction.

It was a sleek two-seater, black, and open to the air. Edward pulled his coat tighter about him.

"It's not the most practical, but it's awfully fun."

Edgar led him to the passenger seat before stepping around to the driver's side. Inside was tight, but plush, with polished wood and supple leather throughout. Edward, not wanting to be caught gawking, turned his attention outward.

The engine fired up with the push of a button. Edward had never seen a car without a hand-crank, nor one that idled as smoothly, and quietly, as this one.

Edgar took advantage of the quietness. "You must not have told Mary anything else about me? She seemed far too warm toward me to know of my misdeeds."

Edward started fiddling with his ring again. "She knows nothing. She's a very warm person, but loyal to a fault. If she had known any of what had transpired between us, you would not have been let into the house."

The engine roared, and with a lurch the automobile began bouncing down the cobbled street.

"It seems like you recovered well enough, though. You have a house of your own, a lovely wife, a stable job."

Edward glared at his brother. "You can say we came from one egg all you want, but the only split that mattered was after our parents' passing. So all that feel-good brotherly love and *coming from one* crap might impress Mary, but it matters little to me."

"It's what matters most," Edgar said. "It's the flaw that cut our heart in two, a wound that we each carry with us to this day. It's the root of everything else. Look at us. We each received something the other did not. You were kind to our parents, I was calculating. You're loyal, I'm selfish. You're easily satisfied, I'm exceedingly ambitious. We're two halves of a whole, but a whole that should have remained a whole. We would have both been the better for it."

"I would have been better off as an only child," muttered Edward.

Edgar laughed. "Perhaps we both would at that."

They drove the rest of the way in silence, the car speeding through the empty night streets. The street lamps ended and the cobblestones turned to dirt, but still Edgar continued to drive.

A while later, Edgar slowed as they neared the only structure within a mile. It was a large brick building, several stories tall, with only a scattering of trees between it and the surrounding fields.

"What's this?" Edward asked, not moving to get out.

Edgar stopped the engine and opened the door. "This is the sum of my travels. All of my gains are contained within. I've brought you here to share it with you." He came around to the other side and opened Edward's door. "You asked me to show you. That's what I'm doing."

Edward stepped out and joined his brother. Edgar led them to a door around the back, secured by a thick padlock, which he unlocked with a key extracted from his vest pocket. A lantern hung next to the door, and Edgar took a moment to light it before continuing on. The flame flickered low, revealing a narrow entryway and a series of warped steps curving down into blackness.

"Mysterious," Edward said, and Edgar looked back with a smile. Edward didn't think it mysterious at all, though—after everything else, it was only fitting that his brother had involved himself with illegal activities, trade in illicit goods, or any other manner of detestable dealings. He had taken a sizable inheritance and parlayed it into a dark business, complete with a remote location safe from prying eyes.

The stairs creaked and groaned. There were a great many more than he had expected for a basement, and the bend continued downward as if circling a wide, deep well, but finally they ended at a stone floor.

"The light won't help much here, I'm sorry to say. Stick close."

"I'm not sure how you expect to show me anything like this."

"There's more light right around the corner. Careful now, it's tight through here. There we go."

Edgar stopped, and had Edward stay right where he was.

With his hands stuffed in his coat's front pockets, Edward could feel the stack of bills safely tucked inside. His thumb ran against it, wanting to count it all. The things he could do with this amount of money—*they* could do. Travel, for one, something that Edgar had enjoyed on money that was not fully his. Now it could be their turn. Mary had always talked of Paris, and Venice. Egypt and the pyramids. The Mediterranean and beaches.

But the money came with a price, something he had long ago forgotten about—dealing with his brother. He had wondered what had become of Edgar, and while for many of those years he dreamt of retribution upon finding him, Mary's kind soul had ultimately led him away from such fantasies. Taking this money would be more than forgiveness; it would be direct support of his brother's actions, tacit agreement that Edgar had been right so long ago, and an understanding that Edward was nothing without his twin.

Edward had worked too hard to jeopardize what he had built up on his own. He had overcome having his life stolen from him once, and whatever his brother was up to now, he didn't need to have that hanging over him once again.

He pulled the stack of notes from his pocket and thrust it forward. *Mary will kill me if she ever finds out,* he thought, but his decision was made. "I've changed my mind. I can't be a part of whatever this is, Edgar."

Small lights flared into existence, one flame after another. Edgar lit each candle in succession. "Interesting choice of words. *A part.* You're right, you know, though I don't suspect in the manner you mean." Edgar waved away the proffered cash, and continued the lighting.

There were dozens of candles in all, each held in a thin, uniquely twisted wrought-iron holder that extended from the ground to chest height. Enough light had started to fill the room for Edward to see that the candles formed a circle, perhaps thirty feet in diameter, near the perimeter of the round room. Both he and his brother within.

"We have been apart for far too long, brother. Each one of us *a part* of something bigger. It is now time to mend our rifts—for our reunion—and I mean that in all possible ways. As you had no choice in our separation back within our dear mother's womb, you have no choice in this matter as well. Too many things have turned to make this happen for me to let you just walk away."

"You're crazy, brother." Edward threw the money into the center of the circle. For the first time he realized something had been drawn upon the ground. In the very middle, a form curved back into itself—one half white, the other black, like two whales locked in a dance. From there, lines stretched out to each candle holder, alternating in black or white. The lines themselves twisted and turned, like the roots of a tree. The candles followed in the same black and white pattern, pairing with the color of the line drawn to it.

"It's an Oriental symbol. Yin and Yang. The duality of existence—of Man. Two halves, interconnected. It's us."

Edgar continued to talk, but Edward stopped listening. He turned to leave, wanting to hear no more of this insanity, and ready to walk all night home if he had to. As he neared the closest candle holder, though, his right hand became incredibly heavy, pulling him to the ground. He stared at the sudden weight as if it were a foreign appendage.

The blue gem of his ring now glowed a bright red, and pulsed in a double beat, as if mimicking a heartbeat. Every inch further toward the edge of the circle brought with it an exponential gain in its weight.

He flashed a glare at his brother. "What kind of devilry is this?"

Edgar's ring glowed as well—the same red, the same heart-like rhythm. "Insurance?" He continued bringing each candle to life, now halfway through the circle.

Edward dug at his hand, twisting and tugging with all his might to remove the ring. It held fast to his finger, tightening with each pull. He dropped to his knees, bending over to maximize his torque.

"Patience, dear brother. Patience."

With every ounce of his strength, Edward rotated the ring beyond endurance, beyond pain. Tears sprung to his eyes and his vision blurred. He screamed in frustration. Tighter—*tighter.* White heat shot through his hand as the ring slipped half an inch.

"Ah, you're eager. I like that! But we'll be getting to that soon enough."

A warm wetness coated both hands. Even through the tears, Edward could see he had torn his own flesh at the base of the finger. Blood splattered onto the ground, mixing with the powdery substance that made up the nearest white line. His whole hand throbbed in pain, and he could not bear to touch the ring.

Maybe now I can slip it off, even if it takes my skin with it.

Edgar stepped past him. "Pardon me," he said. "There we go, that should finish it up."

Edward lifted his head. Each candle had been lit, and Edgar fitted the last one in place—the one he had been using to light the others. The flames gave off an oily smoke, and filled the space with the stink of hot fat. Edward's head swam—a lightheadedness caused by the exertion, the pain, or maybe even the smoke. He stayed squatting in place.

"I feel it too," Edgar said, as if he shared the same dizziness. His cocky smugness had left his voice, and a quieter awe had settled in. "The stars align tonight for just such an event. Look." He pointed upward.

There was no ceiling above them, only a dazzling display of stars at the end of the towering walls that extended far above them. Edward found himself absently wondering how he had missed the tower, or if the building had been built around it.

"It's why it had to be tonight, brother. All of these other magics would be nothing without the ancient stars lending a hand."

"There's no such thing as magic," Edward said, though his own voice had lost any power it once had. A fainting spell danced at his periphery, and he lay back upon the ground to temper the spinning of the room.

"And yet only a minute ago a simple ring kept you from just walking away?"

Hands gripped the shoulders of his coat, dragging him into the center of the room.

"No one magic was real enough. Each culture has a piece of something, but none are complete. I was fortunate enough—*we* were fortunate enough—that I had the means to travel to the corners of the world. Symbols from the Orient and the ancient Norse. Smoke from the American natives. Skills to craft jewelry from both Palestinians and Israelites alike. Powders and spices from India and the Sahara. Ancient tomes from the Miskatonic University library, and the so-called insane scribblings from the Arkham Sanitarium. Each a sliver, a thread needing to be woven into something greater. This here is the final stitching."

Edgar walked the floor, back and forth, and Edward turned his head to watch. The lines upon the ground had not been drawn, but poured—something Edgar did now to patch up the path from dragging Edward, using the tips of rhino horns to trail out fine chalky or charcoal dust. Edgar swayed on his feet as he did this, obviously lightheaded as well, but stayed upright as he completed his task.

"You may be surprised to know our parents are even here with us today. The white lines contain the ground bones of dear Father, and the black is the charred bones of precious Mother. The candles are the rendered fat of both of them. I'm sure you believe I had killed them in the fire so long ago, but it's not true—those were not their remains. I had kept them alive until this week. Much of their life was spent down here in fact."

Edward's mouth hung open, too stunned to speak.

"Just part of the ritual. They were our creators, our gods. They brought us into existence, and they will help bring us back together. It's all academic, of course. You don't need to know how it works for it to do so, and you'll know it all soon enough."

Edgar slipped, tumbling to the ground with a grunt. He staggered on all fours out of Edward's view. "Thank you for your help, though," Edgar said. A hand grabbed his, and his ring clinked against its mate. There was no pain, only more wetness. "I'm not sure I would have had the strength to bring forth your blood. I barely could stab my own hand."

Edward tried pulling away, but had no strength left.

"I owe you this," Edgar said. "I've always owed you. I'm ready to make amends. I'm not only attempting to right the wrongs I have done to you, but also to mend the *first* wrong, the thing that separated us in the beginning."

"I don't want that..." Edward tried saying, uncertain the words came out right.

"But it's not just up to you. Too late anyway."

Words formed on Edward's lips—*don't, stop, help*—but nothing came.

Something shifted in his hand. It twirled around his finger, slipping in and out, intertwining his fingers, splaying them open. It crawled up his wrist, across his forearm, pulling him this way and that. Where it touched, it pressed him firmly against his brother—hand to hand, arm to arm.

He squeezed his eyes shut.

"Brother," he said. Or Edgar said. It all sounded the same in the blackness that swallowed him.

He woke to a lump in his throat, a giant gagging mass that threatened to block his airway. He tried to cough it up, to spit it out.

Instead, he felt himself swallow it down.

Still in darkness, his mind floated in a haze. Nothing responded, as if his entire body had fallen asleep.

Or been left paralyzed, he thought.

"Look who's stirring," Edgar said.

Edward tried sitting up. He felt nothing. Slowly, the darkness gave way to a faint hint of light—blooms of faded color that shifted before him.

"Where are we?" Edward asked. At least he thought he said it. Everything felt numb, disjointed.

"Still in the basement, dear brother. It's early morning according to your pocket watch."

"Can I go now? Are you done with me?" Edward didn't feel up to moving just yet, though his body shifted, and the details of the room began to sweep past his vision—all outside of his control.

"In due time, brother. Though you should know there is no longer any 'I' to speak of. Last night was a success, though not quite what I had in mind." The words sounded strange, as if unspoken. *Had they come from within him?*

A panic rose within Edward, one devoid of any physical reactions—no racing heart, no gooseflesh, no shortness of breath. He had the sudden need to get out, to get away, to be anywhere but here—to be anything but inside this body.

This body that was not his.

"Relax, brother. I, too, am not entirely thrilled by the results. I had hoped our consciousness would have become one as well. Perhaps in time."

His head tilted down.

Edgar's body lay before him, lifeless, a small pool of blood beneath his head. But it was Edgar no longer—Edgar was here, with him—controlling the body they shared. Edward had been left a prisoner in his own head, stuck in the back recesses, unable to do anything but watch.

What will happen to Mary?

"Mary will be just fine," he said—*they* said. Even his thoughts were no longer solely his own. "It's Edward's old clothes, old body. She'll see nothing different but for a more confident Edward. A richer Edward. Perhaps this new Edward will prefer the name Ed?"

He felt the smile pull his face in ways he had never done before.

Why?

"Because I had to. Because I did not have it all. Because back in the seminary I finally realized that I had no soul—it was the one thing not split between us. Now if you don't mind, we have one last part to finish if all of us are going to be one."

Their body bent over the empty shell of Edgar, the sudden movement causing Edward to swoon. "You'll get used to it," he said to himself. Their lips pressed to Edgar's exposed cheek. Teeth tore into the flesh, filling the mouth.

Edward wanted to scream, to cry, but all he could do was chew.

And swallow.

Uncle Sharlevoix's Epidermis

Gregory L. Norris

The big old house on Charrington Road was always dusty, but lately certain rooms had developed a skin, which lay in a film over the walls like on the pudding Aunt Cassandra served when rare guests visited. Uncle Sharlevoix was gone, planted in the ground for just over three years. I was one of the infrequent guests whose callings grew rarer after the funeral, due to the demands of my life.

"Auntie," I said, seated at the oblong dinner table with its scratched rosewood veneer—unintentional tattoos from so many past family dinner gatherings and dropped forks.

"Yes, Cedric?" she answered from over the top of her porcelain teacup, now stained a severe shade of plum-purple from her lipstick.

"Have you noticed anything odd in the house?"

"*Odd?*" she parroted and then considered.

Fretting, her eyes wandered out of the dining room, past the faded though still elegant Japanese patterned paper. I tracked her gaze to the length of wall running behind my back and the imagined direction of my late uncle's laboratory rooms, where a thin coating of living tissue had appeared among the cobwebs and neglected objects d'art—especially in Uncle Sharl's private study, where glass jars filled with cloudy liquid and expired things, and his other scientific hobbies lurked, abandoned by a hobbyist who wouldn't return.

"You mean…?"

"The skin," I said.

"Skin? I suppose that it is."

"So you've noticed it along the chair rail and the wainscoting? Over the wedding cake molding and cornices? Pale, pink, and pulsating, as though the walls are growing their own epidermis?"

The flesh above Aunt Cassandra's left eye ticked from nerves. "Not that I go back there much anymore. This house, big as it is, keeps me occupied."

I drew in a deep breath. Aunt Cassandra's perfume had lost its light floral prettiness and, for a terrible moment, all I could smell was the one foul component included in every brand of ladies' scent designed to accentuate its fragrance.

"Skin," I repeated. "Cells dividing, multiplying, growing thicker and more elastic. Across the walls, ceilings, and floorboards."

To which, my aunt responded, "Well, dear, as your late uncle was fond of reminding us, matter never truly dies—it just changes form."

Uncle Sharlevoix was dead. Part of him, however, had transformed and was growing in scabrous pink patches in the darkest and most mysterious rooms of the big old house. My uncle was, as you can imagine, a strange man. Some would say eccentric, though I prefer the former. Over the course of his life, Sharlevoix Beauregard Smythe worked as a tree farmer, a tree surgeon, a consultant for the state, the state university and, later, a delver into the mysteries of the Universe, both small and vast, unlocking the secrets of microbiology, one of his favorite passions and pastimes. Some of the trees he planted around the Smythe Family estate as saplings are now elder giants with half a century's worth of added rings. At least one of his experiments crawls through the halls and over the walls of the big old house on Charrington Road.

Uncle Sharl and Aunt Cassandra were married forty-two years before a tiny vessel in his brilliant brain exploded, and blood formed bruises, and more of the conduits in his grey matter shattered in sequence, causing the catastrophic breakdown that led to my late autumn morning in the dining room with my elderly aunt.

"Tea, dear?" she asked.

"Don't switch the subject, Aunty," I chastised. "And you know I don't drink tea. I prefer coffee."

"Your uncle loved his tea. A nice, robust Darjeeling with a splash of lemon was his favorite. He claimed it helped him to think."

"I think," I said, "that the house is too big for one person."

And there it was, that other oddity spoken of for the first time since my return following the funeral.

"It may be too big for *two.* Have you thought about selling the estate?"

Aunt Cassandra finished her tea and avoided my scrutiny. "Please do not go there again, Cedric. You'd have to drag me out of this house by my stockings."

"I have no intention of doing that, Aunty, though I wish you'd at least consider the notion. In any event, I'll stick around long enough to help you put things in some sort of order. Clean the place up. Scrape the walls."

My aunt's eyes shot open like old shades drawn too quickly. Her mascara magnified whites and pupils alike. "Oh no, dear, no," she said. "Not about joining me for a time—you know how much I enjoy the company. But Cedric, you mustn't do anything to the skin on the walls."

"Why not?"

"Because…" she said, but then fell silent and raised the teacup to her lips, stemming further discussion.

The house on Charrington Road was a cryptic old place. I summered there as a boy, and maintain there are rooms I remember playing in, like the Pink Parlor—only those rooms no longer exist. Or I've not been able to find them, despite many attempts to map the estate's layout and catalogue contents. The house's cells, I imagine, have multiplied, divided, and regrown new limbs in the form of rooms and whole new wings.

After my morning coffee, I walked outside the back portico and wandered the dead gardens. It was, perhaps, the year's last good morning. A bright, warm November day unfolded, and on a pleasant breeze were reminders of summer: grass and leaves, a hint of floral perfume from October's asters. The wild tangles of overgrown reeds and shrubbery spilled over the stone walls delineating the gardens from walking paths. In the summers of my youth, Uncle Sharl tended the flora with strict geometry, imposing shape, order, and science on the vast green spaces he so loved. Now, all was chaos.

I picked my way through brambles and briars, past the sundial with its sad smile, and the granite bench upon whose seat was carved a single word: *Resurgam.*

"'I will rise again,'" I whispered, and remembered my batty old aunt's cryptic behavior over breakfast.

Uncle Sharlevoix was brilliant, if batty, too. My late uncle, through his research into the unknown properties of the Greater Universe and the microscopic galaxy spirals contained within our genes, was convinced he would discover a way to beat the grave. If he had unlocked such forbidden knowledge before his death, the *Eureka!* moment clearly hadn't struck in the ancient greenhouse wherein the plants that populated the summer gardens were cultivated. Seasons of abandonment had shattered three of the glass panes. Dead leaves cluttered an environment where, in my memory, only green things flourished.

I tried the door. It resisted. I pushed harder and the old wood croaked open. Inside on a corner table stood two clay pots that contained misshapen growths rising up from desiccated soil; thick, gnarled stalks, each having put forth five digits. To my horror, the lifeless plants resembled human wrists and hands, the fingers capped in cracked gray nails frozen in a pose suggesting they'd suffocated while grabbing at thin air.

Vines and shoots, thorns and stamens, everything within the greenhouse was dead.

Not so in Uncle Sharl's laboratory. Yes, it was true that the glass jars filled with formaldehyde and biological remnants were canopic in nature. I lifted one from the credenza upon which it and several dozen others sat. The organ inside, something gray and crenulated, vanished in a snowstorm of liquid dust. Dead things, things pinned to boards and splayed open, insects and arachnids and ugly, expired horrors, stored neatly in rolling cabinet drawers or hung on walls behind glass, but…

On the window shelves, the flora abandoned by Uncle Sharlevoix bloomed lushly in the light of that last resplendent November afternoon. I wondered how the plants could subsist here, let alone flourish, until I heard the buzzing of flies and caught darting, dark afterimages near the windows, smelled the cloying sweetness from the waxy throats of fat flower blossoms, and made the connection. A small ecosystem had formed in a forgotten corner of the house, like the pale pink skin stretched thin over the wall in another part of the room.

Mastering courage, I turned away from the flesh-eating blossoms and willed my feet toward the patch of epidermis, similar to others growing elsewhere in the house on Charrington Road. Perhaps the segments were expanding their reaches, linking up, swelling in layers in an attempt to become whole.

As I neared the section of wall, a shiver teased the nape of my neck. I fought it, failed. The room fazed out of focus as it tumbled. When the world again stabilized, I identified the source: eyes, somewhere in the room—I was being watched!

I caught a reflection in one of those glass cases behind which bugs and beasts were impaled to boards. Eyes, one pair, bright red, leered at me from somewhere in the laboratory. I spun around. The eyes manifested there, close to the window.

The eyes were really flowers, but the sensation of being studied persisted and crawled across my skin, conjuring gooseflesh. Eyes, red and unblinking, drew me into their hypnotic pull. In some disconnected way, I understood that I had fallen into a trance state. My eyes burned from not blinking. At the periphery, the buzz of flies formed a sort of music, itchy on the ear. In counterpoint, individual notes shorted out abruptly as the makers of the melody vanished into tiny pools of deadly nectar in the throats of flowers.

Blink, a voice in my thoughts commanded. My eyes resisted.

It took the slithery sound of the skin moving close behind me to force my muscles out of their paralysis. I sucked in a deep breath, jolted out of my stance, and turned in time to see the skin on the wall reach down toward me, like a serpent in the branches.

The skin put forth a rudimentary limb with one wiggling finger. I gasped a rosary of expletives and stepped clear of its clutches. The skin stretched out, grabbed at open air formerly occupied by my right shoulder, and lost its grip on the cracked ceiling plaster. Gravity launched the skin-snake out of the canopy and flattened it on the dusty floor. The loud, squelching *splat* as it struck hardwood exorcized the last trace of the flower's spell.

Revulsion seized hold of me at the horrifying vision of the skin, wriggling in death-throes, writhing worm-like at both ends as it expanded and contracted. An elastic, agonizing peal rippled up through its layers of skin cells. Several long, tense seconds later, the patch of epidermis ceased pulsing and, before my eyes, went gray and lifeless.

* * *

A stiff wind sent in storm clouds later that same day. By dusk, rain fell in torrents and hammered the old house.

Aunt Cassandra fixed one of her usual succulent dinners—roasted chicken, the skin golden and salty; red potatoes crusted with rosemary from her kitchen herb garden; baby peas and pearl onions; and the old-fashioned chocolate pudding with its filmy top layer for which she became famous among family and friends, with dollops of fresh whipped cream on top.

I stabbed at the skin with my spoon. The thin crust split. The matter beneath was damp and pillow-soft.

"Aunty?"

Aunt Cassandra glanced up from her dessert. She had dressed for dinner in her finest black silk-satins and an ostentatious broach with a glittering opal at the center. "Is everything satisfactory?"

"Above and beyond, dear," I said. "You are, as has so often been said, a culinary genius."

"Thank you," Aunt Cassandra said. She then scooped a huge spoonful of pudding out of her bowl and savored the experience through rolled eyes and a soft moan.

"Aunty, about the skin..."

My aunt's euphoria shorted out. She faced me directly, her eyes narrowed, her lips pursed. "Yes, Cedric?"

"The skin on the walls."

"Yes?"

"What exactly was my late uncle working on when, you know...when the tragedy struck?"

Her mouth twisted into a smile. "The mysteries of life. The conquest of death. Hybridization and cytoplasm, photosynthesis and grafting."

"Grafting?" I asked.

"Yes, dear—the skilled application of one species' branch to another's roots. There are, I fear, things out there still skittering about on the grounds that got loose from his laboratory before he fully understood that which he'd created. I've seen this one abomination...with the loveliest blue tentacles and a face one could almost believe was human, like a child's..."

Her voice trailed to a whisper. Then, as though grasping that she had revealed too much, Aunt Cassandra ground her teeth, stemming further discussion on the subject.

"A nice cup of tea, dear?" she asked.

I reminded her that I drank coffee and offered to clear the plates.

"No, Cedric, why don't you call it an early night."

I returned to my room. The rain beat a somber staccato against the roof and outer walls of the old house. And the skin divided and multiplied in certain dark rooms around me.

The wind howled. Limbs from the surrounding trees crept closer toward the house, driven into undulation by the storm. The effect created in my room mirrored that of black and white stop-motion photography, projected through the windows onto the walls and ceiling.

I lie on my spine and pondered the things I'd seen and heard during the daylight hours. Wooden wrists and fingers, sinister petal-eyes, slithering patches of skin, and obscenities with tentacles and child faces jumped out of my imagination and superimposed over the flickers. My pulse galloped. The urge to switch on the lamp at bedside possessed me, but fear held me rigid.

Between shutter-clicks, a shape formed, grotesquely human, a caricature. I heard it as it completed crawling in from the base of the door and across the floor, its movements wet and sticky. On suction cup fingers, it pulled itself closer—and closer yet. My heart jumped into my throat, lodged in my windpipe. Suddenly, I couldn't breathe.

Closer.

Mustering all of my energy, I bolted upright, reached for the lamp, and turned the switch. Light drove shadows back into corners, and the primitive horror attempting to stand upright, waving jelly limbs that had no skeletal structure, bent backward in panic and wriggled away, making what sounded to my ears like a scream.

The rain fell. A cold November rain, one week later and the world beyond the windows of the old house on Charrington Road would be blanketed in white instead of gray.

When I arrived to the Smythe Family estate, a palace few visited, my main concern was for an elderly aunt living alone in an endless succession of rooms set on a vast, remote plot. My motives were mostly noble in nature, though I admit there was another reason for my visit.

The house was filled with decades of acquired treasures in the art, the silver, the furniture, and objects sharing space with so much dust and, in certain rooms, skin. As one of the sole surviving Smythes, I was due my legacy. I didn't think this as being entirely selfish; it felt practical.

But I soon came to the realization that there was something far more valuable there than original Impressionist paintings and Revere silver. Around the house, in the laboratory rooms, and loose on the grounds were manifestations of my late uncle's scientific genius.

Twice, the pale pink flesh growing, dying, stretching out, had attempted to communicate with me.

"Aunty?" I asked.

"Yes?" said Aunt Cassandra over vibrant eggs that glowed with their sunny sides up, beside ham steaks with seared scarlet flesh and hot buttered toast served on her favorite antique Royal Doulton plates.

"Uncle Sharlevoix...did he write down his ideas?"

"Why yes, he did. Your late uncle kept an extensive journal regarding his scientific experiments and interests."

I picked up a slice of toast and aimed the point at an egg yolk. The tiny sun went nova. Hot liquid poured past the fine layer of skin holding all intact. "Where did Uncle Sharl keep his journal? I've been through his laboratory twice and didn't find it."

"You didn't?" Aunt Cassandra answered. And though she said no more on the subject and, instead, raised her teacup to her lips, I sensed she knew far more than she chose to share.

I followed fresh tracks wound through the dust on the floor and again entered Uncle Sharlevoix's laboratory.

The skin on the wall quivered, pink and gelatinous, inspiring comparisons to jellyfish and juicy fruits and whole galaxies held together by the skin of energy particles. It *was* alive, after a fashion. A life form born of dust and debris cursed by the will to endure against nature's version of planned obsolescence.

Dust is mostly made of shed human skin cells. Like leaves dropped in the autumn, which nourish new plants in the spring, Uncle Sharlevoix's epidermis had birthed something *other.*

I approached the skin and whispered, "Uncle Sharl?"

A muffled sob drifted out of the flesh in counterpoint to the rain's elegy.

I extended my hand, brushed the backs of my knuckles over the quivery mass. Heat and electricity crackled over my flesh. It cooed like a pet, folded its primitive digit around my wrist. Then its grip tightened and all pleasantness evaporated. Pain flared. I pulled away. The skin held on. When it refused to release me, I aimed pointer and middle fingers at its mass and dug.

The skin popped. The gelatinous layer beneath came rushing out in liquid spindles. Wetness sprayed my face. A foul, coppery taste blossomed on my tongue. Energy raced down my throat, tugged at my eyeballs, jabbed oily fingers into both ears. My next desperate gasp for breath came through a fleshy filter.

The room plunged into darkness.

Hours later—or it could have been days—I woke to find myself seated in the chair at the big dining room table, my head resting on wrists. I attempted to swallow, only to discover that my mouth was miserably dry. Water…I had never been thirstier.

Sunlight streamed through the windows. I stretched. The effulgence rained over the skin of my bruised arm. The pain was gone, however. My entire body felt reborn.

In glided Cassandra, who looked radiant in the golden glare. She carried a big book with a worn cover under one arm.

"Finally, you're awake," she said.

"Yes."

Cassandra set the book on the desk. "The journal of fantastic secrets, dear. May I bring you anything else?"

I opened the book to the last page with writing. "Yes, water. And coffee."

"Coffee?"

My eyes fell into the words on the pages; sentences and spells that referenced photosynthesis and resurrection.

"Make it tea, dear," I said, and began to read.

Husks

Angeline Trevena

Elsa unfolded herself from the passenger seat, stretching out her cramped muscles and squinting against the sunshine. She looked around her, seeing nothing but bright fields of corn laid out in every direction. "What do you mean we're here?" She leaned on the car, the metal hot against her bare arms.

"We're here," Harvey repeated.

Elsa gestured to their surroundings. "But here is nowhere. What am I supposed to be looking at?"

Harvey pointed behind her. Elsa turned and squinted through the haze, picking out the faint outline of a house rising out of the corn like a mirage.

"Can you get the gate for me?" he asked, climbing back into the car.

Elsa dropped her sunglasses over her eyes and picked her way along the nettled verge. The wide metal gate was kept closed by just a frayed piece of rope hooked over a pillar. Elsa stood on the bottom rung of the gate, and swung it open. She swept down in a bow as Harvey rattled the car onto the uneven track.

"Hurry up," he said. "Knowing Mum, she's probably dishing up a pot roast as we speak."

Elsa hooked the gate closed, and climbed back into the car, gripping the dashboard as it bounced over the heavily rutted ground. By the time they pulled up to the house, they were both laughing hard.

"My poor butt," Elsa whined, feeling a little travel sick.

Harvey was already on the veranda that ran along the front of the house, beckoning her to follow. She could hear him calling out as he pushed the front door open.

"Mum? Dad? We're here..."

Elsa stepped up into the shade of the veranda, a dusty breeze urging her forward. The front door led into a narrow hallway, a staircase at the end. The living room was on the right, and, on the left was a small dining room with the kitchen beyond. She stopped to scan over a wall of family portraits, smiling at the sight of Harvey as a nerdy teenager.

He appeared at the top of the stairs. "I can't find them." He said, slightly out of breath.

"Don't worry…they probably went into town for some milk or something."

"Their car's still in the garage out back."

Elsa walked to the bottom of the stairs, placing her hand on the bannister. "Then they're probably out in the fields somewhere, or walking the dog."

Harvey rubbed his chin. "Yeah, maybe. It's just so unlike them not to be here when I arrive."

"Missing your red carpet?" Elsa grinned. "They're probably enjoying their lives now that they've gotten rid of you. I'll put the kettle on."

When she brought Harvey's coffee out, he was still stationed at the top of the stairs, his head in his hands.

"Stop fretting," Elsa said. "They'll show up soon enough."

"Yeah, I'm sure you're right."

Elsa watched a moth flicker around the light bulb, its wings batting against the hot glass. A second one joined it. "Can we shut the door, Harvey? This place is filling up with bugs."

He hadn't moved from the veranda since dusk. He hadn't eaten, and Elsa doubted he would sleep. She wandered out, slipping her hands around his waist.

"Is there someone you can call? A neighbour? The local police?"

Harvey shook his head. "Everyone I knew as a kid has either sold their farms to developers—or died. I don't even know who my parents are friends with anymore."

"Maybe they have an address book somewhere." Elsa rubbed his bare arm, his skin pimpled in the cool air.

"Good thinking," he said, turning to let her guide him back into the house.

Elsa went upstairs to bed a little after midnight, and Harvey was still punching in numbers, apologizing for waking people up.

Before Elsa even opened her eyes, she swept her arm over Harvey's side of the bed, finding it cold and empty. She sat up and untangled the duvet from around her legs. Creeping downstairs, she listened to the silence of the house, punctuated only by a ticking clock.

"Harvey?" she called out, not expecting a reply.

The back door to the kitchen stood open, and dried corn husks, like tissue paper, scratched against the floor in the breeze.

Slipping on her trainers, she stepped outside. The sun was already warm and promised another hot day. She spotted Harvey standing by the garage, looking down at something on the ground.

Elsa opened her mouth, but something about the way he was hunched over stopped her from calling out to him. As she got closer, she saw what he was looking at, and her hands flew to her mouth.

The dog was laid out on its side, its body sunk in, skin clinging to its skeleton like it'd been left out to dry in the heat of an afternoon sun. Covered in grit and dirt, the dog's tongue lolled to one side; flies buzzed around it, walking over the pale gums.

Elsa touched Harvey's arm, making him jump. "Is this...?"

Harvey nodded. "It's Chief. We've had him since I was fifteen."

"I'm so sorry. *Now* can we call the police?"

Harvey nodded. "But I want to bury him first. I owe him that."

"I'll make some breakfast. Looks like your mum stocked enough food for an army."

Harvey managed a weak smile. "That's Mum."

Elsa was dishing up fried eggs when Harvey came inside, his arms streaked with mud and his face running with sweat. He washed up in the kitchen sink before sitting down at the table, picking over his food without eating anything.

"Try and eat some of it at least," Elsa said. "If you're going to be running search parties, you're going to need your strength."

"I really don't think I can." He rubbed at his throat. "I can barely breathe." He pushed back his chair and stood up. "I'm going to call the police. Perhaps then I can relax a little."

Elsa ate her breakfast alone, listening to Harvey's side of the conversation on the phone—clipped, staccato responses. He returned, twisting his fingers together in a gesture she recognized.

"There's been some kind of explosion a few farms over. Everyone's going to be tied up there for hours. Maybe even all day. They said they'd get out here as soon as they could."

Elsa stood up. "Then we'll start our own search party."

Harvey tapped the table thoughtfully. "No. I'll go alone. I know the area, and I wouldn't want you to get lost as well. Besides, I need you to stay by the phone in case the police call back."

"Are you sure?"

Harvey nodded. "I'll be fine once I feel like I'm doing something positive."

"Take plenty of water. I don't want to have to come and rescue you."

Elsa leaned on the veranda railing and watched Harvey's figure fade into the haze of the fields. Suddenly the house behind her felt huge. She hesitated in the doorway, a shiver running over her skin. "You're being silly," she said out loud, stepping into the front hallway.

Closing the door behind her, she walked into the living room and switched on the TV, comforted by the sound of it wafting through the house. Even though it was broad daylight, she turned on some lights, too, and then went into the kitchen to put the kettle on—trying her best to fill the house with as much life as a person could by themselves.

She tidied magazines in the living room, organized food in the kitchen cupboards, counted the floor tiles, then counted her steps around the house's interior. She moved a chair onto the veranda and watched out for Harvey. She checked her watch after what felt like an hour, but only ten minutes had passed.

Wandering back into the dining room, she glanced over at the sideboard. An expensive-looking gravy boat that probably never got used stood there amid a few more photos of Harvey as a child—a photo of Chief, a glass bowl containing coins and some keys. There were a few china ornaments, a watch, a half packet of mints. She opened a drawer, hoping to find a deck of playing cards or something to take her mind off the situation. It held odd bits of cutlery and an electric carving knife. The next drawer was being used as a sewing box. The third was crammed with letters, many of them still unopened. There were lawyer's letters, notices of refused planning permission. And then there were other bills, all of them stamped with OVERDUE or FINAL NOTICE.

"You were losing the farm," she whispered. "But did you really do a moonlight flit without even telling your son?"

Leaving the papers on the table, she went upstairs and slowly opened the door to Harvey's parents' bedroom. She poked her head in through the gap, half expecting to see them sitting on the bed. She opened their wardrobe, but everything seemed to be in place. A hairbrush sat on the dressing table, and there was aftershave on the window ledge—even pyjamas folded on their pillows.

Elsa chewed her lip thoughtfully. "Unless you faked your own deaths..." She looked around the room one last time. "Or *didn't* fake them." She glanced up at the ceiling. An image of them hanging from the attic rafters, side by side, gently swaying back and forth, came to mind. She shook her head. *Don't even think that.* She glanced out the window at the garage below, her stomach knotting.

The space between the house and the garage seemed further than ever, and Elsa walked slowly, her legs reluctant. Shielding her eyes, she looked at Chief's fresh grave as she passed it. A crude wooden cross marked it, his name written across the horizontal slat. It was an inadequate memorial to a dog that'd saved Harvey's life once. Elsa had heard the story so many times she could recite it word for word.

Strictly speaking, the garage was actually a barn, accessed through a sliding door the whole height of the building. This door stood slightly open, the gap big enough to show the front corner of a dark blue Volvo. Elsa's heart beat hard in her chest. She wiped her mouth and forced her feet onward, finally closing her fingers around the edge of the open door. The smell of petrol and paint escaped from the darkness inside. Holding her breath, she pulled the door open all the way and flooded the garage with light. It threw a shadow against the back wall, showing something swinging from the beams. Elsa's eyes shot to the ceiling where a group of pheasants were strung up.

"Ha! I told you," she said to the emptiness. "You're jumping at shadows."

* * *

Elsa woke to the shrill sound of the telephone. She stumbled into the hallway, grabbing the phone in clumsy hands.

"Yes? *Hello?*"

Static crackled on the line.

"Hello?" Elsa said again. "Harvey…is that you?"

She heard indistinct voices, the drone of a child reciting some kind of poem or nursery rhyme. The line clicked and went silent. Elsa pulled the receiver from her ear and stared at it.

The front door opened and Elsa spun round. When she saw Harvey, silhouetted against the orange burn of sunset, she sighed.

"Oh, my goodness, you scared me," she said. "You're so late. I was getting worried."

Harvey stepped into the hall and flicked on the light. Elsa blinked against the sudden brightness.

"Did the police call?" he asked, looking at the receiver in Elsa's hand.

"I don't think so." She said, returning the phone to its cradle. "It was static. A crossed line, I think. Harvey. I need to show you something."

She led him into the dining room where the letters were still spread over the table. He sat down and picked one up, barely glancing at it.

He turned to her, his eyes blazing. "You've been going through my parents' stuff? When I said make yourself at home…this isn't quite what I meant."

Elsa stepped back. "They were going to lose the farm," she whispered.

Harvey looked back at the letter in his hand. He slunk down into the chair, kneading his throbbing forehead. "Oh, God…they wanted to build, to update the farm, to diversify. You can't run a farm like you used to, not if you want to survive. They'd already started digging, and laying foundations. They were spending money, but they couldn't see any reason why permissions would be refused. No one overlooks them, and all the other farms had done it in previous years. I knew that things were tight, but I had no idea it was this bad."

Elsa rubbed his shoulders. "You don't think this might have something to do with their disappearance, do you?"

"They're not the kind of people to run away from their problems."

Elsa gestured to the spread of letters. "Does this look like they were dealing with it?" Many of the letters were unopened.

Harvey grabbed at them, screwing them up in his fists. "Why the hell didn't they tell me they needed help?"

Elsa placed her hand on his arm, but he shrugged her off aggressively. "They probably just didn't want to worry you."

"Where are the damned police when you need them?" He jumped up and strode into the hallway, snatching up the phone. Elsa crept past him and sat halfway up the stairs, listening to him scream at whoever had been unlucky enough to answer his call.

It was barely dawn when Harvey shook Elsa awake. His eyes were rimmed with shadows, his hair unkempt. "Wake up," he hissed, closing his cold fingers around her wrist. "They're here."

Elsa sat upright. "Your parents?"

Harvey nodded. "Get dressed."

"Hang on, I don't understand. Have you been out looking already this morning?"

Harvey released her and stepped toward the open door, his hands twitching. "No…they just came home. Come on." He disappeared, and Elsa listened to his footsteps retreating.

"This is weird," she said to the empty room." She pulled on jeans and a top, and went downstairs.

Harvey was standing on the veranda, his back to the door, hands tightly gripping the railing. His parents were in the middle of the farm's drive, looking out over the cornfield beyond.

Elsa touched Harvey's arm, and he turned around quickly, his face set hard.

"What's going on?" she asked.

He looked back toward where his parents were standing, and Elsa followed his gaze.

"What are they looking at?" she asked, goosebumps rising on her arms.

He shrugged.

"When did they get back?"

"I don't know." His voice was clipped, agitated.

"Should I call the police? An ambulance?"

Harvey exhaled, scratching his nails across the wooden railing. "If you think so."

Elsa turned and walked down the veranda steps. She approached Harvey's parents. "Mr. Benton? Mrs. Benton?" Neither of them moved. She walked around to the front of them. Their faces were pale and expressionless; their eyes looked straight ahead, but didn't appear to be focused on anything in particular.

"I'm Elsa," she said, reaching out to touch Mrs. Benton's arm, recoiling as she noticed the skin criss-crossed with red scratches. There was no blood, but the scratches were raised and swollen. They looked fresh.

"Did you see her arms?" Elsa called back to Harvey. He turned and walked back into the house without answering.

Elsa looked into the cornfield. It stood in neat channels, but the tangle of leaves made it impossible to see more than a few rows back. The stalks stood several inches taller than Elsa, and rustled in the breeze—keeping their secrets to themselves.

Elsa tucked her hand into the crook of Mrs. Benton's arm, and tugged gently. The woman resisted. She tugged a little harder, but the woman still didn't budge. "It's okay, Mrs. Benton, you're home now. Please, come inside."

The woman looked at Elsa, her face showing a flash of recognition. She smiled fleetingly, before her eyes glazed over again. "He's going to make you pay," she said quietly, her eyes looking straight through Elsa.

Elsa stepped back, breaking the contact between them. "What?" she stuttered.

Mrs. Benton turned back to the corn and, as if choreographed, she and her husband walked into it.

Elsa stared at the field before turning and running back into the house.

"Harvey?" she called out. She leaned into the living room, gripping the door frame. Harvey was lying on the sofa, fast asleep and tucked under a blanket. "Harvey?" she said again.

He stirred, turning away from her. The creases on his face were deep set; he'd been there for some time. He mumbled and opened his eyes, blinking, and finally focusing on her.

"Is it morning already? I'm so sorry, I must have fallen asleep. I have to admit, though, I feel a lot better for it."

"Honey, I've already spoken to you this morning."

Harvey sat up, rubbing his puffy eyes. "No, Elsa, you only just woke me."

"No...you woke me. Don't you remember?"

Harvey ran his hands through his messy hair. "I don't understand. Let me get some coffee in me first." He stood up.

Elsa held up her hand, gesturing for him to stop. "Harvey...you came and woke me up this morning, saying your parents were back. We had a full conversation on the veranda. I *spoke* to your Mum. They were right there. You were out there with us, and then you came back inside."

Harvey smiled. "You must've been having a dream."

Despite herself, Elsa stamped her foot. "No, I wasn't. I spoke to you."

He reached out and touched her hand. "It wasn't me."

A shiver ran down her arms. "It wasn't you...?" she repeated. Her footing faltered and Harvey gripped her by the shoulders.

"Did you really see my parents?"

"They were out by the corn," she said, flatly. "Then they just walked back into it."

Harvey smiled. "Maybe I'll go and check—just in case."

Elsa followed him outside, still feeling dazed. He wandered over toward the field, looking back at her every few steps. She leaned on the railing and watched Harvey part the corn and step into it. The stalks snapped back into place behind him.

Glancing down, she ran her hand over the railing. There were two deep grooves carved into the wood, where Harvey had scratched them. But, if Harvey was to be believed, it hadn't been him. She was terribly confused.

Elsa ran after him, the corn slapping against her, holding her back. She stumbled through the field blindly, losing sense of where she was or where she was going—or even which way she was facing. Breathing heavily, she stopped and listened to the field around her, hoping to hear Harvey stomping through the corn. Instead, what she heard was a child's laughter—somewhere close. She wheeled around, trying to locate the sound, but it was gone before she could train her ears on it. The wind blew, rustling through the corn, leaving her to wonder if in fact she'd really heard it.

A shiver ran through her body again—panic rising from the tightening knot in her stomach. The corn crowded in on every side, and she screamed for Harvey. Tears flowed over her cheeks, her voice becoming tight and hoarse as she continued to call out his name.

She shrieked as a hand closed around her wrist.

"Why did you follow me?" Harvey asked, still handling onto her wrist. "It's too easy to get lost in here."

"There were scratches..." she said, her voice fading as she shrugged hopelessly.

Harvey slipped his around her. "I won't lose you, too."

Together, they searched the fields until past midday, when exhaustion and thirst forced them to abandon the hunt, in favour of sustenance.

Sunlight streamed through the open bedroom window, flashing off the white bed sheets, intensifying Elsa's oncoming headache. She groaned and pulled the sheets over her head, tucking her knees beneath her chin. It was a cotton sanctuary, and she closed her eyes, recalling the sound of traffic, the smell of wet tarmac and take-out coffee—anything that didn't involve deep green rows of corn and missing parents. She wrinkled her nose as the scent of earth interrupted her daydream—the smell of sodden leaves and wet dog swirling around her.

She opened her eyes beneath the blanketing cotton, the illusion of being home lost. Two eyes were staring back at her—two eyes set in the mud-streaked face of a young girl. The girl's hair was a matted tangle around her head, and her forehead displayed the faded smudge of a purplish-green bruise.

"Don't go into the corn..." the girl whispered. *"You mustn't find us."*

"What—?" Elsa fought backward, kicking against the covers to free herself. In her effort to get away from the girl, she landed hard on the floor, smashing her elbow against the solid bed frame. Scrambling to her feet, she pulled the sheet from the bed and dropped it to the floor in a knotted bundle.

The bed was empty.

She flicked her eyes to the door, which was closed, just as she'd left it.

Running her eyes over the bed, they came to rest on a pillow. A muddy handprint was smeared across it—small, child-sized.

Elsa ran out onto the landing and leaned over the banister to look downstairs. There was no other sign of the child anywhere on the lower landing.

"Harvey?" she called out.

There was no reply.

She crept back to the bedroom, nudging the door further open with her toe. She crept toward the bed and ran her hand over the clean expanse of the bottom sheet. And the now pristine white pillowcase. *No muddy child's handprint...*

"This is crazy," she said aloud. "Or maybe *I* am." She turned the pillow over. It was equally clean on the reverse side.

Downstairs, the cool breeze drew dried cornhusks through the open front door, hooking them around the bowed legs of a side table. Elsa looked down at them, bending and picking one up. She held it close, and then held it up to the light. Spots of blood speckled the crisp husk. Elsa looked out at the cornfield, greyed a shadowed green under a thick, damp sky.

She stepped out onto the veranda, rain misting her hair, catching in it like dew in a spider's web. Harvey was standing in the middle of the driveway, looking blankly at the corn—just as his parents had.

"Harvey!" Elsa called out. But her voice was lost on the wind.

Without turning around, Harvey stepped into the field and disappeared from sight.

Elsa looked back at the husk in her hand and stepped out into the misting rain. She stopped at the edge of the crop, her toes touching the stalks. Taking a deep breath, she parted the corn and followed Harvey into its shadowed depths.

Somewhere a child laughed, and through the patter of rain, Elsa could hear footsteps, running up and down the tall rows of corn, all around her.

"I told you not to come into the corn," whispered a child's voice.

Elsa spun around.

"Now you'll have to pay," said another voice—much like that of Harvey's mother.

Elsa wheeled back around in the opposite direction. "Where *are* you?"

she cried out.

Hands tugged at her clothes. Fingers slipped through hers, and scraped at her legs. Two strong hands grabbed her by the waist, spinning her around.

"Harvey!" Elsa gasped, throwing her arms around his neck.

He held her tight. "Why did you follow me?" he said. "I told you not to come into the corn."

Elsa pulled back.

"*What?*" Harvey asked.

Elsa's eyes slid past Harvey, widening at the sight of the parting corn behind him. Harvey slowly turned, following her gaze. Blood was sprayed across the crop, dribbling down the stalks, pooling in the mud. Harvey looked back at Elsa, his eyes glazed.

"You can't escape this," he whispered.

"You shouldn't have come," came a child's voice again.

Elsa backed away, tripping and stumbling.

Harvey reached out, closing his hand around her wrist, tightening his grip. "You shouldn't have come," he repeated.

Elsa struggled, pulling against him, but he was too strong to break his grip. She dropped to her knees, pain burning up her arm.

"Harvey…" she whimpered.

"He's going to make you pay." Although Henry's lips moved, the voice came from outside of him—light like his mother's—carried on the wind. He twisted his grip, shooting pain into Elsa's fingertips.

A fly landed on Harvey's lip and he brushed it away. He looked down at her, and the fly returned. He flicked it, his eyes flaring with annoyance. A third time it landed, and when Harvey's hand batted it away, he left a smudge of blood across his cheek. For a moment, he looked confused, staring at the blood on his fingers. Then he lurched forward, more blood bubbling from between his lips.

He glanced down, his eyes fixed on where a blade protruded from his stomach, pushed through from behind. His body tremored as the blade was pulled out forcefully.

Elsa screamed, her hands twitching between Harvey's stomach and her own face, not knowing what to do.

Harvey stumbled, his mouth opening and closing, blood gushing forth.

He fell against Elsa, sliding to his knees, choking on the blood bubbling up and onto the ground.

She knelt with him, scrabbling at his arms, pulling him into her lap. *"Harvey! No!"*

He coughed one last time, then lay still.

Elsa's eyes filled with tears, and through the blur, she saw the girl.

"*Why?*" she begged.

"You can't know," the girl said. *"No one can... You mustn't find us."* The girl turned back toward the cornfield.

"No, *wait!*" Elsa reached out for the girl, but her fingers grabbed nothing but rain swept air. "Come back!" she cried—as much to Harvey, as the girl.

Elsa pulled Harvey's body further into her lap, burying her face in his rain-flattened hair. "Don't leave me here," she whispered.

Two boots appeared in front of her, their toes scuffed, the tan leather stained with blood and dirt. A hand pressed down on top of her head, preventing her from looking up.

"You can't know." The voice was deep. "No one can. You mustn't find them."

"What have you done...?" she asked the voice, her eyes blurring with tears.

Jean-clad legs, bloody and dirt-streaked, moved into Elsa's field of vision.

"They're my girls," the voice said.

And with that, a deluge of rain poured down from the gunmetal grey sky overhead.

The Truth

Jeremy Peterson

The gray line that stood so proud and fierce only moments ago, dissipated like a puff of smoke in a Kansas tornado. Private Benjamin Stafford stared slack-jawed and frozen as death charged at him through the murky black haze of war. Battle cries and death wails came at the young soldier from all directions. At his feet, a fellow southerner lay writhing in the sodden Kansas soil. James was his name—Benjamin had cleaned him out in a rigged game of dice two nights previous.

The doomed soldier used both blood soaked hands to clutch his midsection and Benjamin's stomach turned violently as he saw the man's intestines spill out between his fingers in pinkish- brown strands. With eyes still lucid but laced with horror, the dying man screamed for someone named Kathleen. The poor bastard's wife, Benjamin figured. Or, more likely, his mother.

Twenty minutes earlier, just as the Mine Creek came into view, and well before the bullets began to fly, Benjamin felt certain their bad luck was about to get worse. The creek bulged from heavy rains that had been pounding them for days. To Benjamin it signified the quintessential *fork in the road.* He didn't consider himself a superstitious person, but as he stood beneath those black, rolling clouds, he didn't see a creek—he saw a winding serpent with bad intentions. Not unlike the timeless deceiver that slithered through the Garden of Eden.

Benjamin stood on the muddy bank and shuddered. Crossing the engorged Mine Creek with their heavy supply wagons, proved to be a mind numbing exercise in futility. Only the dimmest Confederate soldiers were surprised when the Union chose this time to mount their offensive. The Northern battle cry was chilling as it drowned out the initial gunfire. Not all of the shots landed home, of course, but those that did sent horses bucking in fear and pain, while fellow soldiers collapsed to bleed out on strange soil.

I don't wanna die.

I don't wanna die.

Benjamin repeated the mantra in his head, as he clung desperately to his own will to survive. Overhead, the sky opened up with sheets of cold October rain, as if God was trying to wash away the terrible bloodshed. Benjamin's boots sunk in the mud as the battle raged on around him.

Soldiers to Benjamin's left and right dropped to the muddy earth in slow motion, while their death-wails taunted him, sounding tinny and distant, like they were coming from the bottom of a deep well.

They're shooting at me, he thought, numbly. *They're trying to kill me!* The very notion of this seemed absurd to him. "I don't wanna die." The words that had been swimming in his head slipped out of his mouth in little more than a whisper. Cannon fire erupted next to him spraying him with mud, blood and bits of flesh. "I DON'T WANNA DIE!" He screamed it this time and, with the words, his blank thousand-yard stare came sharply into focus. Benjamin crouched into the mud, instantly realizing his hands were empty. His musket was gone, and he had no recollection of where he lost it. He cackled at the insanity of his situation.

"Help me..." The words gurgled up from Benjamin's left, sounding like they were being spoken underwater. *"Please!"* It was Private James and Benjamin was glad the man had finally stopped hollering for the girl named Kathleen. The mortally wounded soldier stared vacantly into the pounding rain and clinched his fists obsessively, grinding up weeds and clumps of soggy earth. There, buried in the mud at the soldier's side, was the boy's musket. Benjamin smiled weakly and lunged for the weapon.

"Help me!!" the dying man pleaded again as he noticed the figure looming over him.

Benjamin kneeled down and put a reassuring hand on the man's shoulder, "You're gonna be just fine," he lied, his eyes locked on the gun.

"My guts...I can feel 'em," the fading soldier said, his tongue soaked in blood. "I'm gonna die here." He started playing with the hole in his stomach again. One of his intestines had ruptured and the smell was horrible.

"Naw...it ain't that bad," Benjamin reassured. "I seen way wors'en you.

Now, just let me move this for ya," he trailed off, pulling the man's weapon from the sluggish mud. "There, that's better. Now just stay still and the doc will get ya squared away."

"Thanks," James said. Could ya tell my girl—"

Benjamin sprung to his feet and was gone before the dying man could finish.

Benjamin sought cover, but found only chaos. Smoke hung over the battlefield plike a thick blanket—woven with battle cries and dying wails. Through the haze, he saw a gray-clad soldier lying in the dirt, using the bulk of a dead horse as cover. The marksman used the carcass to line up his shot as he screamed defiantly in the face of the charging Union soldiers. There was a satisfying *crack!* and a puff of black powder as the weapon went off. The soldier admired his shot for a brief moment, and then looked in Benjamin's direction.

"Get down!" he screamed over the din of combat.

Benjamin froze briefly as he recognized the shooter as his friend Charlie from back home. "*G'down,* damnit! You're gonna get yer fuckin' head blowed off!" He screamed with a frantic wave of his arms. Benjamin's panic-struck brain tried to process Charlie's request. Finally, he solved the riddle and dropped to the dirt, where he crawled defensively behind his friend.

"To hell with you Yankee bastards!" Charlie screamed with excitement.

Benjamin couldn't understand how his friend could be enjoying this—but he clearly was. He watched Charlie grab another cartridge, open it with his teeth and empty it into his musket. "Come on, Benny. Let's put these fucking bluecoats in the groun—"

That last word died in Charlie's throat—and his hat flew end over end into the air. Benjamin didn't register the splash of warm liquid that peppered his cheeks until Charlie's face hit the ground. Blood pulsed from a hole in the back of the soldier's head and seeped into a muddy boot print that may or may not have been his own. Benjamin screamed in fear and disgust as he crawled frantically away from the dead boy. He could hear the confident cries of the Northern soldiers as they pushed forward.

Run! He thought, as the smell of blood and black powder assaulted his nostrils. Mustering all the courage he had, he began his retreat along the bank of the creek. The echo of war surrounded him as he crouched and ran.

The flat, open field eventually surrendered to a densely wooded area, forcing him to swat branches away from his face, although some made contact and dug red channels across his arms and face. Benjamin ran until his lungs felt coated in ice and his legs grew weak and rubbery. Exhaustion finally caught up with him and he collapsed at the base of a massive oak tree that jutted awkwardly from the bank of the creek. His heart sank as the sound of gunfire and more shouting came from his flank—they were surrounding him.

He pushed away from the mighty oak and splashed through the icy cold water of the creek. An already ragged breath stuck in his throat as the frigid water shocked his system. He trudged on, through the pain. As Benjamin broke from a cluster of trees, the outline of a cornfield came into view. With newfound energy, he continued on.

Clearing the creek's edge, he stumbled into the first few rows of corn, hoping he was well concealed. With a heart full of dread, he turned back to see if he had been followed. The AWOL soldier half expected to see a full line of Union soldiers marching in his direction, but he appeared to be alone. Through the rows of corn, Benjamin saw the creek stretch off toward the horizon and a seldom-used road wrapping around the field and out of sight. Deep wagon ruts that overflowed with rainwater cut through the length of the road—but thankfully there were no soldiers.

Benjamin hobbled deeper into the cornfield until he could literally move no more. He collapsed between the rows with a grunt, and tried to ignore the chattering of his teeth, frozen to the bone by the creek's frigid temperature. With the sound of rustling corn all around him, he drifted off in mere minutes—and slept like the dead—until the Devil woke him up.

He noticed the heat from the fire and welcomed the warmth on his damp clothes. Benjamin lay still as the fire warmed up his body, but did nothing to squelch the icy voice in his head that said something was wrong. *Very* wrong. It was then that Benjamin noticed a man whistling under his breath—breath that brought the stench of sulfur and decomposition.

*I must be dreaming...*Benjamin thought. He recognized the song the man was whistling as a tune his father's slaves had sung on occasion. *I don't like this dream, I want to wake up!*

"Are you going to join me?" the stranger asked in a deep silky voice—a voice that should've been pleasing, but Benjamin found hypnotic and awful. "I'm afraid you slept through midnight snack time," The man said, smacking his lips loudly.

Benjamin reluctantly opened his eyes, and at once had to shield them from the impossibly bright campfire crackling up into the night air. He looked toward the man on the other side of the fire with eyes that had yet to adjust from the darkness. The fire glowed bright but the man seemed to swallow darkness, as if he extracted it from all things dark in the universe. Benjamin could only make out the mysterious man's outline.

"I hope you don't mind that I started a fire," the dark man said with an air of confident nonchalance. "It was no trouble…T'was my pleasure, in fact." This brought a hearty laugh from the man on the other side of the fire.

"Who are you?" Benjamin asked, finally.

"*Benjamin,*" the dark man said, as if he were scolding a dimwitted child. "Of *all* the questions you could've asked, you choose one you already know the answer to. I'm disappointed in you Benny—but not overly surprised, I must admit."

Benjamin, still woozy from his fitful nap in the cornfield, was just as confused as he was terrified. "What do you want?" He asked in a voice he, himself, hardly recognized. He sat up from his resting spot and noticed the cornstalks that were surrounding him when he'd fallen asleep were now dead and lay rotting in a twelve-foot wide circle around them and the fire. The fire was hot and bright, and blocked his view of the dark man on the other side of the wide circle. The kindling popped and hissed as it burned, and the flames licked the outline of the man's formidable frame.

"What do I want," the stranger repeated. "That is a very thoughtful question, Benjamin. I'm glad you asked it." The man stood quiet for a few more moments, enjoying Benjamin's obvious confusion—and fear. "Truth is…I want everything. I want it all, because I *can*."

Benjamin suddenly found it very difficult to breathe. His bladder let loose, and a warm spray soaked the front of his woolen trousers and pooled in the black dirt beneath him.

"Maybe what you mean is, what do I want from *you?*" The dark man chuckled. "What I want—" he stopped briefly, looking annoyingly up to the sky at a crow that was circling and calling out. He casually waved a large hand toward the sky and the crow went silent. Seconds later, it landed violently in a heap of feathers and broken bones next to the campfire. Benjamin cried out in surprise while the dark man went on without missing a beat.

"What I want from you, Benjamin, is something I could *take* from you whenever I wanted, but it's *sooo* much better if you give it to me! Of course I'm referring to your life."

"But I wanna live!" Benjamin pleaded, a tear streaking down his dirt-caked cheek.

The dark man cackled. "Yes, you made that perfectly clear when you abandoned your fellow soldiers and left them to die. Ah, yes, I nearly burst with pride as I watched your unyielding penchant for self-preservation, as you left all your comrades to die in the mud of the battlefield, every bit the coward."

Benjamin wept openly but didn't attempt to defend himself.

"You know, Benny, it felt like a sort of homecoming…" the dark man said, "With you leaving your fellow southerners to die. It reminded me of the time you left those two chickens locked up and forgot to feed them for two weeks. Do you remember that? I certainly do."

Benjamin didn't answer.

"They fed on themselves eventually. They *ate* themselves, Benny! And how you begged your father to let you take care of those chickens—assuring him you'd be a grown up boy. *"I promise daddy, I'll take real good care of 'em,"* you said at the time. "You took care of them all right..." the dark man recalled the incident with an almost prideful lilt to his voice, like a father recalling the exploits of his only son.

"I was only six..." Benjamin said weakly.

"You were *nine*, Benny. Besides, what does age have to do with it? You'll do well to remember, you can't lie to me. Not successfully, anyway."

"It was an accident! I forgot. I didn't mean to leave them unfed. I was just a boy—"

"Yes, of course." The dark man waved his hand, not wanting to listen to anymore of the soldier's rambling. "How about that time you stumbled on old Uncle Uriah forcing himself on one of those little Negro girls, the ones your folks kept out back to do all the things they didn't want to do for themselves. You remember that, surely? Do you suppose that was the only time that happened?" The dark man paused and shook his head. "Do you suppose that little slave girl was even old enough to bleed yet?"

"Stop it! No more!" Benjamin yelled, burying his head in his hands.

"The answer is NO, Benjamin!" the dark man continued. "That little girl *wasn't* old enough to bleed. But she certainly bled that day, didn't she? In fact, she bled a *great* deal. Don't tell me you're going to blame that on your age as well. You were a *strong* thirteen years old at the time. Surely you were old—and strong—enough to prevent a feeble old man such as Uncle Uriah from hurting that little girl! He was the kind of man who had to force himself on little girls, and you could've stopped him if you'd wanted to. Instead, you just stood there and *watched!* You pretended it never happened...but we both know it did. You thought no one else was watching. But I was." The dark man stared intently at Benjamin through the fire. "I'm always watching, Benjamin. Like a *proud* father, supporting your dark dealings."

"My soul...is that what you want?" Benjamin asked, lifting his hands from his tear streaked face. "Ain't that what you're here for? What you're supposed to take?" His lips quivered as he looked at the dark man, reluctantly.

"It's good to see you've recognized your situation," the dark man said, "that you've *acknowledged the corn,*" as your own father would've said. With an outstretched arm, he roguishly gestured to the dark cornfield surrounding them. "The trouble with taking a man's soul, Benny, is that the soul's become rather shallow and worthless." He looked off into the distance wistfully, "At one time, man cherished the soul above all else—that's what made them so damn delicious. But now they're treated like rubbish. Frankly, Benny, you and your kind have taken all the fun out of it."

Benjamin couldn't move. Fear, it seemed, had severed the connection between his brain and his legs. On the other side of the fire, he could see the dark man's countenance shimmer like the surface of the nearby creek. The flame separating them flickered and played tricks with the man's appearance. One moment he looked to be a young man dressed in the dusty grays of a Confederate soldier. Then, a split second later, he appeared to be a middle-aged man with short black hair, slicked back neatly, a pencil thin mustache and goatee adorning his face—dressed in a black, three-piece suit, like that of a lawyer or politician.

A similar transformation took place every few seconds. The allusion made Benjamin feel dizzy and slightly nauseous. "Why are you doing this?" Benjamin asked, his voice hoarse. "Why me?" He suddenly fought off the urge to vomit.

The dark man laughed. "Nobody *ever* thinks they deserve it, do they?"

"What about all the good I've done throughout my life?" Benjamin said. "What about that?"

The dark man stopped laughing as a dog howled in the distance. "So you hold a door open for an old lady at the drugstore, and that makes it okay to peep on Mrs. Harper while she's bathing in the privacy of her own bathroom?"

"No!" Benjamin screamed. *"Stop it!"*

The dark man ignored him and continued. "You say please and thank you to your lovely wife Elizabeth, and to you, that makes it permissible to lay with whores every chance you get."

Benjamin cried and shook his head vehemently, tears and snot flying.

"God, I love this game!" the dark man said, laughing at the irony of his own statement. Eventually he grew silent and listened to Benjamin weep the tears of the damned. He soaked up the soldier's sorrow, just as a daisy would soak up sunshine.

"She's *dead,* Benjamin. Your wife, Elizabeth, died in terrible pain, calling your name. But, of course, you weren't there. Then again, when were you ever *truly* there for her? You've never been there for anyone but yourself. And that's why you're here with me now. Waiting for me to kill you…and eat you from the inside out."

Benjamin tried to stand up, but his muscles were completely without strength. They felt tingly and distant, like they belonged to someone else. He could vaguely hear a dog howling in the distance, but his senses clearly couldn't be relied upon. "You lie…" he mumbled. "I know who you are…and you're nothing but a pathetic, goddamn liar!" With that, he finally found the will to stand up. He stepped forward, toward the fire, and the dark man on the other side of it. "Why should I believe anything you say? You're the father of lies!"

One moment, the dark man was on his side of the fire—acting out a role he'd played countless times before, going back countless ages—and the next he was inches away from Benjamin's face. "I am the *truth!*" the dark man said with a snarl, his lips pulling back exposing long sharp teeth, his eyes glowing with hatred and spite.

At that moment, Benjamin knew it was the truth—knew it as well as he knew his own name. He had done all that the dark man had said. He'd abandoned his brothers in arms when they'd needed him most. He was sharing a campfire in the middle of a cornfield with the Devil himself. Satan *was* real and he was breathing sulfurous decay and death directly in Benjamin's face.

Benjamin stumbled backwards and fell hard onto the cold, muddy cornfield. His sheathed bayonet hung from his belt and dug into his ribs as he landed.

The Devil followed him down, breathing smoke that smelled of rotten meat.

Without thinking, Benjamin unsheathed his bayonet and drove it up into the Devil's chest. Benjamin screamed as steam and scalding black liquid splashed forth onto his arm.

The Devil's eyes grew wide and turned an ash-gray. He stumbled backwards allowing Benjamin the chance to make another move. He sprung to his feet and scrambled toward the edge of the clearing. He was running at full speed when he collided with the first row of corn. It might as well have been a brick wall. Benjamin bounced off the corn as it tore the air from his lungs.

The Devil's laughter filled their wide circle in the corn.

Benjamin clawed at the dirt as he tried desperately to suck oxygen into his lungs.

The Devil watched him squirm and laughed even louder. "Where are you going, Benny? The game's not over yet!"

Suddenly, from outside the cornfield, came a stranger's voice. "What in the *hell* is goin' on out here?"

The Devil stopped laughing and cocked an ear in the direction of the voice. A wide grin spread across his face. In a flash of movement, he effortlessly spun Benjamin onto his back and pinned him to the ground with a knee to his heaving chest. The bayonet was still sticking out of the Devil's chest. With little effort, he pulled it out and flipped it around, gripping it tight. "Looks like we've got company, so I guess our little game *is* over," he said, regretful.

"Please!" Benjamin pleaded, "I'll do better...I'll *be* better. I promise!"

The Devil looked genuinely perplexed for a moment. "We don't want *that* Benjamin." He said, shaking his head, "I'm afraid you've missed the point of this whole thing." He raised the bayonet.

Benjamin saw the gleaming blade and his eyes grew impossibly wide.

"Please..." was the last word to cross the prone soldier's lips.

The Devil plunged the blade straight through Benjamin's heart. Just outside the cornfield, a dog howled with a sound of great sorrow. The Devil sat on top of his squirming victim and enjoyed the ending of the young man's life for as long as he could.

The voice that'd called out to the field spoke again, growing closer.

The Devil looked into Benjamin's eyes and watched his comprehension fade.

"I'll see you soon," he whispered—just as the waning light in Benjamin's light flickered out.

The Devil stood up and looked around the circle. He waved a hand and the blazing campfire snuffed out. The once dead stalks of corn rimming the circle rose up, leaving Benjamin's soon to be rotting corpse the only evidence that anyone had even been there. That and, of course, the roiling stench of sulfur.

The farmer responsible for that cursed field of corn woke unceremoniously to the sound of an ill-mannered dog. *Goddamn mutt,* John Carr thought. Despite the dog's name, Barkley wasn't much of a barker. Truth be told, he was a damned good dog. John crawled out of his bed and fumbled for the lantern. "What in tarnation is wrong with that dog? I've got half a mind to kick 'im in the—"

"Oh dear," the farmer's wife said from her side of the bed, "you know you couldn't lay a finger on ol' Barkley."

"We both know that, woman! Can't a man bellyache under his breath in the privacy of his own home anymore?" He pulled his trousers on but didn't bother with a shirt. "Do ya know how damn early it is? I'm thinkin' m'day starts early enough, thank ya very kindly!"

His wife shook her head, and rolled over and went back to sleep.

"Oh, that's rich," he said to his wife's back. "Roll over and make sure you get your beauty slee, while I'm out in that damned field, workin' m'tail off!" He stepped into his boots and, after a brief moment of internal debate, grabbed his trade rifle from the corner of the room. He didn't think he would run into anything more than a possum or a 'coon—and, of course, old Barkley—but it was wartime and it didn't pay to be caught unawares. He slammed the door on his way out.

"What in thee *hell* is goin' on out here?" he said, stepping onto the front porch. Barkley was running around in circles, barking like his fur was on fire. Every few seconds he would stop and bark toward the cornfield, but he wouldn't go close to it.

"What in Sam Hill is the matter with ya, dog?" The farmer no longer felt anger toward Barkley, especially seeing how terrified the dog was acting. "Somethin' in the corn, boy?" he asked the mutt.

Still running in circles, the dog just kept barking.

John stood at the edge of the field for a moment and wondered why he suddenly felt so uneasy. "It's just corn," he told himself, with a nervous chuckle, finally stepping into the rows of corn. "Who's out her—" He froze as he saw a dark figure wading through the rows toward him. He couldn't understand why the stalks weren't moving around the tall figure—or how the man wasn't generating any noise as he navigated the stalks. He suddenly wished he had stayed in bed.

"Mr. Carr, what are you doing up so early?" The Devil asked.

John didn't answer—couldn't even if he wanted to. The trade rifle dropped from his hand and fell between the rows, where it would remain for a very long time.

"Sorry about the mess in there," the Devil said, motioning behind him to the bloody corpse he'd left amid the shadowed rows of corn. Stepping up beside the farmer, he put his arm around the man's sloped shoulders, pretending not to notice the acrid scent of fresh urine.

"You wanna play a game?" The Devil asked.

"Uh, n-no . . . I'm just gonna go back to bed. Please, I'm just gonna g-go back—"

"*Shhh,*" the Devil whispered. "You're an adult. I can't bear blubbering from a grown man." The Devil guided them both through the corn—although only one of them left footprints in the muddy earth. “You’re going to come with me and we’re going to—”

“No! I know who you are. You c-can’t do this…I’m a *good* person!” John cried.

The Devil sighed. “Ah…you *are* a righteous bastard, though, aren’t you? Thankfully, I don’t play by the rules.” He heard Mr. Carr murmuring the Lord’s Prayer under his breath and dismissed it with a chuckle. “While it *is* true I would rather you had a few more skeletons in your closet, it most definitely *isn’t* a requirement. Besides, there *is* darkness in you. It’s in all of us, no? Now, let’s see if we can find yours...” The Devil looked toward the Carr farmhouse and smirked.

“No! You leave Mary alone…she’s a good woman…she don’t deserve any of this!”

“Well, John, that’s up to you, now, isn’t it?” The Devil said the words, leading the way up to the porch of John’s simple home. “You let me have Mary…and you’re free to go. She’s sleeping. It will be peaceful for her, I swear.”

John hesitated, appeared to consider the offer briefly, and then finally shook his head. “No, take me…”

“Very well,” the Devil said with a sigh. “Noble to the very end, aren’t you?”

John swayed on his feet and appeared to be struggling with consciousness. “C-can I go in, and see her one m-more time? Just once more, while she’s sleepin.’”

The Devil gave him a sideways glance, but eventually waved his claw-tipped fingers. “Go ahead…but make it quick, Johnny-boy. Wartime’s my busy season.”

Overhead, the clouds were hinting it would be another soggy day in God’s Country. Head down, John approached the dusty steps of the porch and started climbing them. The old wood creaked loudly underfoot, causing him to hesitate for a moment. He stood frozen in the center of the porch, sucking in a ragged breath before breaking into a pitiful, all-out run.

He jumped off the edge of the porch at top speed, crossed the old road in two strides and headed for the wooded area across from their farm, without a backwards glance.

The Devil watched the old farmer run off with a knowing smile on his face. "I knew you had it in you, Johnny-boy," he whispered with satisfaction. The Devil mounted John's porch and thought back upon his day's dealings. It had been a journey he knew well. One that was destined to end at this meager farmhouse in the middle of nowhere.

He reached out his long, bony fingers toward the rusted door handle.

"Playtime is over," he said. "It's time to feed."

As the Devil pushed the front door open, upstairs Mary heard the door creak, and with a faint quiver in her voice asked, "John, is that you, dear?"

A dark light lit in the Devil's eyes. "Afraid not," he whispered, ascending the stairs, to what awaited him.

Peter, Peter

Christine Sutton

Moving Day

Lyle Gilbert took the last cardboard box from the back of the car and carried it up to the steps of their new home. *Their new home.* He felt a sense of pride swell in his chest again. He and Nancy had worked so hard to afford this house—and it was finally a reality. They were now homeowners. It had only taken them fifteen years of renting and hard work, but they'd actually done it. No more dreaming.

Nancy walked onto the porch and put her hands on her hips. She wore a bandana around her head with her long, blonde ponytail dangling out of the back. Lyle stopped to admire the curve of her full hips in her jeans. She was still as beautiful as the first day he ever set eyes on her.

"What?" She smiled down at him coyly.

"Don't give me that. You know exactly what—you sexy thing."

"I look like a cleaning lady. Are you telling me you get turned on by cleaning ladies?"

"Only the hot blonde ones," he said with a wink as he walked up the steps.

"Uh huh," she smiled as he put the box down and took her into his arms. "You are a silver tongued devil, you know."

Lyle leaned in and kissed his wife. Her soft lips pressed against his and he felt her melt into him as she wrapped her arms around his neck.

The front door opened and their son, Riley looked out. "Holy crap. Get a room, guys. How am I ever going to have any kind of social life in this dumpy town if I get labeled the weird kid with the nympho parents?"

"You'll be the cool guy with the hot mom," Lyle said in his best stoner voice.

Nancy playfully slapped him on the arm. "Stop teasing him, Lyle."

"Well, it's kind of my job..."

"Seriously, Dad, you're such a dork." Riley tried his best to look annoyed, but Lyle could see the smile he was trying to hide. He was a good kid, unlike many fourteen-year-old boys these days.

"Besides," Lyle let Nancy go with a quick kiss and a pat on the behind as she made her way back into the house, "Listburg is *not* a dump. This is a nice place to live, son."

"Yeah, right," Riley groaned as he sat down on the steps.

Lyle took a seat beside him. "I grew up about thirty miles from here. We're lucky—we got here just in time for autumn, the best time of year. They have all kinds of festivals and stuff. With *pie*. Lots and lots of pie."

Riley groaned again as Lyle put his arm around the boy's shoulder.

"Listen, I know it's been difficult for you. Moving all the way from California to Illinois has to be a bummer, but you know why we had to do this, right?"

"Yeah, Dad, I know. New job…buy a house…better school…blah, blah, blah."

Riley smiled and rested his head on his Dad's shoulder.

"Uh oh, hot girl alert," Lyle whispered, nodding toward the woman and young girl making their way across the street.

"Hey there, neighbor," the woman shouted as she stepped down from the sidewalk on her side of the street.

"Hello," Lyle replied, watching them both walk across the street and up onto the curb in front of where he and Riley were seated.

The girl was carrying a medium sized pumpkin in her arms. It had to weigh about ten pounds, at least. The woman was dressed in a very smart taupe skirt suit with a camisole that gave a pop of hot pink. Her taupe shoes and bag were accented with little gold buckles that matched her earrings and bangle bracelets. She held out the hand that was not holding a delicious looking pie. "My name is Miley, and this is my daughter Jessica. We just wanted to welcome y'all to the neighborhood," she said with a smile that was almost blinding.

Lyle shook her outstretched hand.

"Thank you, that is very nice of you. Are those for us?"

"Why, yes, they are!"

"This is my son, Riley. My wife's in the house; let me get her."

He turned to head up the stairs as Riley moved forward to take the pumpkin from Jessica. Lyle turned back and saw the two teens smile at each other.

"Nancy, we have a guest," he called out.

Riley continued looking down at the ground as he built up the nerve to speak.

"You wanna see the inside of the house, Jessica?"

"Sure. Is it all right, Mama?"

"Sure it is, honey."

The two walked up the steps and into the house, not saying a word.

Nancy passed them and stepped out into the sunlight. "Hello."

"Hello there, yourself. Aren't you just the prettiest thing? I'm Miley, and I made you a pie. Pumpkin, of course." She held out the pie, with a slight swish of her hip.

"Oh wow, it looks delicious. Won't you come in? I can make some coffee."

"That sounds just fine," Miley smiled again as she made her way into the house.

Miley and Nancy sat at the table as Lyle began making coffee for the three of them.

"How nice. A man who knows his way around a kitchen," Miley said.

"Um, yeah. Lyle is great with a whisk, too," Nancy smiled back.

"Yep, I'm a regular Gordon Ramsey," Lyle said, placing three plates and mugs on the table.

As Nancy served up the pie and Lyle poured coffee once it was done brewing, Miley leaned in, suddenly looking serious.

"I know y'all are new here, and I don't want to scare you off or anything, but today is the Equinox, you know."

"Is it?" Nancy said as she ate a forkful of pie.

"Yes. I assume you know the legend? I heard that one of you grew up around here, is that true?"

Lyle grinned. "This pie is delicious. Yes, I grew up about thirty miles up the road. But I don't know about any legend."

"Peter, Peter..." Miley whispered.

"The Pumpkin Eater?" Nancy grinned.

"It sounds funny—but it's no joke. Believe you me."

It was obvious Miley was uncomfortable, but Nancy wanted to hear more.

"What about this Peter, Peter legend?"

"Every season, starting on the Equinox, everyone in town has to leave a pumpkin on their front doorstep...as a kind of offering. If you don't, legend has it Peter will come after you."

"Why is that?" Lyle asked, already getting irritated. He had no patience for this type of hocus-pocus.

"The legend goes that Peter was a farmhand who worked in a pumpkin field over the hill—sometime back around 1900. Well, a few of the kids from town disappeared about that time, and the townsfolk got in a big ole stink about it. The old man who owned the field found a toy belonging to one of the missing girls just outside the little shed Peter lived in. A lot of the people in town refused to believe Peter had done anything to any of the kids. Peter was a bit slow, but he was a sweet man. All the kids liked him and he did odd jobs for the townspeople, for free. Most of them thought it had to be someone else that had taken the kids. People started putting pumpkins out on their front porches to show their support for Peter. If you had a pumpkin on your porch, it meant you didn't believe Peter was guilty. You understand?"

Nancy and Lyle nodded their heads as Miley continued.

"Not everyone in town thought so highly of Peter. One night, a few of the men got together and went out to the pumpkin field. Peter tried to fend them off, but I imagine those men were fueled by a bit of drinking, if you know what I mean. They dragged him all the way into town. The people that had pumpkins on their doorsteps cried out for them to stop, but they wouldn't have any of it. They beat Peter until he could barely move. They burned him with torches, then shot him, right there in the middle of town. The whole time calling him a baby killer and a pervert. Peter cried and swore he hadn't done anything to those kids, but the men didn't care. They killed that poor man for no reason at all."

"So, Peter really was innocent?" Nancy asked. She had stopped eating her pie and leaned in.

"Oh, yes…It was found a few days after they'd burned Peter's body to cover up the murder, that the kids had been taken by someone else. The town banker's adult son, Randy, had a *thing* for kids, if you know what I mean. They found him in his room a few days later. He had the bodies of two little girls and a little boy in there with him—none of them older than six. Randy had loaded up his pistol and shot himself in the head. He'd left a note admitting to having killed the children—*among other things.*"

Miley said the last few words with an exaggerated drawl.

"Since then, beginning on the Equinox, every night until the pumpkins are harvested, people leave a pumpkin on their front doorstep, to show Peter they believe him."

"Wow…that is a terrible story," Nancy shuddered.

"A creepy local legend," Lyle said with obvious disbelief.

"It's more than that," Miley replied, sounding scared. "Other people have refused to leave a pumpkin out and bad things have happened. Trust me…"

"Well, we'll have to take our chances. I refuse to buy into creepy campfire stories. A tale to scare the kiddies. Every town has one."

"No, Lyle, this town has Peter, and the story is true. I'm ashamed to say my Great Granddaddy was one of the men who killed that poor soul. I'm not proud of the fact, but I put my pumpkin out every night in autumn. You can bet your behind on that one!" Miley was becoming visibly upset.

Lyle didn't want to start a war with a new neighbor on their first night in town. "We appreciate you letting us know, Miley. We'll think about it."

"Nancy, please," Miley said, turning toward Nancy who was slowly sipping at her coffee, "…please make sure you do it. I want y'all to be safe. *Please?*" Miley sounded as though she was begging for her life.

"Okay, we'll do it!" Nancy said, unnerved by the woman's sudden change in demeanor.

Lyle gave a huff, but said nothing.

Miley rose from the table and composed herself. Her dazzling smile replaced the grimace of fear that had been there only moments before. She called out to her daughter. "Jessica, let's get on now."

The young girl emerged from the living room with Riley at her side. She smiled at the adults and Lyle thought he saw her reach back and give Riley's hand a squeeze.

"See you later, Riley. It was nice to meet y'all," Jessica said as she walked out the front door. Miley followed, thanking them for the coffee.

Nancy closed the door behind them and waited a few beats before looking back at Lyle with her eyes crossed. "Can you say, *cuckoo?*" she said, circling her ear with her forefinger, sticking her tongue out to one side.

"Locals love their ghost stories," Lyle said, chuckling. "Or they've found a great way to sell more pumpkins."

"Jessica told me all about Peter, Peter," Riley chimed in. "She said the last family who move here refused to put a pumpkin out on the first day of fall, and the next morning they were found dead. The lady had her throat cut and the man had been beaten to death."

"You don't believe that nonsense, do you?" Lyle asked.

Riley shrugged.

"She said at midnight every night during autumn, Peter walks up and down the streets of town, searching for people who think he's a baby killer. If he finds a house without a pumpkin, he goes inside and rips the whole family to pieces."

"Ooooh...ooooh...ooooh," Lyle moaned in an exaggerated ghostly voice, *"Peter is coming to get you!"*

"Knock it off, Dad," Riley said with an uneasy grin.

"I will show you exactly what I think of this little urban legend." Lyle lifted the pumpkin from the counter and raised it over his head. He stood over the trash bin and let it fall into the empty canister. The pumpkin split in two and spilled its insides into the bottom of the plastic garbage bag.

Riley just looked at him for a moment, and then walked out of the room.

"I'm not sure how he took that," Lyle said.

"It wouldn't have hurt to humor the locals and put that out tonight," Nancy scolded.

"It would have hurt. I don't want Riley to be a rube who believes in the boogeyman."

"Well, all you got out of that little stunt is a trip to the trash. I don't want pumpkin guts sitting in the house all night drawing bugs."

Lyle slumped his shoulders theatrically and gathered up the bag to take outside as Nancy went about deciding what to make for dinner.

* * *

11:27 PM

"Get away from that window, Lyle."

"I can't help it! It's like watching a car accident, seeing all these people scrambling to get stupid pumpkins outside by midnight. It's actually pretty funny. We should pop some popcorn and get the lawn chairs out," Lyle said, proud of his idea.

"Yeah, right..." Looking up from her book, Nancy rolled her eyes. "That would be a great way to make friends with the people here in town. *Let me make fun of your hundred-year-old tradition.* That should definitely endear us to the locals."

"If they insist on clinging to some stupid urban legend bullshit, then they deserve to have someone sane make fun of them." He turned to look at her. "What? Are you actually entertaining the idea that this crap might be true?"

"No, of course not. I just don't think we should poke the bear on this one. Maybe we should just settle in and play along. What harm would it do? You know, when in Rome and all."

Nancy jumped when she heard a loud *thump* from outside.

"What was that?"

"Probably a cat or something."

"Doing what, playing handball?"

"Maybe it was some kids trying to freak us out."

"It's almost midnight on a school night."

"Okay, some *truant* kids trying to freak us out."

"Can you just go check it out, please?"

"I just took my pants off," Lyle whined at her.

"Seriously?"

"All right...I'll go check...but I want you to know, that cat is gonna be pissed when I interrupt his handball game!"

"We'll just have to take our chances," Nancy said.

"Don't say I didn't warn you."

Nancy looked over the top of her book and gave him the stare she reserved for the times when he was being especially annoying.

Lyle slipped his pants back on and headed downstairs toward the source of the sound. In an effort to scare away the little bastards who were messing around outside, he opened the front door with a flourish, but there was no one there. He surveyed the neighborhood with pumpkins on all the front steps.

A loud thudding came from upstairs.

"Nancy? Riley?"

There was no answer.

Lyle headed upstairs with a knot in his stomach.

He walked back into the bedroom. Nancy had her eyes closed and her book was resting on her chest. "I didn't find anything, Babe," he said, unbuckling his pants, sitting down on the side of the bed.

Nancy didn't move.

"Honey?" Lyle reached over and nudged his wife. Her hand fell unceremoniously down to her side.

"Come on, Nancy…not funny."

He reached over to take the book from her chest, careful to slip his finger between the pages so as not to lose her place. He recoiled when his finger touched something warm and wet. He reached back and pulled the book away. His stomach lurched when he saw the green vine that had cut through her throat. Blood pooled in the cavities created by her delicate collarbones. The pumpkin vine was still embedded in the angry slice that ran the width of her neck. Lyle screamed, but no sound came out. All rational thought left him, as he struggled to comprehend what he was seeing.

A single thought wiggled its way into his brain.

Riley.

"Oh, my God…Riley!"

Lyle jumped up from the bed where his dead wife rested and raced down the hall. Riley's room was two doors down, but it seemed like miles away. When he finally reached the door with the Misfits poster hung at an angle, he pulled it open.

"Riley? *Son?*"

His eyes seemed unwilling to adjust to the dark. He fumbled for the switch on the wall and when an eternity had passed, the room finally lit with soft illumination from Riley's bedside lamp. The boy was sitting up in his bed, but there was something wrong. His eyes were open in an expression of terror that Lyle had never seen before, even in the worst horror film. His mouth was open wide as if he was trying to scream. A cascade of orange goo and seeds spilled from his mouth, onto his lap. His neck bulged as though the pumpkin guts had been shoved into his throat with so much force that his airway had been impacted. There were deep scratch marks on either side of his neck.

Lyle groaned as he realized Riley had clawed into his own neck to try to save himself. His son had tried so hard to get air into his lungs, that he felt his only option as he was losing his life was to dig through his throat.

Lyle leaned against the doorframe as the realization that his family was dead hit him. Tears streamed down his cheeks as he looked at the monstrosity sitting in front of him.

He heard a sound. A soft scraping from the hallway behind him.

His first instinct was to run. He saw himself bolting down the stairs, hitting the front door, running into the chilly autumn night, and not stopping until he was out of town and away from the boogeyman it played host to. The desire to do just that was overwhelming for a moment. He stood up and turned, ready to tear ass down the hall, but something stopped him. The soft scraping sound was much louder, and was accompanied by a slow, rhythmic shuffle.

Every beat caused his heart to jump as if it wanted to exit through his throat. The thought made him look at Riley again. That same heart felt as if it was being torn in two—one half for his son, and the other for Nancy. *This has to be a dream;* a *terrible nightmare of some kind, brought on by that bitch Miley's fucking campfire story.* He squeezed his eyes shut, and tried desperately to control his breathing. He thought about lying in his bed, ready to wake up from this torture at any second. Nancy was snoring next to him. She refused to admit that she snored, and he refused to admit that he found it comforting. He instinctively chuckled at the remembrance of her crossing her arms and huffing at him for saying she snored at all.

Lyle decided he could not spend another second in the room staring at his mutilated son. He edged himself into the doorway and gingerly poked his head out into the hall. *Nothing.* He didn't see the horrific boogeyman he was expecting, just an empty hallway full of shadows.

He couldn't bring himself to go back into his own bedroom and see his beautiful wife reduced to nothing but a rotting corpse, but he knew he needed to find a phone and call the police. The police would come and help him find out who killed his wife and son. Someone was going to pay for this, and it sure as hell was not some mystical wronged spirit monster from the old west days of Illinois.

Lyle crept down the hall and found the staircase. He walked down sideways, careful to keep an eye above and below, watching for anyone who might be waiting to attack him. Reaching the bottom of the stairs, he headed toward the kitchen. They had not had their phone service installed yet, so his cell phone was his only hope.

He raced over to the smartphone that was sitting on the kitchen counter. It was fully charged. "*Thank you!*" he said aloud, swiping across the phone's glass screen to activate the device. The familiar welcome screen popped up and he fumbled to bring up the dialer. That was when he heard the scraping sound again.

He turned toward the source of the sound and felt his bladder loosen.

There before him stood something he could never have conjured in his wildest fantasy. The thing in his kitchen stood at least seven feet tall. It looked to have the loose shape of a man—but was twisted and deformed. Its arms were unnaturally long and ended in curled stumps that had long razor-like claws. The thing's shoulders were hunched and uneven, its torso simultaneously bloated and gaunt. The legs appeared to be bowed and broken at their middle, and it was obviously a form that had been burned severely.

When Lyle looked into the monster's face, the last bit of sanity he had been clinging to drained away. The edges of his vision grew dark, like the edges of an old photograph.

Atop the gnarled shoulders sat a large bulbous head that appeared to be in perpetual motion just under the leathery skin. The lips were ragged flaps of skin hanging in front of a row of crooked, blackened teeth. Behind those teeth, a chunk of meat Lyle could only assume had once been a tongue writhed back and forth.

But the worst part, were the eyes.

They were milky orbs that bulged from fleshless sockets and looked as though they might pop at any second and cover Lyle in a spray of viscous, gooey acid. He could no longer help himself. Lyle began to scream uncontrollably. The dam of sanity broke and flooded the valley of his mind as his own ears filled with the unrecognizable sound of his own terror. His screams became hoarse as the flesh of his throat was worn down by his own bile and fear. The monstrosity that was known in Listburg as *Peter, Peter,* reached out and stretched its twisted fingers in his direction. The nightmarish hand grasped the top of his head, and the other hand reached inside the rags draped around its body.

The claw emerged with a small pumpkin encircled in its fist.

Lyle continued his soundless screams.

With a quick motion, the monster shoved the small gourd into Lyle's open mouth. It continued to push with obscene force, until Lyle could feel the muscles of his jaw strain, then tear and finally snap. His mandible unhinged from his skull with a loud *crack.* The pain was literally blinding. Lyle's entire field of vision went white, as he was relieved of the burden of actually looking into his attacker's eyes.

When the pumpkin passed his shattered jaw and jammed into his throat, it seemed as though he was being awakened from his nightmare to find something so much worse waiting for him in reality. His world went from white to black, as he thought to himself how happy his family had been in their own kitchen just a few hours before.

The last thing he heard was a raspy voice that sounded as if it came straight from Hell.

"YOU SHOULD HAVE BELIEVED…"

Preservation

"Well, we've earned ourselves one more year," Miley said, standing next to the fire, covering her mouth.

"Do we have to keep doing this, Mama?" Jessica asked, looking like she might be sick. "I really liked that boy."

"There will be others, Jess. There are always others, every year." She watched as Sherriff Whitely threw the last bundle onto the fire. A bloody hand slipped from beneath the sheet, and began to blister in the flames.

"Yeah, next year…" Jessica said. "I can't wait."

Miley looked at her daughter with a hint of sadness in her eyes. "At least we'll be safe until then." She put her arm around the girl's shoulder as they turned to walk away. "Peter, Peter got what he was owed…and we can live free for another year. At least this year there were strangers to take, and not one of our own."

The Old Cider Press

Gregor Cole

The scent of partially rotten apples slowly fermenting in the long grass of the orchard, drifted on the breeze and filled the evening air, accompanied by the distant hum of settling bee hives. The moon, already bright and high, stood against the fading orange glow of the setting summer sun, with the oncoming darkness mere moments away. Soon the only light in the orchard would be from the *Black Lamb* pub up on the hill. It sat there in silhouette like a miniature gothic castle. The sound of merriment and a tin whistle could be heard across the rolling hills, as the locals did their upmost to keep the day alive. Helen, however, was staying in the village and had lost track of time. As summer wore down to its eventual end—the hint of autumn already looming on the horizon—the worst part of all was that the days went from light to dark in a matter of moments. She hadn't even noticed she could no longer see the words on the pages of her book. She wanted to get inside before it got cold, but the early evening air was so pleasantly mild, she really couldn't think of a nicer place to be. So, she took her time and strolled through the rows of cider apple trees, permitting their heady scent overtake her, as she ambled back to her car.

She had no idea that from its high vantage point, the thing in the tree could see her. The hay filled sack of a man slipped from its gallows above the treeline and silently landed in the long grass with a buffeted *woosh*. It was quite a distance from her and moved with the sound of wind rushing through the trees. Helen was startled for a moment when she heard the rush of the breeze pulse around her, but didn't feel it. She could've sworn she saw something move at her periphery—something *dark*. And there was now another smell clinging to the air; subtle over the heady essence of the orchard at night, but there nonetheless. It was the pungent scent of animal dung mixed with wet hay.

Helen was suddenly aware that the sound of the bees droning away in their hives had abated. The comforting sound had been replaced with a strange clicking, like that of wooden blocks being slapped together by school children. Its slow rhythm filled the valley from all sides, echoing through the trees as Helen quickened her pace at the sound, and that of voices muttering around her, which together sent her into a panic. Although she knew where her car was parked, everything was beginning to look the same in the failing light. Helen hurried past rows of apple trees, and for a moment could've sworn she was going around in circles. The clicking of the wooden blocks became louder, as did the muttering. Whoever was in the orchard with her, they were speeding up their rhythm to an all-out gallop, swiftly closing in.

Helen saw a flash of silver up ahead, between a gap in the trees, and the shape of a man appeared in the darkness. She stopped dead in her tracks, her blood freezing as the thing of cloth and straw hopped toward her in an out-of-step zigzag.

The clicking suddenly stopped.

Everyone in the *Black Lamb* tried to pretend they didn't hear the first of the screams. The girl on the tin whistle kept playing her jaunty tune as the locals got louder and clanked glasses together to drown out the girl in the valley below. It was harder to ignore with the second scream. The entire pub fell silent from the shame of letting it happen. Some of them looked at the floor, while others hurriedly quaffed down their beer. The landlord behind the bar coughed into his hand to try and break the silence. More than one person flinched at the sound. Everyone waited for a third scream—but it never came.

"So that's that then, it's over?" a voice asked from the corner.

The landlord looked over to see Old William smoking his pipe. The old farmer looked as weathered as the stone fireplace he was seated next to, all eyes on him.

"Would seem that way." The landlord crossed his thick arms over his chest, and then reached for a dusty bottle of the expensive stuff he kept on the top shelf.

"Such a waste!" Old Will shook his head as he tapped out his pipe into the grate of the fireplace. "Caught a glimpse of her as I was making my way down here. She was a young thing—pretty, too."

The crowd in the pub mumbled and choked down more ale as Old Will re-packed his pipe, staring into the flames.

"If only the crop this year wasn't so bad, then *he* wouldn't have to...Well, it's best not to dwell on it, I suppose." The landlord gulped down a good measure of the dark liquor he'd just poured for himself.

"Best not, eh?" Old Will lit his pipe and muttered under his breath at the fire. "She was a pretty one, mind."

Brandon's motorcycle spluttered as he rolled to a stop in the gravelled gateway to a field on the narrow country road. He climbed off and kicked at the rear tire—"Bastard!" The muffled shout came from inside his helmet, which he slipped off and threw to the ground with a loud clatter. He could see a farmhouse up ahead, and the start of a rolling hillside dotted with amber and green leaved trees. He dragged the lame bike through the gate and propped it up behind the slate wall that surrounded the field. He'd stripped off his leather jacket, leaving his riding trousers, boots and white vest. Before making his way up to the farmhouse, he draped his jacket and gloves over the seat of the prone bike, holding them in place with the weight of his discarded helmet.

The shadowed countryside was alive with all manner of tiny creatures, especially with it being the end of summer and brink of autumn. The fields were thick with produce. Each tree he passed was lush with berries, and hummed with hidden insects. The evening air was still filled with waning birdsong.

"I could think of worse places to break down," Brandon heard himself say, his pace slowing to a stroll, as he took in his surroundings. It was all he could do to stop himself from whistling, something that bugged the hell out of him when other people did it.

On the opposite side of the road, to the drive that led up to the farm was an overgrown gatehouse. It was small and Brandon figured the weeds and vines were the only things holding it together. At the top of the ramshackle awning, someone had cleared the sign of foliage and given it a fresh lick of paint. It read: PENNYWELL ORCHARD – BEST CIDER SINCE 1562. The orchard was surrounded with the same slate wall as the field and farm, but it was built higher, probably to ward off any young scrumpers looking for a free bag of apples.

He was half tempted to have a peek over the wall himself. He smiled at the idea but continued up toward the farmhouse. Around the side of the house a girl was hanging out white linen sheets from a basket on the ground. She was curvy and wore her red hair up in a bun. Dirty overalls with the arms tied around her waist and a black t-shirt covered her from the last drips of water she wrung from the sheets before she reached up to the line to hang them on tip-toes.

Brandon ran his fingers though his sweaty, helmet matted thatch of blond hair to try and straighten up. He didn't want to look a total mess in front of such a buxom farm girl.

Tucking his vest into his riding leathers he called out, "Excuse me…"

The girl's head turned in the direction of the unfamiliar voice.

"My bike broke down. Would you have a phone I could use?"

The girl stepped closer, bowing under one of the washing lines, rubbing her hands dry down on the back of her shirt.

"No phone in the house, but there's one up at the pub. And there's a mechanics in town." There was a country twang to her voice and she smiled as she crossed her arms. Brandon couldn't tell if it was to push her breasts up or not. "My dad's up at the pub, he might not be that drunk yet, and can come pick the bike up for you. You might have to buy him a pint for his trouble, though."

"Well okay…no mobile then?" Brandon suddenly realised what he said may have come over as a pick up line. "Um, so this pub…"

"The *Black Lamb.* Just up on the hill over the orchard. Follow the road up, you can't miss it." She put her hands on her hips after pointing to the black shape of the pub on the rise behind the blond biker that stood in front of her. This time her breasts were pointing straight at him. He tried not to look—or at least make it look like he wasn't looking—but he did look, just a little.

She tried not to look like she noticed but the slight flush in her cheeks gave it away. "You might want to hurry," she said, smiling. She turned her head to try and avoid eye contact and the obvious blush. "If he gets a few ciders in him, my dad won't move from the bar until last orders."

Brandon smiled as he caught a glimpse of her cheeks redden. "I'd better head up to the pub then, I'll see you later."

She watched him walk all the way out to the main road, "His name's Old Will, by the way," she called out, but he only turned around to check if she was watching once. She blushed again, not really knowing why and returned to hanging out the wet sheets.

The road forked off, one part leading down into the valley toward the small village below. and the other ran around the slate wall, up the hill toward the *Black Lamb* pub, which sat on the crest of the hill, overlooking the vast orchard like a great black crow eyeing a worm far below.

The walls of the building were wattle and daws; thick black beams ran past whitewashed panels and the roof was thatched with tar soaked straw. The air around the pub seemed still and hot; the tar gave off an acrid scent that made Brandon's nose run a little.

Behind the heavy door, Brandon found the pub brightly lit with round cage lamps, and cool, not at all what he was expecting. At the bar a group of chortling farm workers quaffed cider and told jokes with the landlord, while a dog curled up by the fire grumbled as a small boy popped from behind the bar to playfully pull at its tail and giggle. There was an old man seated at the far end of the bar packing his worn pipe with a dark tobacco that Brandon could smell from the doorway.

The lads at the bar turned as Brandon walked over and raised a glass and gave a welcoming nod in his direction. The landlord beamed a huge smile, bracketed by thick, greying sideburns, and a sparkle in his eye as he slapped a glass towel over his shoulder and rubbed his hands together. "What can I get you young man?"

"My bike broke down on the road by the farm. A girl at the farmhouse said someone here might be able to help me out—her father." Brandon was rubbing his hands together now like the action was contagious.

"That would be Rosie. Old Will's daughter," the landlord said. He turned to the old man lighting his pipe. "Old Will, this lad's been down on your farm with your Rosie."

The old man coughed out smoke and spluttered while the lads at the bar erupted with laughter. One of the lads called out, "He wouldn't have been the first, Old Will." They fell about once more and a hand patted Brandon on the shoulder from one of the drinking boys.

Brandon blushed at the notion of being with the red haired farm girl and stepped a little closer to the coughing old chap. "So, yeah, my bike broke down and the girl at the farm house said you—"

The old boy at the bar waved Brandon to a stool. "Stop for a quick half and we'll go down to fetch your bike in a bit. No rush. The garage in town doesn't open till tomorrow morning anyway." Old Will puffed away on his pipe and called for the landlord. "Max, a half of Thunder Apple for the lad."

"Oh, but I wasn't planning on staying. I was hoping to be away as soon as possible."

"Well if the bike needs a fix, you'll have to stay the night. We have a room upstairs if you need it, no charge. Might have to get you to change a few barrels, mind." The landlord chortled as he pulled on a pump filling the short, fat glass with a dirty yellow liquid.

"Well, I guess I'll have to stop on if that's the case."

"Good, now where did you say it was this bike of yours?" Old Will tapped his pipe on the bar as the landlord passed over the glass to Brandon.

"It's just behind a gate off the road before you get to the farmhouse, behind the wall."

"No problem, Max can call Rosie and get her to move it to one of the sheds, then tell her to come up here for a drink."

"That's okay by me fellas." Max tottered out the back, still rubbing his hands together. Brandon didn't see too much of a problem with seeing the girl from the farm again, especially if drinks were involved. He took a sip at the sweet smelling liquid. It tasted of honey and fresh apples and was obviously alcoholic. "Good stuff, eh lad, local apples. Had a bumper crop this year and the press hasn't stopped all week." The old man beamed at Brandon as he chugged down his own cider from a dimpled glass.

Brandon caught sight of Max the landlord on the phone. He must've been calling the girl on the farm about the bike. It looked like he was here for the long haul, at least for the night. At minimum he had a glass in his hand and a roof over his head. What was the worst that could happen?

The pub started to slowly fill with patrons, a group of girls from the village, some more lads from the farm, a middle aged couple dressed in tweed and wellington boots that looked like they might have owned some land around these parts. Then Rosie ducked down through the low side door that lead out to the beer garden.

She was still in her black t-shirt and dirty overalls and rolled straight over to her father and flung her arms around him. Old Will jumped out of his skin as his daughter's affection took him by surprise.

"Did you put the motorbike in the shed, my girl?" His eyes floated around in their sockets from the cider.

"Yep, all away, and I gave the mechanic a call and left a message. Should be right to go down there first thing." Rosie smiled a pink-cheeked smile at Brandon, knowing full well he was staying the night at the pub.

"You hear that lad?" Old Will coughed out smoke from his pipe and dropped his hand on Brandon's shoulder. "My Rosie has sorted everything out for you—no worries."

"I can't thank you enough, everyone's been so helpful."

"Don't you worry about a thing, that's what the orchard community is about, lad, family and helping people." Old Will waved over Max the landlord. "Another pint for the lad and one for my Rosie."

"Thunder Apple?" Max leaned over the bar with a knowing look.

"Thunder Apple!" There was a roar from the steadily building crowd in the bar and around back in the lounge and one of the village lads started to play a coffin box concertina. One of the girls started to play on a tin whistle and the lads at the bar started to jig holding their pints on top of their heads as they linked arms and circled the girl with the whistle.

Every now and then one of the lads would make for a cheeky slap to the girl's behind for which she responded with a kick in the shin. An eruption of laughter from the bar accompanied every swipe of the girl's foot as it connected with an ankle or knee or toe.

"THUNDER APPLE!" the crowd roared.

His head swimming with booze, Brandon stepped out of the rowdy pub into the soft air of the late summer night—unaware he'd been followed out. The beer garden looked over the orchard sweeping across the valley below. The faint sound of buzzing bee hives floated up into the night. A breeze wafted the sweet scent of half-rotting apples up to meet him and he breathed deeply as Rosie's hands wrapped around his waist. She was a little inebriated too.

"I never caught your name." She squeezed him tightly. "I'm Rosie."

"Yeah, your dad told me," Brandon said, telling her his name. He tried to struggle from her grip, but not in a way that might offend her.

"So, Brandon, how are you going to thank me for helping you with your bike today?" The girl's hands were everywhere, and the booze in Brandon's system wasn't letting him put up much of a fight. He tried to shake off the cider's effect—play it cool.

"I dunno. What do you want for all your trouble?"

"Trouble," her eyes lit up. "That's what I want. How about you take me for a walk through the orchard." She giggled and pulled away a little, taking his hand in hers and dragging him out of the gate that led to a steep path down toward the orchard. The path was slippery, made of the same slate as the walls that surrounded the orchard and jutted out in big staggered steps. The girl led the way down to the valley and through the first rows of trees. The air was warm and still, filled with the sound of humming bees.

"Where are we going?" Brandon was still trying to get to grips with the alcohol coursing through his veins.

"You'll see. I know a quiet spot out of the way." She skipped like a child around the trees as Brandon staggered after her. He was completely under the red haired farm girl's spell. They stepped through some low hanging branches, into a small clearing, and Rosie danced to its centre, turning to Brandon with an inviting smile. Brandon wasn't aware that the sound of the hives had fallen silent…or that there was something circling the trees around them.

Rosie beckoned Brandon over with a finger, giggling as he approached. His arms were outstretched like a child taking his first steps toward its mother. His arms slipped through hers and around her back and she leaned in to kiss him.

Over his shoulder she could see the thing of cloth and straw break through the trees and make a sprint in their direction. She pushed Brandon into the path of the thing from the trees, as it swung its heavy tin pot around the back of Brandon's is head—the crack of his skull sounded like thunder, echoing down into the valley.

The girl giggled and jumped as Brandon slumped to the ground, his eyes rolling up into his head. The last thing he saw was the red haired farm girl holding the hands of a ragged scarecrow as they danced around his twitching body.

A commotion came from above him, the same kind of murmuring just before a priest stepped up to say Mass. Brandon didn't know what'd happened. All he could recall was being in the arms of that farm girl, then everything around him going black. His head gave him a reminder that it'd been struck—probably when he fell. All he knew was that he was laying on something really uncomfortable, like he'd fallen into one of those ball pits you get for a child's party.

Brandon's eyes flicked open. He couldn't see for the bright light over him but he was more than aware that he wasn't alone. Shadowy figures stood on all sides, muttering and swaying. His sight slowly adjusted, and he focused on the figure standing at his feet—the red haired farm girl. She looked rather different from the last time he saw her. She was naked, except for a red sash she had wrapped around her waist. There were other naked girls standing around him, too. Girls from the pub. He immediately recognised the girl who'd been plying the tin whistle and had gotten her arse slapped by all the local lads.

They were there too—all of them—standing further behind the girls, they were naked, but were wearing black sashes. In unison, they swayed back and forth in time to the macabre rhythm of their moaning, like slow motion ritualistic coital simulation.

It was then that he realised he was gagged and stretched out over a vast wooden trough full of cider apples. He, too, was naked and strapped tightly to the trough, spread eagle, bound at his ankles and wrists.

He saw the faces of Old Will and Max the landlord looming over him. They were accompanied by the sack-headed scarecrow. The evil thing hopped and skipped around the congregation as the two men swung into place a huge slab of wood with a giant screw mechanism over the prone frame of Brandon. They bolted it to the side of the trough with ratchets and locked it down tight. Brandon was *within* the old cider press.

"Now don't go trying to wriggle free. It won't do you any good anyhow."

Max wheezed as he hurriedly tightened his side of the ratchet.

"He's right you know," Old Will said. "Best not get all flustered. What spoils the blood spoils the brew." The old man nodded when his side was fully strapped down. "We have to do this to give thanks to the orchard spirit for the good crop, otherwise he punishes us with bad apples and takes to the women folk." He pointed to the scarecrow that was now perched up on a beam overhead. The scarecrow hissed down at the ritual and barked a dry coughing sound at the men working the press. The evil thing spat dust and straw onto the top of the screw, as the two men pushed through a metal pole and began to walk around.

Old Will muttered to himself, loud enough for Brandon to hear. "I'd rather it be a stranger's blood than my Rosie's."

The heavy lid of the press slowly lowered and Brandon started to struggle in a vain attempt to break free. The chanting began to grow louder as the naked bodies of the circling crowd thrashed together. The thing made of straw and rags laughed like the sound of bottles being broken and it hopped around on its perch.

Brandon screamed through his gag as the cold wood began to touch his belly. He arched, trying to free himself from his bonds, but still the men kept turning the screw. All the weight of the press lid began to bear down on Brandon, pushing him back onto his bed of apples, which felt like wooden cricket balls digging into him. The pressure started to build up through Brandon's body as the apples beneath his writhing body started to split and crush. The juice from the crushed apples poured into grooves around the trough.

Brandon screamed as he felt his ribs bow out, just as his back was pushed through the mass of pulped apples and met with the bottom slat of the wooden press. His head was pushed down into the pulp and his nostrils filled with the sweet smell of the pulverized mess, as the screw top applied maddening pressure to his skull and jaw. He felt part of his skull give way at the same time his sternum did, with a horrific pop. A splinter of jagged bone tore through his scalp. And his world went black.

The men and women above the bloody apple stew cheered at the sound of Brandon's bones cracking and snapping under the pressure of the press. The men operating it didn't stop until it was completely flat. An orange liquid flowed out into another metal trough below the press and Max gave the thumbs up as he pulled a ladle full from it. The crowd went into rapture and the scarecrow jumped down onto the press and joined in the screaming.

"THUNDER APPLE!"

The car pulled into the gravel drive of the Tudor style public house. Melvin and his wife Linda got out and surveyed the surroundings. Melvin adjusted his glasses and put his hands on his hips. "Well, isn't this lovely?"

"Isn't it just," his wife confirmed.

They ducked down through the low door into the quiet of the pub. An old man sat at the end of the bar packing a burnt black pipe with a rough looking tobacco. Behind the bar stood a fat man with thick grey sideburns. He was rubbing his hands together.

"Yes now, what can I do for you good folks?" The landlord beamed.

"Hello there, my wife and I are looking for a room, a girl down on the farm said you might be able to accommodate us." The couple beamed at the landlord.

"Of course, we have a double room upstairs. It's a bit small, but cosy enough."

"Excellent!" the couple said in unison.

"So how about some refreshments? Food and drink?" The landlord rubbed his hands together again, just as the old man with the pipe chimed in.

"Get them two halves of the Thunder Apple," the old man said, lighting his pipe and coughing through a cloud of rich smoke.

"It would be my pleasure," the landlord said with a broad smile.

Katy and the Green Boy

Lori Safranek

At least she had something fun to do when Mom sent her out to the yard to play. She could play on her swing set. What the heck did Mom think a kid could do out here with no other kids, just a swing set and not even anyone to push her higher? Mom and Dad had moved them out here to the country without thinking about Katy. They just said, "We're moving," and that was it. No one cared if Katy hated it here. They just packed up her bed, her toy box, and her stupid nightlight, and moved her here.

Now she had a new bedroom, a dirty yard to play in, and no one to play with. The bedroom wasn't even really new. Lots of kids had slept in it before her, Dad had told her. The house was something like 400 years old, he'd said, or maybe 100. She wouldn't be in first grade until fall, so she hadn't learned about big numbers yet.

Anyway, they moved her here, and she didn't like it one bit. The house was creaky. Mom was busy all the time, cleaning or unpacking or painting. Dad was working on the farm. Back at their old house in Springfield, Nebraska, Katy had a whole group of kids to play with. Neighbors on both sides, plus about a gazillion kids from school. She missed them a lot, even though Mom swore they would be at school in the fall, just like last year. Mom said, "Dear Lord, Katy, we didn't move *that* far! We're still in Nebraska, girl."

She stuck her lower lip out. She was tired of Mom. She was the one who'd said the house would be *so much fun*. It wasn't fun at all. There were no kids; the yard was super tiny, and surrounded by a cornfield. She was definitely not allowed to go into the cornfield, and that was very irritating. *Irritating* was a new word for Katy. She learned it the day they moved here, when Mom said, "Stop complaining, it's really irritating." Katy tried to use it a lot, so she wouldn't forget the word. Then Mom said, "I swear, you better stop saying irritating every other word, or I'm going to go crazy!" So she just practiced it when she was alone. *Which was all the time*, she thought darkly. "I'm so irritated," she yelled at the top of her voice. "Do you hear that, people? I am irritated!"

How dumb. Yelling didn't do any good when there were no people to hear you. But she realized she did feel a little better. She started swinging, using her legs to pump so she could go higher and higher. Not very high, of course, since her legs were short, even for a kid. She was a little afraid of falling out of the swing and getting hurt, not that she would admit it. Leaning back a little helped get the swing to go a little higher.

The next swing brought Katy back so far, she was shocked. Then she felt a pair of hands in the middle of her back. It was a familiar feeling, and reminded her of the old house, where all her friends lived. At first she didn't remember she was alone. She swung back and forth; the hands gave her a push. Midway through swinging forward, Katy realized something was strange. She automatically tried to twist around to see who was pushing her. The swing wobbled wildly and she tumbled out, landing hard on her left side.

"Mommy!" she cried. "Mommy! I'm hurt!"

Landing in the dirt hurt so badly, she was crying. *"Mommy! Mommy!"*

Mom came running out of the house and knelt down beside Katy, who was covered with dirt. She brushed her tears away. "What happened, Katy?" Mom asked. "Did you fall out of the swing?"

"Y-y-yes, but someone pushed me, Mom," she said, sniffling and holding her elbow with her other hand. Mom was looking at her elbow, which was skinned and bleeding. She stood up, and offered her hand to her daughter.

"Come on, honey, we need to wipe that dirt off your elbow," she said. "We'll put some medicine on it, and it will feel better."

"Okay, Mommy," Katy said, standing up. She looked behind the swing set, but it was just more cornfield. Then Mommy was leading her into the house, with her hand on her shoulder. At the door, she looked back again but still saw nothing.

As Mom washed her elbow, Katy started crying again. It really stung. Mom said, "Sorry, kiddo, but you need to be careful. Don't swing so high next time."

She looked at Mom. "I wasn't swinging high. Not until someone started pushing me."

Mom stopped wiping her elbow and tilted her head. "Someone pushed you? Katy, there's no one out there." This was why Katy sometimes got mad at Mom. She never believed her.

"Mommy, I swear, someone pushed me—twice," she said. "I was pumping my legs, but just a little bit, and all of a sudden I felt someone pushing me. I tried to look back to see them, but that's when I fell off the swing."

Mom smiled. "Katy, you're going to grow up to be a writer. You've always got a story for me!" Katy gave up. She let Mom put a bandage on her elbow and then marched angrily out of the bathroom and into her bedroom. She sat on the bed for a while, enjoying being mad at Mom. Then she walked over to the window and looked down at her swing set. She imagined she was still sitting on it, an invisible friend pushing her higher and higher. This time, she just enjoyed the feeling of flying through the air. She didn't care who was pushing her, she just wanted to go high, like the older kids. Katy was smiling, imagining how much fun that would be. Maybe tomorrow her invisible friend would push her again.

Something moved at the edge of the cornfield. Katy jumped a little, and then smashed her face on the window as she tried to get a better view. The tall cornstalks moved back and forth for a minute, then she saw something slip out from between the stalks. As much as she squinted and pushed her face to the glass, she couldn't see what it was. *It might be a dog,* she thought, with a happy skip in her heart. She wanted a dog so badly, but Mom said later. Like always, Mom said later.

Whatever it was, it didn't walk like a dog. It seemed to be standing up like a person. It moved quickly back into the cornfield, just as Dad pulled into the driveway in his old pickup truck. *Daddy was home!*

In the morning, Katy and Mom ate breakfast then watched a video together. As soon as it was over, Mom told her to go outside and play until lunchtime. She whined and fussed a little until she remembered the cornfield. Going out to see what might be in the cornfield would be fun.

Outside, Katy looked at the cornfield carefully. She squinted and looked again. How *irritating.* There was nothing there to be found. She walked over to the swing set and plopped down on the seat. A wind blew through the dry yard and swept a handful of dirt right into her face. She closed her eyes, but still got plenty of dirt in them, and in her mouth. She spit some dirt onto the ground. *Yuck. Stupid farm!*

She finally opened her eyes, blinking them fast to get rid of the gritty feeling. As they started to feel clearer, she realized she was looking at something. It was standing between the swing set and the cornfield. She blinked a few more times, not sure what she was seeing. It looked green all over, but she knew that couldn't be right—only vegetables, like corn, were green all over.

She blinked her eyes again. It seemed to be a little kid, maybe a boy. Katy scrubbed her fists into her eyes and looked again. It was a little boy, but he sure was funny looking. He definitely was green! Even his hair and skin were green. Poor kid.

"Hi," she called out. In a split second, the green boy was gone again, back into the cornfield, leaving a few cornstalks waving in his wake. She jumped off the swing and ran toward where the boy had been. "Hey, come back out! I live here now. You should come out and meet me. Maybe we could be friends!"

She tried to peer through the rows of corn, but all she saw was *more* corn. "Irritating!" she yelled. She decided to walk just a little farther into the cornfield. She took two steps before Mom was at the door. "Katy Johnson, get out of that cornfield!" Katy froze. How irritating. Mom always knew when she was breaking the rules. "I said get out of there, young lady," Mom yelled. "Get out of that cornfield. You know it's off limits!"

Katy turned around and walked out of the field toward Mom, her head down. "I'm sorry."

Mom motioned for her to keep walking, right into the house. "Since you can't follow rules like a big girl, head upstairs and take a nap," Mom said.

"No!" Katy protested. "I'm too big for a nap, Mommy."

"Well, you're not big enough to follow the rules, young lady," Mom said. "Seriously, Katy, that cornfield's a dangerous place. You could get lost in there. It's like a maze."

"What's a maze?"

Mom sighed. "A maze is a path that goes back and forth and is difficult to find your way through. Even a smart girl like you can't figure out how to get out. How scary would that be?"

"Pretty scary," Katy whispered. "I'll stay out of there, Mom. I promise! I don't want to get amazed and be lost forever."

Mom made a choking sound, but still sent her up to her room.

Katy thought she heard Mom laughing downstairs, but she wasn't sure. She really was tired enough to take a nap, so she laid down on her bed and fell right to sleep. She slept soundly until a noise work her up. Something was hitting her window. She listened for a while and guessed it might be tiny rocks, like she'd seen in a video the other day. The prince had tossed small rocks at the princess's window to get her attention.

Katy slid out of bed and went to the window. Looking down, she saw the green boy, standing right below, on the driveway! She started to run and get Mom to prove to her that she had seen the boy, but he was waving at her, gesturing for her to come outside. She knew she'd be in real trouble if she snuck out to meet the green boy, but five-year-old girls sometimes had to follow their curiosity rather than their good sense. So she quietly crept downstairs and peeked around, looking for Mom. She couldn't see her anywhere, so she continued on out the door.

Once outside, she ran to the spot where she'd seen the green boy. He was still standing there, motioning for her to come closer. She kept walking until she realized she was being led straight into the cornfield. She heard her mother's voice in her head, warning her about being amazed. She stopped and when the green boy continued to urge her forward, she shook her head. "I can't," she told him. "It's not safe in there."

The green boy laughed, which was the first noise Katy had ever heard him make. She smiled at him, his laugh sounded like the cornstalks brushing together. Goosebumps swept up her arms, but she didn't run away. He motioned to her again, waving her forward. She stood with her feet planted in the prairie dirt, shaking her head. No way was she going in there. It was a dangerous place, Mom had said. She trusted Mom about scary stuff, not like Dad who was always playing tricks on her, scaring her until she screamed, then tickling her into laughter.

Mom had been serious about the cornfield. Suddenly, the green boy grabbed Katy by the arm and began dragging her toward the field. She was stunned and didn't say anything at first but then she got scared and started screaming for her mother.

Mom was in the kitchen, sweeping the floor. She thought she'd heard her daughter shouting. Had she just been playing some game with imaginary friends in her room? Probably. Her Katy had one big imagination. Before she could begin sweeping again, Mom heard Katy give an ear-piercing scream. She realized it was coming from outside.

Broom in hand, Mom ran out the door, yelling Katy's name. She heard her baby's voice screaming *"Mommy! Help me."* Her heart was in her throat, thinking of all the danger a child could face on a farm. What was happening to her sweet Katy? She spun around the corner of the house, calling out Katy's name. All she saw was corn, so she headed toward the back of the farmhouse. Before she got there, Katy burst out of the cornfield, her hair a mess, scratches on her face and arms and pure fear in her eyes.

"Katy!" Mom screamed, as her baby flew into her arms. They hugged tightly, both crying tears of joy and relief. Mom imagined again what might've happened to her child, and squeezed her tighter.

"Ouch. You're hugging too much," Katy said. "I'm okay now. That boy wouldn't let me go until I started screaming for you."

"Boy? *What* boy?" Mom asked. "Oh for Pete's sake, you're not talking about that silly *green boy* again, are you? Do you know how much you scared me?"

Katy shook her head so hard her pigtails slapped her face. "Nuh-uh, Mom, I'm not being silly. He grabbed me and pulled me into the field. I was scared and started to get amazed before he finally let me go. I just ran down the row, and I was out of there."

"If you're making this up, I will be very disappointed in you, you know that," Mom's voice had a quiver in it.

Katy burst into tears and hugged her mom again. "Oh, please don't be disappointed. There really is a green boy and he really did try to pull me into the field. He *did* pull me in. Look at my arm." She stuck her right arm out and Mom was shocked by the deep green bruises that stood out brightly. She instinctively grabbed the other arm and it was equally bruised. She pulled her daughter tight to her and cried. "My baby! What in the world is in that field? We need to go inside, now."

Katy offered no resistance. Once inside, Mom put ice packs on the bruises and made a cup of sweet tea for Katy. After drinking the tea, she was good and drowsy and when Mom suggested she go lie down, she didn't argue this time. She was happy to be safely tucked beneath the blankets of her bed and fell right to sleep.

Katy was still sleeping when Dad got home. Mom flew out the front door and met him at his pick-up truck. She threw herself into his arms and sobbed while he stood, confused and worried. Eventually she got all her tears out and was able to talk.

Dad led her to the house and they sat at the kitchen table, the same table they ate meals at every day.

"It's Katy. Something happened to her today," Mom said.

Dad started to get out of his chair, although he had no purpose in mind. His instincts told him to go to his child at once.

Mom grabbed his arm and pulled him back down. "No, she's okay now, I'm sorry I scared you. It's just that she went missing today in the cornfield."

Dad slammed his hand on the table. "How many times have we told that girl—?"

Mom shook her head and stopped him. "There's more, honey. Katy swears the green boy pulled her into the field."

Dad, who had been informed about the green boy from the beginning, rolled his eyes. "The green boy, eh? You mean she broke the rules and went into the field, then she fibbed to get out of trouble?" He shook his head and crossed his strong arms across his chest.

"Honey, I checked her arms and they're covered with bruises." She smiled. "She must've put up a hell of a fight. She had green bruises are all over her arms, like someone had tugged on her over and over again."

He frowned. "You're being ridiculous. A *green boy* attacked our daughter? And left *green* bruises? Hon, Katy's being her usual naughty self... disobeying us...making up stories to cover up her escapades. I say she needs to be restricted to the house for a few days. That'll teach her a lesson."

Mom considered it for a minute then nodded in agreement. "That's not only a good punishment, it will keep her safe."

He laughed. "Safe from what? The green boy boogey man?"

Mom narrowed her eyes and put her hands on her hips. "Listen, smart-ass, it will keep her from playing in the field, and that's all that matters!"

Katy fought the restriction but ultimately gave in and spent her time preparing for school to start. Mom had even let her go to the Dollar Store and spend ten dollars on supplies she would need. They had another fun day shopping for new school clothes and going out for lunch in a real restaurant—fancier than McDonalds. Katy had been quite impressed by the cloth napkins. Mom had eventually made her stop playing with her napkin after she made it into a hat and plopped it on her head.

The next day, the school bus picked Katy up in front of their house. Mom was crying, which almost made Katy cry—except she didn't want the other kids to see her cry. So she just waved and said, "Bye, mom!" as if it wasn't the second scariest day of her life. The first was, of course, when the green boy had pulled her into the cornfield. A little shiver moved through her tiny body. Then she saw one of her friends from the old neighborhood and squealed with pleasure, the green boy and the cornfield long forgotten.

She could barely believe the day was over when she and the other students climbed back aboard the bus and headed for home. She was going to love school, with all the fun classes and tons of new things to learn. School had to be the best place ever!

As the bus pulled up in front of her house, Katy hitched her backpack onto her shoulder and jumped off the last step. Mom was waiting in the yard, waving at her and trying not to run and grab her baby up in her arms.

As Katy ran toward her Mom, eager to tell all about her day, she glanced in the direction of the cornfield. Gone. It was all gone. Just stubbles, ugly and brown, stood covering the whole field. *Where had the corn gone?* And, more importantly, where had the green boy gone?

Katy let out a scream then ran to her mother. "Where's the corn, mommy? What happened? Where is the green boy?"

Mom was taken aback. "Well, today was harvest and Dad and Mr. Petersen harvested the corn, honey, which means there's no more corn until next year. You know what *harvest* means, don't you, sweetie? Didn't Daddy explain it to you?"

Katy burst into tears. "They cut down the corn? *Why?* Where did the green boy go, Mommy?"

“There was no green boy,” Mom said gently. “It was just a figment of your imagination, honey.”

Katy swiped the tears from her cheeks. Through clenched teeth she said, “It wasn’t my imagination, Mommy, and you know it! He grabbed me…you saw the bruises. I bet he tried to pull me into the cornfield so you and Daddy wouldn’t harvest it and he could live there forever.”

Mom gave a weak laugh. “Katy, would you want to live with a green boy in a cornfield forever? That’s silly. You’re a little girl and you go to school and you live in our house. There is no green boy and I don’t want to hear about it anymore. Now go upstairs and rest for a while. You have yourself all riled up over nothing.”

Katy gave her mother one last bitter look, then marched into the house and upstairs to her room. She threw herself across the bed and let the tears flow. No one understood. The green boy was *real.* She’d felt his hands on her arms. He wasn’t nice—but he was real. Had the harvest hurt him? She wasn’t quite sure how the machine worked as it moved down each row, picking corn, but she thought blades were involved, weren’t they? Her tears flowed even harder just thinking about it. The green boy could’ve been hurt by the blades—or worse. No way could he have outrun the machine. Katy’s tears went on and on until she finally fell into an exhausted sleep.

While Katy slept, Dad and Mr. Petersen talked over the harvest, which they deemed a “fine one,” staring out at the barren, stubbled field. “Little Katy, my daughter,” Dad said as Mr. Peterson nodded, “Well, she had a little imaginary friend since we moved here. She called him the green boy. Said he lived out in the cornfield.”

Mr. Petersen turned toward his neighbor. “You’re kidding me, right?”

Dad shook his head and laughed. “Why would I kid about this? She thought she saw a little green boy come out of the cornfield. Eventually she claimed he drug her into the field. She had bruises up and down her arms and everything.”

Mr. Petersen coughed and shook his head. “That’s not a good thing.”

“Why?” Dad asked. Kids have imaginary friends all the time. We had to put an end to it when she turned up bruised. We grounded her, making her stay indoors until school started. Then she came home and the fields had been harvested and she freaked out. It all makes me feel sad for the little dickens."

Mr. Petersen pulled his seed cap off and rubbed his nearly bald head.

"Damn I wish you'd have said something earlier," he said.

Dad cocked an eyebrow. "What do you mean?"

Mr. Petersen shook his head. "I hate to even talk about it. It was such an awful time. I was about the age of little Katy when it happened."

"When *what* happened?" Dad asked.

"Well, a family lived here in this farmhouse, and they had a little boy about seven years old. The little boy was fascinated with all the machines we use on our farms—especially the harvesting machines for the corn. His dad warned him to stay away from them, and most of the time he did. His dad promised to let him ride on the harvester when the corn was ready, if the boy behaved." Mr. Petersen sighed and shook his head sadly. "Poor kid ran all the way home from school, even ran straight through this same cornfield. Only thing was, his dad had already started harvesting. Before the boy saw or heard the machine, it was on top of him. Should've cut him up pretty badly."

Dad scowled. "What do you mean *should've?* It had to have nearly cut the boy in pieces!"

"Well, yes, of course, but by time they realized what'd happened, the father had the machine stopped and people were running through the field to get to the boy," Mr. Petersen said. "When they got there, all they found was the boy's clothes, torn to shreds, and his ball cap. The boy was nowhere to be found. People spent hours looking for him, but he was never found. His mother had a nervous breakdown and they sold the farm and moved away. No one's used this field until now."

"Why did you let me use it?" Dad asked. "Couldn't you have told me first? That's creepy. The kid might be buried in the field somewhere."

"Because I didn't believe it myself," the man said. "I figured the boy was badly injured, he died and the family buried him quietly. Cruel busybodies made up the rest."

"The rest? *What* rest? What's the rest of the story?"

Mr. Petersen looked down at his feet for a moment, seemingly lost in thought. At last he raised his head. "Rumor has it the boy lives in these fields—or his *ghost* does anyway. He's been seen a few times running in and out of the neighboring cornfields. Apparently the cornstalks turned his skin green, as well as his clothing. See…it's a ridiculous story. That's why I didn't tell you about it."

Dad was as white as one of Mom's sheets on the clothesline. "Poor Katy, she's been seeing this ghost and we wouldn't believe her. And the damned thing tried to pull her deeper into the field. Was it going to kill her, keep her ghost with him? Damn, the whole thing sounds crazy!"

Upstairs, Katy had her window open and had heard the discussion between the two men. Her stomach hurt, thinking that she might've played with a ghost. The thought gave her goosebumps. Like Dad, she wondered if that ghost wanted to keep her in the cornfield with him. *No way!* She loved her mom and dad and anyway, she was a little girl. She wouldn't die for a long time. She decided she hated ghosts now. She finally went downstairs when Mom called her for supper. Her parents were especially loving to her during the meal, and Mom had fixed her favorite dinner—chicken nuggets. She felt warm and loved and happy again.

No more green boy, and no more cornfields.

After supper, she went to her room and got ready for bed. With her pajamas on, she dug through her books and found one to read. She turned off her light and crept toward her bed, trying her best not to look out the window.

Just as she reached for the covers, she heard a sprinkle of small stones hitting her window. She froze. She was scared to look out the window, but she was, after all, five years old and a very curious little girl.

She slowly edged toward the window and peeked out. He was out there, standing in the stubbly field. In the twilight, she could see his green skin and broad smile. He was motioning for her to come outside and join him in the harvested field. The movement of his hands was nearly hypnotic. For a moment, Katy considered going to the field again. Then she remembered she was looking at the ghost of a dead boy, one who wanted to keep her forever trapped in the cornfield, lost and amazed, just like him.

She backed away from the window and leapt into bed, burrowing beneath the covers. She pulled her pillow over her head and lay there trembling until sleep finally came and rescued her.

Out in the field, the green boy realized she wasn't coming this time. His head drooped as he turned toward the neighbors' unharvested fields. As he walked, his feet sunk deeper and deeper into the dirt, and soon he was up to his waist. Finally, his head slipped beneath the surface of the ground. Hidden, he would remain there, until the next harvest brought more children for him to play with.

The Last Harvest

Jaime Johnesee

Carter hated the Harvest but there was nothing he could do about it today. He tried his best to ignore their screaming and carried on with his task.

"Carter, please!" Abby Van de Geist had been his neighbor for ten years. It broke his heart that she was to be slaughtered like an animal—sacrificed like all the town's virgins older than sixteen. It'd been this way since his people landed on this planet, and some felt it would always be this way.

"Sacrifices are to remain silent." Carter's voice betrayed him as it cracked. He'd long harbored a crush on Abby.

"You can't let them kill me!"

"I can't stop them, Abby. I am just the Keeper. I'm not in charge of Death." Carter handed her the cup of water and plate of flavorless protein mush they fed to the prisoners and sacrifices. He brushed an errant tear from his cheek and moved on to Gladys Mantle's cage.

"I'm not a virgin, Carter! Please, tell them that! I had sex with Byron Hornbeck last year. Please, I'm begging you!" Gladys grabbed his arm and he shook her off.

"It's not my place to tell them." He tried to sound hard. As soon as he finished feeding them, he'd let the Elders know Gladys had been wrongly harvested. It was good she'd said something. They tried to make sure the virgin sacrifices were truly virgins or the Harvest would be worthless. The crops would fail and the town would inevitably die. Carter didn't agree with any of this crap. He remembered the first year after they terraformed Mars. His ship carried the only people willing to live with the natives, the Red Men, while other Earthlings moved on to other galaxies and more Earth-like planets.

Pastor Jenkins and the other Elders had decided Mars would be their new home. The first year was heaven for all the colonists. The Red Men helped them acclimate to their new environment. They brought the colonists clean water, showed them how to blast through the crust of the planet and get to the viable soil below for planting, and taught them how to use the crust to make bricks for housing. All was utopia—until the virus wiped the Red Men out. The flu the colonists had brought with them destroyed their saviors. The Elders told the colonists this was punishment for not respecting the Red Men's gods. So, although they held onto their own beliefs, every year they appeased the Red Men's god—Gilgorath—with the Harvest.

No fewer than five girls Carter had grown up with—that he'd joked with, laughed with, argued with, and played with—would die this year. They would be slaughtered, their blood allowed to mix with the red dirt, their lives forfeit to an alien god. This was the way it'd been for nine years and this was the way it was to be from then on. At least it would be, until someone decided to change things, speak up, and ask questions the Elders themselves wouldn't answer.

Carter believed they were doing this as a means of population control, and to keep the women from taking charge. They never harvested boys—only girls. Of the virgins, most were around sixteen. The ones older than that had freely given their virginity away to avoid being harvested.

Carter's heartbreak was plain on his face as he stole a glance at Abby. He hated to think what a waste of life the Harvest was—so many good people dying for naught—so much death and blood for a god he felt didn't truly exist. He couldn't understand how the Elders didn't see the blasphemy they were committing by going against their own god to kill for this one. Perhaps they never would. To them, Carter believed, this god was just as real as theirs, and deserved the same level of respect. They didn't see how by including the Red Men's god in their lives they were calling their own faith a lie. Their faith preached only one god, a loving caring god that would never have called for sacrifices.

He understood it was important to learn about the Red Men's culture, and to respect it, but Carter and others believed the Harvest was wrong. He wanted to boycott this year. He longed to tell the Elders he would not serve as Keeper. He knew he couldn't, though. He had to hold out until Harvest Day. The plans he and those like him had drawn up would change this barbaric rite forever, hopefully putting an end to it for good. Carter felt people should not have to die for any god, most especially a god that was not their own, a god that would allow its faithful to die from something as insignificant as a cold virus.

The Elders were supposed to be wise. They were supposed to be the ones making all the decisions. At nearly thirty years old, they were truly the eldest of them all and as such Carter and the other colonists felt they should be judicious and understanding of life and its ways. Sometimes, though, they seemed far younger than Carter and any of his group.

As he finished feeding the virgins, he went over the plans in his mind. As he did so, he grew excited to be the one who would lead the battle charge. The first thing he would change, aside from stopping the Harvest itself, would be to stop the DNA pairings. He would allow the settlers to choose their mates themselves. Matching husbands and wives based on DNA might create better offspring physically but the loveless couples raising them would ensure those children would be closer to psychopaths than regular humans.

He was most excited for the moment when he would unlock Abby's cage and ask her to be his wife. His mother and father had lived a blissfully happy life together until the North Mine collapsed. It'd sealed them in and left him and his brother Edam orphaned at the tender ages of nine and four. Carter had stayed in their dorm and raised his brother himself rather than allow the Elders to take him. He knew if any of them got their hands on Edam, his sweet little brother would be warped and used. To lose one's entire childhood at nine years old was a difficult thing for Carter—he'd not had any choice in the matter. If he hadn't signed up for Labor Camp, then Edam would've lost his own innocence in a far more painful and sinister way than just slaving in the mines. Still, even though it'd been a hard life, it'd been a better one than he'd expected after the death of their parents.

Carter clung tightly to the certainty of his plans and the righteousness he felt inherent in them. He believed in his god and felt adopting the Red Men's deity was wrong and destructive to his group's well-being as humans. He and the others like him would change everything. As the cool breeze ruffled his hair, Carter stood strong in his beliefs, even as those around him sat in cages and shouted for mercy and aid.

He walked to the Elder Dorm and knocked lightly on Elder Andrews's door.

"Yes, Carter?"

"Gladys claims her virginity was taken last year, sir. By Byron."

"Bring me young Hornbeck. If he confirms her story, you may let her go." Andrews shut the door in Carter's face and the boy held back a growl that'd been building in him. He was afraid to risk the Elder's wrath, so he choked back his rage, turned on his heel, and made for where Hornbeck was housed.

The Elder Dorm was large and spacious. Each man had a room of their own, a common room to share, a food preparation station, and a space with a shower, sink, and separate toilet room. The rest of the dorms were cramped and it wasn't unusual to see two or three people to a room. They had a small area that was designed to pull double duty as food prep and common space. That space was smaller than one of the Elder Dorm's toilet rooms, and was meant for between eight to twelve people.

The Hornbeck's had maintained a good-sized family and were lucky enough not to have to share with other villagers. They divided up things among themselves and took care of each other in ways that made Carter envious. It was this care that he'd used as an example to raise his brother. And in return Edam showed the same love and loyalty to him—which meant a lot in a place like this.

Mars Colony Two (they never told anyone what'd happened to Colony One) was alone in this galaxy. Occasionally humans from other planets would send supplies that were later traded for the red rock the colonists mined from the depths of Mars. It only happened once every seventy-six days or so, and when the Outsiders came it was always a tense and nerve-wracking time. Everyone was on high alert, prepared to battle the Outsiders if need be. Though few wanted to live on their planet, nobody could discount the value Mars held as a commodity. The thick, heavy rocks the colonists dug out of the bowels of the planet were highly prized as both building materials and to be used for armor. There was a plan in place for Mars Colony Two to expand seven klicks to the south. They eventually planned to open another mine down there and gather more rocks. They were hoping to be permitted use of more rock for their own buildings; the Elders kept everything rationed very tightly. It made the miners angry to see so much of their wares hauled off, while they slept three to a room. Food was also rationed. Most of the time, the colonists went to bed with pangs of hunger in their bellies, while the Elders never knew of such pangs. Times were shaky and Carter planned to take advantage of it. It didn't seem fair the Elders lived so well, while the rest of them scraped by doing the rover's share of the work, and yet still remained hungry.

They decided if there was enough for the Elders to ship off-world, there should be enough for the MC-2s to build at home. The expansion would be the perfect time to do this. By moving south, the opportunity for more sunlight and longer growing seasons would be possible. The softer soil would allow for the rovers to till and plant easier, and quicker. There was a chance for more water and warmer temperatures. The Elders had never allowed them to explore the rest of the planet, even though it'd been entirely terraformed. It was more than possible that some others had settled on the other side of the large red planet, but nobody checked. There could even be more Red Men on the planet, which Carter felt was something worth finding out.

He and his friends wanted to explore their new home and find out everything they could about it. The possibilities of what they could become—what they could do with an entire planet—were endless. They could create larger fields to plow, so more food could be reaped and perhaps traded for livestock. It'd been a good seven years since Carter had tasted real meat. The protein packs were helpful in delivering the necessary sustenance, but they were bland and tasteless.

When they stopped the Harvest, perhaps they'd be able to procreate more and expand further. Unfortunately the Elders had no real idea what they were doing. They only wanted to keep everything under their own control—keep churning out rocks, taking on supplies, and killing off people who might oppose them. Carter knew what they were doing was wrong, and not just the Harvest, which was bad enough. The Elders had stopped caring about the quality of the rocks they delivered to those who were trading with them. As the mine had hit several walls of crumbly dirt they could not effectively dig from, the rocks they extracted grew to be of worse and worse quality. Greedy for the payout, the Elders didn't care if the supply was below par, as long as the demand continued to bring in business. Carter's parents had raised concerns about this issue, and the next day they were *accidentally* sealed up in the mine they'd been assigned to work in. If the rocks had been degrading in quality even then, surely they must be worse now.

It suddenly hit Carter why they'd not expanded sooner. Perhaps the Elders had known those rocks would fail and eventually crush them, so they'd sold them off-world to bring in money, while keeping their own people safe—at least for the time being. The planets the rocks were sold off to may have had less gravity than what the MC-2s dealt with on Mars, though that didn't mean the rocks wouldn't break down eventually. When the rocks finally did fail, those who'd purchased them would blame MC-2, and the whole operation would die—and the entire planet with it.

The colonists depended on the supplies the Outsiders traded with them. If word escaped that the rocks were poor quality, nobody would do business with them in the future. The supplies they did get were rationed thinly among the youth, while the Elders ate, drank, and used the medicines they traded for freely. This worried Carter as much as it did the other rebels. Nobody should be in charge of everything in a society. That was a philosophy that would never benefit the majority, but rather only the few. That was why Carter and the other rebels had planned a takeover. They realized that age didn't necessarily equal wisdom—nor did it equate to good business sense. The Elders would destroy the very thing they'd helped create, possibly without even realizing it. Or worse still, without even caring. Carter cared. His friends cared. That's why they considered themselves the future of this planet. They would be damned if they were going to sit by and allow anyone to destroy their only hope for survival. If need be they'd go off on their own and start their own colony, so long as the Harvest ended.

For the moment, that was their primary goal. They had to stop all the senseless killings of the girls who were virgins by the age of sixteen. If anything, they needed *more* women. Without them, how could they ever hope to reproduce or grow? But they also knew they needed to end the Harvest the right way, with a solid foundation firmly beneath them.

Right now they were sinking and nobody seemed to care, aside from Carter and the other miners. They hadn't been paid for their work for quite some time. They'd dug out the precious rocks at considerable risk to themselves, but they'd never seen payment in the form of even a single extra ration or a larger room. When they realized how things were truly being run, Carter and the others decided they'd had enough. They were going to take over and make things right. If they weren't successful, they would go off on their own, and start their own community. They'd learned mining from a young age, so surely they could set up their own mine elsewhere and sell their own rocks, without the interference of the Elders.

Carter looked up just in time to see he'd walked past the Hornbeck Dorm. He turned around, gave a wry chuckle, and walked back to the door and knocked. Byron answered. Carter asked the boy to follow him, explaining on the way back to the Elder Dorm what'd happened concerning his having had sex with Gladys, therefore rendering her a non-virgin. Byron admitted to Carter that he'd indeed had sex with the girl last year and that he wished to wed her someday. Byron was mortified when he'd been told she was among those to be harvested.

Arriving at the Elder Dorm, Byron explained he hadn't known Gladys had been selected for the Harvest. He'd been unaware of the fact, because he wasn't working the shift in the mine when the list of those being harvested was announced.

"Carter, go and free Gladys." Elder Andrews looked very angry. "You realize, young man, you could've doomed us all by not letting us know you had relieved her of her virginity before she'd been sacrificed?"

"I'm sorry, sir. I had no idea she'd been pulled for the Harvest, or I would have." Byron looked down at his shoe and tried not to cry.

"I think your punishment shall be...Death. Yes, that seems most fitting for such a grave offense." Andrews nodded solemnly.

"You're going to...to...*kill* me?" Byron had given up trying and the tears were flowing freely down his face.

"No. Nothing so easy, I'm afraid. Instead, you get to *be* Death during the Harvest. You get to wield the scythe and take the lives of the girls selected." A cruel grin spread across the Elder's face. It was easy to see just how much he was enjoying meting out the boy's punishment.

Byron's mouth dropped. Carter, who'd been watching through a crack in the door, saw all of this and bit his tongue, so as not to gasp at Andrews' cruelty. Wanting to witness no more of this, he ran swiftly to the cages and freed Gladys."

"You may go," Carter told the girl. "Byron corroborated your story." The hitch in his breathing told her something wasn't right.

"What is it?" she asked, afraid of his answer.

"For not confessing to having had sex with you before the Harvest, he's been named as Death for this year's Harvest." Carter tried not to let her hear the terror in his voice for young Byron's predicament. The ones who acted as Death were never the same afterward. They became cold, calculating—almost animalistic. Most who served as Death later became Elders.

"No!" cried Gladys. "He's a sweet, loving soul. You can't let him do this. Please, Carter, please don't let them do this to him." She fell to her knees and looked up pleadingly.

"I can't stop them from making him Death, Gladys. I wish I could."

"What about..." she broke off and lowered her voice, "the revolution?"

"How do you—?"

"We all know, Carter," Abby said quietly from her cage. "Many of us were in on it before the harvesting."

"Obviously very few people like the Harvest. I wish I could tell you everything would be okay, but I can't say anything more right now. Just hold on, Abby, please. Trust in me." He looked at the girl trapped in the metal cage and knew he couldn't let her down. She nodded her agreement. He reached out and held her hand through the bars before reluctantly dropping it to take Gladys back to her dorm.

"Carter?"

"Yes, Abby?"

"I do believe in you." Her blue eyes stared at him with such love that he knew what she said was true.

"God, please don't let me disappoint her," he said to himself as he turned away to hide the tears in his eyes. He put his arm around Gladys and offered soft words of support, telling her it would be okay. He decided he would do his damnedest to make those words come true.

The siren rang out announcing the end of the day. Men and boys alike came up out of the mine, choking and coughing out the red dust they'd breathed in all day. The majority of them moved to the rinsing complex where the showers were located. A few headed right for the tavern. After dropping Gladys off at home, Carter joined those in the tavern for a pint. With no Elders in sight, they quickly outlined their plan for ending the Harvest and letting the sacrifices go. They'd have to kill most, if not all, of the Elders in order to make their plan work. Several men and women had been elected by the group to run things properly, in a way that the entirety of the colony would thrive after the revolution. Plans had been drawn up, and rules had been drafted. A new world order was about to begin and Carter couldn't contain his excitement. He'd longed for this kind of change since before his parents had been killed. The Harvest would stop. The dorms would be built so that everyone had their own space. They had an entire planet to spread out on—and so they would.

The group had developed new mining processes to make it more efficient. They even had plans to add a crafting building, so they could form the rocks into perfect sized bricks to be used for armor and building purposes. At last, they'd be more than just grunts. They'd fill needs no other planet could.

As they drank, the rebels talked and plotted and geared up for the fight that would begin in mere hours. Soon their lives would change and things would be so much better for everyone involved. They spoke of the pains the Harvest had wrought on them and their families. They talked about the hell they'd lived through and how they wanted better for their own children.

As their gathering amassed more and more followers, they moved from the tavern out into the square. They walked among the cages as Carter and Ethan, another Keeper, released the girls. The crowd took their pick axes, shovels, and rocks in hand, and battered at the cages until the metal groaned and finally gave way. As cage after cage became nothing more than a pile of iron bars, the crowd cheered and whooped. While the pieces that remained of those cages were either broken down further, or turned into weaponry, the Elders emerged from their dorm to see what was happening.

The throng of people turned toward them and, as one entity, ran at those who'd tormented them for the last decade. Hands, feet, elbows, knees, and rocks, rained down vengeance against the Elders who'd ruled them all with fear and blood. The rebels fought fiercely, while the Elders were slow, fat, and not used to being physical. The masses cried out for retribution, for change, and for release of the pain the Harvest had inflicted on them as a colony.

While limbs were torn asunder, bellies rent, and innards spilled, heads burst open and brains dotted the landscape an eerie grey against the dense red soil. The Elders' cries for help went ignored. Nothing mattered to the mob but the complete extinction of the former regime. At the end of the carnage, those who'd been oppressed were slaked of their thirst for violence. The ground saw blood that night, but not a drop of it was the blood of a single virgin.

The Elders' bodies lay broken and torn in the square. Heads and limbs were speared on rods of metal taken from the former cages; grisly artifacts set up throughout the square to signal the rebels' victory. The Elder Dorm was raided and the food rations were passed out evenly. They found a rather large stash the Elders had been keeping from them. Enough that they soon realized the many ways they'd been lied to in the past ten years.

They found Pastor Jenkins diary and read how the original colonists had slaughtered the Red Men on purpose. They'd injected them with the virus to use it to process and sell antivirals to other planets. They were shocked into quiet as Ethan read more of the diary and they learned how the Elders were sick individuals who simply enjoyed the slaughter of young virgins for the sake of it. This had been the Pastor's idea, to get back at the young girls who'd refused to sleep with him. The Elders had never believed in the Red Men's god and the Harvest had been nothing more than a form of sport.

Carter's parents, along with other colonists who'd died in the mine that day, had learned the truth and had planned their own rebellion. Where they differed from Carter and his friends, was only in that they'd not lived as long with the bloodlust and carnage of the Elders. They thought they could reason with the sociopaths, and had tried. Upon learning of the plot, the Elders had forced those who were involved into the mine, then had caused it to cave in, leaving them to die. An accidental solution to a never talked about problem.

As they read the bloody and brutal past their encampment had been founded on, the rebels grew more and more certain they'd done the right thing. They also read about the Red Men and their beliefs. They'd been a kind and good people who truly believed in helping others. They'd never sacrificed so much as a Cratorian Dung Beetle for their god, let alone a sentient soul. The suffering and death brought about in the name of their ways—their god—would've caused them severe and lasting loss.

As the group continued to read the diary, the truths behind why they'd come here, and what the Elders had done upon their arrival, was revealed. The true horror learned from every line, was just how much agony could've been avoided, if only the few had consulted with the many. But, of course, that wasn't the way of the Elders. How could they remain in control, if everyone was made aware of their deceitful dealings?

As they finished reading the diary, they decided, then and there, that going forward everything would be put to a majority vote, assigning different people tasks and duties that would suit them and benefit their aims. This way everyone would work together in a peaceful, less totalitarian state. The more they realized how much the Elders had preferred a dictatorship—as opposed to a democracy—the more they were each convinced that what they'd done with their rebellion had really been for the best. It wouldn't take long to see how much better they'd all be doing with this new strategy as their base tenet.

In no time at all, physically and mentally, they were all happier and healthier. The pieces of the cages, and remains of the Elders, were buried in a very deep mass grave on the outskirts of town, near the mine—a constant reminder to the newly formed colony of all they'd lived through. But, most of all, all they'd accomplished together.

They closed to trades for a while. Instead of selling the mined rocks off-world, they used them to add on to the dorms and even build more; enough for everyone to have their own individual living spaces. As one, they lived and grew and welcomed change and allowed those with concerns to speak freely. Nobody was penalized for thinking differently than those who'd been placed in charge. They went with a majority rules vote and the people in positions of power were elected this same way. And they were only permitted to serve one term, which was fair and worked well for everyone.

When the Outsiders visited, the colonists were less fearful of them and more welcoming. They saw how kind the Red Men were, and how they'd never intended on hurting anyone. The regime of fear and mistrust the Elders had fostered was officially over. Life had begun anew. They'd learned how to exist peacefully with one another, and other societies. Life was vastly different for the MC-2 colonists, and agreeable to all.

Every year on the date of the old Harvest, they set out five plates of food, for the five Red Men who'd originally helped shape their colony. They felt it was a far better way to pay homage to those who'd come before them, than with terror and bloodshed. Instead of the Harvest, they called the newly founded day of celebration *Remembrance,* during which, they would share in food, family, and camaraderie, which had been so lacking in the original founding of their Red Planet colony.

The End

Billy Chizmar

He was the first to arrive. He strolled into the conference room, grateful to be alone. The silence was refreshing after the hustle and bustle of the cubicle-filled office he'd just exited. There was too much noise in this world. Too much clutter.

He sat down at the table and scanned the rest of the empty seats. He was at least a half-hour early, so he figured he had another fifteen minutes to set everything in place.

He smiled.

Lance had been waiting for this meeting for weeks. This was his *chance*—an opportunity of a lifetime. All the major East Coast investors were waiting for him inside that conference room. He walked quickly—excited, confident—but trying to remain in control of his emotions.

He passed the dozens of cubicles and their occupants, seeing none of them. They were nothing to him. A right turn, then a left, the cubicles placed in a hive-like pattern that made sense only to those who'd created it. At the end of the maze, the conference room, and his destiny, awaited him.

He stopped in front of the door, took a deep breath and opened it.

There were no investors inside.

Instead, there was a lone man, sitting at the head of the table, dressed in a gray hoodie and gray sweatpants. Not exactly business attire. The hood was up, hiding most of the man's face in shadow. Only thin lips curled into a cold smile were visible.

The man stood, and Lance tried to find his voice, but couldn't.

The man started walking toward him, and Lance felt a shiver of fear pass through him.

Something is wrong here.

The man stopped in front of him, close enough to reach out and touch. Lance could see the pale skin of the man's cheeks, but his eyes remained hidden. Cold vapor escaped his mouth, even though he remained silent. Lance could smell him now. A musty, earthy stench.

Again, the thought came to him.

Something is very wrong here.

The man slowly reached into his pocket. Lance had had enough. He turned and bolted for the door.

He grabbed the doorknob and pushed, but the door wouldn't budge. He could hear the man approaching from behind. Panicking now, he lowered his shoulder and slammed into the door with all his force.

Again and again.

It finally gave way and burst open—but not into the hive of well-lit, busy cubicles.

Instead, it opened out onto a stretch of complete darkness.

Lance felt a gentle hand on his back and cried out, jerking forward, away from the man's touch. He looked over his shoulder and could see the man standing silhouetted in the doorway. The man's smile widened. He nodded at Lance and gestured for him to continue forward.

When Lance hesitated, the man took a step toward him, and that's all it took to get Lance moving. He held his hands out in front of him and stumbled into the darkness. Feeling his way.

After only a few steps, his fingers brushed against a hanging cord. Lance pulled it, praying for light, immediately wishing he could be back in darkness again when he saw what surrounded him.

He was standing in a long, dim tunnel, which appeared endless.

Lining its two walls were bodies hanging from an indeterminate ceiling. Businessmen. Their fancy suits rotting off them. Along with their skin.

Lance turned back toward the door—but it was gone.

Feeling like he was in a dream, he walked further down the tunnel. He could recognize some of the faces now. The deeper he walked, the fresher the corpses became.

Lance no longer felt afraid. Now he only felt sadness—an odd sort of understanding.

All the missed birthday parties, tee-ball games, and family get-togethers. All the arguments about money and status and promotions. All the lying and cheating and manipulating.

He would never see his family again.

He was *gone.* Erased.

Lance stopped walking. He had reached the last hanging body. What he saw suspended just beyond it—waiting for him—was actually a relief.

An empty noose.

For *him.*

Finally.

THE END.

Dear Diary

James A. Moore

So, here's the deal. I got a call from Demetrius and that only means one thing—he's got work for me. I don't ask questions in advance. I go to Demetrius and we talk, because that's the way you do business with the man. There are people you can carry an attitude with. He isn't one of them. He's the sort of man you say *Yes, Sir* and *No, Sir* to, and hope you don't piss him off too much. Not that it's a problem, really. Me and Demetrius, we're on good terms.

So, anyway, I get to his restaurant and sit down at the table where he normally hangs round, and sure enough, he comes my way. Demetrius isn't tall, but he carries himself like he's a fucking bruiser. He sits down and gets right to it, which isn't his normal style. Most times we at

least chat it up for a while, you know? So I can tell it's gonna be an interesting night.

"I've got something of an emergency, Buddy. I need your help." That's my name, Buddy. Actually, it's Buddy Fisk. Actually, that's a lie. But when I'm working, it's the name I answer to. What I do when I'm not working is no one's business. Let's just leave it at I live in two worlds. *Buddy Fisk* allows me to live in my other world a little more comfortably.

"What's up?" I say.

Demetrius leans back in his seat and stares at me for a few seconds. When he's figured out what he wants to say, he talks again. He's like that. Demetrius is always slow about saying anything at all, because he wants to make sure he has your undivided attention, like there's any doubt, right?

Finally, he tells me the score. "There are four books that were stolen from a good friend of mine. A *very* good friend. Luckily, he found out where they were being sold and by whom. I need them back and I need a message put out."

"Four books?" Listen, I'll be blunt here. I don't work at a library. I do the sort of shit that no one ever wants to do and somebody always has to do. Mostly, I kill people. I kill a lot of people. I don't ask questions, I don't study my targets and get to know them, I just make them dead. My point is…I don't normally get sent out to gather a few books. My rates are too high for that sort of shit.

Demetrius gives me one of those looks; the ones that say I'd be better off not asking too many questions, and I nod my understanding.

"So what's the deal then?"

"I have a name. I know who has the books. You get them, and you take them to this man at this address." He hands me a piece of paper. "When you get done, you come back to me and I give you a bonus."

I got all of the details from the man in charge and headed out. It was going to be an ugly bit of business, and all over some books. You never know what the day will bring, right? I needed light weapons, but just to be safe, and because I was going after something that somebody wanted in a bad way, I took my truck. I have a few cars, but the truck has special accessories. I didn't think I'd need them, but on the other hand, the bonus that Demetrius mentioned was three times what I should be paid for a simple retrieval case, so I didn't much feel like playing around.

My target was a kid named Leonard Gutherie. He liked to be called Trance because that was the sort of music he kept trying to record and sell. He wasn't at the local club for pompous assholes, so I figured he'd probably be hanging out on the street near his house. How did I know so much? Simple. Demetrius had the information waiting for me. How did he get it? I don't know—and don't care. Demetrius has ways of finding shit out. That's enough for me.

I finally found the little bastard a couple blocks from the high school closest to his house. He had about as much reason for hanging at a high school as me, but he also had a thing for younger girls. Good old Trance was twenty-four years old. He was hanging with a few kids when I saw him. It wasn't a problem to park the truck and lock it. I had what I needed on me already. I made sure I was a few blocks further away than was really necessary, because I wanted to scout out the area and it wouldn't do to have my car close by if things went the wrong way. You have to be careful, see? Not paranoid, just careful. Especially when you do the sort of shit I do.

I moved carefully, but not too carefully. I know that doesn't make sense, so just this once I'll explain it. If you are in a public place and moving like you want to make absolutely no sounds, you're probably going to be noticed by every single person around you. Moving quietly takes effort and you'd be amazed how many people over-exaggerate their steps when they're trying for stealth. The idea is to blend in and look like you fit. Need to sneak into a hospital room late at night? Look like you belong there. It ain't all that hard to do. Need to sneak into a locked building and not set off alarms, then you take your time.

Still, I must have done something to give myself away, or Leo had eyes in the back of his head. I was moving along nice and casual, and I saw the four kids all hanging together. Leo was on the trunk of a BMW that probably belonged to his folks. He had a beer in his left hand and his right hand sitting high and tight on the inner thigh of a skinny little blonde girl with braces and a training bra. Long legs and graceful poise like a dancer. If she was a day over fifteen, I'm the ambassador for world peace. Not far away, a couple of teens who looked closer to driving age were just getting ready to go their own way.

Leo looked over his shoulder and saw me. His eyes flew wide open in surprise, and without even blinking, he was up and running in the opposite direction. I hate when the little shits catch on that something is up. I could've probably run after him and tackled his skinny ass, but that's

not why I was there. I had a job to do and he was about to run away. So I pulled out one of my throwing knives and skewered the back of his leg.

Leo went down hard, skinning both of his palms as he fell to his hands and knees, the blade vibrating like a tuning fork in the muscle of his calf. He might've liked trance music, but the sound that came out of him would've snapped a coma victim to consciousness.

Everything started happening at once, and I needed to get control of the situation. The girl still sitting on the Beamer opened her mouth to scream. The two kids standing nearby started to run. Leo let out another shriek. I pulled out two guns. They were small caliber, because I was trying to do this quietly.

The first .22 I aimed at the blonde girl's face. The second one I aimed at the couple of rabbits. The girl took one look at the business end of my little Remington and shut her mouth quick. The other two teens got about as still as statues. Leo kept screaming until I put my foot on the back of his ass and kicked him forward. Then he let out a grunt and a whimper and caught hold of his leg near the knife's entry point.

I leaned in close before I spoke. "Shut up, boy."

Leo shut up—mostly He was still going strong in the whimper department.

"Quit being a pussy. It's only a three-inch blade. You'll live."

"What do you want from me?" He was good at the crying game. He had tears going strong and I swear kids could've taken diving lessons off that bottom lip of his.

"The books you stole." Of course, it's not so easy talking to one person and keeping guns on three others. The happy couple off to the side started moving. I moved the barrel to follow their progress.

"Move two more steps and I'll blow you away." Yeah, it's a .22 caliber. It's also a .22 caliber loaded with glaser bullets. Those are shells filled with gel and with little pellets. The idea is, the shell hits you, and the point opens up. The goo inside comes out while the shell is moving through you. And when that happens, well, it's like detonating a grenade inside the body. Little hole where it enters—and a hole big enough to park a car in on the other side. Okay, that's an exaggeration, but not much of one. The bullets are called *sure-kills* by a lot of people, because even if you just wing an arm, it's probably gonna get blown open or even severed in the process.

I wasn't really kidding, either. Teens or not, innocent or not, I had a job to do. Good thing for the kids they listened.

"Move your asses over to your blonde friend over there. Now." I kept my voice low and calm. No reason to ask for extra witnesses, really, and I had already gotten a chance of that, thanks to Screaming Mimi at my feet.

I reached down and took my knife back from Leo. He let out another yelp, but calmed it down when I pointed one of my pistols at his face.

"Didn't I tell you not to be such a pussy?" Leo nodded real quiet like. "Get up and move over to the car." Leo made a big show of bravely standing up and limping his way over to the car

where his friends were standing. There was a little dark patch on his jeans, but other than that you could barely tell he was wounded.

The little blonde girl started to hop off the car and run to her hero. I told her to sit the fuck back down and then we all got to business.

"Okay, here's the thing. Leo here, he stole a few books from somebody who wants them back."

"I didn't steal them…I found them!" Yeah, of course I believed him. How could I not trust the sort of sleazy little fuck who was into girls half his age and called himself Trance?

"Whatever. Thing is, I want the books back. I get them…we all go our own ways and nobody has to get hurt."

"But, I already sold the books."

I stared at Leo nice and hard. "You already deliver them?"

"No."

"Then you haven't sold them yet, have you?"

"But, the money…"

"Ain't gonna mean shit if you're dead. Where are the books?"

"I don't have them with me."

"So let's go get them."

"Does that mean the rest of us can go?" That was the older girl, who was looking at me with wide eyes and what I guess was supposed to be a seductive look. Probably killed the boys at her high school but to me she just looked like a kid trying to be all grown up.

"What? Are you fucking high? No, no one goes anywhere. Not until this is all done."

"So, what are you going to do with us?" the other boy asked. Not Leo. Leo was too busy looking at the ground and muttering to himself.

I ignored my target for a second and thought about it.

"We're gonna have to take all of you along with us, and that means you two go into the trunk."

"Oh, hell no!" That was the other boy again. He took a step in my direction and I pointed the pistol at him again.

"Did I say there were choices? Go stand with your girlfriend." He glared, but he did what he was told. Testosterone and kids were never a good combination.

The little blonde was starting to fidget, so I gave her something to do.

I tossed her a roll of duct tape and had her tie up her friends. They wanted to protest, but the gun issue was still in play. I made sure she tied them up nice and tight, and then Leo got to throw them into the trunk of his daddy's Beamer. I noticed where his hands went when he put the girl in there, and she did too, but the tape over her mouth stopped her from calling him out for feeling her up.

When they were nice and cozy, I closed the trunk and climbed into the back seat of the car, but only after Leo and the blonde both climbed into the front. Leo was smart. He drove nice and steady, even if he did keep whining. Even his little squeeze toy was starting to throw disgusted looks in his direction.

We didn't talk and get chummy. Aside from Leo letting out his nasal whimpers, it stayed pretty quiet. That changed around the same time the truck came at us. We were on the same street as before, but at an intersection, and out of the little access road to the back of the yuppie strip mall off to the left, comes a garbage truck. Thursday night after ten PM. Who the fuck is picking up trash that late? Answer: no one. The truck came straight for the Beamer and I saw it and so did the girl. She screamed loud enough to show the braces on her teeth all the way to the back of her mouth. I ducked down and braced myself for impact.

The BMW was a big car. The truck was bigger. We got thrown—and hard. I could feel the tires trying to get a purchase, could hear the sound of the back end of the Beamer caving in, and then there was a wall in front of us and the truck's headlights were lighting up the interior well enough that I could've read one of those pocket versions of the Bible with the really tiny print.

The wall stopped us from going forward. But the truck behind us pushed anyway. The rear window and the windshield both blew out around the same time, and I covered my eyes as the glass storm hit.

A few seconds later, I realized I was still alive. It was a good day, because I hadn't even pissed myself and believe me, I'd have felt perfectly justified. Adrenaline kicked into my system and I made myself stay as calm as possible, taking in slow, deep breaths and waiting for the right moment to make my move.

The windows on the side spider webbed, thanks to the makers of Saf-T-Glass. I couldn't see out of the stuff, but the assholes outside, couldn't see in, either. I had the two pistols out and in my hands in record time. I thumbed the safeties, because I wasn't much worried about shooting somebody by accident at that point. I was worried about getting out of the situation alive.

The truck pulled back a little and took something with it from the back of the car. I could hear the metal screaming as the vehicles separated. I could also hear one of the kids in the trunk screaming, but only one. My guess, the other one was beyond screaming. I could see the back of the trunk accordioned up to where the rear window should have been. It was almost enough to make me feel for the kids. *Almost.*

The girl in the front seat was groaning, and the airbags had punched her and Leo in their faces when they deployed. They were already deflating. Over those sounds, I heard the voices that came from the truck. They sounded anxious. Go figure.

So, it isn't exactly like I could go anywhere at that particular moment. The impact had pushed me forward until I was wedged between the front and back seats. Instead of crying—and I was giving that idea serious thought—I slid up as best I could and got my shoulders free. Up in front, the girl was finally losing it, crying for her mother. That part hurt, because, really, I don't dislike kids. I don't have any of my own, but I don't dislike them, even when they're getting older and want to pretend they're all grown up. I only had one person I was supposed to take out. One contract. I don't like it when things go wrong, so I was getting a little bitchy right about then.

I didn't sit up. I didn't climb back into my seat and try to kick open the door, and I sure as hell didn't make any noises. Good old Leo and his sidekick were doing enough of that for everyone.

What I did, was wait.

Somebody pulled on the driver's side door and cursed when it wouldn't open up for him. He cursed in Spanish. I guessed maybe he wasn't local talent. I don't speak much Spanish, but my Latin is still good from back when I went to church every Sunday. I understood the word *book* when I heard it and knew then and there that they wanted what I wanted.

Have I mentioned I don't much like having to deal with the competition?

Leo made some more noise, and started to talk. I think the dumbass was expecting the cops or an ambulance. He said, "Help us! We're stuck in here with—" He stopped talking around the same time the stocky Latin kid reached through the windshield to grab at his face.

I fired once and watched the bullet take off half the head of the kid trying to get at Leo. After that, I didn't stop shooting. Left hand, and the window on the rear driver's side blew out. It was a wasted bullet, but the best I could do at the time. Right hand, and the bullet I fired cut a hole into the second guy out there, who was just starting to reach for his gun. Two more people at least. I fired at the one who was just climbing from the truck, and caught him in the shoulder. His left arm fell away from the rest of him and he wheeled back before he hit the ground. My right hand again and I parted the hair on Leo's head and caught the last of the Latinos in his neck. Leo was still trying to duck and cover, and the girl was screaming again, her forehead was burned from where the airbag hit her.

I didn't have time to kick the door open, so I climbed out the window and felt the remaining glass slide across my jacket and sprinkle down across my neck and back. The loser I pegged as he was climbing down was still alive, and I couldn't take any chances on him calling for anyone else, or risk another member of their little gang trying to pump a few hundred bullets in me. I wasn't prepared for a long drawn out fight. Hell, the only reason I even had the guns at all was because now and then it helps to cover your ass.

I slipped on what was left of the second guy I shot, but I kept my balance, and aimed at the man nearest the truck. He was moaning, but barely conscious. Just to be safe, I hit him again and took out his head. Not pretty, but it definitely shut him up. Nobody ever checked a garbage truck for extra passengers as fast as I did right then, guaranteed. The good news was the truck was empty. The better news was it was still running. The front end was mashed and shit, but fuck it. It wasn't my truck anyway.

I'd been worried about Leo and the girl trying to get away. I shouldn't've been. They were both in the same positions, and they were both crying. I walked over to Leo and slapped him across the face as soon as I'd re-holstered one of my .22s. He blinked and started to say something, but shut up when I pointed the remaining pistol at him.

"Get out of the fucking car and get in the truck." I didn't have time for this shit. We were at a shopping center, and it was closed, and so far I'd been luckier than I had any right to be and no one had come running to see if they could help with the accident. But even .22s make noise, and the two screamers weren't making things any better. Leo sniffed back his tears like a real man and got out. The blonde followed along, still crying, but quietly now.

We were almost to the truck when she said "Wait! What about Hunter and Trudy?"

"Who?" Okay, I was a little dazed myself. I'd been running on instinct.

"Our friends in the trunk." She stared at me like I was a maniac.

"Oh. They stay where they are."

"What?" Her voice was going up into the loud and shrill range. I was liking her a lot less.

"They stay here. I don't have time for them."

"What if they're hurt?" Now she was screaming, looking at me like I was the worst kind of monster.

"I don't fucking care. We have to go."

"I'm staying here!" Her voice fucking echoed off the closest building. She was, I guarantee you, louder than the fucking car wreck had been. So I shot her. One bullet between her eyes. Most of her face vanished in the spray that went out the back of her head.

Leo let out a wail and I slapped him hard enough to stagger him into the side of the truck. I'd had enough of him and of the fucking hunt for the books, so I grabbed his face with my free hand and pointed at his dead girlfriend with my pistol.

"You did that, Leo. That was all you. You stole some books from the wrong person and now she's dead and so are your friends in the trunk and so are the fuckers who were driving this truck."

He tried the crying shit again and I shook my head and slammed the pistol against his mouth and split his lip.

"You shut the fuck up. You don't have time for that shit. We're leaving, now. I'm driving. You're telling me how to get to the books." Leo was shaking like a vibrator set on overdrive, but he nodded his head and did like he was told. I watched him climb in and push past what was left of the guy I'd shot twice. His face cringed and his body flinched when he set his foot in the man's bloody pulp. Still, he was a real trooper and climbed in the truck. If there'd been any fight at all inside of him, it went away when I massaged his face with the hot barrel of the .22.

I used to drive a truck for a living, a long time ago. I knew the gears and how they worked. We parked the truck down the block from Leo's house, and climbed out quietly. Leo came from money. Old money. The same sort that liked to hang around with Demetrius, because they were too fucking stupid to realize how dangerous he was. Why the fuck he stole the books and tried to put them on eBay is anyone's guess, but certainly not mine. Maybe mommy and daddy didn't want to up his allowance.

We got to the front door before I spoke again.

"In and out. We go in, and you give me the books, and I leave. But if you make a false move, or fail to turn off the alarm, I'm going to kill you and your family. Your mom. Your dad. Any brothers or sisters and the family fucking dog. You get me?"

Leo nodded nice and slow and turned off the alarm. Turns out they didn't own a dog, which is just as good, because I can silence an alarm without waking up a family, but a loud dog is a guaranteed way to have more trouble.

We went up the stairs, and now we were being nice and careful, moving slow and quiet, because now Leo understood that his whole family was going to die if he fucked with me. Half way down the hallway to his room, the smell hit us. Listen, ever hit a skunk in the road? My dad did that once when we were driving down to visit the grandparents. The smell was enough to make your eyes water and ruin any appetite you thought you had for over a hundred miles before the road and the wind wiped most of that shit off the car. What we smelled walking past his parents' closed door was like that skunk, only it smelled dead, too. Leo wanted to stop and look, but I didn't let him. I shook my head and brandished the gun. He got the clue and kept going, his chest heaving with every urge to puke that crept through his body.

I'm a little smarter. I breathed through my mouth. The stuff tasted as nasty as it smelled, but at least I could tolerate it. Nothing a few breath mints wouldn't fix, right? We entered Leo's room and he dropped to his knees, sliding his hand under the bed. I knew he was going for the books, but just to be safe, I slid the pistol behind his ear and leaned in close.

"Better be books, Leo. Or you're dead."

It was books. All four of them. One of them was as big as the Manhattan White Pages and bound in leather. There was some weird writing on the front. It matched the description. One looked like somebody had taken the time to bind eight pages of paper between two pieces of sterling silver. No way it was a fake. Like the first one, it matched the description. The next one was small and well worn, like an old family Bible, only I'm pretty sure the gargoyle face on the front never went with a copy of the Good Book.

I reached out and touched the last one. I swear it squirmed in my fingers. That was enough

for me. No way the little shit had a chance to make copies. Even if he'd had the time, he wasn't that smart. Leo looked at me hopefully and I nodded my approval. Then he turned to pick them up and made my job easier. Two wooden dowels, no more than three inches long, and one piece of high-test fishing line between them. Cost to me was about seven dollars if you count the whole spool of fishing line I had to throw out because no one with a brain leaves evidence behind these days. I had the wire around his neck before he could so much as blink, and my fingers almost joined behind him before I started pulling.

Ever choke a man to death? It takes a little time. Leo put up a fight, too, but he was too late to get his fingers between the wire and his throat, and I was too smart to leave him any slack. He bucked and I pulled. He kicked and I stepped out of the way. His face turned red and then purple as the wire cut deeper. The line of blood down the front of his shirt was surprisingly fast as it flowed. I didn't let go until his face was almost black and the worst of the blood flow had stopped.

I was supposed to leave a message, just in case anyone else in his family knew about the books—or any of his friends were in on the gig. I left it. It's my job. I left the garrote where it was. I'd worn gloves when I made it and I wore gloves when I used it. Why take it with me and risk getting myself covered in blood?

I slipped the nylon rucksack out of my jacket pocket and slid the books inside it. No way in hell they were going to hide in my coat, so I ran the sack's cord into my belt and let it rest against my back and ass. I might've looked a little silly, but I knew the books weren't going anywhere without me. After what I'd been through already, I wasn't much for taking chances.

I knew the town's layout well enough. I figured it was sixteen blocks back over to my truck. Not that bad a run, so I got as ready as I could and then I headed out of the house. I was careful. I didn't want to get spotted by Leo's folks. I'd done enough killing already to earn my pay and then some.

The smell that'd damned near left me gagging earlier had dissipated. It still stank, but it wasn't enough to make me want to hurl anymore. Two minutes later, I was out of the house and gulping in the fresh air, glad to be away from whatever the hell had stunk up the oversized residence. I started jogging, nothing too strenuous, because I wanted to conserve my strength. So far the night had been full of just a few too many surprises for my tastes, and I didn't feel like taking chances, especially because I only had a few bullets left in my weapons and the guns in question were already associated with a few too many murders.

I made it two blocks before I realized I was being followed.

It happens now and then and most times, I can chalk it up to my imagination. You work this sort of business for too long and you start getting paranoid. People die, and sometimes their relatives take it personally. So, it's best to be on the alert.

I didn't see anyone, and if I heard them, it wasn't consciously, but I felt the skin on my neck pull tight and the fine hairs lift up into hackles. First rule you always follow in my book is simply to trust your instincts. I trusted mine and started running a little faster. I also started paying attention to what was around me a little better. Weird feeling, that whole *being followed* thing. I couldn't've said where it was coming from, but I'd have sworn there were eyes on me, and they were watching my every move. Worse, I started catching whiffs of the same nastiness that was back at Leo's house. Not strong enough to really make me feel sick again, but bad enough that I wanted to get away from it, or maybe bathe in a bottle of air freshener.

I'd gone about two blocks before I heard anything. I know a lot of people are gonna say no way, because I'd been running for two blocks, but I run every day, and I usually do around five miles, so believe me, two blocks wasn't even enough to get me breathing hard. It wasn't that much of a sound, just some scratching noises, which, when you hear them on the sidewalk behind you, is a little weird, especially late at night. It sounded sort of like a dog's nails scraping the concrete, but maybe a little louder. That'd have been my luck, a big damned dog that rolled around on a dead skunk to get a special kind of odor going.

I didn't want to let whatever was following me know I'd caught on, so I didn't look behind me. But I did flip the safety to the off position on one pistol. Then I started moving faster. Residential areas can make it a bitch to see anything sneaking up on you. Not enough glass, and too many bushes where things can hide, so I did the only thing I could think of to make sure I could get a fair shake and detoured off my original path. I headed for the strip malls a few blocks south of my location. Closer to where I'd been when all of Leo's friends got themselves killed.

There weren't a lot of places open. Thing about your smaller towns is, when tourist season is over, the shops close earlier and the bars that stay open are the ones that nobody with a lick of common sense wants to enter unarmed. I wasn't unarmed. So I moved fast and looked for a good place to duck into.

My luck again—there were no bars. Serves me right for not really casing the area better. In my defense, it was a rush job and I hadn't expected to get into the sort of trouble I was already cleaning up. I mean, seriously, I was supposed to get a few books, not get into shootouts and arguments with would-be good Samaritans.

I didn't see an open bar, but I finally got a look at what was following me. It wasn't a dog. I would've preferred that, because, noisy and vicious or not, I knew a well-placed bullet would at least kill a dog. I only got a look in the plate glass window from a little five and dime on the

corner of Westfield Avenue and Lanier Road. It was night and the only light was coming from the street lamp behind me. So I couldn't see it clearly, but I knew right away I was in deep shit.

It was just a shadow, okay? But it looked all wrong. It sort of looked human, with arms and legs, but it was running on all fours, and it was as skinny as a greyhound. I couldn't see the face, but I could see the hair on the thing, thin and scraggly, like it had the mange or something, and I could see the long fingers of the hands whenever it was bouncing forward. It didn't run so much as it hopped, the legs pushing off the ground and the hands catching the sidewalk and moving it forward before the legs did their thing and kicked again. It made me think of the way kids played leapfrog when I was younger. The same sort of motion, but faster and a lot stronger.

The thing was covering ten feet or more every time it pushed away from the ground and lunged ahead. I felt my balls try to hide away. No way the thing behind me was human, and I

don't fucking care what my eyes were trying to tell me, it couldn't've been human if it had to be. Anyone that skinny would've been dead from malnutrition, you get my point? No way in hell whatever was behind me was too tired to move.

Enough was enough. The thing behind me had to be stopped before it decided to jump on me and start cutting with the nasty claws I saw on its shadow. I pulled both of the guns and turned my body around, my heels sliding a bit as I put on the brakes. See, I'm only good at a few things, but I'm damned good at those few. One of them is hitting my targets. I almost never miss. That's not bragging—just a fact.

There was nothing behind me. There'd been something a second earlier, but in the time it took me to draw and get ready to fire, the thing had vanished. Gotta tell you, I was getting a bad, bad feeling about the situation. I looked around carefully, and then I decided it was time to be somewhere else.

I started jogging again, the books in my rucksack bouncing off my ass with every step I took. It was a bitch compensating, but it was also too damn late to stop and rearrange things. I had maybe fifteen blocks to run, thanks to my detour, and I needed to cover them so I could get to my truck. I tried not to look behind me too often, and I tried to keep my ears nice and clean

and working. I should've paid attention to what was in front of me. Then I would've seen the car before it came after my stupid ass.

The sound of the engine whining in protest gave it away. It wasn't like in the movies, where the hitman is screeching tires and aiming to be seen. No, the guy driving was good and the car was almost quiet, but I was already doing the paranoia mambo, and I shifted my eyes to where the sound was coming from in time to see the little Ford Focus jump the curb and beeline straight for me.

I was already jogging and I think that's what saved my life. If I'd been walking or standing still, the fucking thing would've knocked me into next week, guaranteed. Instead, I managed to get out of the way and watched the Ford hit one of the trashcans they'd nailed to the ground every hundred or so feet around the whole area. The base stayed where it was. The rest of the can and its decorative cover tried for orbit, but only managed fifteen feet into the air before a wall stopped it. I didn't hang around to see where it was gonna land. I hauled ass, cursing the books banging against me with every step I took.

The car kept coming, and I heard the engine revving again. This time the tires let out a squeal of protest. I was close to squealing myself, because whoever was behind the wheel seemed to want me dead and in a hurry.

Soon as I could, I turned around and fired three rounds. One hit the car's grille and then the engine. Another bounced off the hood and from there disappeared into the night. The last one took out the windshield. The car let out a few more rude noises as the radiator spilled hot antifreeze and water along the curb, and then shuddered and died.

I looked around for some decent cover, but aside from another car that'd been abandoned for the night, there wasn't much. Just to add to the fun, the asshole doing the driving kicked on the high beams, the fog lights and the damned spotlight he was sporting, and nailed me in the face around the same time I was looking at the front end and the next thing I knew, I had blue stars filling my eyes and blinding me as I ducked behind my temporary shield.

I heard the car door open and close. I heard footsteps, even over the sound of the radiator hissing its life fluids all over the ground. Then I heard the voice. It was soft and calm and purely business. That scared me more than anything else, because I knew that tone of voice too well. Hell, it could've been me doing the talking, and believe me, there's a reason I stay calm in bad situations. Edgy or angry get you dead.

"I just want the books, Fisk. I get the books and you go away alive."

Yeah. Right. Like I've never lied to a mark before.

"Gonna have to pass. Man's gotta make a living."

"One time offer. Give up the books, or I'll kill you."

I didn't know the voice, and that was a big problem. I don't like it when people know my name and I can't recognize them. I don't like dealing with unknowns. How fast a draw was he? How good a shot? I know the answers when it comes to me and to a lot of other guys, but this one? Anyone who thinks they're the best is either very lucky or a little crazy. There's always someone out there who's better. You just gotta hope you never meet them.

He was good. He knew I was having trouble seeing and the lights on his car made it almost impossible to find him. I finally decided to drop to the ground before I looked any further. Maybe I'd get lucky.

"Hiding won't help, Fisk." He took a few steps in my direction, nice and slow, setting his feet carefully instead of letting them scuff the concrete. Little sounds can give you away, even to a blinded opponent. Here's where he made his mistake. He really thought I was blind, and not just seeing comet trails. I was down on the ground and hiding behind another car. The lights weren't really in my face any more. It took me a few seconds while he was walking carefully and looking for me, but I spotted his legs. After I saw them, I fired twice. One bullet for each shin. My new worst enemy might've been a problem, but after the sure kill bullets blew the bones out of his calves, he stopped worrying about anything but living.

I got up fast, and staggered over in his direction, praying the asshole didn't have a partner in the car. He was on his back by the time I reached him, screaming bloody murder and trying to cover the bleeding stumps of his lower legs with both of his hands. Frankly, I was surprised he had the reasoning skills to even try. Most people, you shoot them like that, they pass out. That sort of pain will put you in shock in no time at all. I know, I've done it more than once. Maybe it was the bullets. The last time I took someone's legs, it was with a saw.

But enough of that.

I looked at the loser on the ground and fired once more. This time I went for the head. He stopped screaming immediately. I didn't know him, even before I blew his face into hamburger, he was a complete stranger. I also didn't have time to fuck around with worrying about him. I had to move and fast, because so far there had been two other groups paying to look for the books I was carrying and I didn't want to be a target any longer than I had to.

I checked my weapons and cursed under my breath. I had seven bullets left between the two of them. Not a good way to stay in my comfort zone, which I was reminded of around the same time I smelled the nasty thing coming after me again.

Now, a few of you are wondering why I maybe didn't take the weapons off the man I'd just killed and I'll give you a simple answer. There's always a chance I'm gonna get busted by the cops. *Always.* It's part of the job description. I finish a job, I lose the weapons I used. Break 'em down and sink 'em in the river or just throw them in a dumpster or five along the way. I don't get attached to any of the weapons, because these days the forensics teams are almost unnatural with how good they are at finding shit out. There are other guys who like to hold on to one weapon. That means I get busted with their tools of the trade in my possession, and I get fingered for every crime they ever committed. I know one guy who did just that. He got busted after grabbing a weapon off a capo in Brooklyn. He'll never see the outside of a jail again.

So I left the additional firepower. It was too damned risky. I didn't jog this time. I flat out ran. Nice steady breaths and good long strides. I wanted distance from whatever was coming after me, because what I'd seen earlier had made my balls want to hide in my stomach, and I couldn't afford to get scared and stupid.

Unfortunately, no one told that to the thing following me. I didn't see it, but I could feel it, keeping pace with me and hiding at the same time, like it was no big deal. I wanted to stay in the commercial areas, but that wasn't going to happen. I had to go back into the neighborhoods to get to my truck and that meant back to where the thing trailing me could hide behind bushes and cars, or even try to outrace me by going through backyards.

Seven bullets. Most cases, I could kill seven people with that many shells, but I had to be able to see it to kill it and this thing liked playing hide and seek.

I got back to where the shrubs and manicured lawns started and I doubled my speed. I also got off the road whenever I could and kept to the grass, because if he could play at sneaking up on me, I could at least keep my footsteps quieter, so I could hear him coming. It was a nice idea, but I didn't factor in the dogs. I don't know if I caused them to go crazy, or if my stalker did, but they went into fits damned near everywhere I went. Not a little barking to warn people away from their homes, but full-scale frenzies.

I saw the door of one house shaking as the monster inside started slamming against it.

Do you have any idea how many people wake up when their mutts start barking? I mean I was carrying two pistols, both small caliber, for a reason. I wanted quiet. Most people hear a .22, they think it's some little shit with a string of firecrackers. I liked to keep it that way.

I saw lights coming on in a few of the houses, but they were too late to spot me. I was moving in a hard run, and by the time most of the locals were ready to look out their windows, I was already two houses away. I could feel my heart starting to pick up speed, and I could hear the sound of my pulse in my ears. I was as alert as I've ever been.

I barely saw it coming.

Off to my left and in the very edge of my peripheral vision, something dark came from behind a sedan. I snapped my head in that direction and saw the thing clearly for the first time. It was hunched down like a dog and doing its weird hopping run again, the head craned at an unnatural angle as it came closer. The face was thin and bony, the eyes sunken into deep hollows. Its nose was like something that belonged on a skull, a deep hole. The mouth was a nightmare of teeth, all of them too long for the rest of the face, with thin lips that were peeled back like a dried fruit rind.

It was dead. I knew that in my heart. The damned thing was dead and moving my way. Shredded pants and a ruined shirt partially hid the gray skin stretched over wiry bones, but bare feet and long fingers sported claws that looked like knives. I took it all in during the second or so it took for the thing to reach me.

Did I scream when it grabbed me? Shit yes—like a scalded baby. I didn't have long to scream before it had me pinned to the ground, though. The feet of the monster pinned down my legs even as I struck the lawn. The hands grabbed my jacket and pulled it into knots. That freakish face loomed over me, and the pits where its eyes hid—if it actually had eyes—pressed close enough to let me see *things* moving in the darkness.

It opened its mouth, and I saw that what I thought were teeth before weren't a part of the original face. They looked like someone had taken blades of bone and rammed them where the teeth should've been. They were yellowed with age, like granny's dentures only worse, and behind them, I could see a dark tongue slithering like a snake in a cage.

"Give me the books." I heard the words in my head, but those dried lips never moved. The sounds were like fingers on a chalkboard. Not really all that high, but they made my skin crawl in that same way.

"*Ahhhh! Ahhhhhh! Ahhhh!* It wasn't my calmest moment. I admit it. I reached into my jacket pockets.

"Give me the books!"

I aimed the guns in my jacket and pulled both the triggers again and again. I didn't know what it was and I didn't fucking care. I just didn't want it on me for another second, if you know what I mean.

Seven bullets blew holes in my jacket and through the thing standing in front of me. Every impact kicked that dead freak like a mule, sending it backward and upward, even as big chunks of dead flesh and bone mushroomed away from its backside. It fell backward and I could see the house behind it through the holes I'd just put into its body.

Listen, I'm not a doctor, but I saw withered organs and parts of the spine blown out of that thing, along with stuff I don't even want to think about. Moving stuff that wiggled as it hit the lawn. I'd almost cut it in half. There was barely even a stomach left on the thing.

I pushed myself across the lawn, the rucksack digging a trench in somebody's front yard, and I let out a few more girly screams while I did it. I also pulled the triggers on both pistols again and again, just in case there was maybe a bullet somewhere that I'd missed firing at the dead fuck in front of me.

No such luck. No more bullets.

So I got up and did my best to compose myself. I don't normally lose it in the middle of a job, but now and then, you just sort of freak out, you know? Having a dead thing talking to me without words, that qualifies as a good reason, especially as it was close enough to hump my leg.

Part of me wanted to check that lump of meat out. I wanted to know how it was moving, and what it was made of. Only a small part, but it was vocal. I had a job to do, but damn, how often do you get to see a monster in person?

It sat up, and suddenly I didn't want to be anywhere around it.

"The books…"

That was all she wrote. I ran—hard and fast.

As I ran, I peeled off my jacket and wrapped it around my right arm, because I thought maybe a couple of empty pistols would have enough weight to hurt the fucker if it came for me again. I didn't bother to check if it was following. I just took for granted that it was right on my ass and ready to take a bite, and then I ran even faster. The smell alone told me I wasn't too far off. Was I panicked? Duh. I was close to pissing myself.

I'd been in a hurry to get to my truck all along, but now I was desperate. I didn't have any more ammo, and I'd already planned to lose the guns, but the truck was different. The truck had a few surprises I could share. I don't know how far I ran. Maybe ten blocks. I was mostly on autopilot, just doing my best to stay alive. I was winded and sweating and still worried about that thing behind me, but after going full tilt for that long, I was getting shaky and clumsy. I couldn't afford that. I figured if I ran any further, I would stumble and that would be the end of me.

I slowed down to a walk at the same time that I finally looked behind me. Nothing. Not a damned thing was back there. Just lawns and shadows.

I didn't know if I should laugh or cry. I'd half killed myself getting away from nothing at all. On the bright side, I was alive.

I kept walking, but I slowed down some more to gulp in a few deep breaths and let my body recover. The only good news was I knew where I was. I hadn't gotten lost along the way. Four, maybe five blocks and I would be back with my truck. I fished around in my jeans until I could find my throwing knife. The way the night had gone, I didn't want to take any chances. I kept the jacket around my arm, too, but I made sure my hand was free.

Four blocks, then three, then two and finally, I could see my truck, exactly where I'd parked it earlier. I could've cried I was so damned happy.

Which was when the dead, stinky thing got me the second time.

It didn't ask about the books this time, it just tried to eat my face. It came from the manhole cover behind me and I would've never had a chance but the sound of the heavy metal lid scraping gave me enough warning. I smelled it and by the time I had a chance to gag, it was on me. Sharp bony claws grabbed for me and I blocked with my right arm. Even then, I could feel the nails punching into my skin. If the pistols hadn't been wrapped inside my jacket, I think those claws would've sunk all the way into my arm. The teeth came for my face and I swung my other arm around, driving the throwing knife I'd used on Leo's leg earlier deep into the roof of its mouth. I knew it wouldn't do any good. I'd hit the thing with enough firepower to drop a fucking elephant. I was just doing what I could with what I had. The thing reared back and hissed, spitting nasty smelling stuff all over me and almost blinding me in the process. One spinning back kick was all I could afford. Its hands let go of my arm so it could dig at the blade in the back of its mouth. While it was doing that, I hauled around and nailed it square in the jaw. Felt like I'd hit a piece of wrought iron, but I saw the jaw snap loose and hang by the tough gray meat around it.

I ran for the truck again, but I didn't bother with my keys. What I was going for was in the back, inside the tool case that was mounted and welded in place. I opened the lid of the case and started pulling out the shit that was in my way. Just to make sure I kept the thing away from me, I threw a hammer at its face. It ducked and spit out the knife I'd stabbed it with. Gotta say, I wasn't expecting that any more than I'd expected it to get up with half its chest gone. I threw a few more tools, just to keep the fucking thing busy until I got my backup artillery from the toolbox. AK-47 assault rifle, fully loaded with a modified Thompson drum of good old fashioned lead. No fancy bullets, because, really, you don't need them when you pull the trigger on one of these.

The thing came at me again and I unloaded the clip. I started low, and it tried to jump, but dodging hammers and screwdrivers isn't the same as dodging lead moving at the speed of sound.

I saw the bones in its leg get chewed up and spit aside. Then, as it was falling, I watched the bullets cut an arc across its hip, stomach, chest and finally its head. I don't much care what you are, you get hit with enough bullets, you go down. I fired and fired, watching chunks of dead freak hop in the air and bounce off the ground like ice on a hot skillet. I kept firing until the drum was empty. Fucker wasn't looking so ready to eat my face when I was finished.

As much as I hated the idea of losing my favorite toy, I kept with my usual policy. The AK-47 and the .22s got dropped down the sewer. I made sure to avoid getting too close to the mutilated pile of rotting meat and bones, just in case it still had any kick left in it, but it didn't seem much like it wanted to move.

My hands were shaking bad when I climbed into the truck. I didn't let that stop me from getting the hell out of the area, however. You think barking dogs wake up a neighborhood, you should try firing off a hundred or so rounds from an assault rifle.

I left the area as quickly and quietly as I could and I made sure not to turn on my headlights for a couple of blocks. I might get rid of weapons like they don't cost shit, but I liked the truck and didn't want to have to replace it.

Half an hour later, I was pulling up at the address Demetrius had given me. Nice house, in the ritzy part of town. But, hey, it's Blackstone Bay. Every part of town is ritzy, right?

The lights were on, so I knocked on the door.

The guy who opened the door smiled like he was looking at a Jehovah's Witness on a mission. He smiled a lot warmer when I told him Demetrius had sent me. He looked about as old as my grandfather, only without the Alzheimer's. Crew cut hair and a healthy body for a man in his sixties or so.

I opened the rucksack as soon as he showed me to the living room and then I put the books on his coffee table, easy as you please. He took each book in his hands and caressed them, like most guys would caress the legs of a lover he'd only been dreaming about for years. The look he shot my way was one of pure joy.

"Young man, I owe you dearly." His voice was soft, but the hand he used to shake mine was like steel.

"Oh, no sir. Not a problem. Demetrius asks me for a favor, I deliver."

"Just the same, if you should ever need a favor in return, say, trouble with the law or just a little assistance, I am in your debt." He gave me his business card. It said his name was Albert Miles, and it had a cell phone number listed. That was it.

I thanked him and put the card in my wallet. Most times, someone gives me a business card, it's in my pocket and then shoved in the trash at the first opportunity, but any friend of Demetrius is the sort of guy I'd like to keep on my good side.

I got back home in one piece, and I called Demetrius to let him know my uncle said hello and that the surgery had gone well. I called him from my disposable cell and I dialed the number for his disposable cell. Never take chances, and you never get caught.

He thanked me, and told me he hoped my uncle liked the get-well-soon package.

When I checked the usual drop point, the money was right where it was supposed to be. A shitload of money for one night's work, and I'd earned every fucking penny of it.

When that was done, I took off my work clothes, took off the fake mustache and wiped away the stage makeup. It was nice seeing my own face again, even if it was pale and looked a little like I'd been through the wringer. I took a nice, hot shower and tried to wash the stink off me. Whatever that fucking thing had been, its smell lingered like a bad break up.

After that, I drank three fingers of whiskey, settled back on my bed and had a crying jag. Killing people takes a lot more out of a person than most people will ever know. I'd killed a lot of people in the last few hours. I don't much like killing, and I don't much like Buddy Fisk, either, but he serves his purpose. The best news is, he only comes out when I want him to.

Next day, I was back to myself and ready to do what I like the most. I love teaching the kids, and I'm good at it. I guess that's about it. I'll print up one copy of this as always, and then delete the file. It wouldn't do to have the wrong people see any of this shit. I never actually mention my name, but there are other people I talk about and they wouldn't much appreciate me letting anyone know what they do with their spare time.

Eaten Un-Alive

David Bernstein

The vampires were starving and the zombie uprising was the cause. Zombies had no rules or limitations, and they spread like a plague. The vampires, having stayed hidden in the shadows for centuries, had kept their numbers small. Discrepancy had been paramount to their survival. The food supply was limitless. Now, humans hid like the dying breed they were, and to make matters worse, the blood bags had become aware of the vampires. The sun-fearing creatures remained hidden no longer, having become as desperate as their cattle.

Remington spat after draining another rabbit. The taste was awful, bitter and lacked the proper nutrition his kind needed. But it would have to suffice until he found a human.

He lay back against one of the moldy bales of hay in the old barn, finally able to relax. The place was in a remote part of the countryside. He'd seen only a few undead in the area, which he'd easily dispatched, though having to rely on animal blood was making him slower and weaker than he'd ever been.

He glanced around him and chuckled at the sight on his left. A pile of white, gray and brown blood-smeared bunny corpses lay beside him. He was Bunny Slayer, a fierce and formidable foe to the furry, grass-munching critters, sucking them dry like a giant vacuum of doom.

Remington had loved cities, New York his favorite, next to Venice. He loathed the countryside. The open fields, the long boring roads, and the lack of food were intolerable, but the cities had all been overrun with the undead.

With the night still young, Remington fled the barn, deciding it was time for a real meal. He'd consumed enough animals and vermin—yes, he'd resorted to that at times—blood for a vampire's lifetime and deserved better. He would go house to house and search relentlessly for food.

It had been two hours since he left the barn and he'd found nothing but rotted corpses and zombies. The pathetic creatures couldn't even figure out how to open a door or climb a set of stairs. One time, for fun, he'd plucked the eyes from a zombie and watched as it fell over furniture and collided into the walls of the house it had been in. He'd laughed so hard that night.

But for such witless creatures, they sure wreaked enough havoc. Zombies were the vampires' cockroach.

Having not seen a human in days, he walked brazenly down the road. Normally, he'd prefer to stay in the shadows of buildings or trees. The world may have changed, but it was still wise to remain hidden, for humans were more dangerous than ever now.

Getting ready to give up, having searched a number of houses and finding them vacant or with undead life, Remington heard a female's voice.

He cocked his head and listened. He couldn't make out what she was saying, another indication he wasn't receiving the proper nutrition, but it was coming from a farmhouse off to his right.

He traveled swiftly and as quietly as possible down the dirt drive, and then hid behind a small copse of bushes. The house's windows were dark, the place appearing as deserted as all the others he'd visited tonight. It didn't mean much of course, as most homes had no electricity. The humans kept their generators and lights off, for a lit home was often an invitation for unwanted guests, both human and otherwise.

Seeing no one outside, he ran up to the front door and began pounding at it.

"Please," he cried. "I need help. My friends were just killed by a pack of zombies." He continued banging on the door until he heard the sound of approaching footsteps on the other side of it. The locks clicked; there were a number of them. The door flew open and he found himself face to face with the end of a double barrel shotgun. A balding, heavy set man with a scraggly beard and wearing jean overalls was holding the weapon.

"Don't shoot," Remington cried, recoiling. He stepped back and hid behind his arms, trying his best to appear like a mortal.

"Dad," a young girl's voice sounded from behind the man. "Let the guy in."

The man kept the weapon trained on Remington, eyeing him with obvious mistrust.

"Please, sir," Remington said, his voice jittery. "May I take shelter in your home?"

"Got any weapons on you?" the man grumbled.

"No, sir."

"Nice and slow, lift your shirt and turn."

Remington did as he was told, trying not to laugh. He truly was on edge, but it wasn't from nerves. It was from the anticipation of the meal standing before him. He could smell the man's blood, the coppery aroma making his fangs want to extend.

Facing the man, he saw a partially open wound on his forearm. The abrasion was small—a scratch—with the slightest hint of a scab forming. Remington dug his fingernails into his palms, fighting the tremendous urge to pounce on the blood bag.

The man backed up, making room for the vampire. "Get in here before we're spotted."

Remington entered.

The man quickly shut the door, but didn't slam it, and then threw each lock in place in an obviously practiced fashion. He then pulled a thick black tarp over the door, covering it completely. "To keep light from showing," the man said.

"Remington nodded and looked around, noticing now how much light there was. All the windows were covered with similar black tarps or some kind of cloth.

"Say, how'd you know we were in here?" the man asked, and shoved the shotgun against his chest.

"I heard a woman's voice," Remington said, immediately wishing he'd held his tongue. Vampire hearing was exceptional and he wondered if a human could have heard the woman from outside. Maybe they'd soundproofed it. And he knew for certain that she hadn't been yelling. If she had, his case for hearing her would've seemed more reasonable.

The man looked at him for a second, as if deciding to believe him, then nodded and lowered the gun.

"Thank you so much for your hospitality," Remington said and held out his hand.

The man didn't move. The gun, although no longer aimed at Remington's head, was pointed at his groin, if ever so casually.

"Not from around here, I take it?" the man asked.

"No."

"Where are you from?"

"The City. New York, that is."

"Dad, stop pestering the man," the female voice said. "He's just lost his friends." A young girl walked into the foyer and stood next to her father. She looked nothing like the bearded fellow. She had soft looking skin, jade-colored eyes and an aura of sweetness and innocence. Her blonde hair was tied back into a ponytail, save a few strands that hung over her right eye. Remington guessed the man was in his fifties, the girl in her mid-teens. He smiled on the inside, knowing he would feed well tonight.

"They weren't truly *friends,*" Remington said. "I'd only met them a few days ago. They picked me up hitchhiking along the Thruway, after my car broke down."

"Hungry?" the girl asked.

Remington fought a smile, his brain screaming yes.

"Actually, no," he said. "I had just eaten before we were attacked."

The man—the girl's father, he wondered—was still eyeing him and it was beginning to get on his nerves. He wanted to rip out the human's throat and begin his feast, but as with any new place, it was always better to know the surroundings. There could even be more humans lurking about, staying hidden. Remington, especially in his weakened state, preferred to avoid surprises.

"None of your companions got away?" the father asked.

"No, they were all bitten, and torn to pieces," Remington said, staring at the floor. "It was awful."

"Enough, Daddy," the girl said. "Come this way, Mister." The girl took Remington's hand in her own and led him to the living room. Candles, along with a bustling fireplace, lit the room. The windows were blacked out, as expected. A deer's head protruded from a plaque above the hearth's mantle. Black and white framed photographs of people, probably long dead relatives, hung on the walls. Toward the end of the row, the photos were in color. The last picture was of the bearded man and the girl, but they were not the only ones in the picture. There was also a boy of about seven-years-old, maybe eight, and a blonde-haired woman who looked like the girl. They were all smiling.

The girl showed Remington to a seat on the couch along the right wall. Hot pain enveloped him. He began feeling very weak, as if the unlife were being sucked out of him. His stomach churned and he was overcome with nausea. He glanced to his right. Then to his left. Finally, he looked behind him on the wall. There, above him, was a cross. It must have been blessed, for normal, store-bought crosses had no power over a vampire.

"I…could I use your restroom?" Remington said, trying to not sound ill.

"You sick?" the man asked, his right eyebrow raised. He trained the shotgun at Remington. "Were you bitten too? Infected?"

The girl came over, her lips forming into a frown, and swatted the gun away.

"Daddy," she said, harshly. "Stop it."

He looked at her as if she were crazy, and then said, "He could be sick, turning into a living corpse."

"Mister—" the girl began.

"My name's…" Remington was struggling, the cross's power draining him. "My name's Remington. Remy for short…if it pleases…you." He was hunched over now, his stomach cramping up, insides feeling as if they were on fire.

"Let's go," the man said. "Do your puking in the bowl. Then I want to see your naked ass. Make sure you ain't infected."

"Pleased to meet you, Remy," the girl said, seeming as happy as could be. "My name's Tilda, and this here mean man is my daddy. "You can call him, Bill."

Remington managed to stand erect. He told the girl it was nice to meet her, and then hurried from the room.

Standing in the hallway, his strength returned and his nausea vanished, but he kept up the charade of feeling ill.

The bathroom was down the hall. Bill followed him to it. Remington closed the door, expecting to be left alone, but Bill had remained right outside. He made fake vomiting sounds and then flushed the commode.

He couldn't risk going back into the living room and worried that there were more crosses throughout the house. He still didn't know if there were others around, though he didn't think so.

Thinking of the color photo at the end of the row of pictures, he wondered where the woman and boy were. Dead? Missing? Or somewhere in the house? Maybe she had left Bill and her daughter and had taken the boy with her.

Remington didn't like this. He was weak from lack of human blood. His mind wasn't sharp. He was thinking too much. He just needed to act, to attack and kill. Once he had human blood in him, he'd feel better.

"Daddy," Tilda yelled from somewhere down the hallway. "Come here. I have to show you something."

"I'm busy, Til."

"Now, Daddy."

Remington grinned. The little bitch was running the show. Daddy's little girl, or little girl's Daddy?

"Mister?" Bill said.

"Yes?"

"Be right back."

Remington listened to the man's heavy footfalls grow fainter as he walked away.

He cracked the door open, closed his eyes and inhaled. His extraordinary sense of smell picked up the two familiar odors of Bill and Tilda. No other human scents were detected, but something rotten was in the air. Possibly meat, but he wasn't sure. The lack of proper nutrition was truly beginning to aggravate him.

Remington would rather have made sure there were no surprises waiting for him—other people, blessed crosses—but the time had come to strike. He would wait until the man returned, then open the door and drink him dry. He'd then call the daughter over, needing her out of the living room and away from the cross.

A few minutes later, the man's thunderous footsteps announced his return.

"Mister," he said. "You done?"

Remington hadn't even begun yet. "Yes. I'm done, Bill. Be right out." A tingle of excitement ran along his pallid flesh. Fangs protruded from his gums as his ravenousness grew to an almost uncontrollable rage. He threw open the door, fangs bared, and sprang forward like a jaguar on prey, only to be struck across the face by the cross that had been hanging in the living room. His face burned, the skin bubbling like the stew in a witch's cauldron.

"Demon of hellion blood," Bill yelled, holding the cross inches from Remington's body.

"I told you he was a bloodsucker, Daddy," Tilda said, standing next to her father.

"You were right, sweetie," her father said.

The girl smiled, as if she'd received an A plus on a test.

Remington had been in worse positions before. He had to keep them occupied, talking. "How'd you know?"

"My little girl here told me," Bill said.

"I mean, how did she know?"

"Never mind," the man continued. "I had my own suspicions, demon. When I watched you go into the bathroom, I didn't see a reflection in the mirror. Thought maybe it was just the angle I was standing at, but then my baby girl here explained a few things."

Remington laughed, even though he could hardly move. He needed to keep the dialogue going for as long as possible. Think of a way out of the situation he was in.

"What things?" he asked.

"Duh," Tilda said. "Like how freaking cold your hand was when I escorted you into the living room."

Remington wanted to stake himself. How could he have been so careless? It was the damn animal blood he'd been living on. It made him stupid, sloppy.

"And then you got sick on the couch," Tilda continued. "I saw the way you looked at the cross. You were fine when you came in, and when my Daddy mentioned the mirror, well, our suspicions were satisfied enough."

"Thought you found a juicy nest, bloodsucker?" Bill asked, and rammed a boot into Remington's ribs.

The pain was welcomed compared to the draining he felt from the blessed cross. He might've had a chance, but with the animal blood being the only drink he'd had, he was at the human's mercy.

"I wasn't going to—" Remington began, but was cut short when Bill sent his steel-toed boot into his jaw.

"Every word out of your mouth is a lie," Bill shouted, spittle flying from his maw. "Get the necklace, Tilda."

"Yes, sir," Tilda said, a hint of glee in her voice.

The girl ran up the stairs. Remington heard a drawer open then close. She trotted lightly back down the staircase and handed something to her father.

"Hold this," Bill said, giving Tilda the cross. "Keep it on him, close."

"I know how to do it, Daddy," Tilda said, and smiled wickedly, clearly enjoying herself.

Bill lifted Remington's head up and looped something around his neck. Part of the item was lifted and held out so Remington could see it. He was wearing a necklace with a plain wooden cross attached to it, the thing obviously blessed.

"We've got a special treat for you," Bill said, and he and Tilda both chuckled.

Remington wanted to pass out, but that wasn't how being in a blessed cross's presence worked. He would writhe in agony for hours, only feeling as if he might die.

Bill dragged him down the hall and into the kitchen. Tilda opened a door and Remington was tossed down a flight of stairs.

"Have fun," Bill said.

"Say hello to Teddy and Mommy while you're down there, Remy," the girl said.

Remington lay at the foot of the stairs, cold, rough cement below him. The door at the top of the staircase shut, leaving him in complete darkness. But like all vampires, he had night vision, allowing him to see in the gloom.

With as much discomfort as he was feeling, he felt a sense of relief, even joy, befall him. They were keeping him prisoner, which left the possibility for escape, at some point. Although weak and achy, he glanced around. If he could gather enough strength, and find something to cut the necklace off—

He froze mid thought.

A rotting-flesh odor washed over him, much like the one he smelled upstairs, only it was stronger now. To his left, something moved. He heard moaning and the shuffling of feet. With much effort, he turned and saw two zombies coming toward him. One was small, like a child, the other, a woman, with stringy golden hair. Teddy and Mommy, he knew. They had been in the house after all, just not the way he'd imagined.

Panic filled Remington's body. He was trembling with fear. He'd been undead for two hundred and five years. He couldn't go out like this, bested by a little girl and her dumbass father.

But there was nothing he could do. His strength was all but gone. He could only laugh, the action turning hysterical as the zombies approached. He was laughing so loudly he thought he might go insane, that was until the zombies began tearing into his flesh and devouring him. Then all he did was scream.

Weeper

Tim Waggoner

"If something is lost, it only gets more lost."

I look across the dining table at my daughter Jessie. She's scooped up a spoonful of peas and is raising them to her mouth. She's only five, and she holds the spoon awkwardly in her fist. She frowns in concentration as she opens her mouth and lowers her head to meet the spoon halfway. Her hand is steady, but several peas fall off the spoon and back onto the plate.

"What was that, sweetie?" I ask.

I try to keep my voice steady, but my tone is strained. Jessica stops raising her spoon and her eyes look away from the peas and focus on mine.

"Is something wrong, Glen?"

My wife sits at the head of the table. I know how that sounds, but there's only the three of us, and I like it when we sit close. Rachael sits between us because Jessie wants to sit next to her mother, and I want to be next to Rachael.

"Nothing's wrong," I lie. "I just didn't quite catch what Jessie said, that's all." I look to my daughter once more. "Can you say it again, honey?"

Jessie's frown deepens, but not with concentration this time.

"I didn't say anything, Daddy."

Yes, you did, I think. *I know you did . . .*

"I didn't hear anything," Rachael says.

Jessie's mouth is closed now, but there's a hint of a smile at the corners. A smile that says, *Ha-ha! I won!*

Rachael's face is unreadable. She's had far more practice at concealing her thoughts than our daughter has.

I want to jump up from the table, pick up my plate of spaghetti and peas, hurl it at the wall, and shout: *You know! You both know! Just admit it!* But I remain seated. I take in a breath and force a smile. "Sorry," I say. "It must've been my imagination."

"Sure," Rachael says.

"I like peas," Jessie says. She shoves the spoon into her mouth, dislodging a couple more peas in the process. They fall to the table, roll off, and plummet with a soft *thump!* to the floor. Normally, I would tell her to pick them up. But tonight I don't say anything.

I scoop up a spoonful of my own peas, put them in my mouth, and start chewing. They taste like dirt. I swallow them anyway and keep eating. I'm halfway through my meal when I hear the sound of the garage door opening.

"Who could that be?" Rachael says, the line phony, too rehearsed. But I've heard it so many times I don't call her on it. She'd only act as if she had no idea what I was talking about anyway.

"There's probably something wrong with the opener," I say. I've said this before. Rachael isn't the only one who's repeating herself here. I know my lines, too.

I think again of what Jessie said. *If something is lost, it only gets more lost.* That wasn't one of her lines, though. That was new. I push the thought away, put my fork down, thrust my chair back, and stand up. "I'll go take a look," I say.

"Can I come?" Jessie's lips are smeared with marinara sauce, and a tiny piece of spaghetti is stuck to her lower lip. This is something else that's new. Jessie's never asked to come with me before. I find this second change in the script even more disturbing than the first.

"Finish your dinner," Rachael says. "Whatever's wrong, Daddy can take care of it." She smiles at me, and I wonder if I really heard her give *take care* a little extra emphasis. Maybe.

I can't return her smile, so I turn and walk out of the dining room. I head into the kitchen which is still steamy from the water Rachael used to boil the pasta, and I make my way to the door that leads to the garage. I'm moving fast because I want to take care of the situation in the garage—I don't want to have to do it in the house—I *can't* do it in the house. I'm not sure how Jessie and Rachael would react, and I don't want to find out.

I open the door and step into the garage. There's an aluminum bat propped up by the door, and I take hold of it by the handle. The light came on when the door was activated, and I can see him standing there, next to my Sonata, which is parked alongside Rachael's Town and Country minivan. His palm rests on the vehicle's hood, as if he's trying to assure himself that it really exists. My car is much newer than he expects, and the difference shakes him now that he's this close to it. I felt the same way when I stood where he's standing.

He looks at me as I start toward him. He knows what he's going to see—he's been spying on us for several days, I'm sure—but he still can't believe it. That gives me the advantage. His eyes widen as I raise the bat and take a two-handed grip on it. He opens his mouth to speak, at the same time raising his hands as if to ward me off.

"Wrong move, asshole," I say, not without a certain amount of pity. Then I swing the bat, putting as much muscle into the motion as I can. I've learned the hard way, that if I don't drop him with the first blow, I'll have a fight on my hands. That's how *I* survived.

But something goes wrong. Maybe I misjudge the distance, or I'm rushing too much. Maybe at the last instant, he senses what I'm about to do and manages to move just a couple inches out of the way. Whatever the reason, instead of hitting him a solid blow to the left temple, the bat strikes him on the left ear. He lets out a cry of pain that's almost a word, but not quite. He stagger-steps to the side, his ear going instantly red, and I'm equally gratified and sickened to see a trickle of blood flow out of it.

Instead of clapping his hand to his injured ear, he grits his teeth, balls his hands into fists, and starts toward me. His equilibrium is off and he sways as he takes one step—then two. I can't let him get his hands on me, make contact. I swing the bat in a left-hand blow, and even though it's not a strong strike, the bat connects with his right temple. He goes down on one knee this time, and after that, it's easy. I just keep hitting until he's slumped onto his side, motionless, his skull caved in, the bat slick with blood and bits of brain. I've got plenty of both on me, too, but I don't care about that right now. All that matters is that I stopped him from getting inside. I hit the wet mess that used to be his head a couple more times for good measure, even though I know it's overkill, and then I drop the bat. It hits the concrete floor with a metallic *tang!* I don't bother to pick it up. I'm breathing hard and my heart's racing. I'm clearly not as young as I used to be.

I step past the body and walk to the wall where the inner garage door control is mounted. I thumb it and the door begins to ratchet downward. The house is located at the end of a cul-de- sac, and none of the neighbors' houses face ours. Even so, I don't want to risk anyone seeing me clean up the mess I just made. I'm not sure what would happen if some witness called the police. Technically, what I've done is a form of suicide. *Can you be arrested for that?* I have no idea, and I don't want to find out.

His Sonata—same color as mine, black, but much, much older—sits in the driveway. I'll take care of it later, like I always do. When the door's all the way down, I return to the body. He's wearing the same clothes they always do: black T-shirt, jeans, and sneakers. The same clothes I wore when I first came here. First *returned* here, I should say. This one is also wearing a dark blue hoodie, though. It was the end of July when I came here. It's early October now, and the days are getting chilly.

I bend over and take his keys out of his pants pockets. The key to my car would work just as well, but I like to use theirs. It feels tidier that way. I pull his wallet out of his back pocket and open it. He has the same driver's license that I do. Same name, same photo. It's due to expire on his—*my*—birthday. I'll have to make sure I don't forget to renew mine. He has the same debit, credit, and insurance cards I do, again with the same name on them. The wallet contains the same junk as mine: old receipts, appointment reminders, loyalty cards for convenience stores and cheap restaurants. It also contains the same pictures. Jessie's baby picture—the first the staff took in the hospital—big-eyed infant with a piece of pink ribbon tied in her hair, swaddled in a thin blanket. A picture of Jessie in a soccer uniform, grinning, displaying a smile with several teeth missing. A picture of Rachael, Jessie, and me taken at the Sears photography studio, less than six months before Rachael announced she wanted a divorce. The three of us looked so happy then. I take the picture out of my wallet and hold it closer to my face so I can inspect it. I've performed this inspection so many times now, it's become a ritual. I look at Rachael's face. I look at her eyes, searching for any hint of unhappiness, but I never find any, and tonight's no exception. I wonder, as I always do, if she was simply hiding her feelings—or if they were still tiny seeds of emotion that had only started to grow back then and hadn't yet taken root. This picture was taken over fifteen years ago.

There are a couple more pictures in the wallet, most notably one of a young lady with Jessie's long brown hair, wearing a high-school graduation gown. I don't look at that one very long. I never do. I close the wallet and shove it back into the man's pocket, and then I stand and go to the kitchen door. I open it just enough to shout, "The garage door opener's broken, but I think I can fix it. I'll be back in as soon as I can."

It's the same thing I say every time, and Rachael replies just as she does every time.

"Okay, hon!"

I close the door. I tell myself I don't have to worry about Rachael or Jessie coming into the garage. They never have before, so why would they now? But I don't know for certain that one night they *won't* open the door and peek out, so I haul ass. By this point, I have the routine down. It won't take me long.

The first step is to cover the body. There are several storage closets built into the side of the garage, and I open one and remove a blue plastic tarp and a pair of rubber gloves. I don't use the gloves because I'm worried about leaving fingerprints or DNA. The point's moot since the body will never be discovered, but even if it was, so what? We share the same fingerprints and DNA. I use the gloves because I like to keep the blood off my hands as much as possible.

The first time I did this I used clear plastic because that was the only kind of tarps in the closet. Afterward, I stocked up on blue ones. I'd rather not have to look at them as I work. It's not that I'm squeamish. Hell, I'd better not be as many times as I've done this. But I know that if I hadn't gotten lucky—if I hadn't been fast enough to raise my arm to block the aluminum bat—*I* would've been dead and wrapped in plastic weeks ago.

I spread the plastic out on the floor, roll the body onto it, wrap it up, and seal it with duct tape around the chest, waist, and legs. No matter how hard I try, I can never keep the body from *looking* like a body wrapped in a tarp. Luckily, the Glens almost always come when it's dark, and when they don't, I put them in the closet and take them out after Rachael and Jessie have gone to sleep.

The garage has a third door that leads to the back yard. I take hold of the "package" by the ankles and drag it across the concrete to the back door. I smear a little blood on the floor doing this, but not too much. I drag the body outside, across the patio, and into the yard. There's a bite in the air, which causes me to shiver. I wish I'd put a jacket on before coming out. We have a high wooden privacy fence, thank Christ, so I don't have to worry about being seen. There are enough trees in the yard to help block the neighbors' views as well. The leaves have begun to turn colors and fall; the yard is covered with them. My shoes make crunching sounds as I walk and the plastic *sshhhsses* across the leaves as I pull it. Before long, the tree branches will be bare, and the neighbors—all of whom have two-story houses—might be able to see me dragging my "packages" if they look out one of the upper-story windows at just the right time. It's something I'll have to consider later. Right now I have a job to finish.

The dining room is in the front of the house, and its window faces the street. I'm confident that Rachael and Jessie are still sitting at the table and not peering through any of the rear-facing windows, looking out onto the backyard watching me go about my gruesome work. I hope not, anyway. If they left the light off in whatever room they were in, how would I know if they were looking?

When I reach the shed, I let go of the body and turn toward the door. I put a combination lock on the door before I moved out, and it's still here. The same combination still works. The lock should be rusted by now, but it looks brand new. I wonder if it will always stay that way. I wonder if Rachael and Jessie will, too. God, I hope so. I'm not worried about leaving the body in the shed. It'll be gone by morning. They always are. I don't know what happens exactly, and I don't want to know. Sometimes I do wonder how many others have been dragged here besides the ones I've brought. This is my seventh, but there must've been others before I arrived. The Glen that attacked me had been ready—waiting. He kept the baseball bat by the door, and he had plenty of plastic tarps in the storage closet. If I hadn't gotten lucky, he would've killed me, wrapped me in plastic, and dragged me across the lawn, as I have him. He would've locked me inside the shed, and I would've disappeared before sunrise, just like all the other bodies. And it could still happen to me one of these days—if I'm not fast enough.

I undo the lock and open the door. I drag the body inside, my nose wrinkling at the smell. None of the bodies remain in the shed for more than twelve hours. At least none of the ones I have put here. It's not like other Glens show up every day—more like once every week or week-and-a-half. There's no reason the shed should smell like rotting meat, but it does. It's a pungent, almost sweet smell that hangs thick and greasy in the air. I always hold my breath when I'm in the shed. I'm uncomfortable with the thought of drawing death into my lungs—especially *his/their/my* death. There are a dozen different air-fresheners on the shelves and floor, but they haven't cut the stink any. If anything, they've intensified it with the addition of their cloying, artificial scents. I tell myself I'll come here tomorrow, after the body's gone, and clean out the damn air-fresheners. But I told myself the same thing last time. I didn't do it then, and doubt that will now. I don't like coming out here anymore than I have to. I mean, who would?

I close the door behind me, fasten the lock, and give the combination numbers a couple spins. I then head back to the garage, my feet once more crunching through leaves that are virtually identical, dried up and fallen away from the trees that gave them life. There are so *many* of them. I watch as one drifts down near me, almost grazing my face.

And they just keep coming, I think. *No matter what you do.*

Too bad the mess in the garage never takes care of itself—that I have to deal with it the old-fashioned way—with water, a mop, and bleach. It doesn't take as long as you might expect. I've gotten good at it over the last six weeks. When I'm finished, I remove my blood-stained clothes, stuff them in a plastic bag, and then put on the spares I keep in the storage closet next to the tarps. Then I take the bag outside and toss it into the shed with the body. I go around to the side of the house, turn on the spigot, and wash my hands and face with water from the hose. When I'm finished, I walk around front. It's time to deal with the other Glen's car.

The house is only a few blocks away from a small shopping center. I drive his Sonata there, and park it. Every time I do this, I park close to the Chinese take-out place. I try to get the same space every time, and when I can't I take the next closest one. It might not matter where I park, but I try not to vary the routine—just in case.

I then walk home. I know from experience that when I leave for work tomorrow and drive past the shopping center in my own Sonata, the duplicate will be gone. I don't know what happens to it. I'm just glad that it's all over.

Until the next time.

By the time I get back home, Jessie's in the bathtub and Rachael's sitting on the floor next to the tub, washing her hair. I'm always relieved to find them alone when I return. I fear that one night I'll come home after dropping off a Sonata and find another Glen has come in while I was gone and is waiting with the baseball bat to kill me. But so far that hasn't happened, and it didn't tonight, either.

I sit down on the closed toilet lid and watch my wife put baby shampoo on our daughter's hair. I've seen this scene repeated almost every night for the last six weeks, but I'm still so grateful to be here that it almost brings me to tears. Before I came here the first time and survived the other Glen's attempt to kill me, it had been fifteen years since I'd seen Rachael bathe Jessie, and no matter how many times I might get to see the two of them like this, from now on, I'd never take it for granted. Never.

Neither of them say anything about the fact that I've been gone so long or that I've returned wearing different clothes than I had on at dinner. They never do.

"Mommy?" Jessie says, eyes squeezed shut and shampoo-covered head tilted back as Rachael scrubs gently but firmly with her fingers.

"Hmm?"

"Where's my dragon?"

The tub water only comes up to Jessie's belly button, but it's filled with various bath toys. Rubber duckies, plastic boats, rubber fishes that squirt water from their tiny circular mouths when squeezed. But one toy is missing, Jessie's favorite. A pink dragon covered with green spots.

This is another new thing. Not once in six weeks has Jessie had a bath without her dragon. At least, not any of the baths I've been present for. I've done my best not to miss any of them.

"I don't know, sweetie," Rachael says. "I guess it's lost. But don't worry. We'll look for it after your bath is over."

Jessie makes a pouty face while Rachael keeps scrubbing. Then she chants in a sing-song voice, "Finders keepers, losers weepers." She repeats this refrain several times, and then frowns. She opens her eyes and turns her head to look at Rachael.

"Mommy, what's a weeper?"

"It's someone who cries," Rachael says. She reaches for the spray-nozzle attached to the faucet by a length of rubber tubing. She turns on the water, gently tilts Jessie's head back, and begins to rinse the shampoo from her hair.

I have trouble sleeping that night. I usually do after I have to *take care* of a Glen, but this is worse. Rachael is sleeping soundly next to me. I consider reaching over and trying to shake her awake, maybe see if I can convince her to make love. Not because I'm especially horny, but just so I won't feel so alone. But I don't do it. Sex with Rachael is uncomfortable for me. I was only two years older than her when we got married. I was twenty-eight and she was twenty-six. But I'm in my early fifties now, and she—at least this version of her—is in her mid-thirties. She's never mentioned the age difference. As far as I know, she's never even noticed it. But I have a difficult time forgetting it. Rachael looks exactly the same as the day I moved out, while I look like ten miles of bad road—gray at my temples, a paunch where my once-flat belly had been. I can't help feeling sometimes that Rachael's gotten the raw end of this deal. But she's never rejected me in bed, in fact she has approached sex with the same enthusiasm she had before her divorce. But I get the sense she's putting on a convincing performance; that somehow it's all an act. Part of me is afraid that this is exactly how it was between us fifteen years ago. I was too stupid then to realize it.

I slip out of bed and walk to the bedroom door. I open and close it as quietly as I can, and then I head across the hall to check on Jessie. Her door is opened a crack—it always is—and I push it open a little wider so I can peek in. I'm wearing a T-shirt and pair of shorts, so I'm not worried about Jessie waking and seeing me. My parents used to sleep nude, and when they got up in the middle of the night, they were sometimes too groggy to remember to don a robe. I'd slept the same way when I lived here originally, but not now. I want to spare my child the sight of my sagging, overweight body.

Jessie's lying on her side, tucked beneath the covers, her eyes closed. She's cuddling a stuffed giraffe, one of her favorite toys. She has a half dozen or so she sleeps with, and alternates them randomly. Tonight is Mr. Giraffe. She looks so peaceful in the yellow glow of her night light. My heart swells with love and gratitude as I watch her sleep, and I think that whatever I have to do to stay in this house, I will. I'll kill an *army* of Glens if necessary. As I stand in the doorway, I wonder where the other Jessie is right now. The one who goes by *Jessica* and moved to California with her husband. The one I haven't seen or spoken to in three years.

It doesn't matter. I have *this* girl now. The Jessie who loved me, who cried when her mother and I sat her down and told her we were getting a divorce. Now that I'd found my way back to this place and time, I was going to make sure this Jessie never heard the word *divorce*, that this Jessie would never cry because her world was crashing down around her. She wouldn't lose…so she wouldn't weep. I'd see to it.

We couldn't keep going on like this. I slipped up tonight, and if I hadn't recovered, I'd be in the shed right now, dead and wrapped in plastic, and the other Glen would've taken my place. He might even be standing here right now, watching Jessie sleep, and thinking how lucky he was. If I wanted to make certain *I* would be the only Glen who lived in this house from now on, I had to do something. But what?

I thought again of what Jessie had said at dinner.

If something is lost, it only gets more lost.

"Not always, honey," I whisper to the shadowed air of her room. "Not always."

I go into the kitchen to make myself a cup of coffee, sit at the small table in the breakfast nook, and think.

One night in July, I came down with a sinus infection. I called my doctor, and he called in a prescription for an antibiotic to the pharmacy I used. I'm prone to sinus infections, so the doctor didn't have any qualms about phoning in a scrip for me. In the decade and a half since Rachael and I divorced, I'd always meant to switch pharmacies. The one we used was in the shopping center close to our house—or rather, I should say close to the house she got in the divorce and let the bank foreclose on. But I never got around to changing pharmacies. I guess I have trouble letting go.

I stopped after work to pick up the prescription and then started to drive away from the shopping center. I should've turned right, onto the street. That was the direction in which my shithole of an apartment lay. But instead I turned left, in the direction of the house. I'm not sure why I did it. It had been years since I felt compelled to drive by the place. Another family had moved in long ago, and whenever I went past there—driving as slowly around the cul-de-sac as I could without looking like some kind of stalker—I just got depressed. But that evening I drove past the house anyway. My head was already throbbing with sinus pain, and I guess I figured since I was already feeling like crap, what the hell?

As I approached the brick ranch with its black roof, white shutters, and steep driveway, the first thing I noticed was that the white ash tree in the front yard was smaller than it should've been—significantly so. The second thing I noticed was that the garage door was up, and a minivan and a Sonata were parked inside. The same vehicles Rachael and I had owned when we lived there. When we were both happy—or so I'd thought.

The third thing I noticed took my breath away. Sitting on the front porch swing with several stuff animals around her, including Mr. Giraffe, was a little girl who looked enough like my Jessie at five to be her twin. It was hot out, and I had the windows down as I drove by. The little girl saw me, waved, and shouted, "Hi, Daddy!"

I drove home, parked in the cramped lot in front of my building, climbed the stairs to my apartment, let myself in, ran to the bathroom, and spend the next hour hunched over the toilet, vomiting.

I made several other visits after that. I drove by the house at different times. I parked farther up the street and walked by. Once I came late at night and did my best peeping tom impression, sneaking up to the house and peering inside the windows. And what did I learn from my reconnaissance? That for reasons I couldn't even begin to understand, my family once again lived in our old house. Except it wasn't old. It was exactly the same as when I moved out. Rachael and Jessie were exactly the same. There was a Glen there, too, but he wasn't young. He was old, like me. I told myself that I'd gone crazy, that I was hallucinating. But it seemed so real. More, it *felt* real. And though I had no conscious plan to do what I did, I must've worked it out somewhere deep inside me, because I always made sure Rachael—and especially the other Glen—never saw me when I paid my brief visits.

One evening I decided the only way I'd know if I was insane or not, was to enter the house and confront my family's age-delayed doppelgangers and the duplicate of middle-aged me. I still had the garage door opener, even after fifteen years. I kept it in the Sonata's glove box along with my registration and some other junk. That letting go thing again.

I drove to the house, parked in the driveway, and fished the opener out of the glove box. Even after fifteen years, it still worked. I pushed the button, and the garage door began to rise. I stepped out of my car and headed into the garage. And that's when the other Glen came out to greet me with the baseball bat.

Now I'm here and he's not.

Can you imagine what it was like for me to step back into a life I'd lost so many years earlier? They say you can't go home again, that what's past is past. And maybe most of the time that's true. But this time it wasn't. I don't know how it works. I'm just thankful I found my way back here—wherever and whatever *here* truly is.

Rachael and Jessie accepted me as if I was the same Glen that had stepped into the garage. And I was, wasn't I? For all intents and purposes, anyway. I stayed there that night, mostly being quiet and just watching my wife and daughter, not taking my eyes off them, as if I was afraid they might vanish the moment I looked away. I knew outside this house, an older Rachael, one who'd remarried ten years ago and lived in Philadelphia with her current husband—an orthodontist whose name I can never seem to remember—and a grown-up Jessie (*Jessica*) lived with her husband on the other side of the country. But here they were, just as they'd been when we were a family. Regardless of how strange it all was, I was glad to be there.

I never returned to my shitty one-bedroom apartment, the same one I'd moved into after Rachael asked me to leave. I continued going to work at the insurance company that employed me. None of my coworkers noticed anything different about me, other than I seemed happier these days.

Sometimes I find myself wondering where the other Glens come from. Do they live in the apartment I abandoned? Do they work at the same company I do? Do we somehow overlap one another when we are all there? I don't know the answer to any of these questions. All I know is that eventually one of them will decide to take a trip down memory lane and drive past the house, just like I did. Then he will realize the house is somehow *the* house, and he'll decide to investigate. Then I'll kill him. I'll *have* to. But someday, one of them is going to kill *me*. That's how I got in here, after all. I suppose I could be fatalistic and decide to enjoy my reclaimed life for as long as it lasts. But I don't want it to end. I lost this life once, and I won't let it go again. Not if I can help it.

Finders keepers, losers weepers.

I'm a Keeper, goddamnit, and I'm going to stay that way.

The question is…how?

I have to shake things up, I decide. Do something different. Can I move Rachael and Jessie to another house? If I did, none of the other Glens would be able to find them. But what if there's something about the house itself that makes all this possible? If that's the case, then I could ruin everything by trying to remove them from this place. After all, Rachael doesn't work and Jessie doesn't go to school. They don't ever leave the house. Maybe there's a good reason for that. We can't move. Sooner or later, another Glen is going to show up and want to play King of the Hill with me. So maybe what I need to do is go to him first. Break the cycle.

I sip my coffee and start making plans.

At five a.m., after several more cups of coffee, I'm sitting behind the wheel of my Sonata, looking at a much older duplicate parked on the other side of the cramped lot. I backed into this space so I have a clear view of the building's entrance. Not that I'm worried the other Glen will emerge any time soon. I move slow in the morning. I don't have to be at work until nine. I'm sure he's lying on his lumpy mattress—no box springs or frame, just the mattress on the floor—sound asleep. On the seat next to me I have a fresh roll of duct tape and the aluminum bat, wiped clean, of course.

There has to be some kind of sequencing element at work here. A new Glen shows up to challenge the Glen in the house because there are always *two* Glens. Inside-Glen and Outside-Glen. But what if the Outsider is dealt with *before* he comes into the house? If the pattern is disrupted somehow, then maybe the cycle will be broken, and then there will only be *one* Glen—me. That's my hope, anyway.

I remove the key from the ignition. I have half a dozen keys on my keychain, and one of them is to my—*his*—apartment. I grab the tape and the bat, get out of the car, and start walking toward the building.

After I killed my first Glen and hid his body in the shed, I wasn't sure what to do with the remains. I grew up in the country, and my mother still lived in the same house. My father died from a brain tumor when Jessie was still a baby. My folks' place was less than thirty minutes from the house, and they had six acres of land. Not a lot, maybe, but more than enough to bury a body. I decided I'd wait until the next night, and when Rachael and Jessie were sleeping, I'd sneak the body out of the shed, put it in my trunk, drive to my mom's house, and bury it at the back of her property—where Dad used to dispose of items too large and unwieldy for the trash collectors to take—broken bicycles, busted lawnmowers, that sort of thing. It seemed only fitting that my *dead self* was like an obsolete piece of machinery that had been replaced by a newer model. At least one that was luckier and a little faster on the draw.

But that night when I opened the shed door, I discovered the body was gone. At first I feared someone had moved it, but the lock had been on the door, and the shed was intact, so no one had broken in. I spent a nerve-wracking couple of days waiting for the police to come knocking on our door, but they never did. I had no idea how this dark miracle was performed, but I was grateful for it. After that night, I disposed of the other Glens the same way, and I intended to do the same for this one.

It's 5:30 AM by the time I'm back behind the Sonata's wheel and pulling out of the parking lot. With any luck, this will be the last time I ever see this place. I'm not going to miss it. As I drive away, I raise my middle finger to the building. It's a meaningless gesture, but it makes me feel good.

The other Glen—hopefully the last Glen—is in the trunk. He was still asleep on his pathetic mattress on the floor when I entered his apartment and delivered several solid blows to his head with the bat. He didn't even wake up. I checked his pulse. He wasn't dead, but I didn't think he'd be getting up and performing dance routines any time soon. He was wearing a T-shirt and boxers, so at least I didn't have to handle my own naked body—how weird would that have been? I bound his hands and feet with duct tape, and put a strip over his mouth. Carrying him down the stairs to my car was a bitch and a half. It reminded me that I really needed to lose some weight. He remained unconscious the entire time. As hard as I hit him, he might never regain consciousness again, but that was fine with me, it would surely simplify things.

It took me ten minutes to get back to the house.

I pulled into the garage and closed the door. I decided not to bother finishing him off and wrapping him in plastic, the sun was due to rise around seven o'clock, and while I don't know for sure how the shed thing works, I know each body I've put inside has vanished by the next morning. I still have over an hour until sunrise, but the faster I get this done, the better.

I leave the bat in the car and pop the trunk. I sling the fat bastard over my shoulder in a fireman's carry. I go out the back garage door and into the yard. Leaves crunch underfoot as I make my way toward the shed. This is the first Glen I've killed—or will soon kill—who wasn't trying to enter my house. Those Glens had been direct threats. But this one had been sleeping in his rathole apartment, minding his own business. Sure, he would have become a threat one day, but he wasn't one yet. So getting rid of him isn't self-defense, is it? It's murder.

So what if it is—I tell myself.

No price is too high to hold onto what I have, and I know that the unconscious man slung over my shoulder would agree with me if he knew what I was doing. That makes it less like murder and more like a personal sacrifice. I'm giving up one aspect of myself to ensure a happy future for the rest of me. When you look at it like that, what I'm doing is almost noble, really.

I'm breathing heavily by the time I reach the shed, and my back is screaming in protest. My heart is *thud-thud-thudding* in my chest, and I think how ironic it *would* be if my overtaxed middle-aged heart gave out before I could drag the other me inside the shed.

I drop the other Glen to the ground, undo the combination lock, and open the door. I glance up at the sky and see that it's starting to turn purple. The stars are beginning to fade, so I don't have much time.

I bend down to grab hold of the other Glen's ankles, and that's when I hear the faint crackle of a leaf behind me. I spin around in time to see Rachael and Jessie. My wife's wearing a robe over her nightgown and my daughter's in her jammies. Rachael is gripping the baseball bat while Jessie holds the roll of duct tape. Before I can do anything—(although, really, what would I do?)—Rachel swings the bat toward my head and light explodes behind my eyes. I don't lose consciousness—at least I don't think I do—not all the way. I do fall, though, on top of my other self. I hear the sound of tape being pulled free from its roll, and over the next several moments Rachael turns me over and holds my hands and feet together while Jessie binds them. My little girl finishes the job by putting a strip of tape over my mouth. In a strange way, I'm proud of her, and if I could speak, I'd tell her so. *Good work, honey!*

Jessie stands back while Rachael drags me into the shed. She then brings in the other Glen, who's beginning to stir but is a long way from coming to. Rachael then steps outside and turns around to face me. Jessie moves to her side. My vision's a bit blurry, but I fix my gaze on them both. I know this is the last time I'm going to see them, and I don't want to miss a single fraction of this moment—as awful as it might be.

Rachael put the bat down when she dragged me into the shed, but she picks it up again now. There is no way I can threaten her bound as I am—not that I would—but it's a wise move, and I'm glad to see her taking the precaution.

"Sorry, Glen," she says.

Jessie looks up at her. "Don't lie, Mommy. We're not sorry at all."

Rachael sighs. "No, we're not. What we are is *tired*, Glen. Tired of being stuck in the past. Tired of being forced to live in your memories. Do you know how many of you have come here over the years?"

"Lots!" Jessie says.

Rachael nods. "One after the other. It took a while before Jessie and I started to become aware of what was happening and what we really were. We understood there were older versions of us out there somewhere. Versions that had the chance to move on with their lives. We wanted that, too."

Jessie scowled at me. "But you wouldn't let us."

"We tried talking to you," Rachael said. "Telling you how we felt, but you wouldn't let us go free. When a new Glen replaced you, we tried talking with him. And when *he* wouldn't listen, we tried again. Eventually, we realized none of you would ever listen—so we stopped talking. After that, we tried killing you ourselves and putting you in the shed. We'd long ago learned how you disposed of your bodies. But each time we did it, a new Glen would soon arrive, and everything would start all over again. So we decided to wait. We hoped one of you would eventually do something *different,* something that would change our situation and make our freedom possible."

"And you did!" Jessie said. She pointed to the other Glen lying beside me. He'd begun to moan behind the tape over his mouth.

Too little too late, pal, I thought.

"Now that there won't be a new Glen to replace you," Rachael said, "you've broken the cycle. We're finally free."

"Free to do what?" I tried to ask, forgetting about the tape that covered my mouth. All that came out were meaningless muffled sounds, but Rachael must've guessed what I was trying to say, because she answered my question.

"I don't know what will happen to us. Maybe we'll keep living and finally start to age. Maybe we'll vanish as soon as you die. Either way, it doesn't matter. Anything will be better than living in the fishbowl you've created."

I nodded to show her I understood, and that I didn't blame her or Jessie. My daughter had been right at dinner. *If something is lost, it only gets more lost.* You can't get it back, can *bring* it back, no matter how hard you try. The best you can do is delude yourself for a time. But everything, including delusions, comes to an end at some point.

"Goodbye, Glen," Rachael says. "Please don't take this the wrong way, but I sincerely hope we don't see you again."

"Bye, Daddy." Jessie waves and gives me a parting smile. Then her mother closes the shed door and fastens the lock behind them.

I lie in darkness and listen to the sound of crunching leaves as Rachael and Jessie walk away from the shed. When they've gone, the only sounds I hear are my own breathing and the soft moans coming from my other self next to me. Tears sting my eyes and slide down my cheeks, and I tell myself it won't be much longer until sunrise. Whatever is going to happen to me next—to *us*—it's going to happen very soon.

I understand now that I'm not a Keeper. I never was. No matter how hard we all try, in the end, none of us really are.

I close my eyes, and continue to cry.

And wait for daybreak.

The Mad Doctor's Bones

Michael McGlade

September 10, 2009

I've dated the human bone (T12 thoracic vertebrae) to the year 1609. It is fire-charred, indicating a particularly gruesome murder. A journal discovered alongside this bone has a final entry for September 10th, 1609. This cold case investigation is coincidentally 400-years-old. DNA testing reveals the deceased is a direct relative of mine. We're blood related. His name was Doctor William Taylor.

Both bone and journal were discovered in a bricked-up fireplace in Aglish Castle in Durrus, a small town (population 5,000) in South Armagh, Northern Ireland.

Detective Austin Taylor
Cold Case Division
Police Service of Northern Ireland

Due to the 2007 banking collapse, personnel in the Cold Case Division has been cut to a skeleton crew. I've been allocated one week to pursue my investigation into the death of Dr Taylor, who died four centuries ago.

Dr Taylor's journal is peppered with references to altar rocks, stone circles, and pagan rituals…all mystical, superstitious nonsense. If I do nothing else on this investigation, I shall dispel the rumours built around the ghostly foundations of Durrus town. There's a rational explanation for all supernatural occurrences, and I don't scare easily.

Newspaper articles state Dr Taylor, many times referred to as the *Mad Doctor,* simply lured his companions into the woods and murdered them before killing himself. No bodies were ever discovered. Wolves could have devoured the carcasses, them still being present in Ireland and not extinct until the 18th century. However, how had the bone and journal survived? Even if Dr Taylor had lighted himself on fire, somebody had been responsible for preserving this evidence.

I believe the journal and bone denotes a ritualistic murder. Someone set upon them, murdered them and hid the bodies. After all, Dr Taylor had been an agent of the British government, employed to survey suitable lands within Ireland for confiscation and redevelopment as plantations. The local population would have been displaced or indentured.

Due to Dr Taylor's death, Durrus town was spared from seizure. Indeed, the place attained a cult mythology, garnering to this day a reputation as a wild, lawless place. It has become a hub for paranormal enthusiasts. Durrus, although suffering a decline in popularity in recent years, is still steeped in this superstitious claptrap.

From the Journal of Dr Taylor, September 3rd, 1609:

His Royal Highness King James decreed I shall continue my sterling efforts to survey and establish plantations in the north of Ireland. I departed Dublin northward beyond The Pale, sixty miles and two days' ride hence, bound for the village of Durrus in County Armagh. I have provisions enough to remain in the vicinity of the Slieve Gullion mountain range for several weeks, locating lands for seizure by the Crown. This is lawless and wild terrain, full of wood-kerne – Irish bandits specialised in attacking English settlers.

Slieve Gullion is a whale-shaped mountain some two thousand feet tall, surrounded by a ring of hills of which the constituent rock type is granite. I suspect it is of volcanic origin. Much of the present landscape owes its shape to the last Ice Age, when the melting ice sheet deposited mineral-rich material in the form of small rounded hills called drumlins. This place will harbour fertile, arable lands, even though the place be heavily wooded when not bog. But bogs can be drained, trees felled. There's good plantation land here, I know it.

I arrived in Durrus town on September 11th, 2009. Durrus is perched on a hill, with a cobblestone square, and a few horse-driven carts jingling around, their straw-y manure still smoking where it lay. There are several well-pruned public gardens, and the Carrigh River rumbles through the centre. No matter where you walk it can be heard chuckling. I booked into a room in Whites Tavern, and after stowing my equipment I went to the bar for dinner. The open peat fire made the small pub intolerably hot. A hundred heaving people had crowded in, and judging by their accents a mixture of locals and tourists. This place reminds me of that pie shop from Sweeney Todd. I've been told that Whites has been in continuous use since Dr Taylor's time, and to think I might be sitting in the very same place he did before setting out to his demise made my stomach churn.

I ordered poached trout and a glass of ice water. The barman said, "Coming right up, Detective."

I could see everyone here knew my identity, like they'd been expecting me. I felt like a watched thing as I took my seat. A band played trad and, when an elderly man began Irish dancing, as the tourists gathered around, all that could be seen was his head bobbing. Didn't deter those at the back from snapping photos—all part of the *craic.*

A square-shouldered man—40s, balding, comb-over—sat at my table.

"I hear you're after the bones of the Mad Doctor."

Silence. Either an inopportune break in the music or it had been staged, I wasn't sure, but all eyes in the room were on me. I cleared my throat, stood and said, "I am here as part of an investigation into the murder of Dr Taylor 400 years ago and anyone with pertinent information should make themselves known to me."

"There's someone can help," he said. "Ginger-haired fellow, minds a pot of gold and you get to him at the end of a rainbow."

Big belly laughs all around.

I sat and resumed eating my meal. The joker, still at my table, introduced himself as Séamus Malloy.

"What exactly is it you're planning to do?" he asked.

"Among other lines of investigation, I'm going to the last known location of Dr Taylor and his entourage—"

"It's in a peat bog, a half-day's walk through dense wood. You'll have to walk, no vehicle transport."

"Sounds like you're trying to scare me off."

He laughed a nervous kind of warble, like a trapped bird.

On the table I spread the tourist pamphlets I had taken from my room. A quick perusal confirmed them as advertorials for unsubstantiated paranormal activities. Hearsay and folklore. They referred to specific areas of supernatural activity in town and the surrounding areas—accessible pagan altars, ghost sightings, haunted buildings—and the Mad Doctor.

A Bermuda-triangle forest, where many have been lost and it is recommended never to enter without local guidance...

"Nice way of saying pay a local to guide you round in circles."

"I believe you're what we call a Doubting Thomas."

"I am. In fact, I don't believe much has changed in attitude here since Dr Taylor's time. Still a silly, superstitious people."

Séamus leapt to his feet, throwing his stool backwards, and once again the eyes of the tavern were fixedly glued on yours truly. He would have made a jump at me had his friend (Áron Quinn, local butcher, chubby as Santa) not pulled him back.

"He means nothing by it," Áron said. "Under a lot of pressure, is all. How about a drink for you?"

"I don't drink."

"Keeping yourself pure?"

That got a good laugh especially from the American tourists.

From the Journal of Dr Taylor, September 6th, 1609:

Stranger still, the only place of worship is a church that lay in a squalid state beyond repair. No one would speak of why this was, and it is a rare sight to encounter on my travels. More pleasing was that frosty beast the Carrigh River raging through the O'Casey estate (them being the largest landowners in the area) before whipping into Kildrum lough, a couple miles off. At the centre of Durrus village, forming part of the central square is a small castle named Aglish by its presiding owners, the O'Casey family.

Paul O'Casey was the person responsible for discovering Dr Taylor's bone and journal in a bricked-up fireplace in Aglish Castle. Having surrendered this evidence to the police, I believe him to be an ally, even though from Dr Taylor's journal it is clear the O'Casey family stood most to gain from his death, because they would've lost everything they owned.

I met Paul O'Casey inside Aglish Castle, and this blustery little man, apple-cheeked and wheezy, took me on a rushed tour before depositing me at the bricked-up fireplace where the evidence had been discovered.

He departed while I conducted my examination. Initial conclusions are that the wall was bricked up recently, and prior to further tests I would guess the wall had been constructed just a few weeks ago. So the evidence had been placed inside the castle. Why? Had they though it was a safe hiding place, never suspecting that O'Casey would begin renovations and unearth their macabre trophy? I will interview the staff, grounds keepers, anyone who had access to this room. Someone had to have seen the perpetrator.

I was peering into the fireplace and a noise blasted excruciatingly loud. I fell to my knees, hands clamped to my ears. This sound—this wailing marching concussion of a thousand trudging boots—reverberating from everywhere felt like a series of doors slamming shut inside my chest.

Paul O'Casey penguin-ed into the room but by then I was off my knees, standing, and the noise had vanished.

"Are you okay, Detective? You're looking a little green around the gills."

"That noise?"

His eyes sharpened, but he shook his head to say he had heard nothing.

"You didn't hear it?"

"It's an old building. Probably just settling."

"No," I said. "This is a noise you would have heard. Why are you lying to me?"

"I'm not. I wouldn't. I called you here to help."

I went to the window and outside a tour bus had arrived and a large group of people were milling around on the gravel courtyard. The window was open and due to my location in the fireplace the sound had been amplified. Nothing but some weird acoustic anomaly, amplified in much the same way that someone in a whispering gallery can hear from across the room.

"Aren't you going to tell me the castle is haunted?"

"It is haunted. Did you...what did you hear?"

"Haunted by whom?"

"The British family that lived here in the late 17th century were slain while sleeping in bed by wood-kerne. They never left here, y'know. Their bones are buried beneath this floor.

"Then I shall return with a warrant to have the floor smashed up."

O'Casey went pale as wax.

I ordered the steak and Guinness pie in Whites Tavern and touched none of it. I knew I should eat, but I'd lost my appetite. My ears were still ringing from earlier. Séamus Malloy sat at a table of Italian tourists and launched straight into this:

"Right on the very topmost point of Slieve Gullion Mountain is the Calliagh Bhirra Lough, which is Gaelic for *Lake of Sorrow.* The ancient Irish warrior Fionn Mac Cumhaill was tricked by a witch named Miluchra. Fionn had fallen in love with Miluchra's sister Áine but, after spurning Miluchra's advances, she decided to punish him. At the lough's edge, Fionn found a young *maiden* who had dropped her ring into the water. Being a mighty warrior, he promised to retrieve the ring and dived in, not realizing the lake was bottomless. Only then did this maiden revert to her true form as the hag Miluchra. Since Fionn had agreed to the pact, and was unable to return the ring, she transformed him into an old man. Of course Fionn eventually managed to find a cure but his hair remained forever white. To this day it's believed the lough is cursed, and anyone attempting to swim in the water will die. Two years ago was the last recorded drowning."

The tourists asked to be driven up the mountain to see the lake. Nice little earner, and all it took was a few minutes of well-polished spiel.

However, as entertaining as the story was, I profess from a purely scientific viewpoint that the lough simply contains a surprisingly strong downwards current, similar to a vortex or whirlpool, which could drown even the most proficient swimmer.

From the Journal of Dr Taylor, September 8th, 1609:

In some fields adjoining the road, I noted a large circular site. The circle, measuring to a diameter of eighty feet, was formed of large upright stones with a much larger stone in the centre, towering above the others at a height of twenty-one feet. Adjacent, and formed in the same manner, was a much smaller circular spot. It was hard to say what the antiquity or exact uses of these circles may have been therefore I cannot pretend to say.

However, it was possible they were of a religious nature. I could not determine as to what faith the site belonged and as such I will henceforth refer to as pagan. Alas, that the antiquity of the customs and manners of Ireland have not yet been fully realized, for I can comment upon my recent findings that they were beyond doubt of great significance. That this was a place of worship was clear, probably where a simple race of peoples offered adoration to some supreme directing Deity. As such, we viewed it with much respect, caring not to withdraw too hastily or disturb any of the ancient stones other than to remove three small specimens for further scrutiny.

The origin, tales, and peculiar rites of these crude circles I must reluctantly bestow upon the antiquarians, as my job was in duty to the Ordnance Survey Board and their mapping of the Slieve Gullion area. However, these ancient monuments of worship were of particular interest to me, rising above the obvious aspects of the aesthetical, historical and spiritual, to the realm of the origins of mankind and, thus, thy self *– our place within the race of humanity. Since their erection, who is it can say how many centuries and generations have been lost beneath the tide of futurity?*

I located this specific circular site and on inspection noted the smell of incense and another powerful odour like burning tar, accelerant, and charcoal. No one was nearby, but the location had been used recently, within the last day, I would say. And the gravel apron had been meticulously cleaned of weeds.

While circumnavigating the circle, I found an object made of twigs. It was no larger than the size of a human head, but the twigs were lashed together into a pyramid shape. I bagged it as evidence, preferring to examine it more thoroughly in the lab, where no doubt I'd find Séamus Malloy's paw prints all over it.

I went to an area known as Calmor's Rock situated opposite Topny Mountain, at the north entrance of the valley entrance to Durrus. Áron Quinn was leading a tour guide.

"I was born just down the road and spent many hours playing around Calmor's Rock as a child, Quinn was saying."

The rock face stretched forty feet above the treeline, cratered with nooks and crannies and places to hide.

"Never guess what I seen the other day, he said."

"A ghost?" I asked.

He glared at me.

"Actually, it was some young lassie starkers naked, with her *faighin* out and everything, getting photographed for some smut mag. Right there she was. Spread eagle. Might still see the indentation of her arse cheek."

He bent forward and studied a curved indentation in the dirt, and the others crowded around, stooped over, giggling.

"You want me to dust for a print?" I asked.

They laughed.

"She was a fine colleen. Would love to make her acquaintance again," Áron said. "You think you *can* – dust, that is?"

"Might take a mould," I said. "Fit her arse like a glass slipper."

More laughs. But Áron reddened. I think he had been serious about the dusting.

"I'll tell you the honest account of a notorious rapparee," he began his spiel, "from the latter part of the seventeenth century."

He pointed upwards waiting until his audience craned their necks to see the wetly black opening in the forehead of the rock face, like a black cavern leading to another realm.

"Cathal Mór Ó Carrachóir headed a band of bloodthirsty villains terrorising planters and natives alike. Before anyone was allowed into Cathal Mór's gang, he had to kill a man. And this cave you see above us was his hideout.

"Being a first generation descendant of the landed gentry, his father lost everything in the Cromwellian confiscations. Embittered, Cathal turned his family's long military tradition into a campaign of vengeance.

"Rapparee-hunting was major business. Bring the severed head, you'd get five pounds. And on his trail was Constable Johnston of the Fews. *Fews* comes from the Irish word *feadha* meaning trees. Now, Johnston was this dark shadow, guilty and innocent were subject to his wrath—he didn't care. The law decreed anyone apprehended by a Government agent suspected of being a rapparee could be beheaded without proof. Keenan, his lieutenant, known affectionately as *Keenan of the Heads*, personally decapitated over a hundred.

"So, Cathal was captured, and sentenced to be hung, drawn and quartered. They stuck his pretty head on a spike above the entrance to this cave."

Leading the way up the steep incline, Áron paused in the chill of the thick trees. People were visibly shivering now, steam puffing from their mouths like we'd entered a freezer.

"They say his ghost haunts these woods. No one ventures into them at night. Never."

It had been particularly cold this morning, with a bright clear sky, and no sun able to penetrate this dense treeline. That's the reason it was cold, not because of some supposed spectral haunting.

"Well," I said, "I'll be going into these woods to trace the last known path of Doctor Taylor."

"I'd advise against it."

"Of course you would, but I'm a trained officer of the law. So, I'll be going where I please."

"Then do it during daylight, leave early and get back before dusk."

"But that would leave me no time there, for it's a five hour walk. No, I'll hike there and camp the night, spend the day, then return."

"Take someone with you."

"Who would dare attack a police officer?"

"Not who—*what.* Something without care for laws, something maybe not even human."

I laughed.

"Good show for the tourists, but that's all this is, a show."

At the top of the rock, while the tourists entered Cathal Mór's cave, I investigated the other entrances, most of which had collapsed or been plugged with boulders to stop the local kids from getting lost inside.

It was then that I saw it.

My hands trembled and I made fists.

This new bone fragment was human, and similar in size to the previous piece I had examined. It matched the discolouration, and completed the sequence – T11 thoracic vertebrae.

They'd left a piece of Dr Taylor for me to find, disrespecting his bones for some sick kick.

From the Journal of Dr Taylor, September 9th, 1609:

My three associates and I had commandeered the company of several young Irish natives to navigate this remote area. To them, it was clear, this place possessed a raw beauty, and I couldn't help but think it would forever haunt me too, for I was moved by the wildness, this primordial innocence. It promotes the type of humility usually reserved for some grand cathedral. All of us were inspired into contemplative, self-reflection for some time.

I entered the forest and hiked toward the last known location of Dr Taylor. I laboured through dense undergrowth for six hours, with nothing but my ragged breathing for company. I felt utterly alone. And lost.

Then sunlight and deliverance.

I exited onto the descent to Kildrum Lake. There was a great stone, of which the narrower end had been placed in the ground and inclined to the west. The natural stone of this place is granite, but this stone pillar was of a hard material that, I presume, had once been finished to a high polish. Dr Taylor had mentioned that he observed the stone used in temples and places of worship hereabouts had not been sourced locally. This particular stone reminded me of material I once saw in Brescia, northern Italy.

Proceeding along the southern shore of Kildrum Lake by a well-trampled track, after gaining the first rising ground a half-mile off, I found more large stones, the first of these being in a triangular shape, supported atop three smaller ones. It was a Stone Age burial mound.

The pamphlets I had garnered from my tavern room referred to this area as Poulnabrone —*Hole of the Sorrows.* It's described as an altar. Nearby was an abandoned settlement called Ballina, which was translated as *Hag's Town.* This word in Gaelic often refers to a witch or female deity. There was supposed to be a small monastery but all I found were some stone ruins that could have been anything, really, maybe just a ditch dividing some farm fields. The pamphlet alluded to the supposition that the monastery was abandoned and razed to dirt by its former inhabitants. Of course it would.

I set up camp in this location and while inside the tent unrolling my sleeping bag I heard movement in the forest, approaching footsteps and crunching gravel. Peering out, I didn't see anybody.

I've got to remain calm and rational. I probably didn't hear anything at all except for some wildlife, some badgers, maybe, as it was almost sunset. Maybe a fox. This *is* a forest after all; I'm bound to hear wild animals.

The sun dipped behind Slieve Gullion Mountain and a chill shadow embalmed the camp. A wolf howled.

Impossible.

Wolves have been extinct in Ireland for centuries.

At sun up, after a terrible sleepless night, I struck camp and proceeded with haste to the last known location of Dr Taylor. Coming to a muddy stretch near the lake's shoreline I discovered animal tracks. The hairs on my neck went up. Those paw prints were large enough to be a wolf's. I gripped my pistol and hurried on.

Within minutes I came to New Church and a large stone circle. The undergrowth and spiked whins with their yellow blotches were so dense that I had to take an alternative route.

I counted sixteen standing stones leading to the lake in two parallel lines. A serpentine passage, formed by parallel stones, connected New Church and the stone circle, and all around was a squelch of low, marshy ground a mile wide.

From the Journal of Dr Taylor, September 10th, 1609:

Beyond (that is to say, to the east of) this great stone circle, a native, opposite whose cabin the circle was situated, informed me that an old woman had resided in the ruins of New Church for many years. Upon her death the capstones were thrown off, which is the present state of neglect in which it is to be discovered. As much as I wish to believe this tale, it is more likely the capstones were dislodged by scoundrels in search of the buried antiquities.

On our approach to the great stone circle, all of our native guides refused to go further and remained at a distance. It was clear they harboured a superstitious respect.

To my eyes, this site had been used recently. I have decided to observe this location all night, for I wish to know who has been conducting ceremonies here.

I followed a rank of sunken standing stones to an incline and then onto a perfectly flat, almost table-like formation of solid granite which stood several yards above the surrounding bog. This was the last known location of Dr Taylor.

In the utmost centre of this flat stone altar I found a small pyramid-shaped object made of twigs lashed together with cord. It was similar to the object I found previously, and I bagged it for later examination. By now my head was pounding and there was pressure enough inside my head I thought my brains might leak out of my ears. The reek of this bog, the black buggy air, the syrupy denseness of each breath I gasped for.

And then I was running, didn't care where, all I knew was I needed to get away from here, from this *place,* and even though my lungs sizzled I didn't dare stop.

A noise outside my tent jerked me awake. I'd travelled as a far as I could but darkness forced me to stop, still miles from civilization. This movement in the trees seemed to be from all around, above and below. The ground trembled like some bass drum.

I gripped my pistol, but didn't dare go outside. The last three times I'd gone out to take a look there'd been nobody there. The noise, the wolf howls, this braying grew louder and louder, the pressure inside my head unbearable. And then I smelled smoke—burning sulphur.

This place is haunted. Haunted. And *malignant.*

Awakening in bed, I was in a room, a modern room, with walls and curtains and carpet.

"Whoever brought me here saved me. I could kiss them."

"No need for that, Detective," Séamus Malloy said.

He'd been sitting there, watching me.

"Where am I?"

"You passed out in the forest."

"How'd you find me?"

"Because we were following you."

I moved to sit but fell back on the bed, limbs like limp spaghetti.

"The forest, it's haunted, those noises…wait, you were *following* me?"

"No point straining yourself trying to get up. The drugs won't wear off for a while."

I groaned and upchucked on the floor.

"You bastard," I said. "You *drugged* me? You won't get away with this—"

"I expect it will be all over the news."

He said it matter-of-factly like he was powerless to change what was about to occur, but in his pale blue eyes I saw the faintest flicker of doubt.

"Séamus, get me a phone, let me call this in, and I'll make sure it's noted on the record that you helped—"

"I'm not letting you go. I can't."

"What, you're going to sacrifice me to some pagan god?"

He dry gulped. I moved but fell back onto the bed, unable to stand.

"This is ridiculous," I said. "You think I'm some sort of perfect sacrifice because I'm a direct bloodline to Doctor Taylor, that I'm some sort of magic portal and by using me in some hokey ritual you're going to rule the world? You're deluded, Séamus. Insane."

"We're going to kill you, yes, we have to. It's why you were lured here."

My stomach roiled and I spit up.

The diary and the bone fragment…

"You planted them to lure me here?"

The door opened and Paul O'Casey entered.

"Why me?" I whimpered. "Is this some ridiculous version of the Wicker Man? I don't drink, don't curse, never stolen anything in my life … dedicated myself to apprehending evil creeps like you, and making the world a better place. And this is my reward? Well, this isn't the Wicker Man, and I'm not some virgin."

"It's all just part of the image. Image is important."

"Image? What are you talking about?"

"What do you think happened to the Mad Doctor?"

"You murdered him and now it's a family business."

"Business," Paul chuckled. "You got that right."

"I'll tell you exactly what happened to the Mad Doctor," Séamus said. "He killed himself and his two cohorts. He went mad."

"Like you, then."

"Fearing we'd be blamed for it, we hid the evidence, made them disappear. And then a strange thing happened—Durrus got a reputation for paranormal activity. People came from all over for the myth, the legend. The supernatural is our industry now."

"You're talking like this is a business."

"We're not superstitious, none of us are. We're just doing this to survive, doing it for business."

I heard it then, the voice, lots of them, all outside the room.

"You won't get away with this. My disappearance will be all over the news."

"We're counting on it. A nice bit of publicity. The descendant of the Mad Doctor kills himself. It's juicy. Should keep the tourist numbers up for years."

"Tourists? You're doing this to get tourists? But the altars, the stone circles, they're being used. I have evidence."

"Perceptions must be maintained."

I thrashed, lurched, slumped off the bed and landed on my face, my arms like lead weights dragging me down, down, down into darkness.

"We're in the middle of the Great Recession," Séamus said. "Tough times. But something like this—the Mad Doctor's relative killing himself—what's not to love about that? It'll bring people here by the busloads."

Outside were masses of people—a whole town, all in this together. They dragged me from the room toward the funeral pyre.

The Guest

Aaron Gudmunson

Supper came late because the combine bitched out. Darryl's mood stood somewhere between ammonia sharp and vinegar bitter. He came stomping toward the table without bothering to wash, snapped up his silverware, and waited for Brenda to bring on the beef. She did so quietly so as not to further upend her husband.

"Lyle Lee!" Darryl shouted. "Darn it, where is that boy? I sent him in half an hour ago."

"In the front room, hon," Brenda replied, giving the potatoes a final stir.

"Gertie finish her homework?"

"Just about. Few math problems left."

Gramps wheeled in, right up to his place at the foot of the table. He glanced over the fare through his petri-dish spectacles, grunted, and began heaping mashed potatoes onto his chipped CorningWare plate.

"Summatter with the combine?" he asked. "Is it the drum?"

"Dunno," Darryl replied. "Just quit outta the blue."

"Better get it fixed quick, son. Harvest don't wait on no man."

"Want me to wheel your old bones out there to take a gander?"

"Quit scrappin', you two," Aunt Bert said, coming into the kitchen.

"Mind your tongue when you address your father," Gramps said.

Bert's laughter chimed like bells. "Pa, you're so grumpy."

Gramps leaned over his armrest to stroke the red heeler who'd wandered up scoping for scraps. "Let's get Grace over so we can eat."

"We're waiting on Lyle Lee," Brenda said.

"Dammit, where is that kid?"

"Hush now," Brenda said, kissing the top of her husband's shiny pate.

"I'll fetch him."

Gertie slouched in with a sigh and slapped her *Practical Mathematics* workbook on the table beside her plate. "I'll never get this crap."

"Language, young lady!" Aunt Bert snapped. Gertie stuck out her tongue when her aunt turned away and snuck a snap bean, munching it behind her hand so as not to catch heck for foregoing Grace.

Brenda led Lyle Lee in with a hand on his shoulder and pressed him into his chair. Lyle Lee's face scrunched.

"But, Ma, I ain't hungry. I wanna watch the ball game!"

"You'll eat your supper and then you'll help your father fix the combine."

"But Ma, the Cards are down two runs!"

Darryl slapped the table with an open palm, jumping the plates in the air. "You know harvest is our busy time. I don't want to hear another whine out of you."

"Yes, Pa."

"This stuff is too hard," Gertie said, flipping through her workbook.

"Get your homework off the table, sweetie," Brenda said.

"I'll help you after supper," Aunt Bert whispered. "Your mama never was much good at figures."

"I heard that!" Brenda remarked, sliding the bean casserole onto a hot pad beside the taters. "Anyway, I was good at the only figure that mattered." She placed a jaunty hand on her waist and swayed her hips.

"She's got you there," Darryl said. His mood had improved with prospect of the impending meal and his wife's saucy swagger.

Gramps covered his eyes. "Good God. Can't you keep that out of public, Bren?"

Everyone had a laugh at this except Gertie who just rolled her eyes. When everyone settled, they clasped hands around the table while Darryl muttered Grace. He had just come to "Amen" when someone pounded at the door.

"Don't that just figure?" Gramps grumped. The dog rocketed from beneath the table, firing a volley of yaps.

"Well don't just sit there, Lyle Lee. Go see who it is," Darryl said, shooing his son from the table. "And if it's Grant Lang, you tell him he ain't gettin' his mitts on his jigsaw till I get my sandblaster back!"

But the man at the door wasn't Grant Lang. He wore an expensive gray suit with a loose blue tie and the shiniest shoes Lyle Lee had ever seen (though the soles were caked in mud). Although Lyle Lee had never met the man in person, he recognized him immediately. The boy goggled. Surely this must be a mistake, or someone's idea of a joke.

"May I come in, son?" the President of the United States of America asked.

Darryl Avery couldn't quite believe his eyes when his son led the visitor into the kitchen. Like Lyle Lee, Darryl at first thought this must be a joke. He'd seen presidential impersonators—and damn good ones at that—on late night comedy shows. Since his first impression was indeterminate (the man *looked* like the Commander-in-Chief, but how could he be right here in this oft-overlooked tract of country?), the man of the house took to his feet, came around the table, and extended his hand. Just as he would greeting any unexpected guest in his home.

"Mom, Dad, meet the President," Lyle Lee said, prideful at having met him first.

When Brenda, who had been pouring milk, turned and saw who stood in her kitchen, she promptly dropped the glass which shattered and splattered across the worn linoleum.

Gramps, Gertie, and Aunt Bert simply sat like ice sculptures in their seats, mouths agape in frozen wonder.

"I apologize for the intrusion," said the President, still pumping Darryl's paw and not the least bothered by its current state of griminess. "I certainly don't mean to disrupt your dinner, but I have an emergency situation."

"What type of emergency?" Darryl asked in an oyster-raw voice. He hadn't voted for this man and in fact often railed freely against him, but now Darryl found he had nothing to say. For the time, anyway.

Brenda, who *had* voted for him (secretly, of course, for she'd never hear the end of her husband's brash admonishments if he knew), found herself instantly more drawn to the man in person than she ever had on television. He looked taller than he appeared onscreen, and leaner. Strong and intense.

Wolf-hungry. She found a complete inability to speak in his presence.

"Yes, what type of emergency?" Aunt Bert echoed, scraping her voice off the bottom of her tongue. Bert rarely had trouble talking to a man even if doing so brought her man-trouble.

"I need to use your telephone, if I may," he said, never losing his politeness even through his evident desperation.

"Be my guest," Darryl said, nodding at the phone on the wall beside the refrigerator.

The President thanked his host and put the receiver to his ear. He seemed to take a moment of recollection before dialing a number. All eyes watched his back. For a moment, the President listened as the line clicked through miles of relays and finally, shockingly, he spoke.

"Groundhog, this is Raptor. Repeat, Raptor. Mission has been fully compromised. I am unharmed, but Escort is down. Repeat, Escort is down. Current coordinates are—" He broke off and turned to Darryl. "Sir, may I have your address?"

Darryl gave it to him and the President relayed the information to the person on the other end of the phone.

"Send transport to this location. Full lock. Repeat, full lock. Call the number on your display with complications." He hung up and turned back to the six people watching him. A rueful smile unspooled on his face. "Sorry about all the code words. It gets pretty tiresome when you can't speak plainly."

"'S'okay," Gramps said, but the pinch in his voice made out as if it were anything but.

When no one else spoke, the President of the United States looked down at the white petals of milk still slowly blooming across the floor. "Oh. Let me help you clean that up."

"No," Brenda said, breathless. "No, that's all right, sir. Gertie, get a mop. Lyle Lee, you pick up the glass and mind the edges."

The President looked at supper laid out on the old oaken table that had seen approximately 9,000 suppers in its sturdy tenure. "That looks delicious. Do you suppose I could trouble you for a plate?"

Everyone scrambled into action. The kids cleaned up the mess while

Aunt Bert began tidying the cluttered countertops. Decorative dishtowels were slung over the oven handle. A pickle jar layered like sedimentary bedrock with bacon grease from a week's worth of breakfasts vanished into the trash. The scattering of crumbs surrounding the toaster were brushed away.

Brenda pulled down the china set from the dining room curio cabinet. They'd last been used six years ago on the Thanksgiving before her mother's passing. Since then, they'd been strictly for display and the women feverishly wiped a layer of dust from each piece before placing it on the dining room table. They fussed for a few moments with the gate-leg leaf, hoping to give the table a longer, more elegant appearance, but in the end couldn't make it fit and gave up.

In the kitchen, Darryl cleared his throat and asked the guest how he came to be here.

"That's a story you'll want to hear, but let me tell it when everyone can listen. It's not polite dinner conversation, I'll grant you that, but you'll need to hear it. All of you." When no one spoke, the President bent to peer out the kitchen window at the outbuildings beyond, their roofs glowing pink in the day's last light. "So what do you farm here?"

With the dining room table set (Brenda silently thanking God they'd been able to find her only linen tablecloth), Aunt Bert ushered the President to the head chair.

"You shouldn't have gone to such trouble," he told Brenda.

"No trouble, sir," she replied, smiling ingratiatingly.

"This is too much," he answered, with his own sterling smile firmly in place. "But I appreciate the hospitality."

"I just hope the food's still warm."

"At this point, I'd pounce on a liverwurst sandwich," he said. "Anything you serve will be welcome and wonderful."

Everyone positioned themselves around the head of the table while the leader of their country looked them over. "You know who I am," he said. "Now I'd love to meet each of you."

Darryl considered standing, but refrained. He didn't want to look like a schoolboy to go along with feeling like one. "My name's Darryl Avery. This is my wife, Brenda and my sister Bertha—"

"Please, call me Bert," Aunt Bert interrupted.

"—and these are my children, Lyle Lee and Margaret—"

"Please, call me Gertie," the girl said, with a sweet smirk.

"—and this old codger is my dad, Lawrence Avery."

"Call me Gramps, if it gets your goat," the old man said, still goggling through his glasses.

"Dad!" Brenda gasped, but the President laughed.

"Gramps it is," he said, then pointed around at each family member in turn. "And Bert. And Gertie. Lyle Lee, Brenda, and Darryl Avery. Did I pass?"

"All aces," Darryl replied. He had loosened up a little.

The old red heeler approached warily. The guest held out a hand to him, knuckles forward, so the dog could sniff it: the correct way to greet a new dog. Most people presented an open palm. Lyle Lee was impressed and told the guest so.

"I've got a way with dogs," he said. "What's this fella's name?"

Darryl didn't say anything, so Gramps answered, his voice full of spice and spite. "Ike."

The President favored him with his full-on smile. "Good name! I like Ike."

"So did I," Gramps said ruefully.

"Now, who's hungry?" Aunt Bert asked. "We said Grace already, but it might be prudent to start over."

"I think that's an excellent idea," the President replied, reaching to grasp the hands of Darryl and Brenda, who sat sitting nearest him. "Would you mind if I spoke it?"

Brenda nearly gasped. If you'd told her yesterday that today the most powerful man in the world would be seated in her dining room, holding her hand, about to eat food she'd cooked, and asking to lead the prayer, she would have laughed herself mad.

Darryl, who'd grown accustomed to saying Grace since his old man found it too bothersome, happily relinquished the chore. The President bowed his head. The words he spoke sounded, to Darryl, more sincere than any he'd said since winning the White House.

When he finished speaking, the guest rolled up the sleeves of his white

Oxford shirt (showing rings of perspiration beneath the arms) and sawed through his roast beef with abandon. When he chewed it, he closed his eyes again briefly as if adding a postscript to his prayer. He opened his eyes and regarded Brenda.

"Ma'am, this is roasted to perfection."

She blushed and smiled down at her napkin. "Call me Brenda, please."

"Brenda it is." The President grinned his easy grin and ladled gravy from the boat onto his hill of spuds.

"How about this trouble you're in, sir?" Darryl prompted.

The President cleaved the air with his cutlery. "It's bad. Very bad."

"I guess it would be if the President shows up alone at a farm in the middle of Nowhere, USA," Gramps said.

Aunt Bert, seated beside him, shushed him with a swat to the back of his liver-spotted hand.

"He's right," the President said. "It's about as bad as it can get."

"Was it terrorists?" Lyle Lee asked, leaning over his plate with a scoop of peas hovering above.

"We don't know what it was, exactly, son," the President replied. "We were cruising at thirty-thousand feet—"

"In Air Force One?" Lyle Lee cut in. The spoon tottered, dropping a few tiny green bombs into the smashed volcano of his potatoes.

The President gave him a quick, tight smile. "Yes, Air Force One. Just my security detail and a few aides. Pilot and Co-pilot. Small staff. We were returning to Washington after visiting the site of the California wild fires—you've seen news briefs about them, no doubt?"

"Terrible business," Gramps said. "We thank our lucky stars our biggest problem is aphids."

"And tractor trouble," Darryl cut in. "Don't forget about that."

The President stopped chewing. "Tractor trouble?"

"Why, not two hours ago my combine stalled out in the back forty."

The President checked his watch. "That was about the time we came under attack."

"Attack?" Aunt Bert gasped. "My God."

"Yes, well, at least I think it was an attack. The jet's electrical system failed. Lights flickering, monitors blinking out. The co-pilot informed me they were experiencing instrument malfunction. That's when Air Force One simply…dropped out of the sky."

Brenda put a hand to her mouth. Everyone had quit eating, except the President who told his story between bites of farm fresh fare.

"Just like that, down we went. But—" He raised a long, slender finger in the air. "—my team is extremely efficient. They're the best. *Were* the best, at any rate."

"You mean they all…?" Brenda breathed.

The President nodded slowly, sadly. He picked a tooth with his tongue. "They fulfilled their oaths. They died so that I could live."

"How did it happen?"

"My pilot attempted an emergency landing in a field about three miles west, but he had zero control. Everything was dead, across the board. My security detail got me tucked into a chute with bare seconds to spare. They said they would find me on the ground. I jumped to safety, landing right smack in the middle of the field. I watched Air Force One carve through the corn two hundred yards away. When I felt certain it was safe, I approached to investigate."

"And?" Gramps said. "What did you find?"

"Everyone on board was dead," the President replied. "Not from the impact, though. My pilot was very good, one of the best in the country. He pulled off a soft landing. Just the same, everyone aboard was dead. As if they'd just decided to all keel over at the same time."

"They must have only been dead a few seconds," Gertie said, the first she'd spoken since the start of the meal.

"You're a smart kid," the President said.

"Tell that to my math homework," Gertie said with a roll of her eyes.

The President winked at her and then looked around at the rest of the people seated at the table. "Gertie's right. Like I said, the emergency landing was flawless. If the crew had died sooner, the landing would've been botched."

"Maybe the impact *did* kill them," Darryl suggested. "Maybe it was rougher than you thought."

The President nodded. "That could be, except for one detail."

"What's that?"

"When I examined them, each body had a filmy residue covering their exposed skin. Like wet spider webs. That's the best way I can describe it."

"Good Lord," Brenda said. "I don't think the kids should be hearing this."

Both children at once protested, but the President intervened. "They must, Mrs. Avery. We all need to be prepared."

"Prepared for what?"

"For whatever did this," the President replied. "In case it comes this way. And if I was the target of their attack, it's a safe bet they might."

"But what *was* it?" Aunt Bert asked.

The guest drew a deep breath, held it, and let it go in a gust. "If you want my professional opinion, ma'am, I think the attack came from an extra-terrestrial source."

"You mean like *aliens?*" Lyle Lee gasped. He'd been smitten with the notion of otherworldly beings since kindergarten.

"That's precisely what I mean, young man," the President replied. "I walked a good three miles before I happened on your farm, glowing across the fields."

No one said anything while the guest took a long chug of milk. He patted away a white mustache with his napkin.

"On the way, I kept my eyes on the skies. No cloud or plane or bird to be seen. No flying saucers either. But—" He paused again to scrape the last of his potatoes from his plate and into his mouth. "—I did see something funny."

"What? Tell us!" Lyle Lee said, his chair standing on two legs as he leaned across the table on his elbows.

"As I walked through the corn, I saw footprints. They weren't many. They were about the size of a large man's, but instead of five toes they had three thin ones. Like bent tines on a pitchfork. And they *glowed.*"

"Glowed? Like a lantern?" Gramps asked.

"More like swamp gas. The kind you see way out over bogs. It had a bluish hue to it, very faint, around the outer edge of each print."

"*Cool,*" Lyle Lee breathed.

"Or maybe very uncool," the President said. "Anyway, whatever downed my plane didn't come after me while I picked my way to your house."

"Sounds fishy to me," Gramps said.

"In any case, there's no need to worry. The call I made was to a contact in Washington. I put out the word. In about ten minutes, an entire convoy of Special Forces should be rolling up your driveway in APCs and M35 Quadmounts. In ten minutes, your house will be the safest place in the world."

Lyle Lee was practically drooling. "This is the best night ever."

"Clear the table, son," Darryl ordered.

"Yes sir," the enamored lad replied, stacking plates.

"Don't chip my china," Brenda whispered, shooing him off.

To the guest, Darryl said, "My apologies. He doesn't have much excitement in his life."

"No apology required. I'll probably be as star struck when the cavalry arrives."

"You seem so calm about all this," Aunt Bert said.

"I'm the furthest thing from calm, I can assure you," the President remarked. "But when a person faces a situation which bears an outcome he cannot control, there's little sense in panicking over it. You gather information, you prioritize a plan, you put the plan into action."

"And that's what you did. And here you are," Gramps said.

"And here I am," the President confirmed.

The telephone rang.

Lyle Lee was the closest, having just set a load of his mother's good dinnerware in the sink. He answered and listened.

"Sir, it's for you," he called, unnecessarily since the President was already striding toward him full-bore.

"Thank you," the tall man said. Into the mouthpiece he barked, "Raptor." He listened while the Avery family gathered in the archway. Then the man codenamed Raptor told the phone, "Keep me apprised. I'm on standby."

"What is it?" Darryl asked.

The guest turned slowly to face his hosts. "That convoy I spoke of? It's having trouble getting here. Apparently all the vehicles stalled on a perimeter six miles out. Whatever downed Air Force One is crashing all vehicular electrical systems."

"Like my combine," Darryl mused.

"You see? I'm not just telling tall tales," the President said.

"We didn't think that, sir," Brenda said.

"I think we can dispense with the 'sirs' now, don't you? You've invited me into your home. We've broken bread together. We're in the same mess. Please call me by my first name." He smiled again. "Or Raptor, if you prefer. I kind of like that codename."

"So what do we do now, Raptor?" Aunt Bert asked, testing out the name and finding it delightful. They moved from the kitchen into the family room where Darryl set about starting a fire. The wind rattled the windows like angry spirits.

"A detachment of marines is coming on foot. They'll see us safely to the transports and evacuate us to Washington."

"Washington? We can't go to Washington," Darryl said.

"Harvest waits for no man," Gramps put in.

"It's going to have to until we can ensure this hot zone is clear," Raptor said.

"Hot?" Gertie asked, shrugging deeper into her sweatshirt. "It's damn *cold* in here." No one mentioned her language this time.

The President nodded at her math workbook. "Numbers giving you trouble?"

"Story problems. They're the worst."

"Want me to take a peek while we wait?"

Gertie's jaw unhinged. "You'll help me with my homework? *You?*"

Raptor chuckled. "Give me a tough one."

The girl picked up her workbook. "'A ladder hangs over the side of a ship anchored in a port. The bottom rung touches the water. The distance between rungs is twenty centimeters and the length of the ladder is one-hundred-eighty centimeters. The tide is rising at the rate of fifteen centimeters each hour. When will the water reach the seventh rung from the top?'"

The President's brow furrowed. "Let me see that."

Gertie handed over *Practical Mathematics* and scowled at Gramps. She knew nothing would give him greater satisfaction than having the world's most powerful man stumped by a 7th grade arithmetic problem. She knew how Pa and Gramps felt about the President; she'd heard them bemoan him during any number of television appearances. Once, during the State of the Union address, Gramps had actually grown so livid that, red-faced and howling, he'd risen from his wheelchair to slap the TV screen and would have fallen over if Pa hadn't dragged his bony old butt back.

The President pulled a fancy-looking ballpoint pen from his inside pocket, but instead of writing the answer to the question he flipped to the inside cover of the workbook as though scouting a spot for an autograph. As he scribbled, he said, "I'm sending a note to your teacher to get a real arithmetic text for your class. That's a trick question."

"How do you figure?" Darryl asked. "It had numbers and such."

"Smoke and mirrors, Darryl," the President replied. "The answer is much simpler than trying to concoct a meaningless equation to solve it."

"So what is it?" Gramps asked, an edge in his voice.

"If the tide is rising, the water won't rise up the ladder. It will raise the entire boat with it. Smoke and mirrors."

"Smoke and mirrors sounds more like your campaign promises," Gramps said and cackled, slapping a knee.

"Dad!" Aunt Bert wailed, but the President laughed along.

"*Touché,* Gramps," he said, holding his side as if he'd heard the world's funniest joke. He was good, in Brenda's opinion. She'd already decided he'd have her vote come the election next month.

The telephone rang again. The President stood. "May I?" he asked Brenda.

"Of course. Be my guest."

He went into the kitchen alone, though Lyle Lee crept behind to listen.

"—possible gray involvement. Hold your position. Out."

"Grays are aliens, right? So they exist? For sure?" Lyle Lee asked from the archway.

The President hung up and drew a deep breath. "Do you smoke?"

"No sir."

"Care to step outside with me while I partake?"

"Would I!"

"Come on, then. I'll tell you a thing or two."

The wind sighed through the corn. The sky had drained of color and the first stars sparked eastwardly.

The President pulled a pack of cigarettes from the same pocket from which he'd retrieved the upmarket ballpoint. He tapped one out, lit it with a silver Zippo, and inhaled. He regarded the glowing ember thoughtfully, then said, "I was supposed to have quit. Voters see smoking as a sign of weakness, though they themselves are perfectly content to go on puffing. So be a pal and keep a secret, yeah?"

"You bet, sir!"

"How old are you, son?"

"I'll be eighteen in two weeks."

The President raised his eyebrows comically. "Just in time for the election."

"Oh, you have my vote, sir!"

The President grinned and patted Lyle Lee on the shoulder. "Thank you, son. That sets my mind at ease. Now if only we can sway your pa and Gramps."

Lyle Lee looked away, into the corn.

"That was a joke," the President said with a chuckle. "Anyway, would you like to hear a story?"

"I sure would," Lyle Lee said breathlessly.

"When I took office, the very first hour of the very first day, I requested the CIA files pertaining to extra-terrestrials be delivered to my office. I was excited. I couldn't wait. That was the curious boy in me that never grew up. Yes, I was once every bit as awestruck by the prospect of alien life as you are now, young man. Quite honestly, it's half the reason I ran for president in the first place. Knowing for sure—beyond a doubt—that we are not alone in the universe would change everything. Life as we know it would cease to exist. Entire religious foundations would crumble. We would become something else entirely. That's why the government keeps such a tight lid on what we know and I'm not just talking about the little green men. Can you understand that?"

"I guess so," Lyle Lee said.

"Is yours a religious family, son?"

"Some. I mean, we say Grace and go to church. Gran-mama—she was Gramps's wife until she died a few years ago—she used to go every Sunday and make us go too."

"Did you like it?"

"It was all right. Most of it sounded like mumbo-jumbo to me. Granmama used to tell me I'd get it when I grew older. Well, I grew older but it still doesn't make much sense. How could a guy turn water into wine? How could he raise the dead and all that?"

"I asked those exact questions when I was your age," the President said. "I couldn't make all the mumbo-jumbo wash with what I believed about aliens. I had to know, just *had* to. But you know that some things are better left unknown, right?"

"Yeah, I do," Lyle Lee said, kicking gravel down the driveway.

"That said, I'll answer your question. If you still want to know."

Lyle Lee pounced. "I do, I do!"

The President took a final drag on his cigarette before dropping it on the porch step and crushing it out. "When I got back from lunch on that first day I found a single manila folder on my desk, marked with all sorts of stamps like Top Secret and Classified."

"What did it say?" the boy asked eagerly. Starlight shone in his eyes.

"Nothing. The file was empty. They hazed the rookie." The President opened the door to go back inside. "The CIA is a lot funnier than people think."

Lyle Lee stopped his guest in the kitchen. "So what about all that E.T. stuff you were talking about? If the CIA has no file on the grays, what dropped Air Force One out of the sky?"

"I never said the CIA doesn't have files on the grays. I only said I wasn't allowed to view them."

"But you're the most powerful man in the world."

"Tell that to the Director of the CIA."

"Don't you have clearance on all classified information?"

"You learn that in school?"

"Yes sir."

"Then your teachers have done you a disservice. They're naïve to think the President is authorized to tour every little dark corner of Washington."

Darryl stood in the kitchen archway, mustering his full height, a shotgun cradled in his arms.

"Pa, what're you doing?"

"Our guest has a bit of explaining to do."

The President did not look concerned about the weapon. "There's no need for that, Mr. Avery. Tell me what's on your mind."

"Back to misters, are we?" Darryl asked with a snort. "That about 'figgers."

"Pa, you can get in trouble for that," Lyle Lee said. He'd maneuvered between his father and the guest.

"I could," Darryl concurred, "if I thought I had a snowflake's chance in Satan's furnace of getting caught."

"I don't follow," the President said.

"Well how about you follow me to the living room? Something you might find interesting on the tube."

They moved into the living room where the 10 o'clock news unfurled its centerpiece story. The President watched in disbelief as live footage showed a quite intact Air Force One landing safely in Washington. His jaw unhinged as the door opened and the President of the United States emerged, waving and smiling for the cameras. The anchor rambled on about the President's return from a successful campaign run to key western states.

"Lucy, you got some 'splainin to do," Gramps deadpanned from his wheelchair.

"I don't need to explain," the guest said. "You heard me on the phone. I had all the right code words. Obviously I am who I say I am. That is an impostor."

"We heard you say some mumbo-jumbo," Darryl said. "It could've been anyone on the other end of that line."

"Honey, for God's sake," Brenda said to him. To her guest, she said, "I'm sorry, Mr. President. Don't worry, his gun's not loaded."

"It can be soon enough," her husband shot back. "And don't call him 'Mr. President' when he ain't."

"I am though," the guest replied. "I can prove it. Air Force One went down three miles from here. I would be happy to take you there."

"Air Force One just landed in D.C.," Darryl said. "You watched it happen."

"Guys, let's just everyone keep a level head here," Aunt Bert said. "I, for one, wouldn't mind a walk. Although I can't say I'm thrilled at the prospect of seeing dead web-faced men."

"You won't see them because they aren't there," Gramps said. His brushy eyebrows had drawn together as he stared through his spectacles at their guest as if at an enemy through field glasses.

"I'm with Bert. Let's go have a look," Brenda said, eager to ease the tension in the room. She wanted more than anything for her husband to abandon his shotgun, loaded or not.

"I've got a better idea," Darryl said. "Call your man in Washington. Groundhog? I want to hear what he has to say."

"Oh, what's that going to prove?" Gramps growled. "It could be one of his accomplices. Anyone who would go to such lengths to impersonate the President must have a brigade of co-conspirators."

"I can tell, Dad," Darryl said. He nodded to the guest. "Dial, mister."

"Very well," the guest said. He led everyone into the kitchen. Gertie still had her workbook pinched between her fingers. Lyle Lee wore an expression of mixed reverence and fear. The guest dialed and waited with the receiver held loosely so that everyone would be able to hear the voice that answered.

"Groundhog."

"It's Raptor."

A moment of silence. "Please relay your identification code, Raptor."

The guest rattled through a string of numbers with powerful punctuation between each digit.

"Sir, how may I be of assistance?"

"We have a situation."

Another silence. "We're aware of that, sir."

"A potentially hostile one," the guest said. "I need transport immediately."

"Sir, the transports have been recalled."

"On who's authority?" the guest said. Sweat glossed his forehead, just beneath his perfectly barbered hairline.

"Sir, on yours," the person codenamed Groundhog replied. "Terminating connection. Your security code has been revoked and were I in your place, I would consider seeking adequate legal counsel. Local authorities have been notified of your coordinates."

The phone clicked dead.

"That's about what I figured might happen," Darryl said. He stuck a hand in his coveralls and withdrew clutching two bright red shells, which he fitted into the double-barrels of the shotgun.

"Now wait a minute," the guest said. His finger blurred, redialing.

The phone only bounced back the reorder signal, a nippy *bip-bip-bip-bip.* In ten seconds, the line had been shut down. He slapped the receiver into the cradle before snatching it up again and dialing a different number. This time it rang seven times before being picked up.

A female voice issued through the earpiece. "Who is this? How did you get this number?"

"Honey, it's me. I need your help."

A long pause. "It's a federal crime to crank call the White House."

"Sweetheart, I'm in big trouble and I need you to send someone to get me."

"This isn't funny," the woman said. In the background, a man's voice asked who was on the line. The woman answered, "He says it's you."

A man came on, his voice perfectly mirroring that of the Avery family's guest, said, "This is the President of the United States. You've had your fun, but if you call back I'll have no choice but to hand the case over to Secret Service for investigation of harassment."

The phone clicked dead again.

The guest did not so much sit on the floor as dropped to it. He leaned back against the refrigerator, which buzzed against his back like a giant steel beehive. "What's happening here?"

"You tried to pull a fast one," Darryl said. "That's what's happening."

"Swindler, that's what he is," Gramps opined.

"Search him, Lyle Lee."

"Pa—"

"Don't backtalk me, boy."

Lyle Lee stepped hesitantly over to the man on the floor who had been promised the young man's vote next month. Tears trembled in his eyes. "I'm sorry, sir."

The guest did not try to stop the search. Even when the boy pulled first the expensive pen, then a package of cigarettes and silver Zippo, then a small-caliber pistol from the man's jacket, he merely stared ahead at the wall. Brenda gasped when she saw the last item. Ike rumbled low in his throat.

"What were you planning to do with that?" Darryl asked.

The guest blinked around. "I took it from one of my agents. In case I met one of them."

"One of who?"

"*Them,*" the guest repeated. "The grays."

"More lies," Gramps said and clucked his tongue. "And so close to the election."

Then the guest said something Lyle Lee would never forget. Years later, lying in bed as an old man with the upcoming election a long-gone chapter in history, his skin would still crawl when he thought of the guest's final words.

"*Who am I?*"

The most recognizable man in the world had become suddenly and completely anonymous.

"We'd all love to know the answer to that question," Aunt Bert said. "Just more smoke and mirrors, that's all."

"I think you'd better go, sir," Brenda whispered.

"He ain't going anywhere but jail," Darryl said. "I'll be a hero for turning in the impostor of the Prez. Might even get my 'pitcher in the paper. What do you think of that, fella?"

But the guest did not reply. Twenty minutes later, the county sheriff, flanked by two deputies, swung by to pick him up.

"I'll be jiggered," the sheriff said as they led him to the white cruiser with the strobing red and blue lights. "Heckuva makeup job, ain't it?"

Darryl Avery spent the next week smug as a bug in a jug as the news reports unfolded. Neither wreckage of Air Force One nor any dead staffers with weird wet webs over their faces had been discovered in the vicinity.

"Din't I tell you?" Darryl asked his wife during these broadcasts. "Din't I say he was bad news? Glad I din't vote for him."

Brenda thought to point out the inconsistency in her husband's logic, but why bother? He'd never understand anyway. There would be no changing his mind.

The sole piece of seemingly corroborating evidence to support their guest's story was a long, wide track smashed through the corn in a field three miles from the Avery property, which Lyle Lee quickly pointed out to his father.

"So something bent a few rows of crop," Darryl said. "That hardly proves a jet crashed."

"He helped me with my homework," Gertie said. "Got an A-plus."

"About the only good deed he did our family, what after eating our food and running up our phone bill."

"Well, what about our combine? Why did it just quit that night?" Lyle Lee sulked.

"You know well as me she started right up next morning," Darryl argued. "Let it go, son, and be glad your old man's still fast on his toes. Hell, it could be the maniac planned on killing us all."

But Lyle Lee didn't want to let it go. He'd bonded with their guest and hated to think the man had duped them. In fact, Lyle Lee remained convinced the man had at least believed he was who he said he was. Undeniable evidence of such had been etched on the poor guy's face as his story shut down point by point. The poor guy who would likely spend years behind bars as just another felon who'd threatened the President.

A visitor from Washington respectfully but firmly requested the Avery family refrain from discussing the incident outside of the immediate family and he would ensure the story kept clear of media attention. He treated Gertie's workbook cover with an ink eradicating solution until the guest's finely scrawled note vanished as if it had never been. Then the visitor placed a folded check in Darryl's hand and bid them a pleasant evening. Lyle Lee never learned the amount of the check, but he could read its value in his father's eyes. It was at least enough to buy a new combine and a few hundred head of cattle. It also covered his and Gertie's college tuition—to any school they chose.

In the years to come, as Lyle Lee cast votes in each election, he would think over what the guest had said to him that night. About the grays. That even without CIA confirmation, he believed they were a real and possible threat to the world. Any species who could navigate the cosmos could possess the technology to compromise vehicular systems which would shut down a combine and crash a jet, right? They just might know how to recreate the fallen craft and exchange the staff with look-alikes. They could have the means to replace the true President with a decoy of their own design, couldn't they?

Well, couldn't they?

The Field

Sara Brooke

The sun blazed in the sky amid the soupy air of summer. Beneath its unforgiving heat, trampled blades of grass tried desperately to survive the onslaught of its relentless rays, as well as the feet of young campers who enjoyed running back and forth through it.

It was late July in Florida and summer camp was well underway. At Camp Happy Smiles in West Miami, the children were enjoying the fenced in yard where brightly painted jungle gyms and swing sets awaited their eager hands and feet.

One little girl in particular enjoyed these outside jaunts. Her name was Hillary James, and she was a quiet sort, always reading and observing. Hillary didn't have many friends at camp—or in general for that matter—but it didn't bother her one bit. She liked being alone.

It was a Tuesday and there was nothing remarkable about the day, but it just so happened that Hillary had decided to take a walk along the perimeter of the yard. It was enclosed by a green chain link fence that ran along the edges of the property. But beyond the fence, the field continued with weeds, darkness, and infinite possibilities.

Hillary was curious about the field. For a child of nine, there were always limitations and boundaries strategically placed in the most frustrating spots, which led to a constant wondering of what lie beyond the borders—of what was "allowed."

Now was one of those times. As Hillary stared longingly at the field beyond, she wondered what she'd find if permitted to explore it further. Certainly the fields wouldn't be vastly different than the well groomed landscape of the playground yard. There were weeds and the occasional pieces of trash strewn irresponsibly in one spot or another. Flies and mosquitoes buzzed from the camp toward the grasses beyond and seemed to be just as happy. So why was she so drawn to what was on the other side of the fence?

Hillary stood for a few moments looking into the distance when her eyes noticed something glinting in the grass. *What is that?* She wondered. *It looks like a ring.*

Moving closer to the fence, Hillary strained her eyes to get a better look. The spot on the ground would only gleam when she caught the light just right. But it was strange and compelling all the same.

"Hillary," a voice called out. "Time to go inside for snack."

Disappointment filled the little girl's heart as she turned away and headed back to the building where all the children eagerly awaited their afternoon sugar fix.

The next day, Hillary couldn't wait to go back to her new spot along the fence and stare out into the field. As soon as the campers were allowed to go outside and play, she rushed over to the fence and quickly looked to see if she could once again spot the strange glinting in the grass.

As she strained her neck and looked around, her fingers tightly grasping the fence, she noticed something else. There was a hole in the network of links that ran along the bottom of the fence. While not large enough to squeeze through, Hillary wondered why she hadn't seen it before.

As she looked away from the hole and back at the field, her eyes widened because there was something dark in the distance. She watched as it moved slowly, stealthily, hidden by the weeds and bushes. It was close to the ground and seemed to be going in circles. Then, there was a shriek and whatever it was moved out of sight.

Hillary looked around to see if anyone else had heard the shrill sound, but no one acted any differently. Her fellow campers continued to yell and laugh gleefully without a care in the world.

Irritated that no one had noticed anything, she looked back at the ground. Once again, she could barely make out something glinting, but her eyes also caught sight of something else.

A *hand.*

Hillary was so shocked that she jumped back and almost lost her balance, nearly knocking over her camp counselor who was now standing directly behind her. The counselor, a bubbly blonde named Sue, was extremely extroverted and not particularly patient with the quieter campers like Hillary. She was quite annoyed when Hillary would consistently stand by herself at the edge of the yard, not listening when they called everyone in for snacktime.

"Hillary," the counselor sighed, exasperation dripping from her voice. "What is it? Are you okay? Aren't you coming in for your snack?"

The barrage of questions was a bit too much for the nine-year-old to comprehend all at once, so she figured it would be easier to answer the one that made the most sense.

"Sorry, Ms. Sue. I didn't hear you call us in. I was just out here... thinking."

"Thinking? Well, it's summer. You shouldn't spend time thinking. You should be out playing, having fun with the other children. Let's go inside."

With that, Hillary allowed herself to be led back to the camp building, but not before she took a quick look back at the hand.

She was startled to see that it was gone.

Hillary had a plan that she'd devised while lying in bed. It was too difficult to explore the field during normal camp playtime, so she'd need to get out there when no one else was around. The easiest way to do that would be to take on some type of special chore.

The next morning she practiced her speech a few times and then went up to Sue.

"Ms. Sue?"

"Hey there, Hillary. How're you doing this morning? We're going to have a great day at the community pool. Did you remember to bring your bathing suit?"

Hillary took a deep breath and, as calmly as possible, delivered the most eloquent lie of her young life. "Ms. Sue, I wasn't feeling so well, so my mom wants me to stay inside. But I was thinking that instead of just staying indoors, I would help out and collect trash in the yard. There's so much garbage out there that it makes me sad. But I'd be happy to clean it up if you'd like."

Sue sighed and thought about Hillary's request. The child did look a little pale. Perhaps it would be better to leave her at camp, than to have to worry about her wandering off in the pool. The grounds were secure with counselors everywhere, so perhaps it was best for everyone if Hillary did stay at camp and get over whatever cold or illness she had.

"Okay," Sue said. "I think it's great you want to help clean up the grounds. You can go out when we head to the pool. But be sure to let one of the counselors know you're going to be out there. I need you to be careful. You can take a large plastic bag with you so that you've got something to throw the trash in. Okay?"

Hillary gave Sue her sweetest smile and nodded vigorously to demonstrate her understanding. Inside, her heart was hammering. Everything was going as planned.

Hillary watched as her unit left the building and filed into a bright yellow bus. She felt a pang of regret for lying to her counselor, but there was no other way.

She'd been left with one of the other units that was staying indoors for the morning and the counselor for that particular group was a very nice woman named Sheila. Hillary liked Sheila better than Sue because she was kind, gentle, and funny. It made her feel badly to be lying to Sheila as well. But there was a mystery out in the field beyond the fence, and Hillary couldn't stop thinking about it. She needed to figure out what was going on.

Was it a hand I saw? Or was it just my imagination? There was definitely something weird going on.

"Here you go," Sheila said, offering up a large black plastic bag.

Hillary took it and smiled, thankfully.

"Thank you, Ms. Sheila. I'm going to go outside and start cleaning up. Is that okay?"

"Sure. Just come back when you're done. Don't stay out there too long. It's really hot today, and you're getting over a cold."

"Okay."

Hillary took the bag and headed outside. She was so excited it was difficult to not skip or run out into the yard. Trying to make things look as genuine as possible, she took her time and even picked up a few pieces of trash along the way.

When she reached the yard, her eyes immediately focused on the fence. It seemed to be beckoning to her as if to say: *Come to me. There's more to see.*

Come and discover my dark secrets.

The youngster couldn't wait another minute. She rushed over to the fence, the trash bag firmly clutched in her hand. When she reached the chain link barrier, she quickly looked out at the field and once again saw the telltale glinting in the grass.

Then she saw something else again too.

It was definitely a hand, lying near some bushes, partially obscured by weeds and shrubbery.

Her heart pounding now, Hillary knew she had to do something. She quickly looked around and didn't see anyone walking by or loitering—so it was now or never.

Positioning her foot on the fence, she pushed her right shoe down on the links, pulling her little body up as high as possible. Then, she lifted her other foot, and carefully pushed herself up some more, until she was at the top of the fence.

It was a long drop to the bottom, so she turned and tried to carefully climb down the other side. It wasn't an easy trek. Both her legs were full of tiny scratches by the time she got to the ground. Once her feet were on the grass, she turned around and felt a bit dizzy. She'd never quite felt freedom like this before. Being an only child, her parents were constantly coddling her and never quite left her out of their sight. But to have freedom like this? It was all a bit much for the nine-year-old.

Hillary decided it would be best to head toward the item that had been glinting in the grass, then carefully check out the object that looked like a hand. It wasn't as easy as she thought it would be, though. The grass was high and a few times she stumbled on a hidden rock or tree limb in the tall weeds.

As she made her way along the field, she was able to get a closer look at the hand. It was lying near a tall bush beneath a palmetto tree. But first she drew closer and was able to identify what the glinting item was. A ring was lying on the grass. It was set with a diamond and looked expensive. Hillary could only assume the precious item belonged to the hand that was connected to a woman who was lying in the grass.

The woman was dirty and wore a sundress that was stained with dark red spots in different places. Her head was turned toward the tree. Hillary wondered if she was dead. She softly whispered, “Hello…are you okay?”

To her surprise, the woman turned her head and moaned softly.

Relief flooded through the little girl at the realization that she was not standing near a dead person, but someone who was alive. She knelt down next to the woman and whispered, “What happened? Are you okay?”

The woman seemed to have a tough time focusing, but lifted up one dirty hand and pointed to the field. When she spoke, her voice was weak and pained. “Get away while you can. It's in there. It gonna come back soon. You've got to get away.”

“*What* is out there?” Hillary whispered. “*Who?*”

Just then, a voice shouted from the other side of the fence. ”Hillary! Hillary, where are you?”

Oh no, she thought. *I'm in so much trouble.*

“Listen, I've got to go back,” Hillary said to the woman. But I'll come back for you. I promise.”

The wounded woman lifted her head and gave Hillary a brief smile. “There's nothing you can do. It's coming to get me. It's my time. Forget this place. Don't come back.”

Hillary shook her head. The whole thing didn't make sense. Why didn't this woman want to be rescued? In all the movies she'd watched and books she'd read, when someone was hurt, they were eventually saved.

“Hillary…where are you?” the voice shouted again. Hillary recognized it as Sheila's voice. She was obviously very worried.

“I've got to go, I'll come back—”

Suddenly, a growl interrupted her. Hillary turned and saw something behind the tree. It was dark and wore a cloak, like the ones evil villains wore in cartoons on TV.

Hillary had never been more frightened in all her life—but for some reason she couldn't move. “Who're you?” she asked again, her voice tiny and terrified.

“It's not your time, child,” the creature said, each word formed in a guttural monotone. “You are observant, so you see what you shouldn't see. But this is *her* moment now. This is the way things must be.”

The creature came closer and Hillary could feel the temperature change and instantly drop. Bursts of arctic blasts hit her in the face and were so foul that she gagged and turned away. When she looked back, the creature was hovering over the woman in the grass and had fully covered her with its black cloak.

"Hillary!"

The constant shouting of her name jarred her back to her senses, and she turned and ran back toward the fence. She quickly climbed the green chain links without giving any consideration to the fact that her legs were now bleeding from all the scratches and bumps she was acquiring along the way. Hillary made it to the top of the fence and then simply toppled over to the other side. Her ankle twisted at an unnatural angle and she shrieked in pain. Turning her head, she was able to register that the hand was gone and that was the last thing she remembered before her little mind mercifully plunged into darkness.

When Hillary awoke, she was lying on a cot in the nurse's station and was surrounded by concerned faces, including Sheila's and Sue's. Her head hurt and her legs ached, but everything else was a haze.

"What were you doing out there?" shrieked Sue. "Do you know how dangerous that was? How could you've lied to me?"

"Calm down," said Sheila. "Hillary, honey, what were you doing out there in the field? It's dangerous back there with all kinds of snakes and bugs." It was Sheila's gentle voice that reminded Hillary of the injured woman and the creature with the hood. She sat up quickly, her head spinning wildly.

"We have to go back out there," the girl said. "She's hurt—" Hillary's head was pounding. She needed to lay back down and rest.

This time, Sue took over.

"Ok, Hillary. We'll go back to the field and check it out. But you need to lie down now. Your mom is on her way to come and get you."

With that, the blonde counselor stormed off, leaving Hillary alone with Sheila and the nurse. Hillary felt like closing her eyes but before she did, Sheila knelt down and whispered in her ear. "Don't worry, sweetie. We'll go check to make sure everything's okay. Get some rest."

Hillary's mother came to pick her up and took her daughter home where she remained for nearly a week. When the time came to return to camp,

Hillary had promised at least twenty times to never scale the fence again and to always follow the rules.

To her dismay, neither Sheila nor Sue found anything in the field. It turns out there was an easier way to get to the back of the yard—by simply walking over from the parking lot. The counselors searched the perimeter but never found anything.

When Hillary finally returned to camp, things seemed *different*. The world was darker and the nightmares she continued having about the creature in the cloak made it hard for her to sleep.

Everything seemed to move more slowly, and she felt older somehow—like her childhood had passed her by in the blink of an eye.

When the campers were allowed out in the yard, she chose to stay indoors and read. And she never shared with anyone what really happened that day. She felt as if speaking the truth might transport her back to that terrifying encounter in the field somehow.

She did return to the fence one final time, however.

It was the last day of camp and everyone was out playing in the yard, for one final hurrah. No one noticed Hillary as she walked slowly to the fence. She moved as if in a dream and felt her feet gliding along the ground. Even though she'd avoided the fence for weeks, there was now *something* calling out to her—pulling her forward.

Standing in front of the fence, she looked out toward the field. It looked the same as it had before, but something was different about it. Now, she could feel the darkness and the cold in the air that traveled through the weeds and bushes. This place was heavy and frequented by a creature that was of the blackest night with its infinite cold embrace.

When the darkness came near the fence, no one noticed as the little girl disappeared in a puff of black smoke. The only thing that remained in the field was a shimmering diamond ring that lay just on the opposite side of the fence—glinting in the bright Florida sunlight.

Marissa

C.L. Hernandez

"I know you killed her, you smug son-of-a-bitch." The whispered words floated out of Reynolds' mouth on a cloud of cigarette smoke as he watched his neighbor hack at a cluster of weeds with a garden hoe. "A woman like that don't just run away."

Reynolds had no evidence to back up his suspicions, but he knew Benson was responsible for his wife's disappearance; there was no other explanation. Marissa Benson was one of the most subservient women Reynolds had ever seen. Soft spoken and gentle-natured, she drifted ghost-like through the mobile home she shared with her husband, tending to his every need and catering to his every whim. Any man would be proud to have a wife like that; however, she was not quite good enough for Benson. Reynolds heard the late-night screams, had seen the unfortunate woman's occasional black eyes, and he heard the metallic rattle and clank of her husband's empty beer cans as she took the trash bags to the curb every Wednesday.

Reynolds butted his cigarette against a fence post and returned his attention to the rototiller and the still-cool spring soil. His backyard garden was coming along nicely; only a few more yards of it needed to be worked, and he knew where he wanted to plant the corn, beans, pumpkins, and potatoes. The freshly turned earth exuded its rich, primal smell as the churning blades of the rototiller prepared it for planting, and a sleek black crow alit on the fence post to watch. As he worked, Reynolds' thoughts returned to the unfortunate Marissa Benson, her eyes in particular. They were the color of a late summer sky, with just a touch of grey. She was such a pretty, dove-like woman; Reynolds hoped he was mistaken about her fate.

"Damned if you ain't makin' an all-fired racket with that machine!"

Even over the rototiller's motor, Reynolds heard the obnoxious twang of

Benson's voice. He switched off the machine and turned to face his neighbor. Despite the early hour, Benson had a can of Keystone in his hand, and he swigged from it as he leaned against their common fence and surveyed the neat rows of tilled soil.

"It beats shoveling it by hand." Reynolds swiped at his damp forehead with the back of his hand and regarded his neighbor.

"That it does." Benson drained his can of beer, then added, "You'll be wantin' to get them seed potatoes in the ground before it gets too hot." He indicated his own yard with a wave of his hand. "Me, I'm going with a flower garden this season. It's lookin' pretty good, don't ya think?"

Reynolds looked. His odious neighbor's yard was a riot of color: zinnias, freesias, and rose bushes all bloomed profusely in their neatly tended beds, and a flat of purple and yellow pansies sat on the porch, waiting to be transplanted. *Of course it looks good, you moron,* he thought, *you're using your dead wife as fertilizer. You probably chopped her up and ran her through a meat grinder so you could—*

"Don't it look good?" Benson asked again as he eyed the other man expectantly and smiled his gap-toothed smile.

Reynolds nodded. "Looks alright, I reckon. You heard from your wife?"

"Nope. Not a word. She done run off to her mother in Utah, I'm thinkin'." The gap-toothed smile had disappeared; Benson's expression was now tense and guarded.

"Been a few days now. You'd think she woulda contacted you by now. You know, just to let you know she was okay."

"She still might." Benson's faded blue eyes narrowed in an unspoken challenge. "You never know what women are gonna do."

I'm onto you, you bastard. Sooner or later, someone's going to contact the authorities. Who knows, it might even be me. It was all Reynolds could do to keep from saying the words out loud. "I gotta get back to my garden," he said. "Nice talkin' to you." He started up the rototiller again and let the blades chew hungrily at the fertile earth.

He was beginning to wish he hadn't planted the corn. It still had a lot of growing to do, but the stalks were tall and leafy enough to make an odd whispering sound when the wind blew. It didn't bother him during the day when he was out in his backyard garden, weeding, watering, and hoeing; in fact it was rather pleasant then. But at night as Reynolds lay trying to sleep, that soft *husssh, husssh* of the breeze-blown corn drifted in through his open window along with the green scent of the vegetable garden. It was as if a lonesome wraith wandered around out there, whispering to itself. He could hear it even in his sleep, and it unnerved him greatly. Corn harvesting time couldn't come soon enough.

He was soon able to harvest some new potatoes, and he did so on a bright, clear morning in June when the early summer sun was already hot, and a trio of crows hurled avian insults at each other on the fence. The dainty white tubers lay cool and smooth in his hands, and he smiled as he wiped away the dirt. Dinner would be new potatoes, boiled, with plenty of butter and salt. He dug about thirty of them, and their weight strained the seams of the old burlap sack he put them in. Reynolds brought his treasures inside just as the seam split, and several potatoes escaped, rolling every which-way over the kitchen floor. Cussing softly to himself, he gathered them up again, wrapped them in the torn sack, and put them on a shelf in his pots and pans cupboard. They would keep for quite some time there in the cool darkness.

Six weeks after Marissa Benson's disappearance, Reynolds was awakened by a variety of voices coming from his neighbor's yard and driveway. He went to the window and pulled back a corner of the dusty curtain. The first thing he saw was a policeman, stalking back and forth across Benson's yard with an air of great importance. A two-way radio broadcast its incoherent static into the cool morning air, accompanied by the sound of a shovel delving into the earth. Reynolds smiled as a slow realization swept away the last remnants of sleep: someone else had noticed Marissa's absence after all, someone had made the call to the authorities, and they were searching for Benson's wife in the flower garden. He craned his neck to the left and saw Benson himself standing next to the common fence that ran between the two mobile homes. He was flanked by two uniformed officers and looked completely unaffected, almost bored, as he watched his beloved flower garden being dug up and torn to shreds. "They finally caught up to you, I see." Reynolds said the words out loud, despite the open window. "Murderin' bastard."

Benson's head turned on his meaty neck, and when he made eye contact with Reynolds through the dusty window screen, his gap-toothed grin spread slowly across his fat face.

The murmur of voices behind the fence grew louder, and an almost palpable sense of urgency rose from the assembly of people in Benson's yard. Reynolds was reminded of a stirred-up hornets' nest and he almost laughed. A young evidence recovery tech in muddy jeans came into view, and the delicate white bones in the evidence bag he carried were clearly visible. The crazy smile never left Benson's face as he was cuffed and led to one of the police cruisers. He went easily enough; there was no struggle, but Reynolds heard the eerie chuckle in his voice when he spoke. "Looks like you kids can't tell the difference between animal bones and people bones. Oh well, your science guys'll figure it out, then you can kiss my ass as I waltz right on out of my cell."

Twenty minutes later, the only sound Reynolds heard was the *husssh, husssh* of the corn as the wind frolicked in the vegetable garden.

Reynolds lounged in his bed that evening, turning the pages of a garden supply catalog and looking at the items therein with only a mild interest. A half can of warm beer sat forgotten on the nightstand beside him, and the hum of an oscillating fan effectively drowned out the whispering sound of the corn. His eyelids drifted shut, and his hands fell away from the magazine, leaving it tented on his chest.

A commotion from the kitchen yanked him out of his near-sleep, and he sat up with a start, his eyes wide and his ears on full alert. He heard it again—a sound like metal cookware rattling together, followed by a stealthy rustling, just loud enough to be heard over the hum of the fan. Something was exploring the pots and pans cupboard, by the sound of things.

Reynolds got out of bed and headed down the narrow hallway to the kitchen. The cracked vinyl flooring was surprisingly cold beneath his bare feet as he slid open the drawer where he kept his flashlight. His fingers raked through a mess of assorted junk—a broken stapler, rusty screwdrivers, half used rolls of duct tape.

Clank! Shuffle!

A rat, most likely, he thought to himself. *Or one of them damn ground squirrels.* It wasn't the first time a critter had run amok in his kitchen, and he was more annoyed than anything else. His fingers curled around the familiar plastic handle of the big flashlight, and he switched it on; its powerful beam spotlighted the cupboard where the pots and pans were kept. He nudged the door open with his bare foot.

Nothing moved inside the cupboard.

He grabbed a leather work glove from the drawer and put it on before investigating further. Rodents had teeth like tiny chisels; they could bite clear down to the bone. He reached in and moved a saucepan aside, then took out a frying pan and a dented toaster and set them on the floor. He shined the flashlight inside and saw nothing but his burlap sack of new potatoes. He poked at it with the flashlight. Nothing moved, squirmed, squeaked, or tried to rip his face off. *Must be a hole back there somewhere,* he thought to himself. *The little bastard done escaped. Time to set out some rat traps. That'll teach 'em.* Reynolds took the sack with the remaining potatoes inside, and set it on top of the refrigerator. Damned if he'd let some flea-bitten rodent gnaw on the rest of his new potatoes. They were smooth, and creamy, and delicately flavored; probably the best damn spuds he had ever grown.

In the morning, Reynolds arose when the sun was nothing but a pink promise in the sky. The garden was a silent study in grey when he went out to water it, and the breeze was still and heavy with the smell of rich earth, and fertilizer, and green growing things. As he directed the hose between the flourishing plants, he had the uncanny feeling he was being watched from the kitchen window, directly above the bean hills he was watering. Reynolds jerked his head up with the sudden, crazy idea that he would see Marissa's pale, dead face peering out at him through the dirty glass. He saw nothing there but a bottle of dish soap.

Yet...had the corner of the faded gingham curtain twitched, just a little, like someone had stepped away the moment he looked up?

He put down the hose and went back inside. Nothing moved in the dim, musty kitchen. *That damn rat, that's all it was.* He scrubbed a hand down the side of his face and sent a weak, relieved chuckle into the empty kitchen. *I'm freakin' myself out,* he thought. *Living next to a murder scene will do that to a person, I suppose.* He returned to his watering, forcing himself to focus on the beans and the pumpkins. Behind him, the corn began to whisper.

"It was cat bones."

Reynolds whirled around, his heart racing up his throat. Benson stood there, lounging against the fence with the rising sun reflecting off his bald head. "Holy shit, Benson! You don't go sneakin' up on a man like that! The hell's wrong with you?"

"It was cat bones, just like I said. They had to let me go, ain't that somethin'?" Benson scratched his ass and grinned, but his usual good ol' boy next door charm had been replaced by an uneasy darkness, and a spark of crazy burned in each eye.

Reynolds nodded curtly. The words he had wanted to say died on his lips when he saw that crazy, funhouse grin. He was more convinced than ever that his neighbor had killed his wife. "I see," he said cautiously. "I hope she's found real soon."

"They won't find her on my property." Benson fumbled a pack of cigarettes out of his pocket and clamped one between his teeth without lighting it. "She done run away to Utah, like I said. Whatever happened to her after she left has nothing to do with me." He stepped away from the fence and turned to face the rising sun. "But you know, ol' buddy, it's the strangest thing. Last night when I got home, I coulda' swore I heard Marissa callin' me, whisperin' to me, like she had a secret."

Reynolds swallowed hard and turned off the water. "You most likely heard the corn blowin' in the wind," he said quickly. "Look, I gotta go. Got a lot to do today."

"Sure thing." Benson turned to go, still wearing his feral grin. "Got a lot to do myself. Them bastards tore the hell out of my flower beds."

Reynolds avoided Benson as best he could that summer. He set an alarm clock for four in the morning and did his watering then, while his neighbor still slept, and at times he would stay out as late as he could, then park across the street from the trailer park and sleep in his pickup until the lights went out at Benson's place. Sometimes he heard Benson talking in his sleep long into the night, muttering his estranged wife's name over and over, and damned if it didn't sound like the corn whispered back.

The rat traps he set in the cupboards sat undisturbed, yet sometimes at night he could still hear something rummaging around in the pots and pans. Once he heard the cupboard door rattling against its frame, as if something was trying to get out, yet still the traps remained set. It occurred to Reynolds that perhaps it was the wind, not a rat that came in through the wall and rattled that wooden door. He took everything out of the cupboard again, meaning to nail the door shut for now; he would look for the hole in the wall and fix it later. The weather would be cooling down soon; the last thing he needed was another draft in this old place.

As he reached far into the back of the deep cupboard with his hand protected by the heavy glove, he felt something round and lumpy that gave slightly under his leather covered fingers. A familiar stench poured out from the cupboard's dark interior, and Reynolds yanked the object out with a little cry of disgust. Even through the gloves, he could feel the slime on the thing. He hurled the object to the floor and scrubbed his hand on his pant leg. His lip curled in disgust as he looked down at what he had found in the cupboard.

A potato in an advanced state of decay lay on the floor. It had slipped through the hole in the burlap sack, and had rolled to the rear of the cupboard back in May. It had been quietly rotting in there ever since. Long tentacle-like vines, and a few albino leaves had sprouted from the moldering root vegetable, and it oozed brownish-green juices onto the floor. A nose-withering, garbage truck stink filled the kitchen, and he was reminded of something his mother used to say when they cleaned out the cellar in the spring: "Ain't nothin' stinks quite like a rotten potato." Yet it wasn't just the smell that caused him to heave the dead vegetable across the room. It was the *feel* of the thing: warm, and flabby, and soft.

And he was sure it had moved.

"Ridiculous," he said aloud, reaching for a plastic grocery bag. "It's just a damn rotten potato. Potatoes don't move." He picked it up by one of its pale vines and glanced at it briefly before putting it in the bag. A little sunlight might bring those vines around; he might be able to salvage the potato after all. He tied the handles of the grocery bag into a loose knot and set it out on the patio. He would put the potato in the ground tomorrow morning.

Benson muttered in his sleep again that night and spoke his dead wife's name in a strangled whisper. Reynolds slammed his bedroom window and slept with the TV on, the volume turned up high to drown out the sounds of his neighbor's nocturnal madness; they were far worse than the sound of the corn.

The sound of the TV drowned out another noise as well: the blue plastic grocery bag on the patio crinkled and rustled as something shifted inside and tried to find the moonlight.

It was toward dawn when the sound of breaking glass tore Reynolds from sleep. The comforting glow of the patio light was gone, and his bedroom was now a singular dark shadow. He tossed the blankets aside and got to his feet, straining to hear while his eyes adjusted to the blackness.

The sliding glass door rattled, just a little.

Reynolds fumbled through the darkness of his room, found the light switch, then hesitated; maybe it was better to stay hidden in shadow. Whoever was out there might run off if he saw a light come on, and Reynolds didn't want to lose his chance to put a round of bird shot in his sneaky ass. It was Benson, most likely; he'd been acting crazier than a shithouse rat lately. He found his shotgun next to the dresser and crept silently down the narrow hallway toward the sliding glass door. Through a rip in the second-hand curtains, he could see the silent, moon-washed patio. Wanting a better look, he moved his face closer to the hole. He heard a dragging sound now, and a low whimper, like a very young child trying to move a heavy garbage bag. Something hit the glass in front of his face, and Reynolds leaped backwards, nearly blowing his foot off in panic.

A pale, slender tentacle explored the sliding glass door, leaving behind a trail of clear slime, then stretched across the cracked cement toward the patio gate. It moved like an octopus tentacle, hunching and knotting as it dragged itself forward. That sliding sound again, and a low, sad whimper. Another tentacle appeared next to the first, then shot across the patio and wrapped itself around the gate. They were as big around as table legs, perhaps seven feet long fully stretched, and smooth, without suction cups. Once more, that garbage bag sliding sound, and the thing those tentacles were attached to came into view.

A lumpy, oval shaped body, the size of a large dog, slid across the cement on its own slime trail. An undulating ripple ran across the top of it, and six more tentacles shot out and writhed across the slime-coated cement. Wrapped around one of them was the blue plastic grocery bag.

The shotgun slid from his hands and thudded to the floor; Reynolds flattened himself against the wall, unable to tear his eyes away from the hole in the curtain. Although fear had stolen his voice, his lips still moved frantically as he soundlessly recited every prayer he knew. If he had been drinking, it would have been more believable. His mind had played some cruel tricks on him before after a long night out, but Reynolds hadn't been drinking; he wasn't even hung over.

The writhing, sliding monstrosity on the patio still resembled the potato it had once been. The color of its body was still the same, light brown and speckled with dirt, and its slithering vine-tentacles were still decorated with creamy, delicate leaves. It had eight vine-tentacles now, four to a side, and its plump, potato-brown body no longer dragged painfully across the cement.

The potato-thing stopped moving then, and its slime coated body tensed. A circle of eight bumps rose up from the main body, and the tentacles stiffened, became more arachnid in shape. A ragged opening appeared at one end of the body, and it formed a grimace as the creature wailed again in its mournful, childlike voice. White, human-like teeth appeared in the lipless mouth, and they began to rattle together, making a sound like manic castanets. The creature crouched low on its spider-like legs, then launched itself at the sliding glass door.

Reynolds had never seen anything move so fast: it broke through the glass and knocked him down before he could reach the back door. The powerful, leaf studded legs grabbed him and spun him around; then pinned him to the wall. The white, human-like teeth chattered inches from his face, and slits appeared in the round bumps on the top of its body. The slits widened, and the bumps became eyes; eight eyes the color of a late-summer sky with just a touch of grey.

"Marissa!"

His voice returned just long enough for him to utter the dead woman's name. There was no mistaking those eyes, even though there were eight of them now. They swiveled in their sockets, all eight of those lovely, blue, very human eyes, and they gazed steadily at Reynolds as he lay quivering and terrified in the confines of the Marissa creature's legs.

She had come back as best she could. It didn't help that her husband had cut her into such small pieces before he had buried her in Reynolds' garden plot. Her vengeful spirit had to use whatever means it could in order to come back from the dead and pay her husband a visit. The wind in the corn was her voice, whispering promises of revenge long into the night, just loud enough for her murdering husband to hear. From the corner of his eye, Reynolds saw a fountain of dirt rise up, then a long green vine with a few small pumpkins clinging to it eased itself up the side of the fence. The end of the vine wavered and hesitated a moment, as if it was testing the air, then it climbed down the other side, dragging its length and a few more pumpkins with it. Next it would be the beans and their tough, sturdy runners that would go over that fence and slither through the dirt over to Benson's trailer.

Like the vegetable garden, Marissa had grown healthy and strong in the rich black soil; all she needed was a little tender loving care.

The blue eyes rolled again, casting a downward glance at Reynolds, and the Marissa creature released him, as if it realized it had the wrong man. His legs shook too badly to stand on them, and he slid across the floor on his ass until he was backed up against the wall again. The eyes blinked, all eight of them at once, and the dark, curled lashes fluttered. A long, shapely vine-leg shot out and scrabbled at the knob to the front door.

Marissa wanted out.

Reynolds' voice escaped him again, and his lips moved soundlessly in frantic prayer as he reached for the doorknob, turned it, and threw the door open wide. Marissa bolted through the open doorway, faster than any creature Reynolds had ever seen, then she scuttled over the lawn, tearing out great chunks of it in her haste to get to the mobile home next door. He watched her go, hearing the sound of her bustling tentacles as they rattled the gravel in the driveway.

Reynolds scooted backward down the long narrow hallway to his bedroom. He reached his TV and turned it on with the volume as high as it would go. Hopefully it would drown out the screams when they started next door.

Mrs. Alto's Garden

Patrick Lacey

"I love your garden," Kristen said as she crossed into her new neighbor's yard. The old woman was kneeling in front of the most beautiful collection of plant life Kristen had ever seen. The woman turned and smiled a warm smile that reminded Kristen of her grandmother.

She held her hand out to the woman. "Kristen Foreman," she said. "I'm your new neighbor.

The old woman stood up quickly, as if osteoporosis hadn't yet taken effect, though that was unlikely. The woman looked ancient, with deep lines carved into her face. She held out a liver-spotted hand to Kristen. "Betty Alto. Very nice to meet you."

"Have you lived here long?" Kristen looked around, noticed Betty's colonial, which looked like it had been painted recently. She couldn't say the same for her new home but she and her husband had known it was a fixer-upper when they'd made a bid.

"Just about all my life. We bought the place when my husband came back from the war. Going on sixty years if you can believe it."

"Your husband…" Kristen trailed off and felt her face turn the color of Betty's tomatoes. Blood red.

"He passed away a few years ago. Went in his sleep. It was very peaceful and no need to say you're sorry, dear."

She gave that smile again and Kristen felt all the embarrassment drain from her face.

"May I ask how you manage to have such a wonderful garden? I've never seen anything like it."

"A whole lot of time on my hands and years of practice. It's just a hobby, really, but I guess you could say I've become somewhat of an expert."

It was an understatement. On either side of the front steps lay two vegetable gardens, exploding with cucumbers and pumpkins and carrots. And the flowers—they were almost beyond description. There were tulips and peonies, petunias and red columbines, all with colors bursting, emitting a pleasant glow.

One of them in particular caught her eye, a small yellow flower with miniature yellow tendrils. Kristen pointed. "That one is new to me."

Betty nodded. "The prickly pear cactus rose. It's native to Arizona and Mexico."

"How on earth did you get it to grow here?"

"Easy enough. The truth is, you can grow anything if you go about it the right way." Betty's eyes floated to the left. "That your husband?"

Kristen turned around. Mike was still unloading the U-Haul. She'd lost track of time. He was not going to be happy. He was already grumpy from the drive and she knew they were in for a fight later. "That's Michael, alright."

Betty waved but it didn't look as though Mike noticed. That or he was ignoring the both of them.

"He's a professor. He was offered a full-time position with tenure at UMAINE. We're from upstate New York. We were hoping to stay local but we couldn't be picky. Money's been tight to say the least."

"Nothing wrong with that. As long as you like peace and quiet and the occasional blizzard, I think you'll be happy to call this place home."

"Doesn't sound all that bad." She smiled but it was empty. The truth was that Kristen would've rather moved anywhere else in the entire world than Maine. She already felt trapped somehow, like the state itself was closing in on her.

"You want to give me a hand here?" It was Mike. "Or would you rather I finish unloading our life's belongings myself?"

Kristen rolled her eyes as if her husband was just cracking a joke. "If you'll excuse me, I've got to be going. It was so nice to meet you."

Betty shook her hand once more. "Pleasure's all mine. Come over whenever you'd like. I've got a wine cellar and I hate drinking alone."

"I can assure you I'll be taking you up on that." Kristen waved and headed toward her driveway.

Mike tossed her a box. She caught it and almost toppled over. When he turned around she spoke silently to his back. *Go fuck yourself, Your Highness.*

Michael stood atop a ladder, trying to screw in a light bulb in the den. He held his hand out but she didn't notice.

Through the windows she could see Betty on her porch, sipping away at something. There was something captivating about that woman but Kristen could not figure out just what it was yet.

Michael cleared his throat. "You can sleep later. Hand me the light bulb, will you?"

Like clockwork, Kristen thought.

The fight she'd predicted earlier was unfolding before her. She understood he was stressed, that he had a ton of work to get done at his new job, let alone around the house, but she'd had just about enough. She'd moved to East Bumfuck for him and for some damned reason he'd seemed to forget that.

She shot him the dirtiest look she could manage. "Why don't you come down off of that high horse for one second and talk to me like a human being?" She handed him the bulb but it slipped through his fingers, falling to the floor and shattering.

That did it.

"What the hell did you just say?" He stood on the ladder, talking down to her on two different levels. "Look, I don't think you understand how much I have on my mind right now."

"Maybe I don't but that doesn't give you the right to treat me like a fucking dog."

He laughed and gave her that shit-eating grin she'd grown to hate so much. "Typical. Let's put the spotlight on you because you've got it so damned hard. Tell me, is it difficult to sit at a computer all day and make boring stuff up?"

"I'm a writer, Michael. They pay me to make stuff up. What do you want from me?"

"A little support. Not too much to ask for I don't think."

"Support?" She chuckled and waved him away, started toward the door.

"Go ahead," he said from behind. "Walk away. It's what you do best."

"You can stop blaming me for how your life turned out, you poor soul. You had to settle for a state school instead of Ivy League. God forbid."

She heard him scream but she'd stopped listening. She stepped outside and looked around, noticed a few peering faces in the windows across the street. *Say hi to your new neighbors,* she thought and wiped at her eyes.

"Everything okay, dear?" Betty still sat on her porch swing, rocking back and forth slowly.

Kristen felt her face flush for the second time that day but it was lost in the darkness. "Yes, I'm fine. I'm so sorry about that. Michael's not usually like this."

"No need to apologize. All men are the same when you come down to it. Some are just better at covering it up." Betty waved her over. "You look like you could use a nightcap."

"That sounds lovely." Kristen crossed the yard and stepped up the front steps of Betty's porch.

The old woman went inside and came back out with an empty glass. She poured wine from an ancient-looking bottle and handed it to Kristen. "Give that a try."

She sipped and closed her eyes. She'd had wine before but nothing like this.

Betty finished off her own glass and poured herself anther. "Smooth, isn't it? I've been saving it for a special occasion but those seem to be rare these days."

"This seems special enough." Kristen took another sip and again marveled at the taste.

"I don't mean to be nosey, dear, but I couldn't help but overhear you saying something about a state school. I take it your husband was aiming for something higher?"

She looked into her glass and fidgeted her fingers along the stem. "His father was a professor at Dartmouth. Michael sent out applications to the top two hundred private universities in the country but not one called him back. I understand how frustrating that must have been but he got himself a job—with tenure track for god's sake."

"My husband worked at the leather factory most of his life. It wasn't glamorous but he worked his way up to Assistant Manager. Sometimes you have to start from the bottom. Just like flowers in a way. Of course he was also an insufferable prick and the world is better off without him."

Kristen turned her head toward the garden, unsure what to say. Even this late the colors seemed to emanate from each bulb, like a miniature version of the northern lights. They were stunning.

"I'll tell you what," Betty said. "How about I give you a hand with your own garden once you're all unpacked? Show you a few of my tricks."

"I'd like that." Despite Betty's comment about her husband, Kristen again felt as though this woman were the embodiment of all grandmothers, nurturing and kind but also full of piss and vinegar. Despite how dreary the rest of the town seemed, Kristen found herself feeling a little better about the move.

"And don't worry about your husband," Betty said. "He'll come around soon enough. Once he removes his tail from between his legs."

Kristen almost choked on her wine.

She woke during the night covered in sweat. The air conditioner stood in the corner of the bedroom, lying on the floor instead of in the window. Michael said something in his sleep and rolled over, his hand cupping her breast. Despite herself, her nipple grew hard and she thought about waking him up.

Walk away. It's what you do best.

She tossed his hand away.

She stood up and stretched and used the bathroom.

On her way back to bed, she caught movement outside. The moon was bright. It lit the entire street, casting long shadows everywhere. At first it looked like a stray dog but then it seemed much too big.

The figure was in Betty's backyard, peering around, and Kristen thought for a moment that it was a prowler. Her heart began to pound. The figure turned toward her and she was sure she'd been spotted.

But that wasn't what made her skin crawl.

It was Betty herself. The old woman walked slowly, carrying a flashlight in her hand, heading toward the woods behind their houses. *Into* the woods, Kristen realized. What the hell was an elderly woman doing going into the woods at this time of night? It should not have bothered her so much but she felt something like dread. She couldn't explain it and that made matters worse.

Kristen watched for a few more moments until Betty disappeared from her view entirely, swallowed by trees and darkness.

Kristen snuck out early the next morning, running out the front door before Michael had a chance to look up from the morning paper. Not that he would've said anything. He loved to lay on the silent treatment, loved to make her feel like she was just a piece of furniture.

From what Kristen saw on her run, the rest of the surrounding streets were much of the same. The houses varied from colonial to Victorian, the yards all neatly trimmed. She made a note to visit downtown later on, hoping it would offer something different.

After a half hour her legs and lungs began to burn. She slowed down, leaning her hand against a telephone pole for support, which was where she saw the two posters.

Below the ad for guitar lessons was a flyer for a missing cat (Oscar) and below that was another flyer for a missing man (Andy Peterson). He'd last been seen over two weeks ago and there was a reward for any information regarding his whereabouts.

His face seemed to watch her from the black and white frame.

She shook her head and started to jog again.

Maybe Andy can come back and take Michael with him.

She laughed but part of her knew it wasn't really a joke. Part of her knew where her marriage was heading if something didn't give.

She rounded the block and began to slow as her house came into view.

Mrs. Alto was tending to her garden. *Does that woman ever go inside?* Kristen thought.

Which brought her back to last night, watching through the window as Betty made her way into the woods. The sweat began to feel like cold rain drops on her skin.

Betty looked up from her work and waved. She wore oversized gloves and there were dirt streaks on her face. "Beautiful day, isn't it?"

"Sure is." Kristen slowed to a stop and tried to catch her breath.

"How was your first night in the new home? Get any sleep?"

"None worth mentioning." She cleared her throat. "What about you?"

Something changed in Betty's expression, almost too fast to notice if you weren't looking for it, but Kristen saw it just the same. A narrowing of the eyes and then it was gone, replaced with that warm smile. "Slept like a rock," she said. "I don't think I woke once."

That night Kristen slept on the couch. It was usually the other way around when they were fighting but she didn't feel up to arguing with Michael any more than necessary. She plopped herself down and pretended to fall asleep in front of the TV until she heard him walk up the creaky stairs and shut the bedroom door.

Eventually she dozed off but she woke after a few minutes to see a flash of light through the window. Her pulse quickened and she risked a look outside.

Just as the night before, she saw Betty, a flashlight in one hand and something else in the other. It was too dark to make out but it was roughly the size of a small pillow.

The woman looked around, trying to spot any unwanted observers, then she made her way back into the woods.

Before Kristen could question her motives, she was throwing on her pants and shoes. She opened the front door and made her away around the side of the house. From here she could just make out the beam of the flashlight.

She kept her distance and followed Betty.

Her first thought was *why the hell are there spotlights in the middle of the forest?* That's what they looked like at least. After twenty minutes of following Betty from afar, they arrived at a small clearing. Kristen was still too far to know for sure what she was looking at, but something a few yards away was giving off light. Not just one color, but dozens, maybe hundreds. It reminded her of a rainbow and she almost could have smiled under other circumstances.

Not here, though, because as she crept closer, wincing whenever her feet crunched leaves, she saw the source of the lights.

Her eyebrows wrinkled and her mouth opened.

It was another garden, much bigger than the one in front of Betty's home. Whereas the first garden had *seemed* to give off light, this one was no illusion.

Every plant and flower was lit by a different shade. There was nothing familiar about any of these species. No tulips or petunias. All were foreign to her as if they were the only ones of their kind in existence. Each one was deformed somehow, with strange patterns covering the petals and some that looked like mutated vegetables.

Kristen squinted and thought she saw a few with eyes and mouths, with teeth. She shook her head as if telling herself she was having one hell of a nightmare.

Every plant and flower and vegetable was swaying and it wasn't from the wind.

She jumped as she heard a crash. When she turned her head to the left, she covered her mouth.

The object Betty had been carrying was not a pillow.

It was furry and fluffy and unmistakably feline.

Betty set the limp body of Oscar onto the ground and picked up what looked like a shovel. She began to dig. A few minutes later, she tossed the cat into a newly dug hole and shoveled the dirt back on. She patted it and picked up another item. Streams of water began to shower over the spot on the ground.

A watering can. *She was watering a dead thing.*

Kristen couldn't watch anymore. Her stomach heaved and she backed up slowly until she was far enough from the garden, then she broke into a run, not stopping until she was back inside her living room.

She nearly made it to the toilet but missed by a few feet. Her supper spilled onto the floor.

Since sleep was no longer an option, she paced until morning then settled for a scalding shower, hoping the heat could somehow take away what she'd seen.

We've got to get out of here, she thought as she undressed. *We've got to move to another town. Hell, I don't care if it's filled with more hicks than this one.*

Except that they'd already closed on the house and moved in everything they owned. She could see Michael's face now as she gave him the proposition.

And she could see two other things in the mirror.

Her skin was ghostly pale and she wore only one earring. She'd been wearing a set of pearls Michael had bought her for their second anniversary, but now there was one missing and her blood began to rush into her ears, because she had an idea of where and when she'd dropped it.

She looked her reflection in the eyes. It wasn't a big deal. There was no way Betty could find a single pearl in the dark. It was impossible, no matter how familiar the woman was with the land.

Kristen kept repeating the words in her head until she was done showering and drying her hair. She could smell coffee from downstairs and she thought now was as good a time as any to talk to her husband, to prepare for the fight to end all fights.

She walked downstairs but stopped just before the entryway to the kitchen. Michael was talking to someone and by the time she registered to whom the second voice belonged she was shivering despite the early morning heat.

Kristen lifted her lower foot, ready to head back upstairs, but the lowest step creaked. She closed her eyes and bit her lip.

Michael called up to her. "That you, Kris?"

She paused, opened her dry mouth. "Sure is." She put on the biggest smile she could manage and walked in to the kitchen. Everything spun around her as she saw Mrs. Alto sitting at the table.

"Morning, dear," Betty said.

"Morning. I see you've met my husband."

"Sure have. You didn't tell me how lovely he was. You're truly a lucky woman."

Michael poured himself a cup of coffee. He was smiling. The look seemed unfamiliar to Kristen. "Betty here went to grad school for English. We've been talking about Wordsworth for the last half hour."

"That's right," Betty said. "I always did prefer books to movies. They're my favorite thing in the whole world. Aside from my garden that is." She didn't look Kristen in the eyes when she spoke the last words but she didn't need to.

Michael sipped his coffee and Kristen tried to signal him with her eyes, hoped her thoughts could somehow drift over to his, but he paid no notice.

Mrs. Alto yawned and stood up. "Well, I've got to be going. Supposed to be a hot one today. My little lovelies are going to need all the water they can get."

She smiled at the both of them, her eyes lingering on Kristen.

She stopped just before the door and turned around. "Oh, I almost forgot. I found this on the ground." She held out her hand but Kristen already knew what was resting in her palm. "Would it happen to belong to you, dear? Looks like something you'd wear."

Kristen held her breath, nodded, and took the pearl earring from Betty's hand.

She watched from the living room as Betty made her way back to her house. When she was sure it was safe, she stopped Michael as he was getting ready to head out the front door. "What's wrong?" he asked.

"We need to talk."

He sighed. "Look, I know I haven't been the best husband lately."

"No. Not about that."

"Fine. I know I snap at you too much, too. Once we're settled in—"

"Michael, we need to move."

A long pause. "What?"

"We can't stay here."

"And why the hell not?"

"It's Mrs. Alto. I don't trust her."

Before she could say anything else, he was laughing but there was nothing funny about it. The shit-eating grin was back, the one that seemed to say *you're pathetic, you know that?*

"I'm being serious."

"Yes, I'm sure you are." He fixed his tie and grabbed his keys. "Look, I've got to meet with some of the faculty at the school. I'll be home late so you should eat without me."

"Michael, I don't think you're listening to me."

"No, I'm not." He left in a hurry, slamming the door behind him.

In the silence afterward, Kristen tried to weigh her options. A breeze blew in through the living room window, the one facing Betty's house. Though Kristen couldn't see anything from here, she still felt eyes on her.

She ran over and pulled it shut then she closed the curtains.

By the time evening rolled around, Michael still wasn't home. Though he hadn't given her a precise time, something didn't feel right. It was just a meeting, maybe a little bit of mingling and ass kissing. It wouldn't have taken all morning and afternoon.

Kristen watched the driveway, her heart kicking every time she saw headlights.

You son of a bitch, she thought. *Here I am waiting for you, hoping I'm just going crazy, when I should be leaving.*

She picked up the phone and dialed the university. It took ten minutes of talking in circles to be connected to his office. The phone rang but it went unanswered.

She went back to the living room window. The driveway stood empty.

It was getting dark.

Though her mind screamed at her, she peeked behind the curtains facing next door. Mrs. Alto's lights were all off. There was no flashlight beam.

Of course there wasn't, because Kristen had imagined all of it. There was probably some reasonable explanation for everything. There had to be. Because if there wasn't, that would mean everything she'd seen in the other garden was real, and that couldn't be.

She paced and tried not to look at the clock until she couldn't take it anymore. It was eight. Michael had been gone for nearly eleven hours. Everything was not okay.

She gritted her teeth and searched for her own flashlight, and then the largest steak knife on the rack. She slipped out the backdoor and made her way into the woods, retracing the path from the night before.

The familiar glow came at her from afar. She winced at first as if she was looking into the sun. When her eyes adjusted she made her way forward, up the hill until the clearing came into view.

The night garden lay before her, hundreds of rotten and deformed species of flowers and plants and vegetables, all seeming to writhe on their own accord, as if to a hidden pulse.

Something snapped at her feet.

She fought back a scream as she looked at the thing on the ground. It was shriveled and misshapen, a squash that had been left out too long. There was a small opening in the middle and she told herself it wasn't a mouth until it tried to close around her foot. She kicked at it, backing away. It lunged toward her and she dodged it, bringing her foot up and then down. Her heel made impact and she felt its body become pulp.

It let out a small yelp.

Something rustled in the clearing and she turned her attention back to the garden.

There was a figure amid the bright colors. It was carrying something much larger than a cat.

Mrs. Alto raised Michael's body above her head as if he were no heavier than a pillow. She tossed him into an open hole, grabbing her shovel.

Deja vu came over Kristen and then she remembered the man's face from the poster. She had a hunch he was not just missing.

Kristen narrowed her eyes, looking for some sign of life from Michael but she was too far away. She tightened her grip on the knife and charged forward, through the slithering things on the ground. The few times she dared to look, what she saw was enough to make his spine stiffen.

A pumpkin-like thing with a dark brown vine squeezing its face like a boa constrictor. A root, vaguely resembling a potato, with bulging and squirming veins in its forehead. A tomato, half burst open, with dark juices escaping as other things lapped at them.

This was not a garden; this was a nightmare.

She dodged as best she could, trying to avoid teeth that should not have been real.

A few feet away from Mrs. Alto, she stopped to catch her breath and pointed the knife at the woman. "Put the shovel down."

Betty continued to toss dirt onto Michael. Only his face and neck were still visible. "Had a feeling you'd stop by, dear."

Kristen took a step forward.

"I don't think that's such a good idea."

Another step.

"So be it." Betty whistled as if she was calling for a dog but instead what came were vines, countless vines that emanated from the ground and wrapped themselves around her ankles, calves, and finally her thighs.

Mrs. Alto smiled. "Now why the hell would you come after your little dipshit of a husband? Is he really worth getting yourself killed over? You ask me, no man is worth a second thought, much less your life. My husband, I thought he was God's gift to the world—at first anyway—but then the years rolled by and he started going bald and gaining weight, and then he took to drinking just a tad too much, and then he got it in his head that he could have me any which way he wanted me. I struggled at first but eventually learned to give in because it hurt less that way. But even farther down the road, you realize you can only take so much from a man before you lose control of yourself."

Kristen tried to kick her legs but they were frozen in place. She looked down at the knife, and tried to steady her hand.

"I used a little bit of Draino, poured it into his coffee. Not enough to kill him but he didn't leave bed for a week. Then I settled with antifreeze and that, dear, did the trick. I thought I would've felt better once he was dead but I just got angrier. So I dug up his good for nothing body and I dragged him out here. I spit on him, kicked him, and then I cut off the one thing left that made him a man."

Kristen tried not to listen. She breathed deeply and readied herself.

Betty tossed the shovel aside. Her face was demonic in the light of the garden. "I buried him here. I'd visit him every so often…to tell him how much I hated him. One day I got myself stuck in a rainstorm and right before my very eyes I saw the strangest thing. A bud peeked out of the soil. I knew then that the best way to make new life is to start fresh. Death is the best fertilizer."

Kristen sliced at the vines. They recoiled like wounded tentacles, slipping back into the ground. She dove toward Betty and brought the blade into the woman's side.

In the distance was the sound of thunder, loud like an explosion.

The things in the garden began to mewl. Each one opened its mouth and turned it toward the sky as it opened up, letting forth rain and lightning. They drank.

Kristen grabbed the shovel and made her way back to Michael but her foot gave out. She looked down to see Betty holding onto it, smiling.

"It's a part of life. *You can't change the natural order of things, dear!*"

Kristen grabbed the nearest vegetable, a cucumber that was covered in thorns the size of crayons. She shoved it into Betty's mouth.

She picked the shovel up again and started to unbury her husband.

"That was delicious," Michael said, grabbing both their plates and bringing them over to the sink. She'd made beef stew, his favorite.

She stood up and stretched. "Thanks for doing those."

"Don't mention it. Would you like to watch TV?"

They sat on the couch. He put his arm around her and she sighed. One and a half months without a fight. He had woken up a different man and she hoped it stayed that way.

As their show broke for a commercial, the light above the couch went out.

"You want to get that?" She asked.

"Sure thing." He stood on the cushions "Could you pass me a bulb?"

Kristen grabbed one from the pantry and handed it to him. It slipped out of his hands, breaking apart when it struck the floor. *How familiar.*

He opened his mouth and then paused. "No problem. I think we've got some spares downstairs."

"Would you mind getting them, dear?" Kristen smiled. She imagined a bulb of a different kind sprouting out of his ear.

The Longing

John Grover

Ethan stared darkly at the adoption agency's rejection notice, but it was Todd's heart that was broken. He hated seeing Ethan in pain or upset, and he knew how much this meant to his partner.

Todd moved from the back doorway where he'd been watching quietly and put his arms around Ethan, squeezing him with warmth. "I'm sorry, Sweetie."

"It's not fair," Ethan mumbled. His voice wavered a bit.

"I know."

"We've been together ten years and five of those we've been trying to have a child. *Five years.*"

"It'll happen; we just need to be—"

"No, it won't." Ethan pulled from Todd's arms and turned to face him. "We have too many strikes against us. It's not just that we're gay. It's my faith, too. They're afraid of it. They don't understand it."

"There are other Wiccans with children, Sweetie."

"Not gay ones."

Ethan crumpled the rejection notice and threw it into the trash bucket by the back door. He walked out to the sun porch and plopped himself into a wicker chair.

Heavy sulking was in store. Todd dreaded the sleepless nights, the awkward silences and the eating binges he knew would follow. He quickly knelt beside his partner and took his hands.

"We'll move to Massachusetts," Todd said, his eyes glowing, his smile warm. "We can get legally married there, and then it might be a little easier to have children."

"We shouldn't have to." Ethan looked out the window.

Todd followed his gaze to their herbal garden. The dying sun bathed it in shades of orange and violet.

"I want to raise a family here," Ethan added, "the place I've lived all my life. We should be just like anyone else. I won't be chased from my home."

"No one's chasing us. It was just a suggestion. I hate seeing you like this."

"I'm sorry, Todd. You know I'm not upset with you. It's just so frustrating."

"C'mon," Todd stood with a sly look in his eye and pulled Ethan from the chair. He loved the way the last bits of sunlight glimmered through his salt-and-pepper hair. "I know something that will take your mind off all this."

They walked hand in hand down the hall of their three-story Victorian home. The hardwood floors had recently been refinished and the walls repainted. They had worked hard to restore the foreclosed property they had purchased together six years ago. Now it was impeccable, from the crystal chandeliers to the Persian rugs.

Todd glanced at his pride and joy on the walls as they made their way. Black and white photos he'd taken of landscapes and portraits of their friends hung in antique frames. His favorite was the black and white of himself and Ethan that rested at the base of the staircase.

A smile lit Todd's face as they ascended the stairs. His hand slid along the hundred-year-old banister until they reached the second floor, where the master bedroom awaited.

To their right, a smaller set of stairs, unadorned and in need of a touchup, twisted up to the third floor, which housed only one room, Ethan's meditation space. His place of sanctuary. A room Todd didn't enter very often.

The antique four-post bed was regal with its silk sheets and myriad of exotic pillows. It felt like a stack of clouds against Todd's skin as he climbed into it with Ethan, allowing it to fold around them.

Todd pulled his partner close, kissed him deeply, and moved his hands softly over his chest. The heat between them ignited. The dance had begun.

Ethan's skin was the color of amber in the candlelight that glowed in the back of the room. Todd could not take his eyes off him. After all these years, Todd was still mesmerized by his man. His senses drank him in deeply. The scent of Ethan was tantalizing; his touch electric. No one made Todd feel safer.

Afterward, they cuddled without saying a word until Ethan looked up from his bliss and pursed his lips.

"What?" Todd asked.

"I'm sorry about earlier. I just get so outraged about it sometimes."

"Sure." Todd ran his fingers through Ethan's hair. "I know how important it is to you."

"Do you?" Ethan's eyes were damp with tears. "When I first realized I was gay, the thing that hurt the most was the thought that I could never have children. I thought it would never be in the cards for me. Gay people don't have children, for Christ's sake. Much later, I found out I was wrong. Since then, I've never been able to get it out of my head."

"It'll happen. Look at David and Phil."

Ethan frowned. "David's sister was the surrogate for Phil. She carried their son. I'm an only child, Todd, and you only have brothers. There's no one to help us. I'm alone in this."

"Hey," Todd took a serious tone. "You're not alone in anything. I'm right here."

"You know what I mean."

"Let's turn in early and have a big breakfast tomorrow."

"I think I want to be alone for a while." Ethan climbed out of Todd's arms and left the bed. He reached for his pentacle necklace on the nightstand and slipped it around his neck. "I want to meditate on this upstairs in my room."

"Okay. Are you all right?"

"Yes my hot Toddie, I'm all right." Ethan smirked before bending to Todd and pecking him on the cheek. "Don't wait up for me."

"Okay." Todd hugged his favorite pillow and watched Ethan leave the room. He heard soft steps above; his eyes traced them across the ceiling until they dwindled. With a sigh, he slid under the covers and closed his eyes.

Todd didn't know what time it was when he heard the bedroom door creak open. All he knew was that the room was engulfed in darkness, and Ethan's side of the bed was still empty.

Todd lifted his head and saw a figure silhouetted in the doorway. His eyes adjusted slowly to the dark. At first anxiety coursed through him, but the voice calmed him instantly. Although it didn't quite look like him, he knew it had to be Ethan.

"I've found it," Ethan said. "I've found the answer to our problems."

"Huh?" Todd mumbled as he tried to make sense of the words. Strangely, a light from the far end of the hall illuminated something in Ethan's arms. It was a book, its binding broken, its cover faded and worn. Todd smelled the musty pages from across the room.

"It took me hours of research and many calculations, but I think it will work. With your help."

"Yeah, okay…whatever you need, Sweetie." Todd squinted and yawned. He pulled the sheets tight over his chest.

"Thank you." The words seemed to whisper from somewhere behind him.

Todd looked up again and saw the bedroom door close gently. Exhausted, he rolled over, already forgetting the odd exchange.

The first thing Todd did when he opened his eyes the next morning was turn and check for Ethan. His partner was nestled beside him, covers pulled up to the tip of his nose, snoring softly.

A smile ran across Todd's lips. He wondered what time Ethan had finally made it back to bed. It must have been late. Todd had most likely been dead to the world, because he had never even heard him return. Ethan was not exactly light-footed.

Todd sat up and grimaced. His back was stiff yet again, and his head ached. Every year seemed to bring some new ache or pain. At just what age had he started getting old?

He hung his legs over the bed, stretched, and rubbed his auburn beard; his morning ritual. Todd was proud his beard had yet to sprout the dreaded gray hairs. At thirty-six, that wasn't too shabby. He gathered his clothes for the day and headed for the shower. He would dress in the bathroom so as not to disturb his mate.

In a cloud of steam, Todd emerged from the second-floor bathroom with its new ceramic tile floor and clawed bathtub and started downstairs. He paused partway and looked over his shoulder at their bedroom. Its doorway was a sliver of shadow.

"Sweetie, *our* breakfast will be ready in a half hour." Todd waited briefly but no reply came. He shrugged and continued on.

As soon as Todd reached the kitchen, he spotted Ethan on the sun porch with his garden apron on and his basket and gardening sheers in his hands.

"Wow, I've never seen you up this early, Sweetie," Todd called.

"I didn't think you were out of the shower yet." A surprised look hung on Ethan's face. "I need to harvest some herbs and flowers for a church service. They have to be gathered while the sun is in the house of Scorpio."

"I see." Todd didn't really understand the intricacies of Ethan's faith nor did he want to, but he accepted his partner's right to believe as he did. Ethan had been a Wiccan since before they'd met.

"Well, have fun."

Todd diced Canadian bacon along with some peppers and scallions as he looked out the back window into the garden. Morning light glinted off the lush grass and foliage in emerald hues.

Through the garden's iron gate, he caught a glimpse of Ethan stepping into a row of gnarled plants and thorny bushes. In the front of the garden was a bounty of herbs and small vegetables for cooking. That's where the scallions had come from and the chives that Todd sprinkled into some beaten eggs.

Beyond that, deeper in, were the strange plants and flowers that Ethan took to church or used in ceremonies. Most of them had strange names that baffled him. Rows of juniper and yew bushes led to monkshood, aconite, nettle, wormwood, henbane, and those were only some of what grew back there. Most were pungent, used for fragrant incenses, while others were used to make anointing oils and charm bags. Ethan had a host of charm bags scattered in undisclosed places around the house. He said they were meant to bring good luck and offer protection.

Todd poured the eggs into a hot skillet and began scrambling. As he slid the spatula into the pan, he jumped. A shudder shot through his body as a shrill child-like scream pealed through the air. The spatula shot out of his hand and flew across the counter. A shiver shook him as his eyes searched the backyard. What a terrible sound. He'd never heard anything like it before. A wail of pain and shock—a desperate call—a protest in anguish. What the hell was it?

Moments later, Ethan came strolling into the house, his basket overflowing with green herbs and wild flowers.

"What was that awful scream?" Todd asked, his heart still pounding.

"Huh, oh, just a couple of cats fighting next door."

"Didn't sound like any cats I've ever heard."

"They were pretty pissed at each other. Listen, Hon, I need to head over to church now."

"Now?" Todd's brow furrowed. "Why now? You never go this early. What about our big breakfast together? You know…the one I'm making for us right now."

"I'm sorry, Toddie, you know esbats are the Saturday before the full moon."

"In the evening, Ethan. Not at first daybreak."

"We can't honor the Goddess without the high priest and priestess together. You know how Caroline gets. She takes her high priestess position very seriously."

Todd had experienced Caroline's ire before, and she was not to be trifled with. She nearly had a meltdown when he and Ethan were seven minutes late to the Samhain celebration the previous year. That was something he would never forget. The narrowing of her eyes, the vein that bulged in her forehead. It was downright frightening.

"You said you'd never make me choose. My religion or you." Ethan stared at Todd with irresistible doe eyes.

"Okay," Todd mumbled. The scent of burning eggs caught his nostrils. "*Shit!*" He turned to rescue what was left of breakfast.

"Thanks, Babe." Ethan planted a quick kiss on Todd's cheek and dashed from the kitchen, cradling the basket in his arms like a bassinet.

Todd heard his partner fumbling in the hallway with his keys, ceremonial robes, and the basket of plants. He followed the commotion and strolled down the hallway just as Ethan stepped out the front door.

He watched Ethan pull the convertible from the driveway and screech off, as if he were meeting Mother Earth herself. His behavior worried Todd. Even for Ethan, all of this was just a little abrupt and disorganized. There was a change in him, and Todd wasn't sure he liked it.

A disappointed sigh escaped him. He turned from the front door and looked up at the picture of the two of them on the wall beside the stairs. Something caught his attention. He looked closer and saw a shadow on the side of Ethan's cheek. It curled around the shape of his face almost like a tendril. He didn't remember it being there before. Turning away, he shrugged it off and went back to the kitchen, and their abandoned breakfast.

Dusk brought deepening shadows as dinner grew cold. Todd kept tapping his foot on the floor while sitting at the dining room table in silence. Only the annoying ticking grandfather clock behind him kept him company. Pockets of deep purple filled the corners of the room. His heart pounded. He called Ethan's cell phone for the third time and got his voice mail yet again.

The front door opened a moment after Todd snapped his cell phone shut, and Ethan walked into the room. His arms were filled with candles, grocery bags, and his gardening basket.

"Where the hell have you been?" Todd stood up and asked sharply.

"I told you." Ethan froze with a confused look on his face.

"That was this morning. It's almost eight o'clock in the evening. This is really inexcusable. Do you know how worried I've been?"

"I'm sorry, Toddie, time just got away from me. It was really important."

"You could've called—or at least turned on your phone."

"I needed peace for my boon. I needed to be totally focused or Lady Moon might not have heard me. I—"

"I don't want to hear it, Ethan. I'm going to bed. Enjoy your cold dinner."

"Really, I'm sorry. But you'll be thanking me. You'll see. We're going to be so happy."

"Whatever." Todd passed by his favorite picture again, and the shadow had now encroached upon part of Ethan's face. He lifted his hand to touch the picture, his fingers trembling. He pulled his hand back, unable to bring himself to touch it. *It's getting old, fading,* he convinced himself, as he stormed up to their bedroom.

It was the dead of night when Todd felt tickling on his cheek—no, not tickling—kisses, sweet kisses. He woke to find Ethan by the side of the bed on bended knee. Golden light spilled into the room from the hallway, and Todd noticed an elated expression on Ethan's face.

"My love," Ethan whispered breathlessly, "Do you forgive me?"

The weight of exhaustion wreaked havoc on Todd and his body. His mind was a fog of confusion, and his senses had retreated hours ago. "Yes," he managed to croak.

"My Toddie…thank you."

"Come to bed," Todd said.

"Not just yet. Come with me. I have something wonderful to show you. And I need your help."

"What time is it?"

"It doesn't matter. Please…just come."

Todd felt Ethan's hand slip into his. It was strong and warm, reassuring. The next thing he knew, he was following his partner out of the room and up the stairs to the third floor.

Todd's eyes stung a bit from the light, but found comfort as soon as they entered Ethan's meditation room. The space was dimly lit with an array of candles. Incense billowed into the room with a pungent yet intoxicating aroma.

"Come." Ethan led him to a red satin blanket spread in the middle of the room. In the center of the blanket was a copper bowl with a black veil draped over it.

"Ethan, what's going on?"

"Life," he answered cryptically.

The incense filled Todd's nostrils while the candlelight seemed to blur around him. In the corner by Ethan's makeshift worktable, Todd noticed the old book he'd seen earlier that morning in Ethan's hands. It lay open and in disarray.

"What is that you're burning? It smells so sweet."

"I hoped you would like it. Sit with me." Ethan pulled Todd down onto the blanket and kissed him. "I love you, Todd."

"I love you too. What are we—?"

"I need your love now…so we can have the child we have always wanted. Our child." He pulled the veil off the bowl and inside a vaguely fetal-shaped plant with gnarled roots soaked in a pool of milk. Its flesh was coarse and the color of human skin.

"What on earth is that?" Todd blinked, thinking he'd seen the roots move slightly.

"It will be our child. Right now, it's a mandrake root. But once we give it our essences, it will become human and depend on us for the rest of its life."

"Is this some type of joke?"

"No, Toddie. Please, I need your blood and semen to mix with mine so it can have life. It will be a part of both of us. It has worked before, hundreds, maybe thousands of years ago. I researched it. I followed all the rituals. And for a while, it will need me to nurse it. Our love will make it grow." Ethan got up and went to his worktable.

"This is crazy." Todd rubbed his face, but his sight blurred even further, and he was beginning to feel lightheaded.

His partner returned with a silver chalice and his black-handled ritual dagger. "Do you love me, Todd?"

"Of course, I do. But this is…"

"Please make love to me, Todd. Our child is waiting. It needs our essence."

"Ethan," Todd's lips were silenced with another kiss from his man. The room began to move around him, and suddenly Todd felt himself grow aroused. In seconds his erection burned and his body sweated. It was more than he could bear. He reached for his now naked partner.

They made love upon the satin blanket for what seemed like hours, beside the copper bowl. Visions twisted and flickered in Todd's mind. In the last of them, he witnessed Ethan pouring the contents of the silver chalice over the mandrake root.

A chill seared his naked body. His flesh cried out for relief. Drained, Todd closed his eyes and drifted.

Bright sunlight burned his eyes. Todd's entire body was wracked with pain. He felt sick to his stomach—sicker than he had ever felt before. He found himself back in bed, but didn't remember how he'd gotten there. He reached for Ethan but his side of the bed stood empty. Had he come to bed at all?

Todd pulled himself up. It took every bit of energy he had to do so. He stretched, barely able to lift his arms, and rubbed his beard. "Ethan?"

There was no reply.

He pushed himself up off the bed and across the floor, his feet shuffling one at a time. He peered into the hall and found it filled with warm sunlight and the sound of birds singing. Had it all been a dream?

"Ethan?" He listened downstairs but heard nothing and smelled no breakfast cooking. He looked up at the third floor. The meditation room door was closed, but Todd knew Ethan had to be up there. He turned down the hall and took the small flight of stairs up to the room. Todd prepared to knock but instead pushed the door open and gasped.

It had not been a dream.

Ethan sat beside the copper bowl with his thumb held over it. Drops of crimson fell gently onto the root, coating its newly shaped body. It was larger, with a bulbous growth resembling a head at the tip. Todd noticed indentations on its surface that might have appeared to be closed eyes and a mouth.

It absorbed the blood and…squirmed.

Todd's stomach churned as he covered his mouth. Ethan looked up and their eyes met.

"Toddie?"

Todd raced from the room, a horrified and sickened feeling overwhelming him. He stumbled into the bathroom on the second floor and vomited into the toilet.

"It's okay." Ethan appeared in the doorway. "I'm just nursing our child."

"It's not a child," Todd rasped. "It's not even human. It's a thing! Oh, God—" He fought the urge to vomit again. "I want to be alone now. I'm sick."

"You'll come around," Ethan said with a smile. "You just need time. When you see our beautiful son you'll be fine."

Todd closed the door as Ethan started back upstairs. It was madness. What was happening? What had become of the man he loved? He stood up and tried to collect himself. Turning the faucet on, he splashed cold water over his face and stared into the mirror. He noticed grey hairs sprouting from his beard. His fingers quivered as he plucked them out one at a time.

Downstairs, Todd sat on the sun porch and stared out into the garden. For hours he sat and thought. Ethan never once stepped foot outside his meditation room. He sat vigilant, nursing his new child. Every now and then, Todd heard footsteps reverberate across the ceiling. His weary eyes scanned back and forth over the plaster until he finally broke down and cried.

Todd waited for Ethan to come downstairs, to get something to eat, to talk, anything, but he never showed his face. When dinner came and went, and Todd ate alone, he knew Ethan was slipping away.

As darkness set in, Todd retreated to the master bedroom and, for the first time in ten years, locked the door behind him. He didn't want Ethan sharing his bed tonight, though he'd bared his soul to this man, placed all trust in him, Todd didn't want Ethan to come back in the night and steal his essence. A stranger sat upstairs, someone lacking reason and logic, someone who could no longer feel or care.

The air in the bedroom was cold. Icy fingers cast gooseflesh over Todd's body, and he shivered as he crawled into bed, pulling the covers over him as if for protection against the night, like a child fearing the closet monster or the thing under the bed.

The quiet that filled the room was unsettling. Todd felt so alone in the house—abandoned. How could this have happened? How could someone as strong and loving as Ethan become so unrecognizable? Ten years. Ten years of sharing, loving, honesty—a bond that no one else could even touch—had all but disintegrated over a single weekend. How could it be?

An earthy smell tickled Todd's nose. Fresh soil and root vegetables wafted through the room. He felt a bit ill again. He tried to sleep but the bed was vast and empty without Ethan beside him. He put his arm onto the empty side and stared at the wall. Tears came again, and mercifully, sleep followed.

Todd was awakened by the sound of crying. A child's cry. He sat up immediately, shaking the fog of dreamland, and caught the last vestiges of whimpering—a mixture of pup and human calls that suddenly fell silent.

Throwing the covers aside, Todd dressed and crept to the bedroom door. He unlocked it hesitantly and pulled it open. The hall was bright with the morning sun. He glanced up to the third floor and noticed Ethan's door was still closed.

He breathed a sigh of relief as he started down the stairs. Todd pulled his cell phone from the small table by the staircase and dialed work. He couldn't possibly face a day at the office with what was going on. He knew his mental state was in no condition to—

As his boss's voicemail picked up Todd glanced at the picture of himself and Ethan one more time and saw Ethan's face totally obscured now. His partner's face was masked by shadow as if he were wearing a shroud, all but erased from the photograph.

Todd left his sick call while glued to the photo. Clapping the phone shut, he lifted his hand again, his fingers inches away from Ethan's distorted face, when he started.

The cell phone erupted in his hand. He answered, and it was Caroline, Ethan's high priestess.

"Todd, you must stop Ethan from what he's doing." Her voice was stern but full of concern.

"Caroline? How do you know…?"

"Ethan showed me the mandrake. I tried to warn him, but he wouldn't listen. He's blind to the possible dangers. I'm calling because I'm concerned; he won't return my calls. Todd, the root feeds on his life force. The more of himself he gives to it…the more it takes."

"Caroline, he is so far gone, I can't even," Todd's voice cracked. His hands trembled.

"If you ever want him back, you have to act now. The more human and alive the root becomes, the more Ethan dies…until there's nothing left of him to give."

A baby's giggle lilted through the house.

"God…my Ethan…" Todd murmured.

"Stop him now, Todd. He'll only hear his love. You'll know what to do."

"I already do," Todd said, looking up the stairs.

He closed the phone and headed back upstairs. His spine went rigid, but he kept walking.

He turned to the foot of the stairs leading up to the third floor and looked up the shallow incline. The ominous door to the meditation room remained closed. Soft light glowed beneath it. The taste of damp soil hung on his tongue. He placed his hand, palm damp with cold sweat, onto the banister and reluctantly started up.

Todd swallowed deeply as he approached the door and took hold of its knob. His skin tingled. Miraculously, the door was unlocked. He eased it open. Icy air escaped the room, and inside Todd saw Ethan sitting in the center of the room with his face cast down. His skin looked strange. He sat on the satin blanket, the copper bowl perched in front of him. Ethan's hands dangled in front of him. Scarlet wounds speckled every finger.

Todd walked quietly into the room and drew closer to the bowl. His eyes widened and his jaw went suddenly slack, as he stared in mute horror at the abomination standing before him.

The mandrake had nearly outgrown the bowl. The gnarled roots on its end grew wild, twisting into the floor beneath the bowl. Its top had shaped into a small head, sprouting with bristles. Human eyelids fluttered, threatening to open. Tiny arms, not fully formed, sprouted from its bulbous body, while a gaping mouth opened and closed like the mouth of a fish, hungry, demanding sustenance.

A gurgle escaped it, and Todd watched in disgust as Ethan picked up his black-handled knife from the floor and prepared to cut himself again.

Burying his repulsion and disgust, Todd dashed forward and took hold of Ethan's wrist as he lifted the knife. "*Enough!*" Todd said sternly.

Ethan looked up. His face was gaunt and the same color as the mandrake root, only paler. His skin was wrinkled, his cheeks sagged, and his eyes were dim, their spark stolen from them. Veins marked a roadmap of anguish across his partner's drawn face.

Todd held strong despite wanting to scream. If he was ever to get his love back, he needed to be the brave one, the firm one, the guiding hand. It had been long enough.

"It's killing you," Todd said, prying the knife from Ethan's weakened hand.

"Our son," Ethan squealed. "Our son is hungry. He needs my fluids."

"This is not our son!" Todd knelt beside Ethan, gently turning his eyes away from the bowl. "Look at me, my love. This *thing* is not human…and it's killing you. Come back to me, Ethan."

Tears filled Ethan's eyes. "No…he needs me. We have a child now. We have to take care of him."

"Keep your eyes on me, Ethan. You know what I'm saying is the truth. This is not your son. This is not the way to have a child. This is wrong. You know it is. Remember your faith. You can feel it. Remember our love. Remember *me,* Ethan."

Ethan's lips trembled. He found no words. No sound came forth. He only stared blankly at the writhing root before him, like a child lost.

"We'll keep trying, Ethan. I promise!" Todd put his hands on his partner's face and kissed him deeply. "We'll never stop trying. We'll have a child one day. *Together.* I love you. Come back to me, Sweetie."

Todd watched as an awakening occurred. Ethan's eyes lit up, and the tears flowed. He collapsed into Todd's arms and wailed. "Toddie...Toddie help me. It won't let me go. It won't let me leave it!"

"It's okay, Sweetie. I'm here now." Todd caressed Ethan's salt-and-pepper hair, glinting in the candlelight, and eased him off the blanket. "Look away."

Ethan turned his gaze toward the wall as Todd advanced on the mandrake, knife in hand. The hideous shrieks that filled the room would not soon be forgotten.

Outside in the morning sun, Todd stood with Ethan as they surveyed the garden together. He picked up a shovel, looked at Ethan and took his hand.

They walked deep into the garden, where the strange plants and flowers grew.

"My gosh, how many did you plant?" Todd asked.

Ethan looked up with tear-filled eyes. "I wanted a big family."

Cornstalker

Lori R. Lopez

The body was dumped from a car idling on a highway between fields of genetic mutations, also known as maize. The driver opened his trunk and slid a drooping form out of the interior, then hauled the corpse into tall dense rows.

"G'bye, brother."

Clapping his hands as if to remove any blood or germs, a killer ambled to the sedan and drove off, swinging a U-Turn. He didn't get far.

Waves of green parted like a sea in a storm—an unhallowed turbulence frothing with chaotic passion, spawning the infernal. A creature stomped out of the frenzy, and sturdy woven limbs planted squarely in the middle of the lane.

What? The man's first impression was disbelief. The road had seemed desolate, paved over a prostrate terrain crushed by stark alabaster sky. Nothing but asphalt, dirt, and corn.

Sunlight dazzling the hood and windshield blinded him. Static disrupted the radio. Sweat beaded a guilty brow.

Wringing the steering-wheel, Grayson Duckweed instinctively squealed to a halt. The thing towered, a hulking beast, fluctuating in a heat mirage. Maybe that was all it was, he surmised. A mirage.

The man perched on the driver's seat, inert, casually attired. A drubbed countenance sifted meager options. One foot exited the brake pedal; his other foot accelerated. The vehicle gathered momentum and for an instant he was euphoric, in a rapturous thrall.

Grayson blinked, exhaling. He would veer around, in case it wasn't a figment.

As he sped closer, details of the uncanny apparition gained clarity. His eyebrows arched and he forgot to swerve, barreling into the obstruction. A brick wall of brawn affronted him, crumpling the sedan's hood. With slo-mo acuity Grayson pitched beyond the windshield—fragments of glass suspended—directly to the creature's embrace.

Life didn't flash, it bombarded. A stream of mistakes hurtled through his mind at that instant. Including not wearing a safety harness. He flew out of the frying pan into the arms of hell.

The behemoth enveloped him in a bone-crackling bear hug, emitting a GRRRR. And a stench akin to loamy rancid tissue, moldering roots and matter, putrefied mulch. The man's senses rebelled. Intellect collapsed, a backward somersault, his brain flip-flopping in a spiral of Vertigo. Consciousness mercifully succumbed to blackness…despite a growing thunder, the blast of an air-horn.

Locomotive wind and steel rushed past. The monster swung a fist and cratered the side of a semi.

The man was flung. Rolling into vegetation, a murderer lay as still as the corpse he had recently discarded.

The big rig careened, jackknifing in a turn so sharp it nearly sliced the truck in two; skidding onto a shoulder, tires kicking clouds of sand into the air. A dimpled trailer propelled across a gray band, metal screeching and bending as the cab of the truck was shoved by the weight and slammed to face the beast. But the roadway was vacant, more or less. The thing was gone.

She couldn't believe it. After all these years of waiting, requesting routes along lanes bordered by this one particular crop. It was all about the corn.

Jane Doe—a little joke her parents had played on her—managed to straighten the semi and back up a distance. Grimly, a bull threatening an invisible matador, she scowled at the highway. "Come on." A guttural challenge.

The woman dapperly cocked her Deadman's Tophat, which was shorter than a medium or regular tophat, and braced for combat. She had, you might say, an axe to grind. In fact, she had an armory. A box behind her seat was crammed with archaic weapons. Jane was prepared to go medieval on whatever the fiend was.

Advancing slowly, the brunette craned to peer at leafy green margins of the road, seeking clues. There were none. Aside from a section where hell appeared to have broken loose, the maize seemed identical in substance, nothing crooked or fractured, only neat ragged aisles with tufts like an uncombed thatch of hair. No shadowy presence lingered in the fringes of parallel fields. It had vanished. Just her luck.

Pausing the truck, pounding a fist on the wheel in frustration, she screamed. Then hunched in the cab exhausted, soaked and drained by adrenaline. It was very disappointing. And yet she had hope. It wasn't all bad. Now, at least, she knew with conviction that she hadn't been chasing a myth. A legend perhaps, but not a mere myth. Oh no. This sucker was real.

Jane grimaced, surveying the stalks. For several years she had cruised the interstates tracking it. The stories were true. Heaving a shudder, she found her fists aching as they squeezed the steering-wheel in a stranglehold—tense due to the harrowing disaster, as well as a confrontation with evil. She willed her fingers to relax, unpeeling them from the wheel. She could've had him, could've squashed him! Something thwarted it....

The woman's mind surfaced, rising out of the dark place that harbored this fierce side of her. A mental brume dissipated, thoughts swimming in hazy confusion. She blinked over at a vehicle abandoned on the highway. A hole gaped in the windshield. Someone had plunged through the glass and needed assistance. Or a funeral. She scanned the road for a body. No sign of the driver.

It complicated things. She would have to talk to the authorities. How could she explain the circumstances? What happened to the car was not her fault. It could, on the contrary, look like she was responsible. A sick feeling of dread in her stomach oozed upward to her bosom, then congested her wits. She had no idea what to tell the police. A sting of remorse added to her misery. Where was her concern for the person who might be lying maimed and bloody?

Jane glommed a cell-phone from the passenger seat. The device strobed off and on. She jabbed keys and held it to an ear. White noise. The battery wasn't low; there was service. "Must be some kind of interference...like the Bermuda Triangle." Reaching for a C.B. radio, Jane reticently called for help. Channel Nine, the police monitor. Static replied, and feedback so loud she dropped the mouthpiece.

* * *

The guy woke, sprawled prone beside a corpse. That didn't perturb him as much as it should. He was, after all, the one who had ditched the body in the first place. He didn't plan to be lying next to it, a regrettable and unforeseen hitch. The man took stock of his condition. There were gashes on his head and upper torso from the aerial stunt of windshield-diving. On top of scarcely knit scabs and bruises from his previous debacle. He felt contused but he had survived, and that was quite a feat considering the dimensions and ugly mug of the beast that prevented his departure. Thanks to that semi showing up. He foggily recalled a horn. If he met the driver, he would have to give the trucker a kiss!

Gratitude quickly plummeted to desperation. Grayson pushed to his elbows, then onto his knees. Staggering aloft, he prayed the sedan functioned. He didn't want to be stuck with this body. It would be awkward to explain. Especially for who it was. Gray refused to get caught red-handed. Literally. Fingers sticky, his breath in gulps, he wiped the dried blood on both palms against his shirt. It didn't come off. And there was fresh blood from his own lesions. He was a mess, a train wreck. Make that a car wreck. His life had never been a carnival ride, fun and dandy cotton candy, the guy ruefully acknowledged. His brother Garson was a pill, and a lousy role model, but that was ancient history now.

Once the murkiness dispelled, he felt certain his car would be out of commission. Half the engine had been totaled into chop suey. He didn't think insurance would pay damages from hitting a monster. Yet that was the least of his worries. It would be discovered in the vicinity of the body, registered to his name! How could he move it discreetly? Or explain dumping a body? Some getaway!

If the trucker didn't see his face, he might be able to report the car stolen.

No, that wouldn't work. They could connect him to the victim. His car would clinch it.

"Quit feeling sorry for yourself. It's going to be a long walk."

Dinged-up, incredibly sore, the man hesitated on the brink of the cornrows to inspect a rural highway. The creature had left. A flood of relief washed over him. Then anxiety slugged him in the belly, knocking his breath out. The truck was parked in the road adjacent to his smashed car. Limping along the crop's rim, he saw a female driver inside the semi's cab. She had probably contacted the police, or an emergency dispatcher.

There was only one thing to do. It could give him a head start. The chance to disappear.

Grayson hobbled back to the body. Wincing, he grasped the corpse's ankles then dragged the dead man farther into the cornfield. The ears of grain would be harvested soon, and it wouldn't be long before a crow-pecked carcass was identified. There would be a search if his brother was reported missing. This accident, the entire situation, had been very unfortunate.

Wearily, the guy shambled from the stalks and waved his arms.

Warily, the lady hopped from her throne to greet the abused fellow approaching. She felt as powerful as a queen in the gleaming black truck. On the ground she was reduced to common stature, a literal come down to earth. "You're lucky to be alive, mister. That was quite a tumble. I didn't see it. I'm guessing from your car."

"Yeah. My head feels twice its normal size." Lacerated, he grinned and immediately flinched. "Ouch."

"I'm Jane. You from these parts? I could give you a ride to the nearest town. Find a hospital to patch you up."

"I appreciate the offer. Jane. But if it's all the same to you, I'd prefer a lift as far as you're going. Or the nearest bus terminal?"

"However you want. Maybe you should have that gouge on your forehead checked."

"It's a scratch. I'd rather get out of here."

She spread her hands. "Suit yourself. What's the hurry?" Trudging on gravel, she escorted the man to the "cockpit" of her semi. Something about him was off. Jane climbed to the driver's seat. The passenger door vented. "Can you make it?" The guy scrambled up, moaning in a tough-guy manner. "I'll report the accident. Did you want to make arrangements for a tow? We could stop somewhere," she proposed.

He shook his battered gourd and dug her phone from beneath his rump, stowing it on the dashboard. "Don't bother. You're helping enough. And you must be on a tight schedule. We should go."

"What about your car?"

"It's old...not worth fixing. Let the locals deal with it," he dismissed. "I'd just like to forget this ever happened, if you don't mind."

Her brow furrowed. The car was fairly new, at most a couple years old. *Must be rich.*

"Okey-dokey." A foot on the brake, the woman pushed red and yellow buttons on the dash. Air hissed. Engaging the clutch with her left foot, she jerked the gear lever then eased the clutch and released the brake. Her right foot on the throttle, Jane shifted repeatedly and coaxed the truck forward. She wasn't going to argue, yet the man did strike her as odd. Of course, she wasn't the ordinariest of people herself. Spending years on the road, obsessed by a peculiar diversion. But he hadn't even told her his name. And he was acting pretty nervous. "So where's the body?"

Grayson stared at her. Speechless. How did she know? She must have seen him remove it.

Minutes were passing. *Say something!*

The guy croaked, "What?"

"Where did you stash the body? In your trunk? Or in the corn?" She blinked at him. "It's a joke."

"Ah! I thought you were serious." The man rubbed his eyes. "I didn't sleep much lately."

"So you had problems *before* you bashed through the windshield?"

Was that another joke? He couldn't tell. His sense of humor had fled. He was glad to learn she didn't notify anyone. "Personal stuff. You know." He shrugged somberly, striving for a nonchalant attitude.

"That's vague. It's okay though. I'm just giving you a lift. No need to tell me your life's story. I don't mean to pry. Actually I do. I tend to be curious by nature. Suspicious and paranoid too." She laughed. "I'm sure it stems from having a name like Jane Doe."

His eyes widened, absorbing the information. "I imagine that could be a burden." He didn't feel like conversing and wondered how to convey the message tactfully.

"Speaking of names, do you have one yourself—that you might be willing to share? Or is it Top Secret?"

"Wow. There's no being laconic or mysterious around you, is there?"

"No." She adopted an accent. "I vill make you talk." Jane flashed him a wink and a grin, then returned her eyes to the road. "We haven't even discussed the elephant in the room. But your name would be a swell place to start."

"Elephant?"

"That thing we saw? You couldn't have missed it. You *didn't* miss it. You ran into it! Telling anyone else about it could land us in a mental ward. That doesn't mean we can't compare notes."

Gray's mood shifted, from evasive to lockdown—slamming every door, sealing the fortress. The guy raised his palms defensively. "I think I'd prefer to walk. You can let me off here."

The woman glanced at him. Discerning he was sincere, she stationed her rig. Air hissed like a disgruntled dragon as the truck glided to a standstill. She swiveled on her seat, vinyl squeaking against denim. "I can be obnoxious. My younger brother used to call me Grendel's Mother. One of Beowulf's enemies? Sorry if I said or did something to insult you…"

"I'm pretty strung out. Not having the greatest day."

"If I promise to be good and not bring up monsters, will you allow me to give you a ride?"

Scantly perceptible, a corner of his mouth smiled. From cynicism and mistrust to begging for the privilege of assisting him. He had that effect on women.

It was fine by her the guy clammed up. He was doing her a favor. She didn't need distractions now. Or passengers! What was she thinking? The creature could be in the area! That had to be her priority. Not some black-and-blue tumbleweed scraped off the side of the highway. She should have let him walk.

Her truck growled forth, an imposing mechanical beast with a lengthy snout, double chrome smokestacks, a thick custom grill. The Mack was designed to rule the road. It had been Johnny's warhorse. Amazing how one could adapt. A former pilot, Jane's hawkish eyes scoured the boundaries of maize, reluctant to forfeit an opportunity. She had trained for this, from lessons on driving a tractor-trailer to the physical workouts and sparring sessions. She was primed for a clash with the barbarian that lurked in the corn. Being polite, a Good Samaritan, was not a component of the equation.

They were each preoccupied, wearing frowns, involved in their own dramas. Then she downshifted and floored the clutch, mashing the brake pedal as she intensely regarded a figure striding to the pavement, framed in the rectangular side mirror at her left. The eighteen-wheeler slowed. She wrestled a stubborn gearstick to Neutral, engine rumbling. The woman displayed a purposeful expression.

"What are you doing?" the Charity Case squawked.

"You won't like my answer. And this isn't the best time to shatter your Vow of Silence." Adjusting her tophat, shifting again, the trucker accelerated in reverse, eyes focused on the rearview mirrors at either side of the semi's cab. She continuously modified the angle with minor turns of the steering-wheel. It was a gutsy maneuver, and she was only going about thirty miles per hour, but that was sufficient to spook her passenger.

"I changed my mind. I'd like to get out!" the man reneged.

"You're welcome to jump. Otherwise, hang on to your hat!" she exhorted as the truck rammed backwards toward the thing by the road.

"What hat?"

"The hat you'd be wearing if you were cool!" Jane smirked. "I'm kidding. Hats don't fit everyone. And if everyone wore them, I'd be less cool."

"You're crazy."

"Yeah. Forgot to mention that. You may wish to buckle up."

Gripping the dashboard with his left hand, the taciturn fellow anxiously fumbled to fasten a seatbelt with his right. He couldn't get the strap to latch.

"It's a little tricky. I'm not equipped for a sidekick. I usually travel alone so I never got it fixed. Inherited the truck from my baby brother."

"How comforting. Just let me out!" her companion pestered.

Jane couldn't see the beast anymore. She had to risk, or squander a chance to flatten her nemesis. "Johnny called his rig The Monster." Chortling, she boosted velocity. The speedometer needle rose to thirty-five. The trailer's drift increased. Jaws clenched, she jockeyed the wheel, estimating her target….

Rigid with fear, the man yelped, "Aren't Monster Trucks the kind with humongous tires? I might feel better about this if you were a guy."

"You did not say that." Gritting her teeth, Jane upped the speed to forty.

Her passenger squalled, "*Whoa!*"

Where was it? The woman shifted, then depressed the clutch and braked. The semi hissed, lagging, throbbing…"You can get out if you want," she invited.

"Hah! That creature's here, isn't it?"

Jane nodded.

She could see the clockworks spinning in his psyche as the twerp debated staying in the cab with a maniac, or enduring another close encounter with the atrocity that dented the motor of his car. "I think I'll stay," was his grudging conclusion. "For now."

"Terrific!" She couldn't be less thrilled. "There's going to be a slight delay. More of a detour. Something I have to take care of." Yanking the gearstick, flooring pedals, she guided the black rig ahead. Her side mirrors were empty. Where did it go? "Come on, you mangy dirtbag, show yourself."

"You want it to come out?" The man glared at her in disbelief. "Sounds like you're provoking it to a duel."

She leaned over the wheel, devout, a crusader, auditing the windows and mirrors. "You bet I am. We have a date. I've been trolling for Husky ever since my brother Johnny phoned to sputter the devil was after him. His final words were about a monster and corn. In a nutshell, that thing out there is mine. I've been hauling loads up and down these corn roads for five years, itching to destroy this creep. Today's the day."

"I object. You picked me up, insisted on giving me a ride." He aimed a finger as bluntly as a gun. "You owe me that. It isn't my fight. If you want to take on King Kong or Godzilla, be *my* guest—but leave me out of it."

"Nobody's forcing you to be here. You're not a prisoner, so be my guest and take a hike!"

"No thanks, sweetheart. I'm not suicidal. Where am I supposed to go with your stalker boyfriend running around?"

"Then stay, I don't care!" Angrily, Jane brought the rig to a gradual halt. Diesel engine idling, she tugged the red and yellow knobs on the dash then snugged her tophat's brim securely down. The woman consulted mirrors on both sides, rested her left hand on the door latch. A distinct click. Vinyl creaked as the lady stretched to grope behind the seats in a metal box.

Smiling, she extracted an axe with a wooden hilt. The slender curved blade flared to points at its cutting edge.

"What are you gonna do with that?" A sarcastic query.

"This is Francesca. And this is Morning Star." She hefted a second shaft topped by a studded metal ball.

"An axe and a mace? Lady, you need a cannon to go out there. Do you have any firepower?"

"I'm old-fashioned. I like sharp things."

"I suggest you put it in gear and drive. If anything happens to you, I don't know how to move this heap," the guy complained.

"I'm touched by your concern. The feeling's mutual."

"I'm just saying, you should think about more than yourself."

"That's fabulous advice, coming from you!" She nudged her door ajar and leaped.

He could hear her plod away and fumed, rummaging in the crate for an implement to defend himself. "This should do it." Selecting a battle-axe with double blades, he opened his door and hopped to asphalt. She was his ride. He would have to provide back-up. An unbrave heart pounded. Damp palms clasped wood as he meekly followed her.

The trucker-slash-knight marched in front of the trailer. Before her a ribbon of pavement was bare. Gait faltering, she examined the verdant fields.

"Maybe you scared it." Grayson's axe lowered. His tone was optimistic.

"You can't scare evil."

The statement chilled him. "Isn't that a bit melodramatic?"

"No." The woman posed, a stylish silhouette, wavy dark hair cascading to her shoulders.

He swallowed. "I get it. You lost your brother? I just lost a brother too. I sympathize. That's no reason to go kamikaze or road-warrior with your truck and try to make mincemeat out of a monster." He admired her backside. He had been too wrapped up in his current imbroglio to notice that she was attractive.

Pivoting, the femme-fatale tromped boldly to her rig. "Shut up and get in!"

He scaled the cab's passenger side, clanking his axe to the floor, and remembered that he owed the truck driver a kiss for arriving like the cavalry in an old Western.

Her blades were propped in the crate, handles jutting. She squinted through the windshield. "I saw something."

Green stalks trembled on the left side of the road.

Pushing red and yellow buttons, stepping on pedals and shifting, the woman excitedly steered the tractor-trailer. A ferocious black semi grumbled off the highway, plowing into corn.

Jane's portable phone catapulted from the dashboard and clipped his cranium. He probably had a new bruise!

"That musta hurt." She made a comical face.

Was that an apology? "I'm glad my agony amuses you. What are you doing?" He seemed to ask her this a lot. "Are you insane?!"

"The sucker's taunting me. I'm sorry about your brother. Was he in the car with you?" She held onto the wheel as the truck jounced unevenly, carving a broad path, mowing stalks into the soil.

Hooding his eyes, the man struggled to concentrate. It was the answer. It might solve everything. "Yeah. It got him. There was nothing I could do." Like the truck, the creature's presence was equally a hindrance and a blessing. He was beginning to see some hope for the future. Then the bubble burst. The cops would never buy such a story.

"You'd be lying next to him if I didn't come along." Her voice softened. "You couldn't save him, so let it go."

"Like you let it go?"

"I lost two brothers. And I let it fester inside until my heart feels like a rotten apple full of worms."

"Eww. Happily, I am not the mourning type."

"What type are you?"

She knew! He detected an accusation. Panicking, jostled by the truck's lurches, Gray pressed himself into the seat. He had to guard what he said, watch every word. How did she know?

An ogre stomped into view. His eyes bulged. *"Look out!"*

In lieu of sheering like a rational individual, the woman zeroed in on the hellion, fueled by a turbo-charged vengeance. "American Indians call him

Cornstalker!" the madwoman shouted. "I call him…road kill!"

Abominable contours became evident. Thewy cords of dank earthen meat, muscle, and straw; features laden with scar-tissue; sullen black eyes and yellow-brown cusps glowered at their noisy careering assault.

Gray hollered, *"We're not even on a road!"*

The beast abided—ponderous, forbidding, limbs splayed—its posture and demeanor brazen, confidence supreme. A bass snarl spat from the cretin's rancid core, quaking and fissuring the windshield.

The vehicle trampled maize in a gear-gnashing buffalo rampage. Then abruptly impacted a solid mass, a mountain of belligerence. This was no force of Nature, it was preternatural and vile. The heavy-duty grill yielded like a porous slice of bread. A horrendous roar launched a shockwave at them, shattering glass. Jane balanced the rig as the windscreen's imploding shards rained.

The entity dissolved, and a rollicking tractor-trailer stampeded over the spot.

Perspiring, his visage wan, intestines straining to come out of his nose, Grayson peeled himself off the floor and slumped on his seat while the semi churned through corn.

"The Boogeyman just punched your truck as if it were made of foam. Then poofed into smoke. You can't harm the wind or cripple a vapor. You have no shot at this." Hoisting the axe he had retrieved. "If a Mack truck has no effect, these weapons aren't going to either! Wake up and smell the fertilizer. You can't win!"

She peripherally eyed the axe. "Give me that, before you chop off your own head." Impatiently the woman snatched then tossed his cleaver into the crate.

The semi clattered on its reckless crop-busting spree. According to the height of the stalks, eight feet, that thing out there must be thirteen or fourteen.

Sagging, wrung out, praying for a miracle to rescue him, Gray lolled his noggin to the side and gave a shrill yip. Then clamped his mouth, orbs popping. He thought he saw his brother, a gruesome specter between the corn. The truck whipped past. Did his mind conjure the image out of guilt? Or maybe this wild romp was a dream, a fabrication. Maybe he was still face down beside his brother after the collision. What if he hit the truck head-on and the monster was a delusion? He blinked at the female. Then studied the instrument panel, the cavity in the windshield. It made more sense.

"What?" She cranked the wheel right. The semi canted like a ship obeying its rudder.

"Nothing. I bit my tongue."

Jane caught him pinching himself. "If you're some weirdo with a pain fetish, I don't want to know," she declared.

He couldn't be hallucinating, he determined. His arm smarted.

The trailer was bouncing and wobbling along the ground, almost capsizing, its load shifting, tires spinning. Dust billowed in plumes. Foliage rustled, slapping windows.

Grayson cringed against his door. "We're going to tip!"

"Don't get your panties in a bundle! I've got it under control," she boasted.

A bang reverberated. The trailer elevated, then wrenched laterally, seized by a wrathful force. The world gyrated out of orbit like a top, crashing off its axis. Trailer and cab separated with a shrieking grind of metal that sent the truck's occupants into a virtual tizzy.

Frantic, Jane subdued the tractor's maelstrom with difficulty, sweeping sideways to an anticlimactic finish. Then urged her truck onward at a more sedate pace. The black cab circled its mangled trailer. "So much for my job." She wouldn't need it after this, one way or another.

"I'm sure you will have no trouble explaining," the guy remarked, "that you're a lunatic!"

She cast him a scathing glance. "It's moments like this, I wish I had installed the Passenger Eject Button."

Green stalks swayed, crunching, pulled below the hood.

"Where are you?" the huntswoman whispered, prowling the field, jarred up and down as the unhitched tail of the vehicle bobbed roughly over soil and plants. She gave her companion a gentler peek. "Sorry about the bumps. It's worse in an unattached semi. The trailer stabilizes its rear end."

He ignored her.

"Hmph. Try to be nice..." she muttered to an obliterated windshield.

Jane froze, gandering countenances.

"What?" He noticed her slack jaw.

"I saw faces—on the corn. Does that sound idiotic?"

"It might," he confirmed.

A sparkle. Activity. Stunned, she gawped at the sky. A sedan arced high, hurled from the road by brute strength, then descended like a missile. They were the bull's-eye. "Jump!" she barked. And bailed out her door as if in flames.

This time he listened, undoubtedly alarmed by her reaction.

The midsized car struck with a percussive clamor, rending, skreighing, partially caving the roof of the cab.

Jane scurried from range. Teetering, the sedan gracefully toppled off the truck's roof onto the hood and thudded to earth. The Monster halted, purring in a grumpy feral whine, tangling with the twisted metal of the car. Laboring, the engine stalled. A tire blew, gored by a dagger of steel.

The woman felt vulnerable. She hustled to a yawning driver's door and climbed to fish over the seat for blades. Glass rubble littered the semi's cab. She reclaimed her short tophat off the floor, tamped it firmly onto her crown. Acquiring a small arsenal from the crate, Jane withdrew to join the guy hunkered amid a forest of leafen stalks. She passed him a pair of weapons, the double axe he had garnered earlier and a warhammer. "The rules have changed. We're on foot. He's coming for us. It's about survival." Jane overshadowed the squatting man, yet was dwarfed by the grain. Accoutered like a medieval guerrilla, she brandished her lethal beauties: Francesca and Morning Star.

"So now we're *trying* to avoid death and destruction?"

"Not completely. We need to be more cautious."

"You need a strait-jacket."

"I never said I didn't. Are you with me or not? There's no Safe Zone."

His legs unfolded, taking the vantage. "I bow to your superior skills. My life is in your hands. This whole thing is on you."

He would remain with the kook for protection, then make a run for it on the highway. She scared him. The quirky dame had some drastic issues. "Ladies first." Grayson motioned, but it wasn't out of courtesy. With an unchivalrous deference, he pursued the "iron maiden" as she led him toward the road, where his car had been disabled...before being thrown at them.

Single-file, they traversed a row of dirt. *This has to be a fantasy,* the guy asserted to himself. *A fairytale.* "So what are we doing, beating the bushes to find a fabled beast? A crypto-critter like Bigfoot? You called it something...."

She paused to respond, her visage solemn. "Cornstalker. It's a translation. Nobody would tell me the original name. They're afraid speaking it might draw the creature. That isn't how the stories go. Trust me, I analyzed every manner of luring demons aside from sacrifice. It appears when brother kills brother."

His mouth was parched. He couldn't swallow. On the inside, bells were keening Red Alert. Outwardly, the man exuded a degree of calm. "Stories?"

"Over the decades there have been occasional vanishings and sightings. I researched in libraries, databases. Questioned experts, anyone I could trace who heard the rumors. There are two basic versions I've gleaned. In one the creature was mustered to attack Caucasians, who were deemed The White Plague. A Plains band of renegades performed a ritual, invoking the monstrosity from the earth like a Hebrew golem to wipe out intruders and free their land. Then the Mowhktii, possibly Mowhkutt, camouflaged themselves with white riverbank mud and lay in tall grasses to ambush a unit of soldiers. A self-serving member, a traitor, sold their location to the foreigners—arriving with the hated whites. A conflict began. Blood spilled. The monster was rallied, but would annihilate both sides, all of the palefaces. Being marauders who defected or were exiled, lacking the dignity of a tribe, the band had no allies, simply enemies. They were seen as a blight, the same as the White Man: bellicose, uncontrollable. They would not be missed. Even the memory of them was erased, except these dregs of a legend." Jane eyed the corn with misgivings.

Gray scoped a circumference of bladed rods. Breeze fluttered tassels. The crop seemed eerily serene. Deceptively placid.

"An opposing version depicts that the monster rose due to the strife of brother versus brother in history and folklore...that it's a demon manifested through numerous forms, infecting regions where the blood of siblings stains the earth. As an example, Atreus and Thyestes were Greek brothers of myth whose rivalry resulted in terrible acts committed upon each other, after murdering a half-brother." Like a sentinel, Jane stiffly reviewed the perimeter.

"Greek mythology? Are you serious?" He raised the iron implements. "Is that why we're standing in a cornfield with antiquated weapons?"

"Cain and Abel. Brother slaying brother. It's background. There have been many such legends. In this variation of the Cornstalker saga, thieves initially summoning the beast did so unintentionally, by accident. They were not Native-American. The men were imitators, deserters from the U.S. Cavalry who painted their skin pure white to hide that it was pale. Some did not agree with the violence against native inhabitants. Others did not wish to fight, pacifists or cowards. Despite their reasons, the band of raiders ended up feuding. Those who didn't kill each other eventually skirmished with the Cavalry, who did not at first know they were white, then exposed their identities and wanted to slaughter them as chickens. Cornstalker crawled out of the roots and sod, composed of dried husks and fibers, the land's bones and tendons. The demon did not discriminate between biological brothers or blood-brothers. It massacred them all." Her eyes strayed to the corn. "Whichever narrative is more accurate, that's what this thing is."

"And you believe a bunch of superstitions?"

She gazed at him. "I've had doubts. Until today."

"Why your brother? Who did he betray?"

"Himself." She turned away. "We need to keep moving, or that truck could clobber us like a meteor."

He extended the warhammer, blocking her. They exchanged stares.

The woman mused, "I'm wondering why it's here now. If your brother was in the car with you, it must blame you for his death. You told me the monster killed him."

His arm sank. She resumed her patrol, features puzzled.

The faces she had seen were smeared white. It occurred to her they might be ghosts of the men from the legend. Not warriors, not braves…merely dressing like them, whatever the shade of their flesh. The woman had scouted these roads in vain, fearing she would never get this close to avenging her brother and vanquishing the demon. Jane inhaled deeply, filling her lungs with the true spirit of the Plains People. Not defined by paint or feathers, by blood or skin color, but by courage and respect. It was a spirit the world could use more of—a wise and valiant spirit that needed to be shared, like a Peace Pipe—spread from person to person, a contagious fire in the heart.

She sighed. If the guy stumbling at her heels was any indication, that would never happen.

There! Jane gasped. A chalky aspect had materialized, tangible, obtrusive in the bamboo-like trunks of maize, then faded. Ground tilted. Drums echoed, haranguing her ears; it was her pulse. A ghastly vision, a painted mask leered. She scrutinized the jungle of stalks. Faces mocked her, coated with white clay, flitting among the dark recesses.

"Don't freak out but I think this cornfield is haunted," she murmured.

The man had stopped when Jane stopped. For once he had no retort.

"Where's your skepticism when I need it?" She grinned, although bathed in a clammy lather, goosebumps prickling.

"The lock on my mind has sprung. This is all too preposterous. I don't think I'm dreaming, so I must have flipped my lid."

Jane tapped his dome of brown curls with the helve of her mace. "You don't wear a hat. Remember?"

"We're both unhinged, delirious. You must have given me your mental illness."

"That's more like it." Unsettled, she peeped over a shoulder. The faces were gone.

"Ghosts disturb you…a demon you're okay with."

"I'm screwy."

"You're a paradox."

"Pain can alter one's perspective."

"You said you lost two brothers."

"Let's go." She needed to heal, mend her punctured layers, not rip open old injuries! Piqued, Jane forged through the umbrage, resting the spiked mace on a shoulder.

He threw his weapons down with a clang. "Not until you enlighten me! Why are we here, armed for World War Zero, which should have been fought back in the Dark Ages?"

Her steps ceased. The woman shut her eyes. This guy was irritating.

"Iron, specifically Cold Iron, is reputed to smite a demon. I recommend you pick those up."

Clinking signaled the man's hasty compliance.

A corner of her mouth twitched.

Jane brooded, contemplating the atmosphere, and mulled her next words. Generally adept at spotting manipulators, she was vexed trying to read him, a bad sign in itself. She couldn't be certain about the man. He hadn't even told her his name! *So many fakes and users,* she reflected, *trying to take advantage...vultures feeding off the carrion of society.* It reminded her of a famous photograph—a buzzard waiting behind a famished African child. The image made her furious. Did that starving kid survive? Was the bird an opportunist, or merely hungry like the human? The world could be harsh, and she couldn't fix everything alone. But she could improve it; she could make a difference.

Shuffling one-eighty, her weapons lowered, she eyed the mystery man quizzically. What was his game? Why was he so secretive? *It takes one to know one,* a voice in her head reminded.

A ring of ghouls soberly encompassed them. She lifted a hand to the side, frowning at her companion. "You don't see them?"

The revenants disappeared. She blinked around in surprise. Maybe her sanity did unravel, a few marbles fall out. She found herself eyeballing the soil and blushed with chagrin. "If I tell you something I haven't told anyone, will you finally tell me your name?"

It was like bargaining with the Devil. Sporting a complacent smirk, he nodded. Then exhibited fingers in a V. "Two things."

Jane skewed her mouth and chin briefly in disapproval. "Okay, but you first." She panned narrowed eyes across the maize.

"Grayson." A tick later: "Duckweed."

She coughed, suppressing a laugh. Then connected it. "The billboards." She had glimpsed ads bearing the name on a series of roadway placards. "Duckweed Corn."

"Eat more duck!"

"As a vegetarian, I am not impressed by that slogan."

"You do realize it's for a grain? Not actual ducks."

"Oh, I get it. I just find it distasteful. Are these your fields?" She twirled the Morning Star like a scepter. "Is this…your corn?"

"Yes." A terse smile. "It was."

"Sorry!" She gave an embarrassed curtsy-shrug for demolishing a portion.

"I'll send you a bill. Get it? Duckbill? My brother called those puns Lame Ducks." His levity subsided, replaced by a morose expression. "And now it's your turn."

"I don't think I can top yours."

"We have an ironclad contract." He boosted the double axe with a wink. "You had best try."

The banter fizzled. She couldn't gauge whether his gesture was in jest or he was calculating where to hack her neck.

A tempest boomed in the distance; a frigid gust raked icy fingers through tresses, brushing her mane; a shiver strummed her like a harp as a lump of apprehension clogged Jane's throat. Clearing it mimicked an ornery ignition.

"My qualms toward ghosts stem from the death of my grandfather," the woman quietly related. "I had never seen a dead person. He was alive and then he wasn't. At age seven that seemed very traumatic. Nothing anyone said could alleviate the grief and terror. Then I saw him in my closet at night, a pallid transparent copy of him. I had insomnia for days, it couldn't be a nightmare. He approached my bed, then stooped to touch my cheek. The hand was like an ice cube. His voice was familiar, yet reedy and bassoonish. He wailed at me to trust with the eyes, not the heart! I didn't understand. I thought he had it reversed. It's the kind of advice that can be switched—to trust with the heart, not the eyes. I deciphered in time that he was referring to my brother Johnny."

"John Doe," the guy interjected.

She transferred Francesca to the hand that gripped Morning Star and rubbed her neck, massaging a truckload of stress. "It was inevitable. My older brother was named Joseph. Joe Doe. It does have a special charm."

"Like Duckweed. We'll call it a tie. Please continue."

Wielding her weapons in both hands, Jane skimmed the corn for waxen countenances. "Doing a school report on Greek mythology, I read about eidolons…astral replicas of the living that may visit their family once they've died. There are tons of theories on ghosts, spirits, wraiths. Every culture has them. I immersed myself in the topic. I never got over my grandfather's visitation." She fanned a fly. The insects were abundant, swarming above the crop, accumulating. There was an absence of birds. Where were the crows? Perhaps the commotion frightened them off.

Grayson tucked his weapons at his side, pinned by an arm, to swat at the pests.

"My grandfather's words stayed with me too, resonating. Still I was blind. My heart wouldn't let me see the vicissitude, the distortions. He was my baby bro. And a criminal..." Jane wet dry lips. She felt cold, so cold her breath frosted. "...running drugs with his truck in addition to legitimate loads. I was oblivious, in denial that my brother could get into trouble. The kid acted normal with me, bright and cheerful." Tears pooled, obscuring her view. "Joe died in a tragic mishap. He rode with Johnny from time to time. The trailer backed over him during a trip. Soon after, Johnny was slain along a highway through the corn. The police recorded my testimony. The death was officially attributed to the narcotics uncovered in his rig. Then why weren't the drugs stolen? And how were half the bones in his body splintered to twigs? I was shocked and blamed myself for not being there more after we lost our parents when Johnny was a teen. He got involved with the wrong sort and quit paying attention to me, just pretending, while I failed to see his transformation. I was suffering and didn't listen to his drunken sobs one night about being responsible for Joe's death." Tears dripped to her mouth; she brushed them with a sleeve of the white cotton blouse tucked into her jeans. "I could have saved him, could've changed him back! I didn't get the chance, and that's why I have to do this. For Johnny. And for Joe."

The guy looked at her gravely. Eyes blurred, she watched his lips part to speak as if through an ocean.

Wind howled and the maize quivered with a deafening agitation that drowned his comment. An ensuing hush, then faint cries were audible.

Sniffing, mopping tears on her other sleeve, Jane held a finger to her lips. She tracked the sounds, anticipating phantasms, her weapons ready. The man traipsed unstealthily after.

Their probe ended at the base of a vertical cross, the bars weathered and gnarled like wormwood. Trussed to the crucifix was a thrashing figure with a burlap sack over the head. Flies hovered. A multitude of large crows lined the ground in reverence—or waiting to pounce and gnaw the bones clean.

Jane gagged; acid scorched her esophagus. She feigned conniptions to shoo the rooks. Cawing, birds and insects scattered. The scarecrow stopped resisting.

"I'll get you down!" She gingerly sawed tethers at the ankles and neck using Francesca. Braids of straw severed like butter. "Help me catch him." She turned to Gray. Also like butter, the guy had melted into the corn, nowhere to be seen.

From underneath the woman sliced plaited strands to unshackle the scarecrow's wrists, and the prisoner collapsed onto her. Jane reeled, sustaining the bulk, arms hugging the torso.

A man stripped the burlap bag off and goggled at her. "Who are you?"

She distinguished a kinship to Grayson. "You're alive!" Astounded, her arms went flaccid, depositing him in the dirt.

The fellow's temple was direly wounded above an ear. Rust-like blotches had saturated a shoulder of his jacket. "More or less. I'm in your debt."

"That's a nasty cut." She apologized for dropping him. "Your brother's gonna be glad to see you. He thought you were dead."

An inscrutable facade. The man dizzily clambered to his feet as she bolstered him. "Where is he?"

"No idea. He can't be far. He was just—"

"What did he say about me?" the guy interrupted.

"Not much. You were both in an accident. But if you weren't killed, why did that thing return?"

"What thing? And what are you doing here? Where did you come from?"

Why the Third Degree? That injury must've addled his brain. Her gut knotted. She wasn't very trusting. He could stand, so she took a step away.

Huffing, fingers tentative, he explored the goopy cleft on the side of his head. "I assure you, it was no accident. I'm Garson Duckweed, by the way. My brother Grayson is a coward and a murderer."

"You've got the coward part right. Jane Doe." She automatically presented her hand to shake. Then retracted it. This wasn't a social affair.

"Does that mean you don't know who you are? Or you'd rather be anonymous?"

"That's my name. It isn't an alias."

He smirked, even more like his sibling. "Nobody's really named Jane or John Doe."

"Well, somebody neglected to inform my parents. Your brother tried to kill you?"

"He didn't try—I was deceased. I met Azrael, the Angel of Death, the Grim Reaper, who jolted me back. Then…I woke up on that cross."

"Brilliant, Jane. You had to give him the double-bladed axe," she wryly admonished.

"Pardon?"

"Never mind. You probably have a concussion. We need to get out of this corn. We're sitting ducks. No offense." The guy did seem less abrasive than his sibling. He was a victim. And taking off like that made Grayson conspicuously culpable. She eyed crevices between the tall plants. Lips pursed, weapons poised before her, Jane sallied with dubious reserve…aware of tiny snappings that flirted with her paranoia. Then braked to belatedly inquire, "Can you walk?"

He hadn't moved, unconvinced to follow. "What's with the Iron Age?" A bloodied finger poked toward Francesca and Morning Star.

Answering a question with a question irked her. Johnny would do that when he didn't want her to know something. He hadn't given her a hint about the drugs.

Jane plastered a smile on her lips like tape, to prohibit correcting that the weapons were from the Middle Ages. She had a question for him: Why did his brother want him to die?

"Are you always this evasive?"

"I'm not being evasive." Flustered, she blurted what was on her mind.

"You should be asking what's in the corn," Garson smoothly deflected.

It wasn't exactly a question, but it did contain one. "Meaning?"

"Maybe it's because I was dead. I thought I saw the corn change into people. If you think about it, a cornfield resembles a crowd of people staring at you. It's creepy."

"Plus, it's like the adage that walls have ears. It's wall-to-wall ears! Perhaps these corn people put you on the cross." Furtively Jane peeked at the opaqueness, the nebulous depths of the grain. And deduced that he had been erected as bait to entice and entrap his brother. The corn didn't do it. "We have to go!" She trod into the vegetation, swinging her axe like a machete.

A dusty shoe compressed a supple object and the woman screamed, thinking it was a body. Jane toed a decapitated scarecrow that had been torn limb from limb, the sunbaked pieces strewn.

As she wended, Jane heard him tramping behind. Wind rattled the stalks. White faces emanated. The cornfield thronged and ebbed. Birds winged in startled flaps. The flies buzzed her ears, smacked her flesh. An illusory flicker. Was it Grayson? Cumbrous vibrations. The creature? She glanced over a shoulder. Garson wasn't there. A suspenseful interval, then he hove into sight. Skittish, Jane trekked in a zigzag. She faltered, disoriented. Which way to the road? The corn spanned in every direction, a maze of deceit and trickery. She couldn't be positive who was stalking whom.

Swallowing a gob of trepidation, the female revolved in a taut circle. Ashen sky above the plants furnished no inklings, no cues, yet instinct blared like Tinnitus that peril was imminent.

A staccato chorus tapped like the cadence of Deathwatch Beetles marking a bedside vigil. Leaves stirred with a tremendous din. Jane turned and collided. "Oh!"

Garson eyed her, speculative. "You've seen them."

"Who?"

"The corn people."

"I don't think they're our biggest problem."

"What is? My brother? I can handle him." The man drew a pistol from his belt. It had been cloaked by his windbreaker.

"What's that for?"

"Insurance. And yours?"

Jane wagged her ferrous friends. "Some travel light. I'm the opposite. Speaking of which, let's pick up the pace. We don't want to be here in the dark."

Tremors rippled. A testy growl split the air. Massive limbs clomped, wading corn, and a matted emaciated giant loomed. The miscreant swiped a fist, cuffing them to the ground, then reached his mitts over the timbered humans and plucked a man from the vegetation. Grayson's weapons thunked to earth as he dangled in the beast's prodigious paws.

Cowering, Garson fired his gun and riddled the monster with lead. Cornstalker bellowed. The ogre thrust Gray as a trophy. A successive hail of bullets. Blood spurted; the man whimpered. He was chucked at Jane and Garson, bowling them down when they were attempting to straighten.

Maize writhed and danced, an army of spindly skeletons, arms flailing. Out of its rows emerged men in paint and feathers, the warbonnets of Plains Indians. They carried lances and wood shields, bows and arrows, carbines and tomahawks. Doleful white visages mimed disinterred zombies, the skin excoriated in patches. Thieves, deserters in life, this band of phantoms whooped, spears and rifles hoisted, and assailed the creature.

While the fracas waged, a woman grappled and wiggled from under dead weight. Kneeling, she donned her hat then collected her irons. Garson, wide-eyed at the center of a paranormal brawl, recouped his faculties to roll Gray on his spine and aim the muzzle of the pistol against his brother's forehead.

"I hope you're breathing, because I want you to feel this!" he rasped—and pulled the trigger.

Click.

The guy tossed his gun at the corn in disgust. He scrabbled for Grayson's double-bladed axe, lying nearby, and hefted it like an executioner.

"Hey!" She didn't know which brother was worse, but she couldn't let him kill an unconscious sibling. It wasn't right. Jane lifted her spiked mace. "Don't make me use this!"

Besieged by ghosts clinging to his limbs, a corn-fed giant bayed at Garson with the temper of a Grizzly. The brute shed the ghouls then surged to scoop the guy in a hug. Ogling the chimera face to face, the man was too terrified to utter a sound. His arms holding up the axe went rubbery. Flagging, the weapon thumped dirt. Cornstalker squeezed until vessels and organs ruptured. Bones were pulverized by a cruel angel dispensing justice.

"Ugh." Jane averted her gaze. Grasping Morning Star and Francesca, her hat jauntily angled, she confronted her demon. The menace rumbled, Garson's remnants at its feet.

The woman pumped her axe aloft but hesitated. Maybe it was time to let go. There were more important things than revenge. She had been living for this moment, not caring about a future beyond it. Now she wasn't even certain the monster was completely bad. She didn't know what to think about anything, or anyone! She lowered the blade. The beast expelled a musty breath that reeked of mildew and decay. It turned to walk away, to vanish again. And be resurrected by another sibling rivalry or spate of violence. She couldn't accept that. She had enough on her conscience.

The female whistled as the creature forded into a green tide, blazing a trail. "You robbed me of my brother!" goaded Jane. "You're no better than any of them!"

Disintegrating, the beast spun back to her. A mouth churlishly snarled. Its orbs melancholic, the monster dared her with an acrimonious grimace.

Stomach constricted, loosing a battle cry and charging, the woman cast her mace. Cornstalker captured it in a fist. Jane rapidly lobbed her axe. Forged on a cold anvil, the hatchet flew end over end, devised and crafted for precisely that purpose.

The demon grunted. A wooden handle projected out of its breast. The blade was buried to the hilt. A glow erupted from the fiend's core. In seconds the mammoth troll dismantled, granulating, filtering to nullity—to Nirvana—with the breeze.

Jane sighed. This heroic stuff wasn't as glorious as they led you to believe. She felt like puking.

Instead of maize, ranks of white-faced warriors surrounded her, flesh untattered, guises intact. Beneath the feathers and paint they were only men. One of them wafted forward, and she recognized her brother Johnny. The young man was a spirit of the corn. She forgot she was afraid of ghosts. Tears sprang to her eyes.

Johnny confessed, "I waited too long to tell you how much I love you, and that you did everything you could. Joe too. Giving me the truck…I repaid you by breaking your hearts, then killing Joe. He found a cache of drugs and promised to keep it secret if I quit. We were drunk. I was blubbering while backing up at an empty rest-stop, and he was guiding me. I ran him down with the rig. I didn't mean to…I told you it was an accident…but I was intoxicated. I put him in the cab with me and blacked out. Later I delivered the drugs and waited for the alcohol to clear my system, then brought him home."

Jane's hands cupped her mouth. Weeping, she tried to touch him… forgive him. Her fingers passed through the specter.

An eidolon assembled beside Johnny. Their brother Joe beamed at them. Radiating a silver sheen, he embraced John. The souls departed.

Groaning and weak, Gray sat up. He had been shot in his right shoulder. A second slug grazed his left thigh. He would live, he assessed. And there would be no fleeing. He had chosen to stay.

The man smiled fondly at Jane. He needed her to know…everything. "That story Garson told you was false. I can't prove it. I'm just asking you to listen to my version."

She whirled. Was that relief on her face? Jane crouched to check where he was bleeding. "Nothing fatal." Her eyes were swollen from crying.

"There's plenty of pain, if it's any consolation."

"Yippee."

"That thing should have been mad about the corn. About what's in it."

"People?"

"Huh? No, you can't see this. Most of it's engineered. Unnatural. That bothered me. I funded private testing, which predicted the corn may cause mutations in generations to come. I showed my brother, and he labeled it a tolerable risk. Tolerable. Like evolution, he cited. Except this is not an improvement! Who are we to decide that? Maybe it will be, or lead to progress somewhere down the road. That was my brother's opinion. Have you any idea how many foods corn is in these days? We disagreed over the direction of the company. I wanted to get back to basics, the way our family started, and dispose of the tainted seeds. Eliminate chemical fertilizers and pesticides. Use rotation and manure. My brother wanted to build an empire by cutting costs and hiking profits. He saw it as a growth industry. My goal was to diversify and go organic, produce healthy crops." Grayson forlornly shook his head. "Words escalated to a physical altercation. He threatened me with a gun. I whacked him with a shovel, then couldn't find a pulse. I tucked the gun in his pants, shoved him in my trunk and drove. Panicking, I left him in a field."

"That was dumb. You made yourself look guilty," chided Jane.

"I know. There were no witnesses to verify it was self-defense. There were, however, employees present when the argument began a day earlier, when I announced the test results and my plan to get rid of the crop. He yelled, ‘Over my dead body!’ The very next day he was dead. Kind of incriminating.”

Jane stood and leaned over him. “Let’s get you to a doctor. We’ll let detectives worry about solving the Whodunnit.” She helped him up. “I believe you, if it’s any consolation.”

He smirked. “It is.”

Side by side, they strolled down the promenade leveled by the monster.

Jane retrieved Francesca and Morning Star. “Just in case.”

They meandered through corn to a highway and scuffed west. “Toward the Hesperides, the garden of the sunset,” extolled Jane, admiring the sky’s pastel hues.

He admired her. “You changed my life, Jane Doe. If I’m not sentenced to life in prison, I reckon I could change a slogan. ‘Our corn is ducky!’”

The woman snorted.

“‘The duckiest’?”

“‘We’re not quackers, we grow corn right!’” She snickered.

“‘Our corn is something to quack about!’”

“‘Get your ducks in a row with Duckweed Corn!’”

They hooted, weaving with mirth in the road. Then cackled riotously as they looked up at an EAT MORE DUCK! sign.

“How about we change the subject? I’ve had enough corn for one day,” griped Jane.

“Excellent idea. How do you feel about soybeans?”

She halted to plant a smooch on his lips.

“Thanks for reminding me. I owe you one.” Gray tugged her close and kissed her, as if they had all night.

Beyond the Trees

Jordan Phelps

Jane stepped out from the back seat of the family van and into the sinking mud that was the parking lot. The crisp, wind-bitten air danced through her hair and past her shoulders, on to the wide field that lay ahead. It was a wind often expected, but rarely appreciated by the small, rural community that gathered here tonight. Only was it appreciated when the moon was full and spirits were high. Only on nights much like this one, when the trivialities assigned to life could be sent past the clouds and beneath the waves to make room for a truer meaning of existence.

Jane walked alongside her parents and her two older sisters, a smile stretched across her face. A sign hanging overhead displayed the words: ***Fall Equinox Festival,*** and painted underneath in orange, red and yellow were the words: ***Welcome Clark County!*** The family passed under this display and into the field, a pleasant feeling of excitement buzzing in each of them.

Jane surveyed the grounds, taking note of several rides, sizing them up. There was a Ferris Wheel, a Tilt-a-Whirl, a giant slide, and even a set of those rotating, plastic strawberries that you sat inside and didn't stop spinning around until you either threw up or passed out—or, even better, caused one of your sisters to. But none of these were really a priority for Jane. Her eyes hopped from ride to ride, eventually settling in the back corner of the field where the grass came to an abrupt stop and gave way to the dark, watchful tress of the forest beyond.

Tucked into this corner was the Haunted House, shrouded in an artificial fog that smelled of sulfur and mystery. Signs were nailed onto the paint-flecked, wooden walls: ***Only three tickets!*** one said, as if it would be a crime against reason to pass by the dying shack. ***Handing out fresh socks at the exit…for when yours get scared right off your feet!*** said another. Even at the age of nine, Jane knew this last sign was lame. Really lame. But, to her, it took nothing away from the house and the mysterious aura that surrounded it. There was something magical about the ride. Something she couldn't easily define or categorize, but something she could feel deeply within herself, as if by some primal method of communication. Each year before, Jane's mother had told her she was too young to go inside, and she was forced to sit back and watch as her sisters went in without her. But that wouldn't happen again. This would be her year.

As she stood there wide-eyed, fantasizing about what she would find behind the walls of the Haunted House, Jane saw something stir back within the trees that hadn't been there before. She focused on the darkness ahead, trying to locate the disturbance—finding nothing, but feeling as if she was being watched. It wasn't until she had partially given up, that she saw something small and powder-white creep slowly back into the shadows of the forest. *Was it a face?*

"Jane! What are you doing?" It was her mother.

Jane snapped out of the trance and turned toward her mother's voice. Her family had claimed a picnic table not far from where she was standing and they sat staring at her with similar looks of confusion.

"Just looking at the rides," she said, biting her lower lip and holding on to her left arm. For a moment, nobody spoke. There were only eyes—watching, questioning. *Interrogating?* She wasn't sure, so she broke the silence with more words. "They look pretty fun this year," she said, poorly feigning excitement.

"It's the same shit as last year," said Mandy, her oldest sister.

"Don't ruin it for your sister," her mother said. She turned to Jane and smiled. "I'm glad you're excited, honey." There was another silence, during which their eyes spoke loudly. Jane's mother became aware that her youngest daughter wasn't really excited, that instead, something had disturbed her—but what was it? Jane knew her mother was wondering exactly that, but she also knew the question wouldn't be asked explicitly. And she was right.

"Let's get you girls some ride tickets," her mother said, standing up. "Richard, can you watch the table?" Jane's father simply nodded, as the rest of the family got up.

"I want to go in the Haunted House again!" said Christa, the middle sister.

Jane was too busy rubbing the coldness from her arms to catch the reference. She checked to make sure her mother wasn't watching her before glancing back at the trees once more. This time she found only stillness there. But it wasn't a pleasant stillness, it was the kind that created a barrier by freezing the field of vision, allowing things behind it to go unnoticed.

Though Jane couldn't see anything, the feeling of coldness seeped even deeper into her body. She suddenly felt naked. Then, for a moment, there was a lapse in the stillness. Either that or her mind had grown impatient and started doodling perceptions for itself. Jane thought she saw something—a pair of dark eyes, watching carefully from behind a shroud of leaves—yes, she was sure of it. They looked needful, almost *jealous*—but of what? They blinked once, twice, never shifting from their target. And then, along with the stillness, they were gone.

When she turned back, Jane caught her father watching her from the picnic table. He grinned and tilted his head toward Jane's mother and sisters, who hadn't yet noticed her absence. Jane ran quickly to catch up to them.

Tickets were purchased and the journey across the festival began. They started on the Tilt-a-Whirl, making a beeline toward the spinning strawberries directly afterward. Christa threw up after the first round, and then they got in line to ride them again. As the girls dashed from ride to ride, their mother followed uneasily behind, trying to figure out what had disturbed Jane so much. But at the same time she was unwilling to ask, for fear of what the answer might be. The truth was, she felt something too. She wasn't quite sure what she felt, but its presence was growing stronger as darkness fell around them.

The line for the Ferris Wheel ended up taking a half hour to get through and none of them seemed to mind. They spent this time watching the colourful lights dance across the night sky, painting vivid images in the darkness, before the mighty arms of the machine brought them down to make room for new riders. The lights changed, but they were always there and always shining—sometimes you just had to look harder to see them.

The three sisters rose into the sky in their tiny seat and became a part of the cycle, floating alongside the lights. The gentle breeze was just enough to bring pleasant autumn shivers. Jane looked over the edge of her seat and waved to her mother who smiled up at her and waved back.

"Look at the moon," said Christa. "It looks so lonely up there. I think I can see it crying." She gazed thoughtfully into the sky before speaking again. "What if the stars are just the moon's tears and the sun comes out every morning to dry them—to give the moon a hug before it moves on?"

Mandy rolled her eyes. "The moon's a rock."

"But what if it was more than a rock? Would that be so bad?"

"I don't know, but it's not," said Mandy.

For a while all three of them just looked up in silence. Regardless of whether the moon was nothing more than a rock, it was undeniably beautiful tonight, and the stars burned around its fully exposed body like flaming specs of emotion. Jane wondered how everything could seem so close from atop the broad back of this mechanical hulk. Each time they reached the summit they were still only meters away from the ground, but it seemed like so much more than that.

"Tell me again what the Haunted House is like," said Jane.

"The scariest thing you'll ever see," said Christa. "You can't go ten seconds without something jumping out at you! And in some rooms—"

"Just let her experience it for herself," Mandy cut in. "It's not even that great."

"Why do you have to be like that?" said Christa. "Can't you just let her be excited for once? Don't listen to her Jane…the place is creepier than grandma's attic."

"There's nothing creepy about that old shack *or* grandma's attic," said Mandy. "What's scary about enclosed spaces? They aren't mysterious. People put things in them and take them out, that's all. Someone always knows what's going to happen."

Christa seemed to consider this comment for a moment, scanning it for truth, and then her eyes twinkled. "But what about ghosts? People can't keep track of ghosts. They can go anywhere anytime and nobody will ever know until they choose to make themselves known."

"Even if ghosts do exist and you ran into one in that *haunted* house—or even in grandma's attic—you can just turn around and leave. Odds are there will be people in the next room ready to talk about it and give you hugs. That's not scary."

Jane didn't want to interrupt. She quite enjoyed listening, not that she had much of a choice. As their seat climbed slowly to the top again the Haunted House came into view, still shrouded in a weird kind of mist. It looked mysterious enough to Jane, but what if there was some truth to what Mandy had said? Now Mandy was looking far beyond the field with her arms crossed, leaning over the safety bar.

"You know what's really scary?" said Mandy, not turning her head.

"What?" Christa asked.

"Look over there." Jane and Christa both looked to the forest where Mandy was pointing, now only an ominous outline under a cloak of darkness. Mandy began to speak, her tone soft, haunting. "Nobody will ever be able to tell you what exactly is in there. It goes on for miles and miles, not interrupted by any one." A gust of wind blew softly through the trees, changing the forest's outline briefly and then allowing it to return to its natural shape. "They'll tell you there are bears and wolves and snakes in there—maybe even mountain lions—but what about all the things they don't tell you about? The things even they don't know. And in a place like that you can't just walk away; it's not that easy. Being out there, away from people and the comfort of knowing, now *that's* scary!"

The girls considered this for a while, none of them able to move their eyes from the forest. Moments ago it had simply been background to the festival—even to Jane, who had finally managed to dismiss what she had seen earlier as a simple misperception—but now it seemed so much closer, so much *bigger*.

In the silence, Jane began to reconsider. Then they were at the bottom of the Ferris Wheel and a man was helping them out of their seat, releasing the safety bar with a loud *clank*.

The sisters sped through the remaining rides and as they neared the Haunted House the air grew dense with fog. Jane could feel her heart pounding, telling her to stay away. But her mind told her otherwise.

"Let's go!" yelled Christa. "There's almost nobody in line!" Christa took off in a sprint toward the ride while Mandy simply shrugged and walked after her. Jane stood in awe, wide-eyed and smiling. Some girls dream of exquisite gardens and castles containing all of the pretty objects they'd ever been told they needed. Jane, however, had dreamt of this. Finally she would discover what leapt and shambled and lurked behind those creepy looking walls. Jane started after her sisters, but before she could gain any real ground, she felt a hand grab her shoulder firmly. It was her mother's.

"Jane, you're still too young." She spoke these words with the calm precision of a skilled assassin, leaving no chance for retaliation. "I'm not comfortable with you going in there tonight." She had planned to let Jane go in the Haunted House this year, but something had changed her mind. She still wasn't sure what it was that had made her feel ill at ease, but she couldn't shake the uncomfortable feeling that seemed to follow her everywhere she went. She felt exposed, as if someone—or something—was watching her.

"Why? You told me I was ready," said Jane. "You can't just change your mind like that." Then Jane paused, looking at her mother. She knew the look her mom was giving her; knew it well. Any attempt to get into the ride tonight would be a wasted effort. Jane didn't whine. She didn't argue. She just hung her head and turned away.

Mandy and Christa had both returned when they realized Jane wasn't following them.

"Seriously, mom? She hasn't shut up about the Haunted House for the past week, and now you're not even going to let her go in?" said Christa.

"It's not like she's going to be traumatized because of it," added Mandy. "It's nothing but creaky floorboards and masks."

"I don't care," their mother said, gazing uneasily past the Haunted House at the darkness behind it. "Your sister isn't going with you tonight and I don't want to hear any more about it. Now go on, and come right back to our table when you're done."

Mandy and Christa lingered there, scanning their minds for some sort of counterargument, but the solemn look on their mother's face eventually caused them to give up. Christa offered Jane a weak smile before they turned away and walked into the mist surrounding the Haunted House.

"Jane…I'm sorry. I just can't let you go in there tonight. There's something—" Jane's mother trailed off, unsure of where the sentence was going. "Do you want cotton candy? Maybe some ice cream? Or we could go on the Ferris Wheel again, together. That would be fun, wouldn't it?"

Without looking up, Jane said "No thanks," and started walking back toward their table. Her mother followed along silently, slightly ashamed, but also relieved. She didn't know why it had to be this way. She just knew it did.

At the table, Jane's father was talking with a friend, mostly about anything other than crops and harvesting. Jane sat down forcefully, the bench letting out a pained squeak as she did so, and then she crossed her arms on the table and shoved her face into them. The two men looked over at Jane and then back at her mother, who shrugged and sat down next to her husband.

"What did you say to *her?*" he asked, a hint of amusement in his voice.

"She's upset because I wouldn't let her go into the Haunted House."

"Why not? You let her watch those scary movies at home. It's a stupid thing anyway." To this question he received no verbal response, just a glare telling him to shut up. So the subject was changed and they discussed pretty much anything other than crops, harvesting and Jane, who still sat at the end of the bench ignoring them with her face stuffed between her arms.

Time passed and Jane grew restless. Sometimes she forgot how boring adults could be, but listening to them in the midst of conversation, always reminded her of the fact. She began to wonder when her sisters were going to come back, but that made her think about the Haunted House again—and of not being in it—and then she felt sad and angry all over again. And how long were her parents going to go about their night pretending like she wasn't even there?

"I have to go to the bathroom," Jane said, finally emerging from the burrow she had created. She got up from the table and started walking toward the row of Port-a-Potties on the other end of the field.

"Wait. I'll come with you," her mother said, half-running to catch up.

"If you have to," said Jane.

They travelled through the crowd, Jane making sure to be a few steps ahead of her mother the whole way. When they arrived, there was a line of people waiting, and they stood there without speaking to each other. Time passed slowly, especially for Jane's mother who wanted to speak, but didn't. Eventually they were at the front of the line and a man had just come out from the Port-a-Potty furthest to the left. He looked at the wash station, decided against using it, and then walked carelessly back into the crowd.

Jane moved toward the stall he'd just vacated.

"I'll be waiting for you over by the wash station," her mother said.

"Sure," Jane said dismissively. She walked in and allowed the door to slam shut loudly behind her, hoping it would make an impression. First, her mom wouldn't let her go in the Haunted House with her sisters, and now she wouldn't even let her walk to the bathroom on her own. What was happening? Jane sat down on the filthy seat and closed her eyes to think.

The sour smell of human waste wafted up from below. It pushed against the walls and the roof, trying to escape into the crisp night air, but the Port-a-Potty kept the evil trapped well. So it waited—waited for Jane to open the door and set it free—even if it was only for a moment, evil always got out somehow.

Jane rose from the seat, and when she went to zip up her fly, her hand brushed against something in her pocket. Strange—she didn't remember there being anything in there. She reached inside her pocket and her hand emerged with a tiny metal flashlight. She clenched it between her fingers, staring at it, feeling its coolness against her palm. Now she remembered. In a moment of weakness, she had slipped it into her pocket, just in case the Haunted House was too scary. But that didn't matter anymore.

Jane opened the door and stepped outside. Her mother was by the wash station talking to a friend and didn't even notice as she came out—which was perfect. Jane dashed behind the row of urinals and sat down on the grass, propping her back up against the plastic wall. A wide smile spread across her face. This would give her mother the scare she deserved. She would just wait here for a while and bask in her own cleverness while her mother panicked.

Jane fiddled around with the flashlight, then pointed it at the ground and turned it on and off a few times. The beam of light it produced was much brighter than she expected. She sat there for a couple of minutes, feeling the dampness of the grass begin to seep through her jeans and not really minding. Then she heard a knocking sound followed by her mother's voice.

"Jane, are you okay in there, sweetie?" she said from the other side of the Port-a-Potty. Jane snickered quietly. There was silence for a few moments, and then a voice came from within. It was a man's voice.

"Lady, you're looking in the wrong place," he said.

Jane had to cover her mouth with her hands to muffle the laughter that followed. This was too good.

"Jane!" her mother called again. "Where are you? Come out. This isn't funny!"

Oh, but it was.

Jane stood up silently. Not far ahead of her was the forest. Its dark boundary stretched all the way across the back of the field. There was no more time to think. Jane pocketed the flashlight and took off in a full sprint, still hearing her mother's voice in the distance. It was only a matter of time before her mother would check around back, and Jane didn't want to be in view when it happened. She made it quickly through the small stretch of field and then hid behind a tree at the edge of the forest. From here, she could see perfectly.

Her mother's calls were growing faint now, partly because of the distance, but also because her mother's throat was getting hoarse. Finally, her mother stepped out from the side of the furthest Port-a-Potty and came into full view. She looked around frantically, still calling out Jane's name as loudly as she could. There was a moment where Jane thought she had been caught. Her mother stopped calling and stood gravely still, looking right at her. Jane stared into her mother's eyes for a long time, not wanting to make the first move. But then her mother took a step back. She didn't just look panicked now—she looked scared to death—like a deer on vibrating train tracks.

Her mother took another step back, this time colliding with the plastic wall behind her. She stayed there for a moment with her back straight against the wall, staring ahead wide-eyed, and then she ran off back into the crowd, calling her daughter's name as she went.

Perfect. This was exactly what her mother deserved. Jane supposed she had run off to get her father. He would be mad, of course, and she would certainly get into trouble, but this was totally worth it. Now maybe her mother would think twice before going back on a promise.

A cold tingle ran down the back of Jane's neck, and then stopped abruptly. But what had caused it? The wind was largely subdued where she stood by the web of leaves and branches, so it couldn't have been that. Jane remembered what she thought she had seen earlier—the eyes looking out from the trees, fixed and staring. But she was sure they were just an illusion, brought on by the fixation of her own strained eyes. Then the tingle came again, slower now, moving all the way down her spine.

Jane spun around and saw nothing but trees and dim outlines. She fumbled around in her pocket, pulled out the flashlight and turned it on. The beam seemed much brighter back in the field. Here, in the shadows of the forest, it did little more than illuminate the trees and the dirt a few meters ahead.

As she stood alone in the darkness, her sister's words began to resonate with her. Sure, the Haunted House would probably have been scary, but in the forest there was nobody to turn to—no way to know exactly what was lurking just beyond your field of vision. And wasn't *that* fear in its most primal form? Being alone and blind? This was the ultimate thrill, not the Haunted House. She had been looking in the wrong place the whole time. Jane was going to get what she wanted after all.

She advanced with baby steps, holding the flashlight straight ahead like a readied sword. The full moon looked down on her from its perch in the sky, shining with the reflected beauty of the sun. It looked both royal and humble both at the same time. At this point, even if she turned around, Jane wouldn't be able to see the light that came from the festival. It was far behind her now.

As she walked on, something white appeared ahead in the distance, far beyond the scope of her flashlight. It looked like the outline of a woman's body, covered in fine silk. The chill came back—tiny icicles pricking randomly at her body—but she continued on. Yes, she was scared, but she was too intrigued to turn back now.

She and the vision moved onward silently for a while, and then the thing stopped and turned around slowly, revealing its face. It was definitely a woman, and she was smiling widely—too widely, Jane thought. Her hair was long and black, only noticeable in the darkness by its radiant sheen. She stared right at Jane, beckoning her with deep, green eyes, and then she seemed to evaporate into the night air. Her smile was the last part of her to go, and for a moment, it hung alone in the darkness like a sickle moon.

Was she a ghost? Jane wasn't sure if the woman had truly disappeared, or if she had just somehow managed to slip out of her field of vision. The woman didn't seem like a ghost; she looked mostly opaque, though the silk mystified her figure. But she didn't seem completely human either—the way she blended in with the moonlight, and her smile lingered in the air.

Jane needed to know more. She trekked on through the leaves and the hard-packed dirt, not daring to look behind her. The moon seemed to be drifting away from her as she continued on. She doubted this was true, but the thought of it made her feel uncomfortable. She saw a small patch of white glowing in the distance for only a few moments, and then it was gone, just like before. Jane kept following it. The woman seemed to be flickering in and out of Jane's consciousness. Each time she reappeared somewhere different, and Jane had to keep changing direction to keep up with her. She had no clue how deep into the forest she was now, and that didn't matter. The only thing that mattered was following the woman in white.

For a moment, Jane thought she had lost her completely. But then she reappeared. This time the woman was directly ahead. She turned around to face Jane. A smile still illuminated her face, this time spreading to her eyes. The expression looked more genuine this time, but still made her feel uncomfortable. The woman turned back around and continued forward. Soon after, she seemed to disappear into an even darker darkness than that which surrounded them.

Jane continued forward. There was something ahead of her, but the beam coming from her flashlight was too weak to identify it. She thought she was getting close. The patch of darkness was beginning to take shape, its outline compressing into a tight rectangle. Then something appeared above Jane. She aimed her flashlight upward, illuminating a large window. Behind this window was the woman's glowing face. She was watching patiently.

Jane now realized that she had been led to an old house, and that the dark rectangle was actually a doorway. The door itself had been ripped from its hinges. She stepped onto the porch and felt the damp, rotted wood give way beneath her feet. There were squeaks coming from below her. They were loud and agitated. A stream of furry things climbed up from below the steps and scurried past her feet. She could hear the sound of crunching leaves as they ran for cover.

The mixed aroma of rot and burning wax assaulted Jane as soon as she entered the house. It had clearly been decomposing for a long time, but where was the smell of wax coming from? A speck of brightness caught Jane's eye somewhere up on the second floor. That was it. A candle had been lit somewhere above her. Jane scanned the main floor with her flashlight; most of it was taken up by a large and desolate living room. The wooden chairs that outlined the room had lost their colour and were now a sad, pale shade of beige. The cushions on top of them had been overtaken with mold and were likely now a hideaway for a variety of bugs, especially those that crawled about on seemingly infinite legs; the kind that always went unnoticed until they were on you, tickling you until you screamed.

In the center of the room was a battered coffee table that looked as if it would collapse under the slightest of winds. To the side of the living room was a kitchen that appeared to be under the same tragic spell. Cupboard doors hung crookedly from rusted hinges, guarding against intruders of the night. Jane didn't dare open any drawers for fear of what might be lurking within them, but she certainly had ideas, and those were bad enough. Beside the kitchen's opening was a tall, carpeted staircase, a mix between its former red colouring and the dark green of the mold that was consuming it. It looked like some kind of morbid Christmas décor.

Jane went to the staircase and carefully started to climb, trying not to place too much pressure on any one spot. The light from the candle became brighter as she neared the top. She could picture the woman in white waiting for her. In Jane's mind, she stood calmly by the window, her wide, cryptic smile illuminated by a single flame. But what did these thoughts matter? She needed only to see for herself.

Jane reached the top and began down the single hallway. She had been wrong about there being only one light. There were several of them mounted along both sides of the hall, each one burning brightly and coaxing Jane to follow, which she did thoughtlessly, as if by some perverse instinct.

At the end of the hallway stood the first actual door she had seen since entering the house. It hung slightly ajar, just open enough to look inviting but not enough to reveal anything. As she came closer, her mental images of expectation began to blur.

Jane pushed the door open with a trembling hand and it creaked slowly backward to reveal the room. A single candle burned atop a small, round table that stood in the farthest corner, and beside it was the woman in white, rocking slowly back and forth in a throne of rotting wood. She looked silently over at Jane and motioned for her to sit down on the carpet, offering the same unsettling smile as before.

Jane backed up a step. *Why had she followed this woman here?* Her venture into the forest was just supposed to be a cheap thrill, not whatever this was. She wanted to leave, but if it was truly within her power to do so, wouldn't she have turned back long before she reached the house? Jane backed up another step, but then she saw the woman's face flickering behind the candlelight once more, and the smile wouldn't let her go. It was a hungry smile. The woman pointed again to the carpet on the other side of the room, just beyond the range of the dim light, and then she stared expectantly. This time Jane complied.

As she moved to her appointed destination, Jane began to see outlines in the darkness. They were the outlines of small bodies, about the size of hers, and they were each sitting cross-legged on the carpet. She sat down and nudged a girl beside her, but the girl made no response. Jane turned around and tried to get the attention of the boy behind her, again without success. He was staring fixedly ahead, in the direction of the woman in white. So were the rest of them.

The woman cleared her throat in an ultimate act of summoning, and then she picked up a thick and dusty storybook from the table and began to read aloud. Her voice was sadly mysterious—hauntingly beautiful. It provided hope, and then took it away, all in one quick breath. She spoke of far-off lands and of bravely irrational warriors and beasts, of dragons that flew over mountains and cornfields, over cities and apartment buildings, rarely stopping to wave or make small talk. She spoke of the things that soared above the clouds on sprawling, golden wings, and also of the things that danced wildly underground in a sea of flames and judgment.

The pages flipped forward and Jane went with them, stopping briefly on mountaintops, on fields of snow and ice, on puny rowboats lost in vengeful oceans. And then the woman in white spoke of life itself. She spoke truthfully, embellishing nothing and making nothing up—there was cheer and triumph, pain and sadness, and as she reached the end, there seemed to only be loss. The woman began to cry deeply, her tears spilling onto the pages like crystalline blood from a very deep wound.

Jane and the other children stared thoughtfully ahead at her, not daring to speak. For a while, the only noise in the room was the woman's sobbing. And then she rose from her decomposing throne, one hand covering her face, while the other clasped the book tightly to her side.

She bent over and blew out the candle, leaving them all in complete darkness. Her sobbing could no longer be heard.

The sudden darkness stole Jane back from wherever her mind had wandered to and she began to form her own thoughts again. Why was she sitting here in the dark? Where had the other children come from? She just wanted to be home now—home with her dad and her sisters and even her mother.

Jane heard footsteps coming from where the woman had been standing. They travelled across the room, each one stabbing into the silence. And then they stopped. There was a slow and escalating squeak as the woman opened the door, followed by a final thump, as she closed it behind her.

Jane stood and ran to it, only to be met by the clicking sound of a key in a lock. She pounded and kicked at the door, her screams filling the house, but none of that made any difference. The woman's cold footsteps continued down the hall and toward the stairs.

After a while, Jane grew tired from her tantrum. She had known its futility from the start, but instinct had led her to try anyway. She slumped to the ground with her back against the door and curled up into a tight ball. Her tears flowed freely and silently, dripping onto her jeans and creating little dark patches that couldn't be seen through the greater darkness that surrounded her. They were like splashes of vodka in a clear pond.

"What's your name?" It was the voice of a young boy.

"I'm Jane," she said, wiping her tears away. She had almost forgotten she wasn't alone. She squinted into the darkness, searching for the outlines she had seen before, but they seemed to have disappeared.

Nobody spoke for a long time, but Jane knew they were there. She could feel the other children communicating all around her. She wasn't sure how they were doing it. They seemed to be releasing waves of thoughts and feelings into the air, then absorbing them through finely tuned and mysterious receptors. Jane felt a weak current flowing through the room that tickled her skin.

"Why are you here?" asked the boy.

Silence. Though she couldn't see them, Jane felt their eyes on her. They were trying to piece together her story—trying to understand. The tone of the room was serious, but she could feel specks of sympathy slipping through cracks in the mysterious current through which they were communicating.

"You don't belong here," the boy said.

"Do *you* belong here?" asked Jane. Her question lingered in the darkness.

Jane stood up and started to walk toward the boy's voice. She remembered seeing at least a dozen other children earlier, if only just their outlines. They had still been there. She reached the other end of the room without finding anyone, so she circled the area a couple times. Still, she found nothing but dust and stale air. Then Jane remembered the flashlight. She pulled it from her pocket and flicked the switch, drowning the darkness under waves of illumination. But there was nothing to be seen, except for the chair and the table that stood plainly in the corner. Jane looked all around her. Still, she found nothing.

"We can help you leave," said the boy. "You shouldn't be here. You aren't like us."

"How?" she asked.

Then Jane felt the current flowing through the air once again. It was getting stronger. The tickling sensation returned, causing the tiny hairs on her arms to spring up. She could feel the thoughts of the children as they streamed back and forth in conversation. The waves eventually became thicker and they zipped across the room argumentatively like angry bees. Jane tried to snatch messages from the air, but she could only feel their residual vibrations. It took quite some time for the waves to return to their natural, faint buzzing. But when they did, Jane knew the argument had been won. The change in current was followed by a sharp clicking noise on the other side of the room.

"You can leave now," said the boy. "It wasn't your time. You weren't supposed to be here."

"But if you can unlock the door," Jane asked, "then why are you still here?" Again, she was only met with silence.

Jane walked to the other side of the room and opened the door carefully so it didn't squeak. Just before stepping out, she turned back and whispered a "thank you" into the darkness. They had appreciated this. Jane felt a pleasant tingle on her arms and a dozen faces attempting to smile weakly at her as she closed the door.

All of the candles in the hallway had been blown out. Still, Jane pocketed her flashlight, hoping to leave without the woman noticing. She tiptoed silently down the hall and then tried to descend the stairs with the same grace. Unfortunately, they weren't quite as forgiving. Jane expected the woman to be waiting around the corner when she reached the bottom, but apparently she hadn't noticed.

As Jane turned the corner, she heard the woman sobbing in the living room. She had lit a single candle and placed it on the coffee table. It shone alongside the moonlight that streamed faintly through the windows, creating an eerie fluorescence that lingered around the woman. Jane moved closer to the open doorway. Now she could see the woman standing, hunched over in the middle of the room. She was facing away from Jane, looking at something in her hand. Even as her tears streamed down, she kept her eyes fixed on the object.

Jane tiptoed again. She was almost to the door—almost out of the house—but now she could see what the woman was holding. It was a black and white picture of a small girl and a young woman with a crescent moon smile. The child was sitting on her lap and the woman was reading to her from a large storybook.

The woman wept uncontrollably. She was caressing the picture now, carefully, lovingly, in the place where the girl was sitting. Tears were dripping onto the photo, blurring its features. Jane felt sorry for the woman. For a moment, she forgot about everything that had just happened. All she wanted to do was ease the woman's pain. She took a step toward the center of the living room, and at the same time the clouds of emotion parted to make way for the glaring brightness of reason. Jane turned around. She knew she had to leave while she still could, and she was so close now—only a few more steps and she would be back in the forest.

The smells of popcorn and cotton candy materialized, begging her to follow them. She was finished searching for scares. She'd be a good little girl from now on. Hell, she wouldn't even go into the Haunted House ever! As she closed in on the exit, she felt the ground compressing beneath her feet. The rotted floorboards were sinking silently under her weight. She took another step forward, and when Jane brought her foot down, it sunk right through the wood, almost as if it hadn't even been there. Jane screamed as her entire leg disappeared into the empty space below the house.

The woman spun around, the silk of her gown and the tears on her face illuminated by the eerie light. She looked at the picture once more and then tucked it away before approaching the struggling young girl. The woman's face was impossible to read. She looked hopelessly sad, but there was something else there. Was it hope? Her lips curled into the same crescent smile that Jane remembered from the forest. It spread all the way to her eyes, which were now bright, wanting. The woman advanced with a ghostly calm.

Jane continued to scream as she tried to remove her leg from the hole. She placed both hands on the ground beside her and pushed upward, causing even more of the rotted wood to collapse beneath her. As she flailed about, attempting to free her herself, a tickle ran up her leg, and then there was another, which was inevitably followed by more. *Rats.* They ran up her body from the space below and leapt from her shoulders onto the floor before scurrying away. Jane's scream became a wail of disgust, but the rats were not dissuaded by it. Some of them started climbing up her neck and onto her head before leaping away to find a new place of darkness to hide in.

The woman was close now. She kept a steady pace as the rats scurried excitedly past her feet. She wasn't bothered by them. They had been sharing the space for a long time. The woman eagerly reached her arms out toward Jane, her smile curled into that same haunting grin.

Jane saw the woman's hands coming toward her and backed away from them as far as she could. Her leg was still stuck deep below the floorboards. She had been too distracted to make any progress. As Jane tried to pull herself out, an especially mean looking rat dropped from the top of her head and collided with her face, its inexplicably wet fur brushing over her lips before it landed on the floor and ran off. Her scream was so loud it caused the woman to freeze mid-step, her hands mere inches from Jane's pale skin.

Jane's body surged with something greater than adrenaline, and the deepest, most primal parts of her brain—those which were summoned by situation and operated under necessity—took control. Just as the woman had regained her composure, Jane lunged away desperately, bringing her buried leg out from its captivity and landing hard on the floor. She scrambled to the doorway on her hands and knees, and finally felt the cold night air against her face. She was out, and she wasn't looking back. She had been seduced by that woman's smile for the last time.

A wretched scream came from behind her as she ran down the steps and into the darkness of the forest. She could feel the woman's agony sailing after her through the night air, but Jane just kept running. She wasn't sure if she was going in the right direction, and right now she didn't even care. She just wanted to get away from the house and the woman. The sound of snapping twigs came from behind her.

Jane felt around in her pocket for the flashlight as she ran, but it was completely empty. It had to have slipped out of her pocket when she was trying to free her leg. She looked ahead, only seeing faint outlines. But Jane knew there was no time to worry about the flashlight now. She had to keep moving. And even if Jane *was* going the wrong way, she would much rather deal with the wild animals, than come face to face with the woman again. At least she understood what the animals were, what they wanted.

Jane was fairly certain now that she wasn't being followed, but she refused to slow her pace. She leapt over small streams, tree stumps, roots that protruded from the ground like gnarled hands. She did all of this, somehow, without falling flat on her face. Something was propelling her—guiding her—talking directly to her and telling her where to step. And then the darkness began to give way to a faint glow. Ahead, the congregation of trees appeared less dense, less ominous. She could see the moon hanging in the sky between two tall trees, beaming brightly. It looked satisfied, although not in a way that Jane could fully understand.

She heard a familiar voice calling her name. It was coming from just ahead of her. And now she saw that the trees were beginning to give way to the wide field of the festival. She was close now, so close make out the Ferris Wheel's colourful lights spinning around through the leaves and branches.

Jane picked up speed, focusing only on the lights and the sound of the familiar voice. Together they formed the perfect beacon, providing reassurance and motivation. As she neared the border that separated the field and forest, she was granted a clear view of the voice's owner. It belonged to Mandy. A smile spread over Jane's face as she made the connection and ran even faster toward her sister.

"Mandy!" she yelled. "It's me! I'm here!" The last words came out in a choked wheeze of exhaustion.

Mandy was still searching for the voice when Jane came rushing out from behind the trees and collided with her. Jane wrapped her arms tightly around her sister, burying her head deep into her baggy sweater, embracing its warmth, its familiarity. Now that she was out of the woods and away from the mysterious darkness that lived within them, Jane allowed the tears to fall. They had built up behind an icy layer of fear that was just now beginning to thaw and give way to the flood of emotion she was feeling. Jane was forced to relive what she had seen through a constant flow of undistracted and curious thoughts. This particular film would play under dim lighting in the cinema of her mind for years.

"When mom told us you were missing, I knew you had gone in *there*," said Mandy. Her voice was calm. She hugged Jane tightly, not expecting a response. And at first, there was none. They stood in silence, Mandy with her chin resting on Jane's head, and her dark, moonlit hair blowing softly in the breeze. But now, as the tears were beginning to dry, Jane finally spoke. Her voice had been stripped of its usual feigned maturity and what remained sounded natural, like it was coming from the frightened nine-year-old child that she was.

"You were right," said Jane.

"I'm sorry I said what I did. This is my fault. I shouldn't have ruined the Haunted House for you. Then you would have just waited until next year—you wouldn't have gone in there." They stood silently for a while before Mandy spoke again, trying to sound casual, trying to hide her own burning curiosity. "What did you see in the forest?"

Jane peeked out from Mandy's sweater and looked up into her wide, expectant eyes. How was she supposed to explain what had happened? Even if she told her sister the truth, Jane didn't think she'd believe her anyway. She just wanted to go back to their picnic table and pretend that she had never left.

"You can tell me Jane. I'll believe you." Mandy's voice sounded sincere. It wouldn't matter how long Jane put this off. Mandy would keep asking. She knew it. Jane decided to tell her, but just as she was about to begin the story, Mandy smiled and started making wild waving gestures in the air. The rest of the family had found them and now they were running over.

"Tell me what happened—before mom gets here. You know she's never going to leave you alone now," said Mandy. She laughed uncomfortably, her eyes still serious and inquiring.

Jane started to speak. She described how dark it was and how the branches looked like they were reaching out to grab her. She told her about the noises, about the coldness—about everything that wasn't anything. This was even harder than she thought it would be.

"But what did you *see?*" Mandy asked, her tone rushed. The rest of the family was almost there.

"Promise you won't tell anyone?" said Jane.

"I promise."

As reassured as she was going to be, Jane opened her mouth to speak. But before any words came out, she saw something at the edge of the forest, just barely visible from behind Mandy's shoulder. It was the woman, her green eyes glowing brightly and her mouth curled into that disturbing grin.

Jane froze. Her mouth was still wide open, unspoken words dangling from the tip of her tongue. She couldn't tell if the woman was crying or cackling—or if she was doing both. The skin covering the woman's cheekbones was red and strained, almost painfully so, and it looked like it would soon rip apart under the pressure of her smile. Tears fell from her dark, green eyes, curving widely around the edges of her mouth in their descent. She slowly extended her arms out from the forest. Her eyes were hopeful, almost endearing, but her smile was filled with blatant and hideous deceit.

And yet, Jane felt herself being pulled in once more. All she could see were those lips, disgusting and alluring, both at the same time. Pain was festering within the woman, spreading throughout her face; and now it was eating at her eyes. They were no longer a beautiful green; they were now completely black, except for small specks of flame that burned wildly at the very back of them.

Jane tried to move toward the woman, tried to reach past Mandy with both arms, but then she was hugged tightly from behind and removed from the trance she was in.

It was her mother. "Jane! Why would you run away like that? And why there? I don't understand it." Her mother's words were panicked, but Jane didn't register them. She was focused on Mandy, who was now staring at her with fear and confusion—and also with interest. Jane glanced quickly over Mandy's shoulder. The woman was gone…Or at least she had decided not to be seen.

"What did you *see?*" asked Mandy again, her voice a low and disturbed whisper.

Now the whole family was watching her, silently demanding answers. What was she supposed to say to them? If she told them the truth, everyone—except maybe for Mandy—would think she was lunatic. Suddenly, everything hit her all at once, the exhaustion, the fear, everything she still didn't fully understand. And at the center of these thoughts, was the woman's face. It was still smiling, watching her patiently from within the forest.

Jane could no longer handle it. She shut down, collapsing onto the grass and allowing the tears to cleanse her bruised and weary mind. Her family stood silently around her, not knowing what to say or do. They glanced down at her, and then back at each other. Each of them was waiting for someone else to make the first move.

Eventually Jane's father hoisted her up onto his shoulders and started walking back toward the festival. His gait was calm but purposeful—that of a man who was confident in his understanding, regardless of its accuracy. The rest of the family watched him carry Jane across the lonely stretch of grass, and soon they followed, remaining about ten paces behind, making no attempt to close the distance.

The forest watched them as they left the festival grounds. It looked pleasant enough to the casual eyes that occasionally wandered over to it. All those eyes saw were branches that swayed gently in the breeze. They saw a wall of leaves painted silver by the moonlight above. They saw the placid cloak that it wanted them to see.

But, behind it, existed an insatiable hunger. The woman was still there, just deep enough into the trees that she could see without being seen. Now all she could do was wait. Eventually another child would stray from the herd, become vulnerable to her allure. And when they did, she would be there with a sick smile carved upon her face.

The Artifact

Nick Nafpliotis

The normally raucous morning commons area at Wando High School was deadly quiet. All the students who usually milled about before the start of the school day were standing completely still, transfixed by the enormous alligator carcass that hung from the entryway awning.

Francesca's first thought was that it was sort of a symbolic gesture, for that Friday's homecoming game was against Goose Greek High School, whose mascot was the same as the dead creature swinging lazily in the air above them.

"Good thing we aren't playing the Fort Dorchester Patriots," her friend Peter whispered while school administrators frantically cut through the crowd.

The joke made Francesca smile and briefly forget the dark seed of fear that had taken root in her mind. A reptile corpse hanging in front of the school was enough to throw off anyone's morning, but the ghastly act's timing and suspect motivations were bothering her far more than she'd anticipated. "Why the hell would someone string up a wild animal representing the other school's mascot on our campus?" she asked as an assistant principal barked at the students to get inside the building.

"I don't know," Peter replied. "It's homecoming week. Crazy stuff always happens around this time of year."

"Yeah, but that shit over there is a whole different level of messed up," Francesca said while looking back over her shoulder. "I'm all for dress up days and getting out of class for a pep rally, but I don't think I'm ready to take my school spirit into animal sacrifice territory."

"That's just because you don't really care about the team," Peter replied with a grin as they entered their first period class. "Maybe if you actually understood the game of football…"

"Bullshit!" Francesca snapped at him. "I'm the one at Powder Puff each year who has to explain the rules to everyone. And unlike you, I actually go to all our home games!"

Peter smiled, reveling in his latest success at pushing Francesca's buttons. She was normally unflappable, but a slight against her athletic, tomboy nature was a surefire way to bring forth the rage.

As class started, Francesca's annoyance was quickly replaced by the fog of dread that she'd felt after seeing the alligator carcass outside before school. Her mind was completely shut off to the teacher's voice, along with everything else that typically ran through it. Not even the temptation of a fully reloaded data plan was enough to make her want to sneak her phone out under the desk. Instead, all she could focus on was the chill that ran down her spine whenever she pictured the dead alligator's eyes staring back at her. When the bell rang at the end of the period, she felt as if she'd been snapped awake from a dream. She absentmindedly gathered her books and headed out the door, moving by rote to her locker.

"Dude," Isabel said while purposefully bumping into her. "What the hell's wrong with you? You look like me after last weekend."

"First of all, if you're implying that I look drunk and/or stoned out of my mind, then that would be you after every weekend," Francesca replied as she got the rest of her books from her locker. "As far as why I look like this, you can replace 'prolific substance abuse' with the freaking dead alligator that greeted everyone as we walked into school today."

"Yeah, that was a pretty horrible way to start the morning," Isabel responded with a sigh. "Who would even do something like that? I know it's Spirit Week and all, but holy shit…"

"That's not what's really bugging me, though" Francesca replied after closing her locker door. "If it really was a prank by a bunch of douchebags from Goose Creek High School, why would they kill an animal that's the same as their own mascot and display it here? Was it some psychotic way of admitting defeat before the game?"

"Who knows," Isabel said with a wave of her hand. "I'm just glad it looks like the only game I ever go to has so much drama behind it already. And speaking of being my only game, are we still going to dig up our artifacts?"

"Hell yes we are," Francesca said with a nod.

The *artifacts* were something that she and her friends from middle school had been trying to retrieve for the last three years. The building where they'd spent sixth through eighth grade had previously served as the high school until just a few years ago, when it moved down the road to a newly constructed facility. The massive historic football stadium, however, still remained in use. In the shadow of that ancient concrete structure was where they'd buried a part of their lives that was long overdue to be unearthed.

A lifetime ago in 7th grade, Francesca's social studies teacher asked everyone to select some sort of object that represented the most important parts of their lives. When the unit was complete, the class put them all into a giant Rubbermaid container and buried it near the stadium.

"Next year, I'll find a day where you can all come back to visit," Mr. Wisson had proclaimed that afternoon. "We'll dig this container up and see how what's important to you in 8th grade compares to what feels important right now."

That summer, Mr. Wisson got a job in another state, leaving the completion of their project in limbo. Francesca and her friends pleaded with their other teachers to help them unearth the container, but none of them were eager to go outside with a bunch of students to dig a hole in the ground.

The people who'd kept in touch during high school always talked about going back and digging it up themselves, but a multitude of varying schedules and social groups never allowed the reunion to take place. This Friday would be one of the very rare occasions when they'd all be in the same place at the same time, sitting right above the artifacts' burial spot.

"Let's just hope whoever is working security that night isn't an asshole," Francesca said before she and Isabel parted ways. "Hopefully, they'll be too busy dealing with shady people to worry about our perfectly wholesome excavation project."

"Hey, now! I'm one of those shady people you're talking about," Isabel shot back, her mock indignation betrayed by a warm smile.

The rest of the school day went along as normal. At the end of first period, the alligator had been removed and retrieved by the town's animal control unit. By the end of the day, the subject of the dead creature hanging from the school entryway had almost completely disappeared, as well.

Stray cats weren't something that people in the affluent town of Mount Pleasant were used to seeing, especially en mass. So when a group of them came charging down the main hallway of Wando High School on Tuesday after lunch, no one was really sure what to think.

Francesca and her friend Alex, who was twice the size of any other student at the school, both had to dive out of the way as the stampede of fur and yowls barreled past them.

"At least no one hung them from the rafters," Alex said, as they got back up. "Those things were moving fast as hell, though. Pretty sure they were quicker than anyone from the team we're playing this Friday."

"Whoever actually let them in the building is an idiot," Francesca added as they started back down the hall. "One of the zillion cameras they have around here will definitely have caught them in the act."

"So I guess we'll know who it was once they're suspended," Alex replied. "Better not have been one of our guys, though. That would be a pretty dumb reason to lose your eligibility to play this late in the season."

Francesca was about to respond when a scream echoed up the main hallway from the Fine Arts corridor. She quickly excused herself and ran toward the sound. A few feet from the band room, her friend Emily was balled up on the floor, her hands and arms covered in blood.

"I was just leaving from putting away my instrument when I saw them," she stammered through tears and gritted teeth. "I tried to pick one up, but before I could, three of them attacked me and ran off."

"It's alright, babe," Francesca said as she helped her friend off the floor. "I'll walk down to the nurse's office with you." As she put her arm around Emily and turned back toward the main hallway, Francesca saw a teacher opening a door and shooing the cats outside. As they charged out into the courtyard, one of them leapt in the teacher's direction, causing him to nearly fall over.

The rest of the day went by with everyone speculating about who had let the group of feral cats into the building. Unlike most of her peers, Francesca was friends with some of the students who were considered likely suspects, due to their checkered disciplinary history. To her surprise, none of them seemed to know anything about the cats—or the dead alligator from the day before.

By the time the buses and cars rolled away from school that afternoon, no one had been suspended. The next morning, there still hadn't been any word on who was responsible, but those concerns were quickly overshadowed by another bizarre occurrence.

Any classes unfortunate enough to have an outside facing window were violently bombarded throughout the day by birds, which slammed into them repeatedly at full speed. During first period, one hit the art room's window hard enough that its head splattered. The sight had upset everyone enough that the entire class was moved into the auditorium.

Francesca's AP History class had tried to carry on through the intermittent distractions, but even their teacher eventually became too rattled to continue with the lesson. For the rest of the period, everyone just stared outside, trying in vain to steel themselves against the startling thuds and frantic squawking. Yet as unsettling as that was, it didn't compare to what the students were greeted by on Thursday morning.

The night before, someone had painted red symbols in various places all over the outside of the school. Some were smeared on the walls, while others had been drawn onto the sidewalk and courtyard area. "Looks like Mrs. Holland finally marked her territory," Peter said to Francesca with a chuckle. "I wonder if this means we'll get to go home from school or something."

"Fat chance," a girl behind them replied. "But if all it takes to cancel class is a few occult symbols, I'll start drawing them every night before we have a test."

Francesca didn't know what most of the symbols were, but she did recognize a few. Pentagrams could be found in abundance along with the Eye of Providence, which was sure to have the kids who believed in Illuminati conspiracy theories going crazy. The scene was made even more surreal by the fact that everyone was dressed up in exaggerated 1980's style clothing for the Throwback Thursday Spirit Day.

Francesca, once again, felt the strange chill fun down her spine she'd been experiencing all week. Being freaked out by the things she'd seen was normal, but the feeling that gripped her now was something much more powerful. Everyone once in a while, it felt as though every nerve in her body was on fire, ready to make her explode into a ball of panic and tears. *Not the best week to start my period,* Francesca thought, as she walked out of the bathroom toward her first class.

Before she got there, a hand reached out and grabbed her from behind one of the vending machines. Francesca screamed an obscenity before realizing it was a friend who'd startled her.

"Damn it, Kristen," she said, after looking around to make sure there hadn't been any administrators around. "This is a really bad freaking week to scare the shit out of people like that."

"I'm sorry," Kristen replied, a slight tremble in her voice. "I just really needed to talk to you for a minute…about Friday."

"Sure," Francesca said. "You're still in for digging up the artifact with everyone, right?"

"I can't," Kristen replied, shaking her head. "And I don't think you should go, either."

"Why not?" Francesca asked, putting a hand on her friend's shoulder. "Is everything alright?"

"No, everything's not alright," Kristen said, her eyes meeting Francesca's with an earnest stare. "A bunch of those same symbols were drawn all over our church last night."

Francesca wasn't a big fan of Seacoast, the mega church half her school attended. Still, they didn't deserve to be vandalized like that. She started to tell her friend how sorry she was, before Kristen stopped her and continued on.

"Our pastor said he believes there's some type of dark presence descending over our town. God spoke to him and said we need to be vigilant against some sort of attack.

"Kristen—"

"Just listen! I know you don't believe in any of this stuff, but you have to admit there's been some pretty messed up stuff happening this week. Those symbols, though, are by far the worst. My mom also told me this morning that the ones on our church were drawn with animal blood. That probably means the symbols here were, too."

"Okay," Francesca sighed. "First of all, it is incredibly hard to take you seriously when you're wearing leg warmers and a headband. Second, I'm pretty sure all of this has just been the work of some messed up kid who needs to be heavily medicated."

"Or who worships Satan," Kristen replied in a quiet voice.

"Kris, anyone I've ever met who claims to worship the devil really just likes to sit around and smoke pot while listening to Marilyn Manson. Also, I highly doubt those symbols were made with animal blood. And even if they were, so what? Are you really going to let some psychotic douche canoe with a weird graffiti fetish keep you from going to Homecoming?"

"My church is having a lock-in on Friday, so that everyone has somewhere safe to go. I'm going. And I really think you should, too," Kristen stated firmly. "I've been praying about it, and there's a really heavy burden on my heart about you being at the game tomorrow night."

"Oh, what the hell, Kris," Francesca said, rolling her eyes. "Now you sound like my ultra-religious grandmother when she's explaining why I shouldn't wear yoga pants. Look, I respect your beliefs and all, but if God really doesn't want me going to the game, he can tell me himself."

"Just promise me one thing," Kristen said, with a resigned glance toward the floor before looking back up again. "If anything happens, try to dig up the artifact container and find what I put in there. It's really important to me that you be the only other person to have it."

"Yeah, okay…" Francesca replied, apprehensively. "I gotta get to math class. I'll see you later." After the two girls hugged and parted ways, the last thing Kristen said gnawed at Francesca's mind. Her friend was pretty religious, but not in the fundamentally nutty kind of way. She'd never seen Kristen this panicked about anything before. And why would she want her to bring back whatever was buried beneath the stadium so badly—especially if she wasn't willing to go on Friday to get it herself? "At least that means God didn't tell her pastor I would die," Francesca muttered as she entered her second period class.

The rest of the school day went by much more smoothly than the day before. The sound of multiple power washers outside would normally be enough to distract everyone from their studies, but the continual hum of spraying water was comforting compared to the violent and bloody bird crashes from the previous day.

As Francesca went outside to eat lunch in the courtyard, she noticed the red symbols were coming off much easier than paint should have been able to be removed. Maybe what Kristen had said about them being drawn in animal blood had been true.

"Fran! Where are you going?!"

Francesca looked back up into the stands to see Andrew and Maddy barreling down the stairs after her. She instantly felt a twinge of guilt about leaving early, especially since neither one of them even went to Wando. The only reason they'd shown up to the game, was to see her and the rest of their old friends from middle school. And to dig up the artifact.

Unfortunately, a lot more people than Kristen were spooked by everything that had gone on that week. That combined with a freak lighting storm that had popped up two hours before kickoff, had scared away the usual full house that would have been there for Homecoming under any other circumstances. Alumni, parents, and the band, still filled up most of the seats, but the normally packed student section was nearly half empty. What had really bothered Francesca, though, was that most of the people who were there had been acting very strangely. She was used to a lot of them being drunk or stoned—but this was different. It was as if they were trying to act like versions of themselves for a play, but not quite pulling it off.

"This is lame," Francesca said as Maddy and Andrew finally caught up to her. "We're already ahead by four touchdowns and it's not even halftime. Also, everyone's so drunk off their asses that you can't even talk to them."

"I'm not drunk," Maddy said, with a glazed-over stare.

"I'm…starting…to see straight again…maybe," Andrew said with crooked smile.

"*Whatever,*" Francesca said, turning back toward the exit. "I'll just meet up with you guys at Drew's party after the game."

Francesca exited the main gate, where the ticket taker gave her an eerie smile as she headed out toward the parking lot. The chill she'd felt off and on throughout the week ran down her spine once again, causing her to stop and look out over the dimly lit asphalt lot.

Maybe I'm just being paranoid, Francesca thought as she started walking toward her car again. She'd managed to snag a space in the front lot, but it was still a bit of a hike to get there. Leaving early did have its advantages, though. For one thing, all the rows of cars she was passing would remain in place, meaning that for the first time all season, she wouldn't have to wait in a line of traffic to leave.

As Francesca continued onward, a large SUV's high beams blinked on when she passed in front of it. The sudden illumination blinded her momentarily, before she was able to spin around and face the vehicle.

"Can I help you?" she asked. When no one answered, she continued forward, the lights clicking off behind her.

"Prick," Francesca muttered as she continued walking.

A few feet later, another set of lights turned on, this time from two different cars on either side of her. Francesca froze, peering through the blinding rays to try and get a look at the occupants of both the cars.

"Do you assholes have a problem?" she shouted, a slight tremble in her voice. After not getting an answer, Francesca kept on walking. Only this time, at a much quicker pace. As she moved down the row of cars, headlights from either side flashed on, following her like a pursuing runway. Francesca's brisk walk soon morphed into a dead sprint, the crisp autumn air shooting through her lungs as she ran toward her car.

When the familiar blue sedan appeared in her line of vision, she pushed herself harder, reaching into her purse for her keys and pointing them toward what she hoped would be an escape from whatever was following her. Before she could push the *unlock* button, every light and sound possible from her vehicle exploded in a cacophony of noise, causing the other cars around it to do the same.

Francesca slowly backed away, where the headlights of the cars she'd passed all remained lit. After a moment's rest, she bolted in another direction, back toward the stadium. She wasn't sure what was going on, but there was something very scary and unwelcome following her through the parking lot. If she could just get back to where everyone else was, she didn't care if her friends were all blitzed out of their minds or not. At least she'd be safe surrounded by the others.

As Francesca ran toward the stadium from a different direction, she could see out of the corner of her eye that the car lights behind her were once again lighting up. They followed her passing relentlessly, as if they hoped to devour her right along with the dark. In the distance, the stadium lights and steady hum of the football crowd pulled her onward, offering the refuge of not being alone and pursued by something she didn't understand.

As she drew closer to her destination, something odd briefly pricked her mind out of its panicked state. The stadium announcer, who already talked too much during the games, was droning on nonstop. In a language she didn't recognize at all. Francesca brushed off what she heard as the result of her frantically thudding heart, which was now beating so hard it pounded inside her ears. She had to get back to where everyone else was, no matter how odd they'd been acting. She wanted desperately to feel safe again.

After rounding the first gate, Francesca charged toward the entrance to the stadium. Behind her, the parking lot was filled with the illumination of headlights, making it appear almost ethereal, despite its seemingly malevolent nature. Francesca finally reached the front gate, where the ticket taker sat bolt upright with his mouth agape. She reached into her pocket for her ticket stub, but stopped when she saw his eyes, which were as black as the night sky around them.

She cautiously passed the entrance and walked toward the concession area, where everyone else seemed to be frozen in place, just like the ticket taker—their eyes as black as his had been. Their mouths, however, continued to spew forth the familiar sounds of a Friday night football game, like a choir of unmoving, human stereo speakers.

Francesca looked toward the stadium, where both football teams, the coaches, the cheerleaders, and everyone she could see, was turned looking in her direction. Their black, dead eyes and slack jaws contrasted sharply with the sounds of people milling about and helmets crunching that should have been happening with a game in full swing. The only noise that seemed totally out of place was the stadium announcer's voice that was still droning on in the alien sounding tongue.

Francesca wanted to run, but the bright lights still shining from the pursuit in the parking lot kept her feet frozen in place. Suddenly, the stadium announcer's words dissolved into a low growl, causing her to slowly back away. When the rest of the crowd joined in with the same guttural wail, she began sprinting toward the back of the stadium, pushing though hands that were grabbing at her arms and hair as she went.

Just as she made it to the back gate that led to the field beneath the stadium, the crowd that had been sitting atop it surged forward. They quickly massed together with her other pursuers to form a sea of black-eyed humanity, bearing down on her with the same relentless energy as the force she'd just encountered in the parking lot. As she fled into the night, something in the space binding her heart and mind screamed at her to run toward where the artifacts were buried. She knew the action didn't make any sense, but the weight of the urge pressing against her heart pushed her legs to their desired destination.

In a brief flash of manic clarity, Francesca wondered if this was just her mind's way of dealing with the incomprehensible evil swelling at her back. Perhaps it was a way for her to experience some form of comfort for a final few seconds before the darkness swallowed her entirely. Band members and fans from the other side of the stadium, now possessing the same black eyes as the others, had circled around to cut off any other possible escape routes. That left the artifact burial ground as the last place she had left to flee to before her life ended.

Francesca's feet pounded hard into the ground, which was still wet from the rain from a few hours earlier. When she got to within a few feet of the burial site, she slid toward it and began frantically digging into the damp, soft earth. Her fingers and nails dug through the soil without a moment's hesitation, tearing away at the grass and dirt despite the black-eye mob that stumbled closer with every passing second.

She remembered Kristen's words. *"If anything happens, try to dig up the artifact container and find what I put in there. It's really important to me that you be the only other person to have it."* Her friend's words echoed over and over again in her mind, as her hands finally met with the top of the Rubbermaid container.

The mob had gotten close enough by then that she could hear their footsteps squishing in the wet soil all around her. She frantically grabbed at the container's handles and hefted it up. After pulling the container out of the ground, Francesca pried open the lid, tossed it to the side, and looked inside, her heart pounding wildly.

The small bags that she and her classmates had marked with their names all those years ago were still there. It didn't take long for Francesca to find hers, which she quickly grabbed and tore open. She held the contents up to her face, experiencing a surprising sense of peace as a smile crept across her face. No matter how terrible things ever got, Francesca's past experiences in life had always given her strength going forward. Seeing and holding a tangible reminder of that inspired a brief glimmer of hope in her—even in the face of a certain end. Then something else caught her eye. The bag with Kristen's name on it.

Francesca tore it open and found a large stained glass cross inside. Its edges where lined with metal which ended in dull, metal points on every side. As soon as she picked it up, the guttural wailing that had being droning on around her, abruptly stopped. The mob was now standing completely still, mouths hanging open, their black eyes trained on the item in her hand.

Francesca stood and turned, staring into the mass of blank faces, which included many people she considered to be her closest friends. As she continued staring back at them, a black mist rose and swirled up from the mob's center, thickening as it moved in her direction. The dark wisps quickly billowed into one cloud of thick, dense smoke, which settled just a few feet in front of her. It then began to take shape into something resembling a snake, but with a lizard's head and legs. In place of arms, flexing tendrils protruded from its elongated body, weaving in and out of the air in front of her.

After a few seconds, the creature raised its long neck and brought its face down close to hers. Instinctively, Francesca raised the cross in response, which caused the demon to hiss and retreat back a few feet.

"What are you?" it asked, in a weird, two-toned voice—one very high pitched, the other repeating the question a split second later, in a low, distant rumble.

"Kind of sick of your bullshit, if I'm being honest," Francesca replied, masking her overwhelming fear with as much snark as she could muster. The smoke creature tried to move forward, causing her to back away. As she did, the black-eyed crowd parted, staring intently at the cross in her outstretched hand. Francesca continued moving toward the side gate near the stadium scoreboard, which had been left open for the team at halftime. She slowly crept backward until she was on the football field, bathed in the glow of the stadium light. The black-eyed mob followed her closely, led by the smoke snake as it hissed in Francesca's direction.

"You're heart," it said, swirling around her. *"It lets all in…yet you do not*

believe in The Oppressor."

"The Oppressor?" Francesca asked, still holding the cross out in front of her. "Do you mean my soccer coach? Because he's certainly an asshole at times, but I wouldn't necessarily call him—"

"GOD!" the snake yelled, grabbing the sides of its head with all of its tendrils. *"I SPEAK OF THE ONE YOUR KIND CALLS GOD!"*

After saying the word a second time, the creature screeched in pain, which caused the black-eyed mob behind it to begin screaming, as well. The stadium lights began to pop and spark as the shrieking continued. By the time the deafening wails had subsided, only a few bulbs remained lit, leaving the field almost completely dark.

"Oh," Francesca said. "Well, I'm not really one for worshipping anyone or anything, unless it's Jon Stewart or James Franco. Holy hell, I'd do terrible things to those two."

"Why do you show kindness to all without an order from The Oppressor?" the creature asked, turning in a circle, which Francesca matched in kind. *"Why is your heart pure?"*

"HA!" Francesca shot back with a smirk. "You wouldn't think my heart was that pure if you saw some of the stuff I've posted on Snap Chat."

"Why do you not drink from my cup of malice your peers partake of so freely?" the creature pressed on, still trying to move its face closer to hers. *"I've sown the seeds of dissent among your tribe. Hatred and mistrust has been cultivated in them, sustained by nothing more than their own differences. It now flows freely through each of them. Even those who claim to follow The Oppressor, willfully deliver my poison to others."*

"Tell me about it," Francesca said, holding the cross out further in front of her. "The leader of FCA is on our soccer team. She can be a colossal bitch, sometimes."

"ENOUGH!" the demon bellowed, causing the few remaining stadium lights to explode. *"You shall be mine!"*

"Your game is pretty weak, good sir," Francesca replied, struggling to keep her hand from shaking. "At least offer to buy me dinner first or something."

"You are a cancer upon my house!" the creature shrieked, clearly becoming frustrated with its inability to rattle her further. *"You show The Oppressor's wretched warmth without mandate toward all who would receive*

it. You do The Oppressor's work without even believing that He exists." The creature's sudden flash of anger startled her, but Francesca buried it, hiding the panic in the pit of her stomach as the snake swirled and seethed further in her direction.

"So let me get this straight," she said, after a moment's pause, "You're mad because I'm not a completely shitty person? That seems like a pretty low bar for something to make you all pissy like this."

The creature emitted another guttural roar, but Francesca shook it off, determined to keep the thing talking until she could figure out what to do next. "And as far as the whole *not believing* thing…I guess you might constitute a decent amount of proof, but that doesn't mean I suddenly see eye to eye with your *Oppressor* about everything."

"Then why do you cower in fear behind the symbol of The Oppressor's son?" the demon asked, as they continued to circle each other. *"Why do you shield yourself with that which you do not worship?"*

"Hey, I'm still willing to accept any help where I can get it," Francesca shot back, doing all she could to keep her voice from shaking.

"Your words do not fool me," the demon smugly replied. *"You are afraid. You will give into your terror and be mine. Your fear is all you have now."*

FEAR.

As soon as the creature uttered the word, something clicked inside Francesca's head. For a split second an argument raged between her heart and mind, one begging her to flee, while the other demanded that she charge forward.

In the next instant, her legs ended the debate, propelling her forward through the smoke-thick air. The demon shrieked and recoiled as the cross came down on its neck, causing the blacked-eyed mob behind it to begin screaming yet again.

Francesca plunged the cross's dull tip into the creature's head, causing black tendrils to shoot up all around it. The wisps of smoke suddenly became solid, snatching and latching onto her back with such force that it caused her to scream out. She continued to push forward, though, burying the tip as hard as she could into the creature as its howl joined with the wailing mob around it.

Seconds later, a bright flash lit up the night sky, followed immediately by a low wave of sound that knocked Francesca to the ground. When she looked up, the demon was gone. The black-eyed mob, which had previously surrounded her like a group of slack-jawed zombies, was sprawled out all over the field. A few of them began to moan, but this time, in the voices of genuine pain and confusion.

"What the hell happened?" one of the football coach's asked, struggling to get to his feet.

For a moment, Francesca wasn't sure what to say. There was no way to explain what had happened to any of them. Was the demon something that had attacked only them? Perhaps there were more out there, reaping and harvesting discord, pain, and hatred among students around the world. Or maybe this was just all too much to process or explain to anyone right now.

"Power surge…" Francesca stammered. "A freak lightning bolt hit the press box. That's why all the lights, and you guys, got knocked out."

"So why are we all on the field?" a band member who'd just gotten up asked with a perplexed stare.

"I don't know," Francesca replied flatly. "I was walking to my car when it happened."

"What's up, slut?" Kristen said with a friendly bump.

Francesca smiled, thankful to see her friend back to her old self. After the *power surge* incident Friday evening—and a weekend of not talking to anyone unless she absolutely had to—it was nice to start the week off seeing a friendly face.

"Oh…that's odd," Francesca replied after turning her head from side to side. "I just heard you say hello to your mom, but I don't see her anywhere."

After exchanging a few more barbs, the girls walked in silence together toward their last period class. Before parting ways, Kristen finally decided to speak.

"So that was pretty crazy what happened on Friday, right?"

"Yeah," Francesca replied, staring straight ahead.

"Sorry I freaked out on you like that on Thursday," Kristen continued, shaking her head. "Although you have to admit, a 'massive, inexplicable lightning strike' does sound a bit like the work of something hellish. Also, the whole thing about no one remembering how they ended up on the field is like, super weird."

Francesca nodded in agreement, not sure what to say. They walked in silence for a few more seconds before Kristen spoke up again. "So I know this sounds pretty stupid considering what happened, but the artifact container… since we never got to open it, can you tell me what you put in there? You never told anyone what was in your bag."

"That's something I'd like to keep to myself for right now," Francesca replied firmly. "At least until I've figured out what it means for my life going forward. We should wait till we can all be there to open our together."

The two girls hugged and walked in separate directions. Kristen back to the life she'd known and Francesca with a million new questions to answer. Her strength, however, would no longer be one of them.

What Lurks Within the Darkest Wealds

Matthew Pedersen

"Well, here we are." I shouted, mostly to wake up my slumbering passengers.

Carolyn, my wife, was the first to rouse. She lifted her head from the pillow held in her arms and looked ahead. "Is that it...?"

"What do you mean, 'Is that it'"? I asked back.

She sat up, rubbing her eyes as she did so. "It's just that from the way you talked about it I assumed it would be…nicer."

"Think you could put that anymore tactfully?"

I saw her put her finger to her chin out the corner of my eye. "Let's see…better maintained?"

"Thanks." I muttered, turning to check on our son. "Hey Adam, you awake buddy?"

A light groan told me otherwise.

I reached over to him and nudged his shoulder a little. "Adam, we're here."

He grumbled a little more. Poor little guy must have been cranky. We'd been driving for nineteen hours straight. I felt a soft touch on my arm.

"Let him sleep, honey," Carolyn said. "We can get a few things unpacked while he's out."

I smiled back at her. "Alright."

I stepped out of the van and took a moment to take in the forest scenery. With a deep breath, I turned to the cabin, which admittedly was a bit run down. Looks didn't matter though; I was just looking forward to spending some time with Carolyn and Adam.

I had a feeling this was going to be one hell of a week.

I carried the last of the boxes inside. The cabin was dark and clouds of dust rose from the hardwood floor as I walked in. The place was definitely going to need a good sweep. From what I could hear, Adam was finally awake, which meant it was going to be tough getting him back to sleep later. I stepped outside. He was running around like an adventurer while Carolyn cleaned out the van.

"Stay where we can see you, Adam!" I shouted. "It's easy getting lost in these woods." I should know, my friend Jason and I were stuck out there for two days back when we were ten.

Speaking of the devil, "Scottie, that you man?"

"Jason?" I snapped around, finding the scruffy bastard grinning at me with open arms. "What the hell are you doing here?" I asked, accepting the hug.

"I'm staying here for the month, clearing my head and all that. How about you?"

"Vacation. I needed to get away from work myself."

"Ah, brought the wife and ankle biter, too, I see."

As if on cue Adam walked over to us. I looked down, finding him holding the leg of my jeans and peaking up at Jason.

"Hey there!" Jason said, kneeling down to face the boy.

Adam retreated a bit further behind me. He was always shy around strangers. "It's okay, he's an old friend of Daddy's."

"Hi—" Adam said weakly.

Jason went through the usual procedures involved when dealing with a five-year-old. Jason was Jason though, and eventually he started going on about some of the old ghost stories we'd tell when we were younger. Those were fun when we were twelve, but Adam was little and it was going to be hard enough to get to bed. I sent him inside to go pick out a bedroom for himself—another quest for my little explorer.

"I'd appreciate it if you didn't try scaring my kid." I said, mildly irritated.

Jason laughed. "Come on, man, spooky legends add a bit of flavor to staying out in the woods. It's one of the few good things about it, besides the quiet."

"Yeah, well the Cannibal-Witch wasn't the most tasteful one."

"I haven't seen the kid since he was a baby, but he looks a hell of a lot braver than you were at his age."

"Whatever—"

"I remember you were up all night after I told you that one."

"Look, you can join us for dinner tomorrow night. Right now we've got a lot of unpacking to do. It's good to see you, though."

Jason held his hands up, taking a few steps back. "Right, right. Don't let me get in your way. But one thing before I leave you. Wait right here…"

Jason ran off, heading in the direction of his own cabin. It wasn't too far—about a hundred and fifty feet away. It wasn't long before he returned. When he came back, he was holding something small and black.

"A walkie-talkie?" I asked.

"Same kind we used to use back when the world was young." He tossed it to me. "Just in case you're not already feeling the nostalgia."

"Yeah, I'm sure I'll need this."

The unpacking went by quickly. Fortunately Adam wasn't anywhere near as fussy about going to bed as I thought he'd be, which gave Carolyn and me a relaxing evening to ourselves before turning in.

After such a perfect night I'd have loved to have slept in the next morning, but there were still things to do before we settled in. Carolyn was still asleep when I'd gotten dressed. Adam, on the other hand, was wide awake when I went in to check on him. I decided to bring him along so that Carolyn could relax. We needed some bonding time anyway. The first thing on the agenda was to get some actual food to hold us over throughout the week. I got Adam dressed and ready to head into town.

It was about eight o'clock, so I decided to see if Jason wanted to come with us. There was a layer of fog outside, which was unusual for a summer morning out here. I didn't dwell on that for long, I simply picked Adam up and walked over to Jason's place.

After a few hard knocks I heard someone stir inside. The door opened, and I was shocked at what I saw.

"Jason—?" I stammered. He was paler than before, and his eyes were bloodshot.

"Oh, hey man. I, ugh, what are you doing here?"

"Adam and I are heading into town, I wondered if you wanted—" I stopped talking, but only because Jason started coughing.

"Nah, go on without me. I feel like shit this morning," he said, wiping beads of sweat from his brow. "Think I'm gonna head back to bed, try to sleep this thing off."

I didn't stay to argue, I just told him we'd be back in about three hours if he needed us. He nodded and slunk back inside without another word. I was worried about him, but I figured it was probably just the flu or something. I hooked Adam up into the van, and then we were on our way, driving straight into the depths of the forest's unseasonable fog.

The town was oddly unsettling. Splitwood was an old family community, the type of place where everyone knew everyone else. The cabins were only an hour's drive from there, so it was about nine when we arrived. Usually at that time there were a few people walking around, but that wasn't the case this morning as we turned onto Main Street. The quiet and friendly town was just plain *quiet.* I didn't really think that at first though, I was just thinking about all the things I needed to get. I parked the van outside the store. I was going to bring Adam inside with me, but something made me feel uncomfortable with that.

"I'm going to run inside and be right out, okay buddy?"

"Okay, Daddy."

I smiled and left the van, making sure to lock it. I looked around a bit before heading inside. There wasn't anyone in sight, although that may have just been because of the fog. It felt like it was thicker than when we'd left. I shrugged and went inside, waving at Adam one last time before going in.

The store was deserted too. Every aisle and section was empty. I called out, but no one answered. Something wasn't right... I sighed, letting my urge to get the hell out of there win over my curiosity. I grabbed what I needed, left some money on the unattended counter, and left. I opened the trunk and put the food in faster than I normally would have. As I was pulling my keys out, I thought I heard something

I turned around, hoping maybe there was another person out there. But no one was there. “Hello?” I called out. Again, no response. Still though, I felt like there was something in the air. It was just soft enough that you'd almost miss it. It sounded, at least to me, like some sort of music. Wanting to get back, I decided to ignore it, unlocking the door and climbing into the driver's seat. Adam was still strapped into his chair, and I noticed he was looking out the window.

“You okay, buddy?” I asked, putting the van into reverse and backing up.

“I saw something...” Adam whispered.

“What was it?”

“Outside, while you were gone…I saw something.”

I turned around and looked at him. He was paler than he usually was and his eyes were locked on the window beside him.

“Adam, what did you see?”

He turned to me as he answered. The look on his face shocked me to my core. “A monster.”

Carolyn was outside when we got back. She ran up to the van when I pulled in.

“Scott, thank God!” She cried as soon as I opened the door.

“Everything okay?”

“No…it's Jason,” she began as I climbed out of the vehicle. “As soon as I got up, I heard your walkie-talkie go off. Jason was calling for you. He sounded awful. I went to go check on him, and...” She couldn't go on.

There was a sick feeling in my stomach. “Honey, what happened?” I asked, as calmly as I could.

“He's very sick,” she said. “I tried calling a doctor, but the phones aren't working.”

“Get Adam inside. I'll go over there.”

She tried to stop me, but he was my oldest friend. I had to check on him. I ran to his cabin and banged on the door. When he didn't answer, I forced it open. I hurried inside, calling out to him. The lights were out and I could hear something coming from the other room. I wound up in the bedroom. The noise came from my right, where I saw another damn door. I pulled it open, and stepped back, horrified. Jason was kneeling in front of a toilet, vomiting, but it was blood. He was puking up blood...

Jason turned to me, his eyes dark and fevered. "Scottie? He asked. I...I don't feel so hot!"

Adam was asleep when I returned, and I was thankful for that. By the time we'd got back from town, he wasn't feeling well. After finding Jason the way he was, I was worried. I was sure it wasn't the same thing though, whatever the hell Jason had.

At least that's what I thought at first.

Carolyn was watching Jason back at his cabin. She was a nurse, so she was the most suited to take care of him. The phones still weren't working, and after seeing the state of the town earlier, I doubted heading over there would do much good. I just sat there, walkie-talkie in my lap, waiting. God, I felt useless...

It was midnight. I was sweating and the sickness I'd started to feel had grown worse in my stomach. Again, I was worried. I'm no idiot; I knew there was something wrong. What happened to Jason, the town, and my family, shouldn't have been happening. Something was very wrong.

I heard a scream, and seconds later the walkie-talkie buzzed to life.

"Scott! Oh, God, Scott, can you hear me?" Carolyn cried.

"Yes, Carol...I'm here. What's happening?"

"T—There's something in Jason's room. He was in there, sleeping. I left him alone, then, oh God, something must have gotten inside. It's clawing at the door!"

"Carol, listen to me. Just run, come back here. We'll figure out what to do about Jason but first—"

A burst of noise came over the walkie-talkie, then Carolyn screamed, and something else was there...a howling sound.

I ran to the bedroom and pulled a chest out from under the bed, something my father had left there long ago. I opened it and reached inside. The shotgun wasn't as big as I remembered it being, but it was heavier than I would've imagined. After checking to see if it was loaded, I ran out of the cabin. I wasn't sure what I was going to do. All I knew was that I was tired of feeling so useless.

* * *

When I reached Jason's place, I kicked the door open and pointed the shotgun straight ahead. Darkness met me, just like before. I ran in, calling out for Carolyn. I didn't hear anything. At least not at first. I ran into the bedroom. The bed was a horror scene. Blood was soaked into its topside and something slimy was lying on top with the torn-up covers. I took a closer look, and saw that it was skin—Jason's skin.

I heard a noise and spun around. What I saw broke my heart, and I truly wished I had died right then and there. There was a creature, a disgusting, diseased looking thing. It was a grotesque mix of a man, wolf, and reptile. It whimpered and snorted as it focused on eating. I'd have pitied it if it wasn't standing over my wife's dismembered corpse. Its dark, fevered eyes looked up at me as it tore into Carolyn's severed arm. It looked frightened at first, but then it lunged at me with a snarl. It was fast—but not fast enough. The shotgun flared and its chest imploded. I stared at the impossible thing and at my wife's body. How did this happen? What *was* this thing?

I wasn't going to get answers, of that I was certain. There was another question though, one that made my blood freeze. Why did I leave my son alone?

When I returned to the cabin, Adam wasn't there. There wasn't any sign that something had taken him, at least not from what I could see at first glance. His sheets were on the floor with blood on them. There was a small trail of it. I followed it as it led me out of the cabin and into the dark forest. The thick fog made it so I could barely see. I kept up with the trail though, desperate to find my son.

My body felt like it was on fire, but I didn't care. I had to find him. Every breath set my lungs ablaze, and every step was agony. A part of me knew I was dying, and another part told me something even stranger was happening.

After what felt like hours I found him, shambling aimlessly through the fog. I ran to him. Even with the fog obscuring him, I could tell he wasn't well. His pajamas were torn to pieces, and what little that was left of them was stained in blood. His skin was pale—almost translucent. When I finally reached him, I grabbed his arm. His skin felt wrong; it was cold and waxy.

I wasn't prepared for what happened next.

How could I be?

I gave Adam's arm a yank and with a sickening, wet noise, his skin came off in my hand. It tore from his limb like a sheath, and what was underneath wasn't human. As though what I'd done had started a chain reaction, my son's body began to fall apart. His skin began grotesquely slopping off. His bones snapped and reformed, and the fresh hide of what had grown underneath glistened, despite the darkness. I fell back as I looked on, the last of my sanity and hope crushed.

When his metamorphosis was finished, Adam looked like a deer—albeit a grotesque, reptilian one. The thing that had been my son turned toward me, its black eyes wide and its leech-like mouth drooling. It barked at me and, God help me, it sounded like Adam. After that, it galloped off, singing in my son's voice.

It didn't get far though.

There was a whistling noise, and suddenly the deer-thing was hurled back. It kicked and screeched like a wounded child. There was something jutting out from its belly, and I quickly recognized it as an arrow. I might have found that strange—maybe even horrifying—but reality had become one grotesque spectacle after another.

And then they came.

At first I heard strange sounding music, and then the stomping came. They emerged from the fog like spirits, creatures that seemed half-man and half-goat. One pressed a pipe made of bone to its bestial face, while the other readied an arrow in a bow the size of a man. Once released, the arrow sliced through the air and found its way through the deer-thing's skull.

As they came closer to their kill, I tried to make myself unseen, propelled by some animalistic urge to survive. As they approached I noticed something. Hanging from the bizarre leather straps tied around their waists there were chains. Each ended in a small metal ball, and from these balls came thick streams of smoke. No, not smoke. *Fog...*

They were making the fog!

My hand hit a branch. Its snap seemed to echo through the air and the monsters' gaze turned in my direction. The archer pulled out another arrow and I acted again on my insane desire to live. I bolted upward and ran—as fast as my diseased body would go. I heard the arrow fly and saw it hit a tree a few feet ahead of me. I kept running, until my legs felt like they were about to give out. I ran until I walked on all fours. I ran…crawled…even galloped…in an effort to survive in these vile, dark wealds.

The Reaping

Chad P. Brown

The crows frightened him.

He failed miserably in his mundane duty to drive them away, about as effective as an unleashed puppy expected to serve as a vicious watchdog.

The crows would defiantly perch on his outstretched arms, throwing their chilling caws at him like bullying children tossing cruel insults. Their dark, ravenous eyes would inspect every inch of him, determined something tastier lay hidden beneath his straw-stuffed facade.

Sometimes, one of the braver ones would sidle up inches away from the burlap sack covering his head, and he would be certain that this time a menacing, curved beak would rip into his flesh. But some veiled power held the carrion birds at bay, prevented them from exploring their suspicions deeper no matter how much they yearned to feed.

The one who ruled over these lands would never allow him to become a feast for the crows. She was ancient, a primordial spirit who could dispense life just as easily as death, depending on whichever one fancied her whim most at the time. She was intimately bound to the cycle of the seasons, revered yet feared by generations of farmers.

In the old lands, she'd been known as the *Cailleach.*

Now, everyone simply called her the Hag.

As hard as he tried to fight it, the images consumed his mind, replaying that distant memory of when he'd seen the man who'd been his father confront her.

As he approached the barn, the man's usually broad and determined steps were hesitant and timid. Overhead, the waning crescent moon hung in the sky more menacing than the blade of a scythe, ready to chop the heads off any stars foolish enough to show their faces on this dark night. The wind picked up for a brief moment, eliciting an eerie, wail like a banshee foretelling the inevitable approach of impending death.

He shivered at the chilling sound.

When the man reached the barn, he stretched forth his dirt-stained, calloused hand, and slid open the creaking door. He stepped inside, shining the lantern around.

"Silas."

The man spun toward the direction of the voice at the sound of his name, the light of the lantern illuminating the figure hidden in the deep shadows. The Hag smiled, her cracked lips revealing misshapen teeth as discolored as dried husks of corn. Her white, wispy strands of hair fluttered in the howling wind rushing through the open barn door. She took a couple of steps forward. The bluish color of her desiccated, wrinkled flesh reminded him of an undiscovered corpse in a long-forgotten forest. Her emotionless eyes were dark pools of nothingness. Behind them, he caught the threatening glimpse of a dormant fire, strong enough to wipe away entire acres of land once unleashed.

Silas placed his hand over his nose and choked down the urge to puke as her foul stench assaulted his nostrils, a combination of rotting wood floating in a pond of stagnant water.

She pointed her gnarled, ancient finger in his direction. "Why have you called me forth on this night?" Her tone dared him to respond.

Silas took a deep breath. "I've changed my mind."

The Hag cackled; her laughter resounding like brittle bones crushed beneath her feet. "You know there is no backing out of our bargain once it has been made."

"I can't go through with it!" Silas thundered at her.

"It takes blood to make the soil fertile. If you want your land to prosper, then you will abide by the ritual just as everyone else has done for countless ages before your meagre existence. The cycle of seven years has come to completion. You have two choices. Either offer the sacrifice, or your land will be as barren as your pretty wife's womb." The Hag hesitated a moment, fixing her menacing gaze upon him. "You know I can make it so."

Silas took a defensive step forward at the mention of Maggie, balling his hands into tight, white-knuckled fists. "Leave her alone!"

"She is with child right now. Did you know that?"

Silas's eyes widened in disbelief, pleading with her to tell him the truth. So many years had passed since the birth of their son. She'd had such a hard time delivering him that Silas doubted Maggie was capable of bearing any more children.

"See, life is a cycle of giving and taking. It is the natural order of things. From death comes birth." The Hag's voice turned seductive, more tempting than a whore trying to lure him into her bed. "Give me that which is mine."

Silas remained silent as he considered her enticing proposal. Children perished all the time, either from disease or accidents or whatever cruel twist of fate decided to snatch them away. He'd brought Maggie here with the promise that they would prosper. But in order to do so, the land needed to produce crops. According to the Hag, they would have more children with one already on the way. Everything would be alright. He just needed to make the one sacrifice, no matter how abhorrent it was. "Are you sure?" he asked in a shaky voice.

A cunning smile crossed her lips. "I promise."

Silas dropped his head and nodded in agreement, sealing the fate of his son.

"At the full moon, Silas. Make sure it is so."

He glanced up to reassure her that he understood.

But the Hag was gone.

He'd followed the man who'd been his father to the barn that night. The words exchanged between the two of them had been vague and incomprehensible to him at the time. All of his attention had been focused on the terrifying appearance of the Hag, which had evoked a fear he hadn't imagined was even possible. As he forced the picture of the Hag out of his mind, the sun dropped down into the western sky, throwing a blanket of darkness over the fields of corn.

He trembled. The night frightened him even more than the crows.

During the daytime, the sinister birds at least kept him company, despite their threatening provocations. And sometimes the little girl from the house would come and visit him. They called her Rachael. Her golden hair reminded him of the bright sun and her infectious laughter was as refreshing as the birds singing in the morning.

But in the dark, he was alone.

On most nights, the moon and the stars cast their dim light down upon him, offering a seeming respite from the enveloping darkness. But it brought little comfort. They produced terrifying shadows, their skeletal fingers reaching out toward him, threatening to snatch him away into a realm more horrifying than any childhood nightmare. Perhaps the darkness frightened him so much because of that final night. He tried to push the horrible memory away, but it bullied its way into his mind, refusing to give him the peace he sought.

The boy followed his father through the fields of corn, rubbing his eyes in an effort to wipe away the lingering sleep. "Where are we going, Papa?" he asked one more time.

His father still remained silent, brushing aside the stalks with one huge hand as he carried a lantern in the other one. The boy had tried numerous times to get his father to tell him where they were going ever since he'd woken him up in the middle of the night and insisted he follow him.

"Papa, you're scaring me," the boy whispered.

Silas came to a sudden halt. "Don't be afraid, Jacob," he replied without turning around before continuing his determined course through the seemingly never-ending fields of corn.

Jacob found comfort in the words—despite remaining in the dark about their purpose—and followed his father through the field without any further interruptions. After a few minutes, they reached a spot unfamiliar to Jacob. A circle of untilled soil about ten feet wide surrounded them. A wooden, cross-shaped construction stood upright in the middle of the clearing, buried deep into the ground.

Silas set the lantern down and turned toward his son. "Your mama's pregnant. Did you know that?"

Jacob's eyes lit up as a broad, tooth-gapped Jack-o'-lantern smile spread across his face. "I'm going to have a little brother?"

Silas chuckled. "Or a sister." The paternal grin on his face suddenly vanished as the air around them grew colder. "Would you do anything for your family, son?"

Jacob puffed his chest out as wide as he could manage. "Anything. I love you and Mama." He paused a moment. "And my baby sister."

"So, you think it's a girl now?"

Jacob considered the question a brief second before answering. "It's definitely a sister, and I'm going to make sure nothing harms her."

Silas's eyes filled with tears. For a moment, a sliver of doubt pierced his heart. He considered taking his family somewhere else, starting over and forsaking his atrocious agreement with the Hag. But he knew she would pursue them no matter where they tried to hide, bringing death and destruction just as she'd threatened.

Silas choked down the tears and focused on the daunting matter at hand.

"As the eldest child, you have an important duty," he began. He noticed how Jacob concentrated on his every word. "I was the oldest in my family. But, just as I realized, it can also be the most difficult job, sometimes forcing the first-born to make unimaginable sacrifices for his brothers and sisters."

"I would do anything for her," Jacob responded without hesitation.

Somehow, even though he knew Jacob had no idea what was going on, Silas found strength in his son's words, so that he could perform the unthinkable act confronting him. His hand crept behind him and brushed against the cold steel shoved down the back of his pants. Wrapping his fingers around the hilt, he took in a deep breath. "I want you to be brave for me. Alright?"

A look of fear flashed across Jacob's face as his confused eyes fell upon the knife.

As the murderous fog dissipated from his mind, he realized someone was standing in front of him. It was a young woman. Her tender eyes elicited compassion, inviting him to lay his head on her shoulder so she could soothe away the haunting memories of the man who'd been his father.

"Jacob."

The sound of her voice comforted him even more than the warm embrace wrapped around a child after a terrifying nightmare. As he gazed upon her, he could only describe her as the perfect mother.

At first, he didn't recognize his name because it had been so long since he'd heard it spoken aloud. Jacob was the boy who'd played in the yard after he'd finished his chores around the farm, the boy who'd skipped rocks across the creek in the evening as he awaited the call for suppertime—the boy whose entire life had been laid out before him as limitless and promising as the fields of corn which surrounded him now.

That boy had foolishly placed all of his trust in the man who'd been his father.

He cast aside the ghost of that little boy. "Jacob is dead," he answered her.

His response surprised him, doubting he could even produce sounds which resembled articulated words. But the voice he heard now was cold and distant, so different from the one of the little boy who plagued his memories.

She smiled at him. "No, Jacob. You still exist, only in a different form."

He scoffed at her words, his laughter more threatening than a violent thunderstorm, intent upon devastating the land. "This is no life." Despite the motherly appearance he'd ached to gaze upon for so long, he recognized the woman for who she truly was. "What do you want, witch?"

The Hag threw off her guise of enticement, standing before him in her true form. "It is time."

"For what?"

"To decide how you will live out your existence in this world."

"My fate has already been determined."

The Hag stepped closer and placed her hand on his straw-stuffed chest. For a brief second, Jacob was revolted by her touch, her fingers more disgusting than maggots feeding on a rotting corpse. Then, agonizing pain shot through his lifeless form. He stared in astonished horror as his body and limbs grew in size, catching up with the seven years stolen from him, as if he were a long dormant crop drinking in the nourishing drops of life-giving rain.

Before he could ask what had happened, the Hag made her proposal to him.

He would become one of her servants, known in the old lands as a *bodach,* who brought children to her so that she could feed upon their young flesh and bones in order to sustain her waning life.

And it would start with Rachael, his estranged sister.

"You will help me reap the harvest, so to speak," she finished with a cackle. "And, in the process, avenge the one who traded your life for the measly corn surrounding you now."

Jacob yearned to taste revenge against the one who'd taken his life.

He nodded his head in assent.

The little girl bolted upright in her bed and screamed. "Papa!"

Seconds later, footsteps echoed down the hallway and the door swung open. "What's wrong, child?"

Rachael fought to control her fear as she gasped for air. "Another bad dream," she spat out.

Silas crossed the room and sat down on the edge of the bed beside his daughter. He felt helpless. Every night for the past week, she'd been having nightmares. He didn't understand what had caused his seven-year-old to start having them.

Jacob had never....

Silas shook his head and cleared his mind of the haunting memories of his son, focusing his attention on his daughter. "Was it the same one as before?"

Rachael reluctantly nodded her head.

"Do you want to tell me about it?" he asked her.

Rachael's timid eyes darted around the room, unsure if discussing her nightmare would make it better or worse. She hadn't shared the specifics of her tormenting dream with either of her parents. The idea of giving voice to it seemed like it would make it more frightening somehow, breathing life into the nocturnal apparition and thus making it real.

But maybe, just maybe, if she told her father about the nightmare, it might help. He would protect her from anything, after all.

"Okay," she finally answered.

It was night.

The full moon hung ominously in the sky, the one that the farmers called the Hunter's Moon. It was frightening, a crimson hue of blood mixed with the pallid color of a corpse.

She walked through the field of corn. The leaves reached out toward her like sinister hands, brushing against her as goosebumps trickled up and down her cold flesh. Given the time of year, the crop should have been bountiful and ready to be harvested. But the ears of corn were withered husks of decay.

She came to a clearing in the foul-smelling, lifeless field. Glancing up, she smiled as her fears were driven away by the sight of a familiar face, the one who protected the land of her family. For as long as she could remember, she'd spent hours playing with him. She would circle around him as she chanted the words to "Ring around the Rosie." When she reached the final part, "Ashes, ashes, we all fall down," she would drop to the ground and her hysterical laughter would echo across the fields as her spinning head gradually came to a halt.

She had as much fun as if she were playing with one of her brothers or sisters. That is, if she had any siblings.

She even had a special name for him, kept hidden from her parents.

As she stared up at the scarecrow, he raised his head and glared down at her with his empty, sunken eyes. The emotionless, cross-stitched mouth grinned at her, a disturbing and terrifying smile with the faintest hint of teeth, more dangerous than the wood chipper behind the barn. His lifeless arms reached forward, revealing black talons on the tips of his gloved hands.

"Jacob," she screamed. "You're scaring me!"

"What did you call him?" Silas interrupted his daughter in a trembling voice.

Rachael hesitated, momentarily regretting that she'd revealed the secret name she'd given to the scarecrow that'd been dearer to her than any imaginary friend. "Jacob," she finally answered her father.

"Where did you hear that name?" Silas bellowed as he grabbed a hold of her and shook her. "Tell me right now!"

When Rachael was born, he and Maggie had sworn to never mention the name of their deceased son in front of her, refusing to haunt her childhood with the ghost of a brother she could never know.

Rachael grew frightened. She'd never seen her father act like this toward her. He was supposed to protect her. "It's just a name I made up for him," she choked out before bursting into tears.

Silas pulled his daughter close to him, regretting his outburst. "I'm sorry, honey," he said in an effort to comfort her, stroking her long, blonde hair so much like her mother's. "I didn't mean to scare you."

Rachael's sobs gradually receded. "Can I sleep with Mama tonight?"

"Of course, you can," he answered her. He cursed his rash behavior as he recognized how his daughter had left him out of the equation which would ensure she slept through the night.

Silas took Rachael's hand and led her down the hall to their bedroom. As she climbed into the middle of the bed and snuggled up to her mother, Maggie stirred and woke up.

"Another nightmare?" she asked her husband.

"Yeah, but she's alright," Silas assurred her as he climbed into bed.

Within minutes, he could already hear his wife and daughter drifting off.

But sleep eluded him as his mind lingered on the name his daughter had given to the scarecrow.

Silas stared up at the effigy hanging in front of him.

In another week, it would be time to harvest the corn. The profit from the crop would sustain his family for the upcoming year, ensuring their survival. Next spring, he would plant again, and the cycle would continue as it had done for the past seven years.

Just as the Hag had promised him.

But the revelation of his daughter's nightmares now cast a shadow of doubt upon Silas's heart. Something sinister seemed to lurk in the fields of corn. He didn't know how to describe it, but he felt as if his family was threatened in some way.

He'd awoken earlier than usual that morning, determined to somehow set his mind at ease. But the light of day brought no comfort to his troubled heart. Instead, he was more frightened as he confronted the source of his daughter's nightmares. The child-like scarecrow he'd placed in the middle of his fields every spring was somehow the size of a grown man now.

"What's going on, Jacob?" he whispered in an incredulous voice.

The wind stirred, gusting through the stalks of corn surrounding him as if in response to his question, a cold and violent answer.

He glanced up at the burlap-covered head hanging in front of him. Silas closed his eyes and the haunting face of his son immediately appeared in his mind, his betrayed eyes begging for an explanation. He wiped away the tears as the guilt consumed him, the shame he'd kept hidden ever since that accursed night when he'd ensured the fertility of his land in exchange for the life of his oldest child.

Even more horrifying, though, than spilling the blood of his son, had been the events which followed afterward.

As Silas stared into the lifeless, hidden face of the scarecrow, his mind flashed back to that night which he'd fought so hard to keep hidden from the condemning accusations of his heart.

"I honestly doubted you would go through with it."

Silas spun around at the sound of the voice, his eyes drawn away from his land drinking up the boy's blood.

The Hag stood before him. The smirk on her face burned through him more savage than any uncontrollable fire. He raised the knife drenched in the blood of his son and sprung toward her, determined to bury the blade into her cruel chest since he didn't possess the resolve to turn it upon his own guilt-drenched heart.

She giggled, a brief sound wrapping around his spine like cold, dead fingers before she raised her hand toward him in a halting gesture.

As the knife flew out of Silas's hand, an unseen force shoved him backward and sent him crashing to the ground beside the corpse of his son. He scrambled away, turning his head and puking. When he'd emptied the meagre contents of his stomach, he wiped his mouth with his sleeve and rose unsteadily to his feet.

"Get out of here, you bitch," he spat out as he glared at her. "Your very presence infests my home!"

The Hag raised her gnarled finger and shook it at him like a parent chastising a defiant child. "If I leave, then you won't complete the ritual and you'll fail to ensure the prosperity of your land, cursing your entire family."

Silas was taken aback, any hatred he'd felt toward her subsiding for the moment. "What do you mean?" He pointed down at the lifeless body of Jacob. "I performed the damn sacrifice."

"His blood feeds the soil," the Hag agreed. "But his body must protect the land as well."

Silas had listened in disgust as the Hag explained to him how his son's body must serve as a scarecrow to protect the crops of his land. He cursed himself for failing to realize how this was a part of the ritual since she'd demanded the slaughter must take place in front of the empty wooden beam. There would be no proper burial for Jacob. Only countless years of disgrace without any rest for his lost soul.

He had been such a fool, but he'd obeyed her demands, nonetheless, to ensure the lives of Maggie and their unborn child.

If tears were possible, perhaps Jacob would have shed them as he listened to the words of the man who'd been his father. The man pleaded for the life of his daughter, the one whom Jacob had grown to love. He begged Jacob to leave her alone, to stop haunting her dreams. And despite the conflicting emotions raging inside of him, feelings which had long been dormant, Jacob refused to be swayed.

As the Hag had said, it was time to reap the harvest.

As a feeling of hopelessness overwhelmed him, Silas shook his head and retreated from the concealed eyes of his son, void of any compassion or understanding and consumed instead with unforgiving accusations.

Rachael strolled through the fields of corn. It was different, though, from the nightmare which had been tormenting her for the past week. Surprisingly, there was no fear or hesitancy in her steps. She wanted to go see Jacob, the scarecrow who was her best friend in the whole world. If she talked to him about her dreams, he would make everything alright. Perhaps he could even make the nightmares go away, something her father obviously couldn't do.

Rachael still regretted telling her father the details of her recurring nightmare. When she'd expected comfort from him, he'd grown angry, showing her a frightening side she'd never seen before or even imagined possible.

And it all had to do with the name she'd given to her special friend, the one who was also haunting her dreams at night. Rachael didn't understand it at all. At least, if she talked to the scarecrow, he wouldn't grow angry with her and scare her even more, as her father had done. Jacob would somehow make sense out of everything.

A crow cawed in the distance. It seemed like some sort of warning.

Jacob expected to see the man who'd been his father carve a path through the field of corn and plead with him yet again to leave his daughter alone. But it wasn't him. It was the little girl, the last person he wanted to see right now.

She stepped hesitantly into the clearing as her eyes avoided looking up at him. From her words and tone, she sought comfort from him, an explanation of some sort. But he was unable to give it to her. He was as helpless as the little girl who stood before him now. *Realize the extent of that which I give to you, Jacob,* the voice of the Hag crooned inside his mind, interrupting his momentary human emotions.

Suddenly, he felt a sensation of power arise inside of him which had eluded him ever since that night when the man who'd been his father had hung him on the wooden beam, a macabre and grotesque mockery of crucifixion.

The necessary sacrifice for the land.

Rachael's words to Jacob were cut short when she spotted a group of birds circling overhead. Her fearful eyes watched in dread as the threatening crows loomed above. One of them broke away from the rest and soared down toward her.

Rachael let out a squeal of fright before turning and dashing through the field of corn. The sound of the crow's wings echoed in her ears like an unimaginable monster inches away from scooping her up in its engulfing beak and swallowing her whole.

She screamed out for Jacob to help her, but the only response she heard was a cold, heartless laugh as she plowed her way through the tall stalks of corn. As she ran, she tried to convince herself that Jacob hadn't been the one who drove the attacking carrion bird against her.

Finally, she burst out of the field and reached the short stretch leading up to the house. And yet it provided no feeling of safety as she'd expected it would once she escaped from the terrifying corn. From her own experience, the crows never ventured outside their comfort zone. But this crow continued past the field, its shadow eclipsing her as it refused to surrender the possibility of feasting upon her.

"Papa," she screamed. "Help me!"

She continued her desperate dash across the taunting fifty yards leading up to the house. The crow cawed at her, a frightening sound which sent her crashing to the ground. She leapt up and took off running again, refusing to glance behind her to see how close the crow was to tearing into her flesh.

Her father burst out of the back door of the house. Rachael almost gave up hope that he would save her when she saw the brief look of fear cross his face as he came to a sudden stop.

To her relief, her father darted off the porch and ran toward her. She jumped into his protective arms. He spun around when he had a hold of her and sprinted back toward the house, burying her face against his chest.

When they entered the safety of the house, the crow averted its path of pursuit and flew back toward the fields of corn.

As Rachael fought to subside her fear, she couldn't help but think that somehow Jacob had forsaken her.

The crow returned, perching on his shoulder like a dog waiting on its well-deserved treat for obeying the command of its master. "Soon," he whispered. "We will feed your hunger soon."

As he stepped down on wobbly legs, Jacob felt like a toddler walking for the first time. Perhaps, if his life had been longer, he could draw the analogy of a drunken man stumbling home from a night out on the town. But his memories were shackled to the mere span of his seven years of childhood. He could still remember taking his first steps, the accompanying fear that he would tumble to the ground intertwined with the driving determination to cross the room. It had been an exhilarating feeling when he'd finally reached his encouraging mother, collapsing into her outstretched arms.

At the thought of his mother, Jacob could've sworn he felt a tear escape from his dead eyes and roll down the burlap sack which had become his everlasting skin. But it was only a raindrop, the beginning of a storm which would bring the final nourishment to the crop before it was reaped. Jacob wondered if anyone would even be left to bring in the harvest this season.

As he made his way through the field of corn, his legs grew steadier. Movement throughout his long dormant body became easier, more natural. He yearned to take off running through the fields as he'd done when he was alive, so young without any cares in the world. But he refrained from following his childish impulse and embraced his purpose on this dark night.

When he reached the edge of the fields, he paused and glared at the house which had once been his home. A feeling of nostalgia rose inside him as the short seven years he'd spent inside the house flashed through his mind in a dizzying array of images. Soon, he would return home like the parable of the Prodigal Son. But he knew full well that no father's open arms would welcome him as he walked through the front door.

Jacob turned his back to the house for the moment and made his way to the barn. Once inside, he strode across the hay-covered floor toward the far wall. The cows and horses shuffled their feet in nervous agitation and averted their gazes from the thing disturbing the ordinary routine of their lives, sensing the unnatural presence in their midst.

Jacob stared up at the tool hanging on the wall.

A curved blade at least three feet in length flashed out from the almost six-foot long, wooden handle. Despite the apparent lack of use over the past years, in favor of more sophisticated machinery, the steel edge was still razor sharp and glared threateningly in the dim light of the barn.

Jacob reached forward and took down the scythe. The weight of it felt good in his hands.

"It's time to reap the harvest," he whispered.

The house was as silent as the unsettling calm of a cemetery—cold and empty. Perhaps, she'd failed to perceive the shroud of death draped over their home for the past seven years. Now, it engulfed her and threatened to suffocate her. She glanced down at the figure in front of her, buried deep in a sarcophagus of sleep, appearing so blameless, yet so vital to the prosperity of their existence. It had always been about the land, which provided the necessary sustenance in order to survive. But that assurance had been built upon the foundation of the most abominable of crimes, an act ripped right out of the pages of the Old Testament. Only this time, Abraham had carried through with the sacrifice of his son Isaac and there'd been no angel to stay his hesitant hand.

She'd awoken from sleep because of the disturbing events in her dreams. But she'd known, somehow, that it was a revelation. There was no doubt in her mind. The story of an accidental death had been a lie. At the time, she'd accepted it as fact. She'd had no reason not to believe the man to whom she'd bound her life. The child growing inside of her had provided further comfort, replacing the one she'd lost.

Now, however, she knew the truth. And he had to pay for what he'd done, even if he'd had the best interests of his family at heart. She would be the avenging angel of death.

Maggie glanced from the knife in her hand to the exposed area of her husband's chest. The two needed to become acquainted in order to make things right.

"Mama, no!"

Before her mother could respond, Rachael sprinted across the room and stood protectively in front of her father, tears pouring down her cheeks. The knife in her mother's hand came to an abrupt halt, averting from the downward motion it had been intent upon.

Rachael trembled with fear, unsure of what to do next as the blade dropped to her mother's side. "It's not Papa's fault," she pleaded. "He sacrificed Jacob so that we could live."

The clank of the knife hitting the hardwood floor reverberated throughout the silent house. As Maggie stared down at her daughter with a confused look on her face, Rachael's eyes widened in terror when she caught sight of the shadowy figure looming behind her mother.

The violent storm thundering and flashing outside was driven by the anger raging inside the Hag's heart, bent on destruction. She'd revealed the actions of the father to the woman and the little girl in their dreams so that she'd receive more sacrifices, the sustenance necessary to her existence. But the little brat hovered in front of her father, trying to protect him, as the foolish woman turned tail and ran away from the gift of taking revenge.

She should've known better than to give the women of the household this opportunity. But it mattered not. Like the sound of a reassuring voice, she heard the approach of death-dealing footsteps shambling down the hallway.

The Hag smiled.

Jacob would reap the harvest, just as they'd planned.

Silas awoke in a groggy state. "What's going on?" he mumbled, sitting up and rubbing his eyes.

Maggie and Rachael were there with confused and frightened looks on their faces.

His eyes locked with his wife's for a stalled moment in time.

He saw hurt, disbelief, and accusations, which he couldn't deny, flashing forth from her piercing blue eyes. He dropped his head in shame. Silas had dreaded this moment for the past seven years, afraid she would discover the truth. He'd comforted his fears with the reassurance that there was no way possible she would ever find out. But he'd been wrong, foolish and arrogant to believe such a crime could remain unaccounted for without any repercussions.

He hesitantly glanced back up at Maggie. The apology and explanation he was prepared to give her, in order to somehow make things right, died on his lips. He let out a gasp as he caught sight of the figure lurking behind his wife in the shadows.

"Son, no!" Silas cried out.

Jacob hesitated for a brief moment when the man who'd been his father told him to stop, the scythe raised over his head so that he could reap the harvest. He felt like a child caught in the act of getting ready to do something bad. The feeling didn't surprise him, though. He was, after all, only a child at heart, despite his post-mortem growth in size and power. Seven short years had been the span of his existence before life had been snatched away from him at the hands of the man who now had the gall to exert his paternal authority and order him to stop, throwing in the insult of referring to him as his son.

Jacob's empty eyes fell upon the woman who stood before him as she turned around and looked directly at him. He saw recognition dawn across her face. Somehow, she knew the truth. He choked down the word *mother* forcing its way out of his lips. She couldn't make things any better. No matter how much Jacob yearned for his mother to make everything right, she couldn't. For seven years, she'd succumbed to the illusion which she'd chosen to accept concerning the death of her son without any questions whatsoever. All because of the child who would replace him.

Jacob glanced down at Rachael, still protectively placing herself in front of the man who was their father. He couldn't blame her. She was as much a victim as he was—a pawn in this game which cursed their family. Besides, she brought him happiness, a sense of belonging to the family which had sacrificed and forsaken him.

Jacob glared at the man, the one he still refused to call father. Even more painful than the blade which had slashed his throat, was the lingering truth that his life had been traded for a field of corn. Hatred coursed through every inch of his long-dead body. It overwhelmed him, driving away any short-lived compassion he might've felt for his mother or sister.

"Reap the harvest, Jacob," a voice cried out, shaking him out of his momentary lapse in the reason why he'd returned home on this night.

He glanced to his left. The Hag was there, hidden from everyone else. The lightning flashed outside revealing the enticing look of encouragement in her hate-filled eyes. She licked her cracked lips with her emaciated tongue, desirous to taste the life-giving sustenance.

The blood of his kin.

Jacob nodded his head in agreement, taking one last look at his family condemned by the Hag. "Yes, it's time," he hissed as he tightened his grip on the scythe and swung the blade forward.

The crows circled overhead. But it was different this time. No unseen power prevented them from digging into the proffered meal of the dead. And yet, they held back, reluctant to tear into the succulent flesh.

One of them, braver than the others, couldn't fight the urge to feed any longer. It dove down and landed on the clearing amid the ripe fields of corn. Hopping around a few times, it glanced from the decapitated dead littering the ground, to the one hanging above it.

The crow cawed, seeking permission from the one who protected the land.

"Feed," Jacob commanded.

The crow obeyed, tearing into the feast of the Hag laid out before it.

Seeds of Change

Brian Kirk

We had just sat down to supper when Pete Boone came rumbling down our drive in his flashy Ford pickup, carving through the thin film of road frost like some harbinger of bad news. It was meatloaf, if I recall correctly, with mashed potatoes. And corn, of course. Come to think of it, that may have been the last honest ear of corn I ever ate. And it was delicious. That season's crop being particularly sweet. Plump, juicy kernels like nature's candy. Almost as though Mother Nature had peered into our future and was offering a parting gift. Or making a desperate plea for us to leave well enough alone.

Pete had only been over once before, just after he'd struck the deal that lowered corn futures well below break-even for most of the mid-size farmers, forcing many to sell off their families land. To him, of course.

Just a neighborly head's up, is what he told me at the time. *Might want to shoot for a bumper crop.* Which I did, driving down the cost per bushel even lower and causing quite a stir among the other farmers who put me in cahoots with Pete. I'm not sure who Pete struck the deal with, but it turned out finer than corn silk for him. The rest of us now have to rely on government subsidies just to get by.

I pushed aside my plate and asked Martha to brew up a fresh pot of coffee for hospitality sake. But Pete just honked from the front of the farmhouse as he'd done before, expecting me to brave the chill evening air over him. Daniel looked up at me then, not disrespectful or nothing, just curious to see what I'd do, knowing the scolding he'd get for interrupting supper. Wanting to see if I'd honor the same rules. He nodded his head when I stood and left the table, as though filing away a new lesson on how the world really works.

"Don't mean to intrude," Pete said as I walked up, his window cracked just a couple of inches.

"No bother," I told him, both of us telling lies right from the start.

"Winter's come early, it looks like," he said from the warm confines of his truck cabin.

"But ain't that the truth," I agreed, then laughed as if he'd snapped off something witty. That forced laugh we offer as an act of submission. Like a dog showing its belly. I hated the sound of that phony fool's laugh, and was relieved Daniel wasn't around to hear it.

"I just thought you'd like to know that I'm switching over seed this season. Going with a new two-in-one GE from Chemsol, called Freedom Field."

I'd heard talk of these new seeds, made by the same scientists who had supposedly created herbicidal weapons for the Vietnam War. I'd seen pictures of the aftermath. Men and women with their skin peeling right off. Babies born deformed, extra arms and whatnot. Inhumane was how it looked to me. Like grown up kids playing with toys they hadn't fully figured out.

Now they were applying their fancy technology to pesticides, engineering the toxins right into the seeds themselves. Having seen all those dead and deformed babies I wasn't too keen on having that stuff engineered into my corn, but I never gave it too much thought. I always just stored and recycled my own seed each season.

"Alright," I said, not sure why he felt the need to stop over just to tell me that.

"Well, I thought you might want to switch over yourself."

"Nah, I've already got my seed stored up," I told him. "I'm all set."

He looked out through his darkened windshield then, as though assessing the road ahead, scouting for detours and road debris. The display lights flashed color in his eyes like you see in a cat at night, and I felt myself tense up, knowing that Pete was working some angle that I couldn't quite see. And knowing that once I did, it would likely be too late.

"Well," he said, still looking straight ahead. "The thing is, is that Chemsol has a patent on them seeds. If they find even a single stalk from one growing in your field, they'll sue you for infringement. And, given the proximity of our fields, I can't see as how to prevent any crossover from occurring."

"How are they going to sue me for seed that I don't use?"

"If it winds up in your field, it don't matter how it got there, they'll find you liable. Trust me."

When my sister was little, still just a teen, she went off and married a man against our family's will. A dropout junky from Madison. Had three of his kids before he ditched her and ran off with someone even younger. We wanted nothing to do with that man, but when she brought those kids back home, they became ours just the same. Yep, some things you own, whether you like it or not.

I kicked at the ground a little, pulled my hair some. All for show, I suppose. I knew what Pete wanted and that I would go along with it. And that I'd wake up in the morning with all the reasons why not lined up nice and tidy in my mind, after it was all said and done. Because once you make an agreement with Pete, you don't go back on it. Not without a cost.

"The best I can do is offer to combine orders. Save you close to fifty percent off, in addition to the legal fees you'll be avoiding, of course." He started to smile, like it had slipped past his guard, and he turned it toward me as if we shared an inside joke. I smiled back, despite myself, and nodded my head like some dumb otter doing a trick for fish, sealing the deal right there.

"Okay, then. I'll add you to the order," he said, putting his truck back in gear. "I reckon you'll want to tell some of the others. Might want to keep the bulk buy between us, though." He flashed a two-finger solute, then rumbled back down the drive. I watched as his truck passed my two silos stocked full of seed and thought about all the old, wasted things that get thrown away, wondering where it all winds up. Landfills and cemeteries, I suppose. I hear there's a pile of trash the size of Texas floating out in the ocean somewhere. And I swear I'll never understand how the big cities bury all their dead.

I did as Pete asked and broke the news to the others. I took Daniel with me for company, but also because I knew he would help keep the conversations civil. He's the youngest of our four sons, the runt of the litter I guess you could say, small and frail and sensitive, whereas the other three are all big and boisterous and ambitious. It's like they gobbled up all the best of our genetics and Daniel got whatever was left behind.

Those three are long gone, left the farm to chase their fortunes and fancy careers. Not that many in town will miss them. People still hold them responsible for what happened to the Sanders boy. Yeah, they may have bullied him pretty hard from what I hear, but it was the girl that put him over the edge. It was her he was fighting with when he swallowed that shotgun barrel. Did it right over the phone, too, which seems pretty clear cut to me. Love and hate may be on opposite sides of a coin, but there ain't much in between.

People are partial to Daniel, though. So, I knew he'd help soften the news. In a way, I wasn't much different than Pete. We both know how to work an angle.

It was Gumper who I was really worried about. He was our local seed cleaner, and if we were going to do away with recycled seed, then we'd be turning our back on his business as well. More than that, Gumper's son is a bit spastic. Frail and twitchy. Walks all knock-kneed with his mouth wide open all the time. Poor kid can't do much in the fields, but he's able to handle the cleaner okay. It was about the only way for him to help his father out.

I sent Daniel to chat up his boy as I broke the news to Gumper.

"What am I supposed to do now?" he asked me. "How am I supposed to make ends meet?"

I told him that I ain't the bank nor the bill collector, just the messenger.

"Lord Jesus," is about all he had to say after that. And he said it again and again and again as he shook his head and watched his son and mine hobble around the backyard.

If there was one thing our town could rely on, it was Jesus, although it was hard to say what the Savior had ever done for Gumper. I'd see him near every Sunday up at the Heavenly Meadows Methodist, too, singing out of tune and snoozing through the sermon, sneaking off every now and again to have a smoke around back. Maybe that's it. Maybe just showing up ain't enough. Maybe you've got to really feel it, be filled with the Holy Spirit. Or, maybe the Lord just has too many people to look after these days. Maybe that's part of what's going on now too.

It was getting on toward dusk by the time Daniel and I got back to the farm. After supper I took a couple of folding chairs out to the edge of the field. Daniel brought out a hot cocoa for himself and a coffee for me. The field was flat and frosted over and the night sky was dark and rich with stars.

I've never understood the fascination with a bunch of flickering lights, but Daniel could gaze up at them all night if I let him. It was like the farther out he looked the more he saw inside himself.

"How many of those lights do you think are satellites?" he asked me.

"Shoot, son. Heck if I know."

"A bunch of them, I bet," Daniel said. "I bet you one day they'll be more satellites than stars." Then he sat up ramrod straight and his eyes bugged out real wide. "Hey, what if some of those stars aren't really stars at all? What if they're, like, alien surveillance stations disguised as stars so they can watch over us? What if one day all those lights turn off at once and the sky goes dark and then we hear the roar of a billion rocket ships coming at us from a galaxy away?"

And that's why I sat out here with Daniel, because the boy's imagination was always more interesting than anything on the TV. And as I sat out there, trying to tell the satellites from the stars, it got me thinking about how different Daniel's world was from the one I grew up in. How science seems to be trying to outsmart nature, and how we don't seem to have much of a say in the matter.

And that's when I realized what we'd done. That we'd given up the control of our crops to companies like Chemsol. And that I didn't really know what it was that they were engineering into those seeds, but I knew what they'd done to those kids in Vietnam. And just like that I knew what I should have told Pete. How I should have said that God's seed is good enough for me, and if he wanted to plant something created by scientists, he could go right ahead, but it was his responsibility to keep it contained to his field. But, of course, it was far too late for that by then.

Besides, there really ain't no way to keep that seed from spreading. I see that now. I think it was designed that way.

Come spring, Pete brought over my bags of Freedom Field seed from the Chemsol company. The front showed rows of corn reaching toward a rising sun with a big 'ole American flag flying high in the field. I placed them in my storage silos where the old seed used to be. Took up far less space, I'll admit, and when it came time to plant, cost me less as well.

And the yield? Biggest I ever had, by far. It was like the seeds had been injected with steroids in addition to the pesticides they'd put in there.

I started to see how maybe Pete had a point after all. Maybe the savings in production could help offset some of the losses we'd seen since corn prices dropped so low. And the thicker the crop grew in, and the taller the stalks grew up, the more I started believing that maybe these were miracle seeds, and that I'd been silly to worry about them being created by scientists. Heck, these scientists were certainly smarter than me. Maybe they actually were smarter than Mother Nature as well.

That was, until I tasted it. Bland as can be, as though whatever provides the flavor had been replaced by the pesticide. It would be fine for cattle feed and fructose corn syrup, but the summer wouldn't be the same without the sweet, delicious kernel corn I'd grown up eating fresh off the farm. So, we ground it into cornmeal and used it to make muffins, and ate it as mush. It wasn't so bad once you added a stick of butter and a shaker of salt to it, I suppose. But it wasn't as good as it gets right off the cob, that's for sure.

School let out, which freed up time for Daniel to help out more around the farm. One of the first things we'd always do once school was out, and the fields had been seeded, was transform one of the empty silos into a fort for Daniel and his friends. I'd make racks for his toy guns and we'd create a command center where they'd set elaborate plans before playing war games in the cornfields. Daniel's imagination would lead them on wild and dangerous missions, rescuing POWs from the Vietcong, pursuing mad scientists while being chased by mutant monsters of their making.

This year, though, Daniel didn't show any interest in setting up his fort. He just kind of shook his head when I brought it up, like I was the child and was acting immature. But kids get older and grow out of things, which is what I figured it was. Then I thought maybe something had happened at school, as his friends weren't coming around like they used to. Gumper's son was the only one I saw with any regularity, and I reckoned that was due to his father's recent lack of work.

It seems like the final bit of child inside you dies when your kid grows up, when he stops being curious about the world and turning to you for answers. It's like a spell gets broken, one that turns back time, and you realize that you're all grown up and heading nowhere faster than the grave.

Well, I tried to get Daniel to show that spark of imagination that kept me feeling young, but all he seemed interested in was his work. Even at night, out under the stars, he'd just sit there all silent, tugging on his lower lip, looking down toward the ground.

Then one afternoon, his mother, noticing the amount of time Gumper's son was spending at our place, invited the boy over for supper. I could tell Daniel didn't really want him there, but I raised the boy to be polite, especially to company, and was surprised by the way he acted toward the boy. Mimicking his tremors and insulting the way he chewed his food like a fish fighting for air. Normally I would have scolded Daniel and sent him off to bed, but the longer I sat there, the less I seemed to care. In fact, the boy's spasms, clanking his silverware against his plate and spilling grits all down his face, started to get under my skin as well. And Martha actually got up and left the table, shooting a scowl toward the boy as if he was being an ungracious guest.

Still, that didn't seem to discourage the boy from coming around the farm every few days, so I decided I'd say something to Gumper next time I saw him at church. Make up some story about the boy distracting Daniel from his chores and that he shouldn't come around as much any more. But Gumper didn't show that Sunday, or the next one. Then I realized that it wasn't just Gumper, the entire congregation seemed to be thinning out.

I said something to Reverend Marin, told him it seemed like fewer people were coming to service.

"Why should they?" is what he said, and for a moment I thought he was testing me to determine my true faith.

"Well," I said, trying to figure out what he'd expect me to say.

To worship The Lord.

For the sake of our salvation.

Because Jesus died so that we may live eternal.

But none of those reasons seemed true to me at the moment. "I don't know," I answered honestly. Then the Reverend turned and looked at me with these cold eyes that I'd never seen from him before. Eyes that didn't seem to care.

"I don't either," he said, and started removing his robe as he walked down the hall toward his office. Heavenly Meadows shut down a few weeks after that, and Reverend Marin left town.

Daniel came to me after we'd learned the church had closed. Asked me if that meant God had left town as well.

"God doesn't just live in the church," I told him. "He lives in your heart."

His laugh surprised me. It was the first time I'd seen him even smile in several weeks. But as it went on I realized there wasn't much humor to it. He wasn't laughing at anything I'd said, he was laughing at me.

"That's what you believe?" he said, then he just stood and left the room, laughing and shaking his head. Had he waited around to hear my answer, he would of heard me tell him "No." God had left town, and if he ever had lived in my heart, he had packed His things and left there too.

I remember sitting on the porch a couple of days before the final harvest, overlooking my acres of corn. Best looking crop I'd ever grown, waving in the wind like some living quilt. And I realized then that I hated it and couldn't wait until it was gone. Gone off to the confinement farms and refineries. To the mills and canned food manufacturers, even though the taste wasn't worth a damn. Gone off to feed the endless machine that keeps driving us toward some undetermined destination that seems more like a dead end.

Daniel joined me and looked off into the distance, but whether it was the corn, the horizon, or the insides of his own mind he was surveying, I couldn't say. We sat in silence, and I could feel the hate building inside him as well. And then that's all I could feel, was hate. For our field and its chemical corn. For Daniel and his newfound indifference. For me and my compromises. For the whole world and its destructive ways.

I saw Gumper's boy come hobbling around the corner of the house as I sat there seething and I nearly screamed at him to go the hell away. Instead I took a shot at Daniel. I took it out on my son.

"Well, look who's here," I said in a needling voice that was more like a finger poke, one that my older boys surely used when picking on that Sanders boy. "Your best buddy is back." Then I stood and walked into the house, dragging a foot and jiggling my hands against my chest, my mouth open wide.

Martha looked up from unloading the washer when I walked in, and I stopped my imitation, expecting to get an earful. But she just stared at me, offering no reaction to my mockery, just looking at me with these faraway eyes before going back about her business.

Now this was a woman who would normally have tanned both Daniel and my hide for acting indecent toward someone as defenseless as Gumper's son, but it was like she couldn't care less. Like it was proper behavior. Then I remembered the way she'd acted herself that night at supper, storming away from the table like she couldn't stand it anymore. And thinking back, I realized that she had been keeping to herself more and more over the last couple of months. And when we were together, she had a way of looking at us, Daniel and me both, like she was evaluating us under a new light. Like she wasn't quite sure she wanted us around anymore.

We packed and unloaded the last of the year's harvest, shipping it off to all corners of the country. I started to collect the discarded seed to be recycled, then remembered what Pete had told me when he'd dropped the pallets off, that Chemsol had manufactured the seed to become sterile after the growing season, so we'd have to place a new order every year.

Without the need to store seed, I didn't know what to do with my storage silos, especially now that Daniel didn't even want them for a fort anymore.

I went over and opened the door to one of the silos to start thinking about what I could maybe use them for. The smell hit me pretty quick, and I knew what it was right away. Then I saw where the empty seed bags had been piled up on the far side. The Freedom Fields, all arranged in a neat little mound.

I know what I should have felt right then. *Horror. Sadness. Anger. Regret.* But I didn't feel any of those things. Truth be told, I didn't feel anything at all. Other than a nagging sense of annoyance over what I knew I'd have to do.

And I didn't waste any time either, reuniting Gumper with his son that same afternoon. I did a better job disposing of the bodies than Daniel did, although I'm not sure it really matters. People will just assume they left town to find a new line of work.

If they even bother to think about them at all.

Either way, I can't bring myself to care. Emotion seems like a faint memory to me, like an old faded photograph where you can't really make out the faces anymore. Whole town's that way too. Everyone pretty much keeps to themselves, just biding time until growing season comes back around. And with the way that seed spreads, there ain't a farm in the state that won't be using Freedom Fields next season, that's for sure.

I'll miss the sweet way corn used to taste, I can tell you. And I'll miss the way it used to be between Martha, Daniel, and me. But it's no use thinking about the past. I have a feeling things are going to be different around here moving forward. More than just here for that matter. But life moves on, as you know, and you press ahead, because sometimes there ain't no turning back.

The Orange Grove

Tim Jeffreys

There had been half a year of waiting. It was now late summer, the fruit ripening on the orange trees. The first Catherine knew of the boy, Jack, was a headache that came upon her one day while she was working in the grove. Like all the women in her family, she'd suffered from foresights. Her grandmother had liked to call them *warnings*, but Catherine preferred to think of them as *clues*. A tingling in her fingertips might mean something good was due, while a headache could only mean the opposite.

The headache built throughout the afternoon, so that Catherine was forced to retire to the house early. When Ira, the gardener, asked what was wrong, she sensed the expectancy in his question—the weight of it. "It's just a headache, Ira," she told him. "Don't worry."

He was standing in a corner of the kitchen, by an open door that led to the cellar. He carried in his arms a box he had brought up from below. He set it down without looking at Catherine. "I've worked for your family a long time now," he said in a casual manner, as he busied himself at the table. "Ever since I was a boy. Been around long enough to know how things work."

Now he raised his eyes and looked directly at her for a moment. His face was tender, benevolent. Perhaps because of his words, Catherine noticed suddenly how much he had aged. His tan, weathered face betrayed a network of lines, and grey tufts of hair were visible beneath his hat. She managed to stop herself from asking: *When did this happen? Why haven't I noticed before how old you've become?* His eyes, though, were bright and intelligent; his sinewy body, as he worked, showed strength.

"It's just a headache, Ira. I told you."

He nodded, but continued looking at her in a concerned way before returning to his work.

The afternoon sun shone in through the window of Catherine's room. No sooner had she lain down on the bed that she fell asleep. She dreamt she saw a young man walking the dirt track toward the orchard house. His walk was slow but determined. He wore black. His wide-brimmed hat was pulled low against the sun, and his face was down-turned, so that his features made no part of the dream. Somehow, Catherine understood that this person would be linked to David, her husband. With the arrival of this young man, something would soon be resolved in the orange grove. As the dream ended, Catherine saw the young man lift his head, as though attempting to look back at her from the dream. The sky against which he walked grew darker. He was bringing this darkness with him, as though it were a part of him or attached to him in some way. Before it engulfed him, Catherine glimpsed the marks on his face, his gloating smile and the wicked pinprick lights of his eyes.

And she started awake with her husband's name on her lips.

At first she was confused to find the day still bright. She sat a while, waiting for her head to clear, then got up and went downstairs. Ira was waiting in the kitchen. His eyes followed her as she crossed to a cupboard. She took a tin from the cupboard and found it empty. She sighed and shook her head. When she moved toward the cellar door, Ira said, "I'll go."

"It's fine," she replied. "I know I'm not much use around here, but I can still get myself something from the cellar."

Ira turned back to his work. After a long silence, he said, "I heard you cry out."

"Strange dream," she told him.

"A nightmare?"

"Not really, just strange."

"Could it mean—?"

"You can go home now, Ira. Thank you for your help today."

"Did your dream have anything to do with—with David?"

Catherine remained casual when she answered, pretending not to know what he was implying. "No, it wasn't about him. It was nothing really." Even as she said this, Catherine was thinking of the young man's face she had glimpsed in her dream. She felt a shiver. "Please, Ira, we've done all we can today."

"Catherine, it will soon be time to harvest the oranges," he said. "It's too big a job for the two of us."

"Maybe." She froze for a moment, looking inward. "Maybe someone will come looking for work."

Ira's eyes examined her. "You think?" After gathering his things he stood in the doorway, looking back at her. "I didn't mention it before—"

"What is it?"

"I found more of the oranges spoiled today. Over on the far side of the grove. All our hard work, Catherine. If he—" He paused, and Catherine found him studying her face again. When he continued, the tone of his voice was no longer casual. In a tense whisper he said, "What you've done....what you did...it will ruin us in the end."

Catherine felt a cold stir in her stomach. Not wanting Ira to notice her agitation, she shrugged, shaking her head. "I didn't mean to do it. It was an accident, that's all."

Ira gave her a lingering look of sadness. "It was no accident."

"Well, what do you want me to say, Ira?" she said, in a barely controlled voice, swinging the cellar door open so roughly it slammed into the wall with a bang, and swung back and closed again. "He...he made me angry."

"I know," Ira said, looking back at her from the door space. "But what you did needs now to be undone, one way or another."

Down in the cellar, searching among bottles and jars by candlelight, Catherine looked out through a dust-covered window as Ira walked away from the house. She felt a sudden desire for him to stay with her, but stopped herself as she made to knock on the glass. She knew if he returned tonight he would continue needling her about her husband.

Alone in her room, Catherine listened to the hot, still night humming. Somewhere distant, she could hear the clock counting off the minutes, weighing the seconds with silences. She lay on one side, covers thrown, her eyes wide open. She watched leaf shadows dancing on the far wall, opposite the window. The darkness reverberated. The clock went *tick...tick... tick....*

For a while there were no other sounds. Catherine sighed, rolled over, and sighed again. Then, faintly at first, she heard the rainfall begin outside.

It pitter-pattered, patter-pittered softly, like weeping. The air cooled. When a breeze found a gap in the curtains and floated across Catherine's body, every inch of her skin rejoiced.

She lay naked in the dark, listening to the rain pick up. Still feeling the heat, she left her bed and crossed to the window. Stillness had fallen over the orange grove. Though she could not see the clock, Catherine knew it was the deepest part of the night, some moment held like a breath. As she realised this, she felt all at once lonely and turned to find David, half expecting him to be there on his side of the bed. All she could find of him was his image. He looked at her from within his frame, trapped like a butterfly behind glass. The picture being all she'd had of him for six months, she found she was about to say, "Who are you?" Shocked by this, she instead touched a finger to the glass and whispered, "Where are you?" Then, frowning, she replaced the photograph on the dressing table.

The night's humidity became unbearable, so Catherine decided she had to be outside. She wanted to feel the rain spatter her face the way it spattered the fruit in the garden. She wanted to open out her palms like leaves to the raindrops. No sooner had this thought entered her head that she had left her room and span downstairs, pausing only to gather up her nightgown out of modesty.

A fat-faced moon floated behind clouds, patch-working the darkness between the trees with silvery light. Outside, Catherine looked toward Ira's cottage, where a light was burning in one of the windows. She thought she saw movement across the lit pane, as though someone had passed before the window, or stepped back away from it. "Can't you sleep either?" she asked in a whisper, before moving forward towards the trees. She paused before entering the grove to lift her face to the rain, to feel it cover her forehead and cheeks. All around was silent, but for the gentle swaying of the trees. She was enchanted by the quiet, the darkness and the moonlight, until a sobering wind struck up from nowhere. She shrieked as she was pelted with rain, finding her own cry answered by another somewhere deep in the grove.

Stiffening, she glanced around.

Was someone else here, amongst the orange trees? She thought of the black-clad young man from her dream, walking purposefully along the dusty road with clouds drawing in behind him. Could he now be lurking in the grove, spying on her?

She was about to dismiss this notion when she heard her name called from further back in the trees. She turned about in the moonlight, listening.

There was nothing but the rain falling. Had she imagined the sound?

Then she heard it again. Clearly this time. Her name being spoken. The voice she thought she recognised.

"David?" she returned, astounded and afraid.

He called out to her again.

Then she was running in the direction of the voice, gripped suddenly by a bounding joy. Her bare feet slid on the wet grass. She was ducking and swiping at the trees.

Finding herself all at once in a dark, shrouded part of the grove, she stopped running, feeling instead of her happiness an icy fear. Her voice was low and uncertain. "*David?*"

There was silence amongst the trees.

Moving forward, she felt a gossamer shroud cover her face. She fought to free herself of it, only to find her hands entangled in the webbing. It clung with a silky softness, and soon she was ripping it from her body and face, fearing that she would become trapped by it, caught.

"David?" she said again, catching the dread in her own voice. Suddenly she cried out, on the brink of hysteria. "*David?*"

He came at her quick and heavy, just a shadow in the dark. He gripped on to her, breathing her name, and she found she was screaming.

"Catherine!" his voice was loud against her ear. "Come to me, Catherine! Come here!"

"But, David," she said in a shrill voice. "You're—"

She heard him laugh, a scornful, whinnying laugh that she had never heard before. As she struggled against him, they turned about and she began to make out his face in the dim light. The rest of his body remained in darkness.

"*I've come back!*" he said. "*Hold me!*"

"No, David! No!"

The moon was inching out from behind the clouds, threatening to light the scene—threatening to give Catherine a sight she had been waiting months for, but which she was now certain she did not want to see—her husband. Still he held on to her, breathing against her cheek.

"Come to me! Come with me!" he demanded. Then when she made no reply but for a low, terrified whimpering, his voice turned angry. She saw the shape of his body moving beyond his face. *"You did this!"* he roared. *"You did this to me!"*

Reeling, shrieking, Catherine fought back the arms that were holding her. Once free, she turned and ran. She ran from her husband just as quickly as she had run to him, and she did not look back, even when she heard the whipping of his arms and legs as he followed, even when his breath was at her neck once again. His desperate pleas pursued her across the grove. Once she was inside the house, she slammed the door and leaned her body against it. Her breath came in sobs. Sliding to the floor, she wept against her knees. She wept and wept. Eventually she calmed. She lifted her head. There were no sounds from outside. Even the rain had stopped. The night was still again.

She woke the next morning in her own bed. The night's activities she could have dismissed as a dream, but her sheets were muddied with dirt and leaves. Something else troubled her that morning. Before she had even left her room, she knew the young man had arrived. She could feel his presence in the house, compelling but also unnerving.

She could not prevent, when she entered the kitchen, the tone of wariness in her voice.

"Hello."

Ira was facing her across the wide oak table. Opposite him, with his back to Catherine as she entered, was the young man. He had taken off his wide brimmed hat and placed it on the table in front of him.

"Catherine—" Ira began. But at once his voice faded into the background. The young man had turned to look over his shoulder. When he saw Catherine, his eyes flashed and a smile crept up one side of his face. He said nothing, only held onto her gaze.

Ira's voice drifted back in. "—looking for work. We could use an extra pair of hands. *Catherine?*"

"Who are you?" said Catherine, still staring at the stranger. Now the young man got up. He spun quickly about and faced Catherine with a grin, ready to charm. "Jack," he announced, bowing a little. "Swift."

"Swift?"

"My name."

She glared as he gestured towards himself. For the first time she noticed the tiny crisscrossing scars on his face.

"You need work?"

"Your gardener said you have need of a picker. And my hands are quick."

"I'll bet they are."

He held out his hands as though she could tell by looking at them how quick they could move. She noticed their tops also were marked.

Catherine raised her eyes to his face. His stare was blue and hard as glass.

"I can offer you room and board. Not much else."

He smiled. "I accept."

Having been fixed on her face, Jack's gaze now travelled downwards. His tongue moved thoughtfully over his upper lip and Catherine realised that she still wore only her nightgown.

"Ira will show you what to do," she said as though stung. "I expect you to work hard."

Before he could reply, she turned away from him, finding the weight of his eyes too much to bear. Hurriedly, though she tried not to show it, she left the kitchen and returned upstairs to her bedroom. There, she caught David looking at her from behind the glass of his picture frame. As though his eyes too were examining her, she took his picture and turned it towards the wall. Removing a shirt from the dressing table, she suddenly realised why she had thrown it there. Now it was too late, she had uncovered the book which lay open on the dresser top. For a while she stared at it, hoping in the back of her mind that it would vanish and she could say it was a dream, and last night was a dream, and she had done nothing to David, he had simply gone away and left her. But the book sat there, open to the very page she had searched for with trembling, vengeful fingers.

She crossed to the window. The morning sun streamed in. She was gazing out over the heads of the trees, thinking over what had happened the previous night. How it all seemed so unlikely suddenly. She drew the nightgown over her head and let it fall to the floor, feeling the sun's rays warm her bare flesh. Turning, she gave a start, for there in the door space stood Jack Swift, like a funeral sign with his black hat perched on his head. There was the trace of contemplation on his face.

"Miss," he said. Again he gave a little bow, before removing himself from her door and crossing the hall to the bathroom.

Ira had once relished a chance to work alone in the grove. Since childhood he had loved the place. Though the work could be hard, he had always enjoyed the tranquillity amongst the trees. As a younger man, working alone, he had daydreamed that the grove was his, that the work he did day in and day out was for himself, not others. Sometimes he cursed his own humility, his nature to know his place. And he felt a twist at his heart for opportunities he had let slip away. More recently, though, he had not felt so at ease working alone in the grove. Some strange event had taken place. Now, there were always shufflings, snaps, and other more ominous noises. The grove had begun to feel like a haunted place. When he worked, he had always to be glancing around, stopping every once in a while when an odd sound reached his ears. There were times when he was certain he was being watched. He never saw anything. He had tried asking Catherine to explain what had happened to David, but she never answered fully—and he, in any case, could not believe what was suggested.

So, initially, it was a relief for Ira to have Jack with him. Here was an extra pair of eyes to keep watch. The first day Ira took Jack into the grove, he could see that the young man was as quick as he claimed with his hands, but he was also just as quick with his chat. Jack spent the day spinning endless tales about his life, so that Ira quickly learned much about him. By the end of their first day working together, he distrusted the youngster intensely and had even begun to grow weary of his non-stop talk, but he had also began to suspect that Jack might be useful to him.

"Chico was your friend?"

Jack stood up straight, wiping his hand across his brow. "Me and Chico were garbage boys together. That's what they called us. We were too young to join a gang—that is, gangs didn't want us—so we had to scratch around for things to eat, places to sleep. Once we lived in a big cardboard box. We used to curl up nice and snug in there while the rain came down. I remember the sound it made on the roof of the box—*dur-um, dum, dum, dum, dum, dur.* It made me sort of happy, that sound."

"If he was your friend, why did you stab him?"

"That was later," said Jack, without flinching. "After we got in the gang. One night we were told to break into this big house. Only Chico got scared, and ran when he heard footsteps. He left me there alone. I almost didn't get away. Had to fight my way out, and I was only a nipper. Well, I couldn't let that pass, could I? They used to tease me in the gang, see. They thought I was a mummy's boy, because—well—it doesn't matter now. But they never teased me again, not after Chico got what was owed him. No one tests Jack Swift."

Ira made no remark, only stood looking at the young man in a thoughtful way. Jack shrugged, returning to his work. Ira would have done the same, but he detected sounds behind him amongst the trees. He turned, beginning to walk in the direction of the noises. Peering forward, he could make out movement not far from where he stood.

Then, "Ira?"

"Catherine."

She stepped from the trees, radiant in a white rough-cotton dress and carrying a basket in one hand. "I thought you two might be hungry. How's the boy doing?"

"He's a good worker. Gets a lot done though he never stops yakking."

Catherine smiled. "I'm glad. I'm so grateful to have you here, Ira. I don't know where I'd be if it wasn't for you and your hard work."

"It's my duty," Ira said, dropping his head a little. "It's always been my duty to your family, like it was my father's. Now that everyone else is gone, well, you and me have to look after each other."

"That's right," Catherine said. She surprised Ira then by placing down the basket and stepping forward to draw him close to her. As she hugged him, Ira's breath caught. With one hand he almost cupped her head, but stopped himself, letting his hand hang in the air.

"Ira," she said then, her voice muffled against his chest. "I'm so ashamed."

"Don't be," he said. "There must be some way we can put things back to normal."

Catherine drew back, looking into Ira's face. "Maybe I could undo it, undo what I did, but I'm afraid to touch that book again. I'm so afraid I'll make it worse. The others knew; my mother knew about those things. They knew how it worked, but I didn't even believe it."

"Your father was a practical man. Things changed after he came here. Your mother changed. Thinking changed. But you are still your mother's daughter, Catherine. You can still—"

"It was just a silly idea. I was angry. I never truly thought anything would happen."

"So much like your mother," Ira continued, as if she hadn't interrupted. "You have everything she had. Sometimes, I think—"

"Hello! What's all this then?" Jack approached, swinging his arms and grinning. He noted the basket sitting on the grass. "I'm starving. What've you got there?"

Catherine slipped away from Ira, leaving her faint imprint on his body.

He caught her arm, and said, "Don't worry. We'll think of something."

A week passed. One afternoon, Catherine was alone in the kitchen when Jack came in from the garden. He had been out working with Ira in the grove and now stood shirtless in the cool kitchen, his body glistening with sweat.

Seeing Catherine, he tipped his hat. "Miss."

"How is the work going?" Catherine asked, diverting her eyes from the vision of moist bare skin. Jack was pouring from a pitcher of lemonade she had put out on the table, and paused to look at her.

"Not too good. This morning we found a whole section of the grove ruined. No good. It looked like something had gone through, eating what it could and spoiling the rest."

Catherine frowned, feeling a heat rising in her cheeks. "What did Ira have to say about it?"

"Wasn't pleased, Miss. He said if this carries on there won't be much for me to do around here."

Catherine watched Jack as he drank. In trying not to notice the soft contours of his body, she focused instead on the light scars that seemed to cover him.

"How did you get so marked?" she asked. "Your whole body is covered in—"

"Not my whole body," Jack interrupted, foxily.

"I wouldn't know about that."

Jack said nothing, only grinned his boyish grin then poured another glass of lemonade.

Catherine turned her back to him. "How do you find me?" she asked then, surprising even herself with the question.

Jack answered at once. "Very beautiful…and strange."

Catherine span to face him again. "Why strange? Because I told you how I dreamt of your coming? Did I tell you also that in my dream you brought storm clouds with you?"

He said nothing, but laughed a little and shook his head. Catherine continued to watch him as he took something from his belt and tossed it onto the table.

"What is it?"

"This? Only my knife. See?" Reaching down, he picked up the object again and drew from the leather sheath a long bowie knife. He held the knife up so that Catherine could see how it glinted in the sunlight.

"I don't like it," she said. "You mustn't bring it in the house."

"It's only a knife."

"No, Jack. I won't allow it."

He smiled slyly. "I used to knife play a little in the city."

"Knife play?"

"For money. You put two men together in a ring with a knife each, and the first one to draw blood wins. And no one's as quick with a blade as Jack Swift." He glanced down at himself, pre-empting Catherine's next remark. "'Course, you need to warm up first."

"Clearly," said Catherine.

Jack reached into his pocket, taking out a few items and placing them on the table top.

"Now what are you doing?"

"Thought I'd roll a smoke? Want one?"

"No."

"It might just save your life."

"Don't be ridiculous," Catherine snapped. "How could it?"

She half-turned to leave the kitchen, but stopped and looked at Jack.

He had perched on a stool at the table and now busied himself with a pack of tobacco and some cigarette papers. She thought for a moment, then said, "Did you ever kill a man, Jack?"

At this he glanced away, abstracted.

"It happens."

"How old are you?"

"I'm twenty," he said, with a touch of pride.

"Twenty years old and you've already killed another man. Or men? How many is it, then?"

Jack shrugged. He fumbled again in his pocket for a box of matches, popped the cigarette he'd made between his lips and lit it. He stared straight at her through the smoke, all the sneaky humour gone from his features.

"Is it really your husband who's destroying the oranges?" he asked.

Catherine took a step backwards, shocked. "What has Ira told you?"

Jack smirked, blowing smoke out the corner of his mouth. "He alludes."

"Well, he has no right!"

Jack shrugged again, looking at her from an angle. "I don't get it," he said. "Why would your husband come here to ruin the oranges? What happened between you?"

"It's...it's none of your business!"

"Ira says there was a picker before me. A girl. He says one day you found your husband out amongst the trees with the girl and they were—"

"Ira shouldn't be discussing my affairs with you! Not you, of all people!"

Though she was flushed with anger, Jack continued to stand calmly looking at her as though by looking he would get all the answers he needed.

"What did you do to him?"

"I sent him away!"

"That all?"

Catherine turned and slammed her arm against a cupboard in anger. When she did a large spider was dislodged and dropped down onto her hand. With a cry she shook it to the floor.

"Oh, horrible thing! Kill it! Kill it!"

"It's only a spider!" Jack said, faintly amused.

"No, I hate them! Get it away from me! Kill it!"

"Relax," Jack said, stepping forward and carefully crushing the spider under his boot as it scuttled madly across the floor tiles. Then he made to reassure Catherine, though she shrank from his touch. He had that devilish look to his face again.

She crossed to the open door, leaning her body against the frame. She let her eyes wander amongst the edge of the trees.

"This grove is full of secrets, Jack. Mysteries."

"So I've noticed," he said, somewhere behind her.

"My parents worked so hard here. They ran everything. When I was a child I thought my mother controlled the seasons. She was so sure of herself, so at home here in the grove. I'm not like her." She laughed dryly. "I'd give everything to be only half the woman she was."

"What happened to her?" said Jack. "She die?"

"She died in a fire. They both did. There was a terrible accident. Oh!" Catherine pressed her hands to her face. "What a mess I've made of it all."

Close to her ear she heard Jack say, "I could help you sort things out a bit."

She turned around, startled by the voice, surprised to find Jack so close at her shoulder.

"What?"

"I could deal with your husband," he said.

"What do you mean?"

He threw a look to the knife on the table. "I could get rid of him for you."

Catherine looked to his face, and could see from his eyes that he was not offering this service for free.

"What do you want?"

He looked at her with lingering intent. "It wouldn't take much."

"Go back to work."

At length, he said, "You sure?"

She hesitated. How his eyes held her.

"Go."

And he was gone.

* * *

Ira had spent the morning with Jack, working deep in the grove. Around noon Jack had insisted on returning to the house to refresh himself. Ira accompanied him as far as a small burial ground. It was situated in a clearing a short walk from the house, and enclosed by a low circular wall. It was here that Jack found Ira when he returned. Ira was busy tidying one of the graves when Jack approached.

"I'm ready to get busy again when you are?" the young man said.

Ira glanced up at Jack, who had stuck a casual pose, shirtless with his back to the sun, his thumbs jammed into his trouser pockets, and his hat tilted back on his head. "You look pleased with yourself."

"Always have been," Jack said, showing his lopsided grin. "What's going on here? Hell of a gloomy place to take a break."

"I like it here," Ira responded.

"Well, that's something," Jack said with a laugh. "Because you'll be taking up residence soon enough, old man." And he turned to the side, not catching the scolding look Ira threw his way. When Jack looked back to Ira the old man was sweeping clean the headstone with his hands. Jack bowed forward to read the inscription. "Rowan Moniz. Loving mother and…" he stopped reading and cocked his head at the next grave. "What about that one?"

"What about it?" said Ira, not looking.

"Going to give that a little attention some day? Looks like it could use a tidy up."

"Someday, perhaps," said Ira, in a low tone.

Shaking his head in mock dismay, Jack stumbled past Ira to the next grave and began raking back the weeds obscuring the stone.

"Leave it," Ira told him.

"I'm going to give poor…" Jack read the name on the stone. "*Robert* a spruce up too, seeing as you've no intention."

"Leave it!" Ira said, in such a harsh voice that Jack jerked upright and backed away from the grave with his hands raised.

Glaring then at Ira, looking perplexed and a touch amused, he called out, "What've you got against Robert here?"

At length Ira spoke, subdued, speaking to himself almost. "That man didn't belong in a place like this. Should never have come to these parts. She never truly loved him. She was a wild bird and he—he put her in a cage."

"What are you *talking* about?" Jack asked, shaking his head and addressing Ira as though he were a man beyond reason. "You're a strange lot. Here's you hanging around the tombstones talking about *who loved who* and *who belonged where,* when all that's down there is *bones!* And then there's *Madam* back at the house. Now, she's a puzzle, she is."

Without lifting his eyes from the gravestone, Ira said, "Did you talk to Catherine about the matter we discussed earlier? How you might be of help to her?"

"I mentioned it," Jack said. "But she's not best keen on having her husband seen off at the moment."

"But we have to do something. He's destroying the grove. This is her livelihood. Her life."

"I got nothing against doing the job, but don't you think killing him's a bit—harsh? He is her *husband* after all, no matter what might have happened between them. Maybe we should try talking to him. See if that works."

Ira stood, looking directly at Jack now. "Don't you understand? He's beyond talking. He's beyond a lot of things. Are you getting cold feet?"

"Never had cold feet in my life. I could do it in a second, but Madam weren't interested in a trade."

"Trade?" Ira's eyes narrowed. "Who said anything about a trade?"

Jack laughed. "You didn't think I was going to do it for free now, did you?"

"When we talked this morning, no one mentioned any trade? How much did you ask for?"

"Only a little bit," said Jack with a sly grin, glancing away.

"Refused, did she?"

"Not exactly. I've a feeling she might budge."

"Well, then," said Ira. He patted Jack on the shoulder. "Maybe we can give her more incentive."

For the rest of the afternoon, Catherine sat grieving at the kitchen table until she was awakened by shouts from across the garden. As she rose to her feet, Ira and Jack burst through the door. Jack was supporting Ira, whose hands were bloodied. The gardener had one arm around Jack's shoulders, and the other arm was also bloody, the shirtsleeve torn open. Both men appeared stricken.

"What has happened?" Catherine cried out.

"Let him sit down," Jack said. There was something in his voice that suggested she was in some way responsible for whatever had occurred.

"I'll be alright," Ira assured her in a small voice.

"What happened?"

"Something attacked him," Jack said. "I didn't see."

"It was David," Ira told her, his eyes holding hers for a moment. A feeling of dread passed between them.

"You saw David?"

"Yes," Ira said. Now his tone too was weighty and accusing. "I just stumbled across him and he attacked me."

"Something has to be done!" Jack put in.

Catherine rounded on him. "Be quiet. Or go back where you came from."

He answered in a spiteful way, "Maybe I will."

They stood in silence, but Jack made no move towards the door.

"How bad is it?" Catherine said, turning back to Ira. When Ira's eyes widened, she knew that he had misunderstood her and quickly added. "I meant your wounds."

"They need cleaning and dressing."

Without another word Catherine began to prepare hot water and some bandages. Jack merely stood by the door, watching. When all the blood had been washed from Ira's arm, Catherine saw the two deep punctures to his skin just below the shoulder. Ragged lines, less serious, ran from these punctures down almost to his wrist.

"Bit me," Ira whispered, as she leaned over him.

Catherine glanced up at Jack. He remained in the gloom over by the door, with only the light of his eyes seeming to stand out. When she had finished binding Ira's inflictions, she crossed to Jack and said quietly, "Alright…"

His face tightened with a grin. "When?"

"Tonight. But you promise."

"I'll keep my part of the deal," he said, looking her up and down. "If you will."

* * *

Night time had to come, there was no avoiding it. After bathing, Catherine sat at her dresser, waiting for a knock on the door to her room. Jack waited a long time, until the early hours, but she knew he would come eventually. All he said was, "Ready?"

The candles she had lit made their combined shadow monstrous on the wall. Their clothes were strewn about the floor. In her husband's bed, Jack made love to her brutally, as though he wished in some way to punish her, for what she didn't know. She could feel the anger in the stabbing movements of his body. When she complained, his body answered that it was all her fault, that she had created the situation. He was all hardness, all urgency, as though he were killing her. All the while, she tried to soften him with caresses. She wrapped her arms and legs around him to reassure. But he would not be stilled. He leapt in her embrace. He pushed back her arms and pounded away at her. He would not relent until they both cried out.

"There," he said when it was over.

He fell away. The candles had guttered. Catherine listened to him breathing in the darkness.

"You do it as though you hate me," she said quietly.

"Of course I don't hate you, Catherine."

Though his voice was blunt, she thought how once he must have been an innocent boy until circumstance had set to change him.

"Why did you come here?" she asked, searching for his face in the gloom.

"Had to," he said. "Had to leave the city. They were out for blood."

"Who was out for blood?"

"Sometimes it goes too far, the knife play. Well…" Jack gave a dry laugh. "Sometimes *I* go too far. But understand, see. When the blood's pumping it's like something else takes over. You don't know what you've done until it's too late."

"I see," said Catherine with a sigh. "You killed your opponent."

"Not just an opponent. He was their champion! And I have to admit, he had me on the ropes! But I got a secret weapon, see. Anger. All my anger can make me strong and fast."

"And heartless, Jack. A killer. What makes you so angry?"

"Well, I suppose it was my mother who started it."

"What do you mean? What happened to you?"

When he didn't answer, she rolled to find him in the dark, but her arms fell on empty space. She thought for a second that he had played some trick on her. Then from across the room she heard him say, "Don't get sentimental, will you."

"What are you doing?" She could see his shape by the window.

"I heard something."

"What?"

He was silent, looking out of the window. Then he said, "I'm going to find out."

Fear wrapped around Catherine's heart. Turning on the light, she leapt from the bed and clutched at his clothes as he tried to put them on.

"Don't go."

"I have to do something!" he snapped.

"No, it's David! He'll hurt you! You don't know what he is!"

"What do you mean?"

"It was the worst thing I could think of! I used the book and it was the worst thing I could think of..."

"Get out of my way."

He pulled his shoes on, then, heading for the door, he paused to look back at her.

"How was it?" he asked.

She answered sadly, "Like rape."

A shadow moved across his face. She thought for a second that she could see the soft-faced boy he must've once been. Then his face filled up with something else—the desire, the absolute need—to do harm.

"Where's my knife?"

"That won't help you."

"It's a start!"

She hurried to block his path as he moved off down the stairs. "It's alright. I've changed my mind. You don't have to do this. I only said it because I wanted you in my bed."

"Liar!" he sneered, sweeping her out of the way. Half way down the stairs, he stopped and looked back at her. "Maybe you did it to get back at *him*, but now I'm going to kill him."

“Wait!” she said. “Listen to me. That book in my room is a book of spells. I used it to change him! What I did was awful!”

“Nonsense!”

“Stop, Jack! I'd rather go myself!”

He laughed, and she felt a prickle of anger.

“I don't care about the grove, Jack!”

He stopped again to glare at her. “You want to live, don't you? You want to eat. Step aside!”

“You don't know what's out there. You don't know what I did!”

He cried out, as petulant as a child. “I want to find out. I want to kill it.”

And he stormed past her, his knife was already bared in his hand. He did not look back.

The leaf shadows moved across the wall of her room. The night was black and silent. Catherine sat by the window, hoping for a draft to cool her, hoping that a little rain might fall.

She pricked her ears at a sound from across the grove. It was Jack. He was screaming.

Catherine bent over the book that was open in front of her. Under her breath, she began to recite what was written on the page. After this, she waited. In time she saw a shadow move across the garden below. Rising, she left the room and travelled downstairs to the kitchen. There was scratching from behind the door.

“Jack?” she said, opening the door a crack.

But crouched on the doorstep was David, her husband. Though he had blood on his hands, he looked like his old self again, like the picture in the room upstairs.

Pitifully, he raised his eyes to hers. She could see that he asked for forgiveness.

“My love,” she said, falling to her knees to embrace him.

On the Quest of the Crow King

Ahimsa Kerp

The orange fruits clung to the branches of the leafless tree with futile persistence. Three crows sat like winged gargoyles in the bare branches. Natalie leaned her head closer to the window of the bus and stared at starkly autumn landscape. The trees were bare and piles of browning leaves gathered at their roots, though further into the mountains, there would be scarlet and yellow aplenty from the oaks and Japanese maples.

"What are you looking at?" Dylan asked, from the seat next to her. It had been his idea to come down to see the autumn leaves at Jirisan, South Korea's tallest mainland mountain. It was her first holiday in Korea, and a four day weekend was a much needed break from eight hours of teaching six-year-olds each day.

Dylan turned to the seat behind them and offered their friends a beer. Marcus, a well-traveled Englishman, gratefully accepted one. Brian and Lisa, who were from Toronto and Vancouver, did not. Beers or not, they were the only foreigners on the bus, and were getting stared at from the *adjummas,* the permed, floral-print clad women just shy of old age who had rewritten the book on entitlement. They had entire sections for themselves on the subways but never felt shy insisting a foreigner rise to give them a seat, or to cut in front of one in line at the market. Dylan had said the discrimination was a lot worse in South Africa, but Natalie was from San Francisco, a city tolerant of all colors and creeds. It took some getting used to. She ignored the pointed stares from the woman across the aisle from her, and slowly fell asleep.

Jirisan was nothing like the Sierra Nevadas, but it abstractedly reminded Natalie of childhood summers under the stars. They were sitting outside of their pension in Jiritown, on a deck above a bubbling creek, and eating a much-anticipated dinner. Natalie added more of the peppery hot sauce to her bowl and stirred it into her *bibimbap.*

"You're mad," Marcus said. "That stuff is really hot."

"It's okay," said Natalie. "I'm from California. We eat spicy food all the time."

Marcus shrugged, indicating that he would not be responsible for her poor life decisions.

"It's my goal to eat some of that before I leave," Lisa said. She had been in Korea for four months and would be there for another eight. "It's so hot though."

Brian's smile signified surrender. "Not me. God already invented the perfect food, poutine, and if it ain't spicy, nothing should be."

Marcus stood up and banged his beer bottle with his chopsticks.

"I have something to say," he slurred. "From here on out, no one shall refer to perfect food unless, I emphasize *unless,* it comes from the place that started life in all your countries. Chips are nearly the perfect food. Tea would be the perfect food, if it was food. But the best food of all is shepherd's pie, with mutton, like my mum in Rainford used to make. My mum was a saint—"

That was as far as he got. Brian had walked behind him while he was speaking and dropped on all fours. Acting on that cue, Dylan had risen. He walked to Marcus and pushed him in the chest, almost gently. Marcus stumbled back, into Brian, and completely lost his balance. He ended in a heap on the wooden floor. His bottle fell beside him and spilled out the intoxicating liquid onto the ground. Natalie couldn't stop laughing.

Marcus rose gingerly. Brian was laughing so hard that he couldn't get up, and Dylan had tears streaming down his face.

"You bastards," Marcus said, but he was laughing too. "You don't want to hear about my mum, yeah? I've taken your point."

As he sat back down, Lisa asked, "Do you think we'll see moonbears?" Moonbears were small, big-eared bears native to the area.

"I don't think so," Dylan said. "There are less than twenty still alive in the wild. Most of them have been harvested for their gall bladders."

"That's horrible," Natalie said.

"People are disgusting," Lisa said. She put her empty glass on the table and yawned dramatically. "I hate to say it, but I'm going to turn in. I'm getting old."

The others rose. Natalie did not feel like sleeping and she gave Dylan a questioning look.

He slid behind her. "Would you like to take a walk?"

"I could be persuaded," she smiled.

"Don't stay out too late, you two. We've got a big hike tomorrow," Brian said. "Korean mountains aren't like walks back home. They're not as high as the Rockies, of course, but they don't believe in switch-backs. The shortest distance is always the steepest distance."

"We also," Marcus announced, "might have to queue. On a bloody mountain." With that denouncement, the group walked up to their hotel room. It would be one room, sans beds, for them all. But there were blankets aplenty, and the floor itself heated up; the room was surprisingly comfortable.

As Natalie and Dylan waved goodnight to their friends, Dylan leaned in close. "Let's get some more beer," he said.

It didn't take long to find a 7-11. Even in this tiny town, there were three convenience stores within five minutes of their pension.

They emerged from the store with cold cans of beer in hand—one in each hand, in Dylan's case.

"Where shall we go?" He opened one of his beers and drank deeply.

"What about up there?" she asked.

He followed her gaze and frowned. "Up there? That's the Buddhist shrine."

Rising from a small hill on the edge of town, a large statue of Buddha sat serenely. They had seen it on their way in and noticed that the Buddha had looked suspiciously Korean. It was high enough out of town that, this late at night, it would be unlikely for other people to be there.

They walked toward the shrine, up to another metal staircase. It was steep and seemed to last forever. Trees and loose rocks covered the hill on either side of the staircase.

"Fuck me. If this is the town, I'd hate to see the mountain," Dylan joked.

Something rustled in the trees above them.

"What was that?"

A large black bird burst out of the tree, past them and up toward the moon. It hung above them for several moments before flying out of sight.

"Hectic," Dylan said. "That was one big raven."

"I didn't think they were nocturnal," she said.

"Well, they're as black as the night. It kind of makes sense."

She frowned but did not argue further.

They reached the concrete platform a few moments later. The Buddha statue was at least twenty feet high, and it stared down at them impassively. They had not seen any more birds, and the only signs of life came from the town below.

"Hey, look over there," Dylan said.

She followed him across the platform, crossing past the Buddha. At the edge of the circle were a couple of mats.

Dylan spread the mats out on the brown earth next to the platform. It was slightly slanted, as the hill stretched below them. But they were mostly out of sight from the stairs, should anyone come up, and the ground was warmer and softer than the concrete platform.

"At last we're alone," Dylan said. "Well, if you ignore the Buddha." He sat down on the mat.

"Finally," she said, slipping into his arms. All she could feel was his warm body against hers. Their mouths met and as his hands found her breasts, she found herself melting into sensation. She was on her back, her tongue in his mouth and her hands wrapped around him when he suddenly stopped.

"What's wrong?" she asked.

"Shhh," he said. "I hear voices. Someone's coming."

"Who cares?" She tried to kiss him again but he leaned his face up. On her back, she could not see anything, so she rolled out from under him and onto her stomach. Dylan was lying on his stomach next to her. The lip of the platform cut off most of their view, but she could see what he meant.

There were three dark shapes coming from the stairs. One was an old man, and the other two were disheveled looking women.

The trio stopped before the Buddha. The man stood with his arms out and legs spread. The women, who looked more like mythological harpies than living people, began wrapping him in rags. They began at his feet, and worked quickly up his legs. Throughout it, the man stood stoically in the moonlight.

Both women were chanting softly as they worked.

"What are they doing?" Natalie whispered.

"I don't know. They keep saying *jerye.* I don't know what that means."

The two continued to watch. The hags continued to wrap the man in long bandages. They had his chest covered, and his arms soon followed.

"Why are they making him into a mummy?" she asked.

"I have no idea what they are doing," he said. "I've never heard of anything like this."

"I don't think we're supposed to be here for this," Natalie asked.

"I've never heard of anything like this," he said again.

The woman on the right, her eyes gleaming in the moonlight, finished tying the rags around the man's head. He was completely covered. She was chanting like crazy now, and moving in an arrhythmic dance. The other one reached to her hip and suddenly had a knife in her hand. The slim metal blade was clear in the night sky.

"What the hell?"

"It's okay," Dylan said. "They will cut the bandages, leave, and then we can get back to what we were doing." He took a discrete sip from his beer.

The haggish woman with the knife was chanting too. The women's voices hung eerily in the air. They moved together, with sweeping steps, and stood before the man. Natalie took a deep breath.

The woman plunged the knife into the bound man's throat. The bandages blossomed crimson blood as the man sank to his knees. The woman pushed the knife further in.

The man's body slumped. His neck and chest were coated with blood that looked black in the moonlight. The women continued to chant and sing, dancing around his dying body with macabre grace.

Natalie held her scream, but could not stifle her horrified gasp. Her voice cut through the silent night with sharp clarity.

Both women turned toward them. Moving with the same eerie unison, they took a step toward Natalie and Dylan, and then another. They did not seem to see the couple yet, but all it would take was a few more steps.

"Let's go," Dylan said. He sprang up, pulling Natalie with him.

As soon as they were in sight, the hags hissed and moved toward them urgently.

"We can't reach the stairs," Natalie said. The women were between them and the exit.

"Who needs them," Dylan said. They turned and fled down the stony slope.

She heard something crash beside her.

"Shit!" Dylan said.

"What's wrong? Are you okay?"

"I'm fine. My beer, however, has fallen to a tragic death."

"You—"

They moved quickly down the hill. Natalie could not look back. She imagined a bony hand grabbing at her, ripping into her shoulders. When they had reached the bottom, just yards away from the paved road, Natalie risked a look behind her and instantly relaxed.

"It's okay. Look," she said.

Dylan stopped and turned. He laughed.

The women were still at the edge of the platform, looking down on them with blunted rage.

"Not so good at running down a mountain, are you?" Dylan called up to them.

"Let's go to the police," Natalie said.

Dylan's answer was drowned out by a low, menacing growl.

"Is that what I think it is?" Natalie breathed.

"Hectic," Dylan said.

A bear stood before them. It was a moonbear, with squirrel-like ears and a short muzzle. It could have looked cute in other circumstances, but there was no doubt that it was challenging them now.

"What do we do," she asked.

"It's just one bear," Dylan said. "We'll go around it."

The bear growled and they were almost instantaneously ringed by bears. They weren't big like in movies, but there were a lot of them. And their manner was as aggressive and threatening as a rabid dog. The lead bear snarled at them and moved closer. Natalie couldn't look away from its sharp teeth.

"We're going to die," she said, her voice flat with shock.

The snarling bear charged them. Natalie closed her eyes. The sound of wings and a loud *caw* brought them open again.

The bear had stopped. Within the ring of bears was another dark ring—a circle of black birds. There were crows everywhere. They were all big, but the bird before her was impossibly large. It was as tall as her, and even more freakishly, it had three legs.

There were many more crows than bears, but the bears were still the apex predator. Natalie suddenly understood why ostriches felt like sticking their heads in the ground. How many crows did it take to fight a bear? Nonetheless, the sight of the large crow seemed to spook the ursine beasts, and the bears turned and ambled away. Within seconds, they had disappeared into the darkness. The crows—the normal sized ones, at least—rose in the air, cawing noisily.

The three-legged crow stood facing the two teachers.

"I'd think I was dreaming, but even my nightmares aren't this scary," Dylan said.

"What just happened?" Natalie asked.

"I just saved your life," said the crow.

Natalie had never been so close to fainting in all her life.

She and Dylan stared first at each other and then at the crow.

"There is not time for this," the crow said. "We have only a brief span, and the Buddhists will try to kill you again."

"Who are you?" Dylan asked.

"Ah, that question would once have never been asked. But the times have changed. I am the King of the Crows."

Natalie laughed.

"Is that so hard to believe?"

"Yes, it is actually."

"Do you not live in an age of science? Do you not trust what your senses report to you?"

"Look, mate, you've been the strangest part of a very strange night," Dylan said.

"Why do the Buddhists want to kill us?" Natalie asked.

"You know why, Natalie," the Crow King said. "You saw what should not have been seen. They want to kill me, too, if for different reasons. I have battled—and largely lost—with the Buddhists for a long time now."

"But…Buddhists are friendly and peaceful," she objected.

"No religion ever spread through peace," the Crow King said. "Religion is an inherent violence, an alien system that controls the way you see the world around you."

"Aren't you a religious figure?" Dylan asked.

The Crow King cawed, in something that sounded like laughter.

"Perhaps at one time, I was. Now I am merely folklore. Being a myth gives you the advantage of—perspective. And the only word left for me now is *shamanistic.* Thou it's such an insufficient term."

A thousand wings lifted into the air as the crows in the trees stirred and rose. The Crow King cocked his head sideways, as though he was listening to something. At last he spoke to the two teachers.

"We haven't much time. Please, pull this feather from my wing."

Natalie looked to Dylan. His expression reassured her—he was as shit-scared as she was.

"Any part of me is a weapon that can be used against them. Take it, and take it to the heart of Buddhism in Korea. There is a large temple on the mountain known as Bukhansan. You will be followed. Do not allow them to stop you. Take it there, and I can do the rest."

"Why don't you do it?" Dylan asked. "We can't exactly fly."

"It's impossible. I can only appear on a night such as this, a full moon. Even now, you are only seeing the vaguest shadow of what I am."

"Why us?" Natalie asked.

"I would not have picked you if you had not already made yourselves a target. Accepting my mission might increase your danger, but either way the Buddhists will be coming for you."

"That makes sense," she admitted. "But it's really hard to believe a gigantic bird talking to me."

"You don't have to believe me. Maybe no one wants you dead. But isn't it worth listening to me in case I'm right?"

She nodded and pulled a feather from the Crow King's wing. It was long—a yard at least—and shinier than any bird feather she had ever seen, even in the wan light of the moon.

The King flew up into the air, though it seemed to Natalie that part of him was still there. And then both parts—or all—of him were gone. They didn't fade so much as stretch and dissolve until he had simply become part of the wind, the sky, the trees—even the ground. She reached out and grabbed Dylan's hand, needing to feel connected to something material. With her right hand, she took the long feather and slid it through the middle of her bra. It slid down to touch her navel. The feather seemed unnaturally warm, but not at all unpleasantly so.

She cried out a little in surprise. "It's really heavy," she said.

"Well it's a feather from a bird as big as a man," Dylan said. "It's a little odd to be jealous of a feather, I have to admit."

"What are we going to do?" she asked him, ignoring his rakishness.

"Ask me again tomorrow," he said. "For now, I need a drink and some sleep."

They retreated to their pension. Natalie kept wondering what she would tell her friends. "Come on," she heard herself telling them. "Wake up. A giant talking bird told me that Buddhists are coming to kill us." That didn't sound convincing—let alone sane—to her, and she had lived through it.

"What are we going to tell them?" she asked Dylan as they ran through the hotel door.

"First we have to figure out what's happening. Then we explain it to them."

The dim hallway seemed longer than before, and far spookier. They moved through it quickly.

"Good, the door is already open," Dylan said. "They must still be awake."

Natalie felt a thrill of dread flash through her. She stopped. "I don't want to look in there."

"Don't be silly. Worst case, they'll be asleep. Best, they'll be awake, with beer."

Dylan stepped into the door. "Yo!" he shouted.

His face drained of color instantly and his body slumped into the side of the door.

"What's wrong?" Natalie asked. She already knew, though.

"What the fuck?" he asked tonelessly.

Natalie stepped forward, her heart pounding in her ears.

Her first thought was that somebody had spilled spaghetti sauce everywhere. As her brain began to comprehend what her eyes were telling her, she felt the world spinning.

"No," she said.

Marcus, Brian, and Lisa were strewn in bits across the room. They had been chewed up and spat out. The walls, floor, and their bags were splattered with blood. Their backpacks and clothing were likewise torn apart. The vision of the sharp bear teeth appeared again in Natalie's memory.

"Natalie," Dylan said, his eyes fixed on the scene before them.

"Yes?" she asked.

"I think we take that fucking feather to that fucking temple and fuck these fucking fuckers up. And we fucking leave now!"

The sun was coming up in Seoul when Natalie woke up. She looked out the window of the cab and saw the familiar skyscrapers and neon signs. Her sleep had been fitful and full of dark dreams. They had been driving for several hours now, though she had no idea what time they had left. Even in as small a place as Jiritown, they hadn't had any difficulty hailing a cab. The driver had not quite understood their request to go to Seoul, but they had pooled their money and offered him three hundred thousand won. *I've never paid 300 dollars for a cab ride before,* Natalie had thought. It was a night of firsts, it seemed.

As soon as she'd sat down on the cold vinyl of the cab seat, she had started shaking. She had been reliving the night again and again and tears streamed down her face. She could tell that Dylan was disturbed, as he hadn't even made any jokes since they had found their friends. He was looking out the window now as well. She checked that the feather was still in place. It still seemed warm, imbued with an energy she could only vaguely grasp. It still felt strangely heavy.

"I'm confused about what happened last night," she said. "About everything."

"That reminds me," Dylan said. He flourished his Galaxy smartphone and tapped away at it. After a few minutes, he said, "Okay, I think we might have witnessed a Buddhist Death Ritual. They're not that common anymore, but for serious Buddhists it's a necessity."

"But why would they try to kill us?"

He typed something else into his phone. "I'm not sure. But it does say very senior Buddhists have utterly private ceremonies, preferably when the moon is full. We may have violated a sacred ceremony."

"Do you think the Crow King was telling the truth?"

He laughed. "I really don't know. If I had to guess, I'd say he was playing his own game, and he just happened upon us. But I don't think he was lying, and at least he saved us from the bears."

"Crows and bears are both totem animals for the Shasta Indians," she mused. "I wonder if they are pawns in this game as well, or if what we saw are even animals at all," she said.

"You mean…they might be manifestations of a deeper, older force, something like that?" Dylan asked. He shook his head. "That's deep. Perhaps too deep for me."

"I don't know. It's hard to think of a spirit older than Buddha, who sees him as an uppity new-comer. If they are real, however reduced, what does that mean for all the other myths we know?"

"Stop," Dylan said. "Please. I am overwhelmed enough by our problem without applying it to the greater world." As he spoke, he looked out the window and his eyes lit up.

"*Yogi-yo,*" Dylan said abruptly, telling the cab driver to stop where he was. As the car pulled to the side of the street, Natalie looked at the grey city.

"Where are we?" she asked.

"I don't know, but we are close to the subway."

"Why not take the cab all the way to the mountain?" she asked. Bukhansan was in the north of the city, surrounded by high rises and greasy from the fingerprint of man.

"I'm not saying we were followed, or we're in danger," he said. "But let's assume it's safer to throw off anyone who might be following us." He got out of the cab and Natalie followed. "Besides," he added. "I'm starving. We can get some food on the way."

They climbed down the stairs into the subway and beeped through the gates with their cell phones. They grabbed more money from an ATM and

Dylan purchased some fish-shaped baked bread filled with red bean paste and a can of beer. It was legal, if not strictly acceptable, to drink on the subway.

Natalie made a face at the bread.

"Don't you like these?" he asked, mouth half-full.

"It's not that I don't like red bean paste," she said. "I just think it could be anything else and it would taste better."

"It grows on you," he said. "Now I think only most things would taste better."

They went down more stairs, and checked the board showing the next subway's arrival. It was coming in two minutes. Natalie looked around. Something unpleasant crawled through her stomach. Though she didn't see anything unusual, she was beginning to feel nervous.

Due to the holiday, there were less people than usual in Seoul. Most had gone out of the city to visit family. But there were still several people staring at her.

"The Crow King said we might be followed," she said. "But even though we are taking his feather to the temple, I keep thinking it must have all been a bad dream, or an elaborate prank."

"It could have all seemed like a joke," Dylan said. "But we know it's not, not after..." He didn't need to finish the sentence. Neither of them would ever forget what they had seen the previous night.

A triumphant fanfare announced the coming train. Within seconds, there were people everywhere. They formed a neat line with relatively little jostling. The doors opened, but something made Natalie turn around and look behind her. She gasped.

A man had just come down the stairs. He looked like a monk, with his simple clothes and bald head. There was something vaguely ursine about his face, and his body shone with a hidden energy. When he saw Natalie looking at him, a predatory grin appeared on his face and he moved toward them.

She stepped onto the train, hissing to Dylan to look behind them.

He saw the man coming, too. "Fuck me, bro," he said.

The subway doors would close any instant, but the man was only moments away.

He took long strides, his eyes never looking away from the pair. Against her will, Natalie saw the strewn carnage of the night before. She could feel her insides being ripped apart, and she stifled the urge to cry.

"We have to go," she screamed.

"Where?" Dylan asked. The only place off the train was even closer to the advancing man. He was close enough that Natalie could see his long, bloodstained fingernails. They looked like claws, and again she could feel her flesh being torn apart by them. Behind the man, a group of *adjummas* was rushing to the subway as well.

The man was three steps away, and then two.

One step.

His foot was up in the air, aimed at coming down onto the subway itself, when he was shoved aside. The four *adjummas* had hurried into the car, and they knocked him aside in their haste to beat the closing doors. They hit him hard enough that he was pushed aside. The last *adjumma* had to jump, and as she landed the doors closed.

The man with the shaved head looked through the glass at Natalie and Dylan. His dark eyes burned with frustrated murder. The subway pulled away and Dylan grabbed Natalie and held her close to him until she stopped shaking.

Even in early October, the mountains resonated with the shrilling of cicadas. There were thousands of the ugly critters in the trees, and their sound rang through the forests and craggy hills. It being a holiday weekend, there weren't too many other hikers around. A summer weekend would see thousands of people in one day, marching like ants along the mountain trails. The absence of people was a boon, but a small one. Both of them were exhausted from lack of sleep, and the trail was straight up, and littered with broken stones. "I'm already tired," Dylan admitted, looking in dismay up the rocky track.

"At least we get to go onto a hike this weekend, after all," Natalie said. She started walking up, into the chirping forest. Dylan sighed and followed her.

After climbing a particularly grueling section, the two of them stopped to catch their breath. They stood on a flat rock that overlooked a steep drop. The sound of cicadas here was loud enough that they had to speak to each other with raised voices. A smiling woman stood beside them. She held a bag of oranges in her hand.

"We'd need guardrails if this were America," Natalie said. It was at least a fifteen foot fall to the rocky trail, and from there it would be nearly impossible not to roll much further. If falling from here wasn't fatal, it was at least a very close relative.

"The rest of the world tends to rely on common sense a bit more than you all seem to," Dylan said.

"That's actually kinda true," Natalie agreed. She'd come to accept the bashing she received as the token American. Besides, most of the things they said were not wrong. "But it is a long way down." She felt butterflies in her stomach as she looked back down onto the steep climb they had just ascended.

"You can tell we've come a long way because there aren't many people left," Dylan said. The trail was atypically empty at the moment. "And I'm beginning to think we should have brought water."

"I'm beginning to think we should have brought beer," Natalie answered, earning a big smile from him.

The Korean woman stepped toward them, offering each of them a small orange.

"*Kamsamida,*" the two teachers said, thanking her in unison.

As Natalie peeled off the thin skin from the orange, the woman's eyes flicked behind them. The woman stepped past them, offering another fruit to someone who had come up behind them.

Natalie glanced behind her and gasped.

Her body took over as she ducked, dropping to the ground on pure reflex.

The bald man leaped over her, snarling.

The adjumma screamed as the man slashed his long nails across her throat. Bright blood bubbled from a messy gash beneath her chin. Her body slumped to the side, rolling partly off the rock. Her oranges fell to the ground and rolled away in an assortment of directions.

Natalie scrambled back to her feet. The bald man had turned his attention away from her, toward Dylan, who punched him as hard as he could. His fist hit the monk squarely in the chest, without any affect.

"Fuck me, it's like punching a rock," Dylan said, cradling his injured hand.

The monk swung a fist back at Dylan, who raised his hands into an X of defense. The claws tore through his skin as well, and he screamed out in pain.

Natalie knew then that they would die there. The Buddhist killer was too fast, too strong for them. Maybe it would be better to jump and take her chances. She glanced down again at the drop.

And then she knew what to do.

Blood dripped from the bald man's fingers as he advanced on Dylan. His back was to her. She ran and dropped to her knees behind him. She didn't even have time to hope, but Dylan was ready.

He stepped forward and swung again at the long-nailed man. At the last second, his fist relaxed and he shoved the creature as hard as he could. Like a rock, the man barely moved, but it was enough to send him into Natalie. His knees buckled, and he flipped back, nearly off the rock.

But as he fell, his fingernails dug into the stone and he arrested his fall. The sound was excruciatingly painful.

"What do I gotta fucking do?" Dylan asked.

Natalie stood again. Her ribs felt sore from where the man had hit her with his heels.

"Let's start by trying this," she said. She moved over to the edge of the rock and stomped as hard as she could onto his hands.

The bald man stared at her with his furiously dark eyes, and then fell off. He landed with a thud and rolled, painfully, down the steep incline. When he had at last come to a stop, his head and body were covered in blood.

They both watched for a long moment, making sure the body didn't move. It seemed as though light was escaping from the man's body.

"That was mighty clever," Dylan said, turning away. "If I had any skin on my arms, I might hug you."

She hugged him anyway. The dead eyes of the woman stared at her from the side of the rock. One of her oranges had been stepped on in the fight and the pulp glistened there, accusatorily.

"That poor woman," she said.

"It's not our fault. We're trying to stop them, remember?" Dylan said.

"We've got to reach the temple before another of those guys finds us," she said.

"Another?" Dylan asked. "Wasn't that the guy from the subway?"

"Not unless he grew different eyebrows and changed his mouth. There is more than one of these men coming after us."

They got back on the trail, and started up the calf-killing ascent again. Both knew they were almost there. They could see the temple ahead of them, up one more steep incline. Her legs ached and she'd never sweated so much in her life. She hoped that the feather didn't get drenched by her sweat. For several long minutes, she concentrated only on putting one foot ahead of the other.

They reached the top at last. Her legs burned and her throat ached for water.

"Why isn't anybody here?" Dylan asked. "Surely Buddhists don't leave for holidays."

Natalie looked around and saw that he was right. The temple, built into the mountain, looked similar to all such temples in Korea. Most had been destroyed during the war and rebuilt, so that centuries-old temples all had the same, vaguely sixties, appearance. There was room for at least twenty monks to live here, and even on a holiday there should have been a few hikers visiting.

"Look at that," she said.

It was beautiful. Rock formations and huge stone boulders formed the foundation of the monastery. Above it all was a fifty-foot tower with a wide base covered with carvings of Buddhas and strange creatures.

The emptiness was eerie. The cicadas were still singing in full-force, however, which felt oddly reassuring. She pulled out the feather; despite her sweat, it remained completely dry. They walked to the tall statue.

"If this isn't the center of the temple, I don't know where is," Dylan said.

"It seems kind of anti-climatic," she said.

As if on cue, they heard footsteps. From seemingly nowhere, a bald man walked toward them. His feet were bare. There was something strange about his gate, and there was a vulgar nimbus of light surrounding him. Natalie wished she could have felt surprised.

"Not again," Dylan said. "Is that a different one too?"

"I think so. His nose is much bigger, and so is his chin."

The man with the shaved head walked to them with slow, steady paces. The first two men had been feral and savage, but this one smiled with a serene sadness that nearly broke Natalie's heart. She wanted to sit on his lap and have him absorb all her melancholy. He held out his hand to her. Imploringly.

"You're not getting this feather," she said.

He looked at her again, his dark eyes compelling her. She looked down at the feather, wondering how important it could possibly be. She raised her hand, ready to proffer the black burden.

The man reached his hand out for the feather. She noticed his long fingernails, crusted with dried blood. *Blood.* She shut the image of the bloody hotel room out of her head as quickly as it appeared, but the spell was broken. She yanked the feather back and held it protectively with both hands.

And then it began growing.

The bald man leaped back warily, and suddenly he was a predatory animal. The feather doubled in size once, and then did so again. It felt like a baton or a sword, and her hand tingled from the energy it held. The man snarled and stepped toward her.

Moving with instinctual action, she swept the feather down at the bald man. He sprang away and growled at her. His black eyes swam with the promise of dark menace.

"What are you doing?" Dylan asked. He watched open-mouthed and unbelieving.

"I'm not sure," she said. "But it feels right."

The thing stepped at her, and she held the raven feather before her as part talisman and part weapon. But the Buddhist spun and sprang at Dylan. Dylan moved back, but he wasn't quick enough. The man's clawed right hand slashed into his chest, ripping through clothes and skin.

"I'll be goddamned," Dylan said in a soft voice. There was already so much blood.

Natalie brought the feather down on the man's elbow. The feather was as sharp as a razor and it cut through the man's arm with precise sharpness. The bald man yipped in pain and moved back. The hand fell out of Dylan's chest and hit the ground. Within seconds, it had changed into a bloody bear's foot. Even in the light of the day, there was a stream of wan moonlight escaping into the air.

The same light was coming from the man's arm now, streaming out of him as though he were dissolving. The mask of humanity was slipping, as his features looked more ursine than ever, and his body sprouted bristly dark hairs.

The bearman roared and rushed Natalie. His one hand was raised in a claw and his open mouth revealed far too sharp teeth. She swung again and lopped off another hand. The surprise in its eyes was unmistakable. Natalie stepped forward, unsure if her feathery blade was responding to or causing her actions. She held it tightly with both hands and swung as hard as she could. It was a simple as popping a Lego man's head off; the man's head fell off with ease. It rolled away, toward the tower, and the handless, headless body dropped.

She felt fatigued beyond reason. There was a wet sound and, turning, she saw Dylan was coughing up blood but laughing nonetheless. She rushed to him. His chest looked like it had been mauled by a tiger.

"Don't laugh. Don't say anything. We'll get you out of this," she said.

"How's that for non-attachment, bitch?" Dylan spoke with noticeable effort at the body before them. He sank to his knees. "Sorry, I couldn't resist," he said to her with a half smile, and then fell face first onto the ground.

Too exhausted and drained to do anything else, Natalie slumped to the ground next to him. The feather floated from her hand, rising into the wind. Except that there wasn't any wind.

That's nice, she thought dreamily.

A shadow fell over her. She looked up, ice in her veins. *Oh, shit,* she thought.

The man they had evaded in the subway stood before her.

"Oh, for fuck's sake!" she shouted. "Just kill me and get it over with!"

But he wasn't looking at her. He was looking past her, toward the tower.

She wearily craned her neck to follow his gaze. The feather had floated higher and higher into the air, until it was a high as the top of the tower. The feather must have grown even more, as it was quite visible, even if it seemed only a small dark ribbon next to the Buddhist tower.

The man before her made a noise that sounded like a whine. She couldn't take her eyes from the ribbon, though. As it hit the stone, it cracked and splintered as easily as ice or glass. Bits of the top were falling down as the splitting ripped through to the tower, descending to the base. Imploding in seconds, the tower crumbled and dissolved upon itself.

She looked in front again and the man was gone. In his place was an out-of-place moonbear. It seemed to want nothing to do with her anymore, and it turned to leave. Then, from the surrounding trees, came dozens of crows. They swooped in on the bear and pecked it and clawed at it. The bear stumbled and then it was covered with crows. It didn't take long, though Natalie couldn't watch. In less time than it had taken the tower to crumble, the bear was killed. His tasty eyeballs were snatched from their sockets.

Dylan's body was growing cold. She felt her eyes closing but fought off the urge to sleep. There was no way she could lug his body down the steep incline. Her eyes were closing. She could hear the flapping of crows' wings all around her.

"It's okay," said a voice. "I think I can walk." She looked up and saw Dylan standing above her. His face was pale, there were nickel-sized punctures in his chest, and his arms were covered with drying blood. "I mean, I've felt better, but it's got to be easier going down than coming up."

She rose and helped him to his feet.

"Can you really walk?" she asked.

"I don't know what happened," he said. "But I dreamed of a black feather, floating in the wind, and then I woke up feeling much better."

"The Crow King?" she asked.

"I think so. Anyway," Dylan said, as he rested his arm on her shoulder for support, "I would have woken up myself. We both know that all the beer is at the bottom of the mountain."

She laughed and led him slowly to the trail. They moved gingerly down the steep grade. The two of them limped down the mountain as the cries of crows and buzz of cicadas filled the air around them.

At the top of the mountain, a thousand crows descended upon the crumbled remnants of the Buddha statue, looking for a single black feather.

Harberry Close

C.M. Saunders

Waterloo Station was an absolute bitch during rush hour. It was an absolute bitch most of the time, to be fair, but everything seemed exasperated during peak travel times. Torrents of people spilled off the escalators leading up from the Underground, shielding their eyes and looking for all the world like rats escaping from a sewer, while others milled around in a perpetual daze apparently unsure of where they were going.

The steady din of conversation echoed around the cavernous hall, and the smell of fresh coffee hung in the air. Tim hated this leg of his journey into work. Not much about the commute was fun. He had spent the past 35 minutes on the central line, squashed into the armpit of an overweight Polish guy who didn't shower often enough. But even that was preferable to the Waterloo interchange. Controlled chaos, that's what it was.

He held his stride the fraction of a second required to allow a little mousy woman to hurry past, and got roughly jostled from behind for his troubles. A skinny bloke in a smart grey business suit muttered something under his breath as he marched onwards.

Tim negotiated a path through the seething crowds, and gazed up at the departure boards suspended on the lounge wall.

Where the hell was the Strawberry Hill train?

He hurriedly checked his watch. This was going to be a close one.

There it was!

Just leaving from Platform 18. Great. That was all the way over the other side of the station. There was no chance of making it. There was half-an-hour until the next one, which would make him late for work again. That would not do. He was already in his manager Turner's bad books for oversleeping last Wednesday, and his job hung by a thread. Turner would absolutely love to make an example of him, the old fuckstick. He would have to find an alternative route. And quickly.

His eyes frantically scanned the boards. There had to be another way.

Maybe get the Twickenham train and change at Clapham Junction? There were trains everywhere from Clapham Junction. The busiest train station in the world and all that.

Then he saw it.

Destination: Haymarket. 08:27. Platform nine. On time.

A direct train to Haymarket?

No way!

Tim didn't even know there *was* a direct train from or to Haymarket. But given that Waterloo Station was such a throbbing hive of activity, it was entirely possible he just hadn't noticed it before. Most people were creatures of habit, and when they settled into a routine that worked they were usually happy to stick with it. Life was more convenient that way. Why complicate things? Especially when you were still half asleep and had somewhere to be.

Whatever. Platform nine.

He had three minutes.

Tim put his head down and weaved his way through the bustling crowds to the ticket stiles. The train was already at the station. He produced his travel card, swiped it, and the gate swung open invitingly.

As Tim slipped through, his eyes were drawn to the guard stationed at the gate, an elderly man with wispy grey hair partially obscuring his face and snow-white stubble peppering his chin. The most striking thing about him was the thick scar running from his temple, down his cheek, and ending just above his jaw-line. Although healed, it was discolored and tugged at the corner of his left eye.

Whenever Tim saw someone with such profound disfigurements, he always found himself wondering what had caused such injuries. In the case of this poor old bugger it looked like some kind of industrial accident, or maybe a car crash. A no-doubt very painful encounter with some kind of immovable object, the damage resulting in a scar so severe that the carnage must surely run deeper than superficial level. It would affect your confidence, character, disposition, temperament, and maybe even leave a blemish on your very soul.

Their eyes met, and the old man with the scar frowned self-consciously. Tim hesitated and instantly felt a stab of shame, like a kid caught with his hand in a cookie jar. The poor old guy must get stared at all the time. Especially in this job, where thousands of people walk past him each day. People could be such dicks. Why not give the guy an office job, away from all the prying eyes?

But here he was, contributing to the man's discomfort. Tim mentally checked himself and tried to move on, but something about the man's gaze held him. And then he spoke.

"Every scar tells a story," he said.

Tim was mortified. Not only had his revulsion been noted, but the man had been offended enough to break protocol, and violate one of the most important social rules that governs modern society. You do not engage with strangers. You look, you even stare sometimes, but you do not engage.

"I…what?" Tim stammered. But the man with the scar simply stared at him through pale blue expressionless eyes. For a moment Tim wondered if the man had actually spoken, or if he had imagined the words. Whatever. The sense of awkwardness was almost overwhelming, and Tim quickly moved through the ticket barrier before it snapped shut.

There was nobody else on the platform, the revelation sending a wave of panic washing over him. The train was about to leave. Everyone else must already be onboard!

He broke into a jog, jumped on the train, and burst through the door of the nearest carriage.

Phew, made it!

He slumped into a seat, breathing heavily. Immediately, the door slid shut, a whistle sounded, and the train pulled gently out of the station.

Throwing his head back, Tim exhaled loudly.

What a stroke of luck! A few seconds later and he would have missed it.

Only then, as the train left the platform and the people waiting there turned into blurs of color as they zoomed by, did Tim realize, how quiet the carriage was. Apart from him, it appeared to be completely empty. He craned his neck, fully expecting to find at least a few people occupying seats at the rear of the carriage. But there was nobody.

"How odd," he said under his breath. He didn't think it was possible for a train to be this empty during morning rush hour in any city, let alone one of the most over-populated capitals in the world. With a sinking feeling, Tim deduced that he must have somehow gotten his wires crossed and boarded a train that wasn't in service. How else could the lack of people be explained?

"Shit!"

Tim shifted nervously in his seat. The only sound to be heard was the low rumble of the train as it sped along the tracks.

How could he be so fucking stupid?

Oh well. Nothing he could do about it now. The train would have to stop soon enough, and then he would simply get off and make his way back into the city. He would be late for work, of course. But maybe he could stay behind for an hour or two at the end of the day to make up for it.

A few minutes later, a station came into view and Tim breathed a sigh of relief. With any luck he could hop on another train and still make it to work on time. Then he could just write this non-journey off as an embarrassing faux pas never to be spoken of again.

But the train didn't stop. It didn't even slow down. Tim gazed longingly out of the window at the lines of commuters standing on the platform as the train thundered past them at full speed.

What the hell was going on here?

Embarrassment suddenly replaced with anger, Tim stood up, holding on to the back of the seat in front of him for balance as the train rounded a bend. It was picking up speed now, and quite obviously wasn't planning on stopping any time soon. He had to find a guard or a driver. Get them to stop the fucking thing and let him off.

He began making his way up the aisle through the empty carriage, eyes darting from side to side. There was nothing to see except the odd discarded newspaper or piece of litter. He reached the door at the end and peered through the glass anxiously. The next carriage appeared to be just as devoid of life as this one. Regardless, he twisted the handle, swung open the door and stepped through.

About half way down the second carriage, Tim realized that his pace was quickening. His breath now came in shallow gasps as his feet pounded the metal floor. By the time he reached the third carriage he was almost sprinting, his path deviating from side to side with the motion of the train. As if to compliment his ungainly lurch, the train seemed to gather pace as he went.

Bursting through the next door, he suddenly had an idea.

The Emergency Break.

Trains were fitted with them as standard. You pull the lever and the train stops. There might be a penalty for using it, but this situation was fast heading towards an emergency. If questioned, he could always fake a heart attack or something.

He spotted a lever fixed to the wall above an exit door, and gleefully yanked down on it, fully expecting the train to come screeching to a halt.

Nothing happened.

Thinking about it, all the emergency stop probably did was sound an alarm in the driver's cabin, which would then stop the train manually, when it was safe to do so.

Tim stood still for a few moments, waiting to see what would happen. But the train didn't slow down. If anything, it seemed to power onward a little faster.

Letting out a grunt of frustration, Tim pulled the lever again.

Still nothing.

It was either broken, disconnected, or the people hearing the alarm didn't give a shit.

Seeing it was a futile task, Tim reluctantly pressed on with his journey.

At the end of the carriage lay another door. There was something different about this one. But what?

There was no window.

The driver's cabin.

At last!

Instinctively, Tim tried the door handle. It wouldn't move. It was locked, or possibly fitted with some anti-terrorist safety feature. So instead, he cleared his throat and knocked politely.

No answer.

He knocked again, this time clearing his throat and adding a nervous, "Hello?"

It was probably against regulations to open the door to members of the public, in the same way as it was on airplanes. Understandable. In the wrong hands a plane or a vehicle became a weapon of mass destruction.

But somebody had to be driving the damn train, right?

Unless...

Unless he was the only passenger on a runaway train, which was right this moment hurtling through the countryside ever closer to a fiery demise. In that case he would be well within his rights to stop the damn thing by any means necessary.

Tim swallowed hard and knocked again, louder this time. "Hello? Anybody in there?"

He was surprised at how small and breathless his voice sounded above the monotonous rumble of the train.

Still, there was no answer from within the cabin.

He gave the door a frustrated kick and, on finding his shoe gave an infinitely louder and more satisfying thud than his balled-up fist, followed it with another. At the same time he pounded against the door, which bowed inward under the pressure.

"Open...this...fucking...door!" he yelled.

Then, without warning, the train started slowing down.

Yes!

Whoever was driving the train must have heard all the commotion. They were probably on the phone to the Transport Police by now, but that would be a small price to pay. As far as Tim was aware, he hadn't broken any laws. Yet. His heart attack ruse was looking more and more inviting.

He glanced out of a window. Yes, the train was definitely slowing.

Feeling more than a twinge of embarrassment, Tim abandoned his protests and walked down the aisle to the nearest door. Through the glass, he could see there was a station outside and scanned the platform for the name.

There it was.

HARBERRY CLOSE.

Where?

He thought he was familiar with most stations in and around London, but it wasn't inconceivable that one or two may have escaped his notice. There were hundreds of them, and some get overlooked if they are not on your regular route.

This station looked like one of the older, less maintained and more traditional ones. Judging by the design, it possibly dated from Victorian times. It, too, seemed to be deserted, making Tim think it wasn't even in use anymore. Maybe it was one British Rail kept simply to accommodate surplus engines or give worn-out trains somewhere to go when they reached the end of their life cycle. Whatever. He didn't care. He just wanted to get off this hunk of metal and make his way back to the city.

The brakes screeched as the train shuddered to a stop. A green button next to the door illuminated and Tim pushed it. For one horrible second nothing happened, and Tim pushed the button again. Then, the door slid open with a tired *whoosh.*

The autumn air hit him squarely in the face as he stepped off the train onto the platform, straightening his tie as he did so. No sooner had he set his feet down on the concrete, the door whooshed closed behind him and the train began pulling out of the station.

No matter. He was glad to be off the bloody thing with the lunatic driver.

He quickly scanned his surroundings. The station was eerily quiet. The first thing he noticed was that it wasn't equipped with electronic arrival or departure boards. Great. Back to old-school timetable reading it was, then. If he could find one. Or even better, an information desk.

Several wooden benches with ornate ironwork were positioned along the length of the platform, where a sign hung above a door reading: WAITING ROOM.

Tim went over and gave the door a shove. Predictably enough, it was locked.

He looked around. At one end of the platform was an EXIT sign, and at the other end, a covered footbridge leading across the track to the other side of the station. Common sense suggested that if trains leaving London used this set of tracks, then trains heading back the other way used the tracks on the opposite side. Using this logic he made his way towards the bridge, footsteps echoing around the deserted station as he went.

Halfway over the bridge, he paused. This was a good vantage point. Unfortunately, there wasn't much to see. And what he could see was uniform and unremarkable. A few streets of nondescript houses, a playground with some swings and a roundabout, some trees, and swathes of countryside stretching out into the distance. The only distinguishing feature was a church with a steeple set against the dreary grey sky. He hurried on his way, across the bridge and down the steps on the other side.

On this side of the platform was an old-fashioned two-story station house. In fact, the station house, the waiting room, and the connecting bridge, were all part of the same gothic structure. Though Tim guessed it stood empty now, in days gone by, the house was probably where the stationmaster or signalman lived. How times change. The modern equivalent of this quaint little station was a soulless, sterile transport hub where nobody stayed longer than they had to. Not even the workers.

Tim walked down the platform, looking for a timetable of some kind, or maybe a helpful rail worker. Typical of the way his day was going, he could find neither. He walked past another deck of wooden benches, noticing that one was badly stained. He didn't stop to find out what with. Against the dark, porous wood surface it looked like varnish. A few drops had run down the legs of the bench and gathered in small maroon pools on the ground. It was easier to just choose another bench to rest on, if he so chose. It wasn't like he was fighting for space here.

As he made his way down the platform, he felt his foot connect with something. Looking down, he noticed a few stray chunks of masonry lying on the ground. Was the building so old that bits were literally dropping off it?

Frowning, he looked up and around and there on the wall, just below head height was a deep gauge. It looked fresh. The stone around the wound was grimy, dark and weathered, while the inside was pale and raw, like exposed flesh.

What the hell could have caused that? He didn't know why, but Tim suddenly felt a prickly tension settle over him making the hairs on his arms stand to attention. There were a lot of things he didn't understand here. A damaged wall and a tiny pile of rubble seemed like the least of them. Not knowing what else to do, after checking it wasn't wet, he took a seat on one of the benches and gazed at the set of train tracks stretching into the distance. Surely it could only be a matter of time before a train arrived to take him back to the city.

The seconds ticked by, and turned into minutes. Tim sighed heavily. He began to consider calling his office and telling them he was going to be late. It would mean incurring Turner's wrath, but it was probably better than not saying anything at all. At least this way Turner could allocate his duties around and get people to cover for him until he got there. Also, Turner would know Tim wasn't still asleep and therefore might be a little bit more forgiving. Unlikely, but possible. He reached into his front pocket and pulled out his phone.

No signal.

Fantastic. Could the day get any worse?

He turned off the handset, waited a few seconds, and turned it back on. It wasn't exactly a high-tech solution, but turning it off and on again worked more often than not on a surprisingly broad range of electronic products.

As he was waiting for the phone to start up again, a sudden sound shattered the stillness. He froze.

What was that?

It sounded like a loud thump, like heavy furniture being moved. Head cocked to the side, Tim listened closely. Next, there was the tinkle of broken glass as it dropped to the floor. It seemed to be coming from behind him. From inside the old station house.

So somebody was home after all!

Tim jumped to his feet and spun around. The main entrance to the house must be on the other side. The only things on this wall were several windows. The windows were set higher than normal, which made sense. If you lived on a train station, you wouldn't want people drifting past all the time peeking in at you, knocking on your door all the time, or just walking in uninvited in the mistaken belief they had stumbled across a very plush waiting room.

Trying not to make his actions too obvious, Tim stood on tiptoe and tried to peer in through the nearest window. However, whatever lay beyond was obscured by a drawn net curtain.

Just then, a woman screamed.

The sound chilled Tim's blood. There were different kinds of screams. There was the shocked scream you emit when you see a mouse and the excited scream when you win the lottery (not that Tim had witnessed that kind firsthand). This was a scream of pure terror.

For a few moments, Tim didn't know what to do. He simply stood still, mouth opening and closing wordlessly. He began to wonder if he had caused the outburst. Maybe someone had seen him looking through the window and assumed he was a burglar. As he was debating his next move, the scream came again. This time, it was abruptly cut short.

That spurred him into action and he raced around to the other side of the house in search of the door. Someone was in trouble. Terrible trouble.

As he turned the corner he saw something that stopped him in his tracks. Blood. At least, it looked like blood. Crimson splashes, as if someone had thrown a tin of paint against the brickwork.

Or varnish on the bench.

Almost in a daze, he reached out, and found the liquid was still wet to the touch. Fresh.

There was more blood on the floor. A small congealing pool, and a trail. As if something had been dragged away from the scene.

But where?

The trail led directly to a tiny brick structure tacked onto the end of the station house, probably originally intended as either an outhouse or a coal shed. Who knew what the owners used it for these days. Probably storage. Tim approached quietly, heart thudding in his chest. The door was ajar, darkness spilling out from within. Slowly, he pushed the door. It swung open a few more inches then stopped, as if stuck on something.

"What the fuck?"

He pushed a little harder and felt the door give slightly. Evidently, there was some obstruction. A mighty shove later and the door was wide open. A bad smell came rushing out to greet him. The rancid, sickly stench of shit and spoiled meat. Now that he thought about it, the smell had been present before, just not as noticeable. Had it been there since he had got off the train? Wafting around?

Worse than the smell was the sinking feeling in Tim's stomach. He was on the verge of knowing things. Revelations that could change his entire life. Things he couldn't *un*know. Did he want to make that leap?

Yes, he did want to make the leap. Because if he didn't, he would always be left wondering. Besides, it didn't seem as if he had a choice.

Taking a deep breath, he ducked his head and stepped into the tiny enclosed structure.

Bodies.

That was what he found. Piled high. Three, four, maybe even five deep at the back of the cramped little structure. It was hard to tell. If they had been stacked neatly before, they must have toppled over and wedged against the door. Now there was a tangled mess of arms and legs, bloodied torsos and hair.

Mercifully, in the near dark, most of the faces were obscured. Except one. A man in a dark-colored double-breasted business suit, complete with waistcoat. The skin of his face had taken on a waxy quality and his eyes had glazed over, while his mouth hung open in a permanent expression of surprise, blue lips pulled tight over yellowing teeth. Splatters of blood stood out on one of his cheeks.

Tim felt his stomach flip over and swallowed back a mouthful of bitter, hot bile. His world swam in and out of focus, greying around the edges, and he could feel beads of sweat standing out on his forehead. He staggered backwards, and his foot landed in something soft and squishy.

What was that?

He forced himself to look down, and saw that he was standing in a small pile of what looked like intestines, glistening white.

That was the trigger. Tim shoved a fist in his mouth, but too late to stop the putrid vomit spraying out around his fingers.

He had never been this close to death before. What the hell had happened here? And perhaps even more pertinently, who had stuffed the bodies in the coal shed and why?

What kind of monster could do this?

The obvious answer to the latter question would be that someone was trying to cover up the crimes. At least, temporarily. Hiding a bunch of dead people in a coal shed didn't seem like any kind of long-term solution. They were bound to be discovered sooner rather than later, and whoever found them would surely raise the alarm. Suddenly, he realized that as things stood, that responsibility fell to him.

With a shaking hand, he fumbled in his pocket and retrieved his phone from it. The device had restarted. But still, there was no signal.

"*Damn it!*"

Then the scream that had first alerted him to all this chaos came again. Closer this time. It had to be coming from the station house. Backing away from the carnage in the coal shed, he found the front door of the house right behind him. Tim banged on it with a fist. "Hello? Anyone in there? Is everything all right?"

It struck him how stupid a query that was. Somebody was screaming and there was a pile of dead bodies outside. Everything was most certainly *not* all right. His question was met with silence. A deep, heavy silence. With a chill, Tim realized that if anything, all he had succeeded in doing was letting the killer or killers know he was there.

Smart move, idiot.

Tim banged on the door again, harder this time, reaching within himself to summon every ounce of confidence and authority he possessed. It was no surprise to find the well almost empty. It had never exactly been overflowing, but this experience was swiftly depleting any reserves of strength and courage he once had.

The door swung inward. It must have been open all the time. Tim half-expected to be faced with a confused housewife wanting to know, quite rightly, what he was doing on her doorstep. But no one appeared. Heart thudding in his chest, he stepped over the threshold.

The moment he set foot inside the house he became aware of the oppressive, menacing atmosphere. He was in a small passage, with a staircase stretching above him. To his immediate right, a door opened into what appeared to be the living room. He took a few steps inside and looked around, taking in as much detail as he could. The first thing he noticed was how dated and old everything looked. Everything was well maintained and spotlessly clean but there was no widescreen plasma TV, or even a bog-standard model. No DVD player, no computer, no games console.

Instead, the only electrical hardware in the room was an old transistor radio standing on the mantelpiece above a coal-burning fireplace. Curiously, Tim felt drawn to it. He felt the hearth. It was ice cold. There hadn't been a fire lit in there for a long time. Next to the radio was a black-and-white photograph in a silver frame featuring what looked like a young family.

Mother, father and smiling son in between them. There was something oddly familiar about the child in the photograph, but Tim didn't dwell on it, putting the sensation down to some weird mental reaction. He was more taken with the dark clothes the father was wearing, the flashes of insignia on the collars making it look like some kind of military uniform. Then, Tim remembered where he was, and concluded the uniform must be that of a conductor, signalman or some other railway employee.

Tim suddenly felt a wave of guilt. He felt like a transgressor. He shouldn't be snooping around other people's personal possessions. He didn't belong here. He had to remind himself that he was no burglar. On the contrary, it was only the desire to help someone in distress that had brought him here.

He stood still and listened. All was quiet, until a dull thump sounded from the ceiling. It came from upstairs. The feeling of guilt was suddenly replaced with a strange combination of excitement and foreboding. He wasn't alone. Somebody or something was moving around up there. But who?

Or what?

Before he realized what he was doing, he found himself searching for some kind of weapon. His eyes settled on the fireplace, and a shiny brass bucket next to it. Sticking out of the bucket, the handle clearly visible, was a poker.

He immediately felt better with his right hand wrapped around the cold iron tool, its weight reassuring in his grip. Now armed, Tim left the living room by the same door he had entered and eyed the staircase. It was laid with a thick, light brown carpet, which should muffle his footsteps sufficiently. He didn't know if whoever was up there had heard him enter the house or not, but he doubted announcing his presence would be a good idea in any case. Instead, he would go for the softly approach and see what was what. Heart thudding, he began the ascent.

By the halfway point, he was afforded a good view of the second-floor layout. Four doors led off the landing, two open and two closed. He craned his neck and shifted his position to peer into the room on the right. He could see a large bed and some furniture, but no people.

"What are you doing?" he whispered to himself, repeating the words like a mantra as he neared the top of the staircase, holding the poker out in front of him like a sword.

The only way to do this was go from room to room, clearing them one-by-one Special Forces-style. The room on the right was closest. Unless somebody was hiding in the wardrobe, it was empty and had a cold, unlived-in quality about it.

Directly opposite was another bedroom, with the door standing open. Judging by the size of the bed and the toys lying scattered on the floor, this room belonged to a child.

The little boy in the photograph on the mantelpiece?

Tim tiptoed inside, the feeling he should check this room more thoroughly in case the kid really was hiding somewhere weighing heavy. Then he saw the body sprawled on the blind side of the bed, lying in a pool of blood. It was a woman.

The mother?

She was facedown. Or, at least she would have been if her face had still been attached to her body. Her head, long blonde hair matted with blood, had been lopped off and had come to rest against the far wall, almost as if it had been kicked there. Her housecoat had ridden up over her thighs, probably in the struggle. In death she had been stripped of all dignity. Tim gagged, and clasped a hand to his mouth.

Okay, enough. Time to get out of here.

Swaying on his feet, he turned to make an exit.

Suddenly, something rushed past the doorway just a few feet away, the sight accompanied by a set of pattering footsteps. Tim let out an involuntary whimper, almost sinking to the floor in shock.

What the fuck was that?

It was a figure.

So he wasn't alone here, after all.

As quick as a flash, the figure disappeared out of sight and Tim heard a door slam shut. He listened for the sound of a deadbolt or a key turning in a lock. It didn't come. Pulling himself together, he ran out of the room in pursuit.

On the landing he paused to study the configuration of the doors. Judging by the direction in which the figure had been moving, it could only be in one room. Where a door that had previously been open, was now closed tight.

Tim approached cautiously, the poker held in the air ready to strike and his other hand held out in front to fend off any attack.

"Hello?"

Far from the confident, authoritative voice he imagined and hoped for, the word came out as a strangled croak. He cleared his throat and tried again.

"Hello? Who's there?"

No reply.

Given the size of the figure and the light patter of the footsteps, he had an idea that he was dealing with a child. The little boy from the photograph. It all fit. He was probably terrified, the poor kid.

Tim made a conscious effort to soften his tone to appear less threatening. "Whoever's in there, look, some people are hurt. We need to get out of here and go find help."

Still there was no answer. Tim was beginning to get frustrated, a sense of urgency building. He didn't know how he knew, but something was about to happen.

"Okay, I'm coming in," he said through the door, almost as an after-thought, adding, "I'm not going to hurt you."

He took a deep breath, twisted the door handle, and pushed inward. The door opened into another bedroom.

It appeared to be empty. It was smaller than the master bedroom but bigger than the boy's. A double bed took up most of the space, and a fitted wardrobe was positioned against the far wall. The impersonal feel of the room, coupled with the slightly sterile feel, and the fact that he had already located the master bedroom and the boy's bedroom, suggested that this must be a spare. If so, it made sense for the boy to try to hide here. He was probably misguidedly thinking that something unfamiliar to him would be just as alien to an intruder, and therefore offer a level of camouflage, not realizing that to an intruder, everything in the house would be equally as unfamiliar so there was no hiding place.

Tim considered looking under the bed, but from this distance it didn't look as if there was enough room under there to conceal anyone. Instead, his eyes were drawn to the wardrobe.

"I know you're in here. I'm not going to hurt you. Why not just come out and we can get out of here?"

Tim thought he heard a creak from within the wardrobe. He reached out a hand, grasped the handle, and pulled.

The boy was huddled inside, knees pulled up to his chest. He looked up with tearful, forlorn eyes. It was, indeed, the boy from the photograph. He seemed to be no more than six years old and was shaking with fear, tousled brown hair plastered to his head with sweat.

"Come on," Tim whispered sharply, holding out a hand. "Come with me."

The boy hesitated, then his eyes widened and he kicked out his legs as he shrank back into the depths of the wardrobe as far as he could. Could he not see there was nowhere left to run? Poor kid must be so traumatized he was seeing danger everywhere he looked.

"Come on…" Tim said again, as loud as he dared. Then, too late, he realized the kid wasn't shrinking away from him, but something else. Something he could see but Tim couldn't. Something behind him.

Suddenly, something slammed into him, the impact knocking Tim off his feet. He landed on his knees, dazed, struggling to process what had just happened. Somebody had body-checked him, sneaking up in his blind spot. While he had been so focused on getting the kid, he had neglected the cardinal rule of combat. Protect yourself at all times. And now it seemed he was going to pay a heavy price for the oversight. Fearfully, he turned to face his assailant. It was a man in a dark uniform, instantly recognizable as the man from the photograph on the mantelpiece downstairs. He was carrying an ax, streaked with gore and dried blood.

Not the kid's own father?

It had to be.

Except he wasn't smiling anymore. Now his face was twisted into a mask of rage, eyes wide and frantic, spit drooling from the corner of his mouth.

From his position on the floor Tim saw the boy crawl out of the wardrobe, past the ax-wielding maniac, and through the bedroom door.

The man let out a grunt and swung the ax.

Tim saw the instrument of death coming toward him as if in slow motion and rolled. He blinked, and a flickering succession of images passed before his eyes. He saw fragments of his other life, his real life, and had time to wonder if he was caught in a dream. Was any of this real?

It felt real enough.

A heavy thump made the earth shake around him, and Tim opened his eyes. The heavy steel blade of the ax was embedded deep in the wooden floorboards inches from his face, the carpet around it pealed back like skin.

This was his chance.

Tim hauled himself to his feet and pushed past his assailant on the way to the door. As he left the bedroom he heard the axman let out a pained roar of fury. As he neared the top of the staircase, he saw the boy almost at the bottom.

"Hey!"

Tim didn't know why he shouted, and he didn't know why the boy stopped. But he did. The kid turned, and their eyes met momentarily. Then the world turned upside down. Tim felt a huge weight on top of him. He was falling, the staircase rushing up to meet him. He threw his arms out to break his fall and landed painfully, the air exploding from his lungs.

Then everything went black.

Tim's eyes snapped open.

Where am I?

His vision was filled with coils of little brown fibers. He had a vague memory of being in danger and falling, or being pushed down the stairs.

Or was that part of a dream?

Waves of pain racked his body. It was difficult to discern where one pain ended and another began.

He wiggled the fingers of his right hand. So far so good. Putting his fingers to the side of his head he felt an egg-like lump protruding from his skull, sore to the touch. He checked his fingers. No blood. He sat up and rubbed his eyes, wincing with pain.

Then he remembered the boy, and the man with the ax.

Scrambling to his feet, Tim tried to look in all directions at once. He seemed to be alone.

Why hadn't the axman finished him off?

Because he was going after the kid.

Tim swept up the poker. He was feet away from the front door, which now stood wide open. Suddenly fearful for both himself and the boy, he staggered toward it. There was a pain in his left side and lower back. He must have injured himself in the fall, but the pain subsided if he stooped over a little. He hoped he wasn't too late. The comparative brightness outside hurt his eyes, forcing Tim to put a defensive hand to his brow to shield them.

What now?

Tim found that selfishly, his priorities had shifted. Now, he just wanted to get away from this place. Let someone else come and sort this mess out. He looked around, his eyes settling on a tattered sign hanging on the wall. Tim's vision swam in and out of focus, and he wobbled slightly on his feet as he strained to make out what it said.

EXIT.

There was an arrow beneath the word, pointing across the platform away from the station house.

He half-walked, half-jogged back the way he had come, past the coal shed full of bodies, and onto the station platform.

It was still deserted.

Because all the people are dead!

Knowing what he did, he could now read the signs. The gauge in the brickwork was made by the ax, and the spill on the wooden bench wasn't varnish, it was blood.

Then he heard it. A whistle. He stopped in his tracks and listened. There was a soft rumble in the distance.

A train!

Not that remarkable given that he was standing in a train station, but under the circumstances the sound was music to his ears. He looked down the track, then up. Nothing.

Was he hearing things? A side effect of the bump on the head?

No. There it was!

Tim almost dropped to his knees in relief as the train rounded a bend in the distance.

Thank God!

But there was a problem. He was on the wrong side of the station. The train would be pulling into the platform on the other side, across the bridge. No problem, there was time. By the time he reached the bridge he was practically running, holding a protective arm across his left side and carrying the poker with the other.

Absurdly, he wondered if he would be allowed on the train with the poker. It wasn't a weapon as such, more a household item, but it would certainly look strange. Reluctant to get rid of it, he decided to take his chances for the time being. Mustn't forget there was a mad man running around.

What if the lunatic managed to get on the train?

By the time Tim reached the top of the steps he was gasping for air. The pain in his side was sharper, more defined, and he bent over further to compensate. He thought he may have damaged a rib or two, and he had also developed a limp at some point. Taking a few seconds to catch his breath, he peered over the top of the parapet to see how far away the train was, gripping the railing with both hands. Then, summoning every ounce of energy he had left, he pushed himself off the railing and continued on along the bridge.

Not much farther now.

Reaching the steps at the far side, he began the descent, paying close attention to where he was putting his feet. The last thing he needed was another spill.

Suddenly, out of the corner of his eye he saw movement.

The boy.

He must have been hiding somewhere, saw the train coming, and decided to take his chances. Now he stood there on the platform in plain sight, just behind the yellow safety line, gazing anxiously at the oncoming engine.

Yes, kid!

Then, all the elation dissipated as Tim spotted a dark hulking shape creep out of the shadows and start making its way toward the boy from the rear. He wouldn't have a chance.

Tim picked up his pace, gripping onto the railing with one hand to stop himself from falling over, aches and pains shunted to some dark corner of his mind where they wouldn't bother him. He looked up once more to see the looming dark figure raise the ax in the air.

"Kid, look out!"

The train was now almost at the station, and Tim wondered if the noise would be enough to drown out his warning.

Just in time, the boy turned. But too late. He crumpled under the weight of the strike, a crimson jet spurting from his head or neck.

"Noooooo!"

Tim's heart sank. Even though he had no real connection to the boy, had never even spoken to him, he felt a deep affinity with him.

The crisp air was filled with the screech of brakes as the train slowed to pull in to the station, moments too late to save the boy. Tim found himself wondering if the driver had witnessed the atrocity for himself. Someone on board must have seen something. If not, the first passenger to get off the train would surely raise the alarm. It was game over for the monstrous attacker.

As if sensing Tim's presence, the man in the uniform turned to face the bridge, a ghastly wide grin painted across his face. Then, he turned back to the bleeding boy and hoisted the ax high above his head with both hands. This must be the dismemberment part. The part he had been practicing all afternoon.

Tim felt a rage erupt inside him, and before he knew what he was doing, he was running at the man, his lolloping stride eating up the distance between them. As he approached, he raised the poker. It was no match for the ax, but it was all he had and a damn sight better than nothing.

Time seemed to slow down dramatically, allowing Tim to see and feel everything around him in excruciatingly vivid detail. He saw the train, large and ominous yet representing salvation. He saw the boy lying on the cold concrete platform in a spreading pool of blood, an awful gaping gash running across his lower face.

And he saw the man. The monster. Fury written all over his face, maybe even insanity. In that instant Tim realized something was broken inside him. Something that could never be fixed.

The ax was coming down.

Realizing he wasn't going to make it in time, Tim threw the poker like a javelin, staggering slightly with the shift in momentum. The metal rod sailed through the air. It seemed to be veering off course, and for a moment looked like it was going to miss its target. Then, as if by some form of divine intervention, it righted itself and struck the man on the shoulder. It was just a glancing blow, but enough to partially spin the man around, send him off balance, and throw the ax off its deadly trajectory. Instead of striking the boy, it hit the concrete platform sending a shower of sparks over the edge. The poker clattered on the concrete platform, spent.

His only weapon.

The train was finally pulling to a halt, brakes screeching. Without thinking, Tim leaped at the man, throwing his full weight at him.

The man took a step backwards, and for a terrible moment balanced on the very edge of the platform, pin wheeling his arms theatrically. As he toppled off the edge into the path of the oncoming train, his accusing eyes settled on Tim and his mouth formed a shocked 'O.'

Then, the train hit.

It wasn't travelling at full speed. Had it been, the man might well have been vaporized into a pink mist under the force of the impact. As it was, the train was in the process of stopping. It reared up behind the man like a giant steel behemoth, then pulled him down. As he disappeared under the wheels, he screamed. Tim averted his eyes, but the eye in his mind, the one eager to see everything, envisioned the cold steel ripping through flesh and pulverizing bone beneath its crushing weight. The scream withered to a fluid-drenched splutter, before dying away completely.

Tim looked down at the boy lying motionless on the edge of the platform. It seemed he was already too late to save him. Blood cascaded out of a huge jagged wound to his lower face where the skin was peeled back to expose glistening white shards of bone beneath.

The train came to a full stop, one of the doors immediately in front of Tim. It was an old-fashioned door with a handle you had to physically twist and pull, instead of simply pushing a button like the newer models. It was the kind of handle Tim hadn't seen for a long time. Feeling numb, he reached out and turned it. The boy's body, and the others, would be discovered soon enough. Probably within seconds. Obviously the train wouldn't be going anyplace soon, with that man-monster trapped underneath it, but hopefully Tim would be able to blend in with the other passengers amid the chaos that was bound to ensue. He climbed a step and entered the carriage, closing the door behind him, only to realize with a sinking horror that the carriage was empty. Completely empty.

No! Please, not a repeat of his last journey.

He hurriedly turned around and tried to open the door, planning to go straight to the driver's cabin and bang on the window until the bastard noticed him. But the handle wouldn't turn. It seemed frozen in place, the door rattling harmlessly in its moorings.

What the fuck?

Something else. There was nobody on the platform. No fuss, no panic, no alarm. Surely, someone must have got off the train?

The driver must have seen the big guy go under the train and activated some kind of safety mechanism, locking everything down. That must be it. Nobody wanted a panic on their hands.

In that case there was nothing Tim could do except take a seat and wait for some kind of announcement. The moment his rear touched the seat, there was a shudder. His breath caught in his throat.

The train started to move.

He couldn't prevent his mind from being drawn to what must be happening to the man trapped under the train. Lacerated flesh and skin, crushed bones. By the time the entire train drove over it there would be nothing left but bloodied rags and pink mush.

So what? The guy deserved it.

But what about the boy, lying back there on the platform?

What about him? There was nothing anyone could do for him now. The best thing would be for Tim to take this short trip back to normality then notify the authorities. He would personally see to it that the whole place was crawling with police and crime scene detectives within the hour. Let them piece together what happened down there. That was what they were paid to do. Tim was a fucking mortgage adviser.

He sat in the seat, trembling, watching the world whiz past the window. Sometime later, he didn't know how long, the train pulled into a station, and people got on. Actual people! Tim had never been so happy to see a disparate group of commuters in his life. At last, a triumphant return to reality.

He began to wonder if everything he had experienced that afternoon had been a tremendously vivid and realistic dream.

Had he just woken up?

No, his body was still tender and bruised from the fall down the staircase at the station house. A light brush of his forehead confirmed the existence of a large hematoma. He would need to get that checked out.

Soon, the train pulled into Waterloo.

This is the final stop. All change, please. All change.

Tim got off the train and started walking down the platform as if in a daze. People brushed past, all on their way to somewhere else. His head was spinning. As he approached the barrier he fumbled in his pockets for his ticket. Found it. On autopilot, he pushed it into the little slot, and the turnstile obediently opened. As he passed through he made eye contact with the attendant, and a sense of familiarity washed over him.

It was the same attendant he had seen earlier that day. The man with the disfiguring scar.

Every scar tells a story.

But there was more. That face. Grizzled and old now, but beneath, Tim saw the face of a child.

The boy from the station house.

He had survived?

Tim held his gaze, and though no words were spoken something passed between them. Some profound sense of empathy and understanding. Questions tumbled through Tim's mind.

How had this all happened? And what had happened, exactly? What had tipped the crazed man, quite obviously the kid's father, over the edge? How many lives had been extinguished that day? Why hadn't he heard about the atrocity in Harberry Close before?

But he couldn't speak. Instead, his mouth gaped uselessly. Sometimes, words are superfluous.

So now he knew the 'who' and the 'what.' Tim guessed he would never be able to answer the 'why' or 'how.' Isn't that just typical of life? There were always more questions than answers. Maybe that was just the way things were supposed to be.

He could take guesses.

Judging by the current age of the man with the scar, the events would have occurred fifty or more years ago. When things of such devastating magnitude happened, especially in those more conservative times, it was easier to simply bury it and move on as quickly as possible. Who needed to be constantly reminded of so much devastation and pain?

The incident could even have happened during the war years, when the country had enough going on to worry about some mini-tragedy at an isolated train station. Perhaps an Internet search would turn up some answers. Then again, perhaps it wouldn't.

"Come on, mate. Are you in or out?" spoke a rough cockney voice. Tim realized he was blocking the exit. A queue was forming behind him. He broke off eye contact with the attendant—the boy he had saved from death in some other time and place—and willed his feet to propel him forward onto the concourse.

He had an idea. Fishing around in his front pocket he withdrew his phone. Now there was a signal. Mr. Turner picked up on the first ring. Without waiting for the man to start shouting about targets and timekeeping, Tim said, "Hey, big shot. I'm just calling to tell you something. You can stick your job up your fucking fat slimy arse. I quit."

Life was just too short.

The Tended Field of Eido Yamata

Jon Michael Kelley

Somewhere in the distance... the faint tinkling of a bell...

In the serenity where he now found himself, Yamata still retained the vista of his previous life. Sitting meditatively, he could recall every moment of that existence with uncommon clarity. However, he did not recognize from those memories the child standing before him, a girl of obvious Japanese descent, about eight years old, wearing a simple knee-length white dress that seemed remarkably clean and bright, given that her bare legs and feet were black with dirt. A rice hat made of bamboo sat confidently atop her head, and hooked in the bend of an arm was an ikebana basket of similar weave. But there were no flowers.

Except for not having a mouth, she appeared normal in every other way.

But then, Yamata had to look no farther than his own desiccated body to know that—*here*—*normal* was not to be the dominant theme. Obviously, the afterlife was amenable to showcasing his wasted form, one achieved in the previous one through self-mummification. But that such a gaunt and withered state had escorted him so authentically into the next realm was rousing some concern, as he could only slightly turn his head, and to a greater degree his right arm.

Am I to remain forever a rigid corpse? He wondered.

As it had for the better part of his life, a yellow robe draped his body, though with much less resolve given his strangled girth.

Interestingly, *he* was able to speak, and had done so upon his relocation; a kindly greeting to the girl. She'd responded only with an unenthusiastic wave of her hand, her brown eyes staring on, mildly curious.

Beyond the girl was a vastness that Yamata was still trying to grasp. And, like the girl, there was nothing he could recall from his previous life to make its comparison; a life spent mostly in the Tōhoku region of Japan's Honshu Island, in search of purification. To all points on the horizon, barren furrows radiated outward from where he sat, a lotus posture that was the very hub for those tilled spokes. He was reminded of a naval flag, one belonging to a country that only had his compulsory allegiance—*The land of the Rising Sun*—its red ensign's beams flaring outward in strong allegory. And similar intentions were at work here, he suspected, as neither from the east nor west did *this* sun rise, but instead beat down relentlessly from a perpetual noon.

Although his time here was (in the vaguest sense) relatively new, the tropes for enlightenment were ageless.

The atmosphere was leaden with quietude, as if becalmed eons ago by some great inhalation and had since petrified while waiting for the ensuing release. Once here, Yamata had intuited an acceleration of awareness. Not the *passing* of time (although there were sequential aspects to the construct), but rather a kind of hastened shedding; a sloughing of absolutes, and things now obsolete, receding away like dreams do upon wakening. And very much like dreams, those references slipped no further than the periphery of his erstwhile life, and lingered there, close by and ready should they be called upon to offer up sobering testimonials. Witnesses to a world that was more devoted to the conservation of falsehoods than to their dismantling. That hell was eternal was just one of those; that death was the end of learning and bettering oneself, another. No fires burned hotter than those of the physical world—the fires of greed, lust, anger, hatred, sickness. Heaven, he believed, was anywhere such conflagrations had been doused.

Not so unlike his previous journey, the one he would begin from here would be chaperoned by contemplation. He would be careful of being too prideful, and to always remember that it was never about what life had denied him, but rather what he had denied life.

Yamata considered again his permanent seat, his cadaverousness, the hushed girl, the vast field stretching in all directions. A field unproductive as yet, aside from the growing anticipation.

And that fixed ceiling of sunshine. On a profound level, Yamata accepted the unfailing brightness as obligatory to the venue, for the most crucial lessons were often the most evasive, and to achieve their understanding required keeping any and all shadows squarely underfoot. That or the enduring sunshine was simply here to nourish what was clearly an imminent crop of inestimable scope, and aspirations.

In what was without doubt a land of extended metaphor, he considered a myriad of interpretations, from the obvious to the abstruse.

Upon those very thoughts, the little girl stepped closer and tipped her basket to allow him to see its contents. Only a few remained of what appeared to be some kind of seed. With much effort he tilted his head and, beyond her, looked again upon the rows, this time focusing on proximity rather than distance. He saw her footprints, deep and purposeful, marching along the soft trenches. Even closer, he saw the tiny indentations where her finger had pushed the seeds into the soil. And he could now see that her impressions weren't just localized but disappeared into the staggering distance—toward a horizon not teetering upon the curvature of a round world—but poised securely upon the blaring infiniteness of a flat one.

A determined girl! Yamata stared at her again and thought she might even be unusually pretty. But the unnatural smoothness below her nose was influencing that illusion. When having first seen the mouthless girl, Yamata thought of her as stage dressing to his soliloquy, a caricature of quiet innocence. A projection, perhaps, of his immaturity in this new place. He now suspected her reason for being here was as much practical as it was chaste metaphor. She was to be, among other things, the assistant to his immobility.

A less liberated person might have called it servitude, but Yamata saw the potential for collaboration, though he was yet unclear as to what his reciprocal role might be. And that she could read his thoughts wasn't entirely accurate, as he believed her to be, to some degree, the very extension of them—of his mind. In essence, his duality.

Regardless, there was no question that those omitted lips accentuated expression in her eyes. She was smiling in her agrarian achievement.

He smiled back, then impulsively wondered: *Does her white dress suggest virtue? Purity? Or, is it to represent the absence of beguiling color?* After all, beyond the gold tint of his robe there was only a monotonous blend of bucolic hues.

Abruptly, the girl gave a sighing motion with her shoulders, slowly shook her head, then began walking a tight circle, eyes down and focused on her dirty feet.

Watching the demonstration, Yamata was struck with the notion that she was communicating her annoyance with him.

Have I become tedious with my musings? He wondered. *That it is not truth I am chasing but my own tail instead?*

If she agreed with these thoughts, she gave no sign.

Finally, he said to her, "Giving into the assumption that you have no name, even if you could speak it, I shall call you Uekiya."

Upon hearing the word, the girl looked up and nodded to the unfailing field, accepting her new title: Gardner. Then she lowered her eyes once more and resumed etching a tight circle into the loamy soil.

Again considering the girl's inability at speech, Yamata recalled a quote from Lao Tzu, the founder of Taoism, and wondered if she was the exemplar for such wisdom: *"He who knows, does not speak. He who speaks, does not know."*

Then, to confirm that she either was or was not, in fact, substantial, Yamata reached out his workable hand for her. Stiffly, she stopped going round and round and regarded the gesture with narrow eyes, then slowly shook her head, as if to say that was not appropriate.

Why? He wondered. *Am I being reminded that something's authenticity doesn't necessarily lie in its solidness?* Or, was there still lingering within him a tactile need, one not quite disassociated yet from his former self?

Then there was sudden growth in the field. Already the girl was bent over and studying the nearest sprout, a thing that vaguely resembled an asparagus spear, no larger than his littlest finger and appearing just as corpselike. A reaffirming sign that this was going to be a harvest most different from any other.

Still bent over, hands on her knees, Uekiya turned her attention to him. Where triumph could not insinuate itself in a smile so it sparkled doubly in her eyes.

From behind him came once again the tinkling of a bell. A declarative echo, perhaps, of his resolve to achieve *Sokushinbutsu,* the practice to reach ultimate austerity and enlightenment through a most ambitious art of physical punishment: self-mummification. For a Shingon Buddhist, it was an enduring commitment. For many years the devoted monk would practice *nyūjō*, adhering to elaborate regimes of meditations, physical activities that stripped the body of fat, and an exclusive diet of salt, pine bark, nuts, seeds, roots, and urushi tea. This tea was especially significant. It was derived from the sap of the urushi tree and highly toxic, and was normally used for the lacquering of pottery. When ingested, vomiting and dehydration followed. Most importantly, it ultimately made the body too poisonous to be eaten by carrion insects and their ilk. If the body absorbed high enough levels, some believed it could even discourage like-minded bacteria.

Finally, when sensing his end drawing near, the monk would have himself locked inside a pinewood box, one barely large enough to accommodate his body, wherein a permanent lotus position was assumed. Some monks would insist on having coal, salt, or even lime heaped around them to stave off the slightest moisture.

Once confined, the practitioner's only connection to the outside world was an air tube, and a bell—one he would dutifully ring every day to let those listening know that he was still alive. When the ringing stopped, the air tube was removed and the makeshift tomb tightly sealed.

After a customary three years had passed, the body was exhumed. Of the many who attempted to achieve such a hallowed state, only a very few triumphed. The majority of bodies were found to be in normal states of decay. However, those who accomplished their own mummifications were regarded as true Buddhas. Highly revered, they were placed into the temples for viewing.

For their tremendous spirit and devotion, admiration was still paid those who failed in their endeavors. But for Yamata especially, that was modest esteem—and certainly not the sort he ever hoped to gain through compromise.

Uekiya had dropped her basket and, arms dangling at her sides, was now staring intently at something behind him. And by the tilt of her gaze that something was alleging to be looming from a great height. Her awe was absolute. Had she the proper hinges, Yamata thought, she would have been left slack-jawed. He then became both exhilarated and frightened. What could exist among these rural and most modest trappings to provoke such veneration? If he were prone to such expectations, he might have believed she was beholding a god.

That she was witnessing a massive thunderhead instead was the likelier explanation. After all, from a parched point of view, threatening rain clouds could easily provoke the same respect as any passing deity.

Moisture. Yes, it would be the remaining ingredient needed to placate the construct's agricultural objective. Being unable to turn his head fully to either side, Yamata's visual range was limited, thus leaving the matter most tantalizing. Yet another clue that the lessons here would not be easily learned.

After what may have been a mere moment or the passing of centuries, the girl reached down and retrieved her basket, her wonderment either spent or the spectacle had finally retreated.

Another burst of growth in the rows, now appearing as a more recognizable plant. Although still spindly and emaciated, the stalks were more pronounced and now home to little brown offshoots that were unmistakably leaves, semi-translucent in their infancy. A quality that he found to be strangely reminiscent, but of what he couldn't yet say.

Whatever relevance this germination had to the setting remained unclear. Yamata continued to employ his wisdom, always mindful that this was by its very nature a land of illusion.

Yamata again reached out for the girl, his compulsion growing fierce. This time, Uekiya wheeled and violently slapped his hand away, nearly breaking off the first two fingers. With utter disbelief, Yamata stared at those digits, both dangling now on withered tendons and pointing obliquely, if not forebodingly, to the ground.

The pain was sudden and intense—and disconcerting. He had not anticipated there to be such measurable discomfort beyond physical life. But he did not react instinctively and withdraw his arm. Instead, he left it out there for her to see. A testament to her brashness, to her insolence.

With something akin to compassion, Uekiya's eyes softened. Then she made her way to the closest plant and began plucking its leaves, placing each one carefully into her basket. As Yamata watched, his curiosity grew into trepidation as he realized that those lucent leaves were exactly the same color and texture as his dried, wrinkled skin. After having gathered only a few, Uekiya stepped up to his extended arm and began carefully applying the leaves to his broken fingers, bringing them back together at their fractures then wrapping and gently rubbing the new tissue into place, manipulating and messaging it until it was indistinguishable from his own layering. When she was through, she turned his hand this way and that, regarding her accomplishments with satisfaction.

Yamata flexed his fingers and found them restored to their original, albeit intransigent, state. But any appreciation of Uekiya's handiwork was quickly dissolving, melting into an anxiety unlike any he had ever known, confirming that the most profound realizations were often the most unsettling.

Within the rows there was yet again another acceleration of growth, this time even more telling as a small whitish bulb had become evident at the top of every stalk, each of those now taller by another eight inches, and with heartier girth.

Are they the rudiments of a flower? Yamata wondered of the spheres. *A fruit? Or are they the beginnings of something I dare not try to imagine?*

His determined outlook, he realized, was growing dim. A dread had begun building in the thick atmosphere, but there was no beating heart to accompany it to crescendo. Just his quivering essence.

And still the plants grew, now four feet high, their bulbs even whiter and plumper, where within those a restlessness festered. As he stared, they disconcertedly reminded him of caterpillar nests, the larvae inside those silk pouches squirming to break free.

Yamata turned his eyes to Uekiya, as if her own might provide some kind of answer, or at least a concerned recognition to his plight.

He balled his right hand as best he could, and vehemently condemned her speechlessness. *"Are you to remain forever silent, or must I say just the right thing, ask just the right question to elicit a response?"* But her attention had once again been drawn to something behind him. Something gargantuan, was still his impression.

It was then when Yamata noticed that something had gone missing from the construct. He searched his restricted view; frantically so. It was vitally important to remember, he was sure. Everything presented here had dire meaning, and was only expected to change or disappear altogether once its purpose had been understood. Or so he expected.

Then there was movement. Of the nearest plant, its bulb had begun weeping milky rivulets; viscous streams trailing down the stalk with the ambition of warmed honey. Then Yamata realized that the discharge was not comprised of any liquid but was made up of hundreds of pale white worms. And maggots. Upon reaching the ground, the creatures struggled in the loose soil, their frantic undulations less confident but still maintaining a fixed progression toward his still and sitting form.

Bent over once again, hands on knees, Uekiya was watching the bugs' advancement with rapt wonderment.

The first worms to reach Yamata reared up and attached themselves to the lowest parts of his feet, then began burrowing through the brown, shriveled skin. Sparkles of intense pain began dancing behind his eyes, and a shrill, strident noise stung his ears; the pinched squeal, he quickly realized, of his own dry voice.

The pain of them entering his body was memorable, but the kind they ignited once inside was astonishingly bright and bellicose. A feast not had on mere shriveled bone and muscle, he feared, but upon a profound and everlasting food source—his soul. And it too screamed. Sounds not birthed from a decrepit throat, but instead the collected resonances of isolation and grim oblivions, now to be intoned upon an unending existence.

The internal writhing of the worms was equally insufferable, and he cried out for a boyhood god; one he had no occasion to revisit, until now.

Finally, mercifully, the pain slowly receded after the remaining worms had inserted themselves. It was a momentous reprieve. But another look at the burgeoning rows beyond confirmed that such amnesties would be fleeting.

Leisurely filling her basket, Uekiya had set about plucking leaves from the offending plant. Yamata stared out across his field, one that was now growing a perpetual supply of sutures; grafts to outwardly mend the external damage caused by an equally eternal progression of the most vile and ravenous creatures.

But what about the internal *damage?* He desperately wondered. *How will she mend that?*

Uekiya was now kneeling before him, messaging the leaves onto the chewed holes in his feet, restoring the dead tissue.

When finished, she went back to staring at the anomaly behind him.

Yamata prayed that the girl was, in fact, witnessing a storm. Prayed for a deluge to drown the crawling masses. For lightning to scorch them thoroughly. For typhoon winds to scatter them to the endless reaches of this place.

Prayed for any blight that would dissuade his punishment.

Once, his great profundity did not abide the generic concepts of an eternal and torturous perdition. Now, he was being forced to reconsider. Ironically, what remained intact of his fracturing philosophy was the reverberation of his most insightful expression; that it wasn't about what life had denied him, but what he had denied life.

And life, it was being made very clear, was not going to be denied *him.*

Despite his most sincere, consecrated motivations, he had accelerated his own death and thereby corrupted those intentions. To tear away the shiny tinsel of devotion revealed the harsher truth of a prideful suicide. But his biggest sin of all was saturating his body with urushi tea. Having done so, he had denied the carrion eaters their due; had disallowed the natural progression of things, and had done so vainly and with utter disregard for consequence.

The bulb of the second closest plant had opened, releasing its own white undulant stream. Yamata looked beyond the advancing worms and out upon the incalculable vastness, and within that silent horror was revealed the thing that had gone missing. The bell. It was no longer being rung. And on some instinctual level, that awakened in him a fear more primal than the worms themselves.

Uekiya's growing devotion to the unseen behind him was inviting its own species of fear. Her wide brown eyes had assumed a tragically revering expression, and Yamata was now on the brink of admitting that no less than a god could warrant such reverence.

But what sort of god captivates a child while hiding behind an atrocity of infinite proportions?

Yamata one last time contemplated Uekiya's absent mouth, and out of all the convoluted, Byzantine reasons he could think of for it not being there, he finally decided on a most austere one. Once in hell, there is simply nothing left to say.

CPSIA information can be obtained at www.ICGtesting.com
Printed in the USA
LVOW07s1704141214

418773LV00004B/800/P